THE JAGGED LINE

A young woman in the Great
Depression makes her place
in Law Enforcement

SIDNEY A BROWN

Dog River Press, Sharpsburg, Georgia
Printed in the U.S.A.

DEDICATION

This novel is dedicated to my Father and Mother, who taught me right from wrong. They both lived through the Great Depression and World War II. My father served in the U.S. Navy during the war. It is dedicated to the men and women who served in Law Enforcement in Campbell County, Georgia, 1828-1931. Many of their names were never recorded in history. We salute their bravery and service to the citizens of the county, some of them giving their lives. It is also dedicated to the staff of Dog River Press for making this project a reality.

ACKNOWLEDGMENTS

The Jagged Line, as all prior Dog River Press publications, is the result of countless hours of proofreading and editing by my wife of almost fifty years, Phyllis S. Brown. Our oldest staff reader, my mother, Melba Brown, has also read each manuscript several times, and contributes in many ways with comments and suggestions.

THE JAGGED LINE - PROLOGUE

The death of Campbell County was drawing nigh as the last minute of December would see it fade into history. It had been carved from the wilderness, and surely its soul would return to the same. Many were bitter to see it die, including Heather's grandfather. He had watched the town of Campbellton die a slow death to Fairburn, the town that he despised so. Had he lived to see the county merge, he surely would have died from despair. Would there be a celebration of the coming merger with Fulton County, or would there be a sense of defeat? No one would know until the time came.

On the night of December 31, 1931 there were no fireworks, no bands playing on the square, and certainly no parade. It was a silent death and a quiet birth. Margaret Selman Duncan, Heather's grandmother, had always burned a small flame of hope in her room for the return of her Marshal. She would not do so on this night, or any night to come. She truly felt that all was lost in the effort to make Campbellton a thriving city and see that the county survived.

"Shall I light the hope light?" Heather asked softly, closing the house down for sleep.

"No, there is no visible hope left. I will keep it in my heart," Margaret replied.

Heather sighed and pulled the covers high for the old woman to grasp in the darkness. She cupped her hand close to the lamp's chimney and blew out the small flame. Darkness filled the room momentarily until the moonlight softly filled the home with a blue hue. The soft glow of the banked fire coals in the hearth provided warmth. The night was filled with sadness as the two women prepared for slumber. There would be no sound of Sonny on his last pass through the kitchen, picking at the leftovers before bed. There would be no sound of Holly making her rounds to each bedside before finally settling down on her pallet in the kitchen. The times were changing.

The absence of Sonny and Polly left a large void in their hearts. They were missed, only to be remembered through the daily chores. The simplest items reminded of their passing. The funeral flowers had long since died. Some had been dried to further remember Sonny in the quiet private moments when the stillness of the house was filled with the sound of one's own beating heart. The spirit of the two lovers often revealed its presence in the darkness of the night with their soft laughter and conversation as they were often heard through the walls of their bedroom.

The kitchen stove was still warm from the evening meal's preparation. Heather stood at the hall doorway and surveyed the room. She looked to see if Holly might have been there. In her vision she was not, but in spirit and her heart the loyal old bloodhound was there, lying on the pallet of old quilts that had not yet been removed. Heather's eyes worked their way around the dimly lit room. She remembered the cut glass syrup pitcher had not even been set on the table since Sonny had passed away. It was brimming full, just as Sonny had liked to keep it. "Syrup pitcher that ain't full's like a revolver that's the same. You might run out 'fore the meal's over and that wouldn't be good, like runnin' out of bullets," her father would say. Heather smiled widely. The remaining cornbread muffins under the screen cover were calling to her, as late as it was. Heather placed several pieces of dried pine kindling into the warm stove and opened the grate ports, allowing air to bring the warm coals to life under what she had just added. The gray stoneware enameled coffee pot slid to a stop under the guidance of her strong hand. A moment of sweets, of cornbread and syrup consumed under the flow of hot coffee, sounded like just the thing at the moment to remember her father and old Holly by.

Margaret was not deaf and her sense of smell was still as keen as a young woman, but her bones were aching and she was tired. She thought she would pass on the exploration into the kitchen, until Heather came to her door.

"Grandmama," she whispered.

Margaret opened her eyes to the dim light that filled the room. "Yes, dear," she said, not moving.

"Come, let's have a syrup muffin and a cup of coffee," Heather whispered softly from the doorway.

"Child, I'll be up all night," Margaret replied. "But what do I have to do tomorrow, but think and write," she said, as she began to stir.

The lamplight created a soft ball of yellow light for the two women sitting at the table. "This is quite nice," Margaret said softly.

Heather poured fresh coffee into two of the best decorated cups they owned. The aroma wafted quickly through the room. Margaret removed the pressed glass lid from the butter dish in the center of the table.

"It sure is soft," she said, looking at the yellow butter from Mrs. Derick's churn.

Heather turned from the sideboard and placed two small plates with a corn muffin each on the table. "Dad told me to do this." Heather spoke with a slight quiver in her delivery, taking her seat.

"I suppose your mother made him do it," Margaret said softly. "They were a pair, like me and your Granddad." Her eyes began to tear up. The two women were silent for a moment. The house settled from the cold outside. "I think it's better than any formal tea."

The syrup pitcher had, in fact, not been used since Sonny had passed. A slight leathery skin was beginning to form, as the surface of the sorghum had dried. The stove popped.

"The fire seems especially nice, doesn't it?" Margaret asked Heather.

Heather nodded. "Yes".

"This is the kind of thing we'd do when your grandfather was alive, and him and the boys would return in the late hours of the night when they had been out handling the business of the law," Margaret said.

The two women ate in silence for a few minutes, and then Margaret spoke. "The Billings woman, a true reporter she is. She'll expect a detailed story from you, since you promised it to her. She believes you've got a rewarding story to share," she said, taking a sip from her cup.

Heather looked ahead into the darkness of the corner.

"What will you tell her? Will you lambast the ones you are upset with, or tell it the way it happened and let the facts and opinions fall upon those who deserve the rewards and those who deserve to be exposed?" Margaret asked, looking at Heather.

Heather looked down and sat in silence.

"Would it help if you told me the story in detail? I could write it for you. I'm up in years, but my hand is still good, better than most that are still in the business. The typewriter is still like new after all these years," Margaret said, looking at Heather and gently resting her hand on her granddaughter's arm. "That old thing has certainly earned its keep and fed all of us many a time."

"Dad would want me to tell the truth," Heather said, looking up now at Margaret. The clock chimed one. "Is it too late?" Heather asked.

"Child, a good story is never too late to tell. I can start on it as soon as you've told it. It will help you get over the bad and emphasize the good."

"Do you need your tablet?" Heather asked.

"Try me, child," Margaret answered, as she sat back in her straight chair.

Heather stood and arranged her gown, then settled down. "I think I'll tell it like I'd expect to see it printed," she said. Heather took a sip from her cup and prepared to begin her story.

"I think you'd best just start at the beginning in first person, and I'll be the judge as to what person it is written in for Miss Billings," said Margaret, with a smile.

The fire was beginning to die. Heather added several more pieces of wood as she spoke of the things that had disturbed her so. Margaret listened intently, as though it were a story for her own publications that had ended many years back. The second muffin went down for each woman during the long, detailed conversation. The coffee had almost thickened from its simmer on the edge of the stove. The clock struck six and the old red rooster stretched and yawned as roosters do, and climbed once more to the top of the hen house and gave its crow to the sun rising in the east.

"My, it's sunup," Margaret said, with a yawn.

"I'm about talked out," Heather replied, yawning.

Margaret stood, with heavy sleep showing in her eyes. "I have aplenty to go on. I've already begun to compile."

"I'm sure you have, Grandmother. I'm sure you have," replied Heather, as she walked the old woman to bed.

A peaceful sleep fell upon the two tired women. One was drifting off to the exciting compositions of a story, and the other relaxing in the peace of mind that she had done all within her power to administer justice to the wrongdoers and the wicked.

CHAPTER ONE

Wild daisies bloomed along the roadside, blending in with the pink running rose where old home places had once stood. Heather was excited to pick up where she had left off at the Sheriff's Department the day before. "It is a beautiful morning," she thought, as she hurried along in the quiet running, burgundy over black 1929 Essex. Heather glanced over at the sparkling fine red dust on the dash. "I'll take care of that as soon as I get home," she thought to herself. A driver sounded his horn in a brief polite beep as he passed and waved. Heather returned the wave. She did not recognize who it was, but she smiled and felt warm inside over the gesture. Campbellton Street was busy with traffic as she came to the intersection, passed the World War I monument, and soon found her parking place at the courthouse. Allison Sweeney had just pulled up.

"Hello, young lady!" said Allison, the older woman of the two. She motioned for Heather to come to her car.

Heather wondered what was up, as she rolled her window almost to the top. She hurried over to Allison's car.

"Something up?" she asked.

Allison looked about. She did not want to be seen forewarning Heather. "The county closing is official. It comes down at the stroke of midnight on December 31st."

Heather was taken back at hearing the news. "I wonder if my father knows it?" she asked.

Allison looked around again. "He most likely suspects it. There's been talk of it for nigh on two years. Why, you know that."

The two clerical women walked into the courthouse. Their hard raised heels sounded on the dark wood floors.

1

"If that be the finest two clerical women I've got, I need ta see Miss Duncan," shouted Sheriff Benjamin Giles.

"Yes, sir!" Heather called out. She waved Allison on.

The sheriff's office door was ajar. Heather stood straight and pushed it hard enough to allow it to fully open. The half glass door groaned, coming to a stop. As it hit the wooden wedge door stop, the frosted glass rattled. Heather had always had trouble with the lettering on the door. The symmetry of the arc was off, as well as the consistency of the black shadowing. It was her belief that it was done as a work off for an artistically inclined inmate.

"I'd think that was Sonny Duncan the way the door opened," laughed the sheriff. He sat behind his large desk. The stench of a cold cigar filled the cool morning air. It even overpowered the strong coffee that was brewing on a single eye hot plate on a small table under the south window. The steam created by the coffee had soiled the large pane over pane window. The sheriff had chosen to paint his office a dark burgundy with glossy white trim. He said it gave him a presence of power and authority, since everyone else had white walls.

"No. It's me," Heather said.

"Come in," said Sheriff Giles. He moved papers about on his desk. The spoon rattled in the empty coffee mug as he moved it aside. "Old Nigger Jeb can change four tires 'fore that son of a bitch can heat a pot of coffee," he said, looking behind him at the hot plate.

"Old Jeb ain't as old as that hot plate," Heather replied quickly.

"Have a seat," said the sheriff, as he extended his hand toward the heavy chair in front of his desk. "I like you! You've grown ta be as sharp as your dad."

Heather took a seat. She could read him like a book, there was something up.

The first drip of boiling water found its way down the outside of the coffee pot and onto the red coil of the hot plate. It sounded off with a sizzle. "All right! She's a comin'!" yelled the sheriff.

Heather kept her eyes on the sheriff. She knew that too much eye contact from a woman made him anxious, self-conscious. He would move about nervously before long.

Sheriff Giles pulled a pocketknife from his brown suit pants and began to clean under his fingernails. He glanced at her now and then. "Heather, I'm sure you've heard all about the county merging with Fulton, and of all the families against it, it's the Duncans. Your grandfather was a proud law enforcement officer and an avid believer in his town and this county." He looked back again at the coffee pot. "Things do change. I've been to so damn many meetings on this merger that my flat ass has begun to concave." He laughed, folding his knife and putting it away. The sound of footsteps came and went as they sat in his office.

Heather's eyes were distracted by a wren outside on the windowsill. The small dark eyes watched her intently. It was at that point she knew that regardless of what outcome might lie ahead, she would be all right. The wrens had always been loved and admired by her grandfather.

The sheriff turned to see what was distracting her.

"Coffee's almost ready," she said quickly. Heather did not want to tell him that her grandfather was sitting on the windowsill.

Sheriff Giles turned his attention to the discussion. "I need you to take today and get your files and records in order. Let Mrs. Sweeney know what you've got, she'll have to finish them up. Campbell County has to downsize to one clerk, and Mrs. Sweeney will be it. She's been here longer than you."

Heather watched him without the slightest expression. Sheriff Giles seemed to be shocked at her lack of reaction. "I can do that," she eventually replied.

The center drawer of the large desk scrubbed as the sheriff pulled it open. He brought forth a tri-folded letter and handed it across the desk to her. Heather leaned forward to receive it. "This is your notice of separation, and inside is a letter of recommendation," he said, leaning back in his chair.

Heather stood. "Are we done?"

"Aren't you going to read it?" he asked.

"Eventually," she replied. At first, she felt lonely, lost and hollow. The small wren sang out from the window and at that point she was reassured once more.

"If you were a man, I'd be in a hell of a mental state about having to let you go. You are a devoted and hard worker. A dependable worker!" said Sheriff Giles.

Heather looked at the man she had once respected. *"My grandmother would knock you flat on your ass for that talk,"* she thought. *"And if Dad knew it, he would explode."*

"Can I go to work now?" she asked.

"Yes," Sheriff Giles said softly. Heather turned to leave. "Don't close the door," he said.

"You're damned right! I'd slam it," Heather said to herself, as she clenched her teeth. "And the badge? Do you want it?" she asked from the hallway.

Allison looked down the hall from her open door as she sat at her desk. She felt sad for the young woman.

"Keep the badge. The county will be gone and it will be useless," Sheriff Giles answered.

Heather left his sight en route to her desk next to Allison Sweeney. She dropped her purse on the desk with a thud.

"I hear you've got your pistol," said Allison, smiling.

"All the time, another in the boot of the car with our trackin' equipment," Heather said in a monotone, taking her seat.

"I'm sorry," Allison said.

"It's all right. I hope Sonny doesn't lose his composure when he's told," Heather said. She was gathering her thoughts in regards to her organization for leaving.

In a few minutes, the sheriff came down the hall with a mug of coffee. His movements certainly were not very graceful for a slim man. Coffee sloshed from the overfilled mug as he came toward them. He stood in the open doorway sipping coffee for a long while. "Heather, I'll be making this announcement officially to your father. I'd like the courtesy of telling him myself, if you don't mind. He too will not be needed after the county is closed, merged, what tha hell ever ya want ta call it," said Sheriff Giles.

The only telephone for the clerk's office sat on Mrs. Sweeney's desk. "I understand," Heather replied. She knew that she was showing anger. Her ears were starting to ring and her scalp was tingling. She exhaled loudly. The sheriff left quietly.

"If it came in with me or Sonny, it's goin' out!" Heather snapped, manhandling the side drawers of the desk.

"I wouldn't take a lot of time on decisions. I'd take what I thought was mine or y'all's," Allison whispered. "You're not mad at me, are you?" she asked.

"Heavens no!" said Heather. "I've been here in this damn paper job since I was fourteen, and that's been too long! Maybe I'll find a place to be a chief or even run for sheriff. Jody is a lawyer in Atlanta and he's my back-up," said Heather loudly, in hopes of the sheriff and anyone else hearing her. She really did not care.

The filing room and vault shared the same wall as the sheriff's office. During Heather's trips to file, she could hear the sheriff talking to someone on the telephone. She stood poised with papers in hand should someone come in. She was there to file, not eavesdrop. The hard plaster walls gave resonance to the slightest sound. "I'm havin' ta let everyone go except for a senior clerk. Yeah, that's right. Even my deputies have to be let go and apply with Fulton," he laughed. "It's a god damn mess ain't it? I just let a young lady in the clerk's office go this morning. She took it rather well. I dread her father though. I'll do that this afternoon in person or by telephone if he doesn't come in," he said.

Heather mouthed, "Asshole!" as she listened.

"My staff down here ain't too large, but they are people nonetheless who will need a job. Well, it could never be worked out that they would just continue to work. I hate it for the deputies, them boys got families. Yeah, yeah, she's a good lookin' young lady. Shoots better than many of my deputies. She and her father are special deputies. They track for us and anybody else with a prisoner escape or a wanted person on the run. Damn good too! No, no, I don't think so. Not this gal, she ain't the kind to put out," said the sheriff to the other party.

Heather had heard more than she needed to hear. She was learning too much about the sheriff. She moved drawers in and out during the time she was eavesdropping to cover her being there. Heather did not want Sonny to get the news secondhand or be surprised by a telephone call. She went straight to the telephone to call him.

"Allison, can I have the telephone a few minutes?" Heather asked.

Allison was busy sorting papers in alphabetical order and assigning numbers to them with the typewriter. "Certainly," she answered, as she got up quickly and stepped out of the office. Heather quietly closed the door.

Click, click, click, sounded the brass yoke on the telephone as Heather held the earpiece to her ear.

"Operator!" said the distorted voice from the local switchboard.

"Heather Duncan here. Ring my house, please." She waited patiently, listening to the mysterious clicks and voices in the background that broke in and out as the operator made the connection.

"Hello!"

"Grandmama, this is Heather. Is Sonny in the house?" she asked.

"He's close, in the back yard. Just a minute," Margaret replied, as she placed the earpiece on the table beside the telephone. Heather could hear Margaret's footsteps as she walked away. "Sonny! Telephone!" Margaret yelled.

"Jesus Christ! Who is it?" he yelled back from the yard.

"It's your daughter," Margaret called out, from the back door on the enclosed porch.

Heather heard her father call out. "Which one?" She smiled at his foolishness.

"Your only one," Margaret answered, as he came onto the porch with a bound.

"What does she want?" he was heard to ask.

"I don't know," replied Margaret, as she followed him to the telephone table.

Heather could hear Holly sniffing and snorting in the background. Wherever her dad was, so was Holly.

"Hey, girl!" said Sonny.

"I'm settin' you up for the better. You need to appear in the sheriff's office rather than get a telephone call," she said softly.

5

"What's happening?" he asked.

"I've been let go and you are next, effective at the end of the year. The county merge went through," she whispered.

"Son of a bitch!" Sonny said, and then there was silence.

"I ain't supposed to tell you this," she whispered.

"I've got your back, I understand," he said. "I'll be there before the end of the day, wait on me to show," he said.

"Love ya" Heather whispered.

"You too!" Sonny replied, as he gently hung up.

Margaret was standing close by, she could just barely hear Heather's voice. "What's happened?" she asked.

"The county merge has gone through, end of the year. She's out of a job and the sheriff is waiting to tell me himself," Sonny replied. He washed his hands at the kitchen sink and sat down in a kitchen chair.

Holly came over and put her head on Sonny's knee. "Girl, we're a couple of numbered individuals," he said, as he rubbed her head. The dog gave a loud sigh.

"Can I ride?" Margaret asked.

"Certainly," Sonny replied. He sat silently for a while, thinking of the years of service to the county.

Margaret freshened up and changed into a newer dress. She soon came back into the kitchen.

"You look nice," Sonny assured her.

Margaret rubbed her hands down her body. "Do I still look like a Greek Goddess, like I did in the pictures back then?" she asked, standing in front of Sonny.

"Yes, I see why Dad fell for you," he said, smiling.

The dependable Hudson that had served them so well during the early years, to Texas and back, through the cyclone, had long been used for other powered adventures on the homestead. The cab sat out behind the barn, resting on stones. It gave a place for the chickens and smaller animals to take shelter from larger predators and storms. The sunflowers over the past years had dropped their seeds and grew once again against the contrast of the black body. The sparrows built in a headlight body every year. A newer Chevrolet Touring model had taken the place of the Hudson. Heather frequently visited the old body to stand and touch it. This was where her and her mother's lives had changed. It was their beginning. In many ways it was a sacred shrine.

Margaret knew Sonny was angry by the way he was pushing the Chevrolet. "Goin' fast won't make it better," she said, looking at him.

"No, but it makes me feel better," he replied. Holly balanced as she sat on the back seat. "Dad would have died, if he weren't already gone. This merger would have likely killed him," Sonny said, looking ahead.

"He certainly hated Fairburn and everyone who pulled up roots and left Campbellton. He certainly did," Margaret said, growing softer as she finished. "He certainly did," she whispered.

"Look at a map! The bastards wouldn't have built a railroad to Campbellton anyway. They are built on straight lines. Atlanta to Campbellton, a straight line to nowhere," he snarled. "Noise! My ass! The train can't run that many times in a day to be a bother to people," he snarled. He sounded his horn and gave a wave to a passing motorist.

"Who was that?" Margaret asked.

"Wilford Hopkins," he answered. "Chester's brother," he added.

"Oh!" she replied.

Sonny had to stop at the intersection in Fairburn. Margaret looked at the window of Kirkpatrick's Pharmacy on the corner. The traffic moved ahead. Sonny saw the sheriff talking to someone on the sidewalk. He sounded his horn and waved for him to come ahead. Sheriff Giles waved back. "I don't care if you listen, Heather too!" Sonny said. He parked the Chevrolet in the sheriff's parking space, pointing at Margaret. "I don't give a damn," he announced, before she could bring it to his attention.

Heather was standing at the door. "That was quick," she said. Holly ran to her and sniffed about. The black Studebaker driven by the sheriff passed by and parked several spaces down. He looked to be displeased over his parking situation.

All three Duncans stood at his closed door, and Holly. "Afternoon! Just the man I need to see," said Sheriff Giles, as he pulled his keys from his pocket. The key found its home and the heavy door opened. "Come in," he said, leading the way. "I don't have enough chairs; I'll get some more."

"Margaret and Sonny can sit, I'll stand," replied Heather.

"Well, all right," replied Giles.

Sonny and Margaret sat down. Heather stood along the wall and Holly sat in front of Sonny, between his feet and the sheriff's desk.

"I understand you wanted to see me," Sonny said, with his badge in his hand.

"Put yer badge on. I don't want it," said the sheriff. "The county has merged with Fulton and I've got to let everyone go except for a senior clerk, and as you already know, that is Mrs. Allison Sweeney."

"So, where does that put everyone else?" asked Sonny.

"I've got to let everyone go, Sonny," repeated Sheriff Giles.

"And Heather is gone as of today. When do I leave?" Sonny snapped.

"I'd like for you and this handsome dog to stay with us until the last minute of December 31st, and then it's all over," said Sheriff Giles. He leaned back in his desk chair. The two coiled compression springs

7

underneath gave out a loud squeak.

Margaret and Heather were silent.

"Shit!" said Sonny, as he wiped his face in frustration.

"There could be something come up, but it won't be out of the wallet of Campbell County after the first of the year," said the sheriff, trying to make the situation seem better than it was.

Sonny took a deep breath and exhaled. "All right, last minute in December, then me and this old girl's gone," he said, as he rubbed Holly's head. The dog turned and looked at him with her sad eyes. "We've done a lot. This dog's done almost twenty years for this county," Sonny said, as he stood to go.

"Like I told Heather, keep yer badge," said the sheriff. He saw them to the hallway and gently closed his door.

Margaret stepped in between Sonny and Heather as they walked down the hall, toward the bright sunlight. "Let me cook a good meal. We need an old-fashioned family talk. I can even do a canned peach cobbler," she said, as she held their hands. Holly led the way.

Heather and Margaret followed Sonny's Chevrolet back home. Holly sat up front with Sonny. The bloodhound was so large it looked like another person in the car from the back.

"Him and that dog, ain't it a sight?" Margaret exclaimed.

The warm afternoon sun was touching the tops of the western tree line, along to the river hills. The rooster had rounded all the hens in close to the hen house and they were scratching for the last discovered grub and interesting piece of grain. The cats were gathered on the back porch steps. Evening was drawing near. Sonny drove in first and took his spot in front of the barn, with Heather right behind. Not an animal stirred as Holly jumped down from the seat. They had grown to know that she was a guardian and they would not be bothered. The newest cat only raised its head as it watched Holly trot up the back steps.

"You two speak up now or I'll fix what I want," Margaret said, as she slowly climbed the steps.

"Makes no never mind ta me, as long as there's hot cornbread. I can eat cornbread and syrup!" Sonny exclaimed.

"I'll help Grandmama," said Heather, as she filled the water bowl for the animals that visited the back porch.

"Shot of liquor's what I need, and a Coca-Cola," yelled Sonny, as he popped the screen door behind him. "The jonquils will be pretty this year! Maybe we should clean off the cemetery," he said, for no apparent reason other than the possible thought of his father and Polly. He came from the pantry with a bottle of Four Roses bourbon.

Sonny and Holly sat by the double windows and felt the cool evening breeze blow into the room as the earth cooled. "God damn at the places we've been, running all over hell's half acre! Ain't we girl?" he said loudly. Holly answered with a bark.

"Sonny, watch your language," Margaret said, as she and Heather busied themselves with dinner. The smell of frying fatback filled the house.

"Save the crispy edge for me," said Sonny.

"You'll break yer teeth on that hard rind," Margaret answered, working the can opener. The can of Argo corn gave her aging grip some problems.

"So, Heather, what are we to do?" Sonny asked, as he took a sip of his drink.

"B.O. Smith down at the Ford place has always said I'd be a fine addition to his showroom," she replied.

"He's looked at you since you were old enough to be in the monthly way," Sonny replied.

"Sonny!" Margaret called out, as she looked at him with her hands on her hips.

Sonny laughed. "It's true, Mother! You can forget Bob Oliver Smith, the dirty old bastard."

"I've been asked several times to come to work for Iver Johnson, in Birmingham," Heather said. She was mixing cornbread batter for the black iron skillet that was warming on top of the stove.

"Oh Lord, child. If you left home, what would I do?" Margaret asked, looking at Heather in shock.

"Dad can look after you," she replied.

"He can't look after himself," Margaret answered.

"I can too! Live off sorghum, cornbread 'n coffee," Sonny cried out.

"Just stop this foolishness until after dinner and you've heard someone with real reasoning," said Margaret.

Margaret and Heather set a fine table. It was heavy with skillet fried corn, home canned green beans, home canned tomatoes, a few pieces of fried fatback, mostly for Sonny; cornbread, butter, and a thin cut pork chop apiece. A pleasing silence filled the kitchen. Sonny stood to light the lamp. It gave a warm pleasant glow to the room. The bright eyes of the cats gleamed in the darkness of the back porch as they looked in.

"That was a fine meal," Sonny said, as he folded the napkin from his lap and placed it beside his plate where the flatware was resting. He poured himself another drink of bourbon and finished the bottle of Coca-Cola.

Margaret stood up and took the bourbon bottle as soon as he set it down. "I'll take that," she said, and headed for the pantry.

"I'd had enough after this one anyway. Thank you so kindly for putting it up," Sonny said with a smile.

"Ank! Wait a minute!" Heather said quickly. "Pour me about an inch," she said, holding out her tea glass.

"My Lord! I've got a bunch of drinkers! When did you start that?" Margaret asked, gasping for breath at the sudden surprise.

"About the third bitter cold night of tracking. Just a little, Grandmama, now and then. I don't do it in public," Heather said.

"I hope not!" snapped Margaret, as she placed the bottle in the pantry. She took her seat. "Now you two listen to me, about this work situation. We owe nothing but the taxes, everything else is something we can control, unless one of us gets down sick," she said, pointing her finger at the two of them.

Sonny smiled. "She's right."

"Let's just lay low as the Negroes say, and see what becomes of this situation," Margaret said. "Heather, you can contact some of the magazines and see if they are interested in any of my past articles and stories. Sonny, you tend to what needs ta be done around here in the way of gettin' this place jam up." Margaret leaned back in her chair and stopped shaking her finger at the two of them.

Sonny sat silent for a moment. "Jesus! I'll do the dishes," he said, pushing his chair back.

"And I shall not stand in your way," replied Margaret, as she handed him her plate.

Heather still had not read her letter from Sheriff Giles. She would do that later. The night brought a soft gentle rain, bathing the new growth and dripping from the eaves of the roof with a mesmerizing sound that could be heard in the silence of the dark house. The tri-folded letter remained on her chest of drawers until she could stand it no more. She slid from her high iron frame bed. Her bare feet touched the soft rug at the edge of the bed. Margaret knew her granddaughter was up by the sound of the naked coil springs with their unique squeak. Heather lit a small lamp and opened the letter. Her eyes moved quickly through the routine wording of a letter of separation. She had typed several since she was fourteen working in her capacity as a clerk. It was the second sheet that spurred her excitement.

"To Whom It May Concern: Miss Heather Duncan has served my department, the Campbell County Sheriff's Department, for almost ten years. She holds until the last day, at the stroke of midnight, December 31st 1931, the classification of Special Deputy. Along with Sonny Duncan, they have tracked and assisted with cases as needed in this department. I would strongly recommend her for the position of Police Officer. However, I feel that she is most suited to fill the vacancy as a Detective, as she understands the art of paperwork and accuracy in such matters. She has a base knowledge of Georgia criminal law. Miss Duncan is very proficient with various handguns. Sincerely, Sheriff Benjamin Giles."

"Well, I'll be," she whispered to herself. "The old bastard." She turned out the small lamp. That night the covers felt different, more comfortable as they were pulled up under her chin.

CHAPTER TWO

Sonny slept light. His legs and lower back bothered him just enough to let him know they could control his actions. The several drinks of Four Roses did not knock off the sharp edge of pain. The house was warm, certainly warmer than a good cold winter night. It would take some adjusting to sleep again in the coming warmer months. He left the door open. Everyone knew he slept as naked as God had presented him. On this night, Holly had left the comfort of her quilt pallet at the kitchen door and joined Sonny at his bedside. The dog was restless too. Sonny heard Holly sigh at his movement and restlessness as he turned during the night. He stepped into his drawers and walked out into the hallway, down to Heather's room.

"Mornin'!" he said, looking in at her lying on top of the covers in her thin cotton nightgown. "My, yer a handsome woman," he said, still looking at her. The thin gown clung to her body with a pleasing profile to any man's eyes.

"Dad!" she barked, as she pulled the covers over her. "What? It's early," she said sleepily.

"It's court day. I'm still a deputy, I guess I should attend and do my part," he said. "Will you go with me? You can help me or visit downtown with your friends that work in the stores. You might come up with a job."

Heather pointed to the letter on the table by the small lamp with her eyes still closed. "Read it," she said.

Sonny ventured over to the table and took the letter. "I'll have ta get my glasses," he said, walking out of the room.

Heather's thoughts were to stay home and be lazy, but they were a pair. Still, her mind wanted for once to stay home. After all, she was not a deputy anymore, in the sense that she was wanted or even to be paid. But it was her father who had asked her, and not the sheriff. She lay quietly,

12

falling deep into the last precious minutes of bedtime.

Sonny put his glasses on and opened the letter.

"To Whom It May Concern: Miss Heather Duncan has served my department, the Campbell County Sheriff's Department, for almost ten years. She holds until the last day, at the stroke of midnight, December 31, 1931, the classification of Special Deputy." Sonny moved his eyes quickly over the letter. *"Along with Sonny Duncan, they have tracked and assisted with cases as needed in this department. I would strongly recommend her for the position of Police Officer. However, I feel that she is most suited to fill the vacancy as a Detective, as she understands the art of paperwork and accuracy in such matters. She has a base knowledge of Georgia criminal law. Miss Duncan is very proficient with various handguns. Sincerely, Sheriff Benjamin Giles."*

Sonny looked up, bewildered. He was not expecting this. He carefully put his glasses down on the table and went back to Heather's room. This time he stopped and knocked. Holly was tired of following him this early in the morning. She stopped halfway and watched.

"Yes," Heather answered.

"Can I come in?" he asked.

Margaret was beginning to move about in her room.

"Yes, come in," Heather answered. She was sitting at the vanity with her back to him, wearing her best white long sleeve blouse.

The two looked at one another in the mirror. "I didn't expect this," said Sonny, placing the letter on the vanity.

"I didn't either," she said, holding a hairpin in her teeth. Heather finished arranging her dark hair. Sonny thought it was beautiful. It reminded him of Polly's hair. He had often combed it for her before bed.

"Do you think I can do it?" Heather asked, looking at him in the mirror as he stood behind her.

"You've always been able to do anything you put yer mind to doing, and yer heart in it," he answered softly. "I'd rather you didn't. You know there's not but one of you, and I can't replace you," he said, looking down and then back up at Heather. He gave a deep sigh. Holly appeared and sniffed at the open cosmetic jars on the vanity's top.

Over the next hour Margaret prepared breakfast, coffee, grits, and eggs. This morning there was toast made from store-bought bread. It was unusual for Margaret not to fix biscuits. She saw the three out the door and watched them from the double windows just off of the kitchen. Margaret had the house to herself. This was her time to do light housework and read a book.

Sonny drove after he whisked the dog hairs from the front seat. The open windows felt refreshing as they rode silently toward town. Sonny really did not know how to address the issue of Heather pursuing a job as a full-time officer. She was certainly able to hold her own physically, but a man three times her size was another issue. Heather was smart and cunning. She was one to use her head before rushing into a situation foolishly. Sonny smiled as he convinced himself that he had raised her well. Her mother would be proud.

"Who's on the bench today?" he asked.

"Judge Delbridge," Heather replied, with her arm resting in the open window. The wind blew loose strands of hair about her face.

"You look more like your beautiful mother every day," Sonny said, looking over at her.

"Thanks," she said softly.

Traffic was already beginning to back up as they approached the intersection. The monument tended to slow traffic as it occupied the majority of the intersection. Some drivers had to wave at other motorists and also people on the sidewalk that they knew, calling out greetings. It was the Southern thing to do. The folks of Campbell County and Fairburn were a sociable lot. On this particular morning a freight truck had taken on a flat tire, on the front at that, making steering almost impossible. Holly barked from the open back window at a few strays she recognized. Some of the old men called back to the dog. If she had arms, she would have waved back. Holly was the pet of the local men who sat in the parks and on the benches along the store fronts. She never left Sonny's side, but when they were afoot, everyone had to pet her soft silky head.

"Damn, what a mess! That poor bastard'll have a time with that tire," Sonny said, as he watched and inched his way through the intersection.

Heather leaned forward, trying to see the flat.

"There's a parking place coming out next to Mrs. Sweeney's car," Sonny said, as they approached the courthouse. Sonny bore down on the car that was backing out to keep anyone else from thinking the spot was theirs. "I see the sheriff is gone," he said, as he pulled in.

"Good, I didn't want to see him anyway," Heather replied, as she opened the car door.

"He has nothing to do with you being let go," Sonny answered.

"Everyone else is working until the last day, why couldn't I?" Heather asked, as she closed the door.

"I don't know. Just make the best of it. That was a hell of a letter of recommendation he gave you," Sonny said, as they walked up the steps together. He held her hand. Citizens were coming out as fast as they were filing in.

It was unusual for Sonny to hold Heather's hand, but she did not pull away. She was proud of herself and proud of her father. Holly led the way. The public always cleared the way for the bloodhound. Those that did not know the dog were in fear of her, due to her size and the ghostly deep eyes.

"Mr. Duncan! What a pretty lady!" an old man called out. It was Willis

Smith, a Confederate Veteran. He walked the streets to be sociable and still wore his medals on occasions like parades and court days.

"My daughter!" Sonny replied with a big smile. "Just as pretty as her mother," he added. He gave the old veteran a pat on the shoulder as they passed.

"I'll see you settled. I can't face the sheriff," Heather said, as they entered the dark hallway and stood in line to climb the stairs.

"Heck with this, let's slip up the back side. Hell, I'm still a deputy," Sonny said, as he pushed her out of line.

"I'm one too, I guess," Heather replied, as they walked around the corner. They waved and nodded at the remaining employees and out of town lawyers as they approached the back stairs.

"Duncan!" a man's voice called. It echoed in the hard hallway.

Sonny turned to look, his hand moving to his revolver out of habit. It was Deputy Roger Rainwater. "Hey!" Sonny replied, easing his hand down.

Rainwater stood in the back door to the clerk's office with his arms full of folders. "You got the courtroom?" he asked.

"I've got it! Me and Deputy Holly," Sonny replied. Holly gave Rainwater a faint woof as they passed.

"If that dog had a pistol, she'd be a hell-raiser!" Rainwater shouted, and then laughed.

The courtroom had been aired. All the windows were open, allowing the cool breeze to flood the room as it filled to capacity with people. The court clerk of the day was Mrs. Ethel Cook. She traveled with Judge Delbridge.

"Mr. Duncan, we are ready," Mrs. Cook said from the bench. "Settle 'em down." She took her seat and reviewed the calendar.

"I'm going to walk over to Kirkpatrick's Pharmacy," Heather whispered to Sonny.

"Take your time and be careful," he replied.

The courtroom was noisy. Heather worked her way through the crowd of people standing in the aisle looking for a seat. She returned to the lower ground level by means of the rear stairs. Heather saw the sheriff on the sidewalk as he was approaching the courthouse.

"Mornin', Miss Duncan," he said, tipping his hat.

"Mornin'!" Heather replied, as she passed. She tried to sound as cold with her reply as she now felt toward him.

Sheriff Giles stopped at the top of the steps and watched the attractive young woman walk away. She knew he was watching. The sheriff hurried to the courtroom and stood next to Sonny. The crowd still was not seated.

"Please! Folks! Sit tight so no one can pick yer pocket!" Sonny said, smiling with his arms raised high. The crowd chuckled at his comment. "Pull it in close, we still have people who need to be seated." His instruction made seats for over a third of those still standing. "Everyone else will need to stand along the walls. Do not stand in front of a window, as you may fall out," he said. He spoke so loudly his voice cracked. The people who were left standing began to take their places between the open windows. A pair of small birds flew through the courtroom.

"My Deputy Holly will make a walk around the room to see that you are where you need to be," Sonny announced. The attendees that had been to court in the past knew what to expect. "Check 'em out Holly, check 'em out," Sonny said, pointing and making a circle in the air with his fingers. Holly looked at the courtroom full of people. The dog proceeded to walk around the room, first up the center aisle and then one complete pass around the outer walls. She stopped and looked out the south windows.

"She says there's a Ford double-parked out here," yelled a man standing against the wall. The courtroom roared with laughter.

Sonny replied, "Give her the keys and she'll go move it."

Sheriff Benjamin Giles laughed too. Mrs. Cook motioned for Sonny to call the court to order.

"All rise!" Sonny announced loudly. The seated citizens stood in silence with the exception of a few who moaned with pain when they stood. "The Superior Court of Campbell County is now in session. The Honorable Judge Albert Delbridge presiding."

Judge Delbridge entered the bench by means of a small panel door behind the bench. "Be seated!" The judge announced. The moans were repeated during the process of resuming seats. Holly returned to Sonny's side and sat down. The sheriff stood on the other side of Sonny and watched the workings of the court. After several minutes, Deputy Roger Rainwater returned up the back stairs and came to the sheriff's side.

"Telephone," whispered Deputy Rainwater.

"Who tha hell is it?" the sheriff whispered back, with a surprised look on his face.

"It's the Sheriff of Meriwether County, Louis Gilbert," replied Deputy Rainwater.

Sonny overheard the conversation.

"Jesus, it must be important for him to call me. I don't even know the man," replied the sheriff, looking at Sonny. Sonny shrugged his shoulders.

Sheriff Giles walked quietly and with as little disruption as possible past the bench and down the back stairs. The call had come in to the clerk's office. Mrs. Sweeney had taken the opportunity to entertain the Meriwether Sheriff with chatter about the weather and spring planting and such.

"Here's Sheriff Giles now." Mrs. Sweeney held the telephone out to Sheriff Giles. "Here's the call. It came in on my telephone." Sheriff Giles motioned to have the room cleared. Mrs. Sweeney indicated to her two volunteer women to hurry out, then followed and pulled the door to. The women stood in the hallway and looked out the open front doors at the street traffic.

* * *

Heather had made her way to Kirkpatrick's where she took a moment to speak to Miss Betty at the counter. She then wandered down the way to the window of Shropshire's Hardware. She cupped her hands and pressed against the glass, blocking the glare from the morning sun. There was a sparkling white General Electric refrigerator. The ice box at home looked like a piece of oak furniture compared to this alluring thing called "The Monitor". Heather stepped in through the open door. Her presence went unnoticed by the proprietor, Mr. Patrick Shropshire, as he was busy with several men around the counter. The ornate cash register chimed frequently. It was seed time in the South.

The refrigerator sat in line with the oak ice boxes, cast iron wood stoves, and porch rockers. The finish was smooth as a new car as she rubbed her fingertips down the sides. It was a marvel to behold. The legs were high, so cleaning would be easy. The price tag was less than three hundred dollars. Heather felt how well finished the cast door latch was. "Rugged," she thought. "It would last awhile." Even the hinges were heavy. She opened the thick door and looked inside. Her eyes followed the shelves from bottom to top. There were three shelves, and even a freezing compartment for ice. "How nice!" she thought.

Her concentration on the appliance was broken. "Mornin', Miss Duncan! Can I help you?" asked Mr. Shropshire, standing a few feet to her side.

"Oh! I'm just looking at this refrigerator," she replied, closing the door.

"I'd like ta fix ya up with one," said Shropshire.

"I think that would be up to my father and grandmother," she answered, clutching her small purse and stepping back.

"Mighty fine unit. The power company will even finance it," he added.

"No, not today. Thank you." Heather worked her way to the sidewalk. "Beautiful jonquils at the Passenger Depot," she said, turning back to Mr. Shropshire.

"Yes, they are brilliant this year, aren't they?"

Heather smiled and walked ahead, continuing to look into windows. The southbound train was approaching the city limits to the north. The hollow, haunting sound of the whistle echoed and vibrated from the large store front windows. Dogs barked on the Main Street and in residential yards as the train passed. Heather stopped to watch. Dark gray smoke rolled from the straight stubby smokestack of the sooty engine. White steam spewed from several places atop the long engine, answered by hissing steam escaping from numerous smaller places in the rollicking arm assembly as the three large drive wheels raced around and around. Fireman Joe Jennings and Engineer Lester Holton waved as they took the engine through town. The coal car rocked in unison behind the engine still bearing the name "A & WP" and its issued number "280".

Heather wondered how long it would be before the steam locomotives would disappear with the advent of diesel. In some ways such thoughts made her sad, seeing the world changing. For some the world stopped for a moment watching the train go by. Many actually glanced at their timepieces out of habit, comparing the punctuality of the train and the known schedule. A youngster who should have been in school rounded the corner of Smith Street on his piece-built bicycle, almost running into Heather.

"Whoa! Slow down!" Heather cried out, as the boy slid the bicycle to a stop on the brick paved sidewalk. He was out of breath.

"I was comin' to tha courthouse," he panted, trying to catch his breath.

"Someone after you?"

"No! No!" he exclaimed, still gasping for air. "There's a nigger guy. Down in the woods. He jumped out and grabbed my bike." The boy was beginning to catch his breath. "He asked me if I knew any nigger girls that would -- " He paused a long time.

"Would what?" Heather asked, shaking his arm. She thought she knew what he was going to say.

"You know," he replied, looking flushed.

"Would what?" she asked louder.

He looked to the street. "Have sex," he said, his voice low.

"What did you say?" Heather asked.

"Have sex," he repeated. "I said no and pulled away from him and got up here fast as I could. I did see two nigger girls walking toward there. I told them to go another way. They said they weren't scared and walked on."

Heather looked around for a uniformed officer. She finally spotted a parked patrol car at the gasoline station at Cole and Main almost two blocks away. "See that patrol car?" She pointed.

The young boy looked ahead. "Yes!"

"You hurry up there and tell that officer. He can go quickly. I'm not on duty and I've been let go," she said, pointing to the patrol car. "Hurry now!" She watched as the boy rode to Moore's Gasoline Station and Garage to go and tell the officer in the store. She did not see who it was, but she saw the boy leading the patrol car toward the woods he had come from. Heather had a feeling about the mysterious Negro in the woods. She hurried back to the courthouse.

* * *

Sheriff Giles took the phone. "Benjamin Giles!"

"Sheriff Giles, this is Meriwether County Sheriff Louis Gilbert."

"I'm pleased to hear from you. How can I be of help to ya?" Sheriff Giles asked loudly.

Mrs. Sweeney and the two volunteer women could hear the sheriff's side of the conversation. The heavy door had become out of plumb over the years and opened a third of its swing on its own after she left to afford the sheriff the privacy he had asked for. The three women looked at one another as they stood motionless and leaned toward the door.

"We are as short on lawmen as anyone else in the state, I suppose," said Sheriff Gilbert. "But we're in a hell of a fix down here."

"What seems to be the problem?" asked Sheriff Giles, as he sat on the corner of the desk. "Hold on sheriff, hold on," said Giles. A citizen had come into the administrative hallway and stood outside the rear door of the clerk's office. Giles laid the telephone down and stepped to the open door.

"Yes, sir! How can I help ya?" asked Sheriff Giles.

"Too late fer court?" the man asked. He was wearing overalls and held a weathered fedora in his hand.

"Up the front steps, right here; left and then right up the front stairs," instructed Sheriff Giles.

"Thanks, sheriff," said the man, as he walked away. The sand pressed into the soles of his work softened brown brogans made a grinding sound on the hard pine floor as he left.

Sheriff Giles closed the door, making sure it bolted. He could see the main door was ajar, but he trusted that he was alone. "I'm sorry, a citizen walked up. We're in court right now."

"Things happen," replied Sheriff Gilbert. "We had a burglary down in the extreme western corner of the county. Nigger broke into a house and stole money, I'm not sure of the amount right now, and a .32 caliber Smith and Wesson pistol. Sum bitch took a car too. Now that ain't so bad, but we suspect the same one robbed a small store on the same side of the county, in Durand, if ya know where that is," said Sheriff Gilbert.

"I know where it is, a good ways from here," said Sheriff Giles.

"It may be the same nigger, don't know yet, but the one that robbed the store was driving the stolen car and someone saw him shoot and kill the storekeep," said Sheriff Gilbert.

"So how does that involve us?" asked Sheriff Giles.

"The Mayor of Warm Springs and his police chief are sitting here with me. They have one officer per shift. I have two deputies for the entire county per shift. I can't put a full-time man on the case and assist Warm Springs with a second car on each shift until we catch this bastard. We are asking if you can loan us a deputy or two until we can catch this nigger."

"We'd certainly be obliged and willin' ta pay wages," added Mayor Cornelius Cunningham, yelling from his seat on the other side of Sheriff

Gilbert's desk.

"Two to the car is what we're trying to do till he's caught," yelled out Police Chief Howard Hawthorn.

"I see," said Sheriff Giles, thinking vigorously the whole time. He had thoughts of sending Heather Duncan. He would afford her a chance and get a joke on the boys down there by sending a woman. He chuckled to himself. "I don't have any extras. You know the county is merging with Fulton at the end of the year. I've been instructed to work my staff down to a senior clerical woman by then. Even my deputies will be let go, but they can reapply with Fulton County after the first of the year."

"I'd heard of that possibly happening, but didn't realize it had gone through," replied Sheriff Gilbert.

"I let one go just yesterday, make a damn good detective! Young, detailed on paper, and knows Georgia law well, outshoots many of the others up here. Even works with our dog tracker from time ta time. Just a God damned good all-round officer," bragged Sheriff Giles, smiling.

"Can you get in touch and send him down?" asked Sheriff Gilbert.

"I certainly can. Now, I don't know if the distance involved and the relocation will be a problem or not, but I'll pass it on today. I just saw 'em in town a short while ago," said Sheriff Giles.

"Mind you, now. It may not be a long-term thing, just until we can catch this nigger," yelled the mayor. He motioned for the sheriff to hand him the telephone.

"Sheriff! Sheriff Giles, is it?" asked the mayor.

"Yes, Sheriff Benjamin Giles," he answered.

"We'll put this officer with my senior man. I mean senior man. Old Jasper Brown is in his late sixties and I'm afraid if he encounters this sum bitch, he won't come out of a fight or a shooting alive. Now, the city can't have that on our hands," said Mayor Cunningham. "I'll see that there's a better rate at the Tuscawilla Hotel or the Huff House. The city can help out on room and board, bullets and gasoline. If he brings his own car, maybe mileage and gasoline money, that's the least we can do for the favor of the officer comin' down and helpin' us," he said.

Sheriff Giles gleamed with his mischievous intentions as he listened.

"Sheriff Giles, you don't know how much this will mean to us. The folks down here are living in fear, arming more than they normally do, 'till we get him caught," said Sheriff Gilbert.

"Thank you, Sheriff!" yelled both the mayor and police chief in the background.

"I'll do it! Best give 'bout three or four days to show up. If there's a change in comin' I'll call ya back," said Sheriff Giles, grinning at his slick deed.

"We'll be lookin' out," replied Sheriff Gilbert. "Thanks so much!" he added.

"You're very welcome! Glad ta be of some help!" Giles said, hanging up the telephone.

The three women stood straight and began to walk in place for a step of two, then toward the open door. The sheriff came out laughing as he walked back to his office.

"Don't dare say anything," Allison Sweeney said, just loud enough for the other two to hear.

"Not a word," they assured her. "But, it ain't right," added one volunteer.

* * *

The young boy stopped at the crest of the hill and the Studebaker driven by the deputy pulled up beside him.

"Down there, just in the deepest part of the curve." The boy pointed.

"What's he wearin' again?" asked Deputy Will Stinchcomb.

"Faded blue bibbed overalls, real old, torn in places. A plaid shirt and a red leather bibbed cap," said the boy.

"Big? Tall?" asked the deputy.

"Deep rough voice. Taller than you and skinny. Blacker'n most around these parts," the boy added.

"Stay close. If'n I need help you can run and tell someone," said Deputy Stinchcomb. He leaned around and looked. "You can run to the ice plant and tell 'em and they can get me somebody," he added.

"I'll stay right here," said the boy. He watched as the Studebaker rolled silently down the slight grade and stopped in the curve. Deputy Stinchcomb went into the woods.

Suddenly the undergrowth came alive. "He's runnin'!" yelled the boy, pointing to the woods.

Deputy Stinchcomb gave chase through the thick brush. The young boy did his job. He raced on his bicycle to the ice plant and burst inside the first open door. "Deputy's runnin' a nigger! Comin' this way! He needs help!" The excited boy yelled as he pointed to the back corner of the plant property. The young boy and several men ran toward the back fence, where they saw Deputy Stinchcomb take the Negro to the ground as he tried to climb over the fence.

Deputy Stinchcomb threw the Negro to the ground and hurled a knee onto his back as he brought one arm behind the downed man. The Negro was slick from the perspiration worked up during the chase. Deputy Stinchcomb was breathing hard too. The nickel-plated handcuffs made a ratcheting sound as they were secured around the man's strong wrist.

"What did I do?" asked the Negro.

The young boy watched from the corner of the ice plant as the grown men ran to help the deputy. They were too late to assist in the cuffing, but

21

did help get the Negro off the leaf-covered ground.

"Thanks, gentlemen!" said Deputy Stinchcomb, as he held the Negro by the arm.

The boy noticed that Deputy Stinchcomb's holster had been misplaced during the scuffle. It was riding with the bottom hung in the corner of his hip pocket.

"What did I do, boss? Why you handcuff me?" asked the Negro.

"Right now, for questioning. If ya didn't run ya wouldn't be cuffed! But ya ran! God damn it, now I've got a dirty uniform. These sum bitches cost me two a week at the laundry, damn it!" barked Stinchcomb, pushing the Negro ahead. The three men followed Stinchcomb to the street. "Call the courthouse and tell 'em I'm bringin' one in." One of the three men took off to make the call. The other two walked down the hill to the patrol car.

"Thanks!" said Deputy Stinchcomb, as he placed the Negro on the passenger seat. Sheriff Giles had the forethought to have a sturdy link chain fastened to the floorboard. The chain was secured over the middle of the handcuffs on every prisoner transported. The chain rattled under the feet of the Negro. He began to get antsy, almost thought about trying to run, but never broke for it.

Wilbur Lemons, a strong, strapping Negro from the ice plant, stood by with his white co-worker Sam Duvall. "I sees thad look in yo' eyes! Yous tries ta run, he'll shoots you dead right dere in de seat! You fool!" Wilbur said loudly, as he pushed the captured Negro back on the seat. The heavy brass-bodied padlock snapped tightly through the links of the transport chain.

The third man, the one who called the courthouse, was Joe Booth. He hurried back into the street and yelled down the hill as Stinchcomb was getting in the car. "They be waitin' on ya!" Stinchcomb acknowledged with a wave of his hand as he sat down under the steering wheel. Numerous workers had stopped and walked away from their labor-intensive jobs to see what the ruckus was about.

Mrs. Allison Sweeney took the incoming telephone call. Without telling the other women, she hurried down the hall to tell the sheriff. The heavy elevated heels of her shoes made a terrible racket as she almost ran down the hall. Sonny heard her footsteps from the courtroom above. Holly even looked around to see where the noise was coming from.

"What did I do?" the Negro asked again.

Deputy Stinchcomb did not reply. He quickly worked his way through traffic and approached the courthouse. The young boy hurried along on his bicycle. He arrived several minutes after the Negro was taken from the patrol car. As Stinchcomb came closer to the courthouse he triggered his siren, just a short wind-up. Sheriff Giles hurried down the hallway and went out to meet his Deputy. Heather had entered the front doors and stood silently watching from the cover of the shadows. Sonny hurried to the windows upon hearing the siren's wail. People standing along the walls looked out the open windows. They saw the defiant Negro being brought in by the sheriff and his deputy, resisting and refusing to cooperate. The Negro tried several times to drop to his knees, causing the lawmen to have to carry him into the courthouse.

"Get up! God damn it! Get up!" yelled Deputy Stinchcomb, as he tugged at the prisoner on the sidewalk.

"Get up! God damn it! Get up!" yelled Sheriff Giles, as he pulled his leather police club from his hip pocket and began to flail on the Negro's shins and knees. The two of them dragged him along. Sonny watched from the second floor.

"Bang! Bang! Bang!" sounded the Judge's gavel. "What's the disruption?" he asked Sonny, who was standing at the window.

"Bringing one in," he replied.

"Close the shutters! Now! Let us get back to the matters at hand!" he said loudly. Bang! Bang! Bang! The judge's gavel sounded.

Sonny hurried across in front of the bench and closed the doors to the rear stairwell. The sound was muffled. Mrs. Sweeney's loud footsteps were heard returning to her desk. She closed all of her doors and even locked them.

"What's happening?" a volunteer woman asked.

"It's a bad one. He's resisting coming in," answered Mrs. Sweeney, as she sat down at her desk. "I've never witnessed one like this," she added.

Heather appeared in the hallway and hurried to open the extra office where they put prisoners for questioning. The room was certainly not a holding cell by any stretch of the imagination. The sheriff looked surprised to see her, but he was glad. The two men were just about winded from fighting with the prisoner.

"My! I'm glad you're here!" said Sheriff Giles loudly. The Negro's toes scuffed along the floor as they pulled him into the room and dropped him on the floor. Heather stood outside and watched.

"Take your guns?" she asked.

"No, we'll be all right this time. He just doesn't understand. He'll come around," replied the sheriff.

"Want me to change out with Sonny?" she asked.

"We'll be fine! But I need to see you," answered Sheriff Giles, as he tucked the leather club into his hip pocket.

Deputy Stinchcomb stood looking at the Negro on the floor as he tucked his shirt back into his pants and arranged his gun belt that had become twisted in the struggle. The prisoner lay silently on the floor.

"Would the presence of the dog help?" Heather asked.

The prisoner suddenly sat up and squirmed hurriedly toward the corner of the room. He had the look of a wild animal in his eyes. The sheriff shook his head, indicating no.

"I thought I'd ask," Heather replied.

"Stinchcomb, you got this one?" asked Sheriff Giles.

Stinchcomb was catching his breath. "I got this one," he replied, as he took a seat on the opposite side of the room, watching the cornered man.

The sheriff took a moment to arrange his clothing from the scuffle. "Come to my office," he said to Heather, as he started to walk ahead.

"Not if it's a problem," Heather replied sternly.

"How can it be a problem, when I'm not your boss?" he replied.

The two went inside and Heather left the door fully open. "What is it?" she asked, as she took a seat.

"I've got you a job offer, or so it seems, at Warm Springs, down in Meriwether County. They've got a crime spree on and need another officer to ride and possibly work as a detective till the fugitive is captured," said the sheriff, wiping sweat with his white handkerchief.

"What's happened down there?" Heather asked. Her interest was piqued.

"A Negro, they think, has burglarized a residence. They know money was taken, a .32 Smith and Wesson revolver, and a car. The same car was seen driven by a Negro at Durand when he shot a store clerk and killed him in a robbery. The county is short and can't give Warm Springs another man or two. Mayor says they will help on room and board, bullets, and maybe mileage and gasoline. I told 'em I'd tell you," said Sheriff Giles, leaning back in his chair and blowing hard from the encounter with the prisoner. "Shall I tell them you'll apply?" Sheriff Giles asked.

"Yes!" Heather replied quickly, without taking time to reason it out.

"I'll call right now," he said, reaching for the telephone. "Close my door as you leave."

Heather thanked the sheriff and left his office. Court was still in session, but the crowd was thinning out. She headed toward Kirkpatrick's to get a limeade. The afternoon sun was warm for the time of year. Her trip down the sidewalk was interrupted by the sound of a car horn behind her. She turned quickly and saw that it was Deputy Roger Rainwater.

"Where ya goin'?" he asked with a smile.

"You leave me alone! I ain't done nothin' to be stopped for!" Heather yelled into his window with a smile. She walked ahead and Rainwater matched his car's pace with hers. Traffic was being held up by his foolishness. He waved the other cars around without looking at them and they obliged.

"Say! I'd sure like it if you'd consider gettin' in," Rainwater said, smiling at Heather. He was not much older than her.

"All right! Only to Kirkpatrick's," she said, as she opened the passenger door and hopped in.

"I'll buy," he said. "Can I?"

"Well, all right," Heather replied.

Deputy Rainwater found a parking place in front of the pharmacy. The two sat together at the counter, building gossip for the local socialites and busybodies that saw them. They laughed and chatted with Miss Betty.

Back at the courthouse, the sheriff was making the call to Meriwether County. "This is Sheriff Giles," he said to the operator.

"I know who you are, Sheriff," she replied.

"I need the Meriwether County Sheriff's office, the quicker the better." He leaned back in his chair, looking up at the molding along the wall of his office. It was almost a full minute before the telephone rang on the other end.

"Meriwether County, Sheriff Louis Gilbert speaking."

"Sheriff!" said Giles.

"Thad be me," replied Sheriff Gilbert.

"Benjamin Giles! Say, I delivered the message and the applicant said be down soon," he said, still evading any reference to the gender of the person he was sending. "Can you pass it on to Mayor Cunningham and Chief Hawthorn?"

"I certainly can," said Sheriff Gilbert, excitedly. "Say, if ya see the feller, tell him there's a lot of loose women down here. Times are hard, turn a buck, ya know what I mean? We just overlook 'em unless there's trouble," laughed the sheriff.

"Well, now! I just might apply myself!" Sheriff Giles chuckled. "I'll pass it on. Good luck and goodbye." He hung up the telephone, grinning. "Like hell I'll pass it on."

"Sheriff, you comin'?" Stinchcomb yelled from the other room.

"Be there!" Giles yelled back. He opened his door and called out to the clerk's office, where the doors were closed. "Mrs. Sweeney! I need a reporter!" he yelled out, as he closed his door and opened the next.

"Oh, my!" sighed Mrs. Sweeney, as she picked up a clipboard and her tablet. "Wish me well," she sighed, as she hurried out of the room, leaving the door open.

Sheriff Giles and Deputy Stinchcomb were sitting quietly in the room when Mrs. Sweeney came in timidly. "Where do you want me, Sheriff?" she asked. She glanced at the Negro who was still sitting in the corner. The animal-like expression in his eyes frightened her. Mrs. Sweeney took a seat facing away from the man's gaze. She had brought several soft lead pencils with her. They were her preferred instrument for speed and mistakes during dictation. She had done hundreds of interviews, but none had scared her as this one did. Her hands shook while she waited for the questioning of the man to begin.

"What's yer name, boy?" asked Deputy Stinchcomb.

The Negro was non-responsive. He looked at the floor.

"What's your name, mister?" asked Sheriff Giles.

The Negro still stared at the floor. "Ain't done nothin', you don't need to know my name," he said, not looking at the two white men.

"Got yer legs beat while ago 'cause you weren't cooperatin'. I was good mind ta have raised a knot or two on yer damn hard head, but I didn't," said Sheriff Giles. He leaned forward in his chair, looking at the Negro in the dark shadowy corner. The large windows flooded the center of the room with sunlight, but passed up the outside corners. "You takin' this down, Mrs. Sweeney?"

"Yes," she whispered, from behind the two lawmen. Her writing was very poor due to nervous hands.

The occasional footsteps and conversations of people departing court could be heard as they came and went just outside the room.

"This lawman who brought you in is Deputy Stinchcomb. He's not apt to go out of his way to apprehend anyone without reason," said Sheriff Giles. "Deputy Stinchcomb, tell us why you tried to question this man."

"I was told that he stopped a white boy and asked if he knew any girls that would put out, not in those exact words, but the same meaning. Then the boy saw two Negro girls heading to where this man had come out of the woods. The boy was scared over being forcibly stopped and was in fear for the two girls that continued toward the curve, down on Aderholt Street. You did do that, didn't you?" asked Deputy Stinchcomb, looking at the Negro. "We still need to know who you are. Never seen you before, and none of the plant men neither," Stinchcomb added.

"Who are you?" asked Sheriff Giles, leaning back in his chair again. "How old were these two girls?" Sheriff Giles asked Deputy Stinchcomb.

"From what I gather, not much older than the white boy, maybe nine or ten," replied Deputy Stinchcomb.

"Did you approach the two girls?" asked Sheriff Giles, leaning forward once more, looking into the eyes of the Negro.

The Negro had not said a word the entire time, he just stared at his feet.

"Last time! Who are you?" snapped Sheriff Giles, slapping his thighs with both hands. He stood up and arranged his shirt and pants.

By now the courtroom was almost empty. The Judge, Mrs. Cook, and Sonny were the only county officials present. There were no people standing around the walls. The spring breeze blew through the large room, carrying with it the fragrance of new blossoms on the fruit trees nearby. Heather and Deputy Rainwater were still at Kirkpatrick's. The town was unusually quiet for a change. Songbirds sang and the distant laughter of children at play set a soothing tone to the business at hand.

"Deputy Stinchcomb, we need to hold this man until we can check on the welfare of these two Negro girls. Let's take him to the jail until we can clear this up," announced Sheriff Giles. "Mrs. Sweeney, you can go. Pull a case number and hold your notes for Deputy Stinchcomb."

Mrs. Sweeney gladly gathered her things and headed for the door. Sheriff Giles stood at the Negro's feet. "Give me yer hands! Pull up! Let's go!" The sheriff reached out, leaning down. Deputy Stinchcomb was just standing up.

The prisoner suddenly exploded with a burst of energized anger and reached for the sheriff's hands, pulling him head first into the darkened corner. Sheriff Giles's head struck the hard-plastered wall and he was knocked out. He fell off to the side and lay in the wedge of sunlight that came through the window. The Negro was on his feet and heading for the door. As he knocked Mrs. Sweeney aside, she fell on her shoulder and broke her thin gold frame glasses. She suffered a small cut above her left eye, having struck a filing cabinet as she went down. Her dress was above her waist, showing her cotton bloomers and tied white stockings. She was down!

The wiry Negro hurried down the hallway, with Deputy Stinchcomb in pursuit. The noise and yelling were heard upstairs. Sonny opened the stairwell door and listened. "I'll shoot you! Stop! God damn it! Stop!" yelled Deputy Stinchcomb, running after the Negro.

Sonny looked at Judge Delbridge. "Go down and see what's happening!" said the Judge. The last of the folks waiting for their cases to come up looked bewildered by the loud noises from below. Sonny and Holly ventured down the steps.

The two volunteer women in the clerk's office had put distance between themselves and the sudden disturbance by running into the back hallway. They were coming out when Sonny and Holly came to the bottom step.

"What's the ruckus?" Sonny asked. Holly let out a woof and sniffed the air.

"The sheriff called Mrs. Sweeney to take notes while they questioned a prisoner. We heard them yelling, cursing and running," one of the women said.

The other one added, "That was after a couple of hard thumps, like someone falling."

"Stay here," Sonny said, as he and Holly walked through their office. He opened the door slowly, to see Sheriff Giles coming out of the room, into the hallway. The sheriff's white shirt was dirty from the floor and he was rubbing his head. "What's happening?" Sonny asked.

Sheriff Giles turned, already showing some physical limitations after his head's encounter with the wall. "Son of a bitch is runnin'! Stinchcomb's after him!" he answered, as he staggered toward the outer open doors.

"Want us to join in?" Sonny asked loudly, as he started down the hall.

"No! Stay with court, this shouldn't be too long," Sheriff Giles replied.

Sonny looked puzzled. This was rare, a corner full of scent and a damn good dog and they are going to do it themselves. He shrugged his shoulders and shook his head. Holly looked up and seemed to question the situation. Sonny gave her a head scritch as they went back up the steps to the courtroom.

"Excuse me," said the Judge to the lawyer in front of him. "What was happening?" he asked.

"They've got one runnin'!" Sonny said, calmly taking his post.

"Continue, sir," Judge Delbridge said to the lawyer who was presenting a case.

Deputy Stinchcomb was barely able to keep the running Negro in sight, even with the instability caused by the Negro's cuffed hands. "Bastard won't get those cuffs off," he said to himself as he ran, jumping flowerbeds, terrace walls, wheelbarrows, clothes lines, and chasing dogs.

Sheriff Giles was able to follow Deputy Stinchcomb by the noise of the barking dogs that accompanied the foot chase. The Negro and Deputy Stinchcomb had gone into a dense thicket some distance behind the courthouse. The sheriff was unable to hear them. The thrashing of bushes and movement had stopped. He knew that the Negro had gone down, hidden in the thick privet hedge and canes. A small branch ran through the dense thicket. If the Negro took to the branch, he would most likely come out on the Fayetteville Road. The sheriff headed around the hedge, able to trot and making good time. He would soon be at the culvert where the branch crossed the road.

The warmth of the afternoon bathed the marshy ground along the small branch. Deputy Stinchcomb crossed one too many downed and rotten Chinaberries. He aroused a large snake. Poisonous? He considered all snakes to be poisonous! His revolver quickly cleared the holster and he fired, missed and fired once more, killing the snake. Chills ran up and down Stinchcomb's spine as he took the time to reload in the close presence of the snake. He was thinking all the time, "Where there's one there's another."

There had been nothing but silence as the sheriff ran alongside the thicket. He arrived at the culvert to find no fresh tracks of the man. Sheriff Giles stood in silence, listening. He could not stay in the roadway. He was in the open and could be seen. Sheriff Giles saw a rabbit run and chose to follow it into the dense thicket. The sheriff pushed the dense canes and hedges apart and was surprised by the fleeing man. The Negro again knocked the sheriff off balance. The two men fought in the thick undergrowth. Deputy Stinchcomb was heading up the branch but was too far away to hear the fighting. Separation often proves to be deadly. The angry front cuffed Negro pinned his adversary to the wet ground and tried to choke him out. The strong section of link chain on the handcuffs pressed against the windpipe of the downed sheriff. Sheriff Giles fought for his life, striking the Negro with every ounce of force he could deliver to the side of the man's head. He tried to gouge his eyes, even ripping at his ears. The frantic sheriff's hand found a rock. He grabbed it and struck the Negro several times before he was knocked off. A painful throat and the lack of breath slowed the downed sheriff. The angry Negro was upon him once more. It was life or death! Sheriff Giles grabbed for his revolver and the strong, leathery hand of the Negro was quick to stop his aim.

Shots rang out! Deputy Stinchcomb stopped to get a direction. He picked up his pace at a full run. The water-filled footprints of the Negro were in his line of vision. The flowing water and the stagnant side pools splashed as he ran full out. He was wet from toe to waist. Mud spattered on his face, and cane leaves cut like a razor as he pushed quickly onward.

The Negro had managed to get a round off into the sheriff. It struck his abdomen. The sheriff still fought, coming to the top of the fight. The Negro fired another round, striking the bleeding sheriff in the neck. Sheriff Giles lost consciousness and slumped to the ground. The Negro, cuffed in front, came to his feet and fired another round into the sheriff's head, just above his right ear. The round rode the skull and exited the back. Sheriff Giles appeared to be dead.

Deputy Stinchcomb knew without doubt that he could be heard as he ran. "Sheriff! Sheriff!" he cried out.

The open windows of the second-floor courtroom gathered the sounds of the gunshots. They were clearly heard. Holly hurried to an open window and looked out. Her gaze to the west told Sonny which direction they came from.

"Go! Go! Go!" said Judge Delbridge, looking at Sonny and the dog. "Be careful!" the Judge added, watching as Sonny and Holly ran across in front of the bench. Their footsteps echoed as they ran through the building. "This doesn't look good," the Judge said to Mrs. Cook, who sat close by. "Continue, please" he said to the patient lawyer.

Sonny and Holly stood at the top of the steps, looking and listening toward the west. There was no way to contact any more deputies. Heck, there were none other than Deputy Rainwater. But there was an attention getter. Sonny hurried to Deputy Stinchcomb's car and turned on the siren. The slow, motor driven device began with a low moan and Holly struck a chord too. Then it peaked with all its power.

Deputy Stinchcomb was closing in fast on the Negro, but he could not see him. The frightened Negro ran to the road and put distance between himself and the downed sheriff. Deputy Rainwater and Heather hurried out of the pharmacy and listened. "Let's go!" said Rainwater. "Hell's broke loose!" he yelled, as he cranked the car. Heather's door closed at the same time he put the car into reverse and turned on the flashing lights. Heather reached over and turned on the siren to clear the pedestrians and traffic.

Clyde Veal from the hardware store ran up alongside Rainwater's car as he backed out. "We heard shots over behind the courthouse!"

"Was it -- " Heather started.

"No! Not yer father's 45!" Clyde yelled, as he was forced to let go of the window ledge.

Deputy Rainwater's driving put two cars to the curb. Curious men hurried toward the courthouse on foot. Sonny stood in the middle of the street. Rainwater slid his car to a stop next to him.

"They're chasin' one! An unknown Negro that Stinchcomb brought in. The sheriff is with him!" Sonny said, pointing to the west. "He may be cuffed! I don't know! Heather, get out and see about the womenfolk, one may be hurt. Control this mob," Sonny added, as they exchanged places. Deputy Rainwater sped off. "It sounded like they came from the old Hickory Flats swamp," Sonny said, pointing. Holly had jumped into the back seat and her head was hanging out the open window.

Deputy Stinchcomb found a sight he had never wanted to see. An officer was down. He turned with his revolver at arm's length, his sweat filled eyes looking down the barrel as he hurriedly looked for the Negro. Stinchcomb holstered his revolver and placed his head on the sheriff's bloody chest. There was a faint sound and he could feel him breathing. They were alone with no way to call out for help. Deputy Stinchcomb stood up and fired three slow shots into the thick canopy roof of the thicket. "God, if ever you help me, help me now," he prayed silently, still in fear of the missing Negro.

"Fayetteville Road!" Sonny yelled. "Did ya hear 'em?"

"I heard 'em!" replied Deputy Rainwater, as he pushed the Studebaker through its full range of gears, making corners and almost rolling the car. The siren wailed!

Heather had hurried inside the courthouse to check on the women in the clerk's office. She tossed her purse aside and pulled her revolver. "Allison! Allison!" she yelled. A woman broke the cold plane of the hall walls. Heather started to bring her revolver up, but saw it was one of the volunteers. "Are y'all all right?" she yelled. The siren on Deputy Stinchcomb's car still wailed outside.

"Mrs. Sweeney was knocked down! She's bruised, but she'll be fine," the woman replied.

The halls quickly filled with men from every walk of life, white and black. "What's happening? We heard shots! What was that? Where is everybody?" Questions burst from the crowd.

* * *

Sonny turned off the siren. There was not a sound except for the laboring of the powerful straight block six-cylinder engine. "Slow down," Sonny said, as he leaned out the window. Another shot rang out.

"The branch culvert!" said Deputy Rainwater.

"Sounded like it!" Sonny yelled back.

The Studebaker coasted to a stop at the culvert. "Hey! Hey! Down here!" Deputy Stinchcomb yelled at the top of his lungs.

"Separate," Sonny reminded, as the two deputies hurried to the thicket with guns drawn.

"Sonny! Roger!" yelled Stinchcomb.

"Yeah!" Deputy Rainwater responded.

"Sheriff Giles! He's been shot several times! Bad off!" yelled Stinchcomb, his voice cracking from the severity of the situation and the adrenalin rush.

"I'll get a doctor!" yelled Deputy Rainwater.

Sonny and Rainwater could not see either of the men in the dense undergrowth. "The Springers, they have a telephone. It's closer than the courthouse," Sonny remarked. He pushed on. Deputy Rainwater holstered and ran for the car. The hard-driven car roared off in the direction of the Springer residence. People were out on their porches or standing in yards wondering what was taking place, especially with gunshots and sirens in the small town. Old Roy Springer was where he always was, sitting on his front porch. He was standing at the railing when Deputy Rainwater slid the car into his dirt swept yard.

"What in the name of God is happening?" yelled Roy, as Deputy Rainwater ran to the porch steps.

"Someone was shot! I need the telephone!" he snipped.

"Well, use it! Ya know where the damn thing is!" yelled Roy. The screen door slammed behind Deputy Rainwater as he entered the dark house. Mrs. Springer was in the back and came forward drying her hands with a flour sack towel. Old Roy shuffled his feet to the dark screen door and looked inside. "This place is the other office anyway!" he yelled.

Deputy Rainwater signaled the operator. "Afternoon, Mrs. Springer," he said, as the old woman approached. "Sorry for the intrusion. I need an ambulance," he said softly.

"Oh, my!" she replied, as she took a seat to listen to his conversation.

"Operator! This is Deputy Rainwater. I need Bishop and Shaw's ambulance now! I'm at the Fairburn end of Fayetteville Road, be a sheriff's car waiting!" he said sternly.

"Stand by," the operator replied.

He could hear her getting Bishop and Shaw on the line.

"I have a person down at the Fairburn end of Fayetteville Road, a sheriff's car standing by," she said.

"Nature of the need?" the man at Bishop and Shaw asked.

31

"Gunshot!" yelled Deputy Rainwater.

"We're on the way," said the man on the other end.

"Is that all, Deputy?" the operator asked.

"Thanks," Deputy Rainwater said softly, as he hung up.

"Who was shot?" asked Mrs. Springer.

"I'm not sure, someone's down in the thicket," he answered, not wanting to let it out. He left almost as fast as he had come.

Sonny talked his way into the thick undergrowth. He found Deputy Stinchcomb kneeling beside Sheriff Giles, who appeared to be lifeless on the wet ground. "Is he breathin'?" Sonny asked.

"Very shallow," Deputy Stinchcomb replied softly.

Sonny felt the sheriff's neck. "There's a faint pulse," he said. They heard Deputy Rainwater's patrol car stop on the road. "Roger! They'll need to carry him out by hand," Sonny yelled. Holly stood nearby. Her keen nose was busy.

The siren of the approaching ambulance was heard. The funeral home was just across the railroad tracks about four blocks away by road, one block by crow's flight. Mrs. Springer had taken it upon herself to call Dr. Cecil Green. The doctor's residence was a few miles away. He too came from curiosity and found it was Sheriff Giles who was critically wounded.

"You all right?" Sonny asked Deputy Stinchcomb, as he was very pale.

"I'm scared. I've never been around this, especially when it's one of our own," the deputy replied, as a single tear dropped from his eye.

Sonny took off his shirt and rolled it up, placing it under the sheriff's head. "There, maybe that'll keep him out of the wet." The ground beneath him was blood soaked. The head wound bled out the most, but all the others were just as serious. The gut shot was busy releasing all sorts of poisons into the body cavity by the minute. The neck wound could leave him paralyzed. The sheriff's eyelids were almost closed, a slight flutter now and then, but never fully opened.

The road soon became busy with the voices of men, and then they all hurried into the thicket. The two men dressed in matching dress suits from Bishop and Shaw looked down on a weak and very pasty Sheriff Giles. Life was slipping away. "Get him on this quilt, we'll have to carry him out, too much twistin' and turnin' ta get the stretcher in here. Hurry!" the man said, as he dropped the open quilt beside the sheriff. The four strong men struggled with the lifeless sheriff and finally got him to the edge of the thicket where the stretcher waited with Deputy Rainwater. His patrol car was running and his emergency lights flashing. The sheriff was heavy, for a slender man. Dr. Green arrived.

"Jesus! Praise God!" said Mr. Shaw. "He's serious! One in the head and the gut, and here in his neck," he said to Dr. Green. The men carried the rolling stretcher to the waiting ambulance.

"Here, take my car to the courthouse!" said Dr. Green, tossing the keys to Sonny.

Bishop and Shaw were ready to roll. They were in full emergency lighting and just shy of the siren, when several men standing nearby hurried into the street and stopped traffic. "Come ahead!" one yelled. The evening sun was going down. Deputy Rainwater led the way to Grady Memorial Hospital, followed by the ambulance made from a modified hearse. Both vehicles were in full emergency status as they wailed past the public standing along the way. Dr. Green was distant kin to Sheriff Giles, making him even more determined to try and save his life.

Deputy Rainwater, intent on his escort to get the ambulance through traffic, teared up at the sight of the citizens already realizing that one of their lawmen had gone down. They stood with a hand raised as they passed. Rainwater hoped they were asking for a miracle from God. He continued to press the traffic to respect the sirens and the ambulance, going through Union City, Grays Alley, Stonewall, and Green Gables, running hard, northbound. Then they raced through Smokey Hollow and Red Oak. Mrs. Springer, being the busybody she was, hurried into the dark house and telephoned the local operator.

"Look! This is Cecelia Springer! I know for a fact that Bishop and Shaw is headin' ta Grady Hospital with a lawman that was shot here in Fairburn. Yes, ma'am! Just down the road from me. They used my telephone. We'd be grateful if you could notify the police 'tween here and there. They need all the time they can pick up," said Mrs. Springer.

"Yes, Mrs. Springer we'll try to do that for you," said the operator. "You realize there is a charge for false reporting," she advised.

"Yes, I do!" shouted Mrs. Springer. "But I ain't doin' it!" the old woman shouted, as she hung up the telephone.

At Cook's Crossing, the deputy's car was joined by a College Park Police unit. College Park passed off to East Point motorcycle units just over the city limits. "Praise God!" whispered Deputy Rainwater, as his nerves were growing thin. He had never attempted such a run in his career. He envisioned Sonny Duncan riding shotgun. "First time learnin' you'll never forget, my old father used to tell me that." Rainwater's hands were clammy and a bead of perspiration ran down the side of his nose. The motor units stayed with Deputy Rainwater all the way to Lee Street, where they pulled to the side. Atlanta never joined. Fulton County Sheriffs never assisted.

Rainwater continually glanced in his mirror at the heavy hearse behind him. His mouth was dry as cotton. He could see Mr. Bishop driving. Sheriff Giles was lying behind the privacy curtain. Dr. Green and Mr. Shaw worked to stop the bleeding. Blood pressure was almost nothing. Mr. Shaw had wrapped the head wound above the right ear and the exit wound at the spine. The sterile cotton wrapping had begun to bleed through. Color was gradually leaving the lips of Benjamin Giles and his eyes were closed. Dr. Green applied pressure to the gut wound with one hand while trying to monitor his patient's pulse with the other. The emergency lights reflected from the plate glass windows of businesses as they sped past, hardly pausing at intersections. The multiple sirens attracted the public and they stopped and watched the motorcade speed by.

In the Whitehall District, Dr. Green sat up slowly and removed his stethoscope. Mr. Shaw looked into the doctor's eyes. "There's no pulse," Dr. Green said softly, as he dropped his chin against his chest. "Son of a bitch." He shook his head. "He's gone. He's gone," he whispered again.

Mr. Shaw released his hold on Benjamin Giles and sat up straight. "A good man," he whispered. "A good man."

Mr. Shaw opened the privacy curtain and spoke to Mr. Bishop, who was still pressing forward to Grady. "Kill yer lights."

Mr. Bishop turned his head quickly. "What?"

"Kill yer lights. He's gone," advised Mr. Shaw.

"God help," whispered Bishop, as he reached down to the console bracket for the toggle switches to the lights and siren. The click of four switches and it was over. Rainwater could not believe what he was seeing in his mirror. He motioned with his hand out the open window for them to continue and they did, but not under emergency conditions.

Deputy Rainwater refused to allow himself to turn off his emergency equipment. He continued to run with every available light and the siren. A hollow feeling consumed his body. He had lost a friend. The receiving dock at 36 Butler Street was manned with two doctors and several nurses. They were ready with every available piece of medical equipment to receive the sheriff and attempt to save his life. Rainwater slid his car to a stop and assisted Mr. Bishop with backing into the space that was open among the other ambulances at the dock of the A & B Wing. The Grady staff swarmed the rear doors of the ambulance as Dr. Green pushed it open. The first Grady doctor to touch Benjamin Giles knew he was deceased.

"He's gone. Lost him about Gordon Street and Lee," Dr. Green announced loudly, over the other teams hurrying about with the sick and injured that were being brought in.

The Grady doctor was a man of the same age as Dr. Green, both having seen many years of service. "I'll check him for our records," he said, as he motioned for them to transfer the lifeless Giles to a gurney. The second doctor quickly began looking at the wounds. Benjamin Giles was received as though he were still alive. Rainwater watched as his friend was rushed through the double swinging doors to a room. Dr. Green entered with the Grady team and stood by. Mr. Bishop, Mr. Shaw, and Deputy Rainwater gathered, standing in silence for the official conclusion. The spring winds blew through the tall downtown buildings, like the gentle winds passing through a canyon, rushing over the three men in waiting. After several minutes, Dr. Cecil Green walked from the swinging doors into the early evening darkness. His silhouetted image stood above them on the raised dock. "Deputy, friends." He nodded. "I need not tell you, but it is official. Sheriff Benjamin Wiley Giles is on record as deceased, April 3, 1931." The men dropped their heads in sadness.

Bishop and Shaw completed the necessary paperwork. They were the first to leave. Deputy Rainwater found a telephone. It was his burden to call the courthouse and advise the deputy on duty, Will Stinchcomb, that the sheriff was dead. Rainwater removed the sheriff's badge and holster, handcuffs and leather club. These would be presented to his wife, Lucinda Giles, at a later time. After the unpleasant task, Dr. Green rode back to the courthouse with Deputy Rainwater. The return trip was far slower, far sadder than the trip to save a man's life. Ahead lay the task of telling a loving wife, jailers, other deputies, and the citizens of Fairburn and Campbell County, all while the numbered hours trickled away to the end.

CHAPTER THREE

The two men rode south in the dark spring night, along the exact route they had just come. There was little conversation. Dr. Green was disturbed over losing a patient. Deputy Rainwater was upset over losing a fellow lawman and a friend.

Heather found Mrs. Sweeney sitting in a chair in the hallway, just outside her office door. Her stockings were ripped at the knees and her dress was soiled from the light oil that was used to sweep the wood floor. Mrs. Sweeney held a cotton cloth to the cut on her head. The building was overrun with curious men.

"I'll be fine, get them under control," said Mrs. Sweeney, from her chair. The two volunteer women stood at her side.

"It's Mrs. Sweeney! Someone's knocked the hell out of her!" a man's voice cried out. The room became a roar of voices all talking at once.

Heather hurried halfway up the first flight of steps. "Hey! Hey!" she yelled. Her small-framed revolver was tucked into her waistband. She waved her arms about and yelled again. The voices began to settle. "I'll tell you what happened! Listen to me!" she yelled out. The room quickly became silent, except for the moaning of the wood floor. It gave, popped, and cracked as the men shifted their weight.

"There is an escaped man," said Heather. "He was being held for questioning and he ran. I saw him being brought in. He is a Negro, faded blue bibbed overalls, real old, torn in places; a plaid shirt and a red leather billed cap. And he's skinny. Deputy Stinchcomb and Sheriff Giles are out lookin' for him now."

"Sum bitch that would hurt a woman like Mrs. Sweeney ain't much count!" yelled out a man from the back. A sea of voices agreed. Heather held up her hands to bring them back under control. The sudden burst of a siren flooded the hallway. The angry men turned to look. "It's Duncan and Stinchcomb!" one man said. "They'll tell us firsthand!" yelled another.

Sonny and Deputy Stinchcomb ran up the steps and into the courthouse. Both men were covered in blood on their clothes and hands. They were flecked with pieces of small trash from the thicket. Stinchcomb's uniform shirt was torn, the white of his undershirt gleaming against the contrasting colors. Holly trotted beside Sonny.

The angry men came to a loud roar with questions. "Let us through!" Sonny called out, as he and Stinchcomb worked their way to Heather's side.

"Who's hurt? Where's the blood from?" someone yelled.

"Don't say a word! Do not even move, for what I'm about to tell you is not good! We need your controlled help! Do you understand me?" Stinchcomb yelled.

"Yes!" someone yelled back.

"Get on with it! Jesus!" another called out.

"We had a Negro held for questioning who escaped. In the fight, the sheriff was shot three times! He is en route to Grady!" said Stinchcomb.

"Did ya get the nigger?" yelled Sammy Kiser, a coal yard Negro himself.

"No! He is still out there," answered Sonny, motioning for the crowd to be quiet. A silence fell over the angry faces.

"When do we do it?" yelled someone.

Stinchcomb waved his arms. "We need you to get lights, lanterns, and if you bring a gun you better realize if you shoot this Negro you can be held accountable. But if he fires on you or the posse, you would be justified in self-defense," said Deputy Stinchcomb.

"We need all volunteers to come back here in thirty minutes. Do not go it on your own! If your name is not on the posse list and you kill this man, you will be arrested until questioned and cleared," Sonny yelled out. "Show of hands for those comin' back!" A wall of hands quickly rose.

"The hardware will give a case of D batteries!" yelled out Mr. Patrick Shropshire.

"And Kirkpatrick's will have coffee and food for the posse! Coffee free, and food at our cost," added Frank Kirkpatrick. He had arrived late.

"Thirty minutes!" Stinchcomb cried out. The courthouse emptied quickly as the angry men left.

"Mrs. Sweeney, can you get home?" Sonny asked from the steps.

"We'll see to that," answered a volunteer woman.

Mrs. Sweeney had begun to weep upon learning that Sheriff Giles had been shot. The women closed the clerk's office and left into the early night.

"How bad is he?" Heather asked.

"I'll be surprised if he makes it. Gut shot, neck shot, and one in the head," Sonny whispered, as he leaned close, touching Heather with his shoulder.

"Damn!" she replied softly.

"I'm washin' up," said Stinchcomb, as he headed for the nearest sink. Sonny was right behind. Heather checked all the offices one at a time, closing and locking each door. Holly had chosen to accompany her in the shadowed rounds of the two-story building. The courtroom windows were still open. The evening birds sat on the windowsills. Heather stood at the first window to the south and watched the hustle and bustle of men up and down Main Street. The ones that had been there were coming back and bringing more with them. She slowly closed them out as she lowered the large paned windows, one at a time. The courtroom was dark and the rising moon was beginning to bathe the countryside and the red brick building with its soft blue light. Holly found a small gray mouse and ran after it as it went down the center aisle. "You're a puppy," Heather said to the aging dog. "You're a big old wrinkled puppy," she said, watching the grown dog play with the tiny mouse before letting it go.

The dark courthouse was taking on a life of its own in the light of the moon. The shadows had grown deeper and darker than they were during the daytime. Sonny and the deputy stood in the hallway drying off after washing away the sheriff's blood.

"I've locked all the doors except for those." Heather pointed to the open double doors facing the business district.

"We'll watch them until the thirty minutes is up, then we've got to move on some sort of an attempt to locate this Negro," said Stinchcomb.

"Can you get us some food from Miss Betty?" Sonny asked Heather.

"Grandmama needs to be called too," she replied.

"I'll do that if you'll drive over to the counter and get us whatever she can fix quick." Sonny handed the car keys to Heather.

"I'll be right back," she said, as she hurried out.

"Put on your holster!" Sonny shouted.

"I will!" she replied.

The two tired men sat down in the doorway and listened to the sounds of the night. "Reckon he'll jump the train?" asked Stinchcomb.

"Ain't no tellin'," Sonny replied. "I'll get my -- " He started to say flashlight from the car, but he realized Heather had taken it to the pharmacy. "I'll get my light when Heather gets back."

Stinchcomb already had his, and a set of leg chains. "There's Roger," he said, standing. The headlights of the patrol car carrying Deputy Rainwater and Dr. Green lit the two men inside the open doors. Rainwater got out slowly. "That's his troubled stance. It ain't good," said Stinchcomb. The two men stood on the top step waiting for the news.

"How is he?" asked Sonny.

"He's not," answered Deputy Rainwater, his voice cracking.

"What do you mean?" replied Sonny.

"He's passed on," said Dr. Green, looking up at the two men.

"I'll be damned," whispered Sonny.

Stinchcomb turned away and went back inside. "What's the plans?" asked Deputy Rainwater.

"We're signing a posse in." Sonny looked at his watch. "Less than ten minutes. Hardware's giving a case of D batteries and Kirkpatrick's furnishin' coffee and food for the posse at cost," Sonny said.

"Keys," said Dr. Green softly, as he held out his hand to Sonny. "Thanks for bringing it up," the doctor said. "Shall I tell Lucinda?"

"Stinchcomb, Roger?" Sonny asked.

"That would be all right with me," answered Stinchcomb, then Roger nodded.

Dr. Green gave a sigh. "I'll go now and do that," he said.

"Thanks," Sonny said softly. "We will not tell until she's been told," Sonny added.

Dr. Green cranked his new model car and backed it into the dark street. The bright yellow headlights bathed the lawn around the courthouse as he circled the block heading down to the jail where the sheriff and his wife, Mrs. Lucinda, lived. It was about two blocks away.

Dr. Green pulled in toward the red brick, multi-story late Victorian influenced building that resembled a house on the corner. The headlights flooded the downstairs living quarters where Lucinda was expecting her husband to come home. It was well past the end of his work day, but she never knew what might keep him late. His primary location was at the courthouse. Some nights he would talk about gossip that he had sat and listened to from a citizen stopping by. He was considered a friendly, very likable person by many. He was a man that troubles could be expressed to and get an honest heartfelt opinion. Major crime was something that never crossed her mind. She was always hearing of small-time petty theft, but nothing violent, not in Fairburn or even Campbell County. Lucinda had five prisoners. She stood in the galley style kitchen and dished food onto the tin plates for the prisoners. Dr. Green was met by the aroma of her cooking as he passed the open window. Brushing the nandinas and hydrangea at the downspout, he stepped onto the porch. A single bulb burned on the porch. He tapped on the door casing with the butt of his pocketknife.

"Just a minute!" Lucinda called out.

Dr. Green could hear her coming to the door.

"The jail foyer is open!" she called out from the hallway.

Dr. Green knocked again. This time she realized it was at the private entrance. "Who's there?" she asked, coming closer to the frosted glass door.

"Dr. Green, Lucinda!" he called out. The small terrier dog was now barking. It had finally realized the noise was not coming from a prisoner upstairs.

The front door opened. The cooking aroma was now even stronger. "Hello!" said Lucinda.

"May I come in?" he asked, holding his gray fedora in his hand. The hat matched his suit very well.

"Certainly! I don't know what come over me," Lucinda said, laughing. The small dog darted about the doctor's feet.

"We need to talk. Are you alone?" he asked. Lucinda looked puzzled.

"No! Jewel's in the kitchen. You know Nigger Jewel," she said.

"Oh, yes! Me and Miss Jewel go way back with her fried chicken at the café," laughed the doctor. "Hello, Miss Jewel!" he yelled, looking toward the kitchen. The house was dark except for a light in the kitchen.

"Howdy, Doc Greens!" a woman's voice called out.

Lucinda looked over his shoulder at the door. "Where's Ben?" she asked.

Dr. Green put his hands on her shoulders. "Sit down," he said, pushing her gently into the yellow upholstered wingback chair. He took a seat in the other one. "Lucinda, this is the hardest part of my profession," he said.

Lucinda broke into tears. "Oh, no! Oh, no!" she said, wringing her hands.

"Benjamin was killed today on Fayetteville Road. The man is still loose, they are looking now," said Dr. Green.

Lucinda cried for a minute or two. "Who killed him?" she asked.

"We don't know, a Negro they brought in for questioning," Dr. Green replied. The dimly lit room was quiet and still. "Can I get the preacher?" he asked.

"No, Ben's with God now," she said. Lucinda was a strong woman. She gathered herself. "I've got prisoners to feed," she said, standing. "Ben would want it that way," she added in a trembling voice. "Where is my Ben?"

"He's at Grady for now. They will call me when they are ready to release him."

"I'll see you out," Lucinda said, as she held the door.

Dr. Green walked toward the open door. "I'm sorry for your loss," he said softly, stepping out into the night.

"Thank you, Dr. Green," said Lucinda. She closed the door and walked to the kitchen.

Jewel was a busybody, she had eavesdropped. She sat sobbing in a kitchen chair.

"I know you heard," said Lucinda.

Jewel sniffed hard several times. Tears ran down her dark face. "I'ze sho' did, Miss Lucinda."

"Ben would want us to carry on. These plates need to be served," Lucinda said, as she slid them into the narrowly spaced shelves in the carrier box on the dumbwaiter. The last plate went in and Lucinda closed the door. "Let's go," she said. The heavy brass keys jingled in her hand as she carried the browned steel ring. The prisoners were on the second floor. Single bulb wall sconces gave a soft glow to the dark varnished stairwell. Lucinda led the way and Jewel followed.

Jewel huffed and puffed as she climbed the stairs. "Lawd, deez stairs sho' gets steeper de mo' times I'ze comes up 'em." Lucinda was silent. "You'ze gwine ta tell 'em?" Jewel asked.

"In due time, in due time," replied Lucinda.

At the top of the stairs, Jailer Henry Roner sat at a desk anchored to the wall. He was reading the newspaper. "Evening," he said, greeting the two women. Lucinda and Jewel stood just outside the line of sight of the prison cells. "Women on deck!" Henry yelled, as he stood.

"Come ahead, Boss!" a trustee yelled out. There were no lights in the cells, only the two single bulbs that hung from the ceiling between the cell bars and the outside wall.

"Come ahead," said Roner. He carried a key to the cells and the drop doors within them. Lucinda carried the only key for the cell block door, the last door to the outside. It was kept locked downstairs in the jail foyer.

"It smells good," one prisoner said.

"Who was that? Jones? You got a nose like a wharf rat," laughed the jailer.

"Hope it's boiled chicken and white rice," another said from the darkness.

"Maybe some greens and sliced onion," another prisoner dreamed.

Roner pushed the top black button on the wall switch and the dumbwaiter was heard climbing toward them. Roner opened the door and the aroma filled the cell block with a strong presence. He handed Lucinda the roster clipboard from the desk.

"Same thing, men. I'll call yer name, you get your meal, answer when I call," said Lucinda. Jewel served as witness that the prisoners were fed. Roner witnessed them being accounted for.

"Jones!"

"Here, Miss!" he stepped from the darkness, against the cell bars.

Roner slid a tin plate of food through the narrow dropped metal door that was open in the cell door.

"Bulloch!"

"Here, Miss!" He stepped forward. Roner slid the tin plate through to the prisoner.

"Thanks," said Bulloch, as he and the plate disappeared into the darkness of the cell.

"Sims!"

"Here, ma'am!"

"Jasper!"

"Present, Miss!"

"And Thames!"

"Here, Miss!" Roner slid the last tin plate through the narrow opening. He noticed that both women looked upset as they stood in the dim light.

The jailer walked down the line and raised and locked the drop doors. The scrubbing of the keys on the metal surface for many years had worn the paint away. There were bare places on the cell block walls, from short men to tall, the range was bare of paint and it too was well browned by the presence of perspiration. "You all right, Mrs. Giles?" Roner asked softly.

"I need to see you downstairs, lock up and come down," she replied. Jewel placed her name on the clipboard sheet for verification of the meal.

Lucinda handed Roner the key to the cell block door. The two women went down the steps to the jail foyer. Jewel took a nearby chair and Lucinda stood. Roner was close behind. "Yes, ma'am," he said, stopping a respectful distance directly in front of Lucinda.

"Keep it to yourself until told otherwise," she said.

"Yes, ma'am," he said.

"Sheriff Giles was killed today," she whispered.

Jailer Roner fell back and dropped to the nearest chair. "Oh, my God!" he whispered. "Oh, my God," he said again. "What happened?" he asked softly.

"That's all for now. In due time," Lucinda said.

"Oh, my!" he whispered, as he climbed the stairs.

"Send down the keys in the dumbwaiter," she reminded him.

"Yes, ma'am," he replied, holding tight to the handrail.

"Jewel, will you be all right goin' home?" she asked.

"I stay with you if you let me," Jewel urged.

"I need to be alone, Jewel," Lucinda said, looking at her friend with an expression of kindness for her concern.

Jewel left for the night in a sprinkle of rain. Lucinda bolted the door to the private residence provided within the jailhouse complex. She chose to release Jewel early, leaving the kitchen with dirty pots and pans. The small terrier bounced along at her feet as she checked all the windows. They were bolted. The back screen door was hooked and the sturdy solid door locked. Henry Roner was on duty until two o'clock. He would then lock the doors behind himself, departing for his rest, to return the next day at ten o'clock. The prisoners were housed and not worked, as they were short stay. Longer sentences were sent to Fulton County, Fayette, or traded to Coweta at a minimal cost. There they would be worked, offsetting their housing expenses.

Lucinda stood in the darkness of the bedroom, looking out from behind the lace curtains that hung over the window. She wondered what she would do with herself after losing her Benjamin. They had met and fell in love as high school sweethearts. He was her first, and she was his first. Lucinda imagined Benjamin looking into her eyes and admitting that he was a man, and that he did indeed look at other women. He would chuckle then blush and say it was normal. "Mind you, now! You need ta be lookin' too!" he would say. "But I've never touched another woman." She believed him, there were never any signs of such.

The sprinkle of rain soon accumulated on the tall window and began to find its way down in the form of tiny diamond-like droplets. She slowly let out a deep sigh as she parted the curtains and looked toward the courthouse. Lucinda trusted that every effort would be made to apprehend her husband's killer. The city streets were alive with the bobbing of flashlights and the whispering of many men. She watched as they swarmed around the jailhouse, not a shrub was left untouched, not a dark corner went unexplored. She heard them move on. "I am truly saddened over the merging of the county," Benjamin had told her in confidence. "We'll lose some of the very best lawmen. I am afraid that there will never be a better group and as dedicated to our citizens."

Lucinda pulled the yellowed ivory shades on the two corner windows in the room. She dressed in the darkness. It seemed fitting since her husband was not there. She was unprepared, there had never been a time when they had talked about this possibility. There was not a grave lot for either of them. She washed her face and arms in the wall hung sink and looked at herself in the mirror. Moonlight had filled the room, giving her a ghostly blue hue. She looked deep into her own eyes. Benjamin stood behind her. Her still eyes moved from her stare, a blink and he was gone. She turned quickly to see for herself, even hurrying into the bedroom. He was not there, but she felt his strength. The high bed they had shared was adorned with her favorite ivory chenille bedspread. They both agreed on its beauty while at a roadside stand in Rome. It glided in the stillness under the power of her arm. Tonight, she slept on Benjamin's side. The sheets were two days old, from the last laundry. His musk slowly drifted into her nose. She bent down and placed her face against the sheets. How desperate she was to grasp for her lover. She lay where he had lain and wept.

* * *

The volunteers for the posse gathered at the courthouse steps. A single bulb illuminated the steps and the faces at the front of the crowd. Heather sat with a registration roster and several pens. Deputy Stinchcomb set loose a Roman candle left from the last fourth. It went high into the damp night air, popping and crackling loudly in flight. "Gentlemen! This is the time! Please register for the posse with Deputy Heather Duncan, you all know Heather. You are to read and understand the clause at the top of the roster. If you kill or injure anyone, you will be addressed as a civilian, the law will apply accordingly. You will be responsible for your own injuries, cuts, scrapes, and bruises that may be encountered. The county will not cover damage to your clothing, cars, or any type of personal equipment."

"God damn! Let's get on with it!" yelled a voice from the back.

"Do we know who he is yet?" asked another.

"We do not know who he is," Sonny yelled back. The registration line had already formed.

The men of the community were ready. They all but pushed and shoved to get their signature on the roster. After the first few, the pen never rested. It was passed from one hand to another as the angry men quickly signed the sheet and formed a line to the side awaiting instructions. In a matter of minutes, a man yelled, "Last man signed!"

Sonny stood at the top of the steps and addressed the anxious men. "We are looking for a Negro," he said.

"A God damned sorry piece of humanity referred to by many as a nigger!" a man shouted.

"Get yer heads and hearts right! There are Negro citizens among us. They stand with us on this issue. Is that Big Abe?" Sonny asked, shading his eyes from glare.

The sea of white faces moved about as they parted for the huge black man to step forward. "I'ze ready, boss man," said a baritone voice. Big Abe stood holding a double-barrel shotgun and a set of homemade chains. The men were silent.

"Big Abe is in charge of the Negro posse. Hold up yer hands!" Sonny called out. Seven had come to help. "The whites will search everywhere but the Negro communities. They know their own better than we do, and you know yours better than them," Sonny said loudly. Several voices agreed with that statement.

"Big Abe and his men are group one. The remainder will form into three groups. How many registered?" Sonny asked Heather. She had the forethought to have numbered the tablet lines.

"Ninety-two!" she called out. The posse mumbled comments about their strength in numbers. Holly sat next to Heather at the table.

"That's about twenty-eight men to the posse," said Deputy Rainwater.

"One posse work downtown and two blocks over in all directions. This will cover the cemetery and the jailhouse. Group two search East Broad and the road to Fayetteville as far out as you can go between now and daylight. The other group take East Broad and the road to Fayetteville toward Union City. No man walks alone, even to return for batteries or coffee," Sonny announced. "Deputy Stinchcomb will go with one posse and Deputy Rainwater with the other. I will be here with Deputy Heather manning the telephone and handling any questions and leads that may come in. If Big Abe needs help, we'll certainly hear his shotgun echo across the buildings," he said.

Big Abe was a longtime friend of the Duncan family. He and his father, now passed, knew Marshal Mathew Duncan and had tracked with Sonny and Heather several times. Big Abe could talk a Negro into surrender, rather than taking a bloody stand.

The posse formed into groups of acquaintances more than numbers. The two deputies moved their cars along slowly as the angry and eager men moved into the darkness with a sea of bobbing flashlight beams slicing through the night. Going house to house, they asked and searched every dark hiding place, cellars, outbuildings, even one widow woman's attic that had access by way of a strong pecan limb. Cats scurried, dogs barked, some even followed and joined in the search. As the posse made progress, porch lights were left on and doors and windows bolted. The dark storm clouds moved to hide the moon. By one-thirty the first of the posse coffee drinkers were sitting at Kirkpatrick's counter. Miss Betty poured coffee as fast as it would make in the large silver bullet-shaped electric urn. The downtown posse expressed to her that she should be mindful about who passed by on the street, and even lock the doors after they left.

Miss Betty pulled a long substantial fork from under the counter. "If he's without a gun, I ain't scared of him. Why, I'll stick him like a rat!" she snapped, placing it back under the counter.

The downtown posse eventually returned to the courthouse, where Sonny and Heather had moved just inside the doors. The telephone had been silent all night. Holly lay dozing against the baseboard in the deep shadows. Sonny smiled at Heather and shook his head as he chuckled at Holly's snoring.

"About the job offer I got," Heather said.

"What?" Sonny asked.

"Sheriff Giles talked to the Meriwether County Sheriff, they were looking for loaners during a crime spree in the county. Warm Springs Police Department is extremely short on officers. The chief and the mayor are looking for me to come and apply," she replied.

"When?" Sonny asked. He acted as though he had never read the letter she pointed out that morning.

"As soon as I can get down there, tomorrow would make them happy," she replied.

"Doing what?" he asked.

"Dad, an officer. They want one to work in the capacity of detective and ride with the day officer until the culprit can be apprehended," she said, sitting with her legs crossed and her revolver on her hip. Her fingers interlaced.

The shadows of the morning darkness washed over the area where they sat. She was a handsome woman, just like her mother, Polly. Sonny sat in silence and looked at her. He finally replied. "I wish you wouldn't go. I can't replace you," he said, leaning forward and touching her on the knee.

"Dad, I've got to try. I've done this clerical work for years, except for tracking with you and the princess over there," she said, looking at the sleeping dog.

"Pay?" he asked, leaning back.

"It wasn't talked about, but they did say room and board help and bullets, and even mileage if I used my car, and gasoline and days. You can't beat that," she said.

"I'll bet I can," he replied, looking at her. "Stay home with me and your Grandmother. Maybe Jody can use you," he said.

Their conversation was abruptly stopped by the roar of Big Abe's shotgun. "Son of a bitch!" Sonny said, as he jumped to his feet. Holly came up with a loud snort and the vigorous flopping of her ears from side to side. "He's on to something!" Sonny added, as he felt for his keys.

"I'm goin'!" Heather said. She began to close up the courthouse. The keys to the building rattled in the darkness as the double doors were closed. The other posses heard the loud report and they were coming as well. Holly was first at the car and first on a seat when Sonny opened his door.

"It's something or Abe wouldn't have fired. Hope they've found the son of a bitch!" Sonny said excitedly. Heather held on to the open window as the speeding car took the corners around the courthouse, crossed the main street, and dropped into the Negro neighborhood. The small area of Blacks was mostly rundown tenant houses. A few were owned by Negroes, but very few. Heather pointed out a low spot in the creek line where she saw flashlights cutting through the fog in the low-lying area. "There they are!" she said.

Holly hung out the open back window. "I see them," Sonny replied, as he stopped the car.

"I've got our lights," Heather said, as she held one out for Sonny.

Two Negro men met them on the path. "Big Abe got to him jest in time. He's still cuffed and was tryin' ta hung hisself," said one of the men, as the small group went down the narrow brush trail.

"Downs heah at tha big chiner-berry tree!" said the other Negro, leading the way.

Big Abe's posse of men had the wanted man on the ground. Abe had already chained the man's hands to his waist, and even shackled his feet. Sonny shined the light on the downed Negro. "Abe, that's him," Sonny advised.

"He wuz tryin' ta hung hisself when weez slipped down tha trail," Abe said. "I had a feelins he'd beez down here sumwhere," he added, dropping a fresh shell in his double-barrel. "I shots de rope in twos!" said Abe.

Heather and Sonny shined their lights overhead. The strong limb of the old chinaberry was barkless from Abe's gun blast. The two other deputies could be heard on the street, higher above them. "Down here!" Sonny yelled.

Stinchcomb and Rainwater ran down the trail. Their lights moved about as they came down the dark trail. "Did ya get him?" one of them asked.

"Big Abe and his posse got him," Heather said, shining her light on the dirty man shackled on the ground. The unknown suspect was so dirty he was almost unrecognizable.

* * *

Lucinda opened her eyes upon hearing the distant shot. Henry Roner was just leaving the jail. He too heard it and stopped to listen. Lucinda knew the darkness was far from being over. Jailer Roner dropped the keys in the locked box and wrote out on his time card. He could only give so much. Henry Roner would soon lay his head down and think of the turmoil to come.

Lucinda slid her bare feet to the rug covered floor. She felt every grain of sand that was on the woven rug, making her way to the window. Her fingers parted the window shade from the casing. The earlier light rain still clung to the windowpanes. She was able to see the dim lights in town the next block over, and the store front of Kirkpatrick's that was fully lit. In her heart she felt calm at the sudden sound of the gun. Somehow, she knew that Benjamin would be vindicated. Her remaining few hours were comforting knowing that the manhunt was over.

* * *

"Big Abe! Help us get him in a car. You can ride next to him," Stinchcomb said, as he rolled the man over to get a look at him. "Remember me? You God damned piece of shit!" Stinchcomb yelled. Rainwater pulled him back. Stinchcomb still wore the torn and gaping shirt.

One of the men pulled Big Abe to the side, in the darkness. "I knows him," said the Negro posse member to Abe.

"Who he beez?" Abe asked.

"He beez Ted Griffith," said the posse member.

Big Abe stepped back into the circle of men. Other posse members were coming at double-time. A few had arrived at the scene. "Missa Sonny," Abe said. Sonny looked at Abe. "Dey say he beez Ted Griffith," Abe whispered. "Not frum deez parts."

The men in Abe's posse shuffled the captured man up the dark path. Numerous flashlights moved about in the early morning darkness. Rainwater led the way and stood by with the car ready to receive their prize. The Negro men powered Griffith into the car. The heavy automobile rocked from the force of the prisoner landing against the closed door on the opposite side. Big Abe sat on the seat during the transport. "I'ze puts on deez gloves, buss you up if'n you tries sumpin!" Abe said with a tight jaw. He moved his big hands about, working the thin oiled leather gloves on his callused hands.

Sonny rested his hands on Rainwater's open window. "Fulton County Tower," he said, tapping the car body with his palms. "Be quick and be careful," he added. Rainwater and Big Abe pulled away. The stray and loose dogs chased after the patrol car for a short distance, barking as they ran. Rainwater ran with his emergency lights on and started out with the siren. He was proud of the catch and wanted folks to know the law was up and about in Campbell County.

"Gather around men! Gather around!" Sonny yelled. The posse that was present, tired and damp from the rain that had soaked the grass and undergrowth, quietly gathered around on the street. Posse stragglers were still coming. Their dimming yellow lights cast small circles on the surface of the street. There was little comment during the wait for Sonny or Stinchcomb to speak.

"We need to count off, form a large circle," Heather called out. The hard shoe soles of the men could be heard scrubbing about on the pavement as the circle was formed. The posse members were impressed by the formality of the occasion. "Count off!" Heather yelled.

One, two, three, four, five, on through ninety-one were called out. "And Big Abe," added Heather. "Makes ninety-two!"

"Posse, we thank you for everyone's diligent efforts and thorough search of your assigned areas," said Deputy Stinchcomb.

"We saw the blood and the grass down at the Fayetteville Road culvert," a voice called out. "Is that where it happened?"

"I've some news that I'll only say once," said Deputy Stinchcomb. The posse was silent. "Sheriff Benjamin Giles passed away earlier this evening from the gunshot wounds he received from the suspect now identified as Ted Griffith." There was an angry outburst of comments from the crowd.

"Tell us more!" a man cried out.

"This Negro was picked up by me down behind the ice plant. He was being questioned about grabbing a young boy's bicycle and was thought to be soliciting sex. Two Negro girls were warned, but we never got the chance to identify them and check their well-being before Griffith broke and ran, knocking down Mrs. Sweeney, and striking the sheriff in the courthouse, then attacking him in the woods, where the sheriff was shot," said Deputy Stinchcomb.

"So that's why he went to Fulton Tower!" a voice barked.

"That is exactly right!" Sonny yelled back. Holly sat next to him in the darkness. "We will tell Mrs. Lucinda of your apprehension," he added. "Please thank the hardware and Miss Betty for making your search a little more bearable," Sonny said.

The posse slowly dissolved into the darkness of the early morning. To the east, the sun was just striking the barren treetops, still another good hour before daylight.

* * *

Deputy Stinchcomb, tired and still bloodstained, went home. He fell across the bed and rolled himself in the top covers. Daylight found Sonny and Heather at the private entrance to the jailhouse. Sonny tapped hard on the side of the frosted glass with the butt of his revolver, dropping it back into the holster. Holly sat patiently at his feet, waiting for the greeting from the terrier inside. The small dog began to bark. Lucinda was still in bed. After all, it was still very early. Nathan Wooley, the second jailer, was already on duty. He was sweeping the jail office outside of the cell block. He looked out the window and recognized the Duncans' car. He stood quietly and listened.

Lucinda opened her eyes to the ray of sunlight cutting a line down the edge of the easternmost bedroom window. The shadow made by the lace curtains bathed the wall, passing over her in its wash. Her heart began to race. "Could it be Benjamin?" she thought, as she robed. Her heart quickly told her she was mistaken, Benjamin was gone. "Who could it be?" The small terrier was at her side. Its paws could be heard tapping on the hard floor as they progressed to the door. "Who's there?" she called out.

Sonny nudged Heather with his elbow. "Deputy Heather and Sonny," she said loudly.

Lucinda looked out the sheer curtain. "Just a minute!" she called out, as she began to unbolt the door. The iron hinges on the old door squeaked from the light rust that had formed overnight. The two dogs greeted. "Hello," Lucinda said, looking around the edge of the door.

"Mrs. Giles, we are here to tell you that the man who killed Benjamin is in Fulton County Tower. Deputy Rainwater and Big Abe took him about an hour ago. He was captured in the creek bottoms in the Negro community," Sonny said.

Lucinda stood speechless for a moment. "I'm glad. Did he resist?" she asked, with her heart hoping for his beating.

"No, ma'am. He was actually trying to hang himself when Abe and his posse came upon him," Heather advised.

A tear ran down Lucinda's face. "Thank you for coming," she said.

"You needed to know," replied Heather.

"Thank you," Lucinda whispered, as she slowly closed the door.

* * *

The newspaper published the following: *"Victim Dies in Race to Hospital"*. Posse of 100 men hunt slayer who shot Sheriff Benjamin Giles. The posse of mixed color scoured the county near Fairburn on April 3rd and early morning of the 4th, for the unknown Negro slayer. Earlier, the Negro was called out in a wooded area near the ice plant, but gave chase. After capture

49

he was taken to the Fairburn courthouse, where he was attempted to be questioned for suspicious activity and comments to a juvenile. The unknown Negro injured Mrs. A. Sweeney, senior clerk, and the sheriff as he broke for his handcuffed escape. Deputy Stinchcomb and Sheriff Giles gave chase. The Negro was discovered near the culvert on Fayetteville Road where he ambushed the lone sheriff. In the fight, the Negro shot the sheriff three times with his own revolver. Sheriff Giles was shot in the neck, above the right ear, and in the abdomen. The lawman was transported to Grady Hospital by Bishop and Shaw. Dr. Cecil Green attended the dying sheriff during transport. The ambulance was escorted by Deputy Rainwater and joined by local agencies as far as East Point and Atlanta. The Fulton Sheriff did not join in. A portion of the posse led by a local known as "Big Abe" (colored) captured the fugitive without incident. The Negro was identified as Ted Griffith. The Campbell County Sheriff's Department expressed appreciation for all the men who eagerly served in the large posse, especially the members of the black community under the supervision of Big Abe: Hugh McCluskey, William Miller, Roscoe Cochran, Green Smith, Henry Brown and Telfarrow Hawthorn.

Ted Griffith, Negro, was accused of the fatal shooting of Sheriff Benjamin Giles of Campbell County on April 3rd. Campbell County Grand Jury to convene next week, when the charge of murder will be made. Representatives of the county advise they will seek to schedule a trial during the same month. Griffith was transported to the Fulton County Tower after capture and will be housed there pending trial. Judge D. Hathcock has appointed Edward Wilkins and Hank Cooper, Atlanta attorneys, to defend the accused."

CHAPTER FOUR

Warm sunlight filled the cab of the Essex. It was made by Hudson, a fine automobile. Heather's drive had been long, longer than she had anticipated. It was mid-afternoon and Warm Springs was ahead. She had plenty of time to reflect on leaving home. She had never been out on her own before. Being raised by strong independent people, she was very confident she could make it without any problem. Her right hand dropped to her thigh where she could feel the folded one-hundred-dollar bill Grandmother Margaret had slipped to her as she was leaving. The folded bill profiled under her fingertips through her slacks. Heather saw her father differently today. The gleam was gone from his bright eyes, even his hug was different. She had left home confused. It was a feeling of worry or even of a last goodbye. The crosswinds pushed the sparkling road dust into the front windows that were ajar. This bothered her meticulous nature.

The countryside was rolling, not as hilly as around home. The trees were budded out, ahead of those at home. Heather frequently thought of Holly, who often rode with her on short trips. She found herself glancing in the mirror to check on the dog that was not there. Her arm touched the canvas satchel that Sonny had given her several years ago. The worn satchel contained her heavy waist belt and matching holsters, one for the Smith and Wesson .38, and a shoulder rig for the Colt 1911. Sonny was insistent about a box of new cartridges for both. Cotton balls from aspirin bottles drifted among the items. She had been taught that hearing was important, no matter if others made foolish remarks about how funny it looked. A tiny can of 3-in-1 oil chattered among the buckles, two pairs of cuffs, and leg chains. Holly's old leather collar was inside. She could smell the musk of the beloved dog as she ran her hand inside to check for the third time to see that both pistols were there.

Greenville was behind her about a half hour back. It was a well-built town, plenty of red brick making for sturdy buildings. She quickly spotted the sheriff's office and jailhouse on her left as she came into the small town. The loop around the square was like an exaggerated loop around the memorial marker in Fairburn.

* * *

On the eastbound Bethsaida Church Road out of downtown Warm Springs, Officer Jasper Brown sat under a large white oak in the yard of the Sulphur Creek Primitive Baptist Church. The large limbs of the tree cast a dark shadow that protected his eyes from the bright overhead sun. He was too comfortable and began to doze off. His heavy head jerked about as he tried to hold it up and keep his eyes open for the Negro, James Lee, and the stolen vehicle. Jasper Brown was the oldest of the few officers the small town had, only one officer on duty at any time. Jasper's ruddy round face and a head of thinning white hair made him look older than his actual age of sixty-seven. He viewed the world through two sharp ice blue eyes. For a man of his age, he thought he still could hold his own. Shoot? A fifty-five-gallon drum did not stand a chance at fifteen yards with either hand. He would hit it every time!

Jasper was still looking at womenfolk and flirting, nothing wrong with his manhood, everything still worked. His legs were a little bowed from his hard years. He carried his left arm out to the side since it was shattered during the World War. Jasper's appetite was great and kept his medium build fleshed out, a little too fleshed. His dear Alice had chosen to move on. She left him for a traveling salesman. The son of a bitch sold sink traps with a clean-out plug. Jasper had turned to drink after that loss, during his off-duty hours. He had never had any use for tobacco. "Only fer bee stings and such," he replied to anyone offering. He refused to associate in a relationship sort of way with any woman who used it. "Smoochin' a tobacco usin' woman is like sippin' from a spittoon!" he would say, with a loud laugh.

Jasper kept the dust and crumbs brushed from his uniform sack coat and pants. The black color made the slightest trash shine. The silver from the domed buttons was beginning to wear through on the back sides and taking on a green patina. He looked down at his powder blue shirt. There was a spot from lunch. "Damn it!" he mumbled, as he picked the spot of dried food away. Maybe he was too hot, maybe he was too still. The black Sam Browne belt that rested at his waist shoved the heel of the 3rd Model Smith and Wesson revolver into his ribs. The nickel-plated revolver's heel had worn a callus on him over the years. He often thought of upgrading to a .38 caliber, as the old reliable .32 S&W Long was becoming obsolete. The upgrade would have to come from his own pocket with the City Council bitching about expenses. Jasper's eyes wandered to the paper wrapped half sandwich on the car seat. It was pimento cheese, his favorite. "Should I eat it now or later?" he thought. That was his biggest decision at the moment.

* * *

The black 1925 Star two-door sedan driven by James Lee sped past the remains of Jake Johnson's burned out grocery two miles ahead. The determined Negro was hoping to pass through Warm Springs without any resistance from local law enforcement. They were slow old men and wanted nothing but a check and to go home. James Lee drove slowly as he approached the outskirts of town. Drawing attention was the worst thing he could do. He had done well for himself, so far.

"This car had a good set of casings," he thought to himself. His old granddaddy used to call tires that. "Tha dumb old bastard!" His granddaddy always told him he would never amount to anything without hard work and knowing the Lord. James Lee frowned at the very thought of the old man. The money he had stolen in the robbery was tucked inside his shirt, what little there was of it, and the revolver was secured barrel first between the seat back and the bottom cushion. The light car bounced as it drifted with the ruts. He knew by the houses he recognized that he was getting close to the Sulphur Creek Primitive Baptist Church.

Officer Brown sat indecisively, glancing at the sandwich half on the seat. He opened the car door and propped his foot on the top hinge. That position only lasted a few minutes, and then he got out and stood up in the open door. The presence of the sandwich worked on his mind. His taste buds began to secrete saliva. The life of the sandwich, which was originally planned for supplementing his evening meal, was about to be cut short. He stood under a large oak tree and the paper crinkled as he unwrapped the sandwich. "Jesus! It sure is good!" he said to himself, after taking a bite. In the distance he saw the Patterson farm and what appeared to be Jud Patterson plowing in the field with his two-mule team. A man with a tractor was well-to-do in these parts. A bluebird caught his eye as it built a nest in an aged fence post along the churchyard. A dog barked in the far distance, a very faint sound as it reached his ears.

Over the crest of the slight hill came a black Star sedan, driven by a Negro. Jasper Brown stopped chewing for that split second as he realized the approaching car could be James Lee, the wanted man. He was not too sure if it was James Lee or not. "Why would a wanted Negro be seen in broad open daylight?" Jasper thought to himself. "That nigger's too smart to be caught that way. He'll be taken in another armed robbery by a storekeeper with the surprise of a cut down twelve gauge." Jasper was not about to waste the remaining sandwich. He clutched what was left in his mouth and hurried to the patrol car. He could not very well just stand there and not check out the vehicle. The engine was slow to turn over. "Damn it! Come on!" he said, from behind the sandwich.

The black sedan passed without incident and appeared to be a citizen of non-interest. The slim Negro and the vehicle fit the bulletin's description of Lee. The patrol car fired and gradually cranked. "Son of a bitch! Come on!" Jasper said, as he finally placed the remaining sandwich piece on the seat next to him. He pulled the patrol car onto the dusty dirt road and sped increasingly closer to the suspicious vehicle. "Maybe the son of a bitch will go through the center of town," Jasper thought, as he shifted the car into third gear. If this was James Lee, he wanted a second car.

The car Jasper Brown drove was a newer one in the small departmental fleet. It was a 1928 Ford, Model A. The driver he was following knew the officer was behind him. Jasper had activated the two side-mounted spotlights, one with a red lens and the other blue. They burned constantly unless he flicked the toggle switch mounted on the flat dash. His headlights were on, and he bumped the car's horn. Besides the lights, whomever he was following had to have seen him under the oak tree. The patrol car was well marked, forest green with black running board and top. The words "Police Department" encircling the city seal added to the recognition of authority. The black Star was not slowing down. The driver had little regard for his authority. Jasper Brown could see the face of the Negro in the mirrors on the car ahead. Jasper's driving skills were good and he hugged the car he was attempting to stop. He was so close at times he was on top of the car's dust. The two speeding cars raised a large cloud as they entered town. Jasper sounded his stock horn again, but went quickly for the siren.

The defiant Negro gave a hand gesture and passed a wagon with a mule that was trying to spook as it met several oncoming cars. The wagon driver cursed and yelled, shaking his fist at the black sedan. The two oncoming cars saw the danger with the mule and wagon, and quietly dodged the car driven by James Lee. The townsfolk of Warm Springs realized at this point that Officer Jasper Brown had a chase on his hands. The two speeding cars were roaring northbound on State 41. In less than a minute, they passed the resort owned by Dr. Roosevelt, as he was commonly called. He was some highfalutin' politician from up in New York state. The Star, with its big four-cylinder engine, was matched by the slightly more powerful Ford that Jasper drove. The Ford's straight and larger exhaust pipe had a distinctive roar. The mechanical gear driven siren of the Warm Springs Police unit raised the attention of people ahead. Workers in the open fields stopped and stood erect, watching for the approaching vehicle far across the newly plowed fields. James Lee was now gathering charges as fast as his Star could take him up the road.

"He's goin' ta need some help!" yelled out Claude Allen at the filling station downtown. "Where's tha chief?" he called out to others in the yard and across the street on the sidewalks. Claude stopped fueling the truck parked at the pump, ran to his telephone, and called for the operator.

"Claude Allen at the filling station! Where's the police chief? Anybody seen him?" he asked hurriedly.

"This is Paulette. I'll contact City Hall, stand by," she said, placing him to hold on the line. She was gone for a few seconds, and then came back with an answer. "The chief is in Manchester," she advised.

"Best try and get the county to start a car southbound," Claude suggested, then hung up.

The telephone rang in the office of the Meriwether County Sheriff in Greenville. "This is the operator. Advise Sheriff Gilbert that Warm Springs has an officer chasing a black Sedan, northbound. Citizens are requesting help," said the operator.

"We've got a car on the square! I'll get him started," advised the woman who answered the telephone. The woman ran out on the porch of the office and began yelling and waving at the deputy across the street. He drove over.

"Yes, ma'am," he replied, sitting in the running car at the edge of the street.

"Warm Springs has got one in a chase coming northbound, citizens ask that we head that away," she advised. The Meriwether car hurried around the town square and disappeared out of sight, heading toward Warm Springs, some twenty or more minutes away.

The Star automobile was running wide open, Lee's foot resting the gas pedal against the floorboard. The Negro was driving the Sedan recklessly at a speed of at least fifty miles per hour. Officer Jasper Brown kept the suspicious car in sight. Too close in his cloud of dust and a wreck was very possible, should the Sedan ahead stop. The piece of a sandwich bounced on the seat next to him. The taste of the sharp cheese and mayonnaise lingered on his tongue. On a straight stretch of highway, Jasper reached down and picked up the sandwich, enjoying the very last bite. He had no idea that the citizens had tried to locate the chief, and that a Meriwether County unit was heading southbound.

The road ahead was a cloud of dust, and it grew larger as Heather continued south. In the stillness of the warm day, the dust cloud hung like the heavy stage curtain at the Roxie. The lead car was a fast-coming black Sedan, driven by a black male. Heather did not slow down since the oncoming car held to its side of the road. The black Sedan suddenly swerved about and a loud thump filled the cab. She flinched, although she knew what had happened. The front seat was showered with small shards of glass. The lead bullet bounced from the front seat and fell to rest on the floorboard. "Son of a bitch!" Heather exclaimed, as she applied the brakes.

The Essex slid to a stop in the road. Heather saw a police car up ahead, see-sawing out of the ditch. The rear passenger side wheel was slightly off the ground. The driver rocked and struggled to get it back into the chase. The mica filled dust sparkled in the sunlight as the narrow tires spun, grasping for traction. Heather was angry about her windshield taking a bullet. Shifting from high to second, she slid the Essex into a quick turnaround. Her dust cloud engulfed the Warm Springs Police car, still in the ditch.

James Lee pushed the Star sedan northbound, soon to be in Harris City. In the small mirrors he could only see dust. The officer pursued him with a fierceness that made him believe he was not out of danger. "Dumb white boy!" he chuckled to himself.

Heather accelerated her car and pushed it into high gear. She had ridden with Sonny several times under the same conditions and knew to keep a distance, but at the same time keep the pursued vehicle in sight if possible. Her hand explored about in her canvas bag for the 1911. She veered out of the cloud of dust. Another bullet struck her windshield. This one was much closer. Heather flinched as it passed over the top of the seat and thumped on the upholstery. "Damn it!" she said loudly. "Son of a bitch! That's enough!"

James Lee saw the car was overtaking him. He fired at random over his shoulder, as difficult as it was. It appeared that the driver was a woman. "A woman?" he thought, looking again. His revolver was now down to four rounds.

Officer Jasper Brown eventually got traction and climbed out of the sandy ditch. "Damn it! Damn it! Damn it!" he yelled, pounding the steering wheel. "Who tha hell was in the lead?" he asked himself, pushing the Ford ahead. The siren wailed.

James Lee continued to glance in the mirrors at the car closing in. "God damn! It is a woman!" he exclaimed.

Heather was close, probably too close. She gripped the big semi-automatic Colt pistol tightly in her left hand. Aiming was difficult. The line of sight would be split second to get a shot off. The slide safety dropped under the pressure of her index finger. It felt strange, but Sonny had taught her to fire with either hand. Heather held her pistol at the ready. James Lee veered to the left in the slight curve, and for a split second she had her Essex straight and fired at the narrow front tire of the speeding sedan.

Jasper Brown was close enough to hear the report of the large bore pistol. "Son of a bitch! Who is that?" he asked himself again. The light Star automobile driven by James Lee quickly began to drift and rock from side to side, after the front tire deflated. Heather applied her brakes hard and removed her finger from the trigger. She waited for another shot. Officer Jasper Brown was at a safe distance behind the mystery vehicle. He made out a female driver in the deep burgundy over black vehicle ahead. "Damn!" he exclaimed loudly. He unsnapped his revolver.

James Lee put his sedan into the freshly plowed field within sight of the Oakland Plantation. A Negro woman hanging laundry saw the police business and hurried for the safety of the large chinaberry that shaded the back yard. In her rush, she toppled a potted geranium on the old kitchen table under the tree. The car driven by James Lee stopped hard and quick, stirring little dust once it mired up in the field.

Heather slowed her car and made a straight approach, giving her a clear offhand shot. James Lee opened his car door. Heather certainly knew he was armed. She aimed and fired. The heavy round punched through the edge of Lee's door, making its exit through the window glass inside and striking the dashboard. Heather was at a disadvantage as she brought the Essex to a stop. "Hands up! Hands up!" she yelled. "Get in the dirt! In the dirt!"

James Lee knew this woman was not to be toyed with, by her fearsome display of grit. He had never seen a woman act with so much authority. He dropped his revolver in the dirt as he raised both hands and dropped to his knees. Officer Jasper Brown stopped his patrol car to the offset of Heather's. He was a little slow. Heather sprang upon the unknown Negro, her pistol held at the ready. "Move and you're dead! You son of a bitch!"

Jasper Brown did not really care who she was at the moment. He did know she displayed a hell of an authoritative air. Heather stood behind James Lee with her pistol aimed at the center of his shoulder blades. One round and she could have severed his spine. Her intention was to kill the bastard, given any further trouble. She looked at Jasper Brown. "Hurry and cuff the bastard. Two bullets through my windshield, someone's goin' ta pay!" she yelled.

James Lee looked at Officer Jasper Brown approaching. Heather lowered her pistol while Jasper Brown placed a knee on James Lee's neck. "Cuff him in the back!" Heather called out.

Jasper Brown looked puzzled. "What?" he asked.

"Cuff the son of a bitch in the back!" she barked. The officer obliged.

"Them's tight," James Lee mumbled.

Jasper Brown kicked James Lee hard in the ribs. "Ain't like slippers, ya nigger!" he said loudly, clenching his teeth. Jasper Brown looked at Heather. "I don't know who you are, and a woman at that! Damn good shootin'!" he said, smiling at her. "This piece of trash is James Lee. He's wanted for armed robbery and murderin' the store owner," he said, shaking his head and talking with his hands. James Lee was still lying in the dirt. Sweat was running from his short hair and dripping on the dirt beneath him.

"Leg irons?" Heather asked.

"If I had 'em," Jasper Brown replied.

Heather set the slide safety on her pistol while she returned to her car.

Carefully she produced her leg irons to Jasper Brown. His eyes gleamed. "Where does he go?" she asked.

"This nigger goes ta Greenville," Jasper Brown replied.

"Leave 'em at your station. I'll be in town until I get my job, or my windshield repaired. Heather Duncan," she said, offering her hand to the officer.

"Warm Springs PD, Jasper Brown," he said, shaking her hand. He was impressed. This attractive, well-built young woman had a handshake like a strong and sincere man. He liked that. For a moment Jasper was actually excited to be standing in the presence of a pretty young woman wielding a gun. His large grin soon sized down to his normal heavy-jowled expression.

"Can you get him to the jail?" Heather asked, running her fingers through her hair and then shaking it about.

Jasper's heart almost stopped upon seeing her true shape as her blouse grew tight. "Oh, yeah! I can get him to there and then some if he gives me a speck of trouble. I'd like ta kill the son of a bitch between here and there. There's even a few old wells before the jail too!" he said, pushing the chained Negro ahead.

"Who's ta blame for the first hole in my windshield?" Heather asked.

Officer Jasper Brown looked down for a split second. "I am! I missed his head on the first and only shot, before I went into the ditch," he replied.

"I know the second was a lucky shot from him," Heather said, pointing to James Lee.

"I've got a Brownie, Target Six-16 that the department passes from one officer to the other. I'll make some pictures and get underway," Jasper said, closing the car door. "Best camera for the purpose," he boasted. James Lee sat silently looking down. Sweat dripped from his head. "Sum bitch sure is sweating," Jasper commented.

"May be on drugs," Heather replied. The officer looked at her with large eyes.

"Your bullet hole, who do I see?" Heather asked, as she ran her finger around the hole.

"I'll have ta do a report and it will be ready by tomorrow. See the county about the second one." He paused. "See the chief!" he added, as he stood with the camera held waist high. He made several photos.

Heather closed her car door and cranked the engine.

"Will I see you again?" Jasper asked, as he turned from making the last exposure.

"You bought yourself a windshield," she replied. The Essex rolled almost silently on the loose pea gravel of the roadway, as the heavy car backed up.

"I'm sure now that I will," he mumbled, realizing if the city did not pay for it, he would have to. "I'm sure now that I will," he mumbled again.

The pretty woman he had been momentarily infatuated with asked, "How far to town?"

"At a leisurely drive, about ten minutes," Jasper replied. He was not so smitten by her beauty now, realizing the windshield would probably come from his pay check.

Heather moved the car gently ahead. She reached up again and touched the delicate holes in her windshield. "Damn it!" she mumbled. Her 1911 found its place safely in the cover of her canvas satchel. The road ahead offered a shady cover from the late sun. She stopped and replaced the two spent rounds in the magazine that occupied the pistol. "Two down, forty-eight left," she mumbled. The hard tires of her car hummed as they crossed the short bridge at Rocky Ford Branch. The drive into the quaint town was peaceful. It took her the entire distance to calm down.

*   *   *

The dusty Warm Springs Police car moved ahead. Officer Jasper Brown and his prisoner were about twenty-five minutes away from the county jail. There was no conversation between the two men. James Lee never looked at the officer, but Jasper Brown certainly kept a watch on the dangerous Negro. The roadway sloped down to the shallow crossing at Handco Creek. Brown's Ford gave rise to a cloud of steam as the hot exhaust pipe skimmed across the clear rushing water.

"Can I have some water?" asked James Lee, looking down.

"Shit! Don't give me that story! I give you a chance, hell! You'd be off and running!" replied the officer. He slapped the prisoner hard on the left thigh. "But I'm sure yer goin' ta tell 'em all about how a damn nice lookin' white woman took yer ass down," he said loudly, followed by a loud laugh. Jasper saw his police lights were still on. He reached over and turned them off as they approached Harris City. The road at Harris City split the trip, one road went to Woodbury to the east, and the other to the west went to Tigner's Cross Roads and on to LaGrange. "You sure I can't just kill you somewhere?" Jasper Brown asked, looking over at the Negro.

James Lee did not reply. He thought to himself, "You white son of a bitch."

The Meriwether County Deputy was approaching at a high rate of speed. He too was running with his lights on. Jasper Brown saw him up ahead at the crossroads. The siren wailed as he took the intersection. Jasper blinked his headlights and the oncoming deputy killed his emergency lights and began to slow down. The two officers met on the culvert at Jack's Creek.

"In a hurry?" asked Jasper, his left arm resting in the open window.

"The townsfolk were tellin' you had a chase comin' north," replied the deputy. Dust drifted across the cars.

"Got me a big 'un!" Jasper Brown pointed to James Lee. The deputy looked at the Negro. "This is James Lee, wanted by y'all for armed robbery and murder," Jasper boasted.

The deputy raised himself up in the seat and looked at the prisoner. "No shit!" he said.

"That be him, cuffed in the back and leg irons," Jasper bragged.

"Need any help gettin' him to the jail?" asked the deputy.

"I've got him," replied Jasper. "Ya should have been there! A woman took him down! I got in a ditch, she took a bullet through the windshield, and then she went wild after this nigger. Had him run in the field south of Oakland Plantation and shot it out with him!" said Jasper. "She's a looker!" he added.

"No shit!" replied the deputy.

"Say! She reminded me of that woman, uh, on that magazine out of Campbellton. The Selman woman." Jasper shook his head in appreciation at the recollection of Margaret's photograph on the cover.

"I must have missed that one," replied the deputy.

"Oh! She was a handsome, trim built woman, racy for her time," Jasper Brown said, shaking his head and smiling as he looked into the distance and recalled Margaret's curves and womanly attributes.

"I'm headin' south, maybe I'll get a look at this woman," said the deputy, as he began to pull away.

"Say! Reckon you could get his car pulled in to the county's garage? Bein' in a murder, I'm sure them lawyers will want to have a look at it in due time," said Jasper.

"I can do that for you. You did make some pictures?" asked the Meriwether deputy.

"I certainly did," Jasper bragged, holding up the box camera.

Officer Brown continued north with his catch. At the crossroads in Harris City, he paused long enough for anyone who was out and about to see his catch from a distance.

* * *

Heather rolled into the sleepy little town of Warm Springs. She crossed the railroad tracks and found herself in Bullochville. They looked like one town to her. She crossed back over the tracks and soon found the police station. Her windshield with two bullet holes was already drawing onlookers. There was plenty of parking in front of the door, along the brick sidewalk. "I'll see about my damn windshield," she said to herself, getting out of the dust covered Essex. There were families in town, even as late as it was, some in wagons and others riding in the beds of every type of truck imaginable. Heather had made eye contact with an old man who was sitting in the last remains of a straight chair in front of a store. He waved with a two-finger salute. She returned a nod.

"They ain't there," the old man called out.

"Oh!" she replied, as she got out.

"Chief's gone home, officer's north on a car chase," he said loudly, not moving from his comfortable position.

"I know!" replied Heather. She walked to the door anyway. He was right, the door was locked.

The men looked at her with excitement. A woman in pants, that was something else. The women looked and began to elbow their men. She instantly became the talk of the town.

"Damn!" Heather mumbled, as she shook the door hard.

"Note pad in the mail box," the old man pointed out, still in his chair. The folded tow sacks he was sitting on touched the sidewalk on one side.

"Thanks!" Heather called back, taking a short pencil and the tablet. "Nine o'clock, here. My windshield was shot out by your officer!" she wrote, then signed the note "H. Duncan".

There were people looking at her windshield from a distance, and eyeing her too.

"Where's the cleanest place to sleep?" she asked the old man.

"Bein' a woman, I'd stay at the J.C. Blakely. It's small, but the widow runs a clean bed," said the old man. He pointed down the street.

"Thanks!" Heather replied, returning to the car. The Essex sat on a slight incline, making the car seat slightly higher than normal. Her pants stretched around her butt as she raised her leg to get in. An old man across the street at the gas station almost swallowed his tobacco.

The Meriwether deputy came into town in a cloud of dust. He saw the Essex with the two bullet holes. He took the opportunity to look at Heather as he drove past slowly and liked what he saw.

Heather backed into the street. "Southern?" she asked the old man in the chair.

"I ain't no damn Yankee!" he replied, looking up.

"No, no! I mean the railroad," she said, smiling.

"Central of Georgia," he said, with a chuckle.

Heather waved and pulled ahead to the J.C. Blakely Dry Goods & Rooms.

* * *

The afternoon sun was close to the tops of the western trees. "You'll get there in time for the evening meal!" said Jasper Brown, as his Ford took the last incline on the south side of Greenville. James Lee only grunted. "I was in Atlanta at the Federal Pen, now that's the big house, where the real criminals stay. Say! You'll be there, if the jury of yer peers don't just hang your evil soul here. It was Christmas of 1919. The guards come around pushin' a big two-tiered metal cart. It had a huge pot on the top shelf and a stack of metal plates. The old boy stuck a boiled turkey neck with a big fork and flopped it on a plate, put two slices of white bread, and for dessert took an orange from the tier below. That's Christmas dinner! That turkey neck looked like a pony's dick!" Jasper laughed. "Imagine gnawing on that!"

The Ford pulled in at the county jail just off the square.

* * *

Claude Allen at the filling station was closing up for the night. Business was slow and everyone had left town except for those who lived among the downtown businesses. Claude wiped the grease from his hands with a rag soaked in mineral spirits as he stood in the open doorway of his mechanic bay. The late sun was creating a beautiful effect on the newly budding treetops toward Pine Mountain. The daily crowd of talkers and Coke drinkers had already come and gone. The well-worn bench where they congregated was lonely. The morning paper was left to watch the night. It had the heavy company of an ancient brick on top of it. Claude saw the Meriwether car go slowly past across the tracks and disappear out of sight into Bullochville.

"Must be a storm comin'," he thought to himself. The scavenging strays were already out checking their alleys and the few trash cans on the main street. The dampened rag went into this hip pocket as he closed one door at a time. The heavy hinges moaned from the load of the old sagging door. A car came to rest on the gravel lot, just a few feet behind him.

"Early, ain't it?" asked a voice.

Claude turned to greet the new arrival. It was the Meriwether deputy.

"Can you go north, just shy of the Oakland Plantation, and get the black Star sedan from the edge of the field? It needs to be taken to the county garage," said the deputy.

Claude looked at him, fastening the heavy padlock. "Can it be driven?" he asked.

"I'm sure it could be, if you change the tire that was shot out" replied the deputy.

"Ride me up there and I'll follow you to the garage, then you can run me back," said Claude.

"Hop in!" said the deputy, opening the passenger side door. The lock on the outside was broken.

Claude Allen locked the door to his small business and sat down in the patrol car. "This'll be cheaper than me pullin' tha damn thing up there. By tha mile, ya know." He pulled the door closed.

The deputy moved the well-worn car out at a considerable speed. They both looked up the long drive toward the resort. "Them's got money I'll bet!" Claude said, as they passed.

"I'm sure they do," replied the deputy.

"Will this thing run?" Claude asked. He had already heard a motor tick, maybe a valve or a spring getting weak. "Never been in one runnin' lights," he said loudly, trying to overcome the wind noise.

The deputy reached down and turned on his lights and then the siren. It moaned slowly, and the longer it turned the louder it got, until it really sounded like the voice of authority. The sheriff's car hugged the road, leaving a cloud of dust behind. It was almost dark. The dust was only seen when the deputy touched his brake lights. The dim dash lights from the instrumentation lit their faces with a ghostly yellow. The heavy car moved under the two passengers with the comfort of a floating sofa.

"It's doin' pretty good!" Claude said loudly. He still heard the tick in the engine.

"It'll run down most any bootlegger in this county!" replied the deputy. They had already run about a mile with the lights and siren on. He turned them off. "No need gettin' tha countryside excited," he said, letting off of the gas pedal. Claude did not say anything about the tick.

The skid and slide marks were still strong in the dirt of the road as they approached. "What happened?" Claude asked, resting his sweaty arm in the open window.

"Jasper Brown got after a nigger and it turned out ta be James Lee. Some woman's windshield was shot out in the chase. He took a ditch and the mystery woman," he grinned and shook his head. "She turned on Lee and run his ass ta the ground. Shot at him, then held him 'till Jasper could cuff him."

Claude looked at him in wide-eyed surprise. He had seen the woman and her car in front of the police department earlier. "That looker?" he asked.

"Did ya get a look at her?" the deputy asked.

"I sho' did!" replied Claude.

The deputy stopped alongside the ditch where the Sedan had come to rest in the fresh plowed field. "Ya missed it!" he said, in a bragging tone.

Claude made his way across the deep ruts in the poor light afforded by the headlights. He looked inside. "No keys!"

"Hot wire tha damn thing!" the deputy yelled back.

"Then I'll see you at the county garage," Claude yelled back. The deputy pulled ahead, leaving him to fend for himself.

The Star was easy to wire. Claude kept a set of small pliers in his hip pocket. A jump here and there and he was listening to a running motor. The light car easily rocked back and forth until the traction wheels got a strong hold of solid ground. Claude eventually caught up with the deputy. The two cars entered the square well after everyone had closed for the evening. The deputy opened the locked gate and Claude drove the recovered Star through, parking it off to the side in the ankle high grass. The ride back to Warm Springs was slower than the one coming north.

* * *

The smooth-running Essex pulled head-on against the high steps leading up to J.C. Blakely Dry Goods & Rooms. Heather stopped the engine and sat looking at the dimly lit business. She rolled the windows up as the dust created by a young boy sweeping the porch above her caused a cloud of trash that was apt to drift into the car. There was little business to be seen. Hers was the only vehicle nearby. The single hanging lightbulb was becoming more prominent as the evening grew darker. Heather tucked her canvas satchel under the front edge of the seat in the growing darkness of the floorboard.

The young boy, consumed by the task at hand, minded every stroke of the blue-handled, Blu-J Broom. The white apron he wore was all consuming. The bib was dropped down in the front and the bottom hem almost touched his feet. Heather stood at the bottom step waiting for him to allow her to pass. She cleared her throat. The boy looked up, holding the broom that was almost as tall as he was.

"Hello! Welcome to J.C. Blakely Dry Goods & Rooms," he said eagerly.

Heather stood looking up. "Are you Mr. Blakely?" she asked, with a smile. The light from the porch bulb glowed across her face.

"Oh, no! I'm just the handy boy," he said.

She took the opportunity to climb the steps.

"Gee! You're pretty!" he said, looking at her as she climbed the steps.

Heather stopped in front of him. "And you're bold to be so young," she said, looking into his sparkling eyes. He blushed and looked down. She reached out and pulled his chin back up. "There's your mistake, keep your eye contact," she said, smiling. "I need a room." She looked in through the open doors.

"Mrs. Blakely will be happy to fix you up," said the boy.

"Thanks!" Heather replied, as she quietly walked into the store.

The store was a large room with merchandise hung from the walls and the ceiling. Aged smoked shelves with divided cubbyholes covered the long wall behind the main counter. There were refrigerated cases on the back inside wall, but no fresh meats. She was alone in the room. The sound of the corn broom outside filled the stillness. "Hello!" Heather called out.

A reply came from the back, down a dimly lit hallway. The aroma of vegetables and fried meats drifted toward the open front doors. "Just a minute!" a woman's voice called out.

Heather stood at the counter and looked at the assorted notions displayed on the shelves. "May I help you?" a woman's voice broke the stillness.

Heather turned. "I'd like a room," she said.

"Be long?" asked the woman.

"I'm not sure, but it could be long. It just depends," Heather replied.

The woman dried her hands on a white flour sack towel. "I'm Mrs. Blakely, widower. I run the business," said the woman.

"I'm Heather Duncan. I'm in town looking for a job," she said.

"I have four rooms, three are taken for the night, two of them are long term," replied Mrs. Blakely.

"How much?" Heather asked.

"One dollar short time without meals, fifty cents a meal. I only serve two a day, breakfast and dinner," said Mrs. Blakely.

"I'd like to look at the beds," Heather replied. "And is there a bath?"

"My place ain't buggy and there's a bath shared for all four rooms. My food is needing me," replied Mrs. Blakely. She handed Heather the key to Room One. "Look at it and let me know, I'll be in the kitchen, follow yer nose," she snipped, as she turned and hurried away. The young boy had come inside and heard the conversation.

"She's busy. She don't mean nothin'," he said, taking off his apron.

Heather looked down. "Where's your shoes?" she asked.

"I ain't got no shoes," he said. "I'll have some by cold weather," he replied. "I'm savin' for 'em."

Heather looked down again.

"Can I show you Room One?" he asked, holding out his hand.

"You may," she replied.

"Follow me. The stairs is not well lit," he said, as he led the way.

"Are you a Blakely?" Heather asked.

"No, I'm a Cotton," he replied, as he climbed the steps ahead of her. The back cuffs of his pants had long since been worn away.

"How much you lackin' on your shoe money?" Heather asked softly.

"I got sixty cents and they cost two dollars for new ones like I want, a dollar for used ones," he replied.

Heather was silent. The aged steps popped and cracked under their weight. A small kerosene lamp was already burning on a table in the hallway. The yellowed wallpaper at one time had been grand. Heather reached out and touched the floral design. It had a soft flocking in a contrasting color.

"It'll be clean. She don't let nothin' get dirty," the boy said, as he put the key into the deadbolt on the door.

The lamp sat next to a small bouquet of early snowballs. The small white blossoms looked yellow in the lamplight.

"What's your name?" Heather asked.

"Buddy Cotton," he said, pushing the door open. He disappeared inside and pulled the overhead chain, causing the single bulb to illuminate the large rectangular room. It had the same wallpaper as the hallway. "You can look, but they ain't no bedbugs, maybe a wood roach now and then, but no bedbugs," he said proudly.

Heather did not take his word, she explored about the covers and the bed frame. She even got down and looked under the high bed. There was nothing but a polished dustless floor.

"She works my butt off. Oh, I'm sorry. She works me hard keepin' these rooms clean," said Buddy. His red hair and freckles were strong in the light of the single bulb.

"I'll take it!" she said, as she stood.

"Her kitchen's clean too," he added.

"I'm sure it is," she replied, heading for the door. "What days do you work?" Heather asked, as they descended the steps.

"Tuesday through Friday, here. I get extra around town," he replied, behind her. Even at his age he noticed her nice figure.

"Can ya get clean water?" she asked.

"For what?" he asked.

"Wash my car twice and dust the inside, I'll give you your shoe money. That will be two dollars less sixty cents. A dollar forty," she said, taking the last step.

"I can wash it at Cold Spring Branch! It's wide and cars can pass by. I can get towels ta dry it off with!" Buddy said eagerly.

"Do you stay here?" Heather asked.

"No, I'm leaving. It's only about two miles out the Boykin Place Road," he said.

"Let me get in my room and I'll take you home, to your driveway," Heather said, stepping into the kitchen. Mrs. Blakely and her other paying guests, all men, were seated at the table. They stood up and eyed Heather hard, with the wolf pack in a cattle corral look.

"Thank you, gentlemen," said Heather. They took their seats and whispered among themselves. "I'd like to take the room," she said.

"Dollar up front," replied Mrs. Blakely.

Heather pulled a dollar from her pocket. "I'll have the bath at eleven o'clock. Be sure you're out and it's aired," she announced. "Clean up after yourselves. No beards in the sink, no piss on the floor or the toilet seat," Heather announced, leaving the kitchen. Buddy looked shocked at the pretty woman's boldness among a room full of men. "May I buy a few items?" Heather asked Mrs. Blakely.

The woman paused and placed her fork on the side of her plate. "That will be fine," Mrs. Blakely replied, as she stood.

Heather followed Mrs. Blakely to the store room. The woman stood behind the counter. "I'd like a penny's worth of crackers," Heather said.

Mrs. Blakely pointed to the tongs and the clear cracker jar. "Four whole crackers!" she said. Heather made herself at home, carefully placing four whole crackers in a white paper sack.

"A nickel's worth of cheese, a small tin of salmon, and a Chero Cola," said Heather.

"The drink is in the box." The woman pointed to the center of the room. The large heavy cheese knife was raised and Mrs. Blakely dialed up a nickel's worth on the gage ring below. She carefully pushed the heavy knife through the sharp orange cheese. It landed on a sheet of waxed paper. Mrs. Blakely bagged the items, except for the cold drink. The bottle sat on the counter with beads of condensation forming. "That'll be twenty-one cents."

"Out of a quarter," Heather replied, as she placed the coin on the counter and pushed it toward the woman. The ornate brass cash register reported the sale with a loud ring.

"And four cents," replied Mrs. Blakely, pushing four pennies back.

"Thank you," said Heather. "Let's get my bags from the boot," she said to Buddy, as they walked out of the store through the front door. The coiled bell sounded off loudly.

"It's Buddy!" the boy yelled. Mrs. Blakely shook her head at hearing the boy, as she had just been in the store with them.

Sparse streetlights illuminated the main street. All the businesses were closed, except those that served food and drink, or provided room and board. "How many places have rooms?" Heather asked Buddy.

"There's this one, then the Huff House in Bullochville, and the Tuscawilla Hotel over there," he said, pointing to the larger establishment.

Heather had opened the front car door and pulled her canvas bag from the darkness. Buddy opened the boot and struggled out two hard-sided suitcases. He closed the lid with great respect for the car.

"We got a Model A, five of us, but it carries all of us where we need ta go," he volunteered. "I like the colors!" he said, standing back and admiring. "Where ya from?" he asked.

"In due time, Buddy," she said, looking back from the steps and smiling. Buddy hurried along. He did not see the bullet holes.

"Most park out back," he said, breathing hard as he carried the heavy bags. They pushed open the dark door of the closed store.

"I'll be out front for now," Heather said, as she led the way. The floor squeaked as they made their way down the hall toward the stairs.

"Buddy! I'm not paying you extra for this!" Mrs. Blakely cried out from the table.

"Yes, ma'am!" he called back. "I'm doin' this cause --" he was interrupted by Heather, who had suddenly turned around.

"Because I'm pretty and you like my butt," she snapped.

The boy blushed in the darkness and dropped his head, holding the two heavy bags. "There's an art to what you're trying to do and you've not gotten the knack of it yet," she said. "You got any sisters?"

"No, ma'am," he said.

"You need to find you a young girl who hasn't any brothers and then try to be hers," she said encouragingly.

"Yes, ma'am," he said, as they climbed the stairs.

Heather bounced the heavy satchel on the bed. Buddy set the two bags down. "Go down to the car, I'll be down soon," Heather instructed. She wrapped the cold drink in a heavy bath towel that had been placed on the bed. It would keep it cold for a good long time, a trick she had picked up from Sonny.

"Yes, ma'am," Buddy said, leaving the room.

Heather took her Campbell County badge and clipped it on her belt, then retrieved her revolver from the canvas bag. She hid the 1911 under the bed pillows. The deadbolt on her room was reassuring, combined with the box lock mounted on the door. Heather bounded down the stairs and out into the night air, where Buddy stood by the passenger side door. "Get in!" she said, opening the door.

Buddy eagerly opened the door and sat down. "Jesus!" he exclaimed, looking at the two bullet holes in the windshield. "Where did those come from?" he asked, running his index finger around each of the holes.

Heather cranked the Essex. "One from Officer Jasper Brown." She pointed to the top hole. "The other from a Negro now in custody." She backed the car into the dark street. "Which way?" she asked. Buddy was still looking at the holes. "Which way?" she asked again.

"To the corner and east. That's the old Boykin Place Road," Buddy said, lowering his window. He ran his hands over the taut upholstered seats. "This is swanky!"

"It gets me there," she replied. The headlights flooded the road ahead from ditch to ditch.

"When can I wash it?" he asked, with his arm resting in the open window. Lightning bugs seemed to rise from the fresh plowed earth and burst forth in all their splendor as far as the eye could see. "They stink! We catch 'em and put 'em in a fruit jar with a rag on top. They get air and stay the night with us in our room. We let 'em out in the morning, maybe catch 'em again for all we know," Buddy said, looking out the window.

The farms and houses were scarce on this road. They were about a mile out of town before the first one came up in the headlights. A large dog ran out. "That's Rosco!" Buddy said, as he raised himself up and looked around Heather. The dog barked loudly as it chased the car. It finally pulled off. "He's a good dog!" Buddy said.

The faint lights from the next farm house came into view. Another dog chased the car on Heather's side, this one bolder than the last. "That's Butch! Get down, Butch!" Buddy yelled. The dog fell back.

"How far?" Heather asked.

"Next place! See it?" Buddy pointed ahead. The faint lights of a small house, far off the road, lay across the starlit field. "It's our place as long as the crops make," Buddy bragged. "Boy! Will they be surprised," he said, as Heather turned the Essex from the narrow main road.

Heather could tell this was a family of hard workers, people who took pride in home and family, by the painted mail box and post, surrounded by irises in different stages of bloom. She saw the silhouettes of people on the front porch. The headlights swept across the small unpainted house. Heather saw a man and at least four children of different ages on the porch.

"That's my Paw! And my brothers!" Buddy said proudly. The silhouettes stood still as the car came to a stop. Buddy took his time getting out. "When can I wash it?" he asked, looking at the pretty woman he had met.

"Even if you don't get to wash it, I'll pay you for your shoe balance," she said, touching his hand that was on the seat. The softness of her hand rushed over the young boy. Long after she had driven away, the touch of her hand still lingered on his. He had never felt anything like it before.

"Hi, Paw!" Buddy shouted, taking the wide wooden steps with a bound.

Heather pulled away with respect, not raising any dust. The small red running lights of the Essex were almost out of sight when it turned toward town.

"Who was that?" asked Buddy's father.

"She's new in town, stayin' at Mrs. Blakely's. She's payin' me to wash her car, two times!" Buddy said eagerly.

"Don't count yer chickens 'fore they hatch," his father said. The small bowl of a pipe lit his face.

The other siblings chattered on about the fancy car and what they could see of the woman driving it.

"Buddy! You did see them bullet holes?" asked his father. "Might be the kind you need ta stay clear of."

"Jasper Brown put one in there, and the other come from a nigger up the road somewhere," replied Buddy, holding the wire pull handle of the screen door. "She's lookin' for work. I think she's a law woman."

"Come on, Buddy! I'm holdin' yer supper," his mother called out from within the small house.

"Yes, ma'am," he yelled.

"You be careful. Get in trouble, I can't pay you out," his father said, pulling on the pipe.

"Yes, sir," Buddy replied, leaving his father on the porch. His brothers followed him inside to the kitchen table.

The father mumbled to himself. "Law woman." He shook his head at the thought.

"Hominy, fried side meat, hoe cake." Buddy's mother set his plate down in front of him.

"Thanks!" Buddy smiled.

"Good day at the store?" she asked.

The brothers gathered around. All had freckles and red hair. They were stair-stepped in height with Buddy being the tallest. Questions abounded as he ate.

"Good day at the store?" his mother asked again.

"Oh, yes! It was a great day," he replied.

"Who brought you home?" she asked, drying her hands.

"A new lady in town. Her name is Heather Duncan. I think I was introduced, but I looked on the room book anyway," Buddy said between bites. He reached for the large can of Brer Rabbit Molasses in the center of the table.

"Clean knife!" his mother reminded. He wiped his knife off on his shirt and she rolled her eyes.

Heather felt sorry for the family, but why she did not know. They were certainly no worse off than most other folks, statewide. There were plenty less fortunate back in Campbell County, what there was of it. "Damn Fulton County!" she snarled openly. The same two dogs gave chase as she passed back by. She had never been without shoes. "That was terrible," she thought, realizing that so many did go without during the summer months.

The parking spot she had left to take Buddy home was still open. The sound of a piano played in the distance and a woman bellowed forth with song. The black figures of many men and a few women could be made out along with the bright spots made by cigarettes in the darkness. The front door to the store was locked. A small sign reminded patrons to use the side entrance. Heather grasped her revolver, pulled it against the back of her thigh, and walked through the shadows of the night to the side entrance. A small single bulb burned inside the glazed window of the double doors.

The rooms were quiet, not a sound was heard. She knew someone was up, the faint odor of tobacco drifted into the stairwell as she made her way upstairs. Her bed and bath were clean. Heather dined on her cold food items from the store below, while she wiggled her stocking feet in the breeze that came through the open windows. The locks were tripped and the extra chair cocked under the doorknob. The crack at the bottom of the door was chinked with a small throw rug, keeping anyone from seeing her movement. Sleep fell upon her in the first night alone in her life's adventure.

* * *

Warm Springs Officer Jasper Brown rolled into the Greenville square about an hour before dark. He entered the square slowly enough for those standing about to see the marked Warm Springs unit passing through with a Negro inside. The businesses on the square were alive with trade, coming and going. Jasper acknowledged those he knew, and returned a nod or a wave to those who acknowledged his trophy.

"Proud of yerself, ain't ya?" James Lee mumbled, looking down at the floorboard.

"Not as proud as I am of the mean woman that run yer black ass ta ground. Why didn't ya shoot it out with her? I bet she'd give ya a third eye and a new asshole before ya went down," Jasper laughed, punching Lee on the shoulder. "Chicken shit!" he added. The tires of the Model A crunched the pea gravel as they came to rest in front of the red brick two-story jail. "You been here before?" Jasper asked. James Lee did not answer. "Well, I think you have. Best not vex these people, they'll bust yer head in a flash and not even stitch it up," he said, smiling as he got out. The closing of the car door alarmed Curley Jones. He stood up and looked out the edge of the tall office window.

"God damn it! Another one! Can't they find a shady spot and do nothin'?" he mumbled, too low for the sheriff to hear as he came down the short hallway from his residence.

"Got another one, Curley?" asked Sheriff Louis Gilbert.

"Hell, yes!" Curley snapped, reaching for his braided sole leather police club. It was a short eight-inch one. Then he saw it was a Negro and he tossed it back and got the twelve-inch one.

Sheriff Gilbert saw him. "Too small or too light?"

"Hard head! An inch an ounce, swingin' damn near a pound," Curley said, tapping his left palm with the seasoned club.

Jasper noticed two operators taking a break at the telephone company, just a hard stone's throw from the jail. "Howdy, ladies!" he called out. They hurried inside.

Jasper opened the car door for James Lee. "Get yer black ass out!" he snapped. James slid off the seat, chained feet first, and then he stood up. "Cuffed in the back ain't funny, is it?" Jasper asked, as he pushed the prisoner ahead. James Lee shuffled along the woven brick walkway. It had already seen so much traffic a shallow dish was evident. "Hard ass walkin'!" yelled Jasper, kicking the Negro in the seat of the pants. Lee stumbled forward. "Don't fall! Sign of weakness! Them boys are lookin' from inside. Them that are white are ready to train yo' black ass, them that's black'll welcome you for numbers," he mumbled, walking behind the prisoner.

"Bring him on, damn it!" yelled Curley, from the darkness of the deep evening shadows.

Sheriff Gilbert stepped out onto the porch. His hands came to rest on his waist. "Who's that?"

"Hell! I figured the news preceded me! It's yer wanted nigger, James Lee," Jasper called out.

Sheriff Gilbert's jaw dropped. "Who got him?" he asked.

"I'll tell you all about that a little later, if you please. It's worthy of a newspaper article," replied Jasper, grabbing James Lee's cuffed hands and balancing him up the three steps. Sheriff Gilbert, wearing his gray fedora, stood to the side and held the screen door off of Jasper.

Curley Jones started barking orders as he tapped the large club in his left palm. "No speakin', 'less yer spoken to! Only answer what yer asked! No man moves without permission! I am the boss! When I am not present, a trustee will be the boss! This ain't no God damned motel! The beds are hard and the pot rim is narrow!" he yelled out. Everyone in the jail, and even Miss Jewel in the kitchen, could hear that another guest had arrived.

Miss Jewel shook her head. "One mo' ta feed!" she grumbled. The meal had just finished, she gathered what she could find to feed the prisoner. There was nothing but cornbread that was slightly molded and buttermilk that had become suspiciously thick from age. She watered that down a bit and stirred it to life. "Conebread and milk, dat's it," she fussed to herself. Her day was done. The devoted Negro woman waddled her way down the hall to the intake area. "Big Mama's on de' flo'!" she called out.

"Well, come ahead!" replied Curley, at the top of his lungs.

Jasper knew this was a show of force. No prisoner had ever been mistreated unless there was a call to be reckoned with. Sheriff Gilbert located the arrest warrants in the filing cabinet and tossed them at Jasper Brown. "Execute these," he said.

Jasper Brown read the warrants and signed on the appropriate line, indicating that the wanted person had been located and placed into custody. "There ya go," he said low, pushing them toward the sheriff, who had taken a seat to watch Curley. The sheriff sat leaning back in a chair behind the desk, resting his arms in his lap.

Miss Jewel was every bit of five feet tall and five feet around, but cook and have young'uns', nine in all, those were skills she had mastered. "Heah beez his foods!" she said, setting the large tin cup of milk and bread on the corner of Curley's desk. "I'ze headin' to de house!" The screen door slammed behind her. Miss Jewel would walk about a half mile out of town, an open folding knife in her apron pocket and a Ray-o-Vac flashlight in the other. The sheriff furnished the light and the batteries for it. She was issued four a month, so she used them sparingly.

Curley instructed Jasper Brown to move the cuffs from the Negro's back to the front while there were three lawmen present.

"On the stool!" barked Curley. He handed James Lee a key for the leg irons. "Take em' off! Slow, or I'll have yer damn head!" James Lee complied, and then held up the leg irons and the key. Curley handed Officer Brown the leg irons and the tiny key. Jasper sat down on the corner of Curley's desk. He could hear the inmates talking from one cell to the next about a new man coming in. Curley banged his club on the bars of the narrow intake door. "Quiet! God damn it!" The cell block fell quiet, but it brought the faces up against the bars. The trustee of the day sat silent waiting on the new Negro to be turned over to him. Curley closed the narrow hallway door leading into the sheriff's residence. He turned the deadbolt. "Close the front door," Curley said, motioning to Jasper. "All I need is some woman to walk up and see this buck's ass," he said, thumping James Lee on the shin with the club. "Strip down!" he ordered loudly.

James Lee forced his tied shoes off of his feet. His socks followed, staying in the dirt filled shoes. "Pants!" yelled Curley, tapping Lee again. The Negro dropped his pants and stepped out. Curley picked them up after he raked them out of the Negro's immediate reach. He shook them vigorously and then searched the pockets by a hard grip and feel. "Shirt!" the jailer yelled. James Lee pulled the shirt over his head, still buttoned. The Negro stood naked, the shirt dangling from his cuffed hands. The single overhead bulb afforded little light and the shadows were deep. Jasper had looked away only to be startled back to the subject of the book-in by the sound of a wire basket hitting the floor. Jasper jumped.

"Ever thin' but yer shoes, hold 'em in yer hand," Curley barked.

James Lee stood naked, still wearing the cuffs. Curley nudged James Lee's manhood with the end of the club. He moved it from side to side. "I thought you Bucks were hung like horses?" He laughed. "Bo Bob! Ready for this one?" Curley asked the trustee sitting in the darkness of the cell block's common area.

"Send him back," a black man's voice replied. The heavy iron door opened under the key control of Curley. The paint on the lock had long ago been worn away from the scrubbing of the keys on the large steel ring.

"Step in! Turn 'round! Put yer hands through de hole! Let de man take dem cuffs off!" Bo Bob said, from the darkness of his domain. James Lee stepped into the cell block of the Meriwether County Sheriff's Jail, known as the Greenville Jail. Curley slammed the steel door behind him. James Lee flinched at the loud clang.

"Way out! That's right!" Curley said loudly, as Lee pushed his cuffed fists, still covered with the loose shirt, through the rectangular opening in the solid door. The cuffs were loose and then free of his wrists with a little effort. James Lee stepped back into the dim light. The cell block was afforded light by the flame of a single wall mounted kerosene lamp with little fuel. On dark moonless nights the cells were cave black. The sound of keys rattled and scuffed on the only door to the cell block. The head high talk-through opened, silhouetting the person on freedom's side. "Bo Bob, he don't look buggy. Dust him down in the morning," said Curley, slamming the door. Bo Bob heard the keys hit the peg on the wall in the office. "There's food when you want him ta have it," Curley yelled out.

"Yes, sir! Boss!" Bo Bob yelled back. "You buggy, nigger?" Bo Bob asked, looking at the new inmate in the dim light. Bo Bob's eyes were adjusted by now and had been for some time.

"Don't call me nigger!" snarled James Lee.

Bo Bob stood behind James Lee and grabbed a butt cheek, clamping it hard. "I'ze knows a nigger when I sees one," he whispered. "You hear me, boy?"

James Lee's eyes watered from the pain. "Yes, boss!" Bo Bob released his hold, still standing behind him. "I'ze call out wid one cry and dat white man will beat yous to damn near def, you understand? I'ze be heres a long time, long adder yous gone, so I'ze not likely ta sees yous on de street," assured Bo Bob. "Find a bed." Bo Bob shoved the prisoner away. "Clothes after powder in de mawnin'."

Jasper Brown took a rag from a small nail on the corner of Curley's desk and wiped the sweat from the cuffs and leg irons. The rag, kept for this purpose, had a faint trace of 3-in-1 oil on it. "Thank you, Sheriff! I'll be goin' now," said Jasper, standing in front of probably the most powerful man in the county.

"Mighty fine job!" said Sheriff Gilbert, standing to shake Jasper's hand. "Mighty fine job!"

"Thank you," Jasper replied, as he walked to the door. "Open or closed?" he asked Curley.

"Open," Curley replied, washing his hands at a nearby wall mounted sink. "Don't bring no more tonight!" he snarled.

"Oh! My ass is goin' to the house!" Jasper replied from the screen door. "And another thing, I asked your deputy to get the car he was driving up here somewhere," he added.

Sheriff Gilbert stood looking at Jasper. "It was surely brought to the county yard," he answered.

"Good night," said Jasper, as he stepped into the cool air of the clear night.

James Lee first started in to Cell Number 1, where he caught a large arm across his face in the darkness. "Not here!" a gruff voice advised. He stepped to Cell Number 3. "Space?" he asked. A couple of voices joined in enforcing the answer of, "No!" He went to Cell Number 4. "Any room?" "Full!" several voices responded.

"Number 2 is open," a voice advised. James Lee looked over the sliding door tracks, finding Number 2 in the dim light. It was a few feet away. "Room?" he asked at the open door. "Only on the floor," said a deep voice that he thought belonged to his own kind. He stepped in. "Thanks," he said, feeling about. "Bunks all taken! Only on the floor," the voice advised.

James Lee, wanted for car theft and the murder of a store owner, found himself naked, wearing only his shoes, sitting on the cold concrete floor of the jail. The dampness that he felt was urine from the spilling of the piss

bucket during the night before. "Damn," he mumbled.
"Thad's yo job in de mawnin," a second voice said.

CHAPTER FIVE

Warm rays of morning sunlight showered the lobby of the Warm Springs Police Department, cutting through the lingering tobacco smoke from the evening before. Heather was without her badge and gun. They had been left in the satchel on the floorboard of the Essex. She looked at the shoddily framed pictures on the wall, none of which matched. The addition of the interior windows had brought the department into the present century. It allowed the officers and staff to see out, and with some reservation provided the ability of the public to see them. Any effort to hide was somewhat futile.

Heather stood with hands on hips, pushing the lightweight suit coat back as she looked at each picture. They ranged from an early framed tintype up to the current chief, Howard Hawthorn. Heather sized him up. She figured him to be in his mid-fifties. The sign advised the department was open for business at 8:00 clock, Monday through Friday. The wall clock, an old but dependable octagon-headed pendulum swung Regulator, ticked and tocked patiently on the red brick outer wall. It was 8:20!

"Son of a bitch," Heather mumbled. "Posted hours not kept, something that infuriated Grandmother Margaret, and Sonny too." She looked around for a place to sit, thinking she needed to de-escalate her growing anger over the wait. Every upholstered piece of furniture was long since dished, and cleanliness was another issue. She was particular about where she put her butt. A hard-topped bar stool beckoned to her from the deep shadows of the eastern wall. She could watch her car and size up the characters who passed by, even those who came and went across the street at the café. The plaster wall felt good to her back as she leaned against it. Thoughts of her approach raced through her head.

"Howdy, Miss Molly! Mrs. Hindman! Uncle Thurston!" A loud voice called from the street. She judged it to be close, although she could not see the person yet.

"Mornin', Mayor!" the voice of an old man called out. She knew it was an old man by the depth and coarseness, along with the breaks in strength.

"Beautiful morning!" the mayor replied. He was now close to the police department door. She could make out the man through the venetian blinds that covered the window of the door. The doorknob turned. Heather focused on it.

"Biscuits leavin' fast!" a woman's voice cried out from the doorway of the café. "Shall I save ya a couple?"

"I'd be obliged!" the mayor yelled back. "I'll only be a minute or two!"

"A minute or two," Heather thought to herself. Her eyes narrowed as she focused on her windshield issues.

The door opened. The short robust man hummed a pleasant tune as he entered. Heather sat still in the deep shadows. The flat top natural straw hat the mayor wore found its place on the arm of the bentwood hat rack that stood just inside the door. The hat swung about the arm, eventually coming to rest. The morning newspaper was under his arm. He tossed it onto the counter just out of the shadow where Heather sat silently watching. He continued humming his tune.

The mayor was beginning to show age spots, especially on his hands and bald head. His white long sleeve shirt pulled tightly across his belly like Wimpy in the cartoons. Heather expected a button to fly at any moment. Even in the poor light, she could see that his pants did not match his suit coat and his attempts to pick the same color only amplified the contrast. She did think his white oxfords were spiffy and fashionable, along with his round wire framed glasses.

"Morning!" said Heather, in a strong and forceful tone.

The mayor, who thought he was alone, jumped at the sound of her voice. He straightened from his slightly slumping posture and looked around in surprise. He found Heather sitting in the shadow.

"Oh, morning!" he replied. "I thought I was alone," he added, looking at Heather. He could just make out that it was a tall slender person in the poor light.

"What can I do for you, sir?" he asked.

Heather ignored the "sir" part. "I'm here for a new windshield," she said.

The mayor held his hand up, shading his eyes. He was at a disadvantage, looking into the rays of the eastern sun. "We don't do windshields. That's most likely Claude Allen down at the filling station," he said.

Heather stood up and walked closer, into the light. The mayor dropped his jaw upon realizing he had called this attractive woman "sir". He began to apologize.

"I'm sorry, madam. In the shadows I thought -- I assumed you were a man," he stammered.

"No, I'm in the right place," Heather said. "The sign says open for business at eight o'clock. Where is everyone?" she asked.

"They work late hours, odd hours. There's an officer on the road now," said the mayor, trying to cover for the tardiness of the staff.

"I'm here to see the chief," said Heather, remembering the name in the framed picture. "Chief Howard Hawthorn." She still stood with her hands on her waist, her coat pushed back. Her suit matched. It was a dark khaki, with brown laced shoes that covered her ankles. Her white blouse had a few pleats in the front, accenting her bosom. The narrow brown suspenders rested to the side of her breasts, making them even more prominent.

"I think he's over at the café," the mayor stammered. "Oh! Pardon me! I'm Mayor Cornelius Cunningham, Mayor of Warm Springs," he said, offering his hand.

"Heather," she replied, taking his hand and shaking it vigorously with a crushing grip.

Mayor Cunningham blinked several times, surprised by her firm grip. "She is strong to be a slender woman. Pretty too!" he thought.

"He's late and I don't have all day. Half hour late, my time is valuable too," Heather said, looking him straight in the eyes.

"I'll see if I can arrange a meeting with Chief Hawthorn," the mayor stammered, making his way to the door. The blinds bumped as he opened the door quickly. "Howard! Chief Hawthorn! See if the chief's in there!" He yelled to anyone who might hear on the bench in front of the café.

"Hey! Chief! Mayor's callin'!" a man yelled into the open door of the café. The man never left his seat on the end of the bench next to the door.

In a minute or two the chief appeared in the open doorway. "Yes, Mayor!" he yelled back, picking fried ham from his teeth with a toothpick.

Heather watched as Mayor Cunningham waved his hand for the chief to hurry. Heather could see the chief over the mayor's shoulder. The chief was taller than the mayor, but neither was the height of her father, Sonny. He would tower over both. The medium built man was in his middle fifties. He did look professional, she was surprised at that. The black uniform pants were creased and the white shirt was starched. The gold badge and whistle chain gleamed in the morning sun. The military billed cap atop his head sported a white body, black patent leather bill, and woven band. The belt around his waist was older than the hat. She immediately sized up the small frame .32 revolver. The mayor hurried the chief along with his hand motions. Heather saw the chief toss the toothpick into the dusty street as he descended the steps. She changed her location within the room.

The chief made his way between the passing cars, waving at passing motorists and the public. "What is it?" he asked the mayor.

"Woman needs a windshield," replied Mayor Cunningham. The chief still had not come into the room.

"A windshield! Send 'em to -- " the chief started to reply, as Mayor Cunningham shook his head for him to stop, before he made the situation worse.

The mayor beckoned the chief to come into the police department. "This is Heather," said the mayor, pointing to where he had last seen her standing. He looked around quickly. Heather stood with her back to the two men but could see them both in the reflective glass on the pictures in front of her.

"Yes, sir!" snapped the chief. Mayor Cunningham shook his head at the chief's mistake.

Heather turned to greet the chief. "Hello, sir! I'm Heather," she said, offering her hand. The chief took it. She gave him the same shake she had deployed upon Mayor Cunningham.

"I'm sorry. I misunderstood yer name," the chief said, trying to regroup from the gender error. She smiled. "What can I do for you?" he asked.

"You can replace my windshield."

"And why do I need to replace yer windshield?" asked the chief

"So, you're not aware of Officer Brown's capture?"

"No, I haven't read the reports this morning and Officer Brown should be on the road," he replied. "Where is your car?" He stepped to the window and opened the blind easily with the dropped cotton cords. "Getting old," he said, smiling. He too thought the woman was a nice package. He had already wondered if she was in a misdirected body, one who liked women. "She'd be a good lay," he thought to himself.

"It's out front and down toward the tracks about three spaces," Heather answered.

The chief and the mayor leaned to see the car. "The burgundy over black Essex?" asked Chief Hawthorn.

"That's the one," Heather changed places again. She could keep these two confused.

"Jesus!" said Mayor Cunningham, opening the blinds further with his hands. "Can I get the reports?" he asked Heather.

"Certainly, as long as I get a windshield." They had to determine her location again. She found it amusing to watch their expressions.

Chief Hawthorn jingled his keys, taking them from his belt. The inner door to the staff room was kept locked. Mayor Cunningham took a seat and gave a sigh. He scratched his head. Heather watched Chief Hawthorn through the window as he stood at the desk and thumbed the stack of reports, incoming mail, and pages pulled from the newspaper. He finally settled on one. The chief's eyes hurriedly read the report.

"Officer Jasper Brown of the Warm Springs Police Department, while on patrol on the Bethsaida Church Road at or about 2:45 p.m., observed an oncoming black Sedan that was driven by a black male. This situation fit the description of a wanted James Lee, who was suspected to be driving a stolen 1925 Star automobile, two door, hard top, color black."

The chief rolled his eyes at the redundancy of the black Sedan and then color black. He hoped whoever Sheriff Giles sent down was better than this. He continued.

"Officer Jasper Brown made diligent efforts to stop the suspicious Star vehicle before the downtown district, but was unsuccessful. The suspicious vehicle turned north on State 41, passing the old Meriwether Inn's location at a continuing rate of speed. The furnished emergency lights and siren that I had at my disposal were in full operation prior to and passing through town. The Star vehicle failed to stop. The patrol car was at top speed for the longest time. On State 41, still northbound, I lost control of my police car at the vicinity of Rocky Ford Branch, after taking fire from the black Sedan."

Chief Hawthorn shook his head at the report starting in third person and changing to first person. Chief Hawthorn had some formal education and had been a writer for a very short time for an Alabama newspaper. Jasper Brown had at best a high school education. Jasper had graduated from the Bullochville High School before going into the Army. He continued reading.

"Officer Jasper Brown eventually got his police car onto the road and continued in chase. His bullet as of the time of firing was uncertain as to where it struck. Officer Jasper Brown soon found the black Star Sedan driven by the wanted James Lee off of the road, just south of the Oakland Plantation. James Lee was taken into custody and transported to the Meriwether County Sheriff, in Greenville."

Attached to the report with a gem clip was a small piece of paper torn from a tablet. *"Chief! Read the additional pages on your desk."* Chief Hawthorn dropped his arms and looked over at his desk. There were indeed several more pages. Heather watched as he hurried to his desk. Mayor Cunningham sighed again. He picked up an old newspaper to entertain himself. The mayor had realized that his breakfast was long gone. It would be a Moon Pie and coffee from Widow Blakely's store.

"Officer Jasper Brown - I ditched my car after being shot at by the damn nigger! I fired back and I guess my bullet struck the windshield of an oncoming car that I didn't see for the heavy dust. Anyway, this woman had turned around and run that nigger to ground almost in the yard of the old Oakland Plantation. She shot it out with him and he was on the ground when I got there! Hod dang! She's a looker! There's two bullet holes, one's the nigger's." Signed – J. Brown

The chief called for the mayor. By now he was so deep into the old article he had to be called twice. Mayor Cunningham hurried in and closed the door behind him. Heather moved to better see both men. She was still in the darker of the two rooms. "We do owe this woman a windshield," whispered the chief. "And maybe a civil suit before it's over," he added.

Mayor Cunningham turned pale and swayed upon hearing the words civil suit. "God damn," he whispered. "How did that happen?" he asked.

"The Nigger James Lee was in Warm Springs yesterday and Jasper got after him. They left town and Jasper chased him to the old Oakland Plantation where this woman had already put Lee on the ground after exchanging gunfire," said the chief.

The mayor fell down into a nearby chair. "Sum bitch!" he whispered. "Best give it to her!" He rested his head in his hand, leaning on the desk. Both men leaned and looked at Heather. She waved and smiled. They drew back like school boys that had been caught stealing a look.

"You or me?" asked Chief Hawthorn.

"I'll do the honors, since it's the city's money," said Mayor Cunningham, as he pushed himself up from the chair.

Heather eagerly awaited their decision.

"We're sorry to have kept you so long, Miss Heather, but we have found what we needed to know in the official reports," said Mayor Cunningham. His tone was that of his official capacity as mayor. "I will have a note drawn up on letterhead for the City of Warm Springs and present it to you within the hour," he continued, followed by a large politician's grin.

"That will be fine. Make sure it is exactly to the manufacturer's specifications," Heather added. "I'd even like to see the crate it comes out of," she added.

"We'd like to see you choose Claude Allen's place. He does good work and gives the city a close markup for his labor," added the chief.

"I can do that," Heather replied.

"May I buy you breakfast?" asked the mayor. "I haven't eaten myself and I'm hungry. Not even had coffee," he said, smiling.

"That would be nice," she answered.

"When my secretary comes in, she will draft that letter promptly on the typewriter," boasted the mayor.

The chief opened the door of the lobby leading onto the sidewalk. He held out his hand, offering Heather to go first.

"Thank you, sir!" she said, as she stepped into the morning sunlight. It was a refreshing experience compared to the stale tobacco laden air of the lobby.

The morning crowd had left the bench and sidewalk in front of the café. The open screenless door caused Heather to wonder about the cleanliness of the place. The bench sitters along the store fronts watched as the three crossed the rough pot-holed street.

"Need to get the county down with the motor-grader and pull the street. It's in bad shape," said Mayor Cunningham to Chief Hawthorn.

The sidewalk was covered for the most part by tin awnings of all different heights, as dictated by the storefronts. They walked into the morning sun. The singing of wrens reminded Heather of the stories of her grandfather. The wide step allowed the three to ascend together, which kept either of the two men from being able to look at her butt.

"What's the specialty?" Heather asked.

"Just good food!" replied the mayor.

"Did I hear clean in there?" Heather asked, laughing.

"It's as clean as we've got," replied the chief. "The screen door was torn down by two drunks a week ago. They do need to get it up, 'fore the Sanitary Police come around."

Heather stepped inside. The small café was long and narrow. The plaster walls were painted a dinner mint green, with dark lacquered woodwork. Three single bulbs hung from the ceiling, giving light to the length of the dining room. The kitchen was in the back. A pass-through window allowed her a peek into the cooking area. From a distance she could tell it was not like her grandmother's kitchen. The few men who remained in the cafe looked up as they entered. There were two business women sitting together. Heather made eye contact and they exchanged cordial glances.

"Have a seat, Miss!" said Mayor Cunningham, pulling out a chair for Heather.

"May I sit with my back to the wall?" she asked.

"Certainly," he replied, as he pulled out another chair. Heather sat down gracefully and the mayor pushed in her chair.

"Thank you," she said.

"Eve! Three coffees, please," Mayor Cunningham called out. He sat down with his back to the street. The chief sat to the side of the table.

"There's the menu." The chief pointed to the blackboard on the inside wall.

Heather looked at it for a moment. "Not a huge selection," she commented.

"Simple fare, simple folks," chuckled the mayor.

Eve brought three mugs strung on one finger, and carried an enameled coffeepot in the other hand.

"Good morning!" she said, setting the heavy mugs on the table top. Not a one matched. The aroma of strong coffee wafted around the table. "Cream's fresh! Sam Hopkins brought it in this morning before daylight. He said that Greenville was abuzz with the capture of the Nigger James Lee."

"That's right!" Heather replied.

"Sum bitch shot out her windshield," said Chief Hawthorn, as he poured sugar into his mug. Heather watched the pencil size stream free fall into the mug. The fact that it flowed so well told her there was some cleanliness to the place, even if the floor did have a plate or two of accumulated breakfast droppings. Biscuit crumbs contrasted against the painted floor of dark oak brown. The wear marks had created a path pattern of their own. A wren had ventured inside the front door and was helping itself to a meal of crumbs. Heather smiled.

"If ya want breakfast food, we're out," said Eve. The men looked surprised.

"Any cold biscuits?" asked Heather.

"We've got them," Eve replied.

"Split 'em, butter 'em, and toast' em out on the grill with the meat press on top and I think we'll do just fine," Heather said boldly.

"I believe we can do that," said Eve.

"That sounds right tasty!" said the mayor.

Heather sipped hot coffee and looked at the Essex across the street. She listened to the two men chattering about city business and local gossip. "I hope whoever that deputy is Sheriff Giles in Campbell County is sending out gets here soon," said Chief Hawthorn, hugging his coffee mug.

"Jasper was talkin' about workin' alone with that Negro running at large," said Mayor Cunningham. He waved at people passing on the sidewalk now and then.

"Butt kissin' politician," Heather thought to herself.

"With Lee in jail, we actually don't need anyone now," said the chief.

That caught Heather's attention, but she showed no emotion. By the second cup of coffee, the toasted biscuits were brought out. They were buttery and golden brown.

"Syrup, strawberry jam, or honey?" asked Eve.

"Some of each!" answered Mayor Cunningham.

"No! No! It's been approved, let's hire whoever he is when he gets here," said the mayor, taking bites of the biscuit.

Heather ate her biscuit with syrup and watched the two men.

"I'd expect him to arrive by today, damn it," said the chief. "Oh! I'm sorry," he said, glancing at Heather.

"Nothin' I ain't heard before," she said, smiling.

"You know about Sheriff Benjamin Giles, don't you?" Heather asked, looking down at her plate.

"No, what?" asked Chief Hawthorn.

"He was killed two days ago. A Negro escaped and they got into a fight, killed with his own revolver," Heather replied, still looking down.

"Oh, my!" Mayor Cunningham said, slowly and softly. His hands stopped, still over his plate.

"Let's get a paper," said Chief Hawthorn, as he stood up.

"Eve! Got a fresh newspaper?" he called out to the kitchen.

Eve appeared in the pass-through window. "Not today's!" she yelled back. She was peeling onions.

"Sit down, we'll get one soon. Let's finish our meal with this nice lady," the mayor suggested.

"Was it in the paper?" asked Chief Hawthorn.

"Atlanta Journal and the Campbell News," Heather answered.

"There's my secretary. Excuse me for a minute," said the mayor, as he tossed his napkin on the table and hurried to the door. Heather saw him talking to an older woman. She nodded her head as though she was taking in everything the mayor was saying. Mayor Cunningham soon returned from the sidewalk.

"A fine lady! She'll have that letter for the windshield by the time we're finished." He took his seat.

"Did Sheriff Giles promise you a deputy?" Heather asked, looking at both men.

"He sure did! The only department that was close enough to send someone down. He said he had a real humdinger. He was to make us a good detective," bragged the chief.

Eve appeared to the chief's right. "Anything else?" she asked, holding a ticket book.

The chief looked at Heather. She shook her head. The mayor replied with his hand up. "No! That is all. And it was delicious!" said the chief, smiling.

"Here's yer ticket," Eve said, holding out the small piece of form printed paper. Heather had not seen one that was pale yellow and brown ruled before. It was different. The chief took it.

"Twenty cents," he said. Eve had walked away.

"Can I pay for mine?" Heather asked.

"Oh, no! I won't have it. The least we can do," replied the mayor, as the chief dug in his pocket for two dimes.

"Did you know Sheriff Giles?" asked Chief Hawthorn, leaning back in his chair.

"I certainly did," said Heather.

A car stopped in front of the police department. Both men watched eagerly. "A salesman!" said the chief. The mayor frowned and they both shook their heads in disappointment.

The dishwasher appeared from the kitchen door and began to clear off and wipe down every table. The dishes and flatware made a horrific noise as they tried to talk. The chief looked at the woman and she moved more slowly and made less noise. "If he ain't here by two o'clock, call up there and see what the holdup is," said Mayor Cunningham. His bald head turned red.

"I can give you the latest on that deputy," Heather said. Both men looked at her in silence.

"How is that?" asked Chief Hawthorn, as he dropped his chair legs to the floor. The woman clearing the tables was busy listening to their conversation. She was attracted to Heather's nice suit and the way she was holding her own with the two most important men in the small town.

Heather pulled the letter of reference from her coat pocket and handed it to the chief. He opened it and pulled out the clean crisp folds, trying to relax them.

"To Whom It May Concern: Miss Heather Duncan has served my department, the Campbell County Sheriff's Department, for almost ten years. She holds until the last day, at the stroke of midnight, December 31, 1931 the classification of Special Deputy. Along with Sonny Duncan, they have tracked and assisted with cases as needed in this department. I would strongly recommend her for the position of Police Officer. However, I feel that she is most suited to fill the vacancy as a Detective, as she understands the art of paperwork and accuracy in such. She has a base knowledge of Georgia criminal law. Miss Duncan is very proficient with various handguns. Sincerely, Sheriff Benjamin Giles."

Chief Hawthorn dropped the letter on the table and sat in silence. Mayor Cunningham reached for the letter and read it. The chief looked shocked, while the mayor wore a faint smile.

"And in your wildest dreams, you never thought the officer foretold could be a woman," said Heather. She sat back in her chair with her hands on her hips. The two business women had started to leave the room but sat back down to listen to the chief and mayor.

The chief let out a deep breath and then a sigh. He was still silent. "I say she's applied, let's give her a try! Hell! Tell us about them bullet holes," said the mayor.

Jasper Brown turned the corner in the dusty patrol car. "Catch him!" yelled the chief, running for the door. The mayor hurried to the window and watched the chief chase Jasper down the street. Jasper finally stopped.

"Yes, sir!" Jasper said.

"Park this sum bitch and come in the café and tell us about this woman," said the chief, as he leaned in the open passenger side window.

"She's a humdinger," Jasper said, shaking his head.

The chief quickly returned to the table. They were joined by Officer Jasper Brown. "Hello, lady!" Jasper said, extending his hand once again to Heather.

"Hello!" she replied.

"Is this the woman who helped with James Lee?" asked Chief Hawthorn.

"She didn't help. When my bullet went through her windshield, she turned on him and gave chase. That Essex outran my Ford in a hurry!" Jasper boasted. "She was all over that Star. Run him ta ground on the south side of the Oakland Plantation, damn near in the back yard. James

Lee apparently came out with his revolver in hand, but she took a shot and changed his mind for him. When I got there, she had him on the ground at gunpoint and had me cuff him. Cuff him in the back! Then she even had leg irons! I ain't never seen anything like it in these parts, anywhere else for that matter, in my policing," Jasper Brown said, bragging on Heather, who was sitting across from him.

The chief looked at Jasper and pointed his thumb back at Heather. "So, you'd police with this woman?" he asked. "Why, we'll be the laughin' stock of the county! The state!"

Mayor Cunningham motioned for the chief to calm down and lower his volume.

Jasper looked at the chief, then at Heather, and then at the mayor. "That's a woman, boy!" said the chief loudly. The two business women who were listening were sizing him up.

"I'd police with her anytime!" Jasper said, nodding his head up and down.

"Jesus!" said the chief. "This is a man's job, son!"

"I think she took both them shots one handed," added Jasper. The officer rose to leave. He felt his stay had run out.

Chief Hawthorn walked around the table in bewilderment. Mayor Cunningham sat still and smiled.

"You'll pay me a man's wages. I want to see the payroll, so I'll know that I'm not cheated," Heather said.

"Why, I don't think that's none of anyone's business, who's bein' paid what," replied Chief Hawthorn.

The other women stood, taking this as their time to leave. One woman stopped and cleared her throat. "Chief Hawthorn, we will be by the police department later this afternoon." The chief looked shocked.

"Why?" he asked.

"We'd like to see the payroll. That is city money and we are business owners and tax payers," the woman replied.

"Yeah! We want to know who's gettin' what," chimed in the other woman. The chief was speechless and looked angry. Heather kept her poker face.

The mayor exercised his power over the chief and took the meeting from the café table to the staff room at the police department. Heather was shown the books and saw the pittance that the officers were paid. However small, it was in line with other cities of the same size. The secretary found Mayor Cunningham and eased the letter that covered the replacement of the windshield into his hand. "Thank you, dear lady," he said, smiling.

"You are welcome," she replied.

Heather sat at a desk and looked over the books. She ran her finger up and down the short list of current and past officers. "Why was this officer paid a quarter more a day than these others?" she asked.

The mayor pulled the book from her gently so he could see who she was questioning. "Oh! He had some college classes in the Navy," he answered.

"I'll take the same pay. I can do bookkeeping and I understand the clerical work in this profession. Besides, I can type sixty words a minute and I'll furnish my own guns," said Heather.

Chief Hawthorn had all but given up, as Mayor Cunningham had apparently taken over the hiring. "Chief! I'm sure you have some questions," said the mayor.

"Just what kind of guns do you have?" the chief asked.

Heather gently pulled the ledger back from Mayor Cunningham. She continued to explore. "I have a heavy waist belt and matching case for my Tower's Double-lock handcuffs, one for extra revolver rounds for my Smith and Wesson .38. It's the new model that just came out. My father paid a deposit on it last year. I also have a shoulder rig for my Colt 1911. A box of new cartridges for both, until I ran into Officer Brown and James Lee. I have two pairs of cuffs and leg chains, too."

"And you are proficient with both?" asked Chief Hawthorn, leaning closer to her.

"I think so!" she snipped back. "Both of my shots in the chase were offhand," she added.

"And they missed!" snipped back Chief Hawthorn.

"I was shooting with my left hand, I'm right-handed and we were moving," she replied defensively.

"And you missed!" he snipped back.

Heather smiled. "I'm not the party buying a new factory windshield," she said.

Mayor Cunningham burst out laughing and slapped the desk top. "I like this woman! She's damn sure got spunk! Say! That was a pretty good letter too! Oh, me!" he said, trying to calm himself in front of his chief.

"Let's hire her," said Chief Hawthorn. "You'll be days with Officer Jasper Brown, whom you've already met. If he works nights, then you will work with him. But! I'm not one to change shifts for the meanness of it," said the chief, as he stepped back from the filing cabinet with a folder of forms. "Fill out this stuff tonight and put it on my desk in the morning. I agree to the pay. You may be asked to help with important reports and correspondence to agencies out of the county. I don't type well." He looked around for his part-time secretary. She had not come in yet. "And my secretary doesn't either. Stand and Mayor Cunningham will swear you in." Heather stood.

"We'll keep it simple. Just say your name when I nod. Raise your right hand. I -- ," The mayor nodded.

"Heather Duncan" she said proudly.

" -- having been appointed Detective for the City of Warm Springs and old Bullochville, do swear that I will truly and faithfully perform the duties of the office to the best of my ability and understanding; so long as I continue in the office and discharge of the duties thereof; that I am a citizen of Georgia and that I am qualified to hold office under the Constitution of these United States and the State of Georgia, so help me God," read the mayor. The mayor was the first to shake her hand. "Easy now! That's my bridge hand! I have to keep it in condition for the wife." He laughed loudly. "I'm so proud! Wait 'till the wife and her cronies hear of this!"

Chief Hawthorn shook her hand, but rather loosely. The scrubbing of a poorly waxed drawer filled the office as the chief fumbled around among several badges. He pulled one from the pile and made sure it said Detective. "Here's your badge! Do you have a holder?"

"I can take my Campbell County badge out and put this one in," Heather replied. The badge had seen long years without proper cleaning. "And my room and board?" she asked, after taking the badge.

"The Huff House over in Bullochville is where we send folks. They are usually acceptable to most and they charge us fairly. Tell them you're working here and they know to put you in the dining room for meals, breakfast and dinner," said Chief Hawthorn.

"And their rates are?" she asked.

"You meet or beat a dollar a day and fifty cents for two meals and I'll pay it, wherever it is," snapped the chief.

"I'm at the Blakely right now," Heather replied. "I'll give the rates in writing to you tomorrow. I do start tomorrow?" she asked.

"Shift change is seven o'clock until four o'clock. Officer Brown drives," he added. "Do you have suitable clothing for a detective?" he asked.

"Suits like I have on now, and canvas pants and thicker blouses for tracking," she replied. "Will you pay for them to be laundered or dry cleaned?" she asked, as she stood close to the door.

"We certainly will, the men get theirs cleaned by the city and we'll buy whatever clothes you need, within reason, while you're here," said Mayor Cunningham, who had walked up beside her.

"Here's the letter for Mr. Allen. He'll get you fixed up in a hurry. Say, I'll get your exact make and model and I'll go down and give him the information so he can order it, maybe have it on the train day after tomorrow."

"Thanks!" Heather said, as they left together.

There was no one in the police department now but the chief. "Bitch!" he said, as he slammed the door to the staff room. Heather did not hear him, but she already knew it would be a hard battle to prove herself. She knew she could do the job.

* * *

The front door stuck as Heather tried to enter J.C. Blakely Dry Goods & Rooms. Buddy Cotton was busy in the back storeroom. Heather could hear him fussing about a cardboard box of nuts that had fallen through due to dampness. He was on his hands and knees gathering them for placement in a more secure coffee can. "Buddy! I hear you!" Heather called out.

"And I see you, Miss Heather!" he replied from his knees, in the dim light. "Can I help you?" he asked.

"I need to see Mrs. Blakely," Heather replied.

"Oh!" he said, sounding rather disappointed.

"If Mrs. Murphy comes in, all four hundred pounds of her, huffin' and puffin', are you goin' ta be as enthused?" the voice of Mrs. Blakely asked.

Heather looked around to see where it came from. Mrs. Blakely was sitting on a low stool behind the counter, taking an inventory of the J & P Coats threads. Now and then a spool would drop onto the wood floor. Other than the first muffled impact, there was little to no sound as it rolled back and forth until it finally came to rest. That must have been the occasional grunt and "damn it" Heather heard before locating the woman.

"I see you're still with us," Mrs. Blakely replied, as she held up a spool of green thread, reading the numbers for the color designation.

"I'm still here, and maybe a long time," Heather said. She held the dirty badge over the counter so Mrs. Blakely could see it.

"Lord help, woman! You're a City Detective?" Mrs. Blakely exclaimed. That brought Buddy out of the back room.

"Can I see?" he asked, running up to Heather.

"Look quick and get about your work. She's not paying a slacker, wasted time is wasted money," Heather said, as she held the badge along with the young boy.

"Wow!" he exclaimed, then turned to go about his work.

"My windshield was shot at yesterday. There are two index finger size holes. Do you have any flat rubber washers, maybe the kind that would be oversized, like a fender washer?" Heather leaned over the counter, just barely able to see Mrs. Blakely.

"About two inch is all I'll have of that large a size. The center hole is about a quarter of an inch. They've been here a while. I hope they're still good," Mrs. Blakely said, as she tried to get up.

"I found 'em!" yelled Buddy. "How many?" he asked, from the dim store room.

"Four, and two stove bolts, about three quarters of an inch long," Heather called out.

Mrs. Blakely shook her head. "I don't know about that boy," she said.

"I do, he'll make you a good employee, given the time and training. He's very likeable," Heather added.

"So, the city threw the money to the Huff House, I guess," said Mrs.

Blakely.

"If you can meet the price you can have it," replied Heather. "The chief said to beat or meet a dollar a day and fifty cents for two meals and he'll pay it, wherever it is." She added, "I don't eat like those men you feed, but I do like my food."

"One dollar a day for room, forty cents for two meals. I only serve two a day, breakfast and dinner," said Mrs. Blakely.

Heather smiled. "Put it to paper!"

Mrs. Blakely noted her price on paper. "One dollar a day for room, forty cents for two meals. I only serve two a day, breakfast and dinner. Signed, Mrs. Blakely, J.C. Blakely Dry Goods & Rooms." The woman grinned, pushing the note over to Heather.

"We'll make a pair," Heather said. "The chief is already not taking a liking to me, because I'm a woman."

Buddy stood in the door of the store room. "Here they are, four washers and two stove bolts," he said, holding his hand out.

"Can you put them in for me, after work?" Heather asked, even though she could certainly do it herself. Buddy eagerly said that he could.

"How much?" Heather asked, with her hand in her pocket.

"A nickel, and dinner is on me tonight," Mrs. Blakely said, with a pleasant smile. "As soon as it's good dark, some of my guests haven't got timepieces."

* * *

It was about five o'clock when Buddy found Mrs. Blakely in the kitchen. "I come in a little early, can I go home?"

"Turn the sign for me, close the front doors, and drop the bell down," Mrs. Blakely replied from the stove.

"Thank you, ma'am!" he said politely.

Heather was in her room completing the application forms and laying out her suit for the next day. The horn on her Essex sounded off almost in front of her room. She hurried to the open window and looked down. It was Buddy watching for her face in the open window.

"Can I put it on?" Buddy yelled up.

"Be easy, washer inside and out, nut on the outside," she called down.

"I understand!" Buddy yelled back. He hopped in the cab and began to carefully work the stove bolt through the red flat washer. He realized that he could not do it without help. There was no way to put the nut and the outside washer on. Heather suddenly appeared in the windshield. She held the short bolt and began to work the outside washer around the iron body, then the nut was secured thumb tight.

"There! We did it!" Buddy said, sitting back and looking at their handiwork. "Can I have a ride home?" he asked.

"This won't be for every day. I'll be working tomorrow. I'll be riding with Jasper Brown until I get to know the land," she said, motioning for the boy to move over. The two holes were almost center of the windshield.

Heather remembered where the lad lived and needed no directions. "What'll that do?" he pointed to the compressed washers.

"Keeps the rain out and it'll help keep it from falling in on us," she replied.

"Oh!" said Buddy. The same two dogs chased the car again and Buddy yelled at them by name. Heather smiled at his antics.

*   *   *

The table that evening was filled with chairs, not another one could be pulled up. The men introduced themselves, as did Heather. They were astonished to see a woman of the law enforcement caliber in such a small rural Georgia town. Some acknowledged they had heard of women working in the larger precinct houses, such as Detroit, Chicago, New York, but Warm Springs was a first for the South, to their knowledge anyway. Heather told of her and Sonny's exploits, the dogs they had worked, and the bad men they had captured. She held off on her grandfather's exploits in Campbellton. She thought that would be too much of a reputation to fill. Amongst the clamor of cross-talk and the striking of flatware, Mrs. Blakely and Heather were the only two women. The men took the opportunity to try and outdo each other in their politeness and tall tales. The best was that of a man to Heather's right. He introduced himself.

"Miss Duncan, Detective, I guess I should say! I'm from London, as my heavy accent will always tell on me. This profane nickname of 'Squirrel E. Bastard' is derived from the lack of formal education and their pronunciation of my proper given name. Squire Lee Bouchard, the Bouchards from the Dark Hall District," said the thin, frail built man. Her father would have considered him a twig. He looked more like a praying mantis sitting there, compared to the robust men from the South.

"I'm pleased to make your acquaintance," Heather responded. "I shall call you Squire," she said, nodding politely.

The sharp rapping of a glass filled the room. "Tomorrow morning there will be a shift in seating. Detective Duncan will be seated next to me, as I find it hard to discuss various topics at such a distance as the length of my table," announced Mrs. Blakely.

The warm tub bath felt very relaxing to Heather as she soaked that night. It had been a couple of days since she was able to have such a luxury. The men were cleaning up behind themselves in a very thorough manner, which certainly pleased her. She dried and dashed silently to her room, opening the door with the key she had strung on a cotton string found around the bundle of newspapers during the day. The lamp burned very low against the outer wall, being careful not to create a shadow for the street urchins below, a cautionary trick learned from Grandmother

Margaret. She explored the stamped tin plates comprising the ceiling above her. Her eyes grew heavy as the occasional brown cricket chirped to any of its kind that were listening.

CHAPTER SIX

Tiny raindrops glistened in the morning sunlight, sparkling like millions of diamonds as they fell to the thirsty earth. Heather left the shallow porch of J.C. Blakely Dry Goods & Rooms with an excited outlook on her new adventure. It was her adventure. She would be responsible for making it successful. "Sink or swim," she thought to herself, standing on the sidewalk. Her gun belt felt familiar, comfortable one might say. The large Smith and Wesson double-action revolver rode high on her hip. It was balanced by the handcuffs and ammo pouch on her left side. The dark brown suit coat covered it well. Her polished brown shoes repelled the raindrops as she waited for Officer Jasper Brown to come by. The sun was still shining and the rain was all but over. Heather thought of Margaret. She would have called it a garden shower, just enough to wet the crusty earth.

The business women from the café the morning before waved at Heather as they passed on the opposite sidewalk. Heather waved back and smiled. Buddy Cotton whistled at her from behind the broom display that he was rolling out from the store onto the porch. Heather gave him a smile and a ladylike wave. Buddy blushed and ran back inside. The horn on Officer Brown's Model A Ford sounded loud and long as he came up Main Street from the Bullochville end. The two tiny towns almost adjoined one another. Heather waved, hoping he would stop blowing the horn. She was drawing enough attention just standing on the sidewalk. Few women dressed in business suits based around slacks like a man. She felt that many people were looking at her for that reason alone. Certainly, the gossip had already spread that the city had hired a woman to be the City Detective.

The mayor passed by, riding in the passenger seat of a bright blue Chevrolet going slowly down the other side of the street. Mayor Cunningham yelled, "Mornin', Detective Duncan!" waving his hat around. Heather returned a quick three-fingered salute and smiled. She watched the mayor grin and slap the man who was driving on the arm. Heather felt that she had at least one friend in City Hall. The Warm Springs patrol car stopped in front of her.

"Get in!" Jasper said, leaning toward the open passenger side window.

"I didn't think I'd stand here!" Heather said, as she opened the door and sat down.

"My, you do look nice!" Jasper said, still looking at her.

"Nice as in professional, or as in your manhood is about to control your brain?" she asked, giving him a steely glare. His balding head turned red.

"In a professional way," he said, shaking his head.

"We'll be good friends, at work and in time of need, but my folks raised me with the motto of don't sleep with it unless you'd get up to it every morning for life," she said, as they bounced along toward the police station. "Don't let that hamper your conversation and good nature," she added.

"I'm divorced," he replied, pulling into a reserved parking spot marked with a faded sign. Jasper set the brake and left the motor running. "I'll be right back!" He hurried into the police department and quickly returned with a big grin.

"What's up?" Heather asked, as he got in.

"Chief's secretary said to head to Meriwether County Courthouse, there's to be a meeting to bring all the departments up to speed on this Nigger James Lee," he said, pulling the car in gear and looking into the side mirror for a chance to pull out. "This is big! We don't get to leave town much, not for joint meetings anyway. I'm just takin' you because the chief and the mayor have already gone."

"You think so?" Heather asked.

"That's what she said," Jasper replied, taking the railroad tracks in second gear.

"I saw the mayor just a minute before you started blowing the horn," she said, looking out the window. "He was headin' into Bullochville."

"The big boys'll maybe have teacakes or gingerbread made by Miss Jewel. She's the jailhouse cook, a huge old nigger woman, but damn nice!" Jasper said.

"What's that place? With the Meriwether Inn archway?" Heather asked, leaning to look up the long tree-lined roadway.

"That's where the warm springs are, the mineral springs. I think it's magnesium that's so high in the water that attracts people. The water is warm, downright hot, all the time," Jasper said, glancing at his pretty partner. "It's been there since the Injuns', then about 1830 a David Rose acquired the land and built the first place. And then about 1840, rich bastard, Charles Davis, built a huge fancy Victorian place, rooms ta rent, all three hundred of 'em." He waved at an oncoming car. "You could dance under a pavilion, had a bowlin' alley, and a tennis court. I'm not sure, but

I've heard a trap shoot!"

Heather arranged her suit coat and sat back for the long ride. "Who polices the town while we're gone?" she asked.

"Themselves!" Jasper replied.

"Is the resort in the city?"

"Yes! In 1924 some politician, from New York, I think -- uh, Franklin Roosevelt, crippled feller, discovered it, and he come down so much 'til he finally bought the place. He's got that polio. Most folks are scared of it, think they can catch it. Doc Waddell said it's catchin' and he thinks it'll come about that it's carried by people and spread by nastiness," Jasper continued.

"Poor sanitation." Heather bolstered his attempt.

"Yeah!" Jasper replied. "There it is! The place where you took Lee!" Jasper pointed out, leaning forward closer to the windshield. He grinned and winked.

"If only you knew the things my family has been in," she thought to herself, looking ahead.

"That property is the Oakland Plantation. It goes back to the early 1800's too!" Jasper said. He saw the old Negro granny woman in the yard. He sounded the horn and she returned the greeting with a wave. "Her and Jewel, two of a kind, good ole' niggers!" Jasper said, smiling.

The loose free-floating boards of the narrow-planked bridge over Handco Creek made a horrendous clatter as the speeding Ford crossed. Dew drops sparkled in the delicate webs of writing spiders that made their homes up and down the alder covered banks. Deep green waters rushed along the shallow mossy banks. Heather spotted a big turtle on a bleached tree that lay in the east side of the swift moving water. "Big turtle!" she said.

"You'll see several folks fishin' for 'em while yer here," Jasper said, steering the Ford to straddle a large dished spot in the road. "That damn place'll put ya on the roof if'n ya hit it hard," he said, shaking his head.

The two rode without speaking until they reached Harris City where Jasper had to stop for traffic at the intersection. Heather sat patiently observing the sights. There was not much to the tiny place. A natural rock store on the west side of the intersection seemed to make up most of the community's excitement. The vast majority of the people were gathered there.

"Damn it!" Jasper said, holding the steering wheel with both hands.

The large old chain driven White truck that was slowly crossing was loaded with three sections of tree trunks destined for the sawmill less than a mile to the west.

"Now there's a sight," Heather said, as she climbed out of the cab.

"Where ya goin'?" Jasper asked.

"Standing up to see this," she answered.

Jasper looked at her back side as she came off the seat. He shook his head, liking what he saw. Jasper realized he was her father's age and needed to come to terms, curbing his thoughts and desires.

"A rare sight! I've only seen a single team still workin' up home," Heather said, standing in the open door. The gentle morning breeze blew her soft hair about her face.

The triple team of oxen walked slowly with muscles taut, pulling the relic of a pole cart. "That's got ta be a four-and-a-half-foot diameter log," Heather exclaimed, looking back at Jasper. He could see the childlike excitement on her face. As the team cleared the intersection, he saw a photographer dismantling his camera and wooden tripod from a location in the short grass across the way. As the marked police car moved ahead, several locals waved.

"Friendly folks," Jasper said, waving back.

The north side of the square was filled with law enforcement cars, some marked but many unmarked. The cars were as old as 1920 and as new as 1930. Most were Fords or Chevrolets. The courthouse steps were filled with men smoking and exchanging experiences. Laughter broke the continual string of exaggerated truths. Heather quickly saw that she was the only woman. Mayor Cornelius Cunningham laughed and slapped backs as he stood on the top step with the Mayor of Greenville. Greenville Police Chief John Nolly stood close to his mayor, with Chief Hawthorn nearby. Heather asked Jasper to stall until they started inside.

"Why?" he asked.

"Smoke! It bothers me," she replied. They waited in the car.

"Did I tell ya about my kissin' a woman who used tobacco?" he asked, looking at her. His blue eyes sparkled.

"No!"

"It's like sippin' from a spittoon!" he said, slapping the seat and chuckling.

"That's gross!" Heather exclaimed.

"Damn right! I don't smooch on no tobacco usin' females," he said. "Men neither!" He added, pointing his finger at her. He watched the crowd.

"How large is the Greenville department?" Heather asked.

"Four and the chief," Jasper replied. "Now they're a strange bunch. They don't do anything unless they are called out." He paused. "Like they don't get into anything on their own. They just respond. This nigger case, they'll just look out for Greenville, they won't get involved." Jasper looked for a place to park. "They don't get out of the city limits," he added.

Parking was limited. Jasper had parked the car across the square, out of the assembly of law enforcement cars. They could see the courthouse doors and the Greenville jail. "There's Ambrose Watkins, Meriwether Solicitor General, and Louis Gilbert, Meriwether Sheriff." Jasper pointed toward the jail. The two men wore suits and carried folders. Heather could see the sheriff's revolver now and then when the wind blew his coat open. The two men walked briskly toward the courthouse.

"This is good! Let's go!" Heather said, opening her door. Jasper followed.

Ambrose Watkins saw the woman with the Warm Springs officer. "Is that a woman?" he asked Sheriff Gilbert.

The sheriff leaned back and looked around Ambrose Watkins. "It damn sure is," he said. "Your eyes still work."

"She a guest?" asked Watkins.

"Hell if I know," replied Gilbert.

Heather and Jasper hurried to close the gap.

"Mornin', Jasper!" said Sheriff Gilbert.

"Mornin', Sheriff!" Jasper called out. Heather was silent.

"Who's yer guest?" the sheriff asked.

"Gents! This is Detective Duncan." Jasper grinned.

"From what big city?" asked Ambrose Watkins.

"Warm Springs!" Jasper replied.

Both men stopped and turned around. "What?"

"Heather Duncan!" Heather said, extending her hand to the sheriff and the solicitor general. "Nice ta meet ya," she said, shaking their hands.

Sheriff Louis Gilbert almost let his cold wet cigar fall from his mouth in surprise.

The four walked along. "Where ya from?" asked Ambrose Watkins.

"Campbellton, Campbell County," Heather said, from behind them. They walked in silence down the edge of the street. The occasional car and delivery truck passed.

Ambrose Watkins stopped and turned to Heather. "Any kin ta former Marshal Mathew Duncan?" he asked.

Heather stood with her hands on her waist. "Grandfather," she said, smiling. Ambrose Watkins did not reply. He turned to Sheriff Gilbert. "She's more than looks, takin' after him," he said, walking ahead.

Jasper looked surprised. He had heard and read about the hard, honest lawman. He felt even more assured of his new partner. Heather and Jasper walked behind the two men. Heather really did not want attention based on the novelty of being a woman in law enforcement. The gathering of men saw her on the walkway right behind the sheriff and the Meriwether Solicitor General. Many thought she was with them, until they realized that the officer with her was Jasper Brown of Warm Springs, and that made them curious.

A few of the lawmen had started to file into the courthouse. "Let's get this underway, gentlemen!" yelled Sheriff Gilbert, tossing his stubby cigar aside. A blue jay darted down from the scruffy struggling white oak to check out the curious object. It was so offensive the jay did not even attempt to peck at it. "Inside! Inside!" the sheriff yelled, waving his hands as if he was shooing chickens to the pen. Due to fire laws, only chewing tobacco was allowed inside, so that ruled out the vast majority of the men. Only a few gathered a polished brass spittoon as they entered. The spittoons were cradled in an oak floor rack, much like bowling balls. The solicitor general, sheriff, Jasper, and Heather were the last four to enter. Jasper motioned for them to take a seat in the back row.

"I need to be next to the chief and the mayor, and you need to be with me, since we're partners," Heather whispered, pulling Jasper from the back row, just before he sat down. His revolver and belt buckle scrubbed, drawing attention to them as they walked down the aisle. Mayor Cornelius Cunningham and Chief Hawthorn were sitting on the front row and the bench was full, until Heather and Jasper arrived. Jaws slacked, mouths opened, and eyes blinked, focusing on the woman in the suit. Heather stopped next to the mayor.

"Mayor," she said, with a smile.

"Detective Duncan," Mayor Cornelius Cunningham acknowledged. It was all he could do not to break into a smile. Chief Hawthorn looked straight ahead.

"Sir, may I have this seat?" Heather boldly asked the well-dressed man sitting next to the mayor.

The man stood quickly. "Certainly, Miss," he replied, as he motioned for the man on the end to drop to the row behind. The whispering had already begun. The full room sounded like a convention of school boys. Before sitting, she made sure to fan her suit coat, revealing her gun and badge. That really got the room abuzz.

Meriwether Sheriff Louis Gilbert sat down at the heavy dark stained table. Ambrose Watkins was next, but he chose to stand for a moment longer. "Gentlemen! Let's get the mystery put to bed once and for all," he said, pounding the table with the ash gavel. Bang! Bang! Bang! It sounded off in the large hard surfaced room. There was almost an echo. "Mayor Cornelius Cunningham or Chief Howard Hawthorn, please tell us who this attractive woman is. Hell! If she was ugly as a muddy rail fence, put us at ease," he said, extending his hand toward the two men from Warm Springs.

"Me? You?" asked the chief.

"You may do the honors," said Mayor Cunningham, smiling and elbowing Heather.

Chief Hawthorn stepped to the platform and stood by the table. "Gents! We -- well, the city, put out a call for help. Our police department is small, and when the James Lee atrocities commenced, we decided we needed a detective. Former Sheriff Benjamin Giles of Campbell County was kind enough to send down this officer," he said, bobbing his head up and down. "And I, we, thought it was a man coming down, but we've got this -- " he paused, " -- rather attractive young woman." He pointed at different ones in the audience. "I believe she won't put up with any crotch driven crap and crude remarks. I believe her to be as competent as or more so than many of you or your officers back in your jurisdictions," he said. He was silent for a moment, letting that sink in.

Mayor Cunningham promptly stood and looked at the gathering. "She handled us hard, got her right pay for her qualifications, brings her own equipment, and I'll let my chief tell you the rest!" said the mayor as he took his seat. Heather blushed.

"The city has bought this woman a new windshield. For what, you say. I want Officer Jasper Brown to tell you about it," said the chief, motioning for Jasper to take the floor. Jasper stood up next to Heather.

"Stand up," whispered the mayor. As Heather stood, several gasped at her attractiveness.

"Jesus!" someone muttered. Chief Hawthorn quickly pointed and there was silence. "Roll yer tongues in boys! She'll cut it off, and well, where she'll probably stick it on you, it won't taste so good," he said. The men laughed.

The same voice said, "I'm sorry."

Heather gave a nod.

"I was chasin' James Lee north on the Greenville-Manchester Road. Took a shot at him. He shot at me! Well, my shot hit the oncoming windshield that I didn't see for the dust. It was this woman, now my partner." Jasper swayed with pride. "I took a ditch, she turned and chased him down, James Lee, shot it out and had him on the ground when I got there. She caught James Lee for us!" Jasper said, smiling and nodding. "This is Detective Heather Duncan. Her granddaddy was -- " Heather elbowed Jasper to stop.

Ambrose Watkins chimed in, "Marshal Mathew Duncan of Campbellton." That brought comments and agreeable nods from the group.

"Damn fine lawman!" said a man.

Heather swelled with pride. "Thank you, thank you," she said. "Now that Lee's in jail, I'll be working whatever cases come up with Jasper Brown and the other officers. Thank you!" She took her seat.

* * *

Curley Jones had just relieved the night jailer and was inside the cell block conducting a head count. "Step up!" he yelled. The prisoners who knew what he wanted did so immediately. James Lee tended to lag behind in reporting to the bars. Curley walked up and down the short cell block looking into the dim light at the prisoners. No one put their hands on the vertical bars except for James Lee. The other prisoners squinted and turned their heads. Curley saw the black fingers on his jail bars. They were immediately struck with the club, making a solid thud.

"Shit! Damn it!" James Lee shouted, as he drew his bruised fingers back, placing them under his arms. He bent over in pain. "That hurt, you bastard!" The other prisoners knew what was next.

"Boy! Who told you that you could touch my jail bars?" Curley yelled.

"Nobody, boss," James Lee mumbled.

"Boy! Who told you that you could talk in my jail?" Curley yelled, striking the bars over and over with his club, like a mad man in a state of panic. "Another word and I'll open this door and beat you senseless!"

The sheriff's secretary, Mrs. Dixie Van Wormer, had entered the office, greeted by the jail check and stale air. The odors of the cell block had drifted into the book-in office during the damp night. She opened the doors and windows for ventilation. Dixie sat down and began her work as she had for the last fifteen years. She had seen sheriffs come and go. The morning sunlight shone brightly over her shoulders.

James Lee stood naked in the cell except for his shoes. He was able to see his cell mates, four other Negroes.

"De-bug Lee and suit him out. Then let him mop the piss from the cell floor," Curley said to the trustee.

"Yes, boss!" replied Bo Bob.

Curley Jones stepped back into a small bit of civilization, there in the jail office. "Good morning, Mrs. Dixie!" he said cheerfully.

"Mornin'!" she replied.

"Lovely dress," he commented.

"Same one for three years, Curley," she replied, as she looked over the stack of mail. An early gardenia was on her desk, among the wire baskets of paperwork to be filed. "Meetin' at the courthouse?" she asked.

The jail keys rang out as Curley tossed them onto the wall hook. "Joint meeting among the agencies," he replied, opening the morning newspaper. "Miss Jewel's been gone. Coffee and teacakes," he added.

"Maybe she saved us some," replied Dixie.

* * *

"Sheriff, do you want to tell them about the case?" asked Ambrose Watkins.

"You do it. I may tell too much," the sheriff replied, keeping his seat.

"Gentlemen, I would hope that all of you are aware of the demise of Sheriff Benjamin Giles. He was killed by a Negro who was being held for questioning and then broke and ran. In the chase, the sheriff was ambushed and killed with his own revolver. He died on the way to the hospital. That is right, isn't it Detective Duncan?" he asked, looking at her.

"Yes, that is correct," Heather replied.

"Please remember his widow in your prayers, and I'm sure we will learn of funeral arrangements by way of telephone or newspaper," said Ambrose Watkins. He turned and opened the folder he had carried from the jail.

"I will give you a brief coverage. The Negro James Lee burglarized a residence in the community of Odessadale, on the Dodson Road, close to Flat Shoals Creek. There was no one at home during the entry. He stole a small amount of money. We are still asking for the exact amount, from the victim. We hope to have that at some point in the very near future. Lee also stole a .32 S&W blue steel revolver, along with a car. The car was a 1925 Star hard top, two-door sedan, black in color. This was recovered, along with the .32 revolver, by Warm Springs Officer Jasper Brown. Chief Hawthorn, he did a good job, as well as the detective, as I understand yet to be employed. James Lee is in our fine drab establishment known as the Greenville Jail," he said. Several chuckled. "We will hold him there without bond until his trial. Now! After stealing the car, money, and revolver, he drives to Durand, by way of the Tigner Road. We have a witness that puts him entering Durand by that road. Lee enters town by the Mabry Road where he waits until the store of Herman Pickens is empty of customers. James Lee enters and robs, killing Herman Pickens in the street in front of the store." He took a seat on the edge of the heavy table.

"Well, there is something to be said for skipping school," he said. "James Lee is seen and identified by a young white boy hiding during school hours in the basement of the hardware across the corner from the store. He, the boy, sees James Lee from the small barred window under the front and side porch of the hardware. He is unnoticed by James Lee. The young man and his parents will be at the trial. He is old enough to be a reliable witness. His name at this time is withheld, for his safety. As you know, the county patrols Odessadale, and Durand, Raleigh, Woodbury, and a slew of towns north, Gay, Alvaton, Luthersville, Lone Oak, to name a few. Warm Springs and Manchester have police departments." He smiled. "Heck! You know all of this. The Campbell County Sheriff, Benjamin Giles, is contacted about the possibility of sending deputies on loan to assist in bolstering the Warm Springs Department, as the Meriwether Sheriff has no additional to contribute and neighboring counties are on high alert to watch for the suspect who is still not located at that time. They are trying to prevent another murder by spreading the word and being as visible as possible," he said, standing.

An officer raised his hand. "Dan Wagner, Harris County, Sheriff's Department. Where was Mr. Pickens buried?"

The sheriff pointed to the man. "The McKey Cemetery, his wife is a McKey."

"Thank you, sir. We had folks wondering, and if the family was in

101

need."

"I don't think they are in need. I will express your concern in passing to his widow," replied the sheriff.

Ambrose Watkins asked, "How many are in here from the newspapers?" He pointed across the audience. Three hands were raised. "You have enough to publish a story. My office is the official source for information. Don't hound the sheriff's deputies or local police officers."

Mayor Cornelius Cunningham gradually raised his hand. "Yes, Mayor," said Watkins.

"May I make light of the situation for a moment, with my telling of the Warm Springs facts?" he asked. Chief Howard Hawthorn looked down. He knew he was probably going to be embarrassed.

Miss Jewel had been listening from the door to the council chambers. The door was slightly ajar and the aroma of coffee and her teacakes escaped into the courthouse. Sheriff Gilbert yelled to her. "Miss Jewel! After this!"

"Yessa, Shuriff! I'ze ready," she replied, from the narrow opening in the door.

Mayor Cornelius Cunningham stood, his hat cocked on his head. "So, this woman is traveling southbound on Greenville-Manchester Road and she takes a bullet in her windshield. Now, that pisses her off! She turns around and gives chase to tha bastard. Runs him ta ground at the Oakland Plantation. They exchange gunfire. Our officer arrives after he gets out of a ditch and finds the wanted man face down in the dusty road. She even insists that he be handcuffed in the back. Now we've got a woman detective and Sheriff Gilbert's got James Lee," he said, taking a slight bow. The audience laughed.

Chief Hawthorn stood, joining the mayor. "We even paid for her windshield and had breakfast with her, before we knew she was our applicant," he said, laughing.

"She's a slick business woman," said a lawman.

"When yer tired of her, we'll beat yer pay!" yelled another. The moment was light.

The courtroom broke into a roar of conversation, much directed at Detective Duncan. The mayor and the chief seemed for the moment to be the center of attention. The chief was enjoying it. The lawmen hurried into the council chamber to partake of the coffee and teacakes. Miss Jewel sat nearby in the corner and gloated over her presentation.

The afternoon sun felt warm as the lawmen slowly dispersed and returned to their jurisdictions, each with the peace of mind that for now a murderer, James Lee, was in custody, where he would stay until trial. They all hoped he would hang. A man of his caliber was certainly not worthy of prison, and would be a terrible risk in a chain-gang camp. Jasper and Heather had a conversation with Miss Jewel. She slipped Jasper a few more teacakes off to the side.

The north side door of the courthouse opened and they found the patrol car was a resting place for a few pigeons that had found the tall courthouse and called it home. "Shoo!" Jasper yelled. "Damn nasty things!" he shouted, waving his arms.

"It was a good meeting. I think it went well," Heather said.

Jasper looked at his watch. "Soon be quittin' time," he said. "We can finish it out in town."

The two sat in the shadows of the downtown buildings, moving several times from the warm sun. Heather took the opportunity to write a post card home.

***

Bo Bob opened the cell where James Lee still nursed his fingers. "Git yo' black ass out cheer!"

James Lee looked at the trustee. He walked with his fingers under his armpits and mumbled at the Negro trustee. "Yous remembers I kin buss yo' head myseff," Bo Bob advised. The prisoner walked ahead down the narrow passageway, the thick red brick outer wall on one side and the cold dark painted cell block on the other. James Lee came to a narrow-barred door. "Pulls dat do' open. Widout yo' shoes," Bo Bob instructed. James Lee slid his shoes from his feet and stepped into the small heavily barred shower cage. He realized he was outside of the jail. But there was no way out of the shower cage.

"Dey beez soap! First wadder, yous lather! I call second wadder, yous rench!" said Bo Bob, reaching for a gate valve on the wall. The valve screeched as it opened under the force of Bo Bob's brown leathery hand. The first water fell hard into the cage. James Lee felt its power as it struck him, almost knocking him to his knees. "Soaps, nigger! Soaps!" yelled Bo Bob. James Lee could hear cars passing on the roadway, but he could not see them. "Ready nows!" yelled Bo Bob. James Lee stood straight and the second deluge of water struck him. "Flick it offs! Weez ain't got no dryin' towels," Bo Bob said, motioning for James Lee to step back inside. The prisoner stood naked and held his dry shoes. "Back toos where yous come frum," said Bo Bob, nudging James Lee with the club. Lee hurried ahead. "Shakes it off! Yo' suit'll be waitin'!"

James Lee was relatively dry by the time they walked back to the cell block. His clean suit of black and white horizontal striped woven cotton was the cleanest thing in the cell, other than him. Lee looked at the other three Negroes sitting on their bunk, playing cards. The heavy steel door slammed behind him. It was the loudest noise he had ever heard.

"Beez mop up time adder while," Bo Bob said to the prisoner, as he walked away.

CHAPTER SEVEN

When the cities of Warm Springs and Bullochville joined as one under the name of Warm Springs, a better jail was constructed. Many argued over the establishment date for Warm Springs as a city. Some folks say it was 1832 when the first formal construction took place at the spring site. Others say it was 1849 when the first Post Office was appointed by Washington. The Police Department at Warm Springs occupied the expansion room behind the building.

The depressed economy provided an abundance of available skilled labor. Those that were not farmers were in a hard way, food and shelter were at a premium. Mayor Cunningham got a unanimous vote to reconstruct a pug mill and a brick kiln on the vacant lot behind the city hall. The mill and kiln, in the right hands, would allow the city to have the brick needed to enhance the present jail. The desired red clay was not readily available. It was hauled by mule and wagon from various locations. The two most commonly dug sources were in the headwaters of Warm Springs Branch and Cold Springs Branch, both just north of the city. Once the brick operation was in full swing, the eight men used four wagonloads of clay daily.

The four current cells had been built when the second building was constructed back in 1893. The outer walls were only three bricks thick and indications were found that there had been attempts to dig out of the poorly fired bricks. City Council had approved the outer walls to be increased by two layers of newly fired bricks, and the interior walls were all to be five layers thick. The brick operation was run as a small work camp. The skilled brick-men lived in shanties and worked from "can 'till can't" and even on Sundays when the kiln was under fire. For this reason, there were no prisoners housed at Warm Springs at this time. The city court could only try misdemeanor offenders. The felony cases went to the jurisdiction of the county.

The late afternoon sunlight showed signs of its defeat by the onset of darkness that eventually comes to the world outside, and even more so to the inside of the jail. James Lee listened to his cellmates. He seldom contributed anything to conversation. No one knew where he had appeared from. Before the trial, many would wonder if he was Satan himself. Jesse Jones from Luthersville was in for theft of canned goods taken from a delivery truck. His charge was just shy of felony class. Ephraim Myers, an ebony black man with one eye drawn, was from St. Marks. Myers was known well by the local prison system. He had taken the opportunity to steal two new tires from the open-air rack outside Wylie James's Garage in Rocky Mount. James had gone to the outhouse when no customers were present and Myers was seen by a passing motorist running from the high grass on the Rocky Mount-Oakland Road carrying the two tires. Myers had left a trackable trail in the tall dry grass.

Oliver Queen was from Rocky Mount. He was crafty enough to borrow a truck and ride the countryside siphoning gasoline from farm equipment and unguarded parked cars. The attempt that got him caught was at the Warm Springs Hotel, in the back lot. An unnamed napping patrolman observed suspicious activity and moved quietly in the night, finding Queen's two feet sticking out from under a delivery truck. Oliver Queen was a lean, tall, crafty fellow.

Cyrus Dickey had been observed driving and unable to keep the car in between the ditches, out on the Oakland Road, almost to the covered bridge at White Oak Creek. He was heading northbound, soon to be into Pike County. He was caught in a ditch, sleeping in the running car. There was a volume of spirits found in the vehicle.

James Lee slept on the floor, against the bars. This time he had permission to touch Curley Jones's bars. His bed was a wool blanket, and his shoes served as his pillow.

Myers was favored by Bo Bob and was allowed to have a candle. It was lit by the attending jailer at the request of Bo Bob. The five Negroes played cards into the wee hours of the morning. James Lee had won favor and was allowed to join in after the first week. Lee had volunteered to take on the job of emptying the piss bucket every morning and mopping the floor when allowed to do so. This chore only occurred about every three days, regardless of the spills. The ten remaining prisoners were white. They would contribute nothing to the events, other than intense hatred for the Negroes.

James Lee appeared to be eager to break his long days with any chore that would get him out of the cell. He had even volunteered to empty and wash the piss buckets of the other three cells, all made up of white men. Bo Bob did not care who did the demeaning task, as long as it got done.

James Lee was seemingly out of his cell more than he was in. He noted the going and coming of meals and the times. From his cell he could see the street traffic as it passed about fifty yards away on the Greenville-Moreland Road.

* * *

"Mornin', Mayor!" Detective Duncan called out from her side of the patrol car. Officer Jasper Brown had driven around behind the police department and city hall to see the progress. His justification was that alleys had to be watched just like streets, and he was right.

Mayor Cunningham stood wiping sweat from his brow. "Morning, officers," he replied, catching both at once.

Jasper waved as he leaned over the steering wheel and looked at the progress. "Coming along nicely!" He yelled back to the mayor.

"Have a good shift," replied the mayor. That was his way of indicating that he was busy for the moment. Later, he might be caught playing checkers at a board spread anywhere in town. The incoming train shook the earth as it passed nearby.

"Tell me about the Durand shooting," Heather said, looking at Jasper.

"The witness, the young boy, said the nigger, James Lee, came out of the store into the street. Lee had a bag of money in one hand and his stolen revolver in the other. Herman Pickens, not to be robbed, ran after Lee with a shotgun he had managed to get from behind the counter. Mrs. Pickens later said they kept the shotgun hidden under the counter hoping they would never need it, but the day came. The stolen car driven by Lee was parked with the tag toward the hardware store, across the street. Herman got to the steps and started to draw down on the nigger when Lee shot him twice in the chest. The shotgun went off and filled the hanging Canada Dry sign full of holes. Men from the hardware heard the gunshots and ran out to see. When they got to Herman, he was already dead. The young boy came out of hiding when the deputies got there. That was Sheriff Gilbert, and I'm not clear on which deputy," said Jasper. He had driven out on the Bulloch-Bonner Road to Judson Road. There was no one coming, so Jasper swung the car around and headed back toward town. "Where's this road go?" he asked.

"Manchester Highway before we turned around, now toward town and then to Durand, given ya keep on the main road," Heather said, taking in the houses and small farms along the way. "We're well outside the city, that's for sure," she added. "I need to know where all the clean toilets are. I have no intentions of going to the woods, if it can be avoided."

"Most folks in town don't have toilets for the public. Those that have the space have two, as you know. Well, really three," Jasper said.

"One for the white men and white women, and then one for both sexes for the Negroes," Heather said, looking at Jasper. "I'm an officer of the law and I don't consider myself as the general public," Heather replied.

* * *

The screen door to the sheriff's office moaned as it was pulled open. Secretary Dixie Van Wormer stopped her work and looked up. The inside door was opened slowly. She knew by the lack of announcement it was Erastus Cobb, Meriwether Superior Court Judge. Cobb was a hard old man. He had seen many a rough term in his years as Judge. His thin oxford shoes carried in the grit from the yard. His six-foot frame was beginning to stoop. The tiny blue eyes and large heavy lobed ears gave a stark contrast to the snow-white hair and sharp facial features. Dixie had seen the same gray suit with faint vertical black stripes for many years. The cuffs of the Judge's white shirt were tattered from wear. His wife, Emma, had carefully whip-stitched the worn spots to get more wear from the garment. Dixie did not feel any pity for him, she had only three dresses to her name that she could wear to work, and a closet of worn out house dresses. Holding his seat, she knew he had to be well paid.

"Good mornin'!" said Erastus Cobb. "Where's Curley?"

"He's in the kitchen with Miss Jewel, probably bringing our coffee up," she replied.

"That's fine. I'll sit down and wait. No hurry. I need to see the Nigger James Lee," said Cobb.

"Me and Bo Bob can get him to the bars," Dixie said, looking at him over her papers.

"No! Curley needs to be present," he replied, resting his hands on his knees as he sat in the worn cane bottomed chair. "This sunlight feels nice," he said, with a slight smile.

They could hear Curley talking to the sheriff and Miss Jewel. There was laughter and a loud outburst. "I hear them now," said Cobb, watching the narrow door that entered into the sheriff's residence.

Curley swung the door open with his butt. "Here's yer coffee, Dixie!" He closed the door behind him with his foot. The face-mounted deadbolt clicked. The Judge watched. "Hello, Judge!" Curley said. "Sheriff know yer here?"

"No, I just got here," replied the Judge.

"Sheriff! Sheriff!" yelled Curley, standing with his back to Judge Cobb.

The heavy, hurried footsteps of the sheriff were heard. The narrow door swung open. "God damn! What is it?" he barked.

"Judge Cobb's here," said Curley, sipping on his hot coffee and looking over the cup at the sitting Judge.

The sheriff's tone changed. "Good mornin'!" he said. "What can we do for you?"

Judge Erastus Cobb slowly stood. "James Lee. Need ta see him."

"Bring him to the bars, Curley," said Sheriff Gilbert. Curley opened the heavy metal door and called for Bo Bob.

Bo Bob had already heard the talk and was standing just to the side of the door. He stepped out of the shadow. "Yes, Boss!"

"Take the keys and get James Lee out. Judge needs him," Curley said, sipping his coffee as the cool air rushed by his face, carrying the stench of the overcrowded cell block past him.

"James Lee!" Bo Bob yelled.

"Here, boss man!" replied Lee, from the dim light of the cell.

Bo Bob worked the heavy ring of keys and opened the cell door. "Judges Rat-tit Cobb's heah ta sees you."

"Comin' out, boss!" yelled James Lee.

"Comes ahead!" replied Bo Bob, stepping aside.

James Lee walked to the narrow intake door where the Judge stood. Erastus Cobb stood silently, looking at James Lee. He looked from his feet to the top of his head. "What happened to yer fingers?" he asked.

"Closed 'em in tha door, sir!" James Lee replied. Bo Bob stood out of the Judge's line of sight and tapped his palm with his club. He dared Lee to say what actually happened to his fingers.

"I'm here to tell you that the arrest warrant, as you know, has been executed. You are charged with armed robbery and murder. The murder of storekeeper Herman Pickens of Durand. As soon as the sheriff's deputies can tie you to the burglary of the residence where you took money, the murder weapon, the .32 revolver, and the Star automobile, you will be charged with those as well," said the Judge. "But with murder, those won't make much difference if you're found guilty," he added. Sheriff Gilbert sat on the corner of his desk and watched.

"Do you have anyone you want to contact?" asked the Judge.

James Lee shook his head.

"I can't hear a head shake, answer my question," barked the Judge.

"No, sir!" James Lee said loudly.

"Mrs. Dixie, are you getting all this down?" asked Judge Cobb.

"I am," she replied, as she took the conversation down in shorthand.

"Can you afford a lawyer?" asked Cobb.

"No, sir!" James Lee said loudly.

"We've got some time, before statute runs out. I'll be back and we'll talk about that," said the Judge. He stepped away from the stench of the jail door.

"Put 'im back, Bo Bob!" barked Curley Jones. The other prisoners watched from their cells. The men that were seasoned in the system were becoming suspicious of James Lee.

* * *

"My grandmother back home would call this a blue bird sky. The deep blue sky, filled with beautiful brilliant white clouds like popcorn," Heather said, leaning forward and looking up. She was close to the windshield. "I need to run my Essex. What are you doing right after work?" Before Jasper could answer she added, "This ain't a date."

"Oh! I didn't think I could be so lucky," Jasper said, followed by a loud deep sigh. He turned the patrol car from Orchard Lane onto Main Street. The town was busy with folks who had come to trade. The automobiles were taking second place to the wagons that were parked along the street and down the alleyways. "Hard times brings the old ways out in folks," he said, easing the car ahead. The occasional young boy and his dogs ran across the dusty street.

"Up home school would be lettin' out for plantin', those that still farm," Heather said, taking in all the different faces. The weathered, leathery faces of both men and women, young and old, watched her as they passed. Some of the women and girls managed to give her a slight smile. She could see the hard times in their faces. "Jasper, is this area depressed?" she asked, turning to see a large red jenny mule.

"Depressed?" he asked.

"Poor folks," she replied, turning about, looking at the people.

"Some go to bed hungry, many wear two sets of clothes until they're threadbare. Women folks have a Sunday dress," he said. "I'm damn lucky to have this job, but it's hard to arrest a man in such hard times," he said, stopping the car to allow a one-horse wagon to swing wide in the street.

"I want to get out. I see some women. I need to let them see that I'm here and I can be approached at any time," Heather said, pulling on the door handle.

Jasper parked the patrol car across three spaces, in order to pull away if they were needed. He set the brake and turned off the engine. "We need to make a scene when we do get a call," he said. "We're always responding to what has already happened." He stood in the door trying to get his legs back. A small boy and his sister suddenly ran up to Jasper.

"Hi!" said the young boy. He appeared to be less than five years old.

"Hello!" replied Jasper, looking down. The boy's sister stood silently looking up at the officer. Jasper felt funny. He did not know what to do or say from there. "Uh! Have you met the detective?" he stuttered. Both children shook their heads.

Heather walked around to Jasper's side of the car. The small boy looked up with surprise to see a woman dressed like a man and wearing a gun and badge. He eventually smiled, as did his sister. Heather offered her hand to the little boy's dirty one, and then to the girl. "Hello! I'm Detective Heather Duncan," she said, smiling.

The dusty faces of the two children smiled, but Heather could see stress deep within their eyes. Cars passed, and several wagons. "Are you hungry?" Heather asked. There were tears long before the answer that finally came. They nodded their heads "yes".

"Hey!" A gruff voice called out. Heather looked up. The two children flinched. Heather took them by the hands. "Jasper," she whispered.

"They're fine! No harm! Just visitin'!" Jasper yelled back to the rough bearded man standing by a wagon across the street.

"Don't be a bother!" the man called back.

Heather knew she had a nickel in her front right pocket. That was to be her mid-day meal, but these two looked like needed it more than she did. "Come, let's go to the store," she said, stepping out, still holding the two small hands. Heather took short steps, allowing the young children to keep up with her. "Jasper! Let's see what T.C. Handley's store has today," she said. Jasper hurried to catch up. Handley's store was within sight of the gruff father's wagon.

The sidewalk was full of people and dogs. The dogs sat along the edge of the raised boardwalk. Some lay in the shade while others sat in the warm sun. Heather had not been inside Handley's store. It was a poorly lit place, busy and dark. The store room quickly grew dim after the sunlight had reached as far as it could through the main window on the front. There were no other windows, and only a single bulb hung over the cash register. The open back door created a bright rectangle in the rear of the long narrow building. The crosswind brought the bite of guano, onions, turpentine, and seasonal fruits to the front.

"Jasper, I need all I can get for as little as I can spend," Heather said softly.

"This is the wrong store for that. This old lady's a bitch," he replied.

"Stay with me," Heather said kindly to the two children, stilling holding their hands. Customers were being held up by their slow walk. She heard a loud impatient sigh behind her. "God bless the children, for they are the seeds of the earth, Mathew Duncan, Book One," she suddenly said loudly. She looked over her shoulder in the direction of the impatient man. He backed off.

"Afternoon, Mrs. Handley!" Jasper cried out to the darkness.

"Afternoon, Jasper Brown!" a woman's voice replied. They looked about to find the woman high atop a rolling ladder. Her full dress was tucked between her legs.

"Help yerself," she called down.

Heather looked up at the busy woman. "Mrs. Handley?"

The old woman looked down at the younger woman's voice. Their faces were bathed in the faint light. "Yes," replied the woman.

"I'm Detective Heather Duncan, of your city police department. I need some marked down fruit. Do you have any?" she asked.

"Maybe," Mrs. Handley replied. She was busy looking into a wooden crate. "Along the cooler wall. You pick it out and I'll see if it's ta be marked down," replied Mrs. Handley.

"Nice ta have met ya," Heather replied.

Jasper talked to several customers while Heather picked among the last of the winter apples. Some were still paper wrapped. The children smiled as Heather handed them each two apples, one red and one deep yellow. "Don't eat it yet. I've got to pay for it first," she said. Mrs. Handley had returned to the floor where she waited on customers. Many customers were lined up to trade produce, eggs, even butter against their tabs. Jasper walked up.

"Get me two cans of Vienna sausage and a penny's worth of cheese and crackers for these two," Heather said. The little girl was pressing the yellow apple to her nose. Jasper hurried the gathering process. Heather and the two children stood quietly in line. There were several people ahead of them.

"So, yer tha new lady po-lice," a man turned from the line to say, looking at her from head to foot. He had the look of a hungry wolf.

"I am that!" she replied.

"I'll be sure ta call fer ya if'n I need somethin' detected," he said, rather snooty like.

"You do that!" replied Heather.

The line moved along. Heather heard a woman behind her clear her throat. "Miss," the woman said.

Heather turned. "Yes?"

"The womenfolk that know yer here really appreciate you comin'," whispered the weathered woman. Her sunbonnet was pushed off of her head.

"Thank you!" Heather replied. "I'm here for everyone."

Jasper broke in line, his arms loaded with the items Heather had requested. "I got it," he said. "We need ta be out on the street. I think some kind of disturbance is developin'. I heard the familiar sound from the front doors." He looked ahead. "Excuse me! Can we pay so we can get on patrol?" he asked loudly.

Mrs. Handley motioned them to the front of the line. "Thank you, ma'am," said Heather.

"Them's tha Harper young'uns," said Mrs. Handley, as she wrote out a receipt. "Couldn't be taken from a nicer bastard," she mumbled.

Jasper was at the front door. "I think we need to hurry," he said excitedly.

Heather handed each of the two children a brown paper bag. "Now you can eat your apple," she said, smiling. The dirty faces looked up at her and slowly grew timid smiles.

Heather could now hear the noise Jasper had been jabbering about. She hurried the two children along toward the front doors. Heather saw the light one-horse wagon rock as the bearded man shoved a woman into the side of it. The yelling was not to be tolerated, much less the abuse on the woman. Heather assumed it to be his wife, the mother of these two children.

"This'll take both of us," Jasper said, looking at Heather.

"No, you keep these children. Take 'em around the corner. They don't need to see this," Heather said, pushing the pair toward Jasper.

"You sure?" he asked. He was not too sure of the situation. He had talked to old man Harper before about beating on his wife. Jasper sat the children down on the corner of the porch where he could watch his partner. The hungry children quietly enjoyed their food. They never turned to look at the loud argument. They had seen it all before.

"Let me through!" Heather barked, as she touched the folks on the crowded sidewalk. They parted for her passing, many taking a second look upon seeing that it was a woman. "Let me through!" Harper pushed his wife against the wagon and addressed her with a horrific selection of demeaning words. The woman began to cry as he shook her about. He shook her so hard her bonnet came off and hung around her neck. The top button of her faded dress had torn away and allowed the loose dress to fall from her shoulder.

Detective Duncan stood on the top step of the store and called down to the angry, violent man. "Harper!" she yelled. The public watched her and began to whisper, wondering just what this slim young badge wearing woman could do to a man of Harper's size. "Harper!" Heather yelled again.

Still holding his wife by her arms hard enough to leave bruises, Harper looked around. His mean face glared at the law woman on the steps. "What?" he yelled.

"Let her go!" Detective Duncan yelled.

"No badge wearin' big city bitch goin' ta tell me what I can do with my wife! Ain't you tha one that walked away wid my young'uns?" he said loudly, shaking his sobbing wife.

Detective Duncan checked her handcuffs. "Come to me, Mr. Harper!" she barked. The townsfolk stood silently and watched. Many would have bet on Harper, he was a grizzly of a man. Jasper watched and worried.

Harper pushed his wife into the wagon once more. "I'll come ta ya bitch!" he said, taking a step toward the detective.

Detective Duncan jumped from the top step, grabbed Harper's throat with her right hand, and clamped down with a mighty grip. She squeezed with all her might, so tightly that her forearm muscles were quivering. Her left hand grabbed an ear amongst the long hair and began to twist and pull. Harper gasped for breath under the crushing pressure on his throat. All he could muster was a groan as he hit the dusty street with the detective on top of him. Whispers arose from the crowd. First one woman came to the side of Mrs. Harper, and then another. Jasper could not stand it any longer, he ran to his partner's side. Heather rolled Harper on his stomach and cuffed him in the back. He still moaned and gasped for breath.

"God damn! I think my windpipe's crushed," said Harper, blowing dust as he spoke. Harper had sucked down a goodly amount of dirt. He spit and coughed.

Heather got up from her hands and knees. "Damn lucky you're in town! You should be shot! You asshole!" she barked, kicking Harper in the ribs a couple of hard times. The women gasped at her display of anger. The men grinned and liked what they saw.

Jasper entered the thick crowd. "You all right?" he asked, catching his breath. Jasper rolled Harper onto his back.

Mrs. Harper sobbed, as she was offered comfort by the two women. "He'll kill me for sure," she said, wiping tears.

Detective Duncan bent down and looked at Harper. "Can you hear me?" she yelled.

"God damn! I ain't deef!" he replied.

Heather stood and began counting the people in the crowd. "One, two, three -- and up to the thirties," she counted. "Did everyone hear this man? He said he ain't deef," she said loudly.

Laughter came from the crowd. "He may be dumb, though!" one man yelled out.

Heather bent down once more. "Mr. Harper! You are goin' to the jail tonight. I'm seein' that you understand me and I mean exactly what I say. When I'm in this town, you touch this woman who bore you two children, I'll beat you senseless. Do you understand?" she asked loudly. Harper remained silent and looked at her. Heather kicked him in the ribs again. Harper's big ribcage sounded like a ripe melon as her shoe found its place.

"Ugh!" he grunted.

"Answer me, you dumb son of a bitch!" Heather yelled.

"I'll kill you! You bitch!" Harper said, as he rolled around trying to get to her.

In a flash, Heather pulled her revolver and held it a foot from his face. "That's a threat! These folks heard it! I can shoot you, you bastard!" she snarled. Mrs. Harper looked shocked.

Harper shook his head now that he understood her intentions. "Get him in the car! We're going to Greenville!" Heather said to Jasper. Jasper sat the large man up and helped him to his feet. Heather leaned in close, letting Harper feel her warm breath. "You stop tobacco use and feed your family, or so help me God I'll kill you at close range. I tracked a wanted murderer down and shot him takin' a shit in the woods," she added, which was a convincing but frightening lie. Heather fell back and kicked him in the butt. The dust billowed like a cloud. "Shot him in the back of the head! Never knew I was there," she whispered in his ear. Mrs. Harper saw her husband turn pale with fear. "I want to talk to his wife," she said to Jasper.

"Take yer time, old Harper needs to think about his actions," Jasper replied, as he closed the door.

Detective Duncan introduced herself to the battered woman, as the two children ran up with their leftovers in the paper bags. "Can you fend for yourselves?" asked Heather, gently touching the woman's bruised face.

"Yes," Mrs. Harper sobbed.

"He'll be gone for as long as I can convince the Judge to keep him. I'm asking for an order for him to stay away, unless you let him back," Heather said, dusting her suit off. The crowd began to go about their business. Several men gave the detective a pat on the back for a job well done.

Mrs. Harper hugged her two small children. "I took it upon myself to feed them, I hope it was all right," Heather said, rubbing the heads of both children. They looked up and smiled.

"He's beat on me all my married life," said the woman softly, looking down in shame. "I'm really afraid for the day he gets out," she added, looking at the detective.

"You go home and run your house like you wish. I'll deal with him," Heather said, giving the woman a one-armed hug.

The two women who had stepped forward were still close by. Heather turned to leave.

"Detective!" One of the women called out.

Heather turned. "Yes?"

Jasper stood by the patrol car looking at his watch.

"We are glad you're here," the woman said.

"And I'm glad you stepped up to help," said Heather.

"May we call on you?" asked the other woman.

"Any time, at the police department. If I'm not in, please leave me a note that you stopped by," said Heather. She knew she would most likely not be there when they called, as her place was on the streets.

The detective dusted her suit off again as she walked toward the waiting patrol car. "It's about time!" Jasper said, shaking his keys.

"We've done a day's work," Heather replied, as she sat down in the car and closed the door. Harper was sitting cramped in the back seat. "Slide behind Officer Brown!" she barked. Harper grunted and moved over against the door. He was a back seat full.

"You bitch! I think you've affected my speech," he grunted, looking at the detective.

"Mr. Harper, when you get out, you will be served with a court order. That order should say that you will walk away from your home and not return. That is severe, and most wives that are beaten let the son of a bitch, in your case, return," Heather said, sitting sideways looking at the cuffed man. "I'll pass your troubles on to the local preacher, expect a visit from him and his deacons," she said, pulling out her revolver. Harper looked surprised. "You make a sudden move and I'll kill you where you sit. That will be put on the police report as an attack on the driving officer," she said with a smile. Jasper looked over at her as he was passing the roadway to the Meriwether Inn.

"There'll be no trouble," said Harper, closing his eyes.

"You've closed your eyes, but I know your ears are still open. If I can find a Ku Klux Klan officer, I'll ask that they visit you, a secret meeting, most likely in the darkness of night, and tell you about the love a man should have for his wife and children. They make their calls in the night so they won't embarrass anyone. I think that would be as comforting to you as a fifty-count dose of Ex-Lax, after a pound of cheese." She tightened her lip as she looked at the prisoner with his eyes closed. "Up home, I could've gotten you in the darkness of night," Heather said, nodding her head in an assuring manner. Her revolver was on her thigh.

Jasper looked over at her. "Are you for real?" he mouthed silently.

Heather nodded her head, "Yes."

The run to the Greenville jail was fast. Both officers wanted to get home at quitting time. There was no time lost on the book-in of Harper. Bo Bob shined at another prisoner to control, but Curley Jones bitched, as the late arrival would keep him after hours.

* * *

In the days that James Lee had been incarcerated, he had managed to make numerous trips to the toilet outside of the jail. His ankles were shackled with a road chain, giving him just enough slack to make about three-quarters of a normal stride. The set that Bo Bob tossed down for him to put on still had the center clip for the added ball weight. The ball weight was missing. James Lee fastened the restraints over his jail suit, as this helped with the chafing of the bare metal on his dry skin. The first time James Lee was in the system in Milledgeville, the ankle restraints had worn the skin from around his ankles. The dark Negro skin contrasted with the bare flesh of red.

On the mid-morning trips carrying the piss buckets, sometimes all four, two in each hand, James Lee observed the late Victorian house on the side street. The owner ran a fruit stand along the sidewalk. The fragrance of the early fruits for sale was detected by Lee's keen sense of smell. The imported bright yellow bananas particularly attracted his attention from afar. His desire for several of them overcame the odor of the mixed piss in the buckets that he carried, sloshing along toward the toilet. At no time was he out of sight of Bo Bob, and Curley Jones was notified when there was a man shackled and heading for the toilets, a distance away under the dark green chinaberry trees. James Lee watched the fruit stand customers as he poured out each bucket. It was generally only one or two customers at a time. They often left their cars running. This was verified as Lee rinsed out the buckets at the yard spigot. He could hear some of the cars and could see the exhaust raising a faint dust from all of the running cars. James Lee found a small dry matchstick size piece of chinaberry limb at the toilet door and eased it into his cheek.

James Lee had studied the ankle chains that hung within sight of cells two and four, for as long as there was sufficient light to see. During the night he worked the dry twig down to a small wedge by scrubbing it vigorously on the dry concrete floor. His other cellmates noticed his intense efforts on something.

"Wad yous doin'?" asked Oliver Queen, from the top bunk.

James Lee never broke his efforts as he scrubbed the small piece back and forth along the unpainted spot on the floor. "Toothpick!" he said, in a loud whisper.

"Toothpick, my ass! Yous beez up ta sumthin'," said Cyrus Dickey, closest to James Lee.

"Curley Jones dun shots fo' runnin', niggers! Yous just beez numba fives," whispered Ephraim Myers. "Dat's in de lass two yeahs," he added, turning onto his back.

James Lee followed a spot of moonlight that managed to work its way into the dark cell block. When morning came, Lee once again volunteered for piss bucket detail. When he put on the ankle chains, he would wedge the small piece of wood in the ratchet teeth and force a hold, just long enough for him to get out into the yard of the small compound. The ten-foot Anchor Fence was mere child's play for the lean young Negro. He had read the metal sign that declared the manufacturer of the fence, *"Anchor Fence",* and scoffed. "They ain't made a fence I cain't scale," he thought to himself. The four strands of taut barbed wire were a simple overhanded jump to clear.

"Bo Bob! Ready for piss bucket detail?" James Lee called out.

"You beez at ease! I'ze gets to it," Bo Bob called out from the intake door, where he was looking out at Mrs. Dixie coming up the walkway. She was an older woman, but all he got to see, except for Miss Jewel. Curley Jones was eager to get coffee for him and Mrs. Dixie, as he had for many mornings. He heard the stove top clink and rattle. Curley knew Miss Jewel was in the kitchen.

"I'm goin' back," Curley said to Bo Bob. "You got the detail?" he asked.

"I'ze gots it, boss," Bo Bob replied. He took down the ankle chains from the peg and walked back to cell number four where James Lee stood waiting with the tiny wedge in his jaw. The other Negro prisoners sat silently. The whites did not know what was up.

"Bo Bob! Got a piss nigger, I see!" yelled one white prisoner.

Bo Bob grinned and shook his head in agreement. "Ands a good 'un toos!" he said, tossing the ankle chains to the bottom of the bars where James Lee stood. Bo Bob pointed to the whites. "Yous beez doin' it tomorrow!" he said, pointing his club at the cell blocks where the whites looked on.

"Yes, sir! Bo Bob got a piss nigger!" the white prisoner said again.

James Lee pulled the chains under the bars and put the restraints on. He slipped the tiny wedge into the ratchet and swung it home. "Ready, boss!" he reported, standing straight.

"Same thin' boys! Slide 'em out quick!" Bo Bob called, as he levered the controls. James Lee stepped out with the piss bucket for cell number four, and the other three buckets from one, two, and three slid out of the bar line. The vibration of the sliding buckets on the hard floor splashed the piss about, making it even more odorous. "Close 'em up!" Bo Bob yelled, pushing the control lever to secure the cell doors. Harper was the fifth man in cell number three. The four already in were unhappy, and so was Harper. He, like James Lee, took a blanket to the floor.

It was all James Lee could do to keep his enthusiasm from showing. He shuffled along in front of the trustee, Bo Bob. Every few steps James Lee would make a sharp grunting sound and bend down slightly. "Yous all right?" Bo Bob asked, from a short distance behind Lee.

"Just a little gas, I guess," James Lee replied. This continued to the back door. "Ready, Boss!" Lee said loudly, bending down and moaning. Bo Bob walked up behind him. James Lee exploded on the old man. He grabbed his club and struck him about the head and shoulders as fast as he could swing the homemade club. The old man went down without a sound. James Lee pulled at the keys in Bo Bob's clenched fist. The old trustee would not give them up. James Lee stomped his hand and took the keys. The back door moaned and swung open. James Lee could hear Curley in the kitchen flirting with Miss Jewel. Her laughter was loud, just what he needed. The wedged side of the ankle cuffs pulled loose. James Lee took the pointed end of the ratchet arm and poked two holes in his pants, about the knee. The restraint slipped through the cotton fabric and fastened. He looked about for others in the compound. There was no one.

The Anchor fence rattled with its own unique sound as he leaped upon it and began to climb. There was no one on the street, not even a car passed as he scaled over the top strands of barbed wire. The tall Johnson grass made good cover as Lee crawled up the steep road bank toward the fruit stand. The operator sat with his back to the escaped Negro. James Lee ducked down. Bo Bob had come to and was beginning to yell out.

"'Scape! 'Scape!" he yelled, as he rubbed his bleeding head. Bo Bob found himself lying among the toppled piss buckets.

A 1925 black and red Nash came from the direction of Luthersville. James Lee watched as it slowed down and stopped at the fruit stand. "Easy take," James Lee mumbled. He watched an old man get out. "Easier take," he said, as he started across the street. He ran in a crouched posture toward the running Nash. The old Veteran carried a black lacquered cane and even limped.

Curley stopped and listened. Sheriff Gilbert was gone. "Was that Bo Bob?" he asked Miss Jewel.

"I'ze believes it wuz," she said, her hands in the dough tray.

Curley heard the cry again. "'Scape! 'Scape!" Curley ran for the kitchen door, just a few feet away. The door to the compound was locked. He shook it hard. "God damn it! Son of a bitch!" he mumbled, as he tried to find his keys on his person. They were not there, they were on his desk. "Shit!" he yelled, as he ran through the sheriff's residence and into the office. "Got one escaped!" he yelled, as he grabbed a shotgun from the wall rack. The hallway floor popped under his running feet.

Bo Bob was sitting in the compound a few feet from the back door, holding his bleeding head. "Lawd! On de Greensville-Luthersville Road!" Curley hurried to open the back kitchen door. His keys rattled as he tried each one, as under stress he had forgotten which key it was. They were all from the same blank.

The Civil War veteran was Ellis DeFoor, a child soldier. He was too old to be driving, but folks recognized him and gave a wide berth. DeFoor was in a linen summer suit, too early, but already in it. A wide-brimmed brown hat sat atop his cotton white hair. The chin whiskers were combed and shaped into a point. "Mornin', Bob!" said Ellis, as he wobbled about in his attempt to get his legs back after the drive from Moreland.

Bob Sims turned to look as he was folding his morning paper. "Look out!" Sims yelled.

James Lee pushed his way between DeFoor and the running Nash. Not to be taken without a fight, the black lacquered cane rose into the morning air. Ellis DeFoor got in several good licks before James Lee struck the old man. DeFoor fell to the ground, striking his head on an old mounting block that was just a few steps away. Bob Sims stood in total fear as he and James Lee made eye contact. Curley saw the escapee and tried to get a shot off, but due to the steep road bank there was no way without pellets striking the fruit stand and even the windows of the house behind it. Curley cursed and jumped up and down in the compound.

The Nash rolled away with James Lee behind the wheel. Mrs. Dixie was already on the telephone trying to locate the sheriff and any of the deputies, by their assigned patrol routes. Dixie leaned against the office window and saw the speeding car take to the courthouse square, where she lost sight.

"Bo Bob! God damn it! I ought ta kill you!" Curley yelled at the Negro trustee.

"Yessa," Bo Bob sobbed, still sitting in the grassy compound.

Curley ran back through the kitchen and out the front doors. Now he looked back, he really did not know why, maybe to see the stolen Nash go by on the street. He stood silently and gritted his teeth. "Dixie! Call for a doctor at the fruit stand, and then to Bo Bob," he yelled at the top of his lungs.

Mrs. Dixie called, as he had ordered. She could hear Curley cursing out front. "Damn it! Damn it! Shit!" he said, kicking the concrete walkway.

Sheriff Gilbert soon arrived. He found Curley at the fruit stand with the doctor. "Who is it?" asked the sheriff, as he hurried closer. Townsfolk were gathering.

"Mr. Ellis DeFoor. He's dead," said the doctor.

"God damn," mumbled Sheriff Gilbert, tossing his wet cigar in the yard.

James Lee hurried to take off the prison shirt. He tossed it in the floorboard. He slowed the powerful Nash down and laughed at those he had left behind. The dust rolled behind the long soft top Sedan as it hugged the ruts on the narrow Tigner-Greenville Road. James Lee was heading west.

CHAPTER EIGHT

"Damn it, Bo Bob! Hold still, yer like stitchin' up a resistin' mule!" Doc Augustus Hubbard fussed. Hubbard's six-foot height towered over the small Negro sitting before him on the back porch of the kitchen. Miss Jewel stood by with clean towels and a pan of scalding water.

"Sho' did a jobs on yo' head," she mumbled, looking down on the remaining gaping wounds. In some places she could see white shining through. "What's dat white?" she asked.

"That's his skull," mumbled Doc Hubbard. He took a moment to spit tobacco into the yard. Bo Bob moaned. "Have ya got any whiskey?" Doc Hubbard barked.

"I'ze gots a bottle hid," said Miss Jewel, looking around for Jailer Curley Jones. He was nowhere in sight. She hurried to her hiding place, soon returning with an almost full bottle of whiskey. "Here," she said, holding it out to the doctor. Bo Bob's mouth was already watering over the thought of a drink.

Doc Hubbard stopped for a moment, a stitch knot still to be tied. He took the bottle. Bo Bob had already wet his lips. "Thanks!" barked the doctor, just before taking a large gulp. "Damn! That's good!" he said, licking his lips. He pushed the bottle back to Miss Jewel. Bo Bob's heart sank, as the drool dripped from the corner of his mouth. The rough doctor pulled at the stitch knot. The sting was harsh. "You can hide it back," he said, looking around for Curley or the sheriff.

Sheriff Gilbert stood at Dixie's desk and thumped his index finger on it. At times the finger moved so fast it was almost a blur as he looked into the distant horizon. The window faced the setting sun. The jailer Curley Jones walked the outside compound checking every barred window and door. The perimeter was secure. He finished at the back porch, where the doctor took the last three stitches on Bo Bob. Miss Jewel saw him coming up but

120

did not say a word. Things were already bad. Doc Hubbard knew Curley's walk. "How long this old nigger got left?" he asked, without looking up from his work.

"Three months and two days," Curley replied, as he took the bottom step. "God damn, what a mess," Curley said, looking down at the Negro's head. "Will he live?" he asked.

"He'll live, but he needs to be isolated for at least a week. I can't tell if he's got good vision without getting him checked out," the doctor replied, dropping the needle and a small amount of trailing thread into the bloody pan of water on the top step. "I'd like to see this nigger at home," he added. "Where's the sheriff?" he asked. Bo Bob smiled, still looking down.

"That won't happen," replied Curley.

"If I say he's apt to die in this jail, it'll damn sure happen," snapped Doc Hubbard, wiping his hands on the clean towel Miss Jewel held out to him.

The injured Negro was led out of the jail in ankle chains. His uniform was bloody. Doc Hubbard was on one arm and Curley Jones was on the other. The prisoner's time would be finished at his weathered old rough and tumbled farm house in the edge of Beaver Creek swamp, west of Alvaton. Curley closed the door on the new car very carefully.

"Bo Bob!" Curley said loudly.

"Yessa, boss," the Negro answered.

"One of us apt to check on you anytime, day or night. You best be there. Ya hear?" asked Curley.

"Yessa, boss," the Negro answered.

The new 1930 teal blue Chevrolet Coupe owned by Doc Augustus Hubbard was seen leaving town with the Negro prisoner, Bo Bob. The Alvaton Road was a rough and bumpy road leaving town to the northeast.

"Dixie!" yelled Sheriff Gilbert. He jumped, realizing she was sitting at her desk, where he stood. "Call the newspaper. Ask if they're part of Associated Press," he said. "Then call the solicitor," he added. "I think he needs ta come over here."

Curley came into the office and tossed the bloody club that had belonged to Bo Bob on his desk. Sheriff Gilbert looked at the irritated man. "Best tag it for evidence," he said, as he patted his coat pockets for another cigar that was not there. Dixie was heard in the background making the telephone calls. "Curley! Get me a shotgun out," said the sheriff. "We need to be sure they're on lockdown." Curley pulled keys from his pocket and opened the gun cabinet that was built into the plastered wall.

Soon, the heavy jail door opened and Curley called out. "Strip down boys! Take 'em off!" he yelled out. There was a faint mumbling of discontent from the cells. Every inmate hurriedly took off their clothes and tossed them in front of the cell bars. The naked men stood back from the bars waiting on the shake-down. Under the armed guard of Sheriff Gilbert, Curley handled each small pile of uniform clothing, tossing them one by one back against the bars. "Dress when ya get 'em," Curley announced, continuing to search. He felt there would be nothing, but formality was paramount. He started to inspect the clothing of Cell No. 3. "Anyone knows something, they'd best tell," Curley said, being as thorough and quick as he could.

"For damn sure," said Sheriff Gilbert, racking the Winchester Model 97. The sudden loud motion placed a round in the chamber and sent chills down the spines of those men who had been fired upon, or better yet, hit by the flesh tearing balls of "00" buck. "You let us put James Lee with you, by not speaking up, we'll charge the cell with accessory to whatever this God damned nigger racks up. He's already struck Ellis DeFoor and he's dead," said Sheriff Gilbert. "He killed him right out there." Gilbert pointed in the direction of the west wall.

The four Negroes looked at one another. They still stood naked awaiting their inspection. Without a word of agreement, Ephraim Myers nodded his head at Oliver Queen. "Tells de man," he said.

"Do I hear talkin'?" Sheriff Gilbert yelled. His shotgun butt rested on his hip bone.

"Yes, boss!" several Negro voices answered.

"We knowed he wuz wukkin' downs uh small piece of wood las' night. Sayed it wuz a toofs pick," said Oliver.

"You boys get a feel for where he's headin'?" asked Curley, holding up clothing and feeling every inch.

"No, boss," Oliver answered.

Sheriff Gilbert walked slowly in the common area between the cells. He looked into each cell. The eyes he looked into realized that he of all men could control their sentence or death. The judicial system was partial to believing a sheriff over an inmate. Many a man had pissed off the sheriff and gone missing. "Curley! After feedin' time, give 'em a lamp here in the center for a while. I'll get some better cards for you all," said the sheriff. Several voices replied, "Thank you, boss!"

Alfred Huffman from the newspaper, along with Solicitor General Ambrose Watkins, waited in the office. Dixie was skilled at roughing out newspaper releases. She had already started. The typewriter clicked, clacked, and hammered the letters one at a time under the guidance of her fast-moving fingers. Huffman stood by quietly and read. The sheriff's secretary had titled the release "Murderer Escapes!" Huffman was distracted when the jail door slammed shut and Sheriff Gilbert and Curley Jones entered the room.

Ambrose Watkins, the solicitor, looked at the two lawmen and gave a loud sigh. "Make it short and to the point," he said, sitting down in the metal frame chair beside Dixie's desk.

Curley started, but Sheriff Gilbert motioned him down. Curley sat down at his desk. "Lee took the piss bucket detail again this morning. Apparently, he had wedged a small sliver of wood in the ankle cuffs, gettin' 'em ta hold. He sprang on Bo Bob at the compound door. He took Bo Bob's club and damn near killed the old nigger. Lee made the fence and rushed Ellis DeFoor at the fruit stand. They fought and Lee struck the old man. He fell, striking his head on the old mounting block. Lee was seen leaving in DeFoor's 1925 black over red Nash. Witnesses said he went west, toward Odessadale or even Hambyville," said Sheriff Gilbert. He stood with his arms folded looking out the window behind Curley. The solicitor bent forward and rested his face in his hands. Curley looked away from the sheriff. The clock tower at the courthouse chimed out one o'clock.

"Dixie! First two calls need ta be Troup County Sheriff and Chief Hawthorn in Warm Springs," Sheriff Gilbert barked. "Do you agree with me that this son of a bitch is dangerous and should be brought in at all cost? I mean dead or alive!" shouted Sheriff Gilbert, as he looked down at Solicitor Watkins.

Watkins sat up straight. "You can't use dead or alive. That went out years ago," he said, opening and closing the drawers of Curley's desk.

"It damn sure makes me feel better!" snapped the sheriff. He cleared his throat. "If I don't get a cigar, I'm apt ta go berserk," he added. Curley leaned out of the way and remained silent.

Dixie made the calls quickly. "Hold on, I'll ask," she said. "Chief Hawthorn wants to know if he needs ta put day watch out of the city, if the mayor and council approve?" she asked, looking at her boss.

Sheriff Gilbert looked at Watkins. "What do you think?"

"We need all the help we can get. Hell, they hired the woman to work the extra coverage. I say, let 'em do it," answered Watkins.

"Chief, put 'em out," Dixie advised. "I'll call the favorite hangouts and try to raise the deputies," she said, pulling her finger down the mechanical indexing telephone tablet.

"Tell 'em what you know, and tell 'em for God's sake if they have ta nap, come in here to do it. That's all I need, is a deputy shot in the head while asleep on the road somewhere," said the sheriff, as he shoved an empty chair against the wall.

* * *

Doc Augustus Hubbard slowed his new Chevrolet almost to a stop and turned into the long winding farm road that led to Bo Bob's. "Bo Bob! Ya with me?" he yelled. Bo Bob was asleep and drooling all over himself as he leaned against the window. Alvaton Road was a rough and bumpy road, but the injured man had slept most of the way. The Negro suddenly waved his hands about, grasping for the door handle. Doc Hubbard stopped the car and leaned over, opening the door. Bo Bob leaned over and tried to puke. There was little to nothing there. The dust from the road rolled into the open door.

"Bo Bob, you all right?" asked Doc Hubbard, as he pulled the man back into the seat. The Negro nodded his head, "Yes."

Doc Hubbard wanted to get him out of his new car. There was nothing like having a new car covered in puke. "Which place?" he asked, as they bounced along.

Bo Bob held up three fingers. "Third place," replied the doctor. "I see it! Faded blue barn?" he asked, looking once again at the injured Negro. Bo Bob nodded his head. The Negro behind the plow looked like a younger Bo Bob. Doc Hubbard waved his hat out the window and sounded the horn. The lad stopped the mule and headed toward the house. "I see yer lady in the yard, Bo Bob," said the doctor. The injured man smiled as he sat leaning against the door.

The new teal blue Chevrolet caused quite a ruckus as it turned into the yard. The small weathered house was nothing more than a rough shanty. The toilet in the hedge row was leaning badly, probably held up by the ancient bushes. A mixed yard full of chickens scurried about, taking cover under the house. The house sat on high native stone pillars. Doc Hubbard could see under the house to the back where two girls ran up the steps. No one approached the unknown car. Emma looked out from behind the dark, heavily oxidized screen door and Tom stood off at the edge of the smokehouse. The retarded son sat on the front porch and watched. Doc Hubbard shook his head and took on a tear in his eyes. "How God puts hardship on us like that I'll never understand," he thought to himself, knowing through his experienced eyes what he was looking at. The retarded son sat with his head to the side and his body gave a slight quiver.

"Bo Bob, we're home," Doc Hubbard announced. He opened his car door and got out. "Miss Emma! Dr. Augustus Hubbard! I've brought Bo Bob!" he yelled, as he walked in front of the car. Even the three dogs had run under the high house. They were coming back out now. The screen door spring screeched as Emma quickly pushed it open. She ran toward the porch steps, but suddenly turned to get the retarded son. The two came to the car where Bo Bob sat. Young Tom had already seen the condition of his father. The two neat and clean daughters hurried out.

"It's Daddy!" one called out, as they ran to the car.

Emma stood the retarded son by the remains of the yard gate. "Why is he here? Lawd! What's happened?" she asked, as she opened the door and hugged her bloody husband.

"Let's get him in the house," said the doctor. "Easy now, he needs help," he said, walking slowly ahead of the family. Petunias had begun to sprout in the many flower pots along the walkway and on each side of the front steps. The screen door moaned as the doctor opened it. "May I come in?" he asked.

"Whoop yo' butts if'n yo' don'ts!" Emma answered. The ankle chains were dragging as Bo Bob shuffled along.

Emma and Tom helped Bo Bob down into his chair. The overstuffed wingback had white doilies on the arms and back. The old Negro gave a sigh as he sat down. Doc Hubbard pulled up a five-gallon lard bucket with a cushion on top and sat down next to his patient. "We had a bad nigger to escape this morning from the jail in Greenville. He overpowered yer husband and, well -- damn near beat him ta death. These stitches need ta be kept clean and when they start ta scab and pull, just clip 'em out with yer fine sewin' scissors," the doctor said, reaching up and touching the largest one on Bo Bob's head.

"Who beat my Daddy?" asked Tom, standing nearby.

"It was a God damn -- excuse me," Doc Hubbard looked around. "-- bad nigger, James Lee. He's the one that was wanted for the murder of the Durand store clerk. Now he's killed old Ellis DeFoor this morning and beat Bo Bob here," he said, holding his hat in his hands. "Does the son," he looked at the retarded one, "understand what we are saying?" he asked.

"He beez all right. Weez tell him when yous leaves," said Emma.

The doctor stood. "Keep him in the house and he can't leave. These chains, I'll take them off, but if he's seen out of here, I'm in trouble. This may finish his time," he said, running his fingers inside of his coat pocket. He found a key and bent down, unlocking the ankle cuffs. "Now, that's better!" he said. "Hang these were ya can find 'em. If the sheriff comes, you better get 'em back on," Doc Hubbard said, holding the heavy restraints out to Tom. The young Negro snatched them.

"Looks a heah, nows! Doc Hubbard's hopin' us! Don't beez dat a ways toward him!" Emma said, pointing her finger at her son.

"Sorry, sir," Tom said softly.

"Accepted," replied the doctor, as he slowly made his way to the door. "Fine looking young women, Miss Emma!" he said, putting on his hat. The two girls giggled.

Emma took the lard bucket seat the doctor had vacated. She was patting the sweat from her husband's brow with her white handkerchief. "Gods bless yous!" she said.

"I'll see him in a week, right here," replied the doctor.

*　*　*

"Sheriff, I've got my rough out done for the news release," Dixie said, holding up a sheet of typing paper.

"Read it, please!" he replied, as he stood at the front door looking out on the town square.

She cleared her throat and took a sip of her cold coffee. "Murderer

Escapes! On the morning of, today's date," she said, looking at the sheriff standing at the door. "Negro, James Lee, brutally attacked Greenville Jail trustee, Bo Bob Huggins, leaving him severely injured. Lee scaled the compound fence and accosted Ellis DeFoor of Luthersville. DeFoor struck his head in the struggle and was pronounced dead by the arriving Doctor Augustus Hubbard. The escaped prisoner took DeFoor's 1925 Nash and is believed to be heading in a westward direction, from the Greenville square. The vehicle is a black over red soft top.

James Lee is a dark Negro, 5'10" tall, weighs 140 pounds, short clipped black hair, brown eyes with yellow, large flat facial features. Last seen wearing a prison uniform and brown brogans. The escapee is possibly armed and dangerous. Any sighting or known location should be called in to Sheriff Louis Gilbert, Meriwether County."

"That sounds fine ta me. How 'bout you?" Sheriff Gilbert asked, looking at Ambrose Watkins.

"We need to list the known charges at this time," he said.

"So, I'll put in existing charges, prior to escape, were armed robbery and murder. The murder of storekeeper Herman Pickens of Durand," Dixie said. She rolled the thin sheet of paper back into the carriage of the typewriter.

"We can get that out almost nationwide tonight, even a picture if I had one," boasted the reporter, Alfred Huffman. Huffman was a thin wisp of a man. His dark hair, bathed in Vaseline tonic, lay close to his head. The man's small ears supported gold wire rimmed glasses. Dixie had always noticed that he wore his pants too long, sometimes they hung on his oxford heels. "The Associated Press that we belong to is a powerful thing," said Huffman, taking notes on his spiral wirebound pocket tablet.

"As powerful as a twelve gage, when I shoot that nigger?" asked the sheriff. "As powerful as me when I beat the livin' piss out of him for whoopin' old Bo Bob Huggins?"

The young man was embarrassed by the sheriff's strong language. He stuttered, "Well, sir, I don't know about that."

Sheriff Gilbert got close to the young man. "Ever beat a man?" he asked coldly, looking him in the eyes.

"No, sir!" said Alfred Huffman.

"There's nothin' like it when yer right!" snarled the sheriff.

"Jesus!" said Ambrose Watkins. "I'll be in my office. I'm applying for warrants," he informed the sheriff. The solicitor closed the door behind him. Curley watched him walk across to the courthouse square and go up the steps on the east side.

* * *

The morning had begun with a song from a pair of bluebirds at Heather's window. They were sharing the railing with the wrens that lived in the rafters. This morning she would walk down to the police department and familiarize herself with the secretary and the filing system, as directed by Chief Hawthorn. Jasper would be on his own. Having a female in the car had cramped his natural style, burpin', fartin' and coughin' as he pleased. He was looking forward to having some alone time. He was already on the road when Heather stepped out onto the sidewalk. "What a beautiful morning," she said to herself. She thought of her father, Sonny. "Beware of beautiful mornings, they turn into shit!" he often said. Heather laughed out loud. Other people on the sidewalk looked at her with a reserved expression.

Heather met an old man who was arranging himself on the store bench where he had apparently sat for years. "Mornin'!" he said, smiling at the neat young, badge wearing suited woman approaching him. Heather nodded and smiled. "Mark Twain said, everybody talks about the weather, but nobody does nothin' 'bout it," the man said, laughing. His newspaper was folded under his arm. He wiped the bench with his handkerchief before sitting down.

Heather stopped for a moment, just long enough to converse politely. "I say, leave the weather as it is. God sends it, be thankful for it, good or bad," she said.

A couple passing agreed with an, "Amen!"

The door rattled as Heather opened it. The chief's secretary looked up and waved. Heather smiled and walked into the staff office. The workers out back could be heard laying the new bricks. Their trowels made scraping sounds as they worked the sandy mortar. Jasper stopped in to say hello, but soon left, since the chief was in and about town. At eleven thirty Heather looked up to see the face of Buddy Cotton pressed against the outer window of the lobby.

"Excuse me!" Heather said, as she stepped away from the filing cabinet. "Let me see what this young man wants."

Buddy stood by the front door. "Yes, Buddy! What is it?" Heather asked.

"Mrs. Blakely wants ta know if she can skip yer sheets today? She's got the chance to feed several more salesmen this evening. They're not stayin' but just eatin'," he said, waiting on her reply.

"You tell Mrs. Blakely that my sheets are nice and smooth, not dirty at all. They'll make it until next time," she said. "Hurry along, now," she said, gently nudging him off. She watched as the young boy hurried down the street. He looked back several times. She waved and he stopped in traffic and waved eagerly. It was about half past one.

Chief Hawthorn came into the office. "Is she ready to work?" he asked the secretary. He tossed his uniform hat on the desk.

"Oh! That she is!" the woman replied. "Like a fish to clean water, she is," the secretary added. The telephone rang.

"Warm Springs Police Department, Detective Duncan speaking," Heather said sharply. "It's for you Chief," she said, waiting for him to take the telephone.

"Chief Hawthorn!" he said. "What?" he snapped. "When?" He looked around. "What time?" he asked. It was Dixie from the Meriwether County Sheriff's Department. "Should I put the day watch with my detective on it, out of the city?" he asked. "I'll certainly do that!" he said. "Thanks for lettin' us know." He slowly hung up the telephone.

"Trouble?" asked the secretary.

"James Lee has escaped this morning," said the chief. He looked pale.

Heather closed the filing cabinet and tugged at her holster, placing it on her hip. "Take my car and stay in town. I'll call around and try to find Jasper. We need to meet," said the chief. He held out his car keys.

The meeting that followed would set the tone for Heather's work performance. When she left the station, she knew the job was taking a deadly serious turn. She quickly drove the city streets looking for Jasper.

CHAPTER NINE

The small staff room of the Warm Springs Police Department roared with conversation and excitement. Heather was last to enter the room. The majority of the town council was there, sitting on every available chair and even desk corners. Mayor Cornelius Cunningham waved his arms and appeared to be defending something in his conversation. Jasper stood at a desk with his back turned. The three shotguns before him were lying among a slew of 12-gauge red paper shells.

Chief Hawthorn yelled, "Settle down!" He whistled and waved. Heather stood close by. "This is an important meeting and you need to listen," the chief added, looking at each person in the room. The councilmen settled down. Jasper raised his hand, waving to let the chief know he was listening. The retaining catch on the shotgun clicked as each shell rim passed into the tubular magazine. For a few seconds, it was the only sound in the room. Heather noticed that each time it clicked, the councilmen blinked, as though a civil suit was knocking at the door.

"In spite of all we are able to do, we are almost at day's end. Four-thirty is upon us," said Chief Hawthorn. "Frances, you are taking this down?" he asked. She nodded her head in the affirmative, holding up her tablet. "As Sheriff Louis Gilbert advises, a murderer has escaped. This morning Negro James Lee brutally attacked Greenville Jail trustee Bo Bob Huggins, leaving him severely injured. Lee scaled the compound fence and accosted Ellis DeFoor, of Luthersville. DeFoor struck his head in the struggle and was pronounced dead by the arriving Doctor Augustus Hubbard.

The escaped prisoner took Mr. DeFoor's 1925 Nash and is believed to be heading in a westward direction, from the Greenville square. The vehicle is a black over red soft top. James Lee is a dark Negro, 5'10" tall, weighs 140 pounds, short clipped black hair, brown eyes with yellow, large flat facial features. Last seen wearing a prison uniform and brown brogans.

The escapee is possibly armed and dangerous. Any sighting or known location should be called in to Sheriff Louis Gilbert, Meriwether County, or myself, here at the police department. The existing charges, prior to escape, include armed robbery and murder of Herman Pickens of Durand," said the chief.

A hand went up. "Put it down!" snapped the chief. "We have employed Heather Duncan from Campbell County Sheriff's Department, as you know, to help us cover our city, all prior to his first capture. This is the young lady," he said, looking at Heather. Heather smiled and nodded. Mayor Cunningham grinned.

"Those who haven't met her, you're in for a treat. She ain't no pushover," said the chief, looking at her with a smile. He was certainly more amiable now than when they first met.

Jasper pushed in the last shell. "That's for damn sure!" he agreed. He left the action open on the shotguns and set the last one back in the wall rack.

"Is he apt to come this way?" asked one man.

"How the hell do I know which way he's apt to go?" replied the chief. There was laughter from the group.

"Boys, we don't have any way of knowing where he'll be. This nigger's like a mad dog! Can you tell which way one will stagger next?" asked the mayor. "No!"

"Mayor's right. Please be aware that you may see a Warm Springs Police car outside of the city, could be way outside the city," said the chief. He tugged at his waist line, arranging his slacks. "Sheriff Gilbert has verbally deputized the Day Watch officers so they can assist legally. This will not be an overnight case," he said, sitting on a desk. "You councilmen need to tell everyone you know, lock yer outbuildings, lock yer doors all the time." The men gasped at that statement. "Take a wire from your vehicles that you're not able to lock up. This nigger is a demon," said the chief.

"Thank you for coming!" said Mayor Cunningham. Heather shook hands and introduced herself to those who were interested. She took comments of her beauty, her revolver, and her badge. Some were overheard about giving her a home, should she need one. She was sure there were some underlying sexual thoughts. The staff room cleared out. Frances even called it a day. The rays of the early evening sun cut through the darkness of the lobby, illuminating the tiny floating dust particles. Heather had noticed over a period of time that the sun individually lit the photograph of each past chief that hung on the wall.

"Chief! I'm headin' to the house, myself," said the mayor. "You po-lice be careful," he said, winking at Heather as he placed his hat on his head.

* * *

Alfred Huffman hurried to his office where he announced the big story.

The telegraph unit soon transported the approved story to all the cities that were associated members. "Think about it! All this happening here in Greenville, Georgia and now at this very moment all of our major sister cities know about it. LaGrange, Columbus, Augusta, Macon, Atlanta, and heck, up in the northeast as well, Charlotte, Boston, New York," he said, rocking on his heels as he watched the unit sending.

"Calm down." A voice came from the dimly lit corner of the press room. It was the oldest reporting member of the newspaper, Buford Stokes. He wore an elastic visor over his eyes. There was no hair on his head, just large wrinkled ears that stopped the elastic from continuing to fall. The old man's feet never cleared the floor and bedroom slippers on his feet made a "chew, chew, chew" sound depending on how fast Buford moved in the office. His favorite haunts were trailed by a worn path on the dark stained and varnished wood floor. There were three main scuff trails, one to the food table, one to the toilet, and the last to the cash register at the main counter. Alfred expected him to be found dead at his desk someday. Buford would sit for several hours appearing to be motionless to those watching, but by press time he held up a stack of finished stories.

"Keep the cam-rey handy, best take it with you, even to home," said Buford, to the younger Alfred. "I'm putting you in charge of this story, get some good pictures, but be reasonable with the amount of film. It's expensive, money's hard ta come by," he reminded.

"Yes, sir!" Alfred said eagerly. "Can I get a press car?" he asked.

"You'll be paid mileage, just as always," Buford said, shaking his finger at the young reporter. "Stay here long 'nuff and you'll get a company car," he said, fading in volume as he shuffled to his desk in the far outside corner of the dim room.

"When I own the place," Alfred replied, in a faint whisper.

"Probably so," answered Buford, over the sound of his heavy swivel chair, humping up to the desk well.

Alfred looked at the wall clock. It was an ancient octagon headed Regulator. It could be heard with each tick and tock all day, and even its chime in the passing of the silent hours along the sidewalk. "You goin' home?" he asked, looking back at the old reporter.

"Didn't get here until six thirty this morning," said Buford, looking at the clock. "A while longer," he said, picking up his yellow pencil.

"Good night!" said Alfred, as he turned the sign from open to closed and locked the door behind him.

It was a pleasant night, just warm enough to roll his sleeves back a turn or two and enjoy the walk to his small apartment behind the pharmacy, off of the square. He carried his leather briefcase in one hand and the large square leather camera bag in the other. It was a heavy load, but he was proud to be seen with it. He made a point to let the girl at the pharmacy lunch counter see him looking in the window. She waved. He returned the same with a big smile, just before departing from the deliberate stop.

* * *

Chief Hawthorn sat down at his desk and motioned for Jasper and his detective to join him. "Pull up a chair," he said, pushing one toward Heather.

"Thanks," she said, taking the seat.

"I'd ask that you advise Mrs. Blakely of our need for communications, her telephone may be ringing. I'll give you a Confidentiality Agreement Form," said the chief.

Jasper leaned over and whispered to Heather, "A CAF." He pulled back and smiled.

"I figured that," Heather winked at her partner. The chief rolled his eyes.

"Get it signed, keep the original and give her the carbon," said Chief Hawthorn, as he handed Heather the two sheets with the carbon between. She handled it easy, knowing the slightest pressure would cause the carbon to leave a mark on the copy. Heather put the copy aside.

"Any thoughts on catching this Negro?" the chief asked, looking at his detective.

"Until we get a lead on where he is or where he is heading, all we can do is patrol and wait," Heather said. She crossed her legs and dug a small pebble from her shoe sole with a bone-handled pen knife that she had pulled from her pocket.

The night officer came in the back door. "Haven't I told you to always use the front door?" yelled the chief. The officer stood still with a shocked look on his face. "God damn it! If you can't follow orders, you could just get fired! Please come in here!" The officer stepped from the darkness of the back doorway.

Detective Duncan stood up. "Heather Duncan, Detective. Glad to meet you," she said, shaking his hand.

"Likewise. I'm Edgar Peterson," he said, releasing her hand. Edgar saw the three shotguns in the rack. "What's up?" he asked.

"You haven't heard?" asked Jasper.

"Heard what?" replied Edgar.

"That Negro, James Lee. He's escaped. Almost killed old Bo Bob Huggins and did kill Ellis DeFoor from Luthersville," Jasper said, sitting in his chair and looking up at Edgar.

"Shit!" Edgar replied. "So, I guess I get a shotgun tonight?" he said, taking a seat on the nearest desk.

"You'd best have strong batteries for yer flashlight and don't take any chances. Anything suspicious and you call Jasper first, he'll call the detective, if needed. They both have a car apiece. Heather stays at Mrs. Blakely's place," said the chief.

"I'll jump a call with him, if I'm closer than Jasper," said Heather. "Call Mrs. Blakely, she can get me," she urged.

"You don't think nothin' about her ability. She's the one that run the son of a bitch ta ground on her first day, shot it out with him!" Jasper bragged.

Edgar shook his head. Heather saw disbelief in his eyes and body language. "I'll do that," he replied. He got up and took a shotgun. Heather saw that he checked for shells in the magazine tube.

"Edgar!" snapped the chief. Edgar turned to look. "You be extra careful, and use the front door," he said, smiling. "Jasper, shut the lights down to a soft glow and let's close up," he said, as he headed to the door.

"Will ya have dinner with me?" Heather asked Jasper, out on the sidewalk.

He blushed. "I can't afford that," he replied, with both hands in his front pockets.

"It's an invite. I'm sure Mrs. Blakely can thin it out," Heather smiled. "I want to drive my Essex, keep it moving. We can go see if we can get into trouble," she said, smiling. "We'll have our guns. Not very long, ten miles or so."

"I'd be happy to," smiled Jasper.

* * *

James Lee stopped the big Nash at the narrow plank bridge over Walnut Creek. The afternoon sun was high overhead. He had not seen a car or anyone for that matter, on the road or in the fields along the way. He pulled the hand brake and set the large car in neutral. He checked the mirrors before getting out. A gray heron flew away silently. The only sound was that of the engine running and the "putt, putt, putt" of the exhaust. He took the prison shirt and filled it with several pieces of rock from the road, tied a knot in it, and tossed it far out into the dark waters. There was a loud splash. James Lee watched the tiny bubbles as the shirt took on water and quickly sank to the bottom of the swampy creek. The ankle cuffs that were still on his right leg rattled as he moved about. They had to come off, and soon.

Flat Shoals Creek was up ahead, and then the old Tigner Cemetery. Past the cemetery was the Davenport Plantation, or what was left of it. Most of the Negroes had been gone from there for years. The farmers left to work the place were ruffians, white boys that would just as soon cut his ass as to look at him. James Lee worked the Nash around the Davenport property by the rambling roads and wallows called roads. For an hour or so he hid the car behind the Arbor Chapel. The thick magnolias gave cover for the automobile, while he worked frantically to free himself of the remaining restraint. The churchyard had a well in front. The water was clear and cool to his thirsty dry throat. He looked at the homemade dipper. It was half of a sanded coconut shell screwed to the end of a broom handle. "Reckon drinkin' after white folks won't give me no disease," he thought to himself. The cold water rushed over the edges of the dipper and ran down his neck.

James Lee hurried from the well to the cover of the deep green magnolias. He sat on the running board and tinkered with the ratchet lock. He wiggled and tugged but nothing, not even the jailhouse tricks he had used in the past, seemed to move the lock. "Damn it!" he mumbled. He was getting a headache from bending down so long. Lee realized he was not alone. His heart raced. It was so loud he was sure it could be heard. There was someone at the well. He lay flat down and looked under the heavy branches of the magnolia. All he could see was from the knees down. Whoever it was gave no indication of knowing he was there. James Lee heard the well cover slide to the side and eventually the windlass lowering the bucket.

The windlass squeaked as it raised the metal bucket filled with water. There was the loud snort of a mule. He still was not sure if it was a Negro or a white boy. A small seed eating gray mouse got his attention as he lay under the dark limbs, watching. James Lee slid forward to get a better look at the person at the well. A better look he would never get. The sudden loud "thump" of a water oak acorn reported from the engine bonnet. Lee jumped. "Shit!" he thought, as the man at the well curb stood straight and looked about. The church had a shingle roof. That was the sound of metal! Sweat dripped from the shirtless Negro, as the small pieces of trash stuck to his body. The legs by the well soon walked out of sight and the moaning of a wagon was heard rolling to the west.

James Lee did not know how long he had been there, but by the feel of the bonnet it was probably a couple of hours, as the engine was almost cold. A narrow path of road led from behind the church toward the white folks' cemetery. He knew that heading west like he was, there was no one to be the wiser of his escape for several hours, or until the newspaper was thrown in the morning. The Nash cranked effortlessly and took the narrow path past the toilets and on toward the cemetery. His next risky encounter might be ahead at Tigner's Crossroads. As Lee approached the crossroads, he could see the one room store. There were several cars in the lot, but no one in sight. Maybe it would stay that way until he could make his left, on toward the abandoned church at the old Stovall community. There was a cloud of sandy dust rising behind the heavy, fast running car. The angular setting of the restraint was beginning to cut a blister on his ankle, even through the heavy, canvas-like pants. The bridge over Sulphur Creek rattled as he crossed.

"Jesus! Shit!" he said aloud. An old white man stood on the porch of the store. The old bastard looked at the Nash like he knew who was coming. The old man threw up his hand and waved as James Lee took the corner west in second gear. He sounded the horn several short bursts. "Holy shit!" he said, looking back in the mirror. "Maybe that won't raise suspicion," he thought. He was driving into the sun now. The Nash rose and fell gracefully with the roughness of the road. Through his fingers he got a glimpse of a clothesline. There were shirts blowing in the breeze. "Thank you, Lord!" he said, slapping the steering wheel. The small unpainted house was surrounded by chinaberry trees and the driveway was lined with cottonwoods. There was not a person in sight, or a vehicle anywhere. He leaned and looked closer. There was no smoke coming from the chimney. "God damn!" he said loudly. There was an oncoming car. He took the road to the left, putting him away from the window as the car came closer. He slowed as though he were stopping at the house just ahead. James Lee saw the passing car go out of sight. The Nash spun in the soft dirt as he hurriedly backed onto the main road and took the right toward the clothesline.

A large blue tick hound was sprawled on the front porch. It hardly raised its head when Lee stopped the car. The front door was closed, and the yard was open all the way around the house. "Make it easy," he said to himself, as he released the clutch and drove into the swept dirt yard. The heavy car rocked as it jumped the shallow ditch, filled with black ashes from leaf burning. He laughed as he drove around the house. The edge of the rear bumper struck the black iron pot and turned it loose across the yard. It rolled several times, spilling its watery contents. James Lee laughed. He drove under the clothesline, took two shirts, and pulled away toward the road. The prop stick fell from the line and the clean laundry took to the dirt covered yard. "Dumb ass white folks!" he shouted, as he worked his way into a shirt. It was too large, but it was a shirt. He was beginning to think of an Acetylene torch, as the restraint rubbed his ankle. The hound never left the porch.

James Lee was in a more confident frame of mind now that he had a shirt on. He felt less conspicuous to anyone he might see along the road. His stomach growled with hunger. The morning's grits and red-eye gravy, sloshed about by black coffee, had run out long ago. "Burned dat up on de fence," he chuckled to himself. The gasoline gauge was getting very low. Maybe the closed Berry's Mill site would be a good hideout until after dark. He had heard that his folks did not fish there anymore. When the high water of 1905 came through and the raceway was damaged, the big snakes had washed in with the high water and chosen to remain. James Lee did not like snakes, but to save his hide, he would just watch his step. Besides, he could piss from the running board, there was really no reason to get into the high grass.

Stovall was right up the road. He knew a road from Odessadale went down into the sleepy little community. It too was named after some white bastard. Lee did not know what Stovall, just another wealthy white son of a bitch. He was seeing more and more people, and they were all white. James Lee was beginning to think that his kind were not to be seen in Stovall. A Model A truck suddenly pulled close behind him. He saw it in his mirror. A quick glance, not too long, he did not want to be seen. Stovall had enough houses and there was apt to be a telephone in some of them. The small truck turned off as quickly as it had appeared.

"Damn!" Lee exclaimed, exhaling deeply. His nerves were being tested. "God damn!" he said aloud, as he saw a couple standing at their mail box. They stood looking toward his oncoming car and waved as he approached. Lee waved but looked straight ahead, making no eye contact. In the mirror, he saw them watching as he passed. James Lee's left turn was just ahead. The road was worn from the banking cars taking the turn without slowing. There was a mule and wagon loaded with dried field corn, just as he made the corner. He slowed to second gear, then down to first. Ellis DeFoor had tucked a piece of laundry cardboard into the roof brace. James Lee quickly put it into use as a sun shade. There was no sun, but if he kept his hands below the windshield line, the white farmer would never know who was driving the closely following car. The farmer turned and looked back, giving a neighborly wave. Lee could not afford to reply.

The slow wagon had nowhere to pull off and there were two other cars behind him, a Ford and a Chrysler. He thought that was odd, Chryslers were seldom seen in these parts. The farmer motioned that he was turning off up ahead. James Lee pulled the shirt sleeve down over his hand and placed his arm in the open window, which made him look as though he was a patient man. The welts and bruises the old man and his cane had put on his head and neck were tender and sore. Lee rolled his head about, stretching the tightening muscles. At the next field road, the small wagon rocked from side to side as it left the main road. The gray mule laid its ears back and pulled the load up the slight incline toward the whitewashed barn. James Lee watched as a wife and several children ran out to meet the wagon. He had never had that experience.

The two cars behind Lee were pushing to make time. He sped through the gears and left them in a cloud of dust so as not to hold them up. Keeping watch on their location, he saw that both cars took the first left road and from there he was alone. His heart rate dropped. The sweat of his brow had begun to bead up in the tense situation. James Lee crossed Sulphur Creek once more, this time without a bridge. The splash under the large flat-bottomed car soaked the exhaust manifold and a cloud of white steam rose, quickly drifting on the wind. The rambling creek had many branches. The next road went by Berry's Mill and eventually to Hambyville in Troup County.

* * *

The presence of an extra guest somewhat angered Mrs. Blakely, until Heather caught her alone in the kitchen. The sizzling sound of chicken fried pork chops filled the hot room, along with steam from the very last of the mixed greens from the small garden that grew in the fenced area out back. "I'll pay for his meal," Heather said, standing close by the busy woman. "It's unusual circumstances," she added.

Mrs. Blakely drained the boiled white potatoes for mashing. The steam billowed upward from the heavy cast iron sink. "If a regular misses, there'll be no charge," she said, squinting as the hot steam surrounded her head.

As luck would have it, there was a no show. The meal was very impressive to Jasper. "A delightful meal, Mrs. Blakely," Jasper said, folding his napkin and placing it next to his plate, where the flatware was crossed.

"Thank you, sir! It was a pleasure to have you," Mrs. Blakely replied, as she cleared the table.

"Can I impose on you to read and sign this confidentiality form?" asked Heather, as she held it above the plates.

"I'm familiar," she said, motioning for Heather to hand it to her. "What brought this about?" she asked, wiping her hands on her yellow calico apron.

"I'll be getting telephone calls here from the chief, and possibly other agencies," Heather said. "What's discussed and who calls is to be kept confidential," she added. Mrs. Blakely signed the form and handed Heather the carbon and the original.

The other boarders sat listening. "The Negro, James Lee, that was captured several days ago, has escaped from the Greenville Jail. He's a dangerous man," Jasper said. "He was known to be driving a black and red Nash. Killed a man from Luthersville to get the car," he added.

The plates rattled as Mrs. Blakely placed them in the enameled dish pan. "Who did he kill?" she quickly asked.

"Ellis DeFoor," Heather announced.

"My, my!" the woman replied, shaking her head. "The world's full of evil."

"A fine meal, ma'am," said Jasper. He brushed a few crumbs from his pants when he stood.

"I'll be in later. We're riding out toward Durand. We'll be on the Durand Road if anyone tries to find us, just a look-see," Heather said. "My Essex needs to be run," she added.

"You be careful, Miss," added a boarder whose room was across from hers, on the back side.

Both Jasper and Heather were still in their work clothes. Jasper hurried ahead, finding his way out the side entrance. The single bulb was out. He reached up and gave it a slight twist. "Now, that's better," he said, as the light glowed in the narrow alleyway.

The Essex cranked on the third rotation. The smell of raw leaded gasoline gave a unique sweet smell to the dampening night air. Heather unlocked the passenger door from inside. The headlights made two overlapping circles against the nearby buildings.

"Let's go!" she said, working the transmission into reverse. The cold gears gave a slight groan. "North a little piece, then left onto Durand Road." There were no other cars out. Heather took the opportunity to move along. "Did you bring a flashlight?"

"Shit! No!" Jasper replied, looking at her face, softly lit by the instruments. They rode in silence, looking into the distant landscape for anything profiling a questionable object. "First right," he pointed. Heather took it. "Left, Seven Branches, goes to a little place called Midget." He leaned closer. "Just a crossroads," he added. "Say! Did you see the advertisement in the local paper and the display in all the stores that sell overalls?" he asked.

"I did, but didn't pay any attention to the details," she replied. The Essex rose and fell, rocking from side to side on the winding road.

Jasper pulled his spiral wire bound pocket tablet from his shirt pocket. "This comes out at a crossroads above the Ward cemetery. It's in the open field." He turned toward his window looking into the moonlit night. "Not a good place to hide," he remarked. "Damn cemeteries all over this country." He began flipping pages in the tablet.

Heather stopped the Essex at the intersection. She looked up and down the road, which ran north and south.

Jasper pointed across her face. "See the Ward cemetery?"

"I see it," Heather replied, gently pushing his hand down.

"Turn south and we can make the loop, right back to town," Jasper suggested. Heather turned south, but drove slower. "Anyway! The Duckhead Brand has a slogan contest," he said, grinning. "I've got the winning slogan. I think I can get the fifty bucks," he said.

Heather smiled and rolled her eyes. Jasper did not see her. She really was not interested. "Let's hear it," she said politely.

Jasper leaned down closer to the courtesy light on the dashboard. He cleared his throat. "Here goes," he said.

"Well, let's have it!" she said.

> *"O'Brien Brothers are honest men; they do the thing that's fair-*
> *They make the Duckhead Overall; that stands all kinds of wear.*
> *You folks that do all kinds of work; just buy the Duckhead Brand;*
> *And use them rough, ta hunt and fish; for they will surely stand.*
> *The dye is good and never fades; the buttons don't pull out;*
> *The seams hold fast and never break, the thread is strong and stout.*

The Duckhead Brand of overalls, your wife will never find,
No use for needle and thread; it's for the other kinds!"

"Well, what do ya think?" Jasper asked, grinning. He leaned back in the seat with the look of a winner on his smiling face.

Not wanting to hurt his feelings Heather replied, "Not a better one have I heard." She had only heard one, and that one was his.

The two Warm Springs officers called an end to the joy ride in the pleasant spring night. Jasper Brown drove home in a very mellow mindset, after the evening of a good meal and the company of a young woman. Tonight, Jasper would use extra caution. He drove all the way around his small house. All appeared to be secure, just as he had left it. As an extra measure, he raised the bonnet on the patrol car and removed a plug wire. He placed it next to the ignition key on the kitchen table, close to the back door. Jasper closed his eyes knowing that the windows were secured with a cross nail, only allowing for a modest amount of circulation, and the added straight chairs under the front and back doors would create resistance, should he sleep through an attempted intrusion.

Heather read from a novel and then went to bathe once the menfolk had had their turns in the shared bathroom. In her camisole, she plucked and shaped her eyebrows in the magnifying mirror that hung from the wall over the pedestal sink. The black barber scissors she had brought from home snipped the new growth from her hair as she tried to maintain its cut as long as possible. She admired her long thick lashes and knew that she got those from her dear departed Mother. Silently Heather removed her silky garment and stood looking in the sink mirror. She turned one way and then the other as she looked at her bare bosom. Grandmother Margaret's words came to her. "You know you're young when the girls look ahead, and then you're old when they look down." Heather smiled. Hers were still looking ahead.

The building was quiet. Not a sound was heard from the other boarders. The sound of a passing car was occasionally heard. Thoughts of the wanted Negro went through her head and how they might catch him. She placed a large bath towel on the floor between the tub and the sink. Her naked butt dropped to the soft towel and she began to exercise, starting with sit-ups. These would turn into push-ups before her session would end. The counts softly blurted out as she finished each one. Her sit-ups were at seventy-five before she began to tire. She could only do forty push-ups. At thirty-eight her arms were trembling as she committed to an even number. "Thirty-nine, and forty," she said, rolling over onto her back. Heather lay tired and naked, looking up at the ceiling. The single bulb hung on its fabric wrapped, insulated cord. A tiny candle fly clung to the brown cord and gracefully walked upon it. When the tiny bug flew across the warm bulb, it cast the shadow of a much larger creature. It made the impression of a large butterfly upon the white painted wall.

Heather bathed in the large claw-foot tub. Her thoughts were to write home with the latest news. In the quiet of the night the letter was started, but never finished, before she fell asleep. The letter fell to her side.

In Hambyville, the Dry Goods and Hardware run by Benjamin Hill had closed later than normal, due to the number of customers coming in. Hill left that night as a satisfied businessman. He had not had a better day since before the depression. Mr. Hill and his small Terrier dog, which he called Skippy because he was peanut butter brown, had checked and shook all the doors. Each was found to be locked and chained. The only gasoline out was twelve gallons still in the globe topped pump, where a disagreement had taken place over the price. Even the pumps were chained. The single bulb that hung under the drive under porch was turned off, and a single bulb was left burning over the cash register. The bulb's location created shadows if anyone was in the store. Benjamin Hill and Skippy left for the night in his black Model A truck. Skippy stood on the seat, front paws on the dashboard, as the small opening in the windshield pushed the fresh night air against his whiskered face. Benjamin's face was illuminated by the occasional glow when he pulled on his pipe. The comfortable man pointed out to his small dog the distant lightning that lit the southwestern sky.

* * *

The turnoff down to the old mill was grown up in weeds, but with almost a hundred years of use, the road was cut deep into the earth. James Lee stopped the Nash and looked toward the mill. There was not much left except for the huge pecan trees that had thrived after the high water. The skeletons of weathered treetops rose from the grass. The remains of the damaged raceway were down there somewhere. The rapids and the waterfall could be heard but not seen due to the growth of wild plums and crabapples among the waist high grass. The remains of the tall rock foundation offered him a place to hide. It was almost good dark. James Lee was a man of luck. He had no trouble in backing the Nash down to the lower side of the foundation. He was hidden from the road above and from the open fields across the creek. He still fidgeted with the irritating restraints, as he waited on the darkness of night and deep sleep to fall upon the countryside. The baritone voices of the heavy pond frogs carried a rhythm in the stillness.

James Lee was tired, hungry, and in pain from the restraints. He fought sleep in the darkness. His hiding spot in the shadows of the foundation and the tall grass was cozy. Frequently he dozed off, only to be startled awake by the scraping of bony, skeleton-like fingers grasping the edge of the open windows. It turned out to be the blades of the tall grass swaying in the wind. Now and then he would be alarmed by the passing of headlights on the road above him. Some came from the direction of Hambyville, while others went toward the small town. By the stars and the ending flow of traffic, he decided it was time to move out. The sudden sound of the smooth-running engine caused the frogs to stop their conversation. The crickets followed, and even the occasional call of the night bird stopped. The hard narrow tires spun on the damp grass, trying to gain traction on the steep incline.

James Lee had no idea who he would burglarize. He was over the county line in a short quarter of a mile. The distant farm houses in the darkness showed no visible signs of people. Darkness and deep shadows filled the Troup County countryside. He was so far from LaGrange, he felt there would be little chance of encountering the law. A mile before Hambyville, he encountered an oncoming set of headlights. If he was lucky, a long driveway was up ahead. He could make it before the headlights filled the cab of the stolen Nash. Lee killed his headlights and pulled in, making sure to keep his foot clear of the brake light. The vehicle quickly passed and went out of sight. Lee pulled out and drove on in darkness. The escaped Negro was like a black cat on the hunt.

The target would have to meet his criteria: cover, isolation, and darkness. B. Hill Dry Goods & Hardware would be the first to fill them all. The back side of the store was nestled in a thick pecan orchard. The front was dark too, and with the filled globe tank, the required gasoline was easy pickings. Lee carefully drove the blacked-out Nash to the back of the dark store lot and stopped the engine. There was silence except for the expansion and contraction of the engine. Lee quietly closed the car door and cautiously ventured into the darkness of the open shed. He stumbled into the ends of racked boards, cutting himself above the left eye.

"Damn it!" he exclaimed, as he stopped abruptly against the board's squared end. Warm blood ran down the side of his nose. He felt it with his hand. Inching along, Lee soon found himself feeling an Acetylene torch. He smiled. The exploring hands of the escaped prisoner eventually found the striker. He thought he heard someone inside. James Lee listened, leaning toward the wall of the store. It was a compressor unit running. It bumped like someone stirring about. The deep darkness under the shed came to life with the flick of the striker. The fast, repetitive striking of the small flint on the hardened steel rod allowed Lee to find the oxygen and the Acetylene valves. Regardless of the torch tip, he knew that once it was adjusted, he could cut the ankle cuff from his leg.

Equal turns on the two tanks and a flick of the striker at the torch tip ignited the yellow hot flame. A car was heard on the road. James Lee pushed the torch to the earth, under the cover of the junk around the work bench. The car passed, but suddenly stopped. Lee's heart raced. He was ready to run for the car in a split second, if need be. The other car moved on. "God damn," he said out loud. He applied the torch tip to the restraint and pressed the lever. The added gas pushed the molten steel away. The intense heat raced around the cuffs and began to burn his pants and then his ankle. He knocked the hot cuffs with the torch head. They fell away, but his prison pants still burned. The torch head struck the ground as he tried to pat out his burning pants.

The wood doors under the dark shed were only locked by a padlock. That was easy work for the torch. James Lee slowly pushed the doors open, just enough to enter, then he closed them. The single bulb over the cash register gave enough light for him to scurry about. A large mouse ran across in front of him. Lee soon located a stack of khaki pants. He tossed them one or two at a time onto the floor until he found his size. He tucked two pairs in the back of his waist for later. The warehouse space of the store was littered with empty wooden crates and boxes. The first wooden crate was an Armour Meat Company box.

"Just what I need. Sturdy enough to hold lots of canned food," he thought.

The old trick of leaving a light on for shadows did not work unless the burglar rose above the counter height. Lee stooped over and hurried for the canned meats, beans, and even a hunk of cheese, in the front part of the dimly lit store. The shallow woven basket behind the counter, with no dog, gave rise to his suspicion. "Am I alone?" he wondered, going about his business. He took three of the biggest drinks from the cooler. The cash register was ready for the next day. It held only ten dollars, five in ones and the rest in change. His front pockets bulged with the heavy coins. "Every store has a hideout gun," he thought to himself. Remaining crouched down, he ran his hands under the counter and into every deep, dark cubbyhole. "There it is!" he whispered. James Lee drew his hand back, grasping a top break Harrington & Richardson Arms revolver.

He duck walked into the circle of light made by the hanging bulb. "Harrington and Richardson Arms Co., Worchester, Massive-two-tits," he said, laughing. "38 S&W," he added, pointing the revolver about, first at a candy jar, and then at a calendar featuring a well-built white woman in a short red gingham skirt and blouse. It was a fine piece, blue steel, checkered black gutta-percha grips, a six-inch barrel. "Shit!" He realized it shot black powder shells. "God damn it!" That sure narrowed down his chances of getting cartridges just anywhere. He ran his hand back into the darkness where he had found it. His fingers explored. "There they are." He pulled up two full boxes of 38 S&W cartridges. "That's a hundred rounds! That should be enough!" he thought.

When he pulled the doors closed behind him, he heard the barking of dogs in the distance. James Lee stood motionless, listening. He remembered that many of these white boys lived on property or just a short distance away. They seemed to be possessive of their wares. The gasoline pump was ahead on the gravel lot. The crate was left on the steps while he slipped down the side of the dark building to get a better look at the pump filled with gasoline. His feet and legs were gathering dampness from the tall weeds. If a car came from Berry's Mill, he would surely be seen standing against the building. His heart raced as he surveyed the pump. A smile came upon his face. "Dumb white boy!" he muttered. The crank handle on the pump was chained, but the hose and nozzle were open to the world. This was not Lee's first time stealing gasoline from an outdated pump like this. The pocketknife display, back inside, was short one damn good Case knife. He was prepared to cut the red rubber hose at the nozzle and run the red gasoline into the fuel tank of the automobile.

James Lee boldly drove the Nash from the dark pecan orchard to the pump and began to fill the gas tank. The twelve gallons could not flow fast enough. The anxious Negro danced around, hoping the fuel would flow faster. The large revolver was stuck in the front of his pants. There were other lit stores, several across the street, and white folks sleeping in their homes, all in sight of James Lee's acts. Eventually, the refueled Nash roared away into the night. He headed south out of the small town, in hopes of finding cover for the night in the community of Weatherford. The crafty Negro looked back on his tact. He had even returned the nozzle to its rest on the side of the old pump. It would be hours before the store owner discovered the missing fuel. The crate of food and the two pairs of pants sat on the seat next to him.

James Lee kept moving with no hard and fast plan. He knew that putting distance between himself and Greenville was his best plan. He did not know exactly where he was or where he was going at times, but he continued to move farther away. The bright headlights of the Nash headed south, possibly into Harris County, until the left-hand turn came up. Lee stopped the car and sat looking around. "Straight ahead is the general area of Pine Mountain and Harris County, to the left is the small forgotten community of Weatherford," he thought to himself. The intersection was filled with houses and headlights were coming brighter on the horizon. He chose to turn toward Weatherford. In a matter of a few minutes, Lee was in the sparse settlement. There was nothing resembling commerce, just several rundown frame buildings and a small cemetery. The buildings were too risky to pull behind, broken window glass and possibly nails, just waiting for his tires to come along. Once again, he chose to park in a small cemetery. Moonlight broke from behind the heavy forming clouds that passed overhead. He stood in the silence and rubbed the blistered ring on his leg, where the restraints had raised the skin and the heat from the burning pants dried it out. The gentle pressure exerted from his own fingertips felt soothing, as he rubbed his ankle, propped on the running board.

The haunting stillness of the night was amplified by the lightning to the southwest. There was no thunder to be heard, only the occasional flash. The obelisk tombstones and the carved statues that reminded those yet to come demanded respect as they cast their shadows across the smaller markers. James Lee often stood with his large yellow eyes wide open, looking about for someone or something that he felt was there, watching in the night. In the moonlight and lightning, he saw the deep shadow of a leaning crypt. It was the perfect place to hide his prison pants. He removed his brogans as he sat on the car seat, and then hurriedly removed his pants, tossing them aside in the floorboard. The new khakis fit nicely, and he had the second pair for later. He stood arranging his shirttail inside the new pants, thinking how much nicer he looked. "Almost like a business man," he thought.

Big raindrops began to strike the car. Each one made a thumping, spattering sound. "Many more of those and the grass will be too slick to pull back onto the road," Lee thought to himself. The Negro rolled the prison pants tightly into a small roll and hurried toward the leaning crypt. Between the car and the crypt, a rabbit broke and ran. It laughed as it left, nothing visible but the white cotton tail darting about in the moonlight.

"Shit!" Lee said aloud, as his heart raced from the sudden start. "Whosoever you beez, yous got sum pants," he said, poking the rolled pants into the opening of the crypt. The pants made a scrubbing sound as he forced them into the dark hole created by the large leaning stone. He jerked his hand back and shivered, thinking about what he had just touched. If someone had taken the pants from him, he would have died right there, alone in the cemetery, with a crate full of canned meats, three belly washers, and a stolen car. He ran back to the car. The headlights were a warm and comforting sight as they flooded the cemetery with a bright yellowish light. James Lee pushed on toward Midget. As a boy he had helped roof a church, maybe it was still there.

The road was going steadily downhill, hardly enough to notice, but all indications were that a stream was ahead. The headlights eventually reflected upon a black mirror-like body of water. He slowed the car. Ahead was a wide stream, how deep there was no way to tell, but he could just barely make out tire tracks on the opposite side, and a rocky grade. Lightning flashed again, illuminating a weathered tree trunk just across the water. For that split second, it looked like a man was standing on the bank. He pulled the revolver close to his side. For what comfort it was, James Lee rolled his window up, and started across the dark still stream. The water was almost up to the running boards. The taillight reflected on the wake of the water as he slowly drove through. The hot exhaust pipe sizzled and popped as it billowed a cloud of white steam into the winds of the coming storm.

The rain was falling harder. James Lee was relying on landmarks as much as roads to get him toward his end goal. At the next intersection he made a right turn, heading south. If all went well, he would be in hiding for the rainy night. Lightning flashed. He pushed the car harder, overrunning the turn he should have made. In his efforts to back up, he got a wheel into the sandy ditch. It almost cost him the car, as it took a lot of skilled rocking back and forth to finally get back onto the road. It was well after midnight. The large raindrops glistened in the headlights. At the turn, a mailbox leaning against the wild plum bushes had a faded-out number and the road name. "Tucker Road." Lee smiled. That was the road he needed.

The rain was coming in sheets now, and lightning lit the countryside with its blue hue for a fraction of a second. He saw the old church up ahead. It was not what he was hoping for, as the church had fallen into disrepair, and a large red oak had fallen during a storm years ago. Even the limbs of the fallen tree were rotting. The pasture grass had taken over the yard, and the toilets were collapsed. The headlights illuminated his salvation for the night. The red oak had created a large root ball when it fell across the small church. The root ball was the ideal place for him to hide the stolen car behind. Just beyond it was a pine thicket. The Nash was backed successfully between the root ball and the thicket. There were no other houses on the short road. Midget was behind him and Harris County was to his left. The freed Negro settled in for a meal of canned meat and a good night's sleep. He grinned at the thought of the law out in the stormy night looking for him. "Maybe they even have the dogs out! Who knows?" he thought, as he closed his eyes.

CHAPTER TEN

Benjamin Hill and Skippy arrived at the store just before dawn. Skippy stood on the seat, front paws on the dashboard of the black Model A truck. Skippy was eager as always to get to the store. Benjamin ran a small hot bar of sage pork sausage and oven hot biscuits. There were only two pans of biscuits cooked, and by the time the doors opened, the regulars were there to get them. At a nickel apiece, they went quickly. The morning sky glowed deep orange. Benjamin's face was illuminated in the shadows occasionally when he pulled on his pipe as he unlocked the front doors. Skippy hurried right into the dim light of the store. He came out as fast as he had gone in. Benjamin took note of that as his pal stood on the top step and growled. Benjamin was not stupid. He had been robbed and burglarized before, but it had been several years ago. When times were hard, theft became worse. In some ways he was expecting it, but a robbery was something he would be ready for. He was a veteran of World War I and he was of the mindset that God damn it, he was keeping what was his.

The storekeeper swooped the small dog up under his arm. "Son of a bitch! We've forgot something!" he said loudly. Skippy was shaking. Benjamin swung wide, out of view of the open door. He could see the path that had been made in the tall dewy grass alongside the store. He carefully walked to the shed with the double warehouse doors. From a distance he could see the lock was missing. "Shit!" he whispered to Skippy. The dog licked his lips and was about to bark, until Benjamin held his muzzle. "Be quiet," he whispered. He turned back to the truck parked under the first large pecan tree. He had always parked there, the grass was dead. Chester Grubbs pulled into his feed store lot. Benjamin waved, motioning him over.

Chester came across the road. "Ain't you got legs?" he asked, midway of the dusty road.

146

Still holding Skippy, Benjamin replied just above a whisper. "I've got a burglar in the building, or he's been there. And my pistol's inside," he added.

"Well, I'll get my shotgun and an old Winchester and we'll just see who the hell's in there. Punch a few holes in the son of a bitch," Chester said, as he hurried away. He quickly returned from his small office with a gun in each hand. He gave the Winchester to Benjamin. Skippy was on the truck seat watching from the open window, tail wagging. If dogs think, he was probably saying, "That sum bitch better not get 'tween me and my meal."

"You watch the back doors. I'll go in the front," Chester whispered. The two men hurried into place. Chester stood at the front corner of the building until Benjamin got close to the warehouse doors. Chester was also a veteran. He eased the door open enough to get inside. He was a larger man than Benjamin. His wife was a good cook, and office work had caused him to spread over the years. Chester knew enough to get out of the open door. He stood to the side for a moment or two, allowing his eyes to adjust to the darkness, and then carefully moved across the end of the aisles. Chester expected to be rushed by someone every time he looked down another aisle. He saw the floor full of papers and cigar boxes at the register, and the pants on the warehouse floor. Benjamin stood at the ready, just waiting for someone to rush out of the closed doors. Skippy touched him on the ankle above the sock line and Benjamin almost fired the gun when he jumped.

"Damn it! You scared me!" he said softly, to the small dog. Skippy looked up and wagged his tail, with his bright pink tongue hanging out and his eyes narrowed to show concentration.

Chester eventually turned on every pull chain light in the store that he could find. Whoever had been in there was gone. He slowly opened the warehouse door and let his shotgun barrel lead before he opened it fully.

"They in there?" yelled Benjamin.

"Gone and left ya a mess," Chester replied, opening the doors. Skippy ran inside.

"Chicken shit bastard!" Benjamin said loudly, lowering the hammer on the lever gun.

The stove was cold, sausage was not cooked, and Benjamin's customers were arriving. The men gathered in the front of the store after all the doors were open. One of the cars on the lot was a Troup County Sheriff's car. That was luck. The tall deputy walked inside, meeting the two men bearing guns. "Damn! Y'all bear huntin' or lookin fer rats?" he asked jokingly.

Chester took back his Winchester. "Call me if you need anything," he said, as he headed toward his own place.

"Burglarized during the night! Damn it! Chicken shit son of a bitches!" Benjamin said loudly. The early customers began to cross-talk over the deputy and Benjamin.

"No biscuits today," Benjamin said, looking sad.

"If I can make a pot of coffee, I'll bet a box of Moon Pies'll do under the circumstances," said one customer.

"You guys know where things are, put yer money on the counter before you leave, and any wrappers," replied Benjamin. Soon the aroma of coffee filled the store.

"Let's look at what took place," said the deputy.

Benjamin showed what was disturbed and what was damaged. "They cut the lock with the torch, came in the warehouse doors. I think I'm missing some pants, and judging by the way the register area looks disturbed, the bastard's got my revolver," advised Benjamin. Skippy had broken away and was tagging along.

"Was this like this before?" asked the deputy, as he pointed to the canned meats, some of which had fallen onto the floor.

"No!" Benjamin answered. He stooped down and arranged the display. "These were all fronted before we left," he said. "There's five missing of the corned beef," he added.

"We? We who?" asked the deputy.

"Me and Skippy," Benjamin said. He hurried to the cash register counter and began to take stock of what was missing. "Yep, God damn pistol's gone!" Benjamin snapped, striking the top of the counter. Skippy jumped.

"Any money?" asked the deputy.

Benjamin moved the register tray. "All my opening money, ten dollars, five bills and five in coins," he said. "Damn it!" he said, gritting his teeth. "Shit!" His morning customers began to leave quietly, one at a time, putting money for what they ate on the center of the counter.

"Pants, ten dollars, food, and a revolver. What kind?" asked the deputy, as he took notes.

"It was a top break, Harrington & Richardson! 38 S&W!" he yelled.

"Be calm, Benjamin. I can hear fine," said the deputy, still writing hurriedly.

"It was a fine piece, blue steel, checkered black gutta-percha grips, a six-inch barrel. "Shit!" said Benjamin.

"Shit what?" asked the deputy.

"There's two full boxes of shells gone too!" answered Benjamin, as he bent down looking under the dark counter. He was breathing hard from stooping and anger.

"See anyone afoot when you left? Meet any cars?" asked the deputy, looking out into the bright morning yard.

Benjamin thought for a few seconds. "No!" he replied.

"I need the telephone," said the deputy.

"I ain't got one of the damn things, but tomorrow I will have," replied Benjamin. "Chester Grubbs's got the only one in the vicinity."

"I'll go over," said the deputy. "Put up some signs, 'dog inside'. Double chain the doors, and by the way, keep the torch inside," he said, winking.

Chester Grubbs ran a third-generation family business and was a successful man. He was one of the first in the small town to have a telephone. The Troup County Sheriff's Deputy hurried across the road. The morning traffic had picked up and commerce was in full sway at the businesses there in Hambyville. Chester saw the deputy coming. He knew it was probably for the use of the telephone. The deputy's Wellington boots made a heavy thud as he took the steps in a hurry.

"Good mornin'!" said the deputy, looking in at Chester, who sat at his desk.

"And a good morning to you!" Chester replied. "What can I do for you? Scratch feed? Rabbit feed? Hay? Oats?" he asked, stalling the lawman from his business.

"No, sir! I'd like to use the telephone to call the department." He had already spied the telephone on the desk, almost covered with the morning newspaper.

"Do I need to leave?" asked Chester, as he pushed back in his heavy swivel chair.

"No, you're fine," replied the deputy.

Chester leaned forward, looking at the brass name plate on the medium brown uniform shirt. "A. Thigpen," Chester said aloud, leaning back. "From 'round here?" he asked.

Deputy Thigpen stood anxiously awaiting the use of the telephone. "Married one of the Perry girls, from Durand," he replied. "May I use the telephone?" Thigpen asked once more.

Chester moved the morning paper. "Certainly."

"Dial out or operator?" Thigpen asked, holding the receiver. He saw that there was a rotary dialer.

"Pray tell! We're out in the sticks, son!" Chester laughed. "Dial 'O' for Suzie!" He laughed loudly. "Now, she'll listen to yer conversation if you don't call her down right off."

"Thanks! I'll do that," replied Thigpen, placing his fingertip in the hole for the 'O'. He gave it a stout turn until the dial stopped.

"Operator!" A woman's voice was heard.

"Get me the Troup County Sheriff's Department, please. Is this Suzie?" asked the deputy.

"Yes, it is," the woman replied.

"This is Deputy Alonzo Thigpen. Close the line when I'm connected, please. This is official business," he said, looking down at Chester.

Chester smiled. "That'll just kill her. She's a busybody," he snickered.

He covered his mouth, hiding his smile.

The call went through, with a few suspenseful clicks and clacks of circuitry switching. "Troup County Sheriff's Office! Sheriff Jacob Ector speakin'."

"Thigpen here! I come up on a burglary this morning over here in Hambyville," he said, glancing out the dusty window behind Chester's chair.

"You'd come on in here and not been after one of them damn sausage biscuits from Hill's place, you wouldn't have a damn case now, would you?" shouted the sheriff.

Thigpen's face blushed. He tried to ignore the outburst. "It appears that the store was broken into during the night, took a .38 revolver, two boxes cartridges, canned food, and two pair of pants, Hill thinks. And ten dollars in bills and change from the register," Thigpen said. "I hear ya breathin', Suzie!" he said slowly and forcefully. There was a sudden click.

"Who the hell is Suzie?" asked the sheriff.

"The operator over here," Thigpen replied.

Sheriff Ector's eyes searched over the papers on his desk. There was the latest bulletin from the Meriwether Sheriff. He was silent. Thigpen waited on a reply, as it was the sheriff's habit to be doing something and not responding, but when he did it was worthwhile. Sheriff Ector read the bulletin again.

"Two pair pants?" he asked.

"Yes," answered Thigpen.

Chester left the office to make a sale. The deputy took his seat.

"And they cut the lock off the door," Thigpen added.

"You go look around some more and I'll bet you'll find more than a cut lock," said Sheriff Ector. "Now, listen up. This food, pants, money, and a gun sounds like the escaped Negro from Sheriff Gilbert's jail in Greenville. Look some more and call me back," he added. The telephone went dead.

Deputy Thigpen yelled and waved to Chester, expressing his thanks for the use of the telephone. Skippy was standing at the open door of the store watching the business on the lot. A green Ford was fueling at the same pump that was in dispute on the previous afternoon. The driver came in to pay. "I got six gallons from the pump on the east side," said a man in overalls.

"That pump had twelve gallons in the globe when I locked up," replied Benjamin, looking over his thin wire framed glasses.

"Six gallons," replied the customer. Thigpen was watching from just inside the doorway.

"Twelve gallons," said Benjamin. The customer remained silent and shook his head, no.

"Mr. Hill, the globe was empty when I came in this morning," replied Thigpen. "That's one of the things we look for, just out of habit. We've found pump locks cut and nozzles lying on the ground before."

"Then the bastard's driving a car or something and took twelve gallons of gas!" snapped Benjamin. "Six gallons!' he said, pointing to the customer. There were several customers in line to pay for items. "Damn it!" mumbled the storekeeper.

Thigpen made a note of the missing gasoline and quantity in his notepad. "Sir, I need to look around some more," he said, pointing to the back of the store.

"Go ahead," Benjamin sighed. He started once more to tell of his misfortune to the customers that were gathered. Skippy sat in a sunbeam on the doorstep.

Deputy Thigpen wormed his way among the aisles of merchandise and then into the warehouse, where most of the larger hardware items were kept. There were plow points and mule collars, and buckets of all sizes hung from strong nails on the rafters. The only light on a sunny day came from the shallow windows along the ceiling line on the west wall. He opened the warehouse doors and looked for signs of forced entry, but there were none. The hot spatters of molten lock had been blown against the dry wooden door, leaving small black charred marks. The cut lock lay nearby in the gravel. His eyes searched for footprints, but there were so many under the shed that it was impossible to single out any particular set. Thigpen knew the same would hold true around the gas pumps, so he did not go and look. The Acetylene torch hung from the steel rolling rack, just to the right of the wooden steps. There was a possibility that a good thumbprint was still on the thumb lever.

Thigpen rubbed his face with his hand, thinking of what he should do. Should he risk calling out the only scene technician they had for one "maybe" thumbprint or just leave it alone, he thought. Even then, that was old Doc McCay at Liddell's Rexall, on South Hines in LaGrange. Sheriff Ector guarded the print dusting powder like an evil hawk. Skippy suddenly stood beside him at the work bench. "Hey, little guy! What are you up to?" asked Thigpen, looking down at the small Terrier. He had made a habit long ago of not touching dogs, as he had been snapped at one too many times. Skippy returned the conversation with a look, and then trotted off toward the pecan orchard. "Hey! Wait, I'll go with ya!" the Deputy said, pointing at the small dog. Skippy explored and sniffed about as they made their way through the heavy metal racks of steel piping and lumber.

Skippy always kept ahead. It was a dog's way, to be in front. The dog stopped and sniffed at the end of the wood rack. Thigpen was still approaching. He had stopped to admire an air-drying piece of some kind of wood. He thought it might possibly be cherry, or maybe a huge slab of pear. He was not sure. The house wrens and sparrows darted about under the shed, laying claim to their territory and nesting rafter rights. Thigpen had forgotten to note what time he arrived and found the case. He had just put down opening time. That was 5:30. Thigpen was beginning to get "yawn-i-fied". He smiled wide. That was his great-grandmother's word for yawning almost continuously. He shook his head and smiled, thinking of the old woman. She had passed away when he was just a small boy.

The deputy squatted down next to the sniffing dog. He nudged him away, risking being snipped, but part of the job. There was dried blood, just a drop or two, on the dirt under the end of the two-by's that rested at eye level above. "Shit!" he mumbled to himself. Skippy had moved on, finding a tree to mark. That gave the tiring officer the urge to pee himself. He thought he could hold it until he got back inside. The small spots of dried blood were dark, but they were fresh. He knew because the gnats and flies had not discovered it yet.

Thigpen was trying to get off the road. The shift work was hard on a person. He had read every police magazine and book he could get. Going to any training was damn near impossible for a local boy. He seemed to know what needed to be done on the scene, but did not have the tools to work with. The ones who seemed to have gotten ahead were medical or lawyers that had fallen out along the way. They got ahead with a college degree, even with limited interest in the law enforcement profession and no interest in the ability to shoot.

He was startled upon hearing the sudden voice of Benjamin calling from the warehouse doors. "Find anything else?"

"Can you bring me a clean cup or a clean can to cover up some blood spots?" Thigpen asked, standing guard.

Benjamin quickly turned and hurried back into the store. He soon returned, bringing a short stack of paper cups. "These do?" he asked, holding them out to the deputy.

"They certainly will. I need -- " he thought for a minute. " -- piece of wood, a block heavy enough to hold the cup over these spots, to keep them from blowin' away," said Thigpen. Benjamin hurried to the scrap barrel and retrieved three thick blocks of wood.

"Thanks!" replied the deputy. "Now, that's covered," he said, standing. "Don't go on out, let me work the scene."

"Oh! I'll stand right here. What'll happen with the blood spots?" Benjamin asked.

Deputy Thigpen stood at the end of the shed and looked out into the pecan orchard. "I'll probably get it in the clean cups and take it in to Doc McCay and see if he can type it."

Thigpen looked into the orchard for the longest, without moving from one spot. "God damn it! I don't even have a camera. The county's equipment poor," he said, looking down.

"Hell! I can get a camera from someone here in the neighborhood," replied Benjamin. "And I sell film!" he added. He sounded excited that something was happening on his case. "I'll go make some calls!" Benjamin hurried away. Skippy ran to join him. The small dog's paws raised the dust as he tried to catch up with his master.

Deputy Thigpen went back to the place where the cups guarded the blood spots. He looked up out of curiosity. He pulled his readers from his shirt pocket. They were half-glasses. The optometrist said he could get drug store ones or he could give "hand over fist" amounts for stylish ones. Thigpen chose what he could afford, so he had a cigar box full of cheap readers at home. Some were even red rubber frames so he could find them easier, but most were black or tortoise shell. He studied the end of the plank that stuck out the most from the heavy stack. As he squinted his eyes and turned his head, he eventually discovered a tiny looking piece of skin. "Is that skin? It's too black, probably trash," he thought. Then he looked again. It was dark brown. "Negro skin!" he said aloud. His heart raced. "God damn it! I need tweezers," he said out loud.

"Hell! I've got them too," Benjamin said. The deputy jumped. He thought he was alone. "Did I scare ya?" Benjamin asked.

"I'm not really jumpy, I'm just tired and still gatherin' evidence," replied the exhausted deputy.

"A camera's on the way, and a man to operate it," Benjamin advised. "Be right here!" he added. "What else might you need?" he asked.

"Index cards, a black crayon, clean rollin' papers! And several envelopes," replied Thigpen.

Within a few minutes, a black Plymouth rolled onto the lot and pulled up to the business end of the shed. A woman got out. "I'm here!" she said.

"Who might you be?" the deputy asked. Benjamin was not back, as there were several customers in the store. Thigpen still stood guard over his findings.

"Pansy Bowen, photographer," said the short round matronly young woman. "Benjamin said there was a need for a camera. I've got one, but I use it," she said, standing by her car door.

"Can I have the film?" Thigpen asked.

"After I develop it," Pansy replied.

"How close can you get?" asked Thigpen.

"What are we photographing?" she asked.

"Blood spots and then a piece of skin on the end of a board, and maybe some more stuff," he said.

"It ain't a baby portrait?" She sounded surprised.

"Far from it," he replied. Benjamin came into the shed area.

"There's my girl!" Benjamin said loudly, holding the items the deputy had asked for. "Crime scene, girl!" he smiled.

"Jesus, Benjamin! I don't do that," she said angrily.

"Hot biscuits, gasoline," Benjamin said, trying to put on a pouty face. Skippy even gave a sad little whine.

"Miss, the county is in a world of hurt, and I need a person to photograph the stuff I point out. It should only take a few minutes, and not even a roll of film," begged Thigpen.

The young woman sighed and began to take her equipment from the trunk of the car. "What's first?" she asked.

"Please make the best picture of the store front showing the business sign, then one from this side showing the shed. Make one from the back here too," instructed the deputy. Benjamin stood by watching the deputy, as he looked out for customers. "Be sure to show the gas pumps too!" he added.

"This is number one, the blood spots, the skin I found up here is number two," Thigpen said, as he carefully drew the numbers onto the index cards. He placed the card beside the evidence.

"I'm ready," said Pansy, as she stood behind the two men.

"Right here, as close as you can, and focus on where my pencil point is," said the deputy, as he kneeled down by the blood.

The lens of the big twin lens reflex made a crisp sound as it exposed the film. "Okay!" said Pansy, advancing the film with the fold out hand lever.

"This right here," said Thigpen, as he pointed to the skin with his pencil. She moved in and out, getting her stance steady, then made the photograph.

"Benjamin, close the doors." He thought for a moment. "Lay the lock back where it was found and let her make a picture of it. Then close the doors, put the lock in the hasp, and get a picture," he said. "I've got to gather this evidence," Thigpen advised, as they walked away.

Deputy Thigpen gently picked up the three pieces of granite gravel with the blood spots and placed them into the paper cup. He plucked the small piece of skin from the end of the board with the tweezers and placed it on a clean rolling paper. He had seen how the books and magazines had shown a fold called a pharmacy fold that kept things from escaping easily. He did his best to fold the skin in the paper in that manner. The skin paper was secured in an envelope and sealed. "B. Hill's Store Hambyville, skin". Pansy and Benjamin were talking at the work bench.

"I'll put this in my car," Thigpen said in passing.

The baby photographer stood by her car as the deputy returned from his. "One hour and these will be ready at my lab," she said.

"Where's that?" asked the deputy.

"A mile down on the right, sign's got a baby on it," she advised. The heavy woman was a seat full, not a lot of room between her bosom and the steering wheel.

"Thank you, I'll be there. Any money?" he asked.

"No, Benjamin's got it covered," she replied, as the car cranked. Deputy Thigpen watched as she drove out of sight. He could not remember a sign with a baby on it. He walked to the pecan orchard scratching his head.

The search in the rear of the store revealed where an automobile had circled around and parked in the orchard. The grass that was pressed down from walking on it had almost recovered. Thigpen felt good about his findings. He hurried toward the store. His yawning was worse, since the last burst of adrenalin played out. This time the steps seemed to be taller. The deputy stopped halfway and looked back under the work bench. "Son of a bitch!" he said, returning to the bench. On his hands and knees, he pulled out the ankle cuffs that had been cut off with the torch and the chain that connected them. There were several pieces of burnt fabric. "God damn it!" he said to himself. "She's already gone." He gathered the evidence and placed it in a brown paper bag, making note of the details in his report to come.

Thigpen hurried into the store. "I know who yer burglar is," he said, heading hurriedly for the front doors.

"You do!" replied Benjamin, leaning over the counter, watching the deputy hurry across the street to Chester's telephone. "Damn it! There'll be a telephone in here tomorrow!" he said, pounding the counter with his fist. A shopper looked around a display at him.

"Can I use the telephone again?" the deputy asked Chester.

"Certainly," he replied, pushing it toward him. "Shall I leave?" Chester asked.

Deputy Thigpen shook his head no and dialed the operator.

"Operator!"

"Suzie?" he asked.

"Yes," she replied.

"You listened in this morning and I'm listing you in my report as a witness. You listen this time and I'll get you for interference," he said calmly. "Get me the Troup County Sheriff's Department, please."

The call went through with the same suspenseful clicks and clacks of switching circuitry.

"Troup County Sheriff's Office! Sheriff Jacob Ector speakin'," said the sheriff.

"This is Thigpen!" Before he could get a word in, the sheriff started.

"You know you work at the leisure of the sheriff?" he barked. Thigpen thought that he did, though more like working while the sheriff leisured, but he did not say anything.

"I know who broke in," Thigpen said.

"Was it the escaped Negro?" barked the sheriff.

"I found blood where he or somebody walked into a board in the dark and cut themselves, probably in the face. I've even got a tiny piece of what looks like dark skin," said Thigpen.

"Negro skin?" the sheriff snapped back.

"I believe so, by the naked eye," Thigpen said. "I've even got the cut off ankle cuffs," he said, smiling. Chester sat at his desk acting like he was running a list of numbers on the comptometer. One hand guided his eyes on a sheet of paper while the other index finger hurriedly punched buttons. The deputy knew Chester was listening.

Sheriff Ector leaned forward sitting at his desk. "Go home and get some sleep. Get the blood and skin to Doc McCay as soon tomorrow or tonight as you can. I'll call the Meriwether Sheriff. Good job, son, good job," he said. "Alonzo!" he said loudly, then paused for the longest moment. "Thanks, for the good work. Go home! Don't worry about Granny Thompson callin' in. She ain't seen a county car all morning and it's only 9:30. I'll get in my god damn car and drive by the old biddy's house. Ya know all she's got to do is watch for the mail and make sure we get a car down her street," said the sheriff.

"Yes, sir!" Thigpen replied. "Thank you, sir!" he added, before hanging up.

Deputy Thigpen returned to Benjamin Hill's store and advised him of the likelihood that they now knew who they were looking for.

"We'll be in here tonight," snapped the angry Benjamin. "Me and old Skippy'll get his ass!"

"Sir, go home! Padlock the doors and chain what you can, get the tools and torch from the shed and workbench, and go home," the tired deputy advised. The short trip to the baby photographer's place was tiring, but the photographs were well worth the effort. They would be valuable evidence in court.

* * *

On this beautiful morning, Heather and her partner Jasper Brown had met at the café. While it appeared to be a meeting place for those in control of the city government and business, they chose to meet there, regardless. Heather carefully crossed the busy street. Jasper was already there and had parked the marked unit in front. Even that angered some folks. Police cars should be parked away from the best spots, saving them for the citizens. Jasper stood under the shade of the shallow porch, speaking to citizens who passed by.

"Mornin'!" Heather said, bouncing up the steps. Jasper noticed her well gathered bosom move as she came up the steps. After all, he was not dead yet.

"Good morning," he replied, touching the bill of his uniform cap.

"Spiffy bastard," Heather mumbled. "Maybe I need to get out my Fedora," she said, just for him to hear, as citizens hurried by. A couple of dogs chased a cat across the busy street. "That cat's just toying with those dogs. That old Tom'll time it right one morning and those two dogs'll be hit by a car." Heather had left her suit coat in her room. The white pleated front blouse went well with the brown slacks and her matching dark brown leather. She saw Jasper looking. "Nice, isn't it?" she said, striking him on the upper arm like a schoolboy.

"Darn! That hurt," Jasper said, grabbing his shoulder. "Bitch!" he said in a low voice. "Ya knocked a second biscuit in me," he said, limping toward the café door. "What if we're seen?" he asked, stepping inside.

"Hey! They've changed the tablecloths. They were red gingham the last time," Heather remarked, pushing Jasper deeper inside. The patrons looked up. "Find a seat out in the open," she said. He paused. "Do it!" she whispered.

Jasper took the first table that was cleared. As they expected, everyone looked at them. It was like they were stealing from the public, or so the officers felt.

"Morning!" Jasper said loudly, as he pulled out two chairs. Heather abruptly pushed them back in and pulled out the other two. She smiled at Jasper. He sat down with a questioning expression as to what he had or had not done.

Heather leaned toward him. "Never sit with your back to the door. Sitting here you watch my back, to the kitchen, and I've got yours to the street.

"Oh," he replied in a soft whisper.

"What will it be, officers?" asked the waitress. She held two mugs on her finger, and a hot coffee pot in the other hand.

"My, it looks nice," Heather replied, smiling. "I'll have coffee and a sausage biscuit."

Jasper replied, "I'll have the same, but put a buttered biscuit on there too." He smiled at the waitress. She winked. Jasper's head, where the hair had been thick at one time, turned red. "That's Esther," he said, reaching for the sugar.

"Here comes the chief and the mayor," Heather said, leaning from one side to the next, looking around other patrons. The small place had a soft roar of its own.

"Crap!" Jasper replied, looking toward the door.

"Follow my lead, just be polite. I'll handle this," said Heather. "And don't kiss any ass," she whispered, touching his shaking hand. Jasper's spoon hand began to shake and the spoon struck the side of his mug several times before he could lay it down. "You get rattled like that in a shootin' and you'll be in a damn box," Heather whispered, kicking his foot.

The Chief and Mayor Cunningham came in the single door smiling and greeting everyone, some longer than others. Heather noted the suits and ties got more words than the men wearing overalls. "Politics," she said to herself. The hot food was placed before them. "Thanks!" they both replied.

As Heather had expected, the two men stopped right in front of them. "Well! Good morning! Our patrolling officers have decided to join us," smiled the chief. The mayor smiled at Heather.

"We'd ask you to sit with us, but we're expecting some folks to bring us some information on James Lee." The soft roar of conversation dropped to silence once that name steeled upon their ears.

"Oh! Just get him in cuffs," replied the chief with a smile. He stood and tapped the back of the vacant chair several times as though he was thinking of what to say next. Heather bumped Jasper on the shoe once more.

"I'm surprised they're not here already," Jasper said, looking toward the street. "We'll give 'em a few," he added, taking a bite of his biscuit.

"Keep us informed," said Chief Hawthorn, as he went to join the mayor at another table, far away in the corner.

Heather added yellow mustard from the jar on the table to her sausage biscuit.

"I like jelly on mine," Jasper said.

"If I was at home, it would be good sorghum syrup," she replied.

"That is good when it's cooked past green," Jasper said. Heather could see he was beginning to relax a bit.

Officer Edgar Peterson burst out of the police department onto the street followed by Frances Goulding. They were looking up and down the street for any sign of the chief. Heather saw them. "I think our information is almost here," she whispered. "Look at the street." Jasper turned and saw Peterson stopping traffic to get across.

"Chief! Chief!" called the night officer, as he hurried into the café.

Chief Hawthorn stood and waved. Peterson hurried over to him as Jasper and Heather watched. They were not sure Peterson even saw them. Besides, if it was a call, they should be first to hear it.

"Troup County called," Peterson gasped.

"Outside," said the chief, grasping Peterson's arm. The excited man stopped talking. Heather nudged Jasper and they too headed for the door.

"What is it?" asked the chief. The two day officers stood close by.

"Sheriff Jacob Ector called and said there was a burglary in Hambyville that we might want to be aware of. It sounded like the escaped nigger," Peterson said. The chief looked at Heather and Jasper.

"I guess we've got his telephone number?" asked Heather. She saw Frances standing on the sidewalk. "Frances all right?" she asked, looking in her direction.

"She's got kin over there. She's a little shook," replied Peterson.

"We've got it! Go home! Some of us'll see you tonight," said Chief Hawthorn. Officer Peterson crossed the busy street and disappeared into the police department. Frances followed.

The three law officers stood on the porch, being careful as to when they spoke. Information getting out at the wrong time could spoil a case, or make it longer. "All right! You two know what to do. Jasper, she's in charge on this one," said the chief.

"I understand," Jasper said, respectfully.

"We're still looking for our contacts. I'll give 'em a few more minutes," Heather said, pulling at Jasper to join her inside, where their meal sat waiting on the table. The chief went back to join the mayor, who had gathered another guest at the small table.

Esther had topped off their coffee. Jasper leaned toward Heather. "Shouldn't we be going?"

"Eat up, it ain't going nowhere, remember it's already happened," she replied.

The two expected guests bearing information never came. The two officers paid for their breakfast and headed toward the telephone.

"Mornin', Miss Frances," Heather greeted. Jasper smiled as he took a seat on the edge of the back desk. Heather sat down at the telephone, several desks away. "Do I need a number for Troup County Sheriff? What's his name?" she asked, holding the receiver.

Jasper was answering her question that was directed to Frances. He vigorously shook his head. "His name is Ector, Jacob Ector. Just tell the operator to connect you," Frances replied, without looking up from her opened mail.

"Thanks!" replied Heather.

The Warm Springs Detective was soon connected with the Sheriff of Troup County. He advised her of the burglary location and told her in great detail what his deputy had discovered on the crime scene. The sheriff tended to speak highly of his man's work and how continued diligence had built a good strong case once the offender was captured. Heather thought the bragging was a little heavy, as Campbell County always expected every officer to make the best case possible. Good cases meant longevity in office. Jasper listened as she signed off.

"We're going to be in Troup County, Benjamin Hill's store," Heather advised, hoping that Frances was listening as she read the mail.

The police department's lobby door was tight due to the dampness of the rain from the night before, as little as it was. It slammed hard when it was pulled shut. Heather saw Frances look up. "Hambyville, the store of Benjamin Hill," Heather said, as she opened the car door.

Jasper tended to race the engine every time he cranked it. Heather wondered why, but never said anything. Jasper drove. Heather leaned down and looked at the fuel gauge. "Seein' if we've got enough fuel," she said, sitting back in the seat. The traffic in Warm Springs was heavy.

"Shall I move 'em along?" Jasper asked.

"Just a nudge," Heather replied.

Jasper turned on the siren and all his lights. The foot traffic jumped and became startled, stopping in their tracks. The automobiles pulled to the right, but several stopped where they were. "Dumb asses!" Jasper said loudly, as he had to back up to go around the first car. "Only sixteen miles or so, and it ain't no direct way ta get there," Jasper said. His window was down. Once they turned onto Seven Branches Road, Jasper turned off all the lights and the siren. He caught a faint whiff of Heather's perfume.

"Honeysuckle?" he asked, looking toward her. Damn she was a pretty woman. If he was a younger man, he'd gnaw his arms off to get next to her. Damn!

"Left over from another wearing," she replied. The wind blew her short hair about, but her cut and style never lost its shape.

"If I wuzn't here, could ya get there?" Jasper asked.

"Seven Branches Road to Midget, on to Weatherford, north on McGee's Pond Road or west to County Line Road, on into Hambyville," she said loudly. "Raise the damn window! I can't hear ya for the wind." She gave her lowered window a crank or two. "Tha high road would be through Durand Sulphur Springs and into Weatherford," she said. The city issued twenty-eight Ford bounced along the rough roads, few were paved.

Heather leaned over and switched on the motor driven siren. Jasper looked puzzled. The low moan growled and eventually became a sturdy constant pitch as the device wailed. "God, that takes me back home!" she said, smiling. Heather leaned deeper into the seat with her eyes closed and smiled.

"Can I turn it off?" Jasper asked.

"I guess!" she replied quickly. "We'd run ours and Holly, our only and best trackin' dog, would hang out the back open window and try to imitate it. She'd start out with the lowest moan and then bring it up to a hair raisin' howl. She was somethin' else!" Heather said. The shadows of the trees flickered across their faces as the strong running Model A clipped along.

Between Midget and Weatherford, the two unknowing Warm Springs officers were less than half a mile from the escapee James Lee. He still sat napping in the stolen automobile. Around 10:30 the two officers saw Hambyville up ahead. Benjamin Hill's store was busy with customers and curiosity seekers, as word of mouth and telephone had traveled quickly. Sheriff Ector had vowed to bring this escaped Negro to justice for the crime committed in his county. He had contacted two of the most powerful radio stations in the area, WPAX in Thomasville and WFDV in Columbus. His intent was to contact WSB in Atlanta, located on Forsyth Street, but he had failed to do so at the time. That was on his "to-do" list. The pecan tassels were blowing across the unpaved lot, even as the cars came and went. The spring winds this year were still strong.

"Hard winds, good crops," Jasper said.

"Hadn't heard that one. Makes sense though," Heather replied. "Park in front if you can, let folks know we're on the job. The sheriff didn't say anything we didn't hear this morning from the chief," she said, looking over at her partner.

The people of Hambyville were surprised to see a Warm Springs Police car in their small town. Some stood and watched as they passed, others greeted with a wave of the hand. The officers smiled and nodded, returning waves in many instances. After all, they represented the city government of Warm Springs.

"Here's one!" Jasper said, as he headed for the empty parking space in close proximity to the front steps.

"Look!" Heather pointed at Skippy sitting on the top steps. The small dog began to wag its tail as the officers came up the steps. Heather made over the cheerful dog and quickly had a trot along partner. The store was busy with customers, probably more socializing than buying. The countertop radio was aglow in the dim light. Jasper started introductions, but was stopped by Mr. Hill. "Listen! Just a minute!" he shushed.

"Time now eleven o'clock, one hour 'fore Grandma's beans and cornbread. This is WPAX from Thomasville, Jaw-ja! News of the hour," said the radio host.

"This is it! Listen up!" Benjamin Hill yelled. Everyone quieted down. The only sound was the wind around the corner of the building, a car that passed, and the tiny claws of Skippy walking toward the food bowl under the end of the register counter. Tick, tick, tick, they sounded off on the floor. Heather smiled. It reminded her of home.

"Yesterday we broadcast that a Negro, James Lee, had escaped from the Greenville Jail. He badly injured a trustee and assaulted Ellis DeFoor, of Luthersville. DeFoor struck his head in the struggle and was pronounced dead by the arriving Doctor Augustus Hubbard. The escaped prisoner took Mr. DeFoor's 1925 Nash and was believed to be heading in a westward direction, from the Greenville square. The vehicle is a black over red soft top. James Lee is a dark Negro, 5'10" tall, weighs 140 pounds, short clipped black hair, brown eyes, with yellow, large flat facial features. Was last wearing a prison uniform and brown brogans. The escapee is possibly armed and is dangerous. Any sighting or known location should be called in to Sheriff Louis Gilbert, Meriwether County Sheriff, or your law enforcement officers. The existing charges prior to escape were armed robbery and murder of Herman Pickens of Durand," said the radio announcer. Benjamin Hill put his thumbs behind his suspenders and smiled. "This portion of the broadcast is brought to you by LUX! Like the wardrobe mistresses of Broadway, women everywhere use LUX for silk stockings! They know rubbing with cake -- " the patience of Mr. Hill got the best of him.

"God damn it! Let's here tha news!" he yelled, shaking his head from side to side with impatience.

" -- whether flakes, chips, or cakes contain harmful alkali that may fade lovely colors! So, to make sure of extra wear, use LUX! Now, back to the news. The Humbyville store of Benjamin Dill was burglarized last night. From all indications of items taken and evidence found at the crime scene, the same wanted fugitive is believed to have committed the crime."

Mr. Hill made a face at the slaughtering of the town's name and his. "Benjamin Dill! Shit!" he said, turning the radio off. There were chuckles from the customers. "Yes!" Hill said, looking at the uniformed officer and the suited woman.

"Officer Jasper Brown, and this is Detective Duncan, Warm Springs Police Department. We are acting as Special Deputies for Meriwether County," Jasper said, extending his hand to the store owner. Heather did the same, and then she took over.

"We'd like to be shown the crime scene, and hear your story," she said. She could feel the examining male eyes looking at her, from her shoe soles to her bosom. They did not get much higher. She kept her arm and elbow against her revolver while in the crowded store. A small girl and her mother emerged from an aisle. Heather made eye contact with the timid young girl and they exchanged smiles. Benjamin Hill began his long and detailed story, which certainly told more than either of the officers needed or wanted to hear. The detailed account by Hill took almost thirty minutes, before they returned to the front of the store.

"Any photographs?" Heather asked of Hill.

"Yes, there was. The deputy had a photographer from down the road to make photographs under his direction. Those should be at the sheriff's office," replied Hill. Skippy stood and pawed on Benjamin's pants legs. It was noon, time to eat.

Heather asked to drive and Jasper obliged. "What's next?" he asked, sitting on the passenger side, his arm out the open window.

"Somethin' tells me that the son of a bitch didn't continue west. Let's work our way back by stopping at all the crossroads and talking to those we see along the way. It may take a while. Anyone with a telephone could let us tell them where we are," she said, backing the car carefully on the busy lot. For the next six miles there was no one to be seen in the fields or even on the front porches. It seemed as though everyone had vanished. "We'll find someone at Weatherford," Heather said. She was angered over the fact that there was no one, no matter how hard they looked. Housewives could be disturbed, but she wanted those out and about, who had talked to others this morning. The angry detective pushed the city car hard.

Jasper held on to the jolting and jostling Ford. "You pissed at me?" he asked loudly over the window noise.

Heather shook her head. "No. We need to talk to folks! This nigger's probably close by. He's apt to go to ground during the day and move at night."

"Oh!" replied Jasper, looking ahead. They rode in silence for a while, both looking for field workers and businesses along the way.

"Could ya read that sum bitch?" Heather suddenly asked, looking at Jasper. He had never seen the anger in her eyes like this before.

Jasper shook his head. "No". Jasper was almost scared. "No!" he repeated.

"He doubted me! He's on the telephone right now," she said, her lips tight across her teeth.

"He ain't got a telephone," Jasper replied.

"Then he's wherever there is one!" Heather turned and looked out the window. Jasper sat silently.

* * *

Skippy was rushed across the road under Benjamin Hill's arm, to Chester Grubb's office. "I need tha telephone!" Benjamin said, putting the small dog on the dusty floor.

"Another problem?" asked Chester, pushing back in his chair. The customers had just about died out for the day.

"Did you see the two Warm Springs officers that were at my place?" he snapped, leaning on the counter.

"No, but I heard there was a damn pretty one," Chester replied.

"That's a god damn joke! A woman doin' a man's job! And law enforcement! Son of a god damn bitch!" Benjamin shouted and pounded the counter.

Chester did not disagree as strongly as his neighbor. He surrendered the telephone with the gesture of his open hand. "Shall I leave?"

"No, it's yer telephone!" snapped Benjamin. Chester sat quietly and listened. "Get me the Meriwether Sheriff!" Benjamin barked. "Yes, In Greenville!" He covered the mouthpiece. "Dumb bitch!"

"Best be careful what ya say, them words can bite ya in the butt," said Chester, sitting with his fingers laced across his stomach.

"Damn it, damn it!" Benjamin barked impatiently.

"I heard tell of a guy in the first World War, told one of them Filipino broads ta hang on his," he was stopped by Benjamin's talking.

"All right, I'll hold," Benjamin barked again.

"Anyway, she wasn't a woman of the night and took in ta whoopin' his young ass, with that marry-tal arts hand fightin'," Chester warned.

Benjamin stood straight. "Okay!" he said.

"He wears false teeth today, and has bad aches in his ribs when it's cold

163

and damp," Chester hurried on.

"Is this the Shurriff in Meriwether County?" asked Benjamin. "Well, good! This is store owner Benjamin Hill over in Hambyville, Troup County. Appears you or somebody sent a woman detective to my place, said they, him, the other man officer, were Special Deputies of yorn," said Benjamin.

"They are. Yes, they, well, the woman, it's a joint effort with us and Warm Springs. She's well-qualified and sent down from Campbell County," said the sheriff. Chester could just barely hear the sheriff's voice.

"I don't want no woman workin' my case!" shouted Benjamin. "Do what?"

"It's not your choice, Mr. Hill. The world we live in is slowly changing. I guess it's made it to our end of the state," said Sheriff Gilbert.

"It ain't right, a woman doin' a man's job!" Benjamin yelled. Chester tried not to smile at Benjamin's frustration. Skippy had curled up on a sack of grain in the corner. The dog was ready to stay awhile.

"Take her off!" yelled Benjamin.

Sheriff Gilbert leaned close to his telephone. "Listen, Mr. Hill. She's working yer case and my case; our case, just like any other qualified officer. DO YOU HEAR ME?" he asked, in a steely tone.

Benjamin Hill's face turned pale. "I don't like it, but I hear you," he said.

"Have a good day, sir!" said Sheriff Gilbert, then the telephone went dead.

Benjamin thanked his neighbor and then grabbed his dog and hurried across the road.

* * *

"I can feel it in my bones. I know that's exactly what he's done," said Heather. She slowed the speeding Ford down. "There's a man." He was plowing a five-acre plot with a gray mule. His lunch pail and water bucket were tucked under the shade of a blooming wild plum by the roadside. Heather waved as she dropped one set of wheels onto the grass bordering the shoulder.

"Ways from home!" said the sweaty man, wiping his brow with his shirt sleeve. The straw hat he held was about to come apart.

"Get out," said Heather. Jasper hurried to comply. He had seen her pissed off look, and certainly did not want to see it again. He went to meet the man, who was walking toward them.

"We're on a case for Meriwether County," Heather yelled out.

The steel framed plow had rolled the rich dirt, making it difficult to walk. "How can I help?" the man asked, extending his dirty hand to both of them. "My, what a pretty law -- uh! Law person," he said, smiling. Heather returned the smile.

"We're Special Deputies for Sheriff Gilbert. There was a break-in at

Hill's store in Hambyville," she said.

"I know Benjamin Hill," said the farmer, resting his hands on his waist.

"Wet ta plow, ain't it?" asked Jasper, poking the dirt with the toe of his shoe.

"My place's been turned once last fall and it slopes good," replied the farmer.

"Twofold, we think the person who broke in is the same as the escaped Negro, James Lee. He took a 1925 Nash owned by Ellis DeFoor, from the Luthersville area. Lee is believed to be heading in a westward direction, from the Greenville square. By what was found and taken from the store last night, we feel that James Lee is in the area. The vehicle is a black over red soft top. Lee is a dark Negro, 5'10" tall, weighs 140 pounds, short clipped black hair, brown eyes with yellow, large flat facial features. He is now wearing khaki pants and probably a different shirt and brown brogans," Heather said, looking past the man toward the edge of the fields.

The farmer scratched his head. "I ain't seen anyone like that, and only three or four cars been by this morning, and they were all neighbors," he said, putting his hat back on his head.

"This is your land?" Heather asked.

"Oh, yes! Third generation, right here," he bragged. "Almost ninety acres."

Jasper looked about. He walked down the road a short way, looking for fresh trash and such.

"If you were thinking of hiding until nightfall, where would you go?" Heather asked, standing with her hands on her waist. She looked up and down the narrow road.

"I'd tuck it in an overgrown cemetery, but ya know how spooked them niggers get," the farmer laughed. "They most likely wouldn't be there."

"I'm not from here, up Campbellton way," Heather said.

"Hey! I know where that is, Sheriff was shot and killed just a few weeks ago," the farmer replied.

"That's right. I was a Special Deputy there and my father Sonny Duncan and I tracked for us and anybody else that asked and paid expenses," Heather said. "Where might some hidden church be?" she asked.

The farmer thought for a moment, rubbing his chin. He began to talk, pointing his finger in the direction of the churches he was describing. "Every one of these roads, goin' back toward Midget, has a church or what used to be a church," he said, his brow wrinkled. Jasper had walked back up. He stood listening. "The woolliest one I'd say is Cold Spring Chapel, been closed for many years. I don't even know if the building is still standing. I do know the cemetery is in pitiful shape, young pines, wax myrtles, hawthorns, and damn pink running roses. That's the only thing I know that'll stop a mule. They won't go through the damn stuff," he said, twitching his head to the side. He saw a burst of excitement in the woman law officer's eyes. He felt as though he had helped.

"And yer name?" Jasper asked.

"Why?" the farmer asked quickly, stepping back.

"For our report," Jasper answered.

The farmer smiled and held up both hands, "Keep me out of it, just glad to help." He started walking back to his mule.

"Thanks!" Heather said, giving him a wave and a smile.

The hot Ford cranked quickly. "Did ya get anything?" Jasper asked, riding shotgun.

"Cold Spring Chapel. Do you know where it is?" she asked, pulling into second gear.

"Back the way we came, but south toward Harris County," Jasper answered.

* * *

The rain during the night had washed all the tracks made by the heavy Nash, making them appear old, or disappear entirely. James Lee woke at dawn to see a big buck grazing a few yards in front of the car. The freedom to move his legs about felt good. He gently rubbed his blistered and sore ankle from time to time as he sat and watched. The days were the hardest. He was most apt to be discovered by anyone walking, and in the worst case damn school age kids slipping off to fish. They would take every pig trail and shortcut before they would the roads. Lee had been tormented all during the night by falling limbs and hard acorns striking the car with a loud bang. He was frequently startled from his light slumber. In spite of the rain, the Nash had cut deep ruts in the floor of the young growing forest. He realized he would have to move.

Not knowing where he was going, James Lee chose to drive south toward Harris County. The narrow tires on the Nash gently turned under the power transmitted by the clutch that he rode ever so carefully. Onto the road he came. "Shit!" he said to himself. The road passing the church was well maintained. The last of the winter pine needles had fallen during the night, covering the road with a very thin layer. He could instantly see if there were tracks of anyone passing without his noticing. Lee was lucky, as there was not a needle disturbed.

The rural road was quiet and unassuming. The feeding birds darted across the road as he traveled along quietly. Lee held the car in second gear, why he really did not know. His exploring eyes moved about, looking for a place to hide. The red clay banks rose and fell along the window line, not a pull off of any kind did he see. The driver's side window was down, the engine noise echoing from the road banks as he moved south. Suddenly there was a loud clattering and popping up ahead. The Negro began to stop as a heavy pulp wood truck topped the rise. The two almost ran head on, but not before James Lee was able to swerve and drop down behind the cover of the dashboard. The heavy, loaded truck roared by, slinging loose sand and gravel that struck the car. "Son of a bitch!" Lee exclaimed, rising up from the dashboard. "Damn asshole!" he shouted, looking at the loaded end of the truck going out of sight. The near-miss worked in his favor, as it certainly covered his tracks back to the old church and gave him a better chance to hide the tracks that he was sure to make up ahead.

James Lee's eyes moved from left to right, constantly looking for a quick hide. "Heben hope de' black child," he whispered aloud, as he saw the parking spot for the heavy truck, and where it had apparently turned around, or at least had been loaded. A narrow, root covered roadway rose high into the budding woods. Lee carefully backed the Nash high on the green hillside, where he would sit until dark, then he would continue on to seek assistance from a friend. The green foliage was still, allowing a view of the road he had come from, but not behind him to the south. He would sit quietly and listen. Lee dozed in the warm sun. At one point he chuckled about the debate of what part of the body was in control, the brain or the asshole. He laughed, knowing the eyes often played a strong part in the equation. Throughout the daylight hours he marked all the surrounding trees, and even managed to drop pieces of labels on the leaf-covered ground. These were all signs a tracking dog could hit on.

* * *

The eager deputies moved along, watching the shoulders of the road for signs of a pull off, but none were to be found. "Right here, right here!" Jasper pointed. Heather took the left turn. The road was narrowing. Heather stopped the patrol car and they both leaned forward, closer to the windshield.

"Heavy truck tracks," Heather said, gripping the top of the steering wheel.

"Pulpwooders," Jasper said softly, sitting back in his seat.

"How far?" Heather asked.

"If the leaves weren't out, ya could see it from here," he replied.

"Get over here and drive," she said, setting the brake and starting to get out. Jasper exited the car.

"Why?" he asked, as they passed at the rear of the Ford. He sat down under the steering wheel.

"I'll do some strange things before we're finished. This is the first. I'll ride on the running board over here. When you get close to the church, say almost on it, go very slow, like you're looking. I'll hop off and work my way down through the woods. Listen! You go past the church at a good clip, turn around and come back. Stop short and get out, use the car for some cover," Heather said. "Do you understand?" she barked.

Jasper nodded his head before slowly moving along. Heather held the door post and the rooftop as she hid on the side of the car. Jasper had never seen this approach, but he had never been after an armed double murderer. The tactical plan was well executed. Heather hurried quietly through the woods, toward the overgrown church yard, where the red oak and root ball concerned her. She saw Jasper behind the engine compartment. She would give him credit for that, it was the most solid place he could be for bullet deflection. The old ornate tombstones provided excellent cover as she worked her way closer to the ruins. Jasper began to wave and make hand gestures. Heather stopped and looked at him. "Nobody there!" he called out. She holstered her revolver and worked her way to the easier walking on the roadway. Jasper met her.

"There's car tracks," he said low, looking about the rolling countryside.

Heather headed toward the root ball to investigate. Jasper hurried along beside her.

"Certainly, someone was here," he said, looking at the car tracks on the matted straw covered ground. "Whoever was here did a good job," he said, pointing to the tracks. "In and out the same set."

"How far's the county line?" Heather asked.

"Down the road a piece," he replied, holstering his revolver.

"So how fer's a piece?" she asked.

Jasper blushed. "Almost a mile, no more."

"You drive, I'll look for signs," Heather said, walking toward the car.

James Lee actually heard the closing car doors, but could not see who it was or how close they were. Sound travels up high. The two officers worked the road slowly, but they were unable to pick up on anything that was a sure sign. The heavy pulpwood truck had done an excellent job of cutting a deep track down the road, and even in the turn-around or loading site.

The road came to a dead end. "Harris County!" Jasper said. "Take a right here and we can loop around to Midget, then home," he said, turning the steering wheel.

James Lee was a lucky man.

CHAPTER ELEVEN

Sheriff Louis Gilbert of Meriwether County pressed his men into attentiveness, alertness, and dedication to capture the escapee James Lee. It was rumored that Gilbert promised a promotion for the man who brought him in, dead or alive. Troup County Sheriff Jacob Ector was using every means at his disposal to make the citizens aware of the impending danger of the escaped killer. He had taken it upon himself to meet with the Harris County Sheriff, giving him firsthand knowledge of the dangerous man. Benjamin Hill was angered about the woman detective that was assigned to his case. He felt that he was being neglected.

Detective Duncan and Officer Jasper Brown checked every cemetery between the Harris County line and the edge of Warm Springs. There was not even a tire track or a footprint to raise suspicion. The end of the work day was close at hand.

"Sum bitch gets over Pine Mountain we've lost him for sure," Jasper said, using caution at the intersection of Durand-Warm Springs Road. Heather sat and scraped beggar-lice from her slacks. Jasper watched as she ran the blade of her pocketknife under the attached pests. "They were bad this year," he said. The flat blade glided smoothly along her firm thigh. "I'd have picked 'em off," he thought to himself. Heather's presence stirred emotions he had almost forgotten about, more exciting than a Saturday night at Esther's small house, tucked away on Rocky Ford Lake. Jasper looked out the window trying to get his thoughts back where they should be. The cooling evening air amplified Heather's very faint perfume.

Heather's thumb pushed a load from her blade, out the open window. "We didn't check in. I guess they think we're dead," she said, continuing to lift the flat green seedy bastards from her slacks. The strong wind gusts pushed the car about. Downtown traffic was all but gone. Only the café and the last open hardware store had customers. "Slow," she commented.

"At times," Jasper replied. He waved at Claude Allen as they drove past the service station.

"I hope he'll get my windshield soon," Heather said, tossing the last known beggar-lice out the window.

"Take ya to your place?" Jasper asked, crossing the railroad tracks slowly. The car rocked from one side to the other as it rolled over the worn steel ribbons of commerce. "That Roosevelt guy, out at the Meriwether Inn, he comes in on these same tracks, all the way from New York City," he said. The tires of the Ford slid ever so slightly on the polished rails of the train track. The evening sun had almost set in the western horizon. Tones of orange and vermilion streaked the sky as darkness overtook it. The cat that had taken the two dogs across the street that morning sat confidently on the porch of the café. Its keen yellow predator eyes squinted as it watched them ride by.

"To the department," Heather said, folding her knife closed. It gave a crisp snap.

Jasper had never known a woman to carry a pocketknife, much less a revolver; that in itself was attractive. The headlights bathed the store fronts as Jasper turned the corner. "Why here?" he asked, looking at her. Her profile in the darkness of the evening was alluring.

"Check for any calls that come in, or messages," Heather replied. By the time she had answered they were there. "There's something on the front door. I'll get it!"

A folded sheet of writing tablet paper was secured in the crack of the door. Heather did have the courtesy to return to Jasper's car window to read it. "Call Chief, information on pulpwood truck about black over red Nash. Frances," Heather read aloud. Jasper stopped the engine and set the brake. His ring of keys jingled as he hurriedly pulled them from the brass snap on his duty belt. The department was dimly lit by one single bulb that burned in the desk lamp on the secretary's desk. Heather hurried ahead, opening the staff room door. Another note of the same was on the telephone.

"Get me Chief Hawthorn," she said to the operator. "And close the line after we're connected."

"As always," replied the operator. Heather rolled her eyes in disbelief of the statement she had just heard. Jasper once again found his place on the corner of the far desktop where he sat and listened. The headlights of the occasional car flooded the small room with light. The laughter of the brick men could be heard faintly against the back wall.

The phone line was a little slow to connect. "Hawthorn residence," answered a man's voice.

"Detective Duncan," Heather replied. "We got yer note," she said, sitting down gently on the desk.

"We had a telephone call about midday. A pulpwooder was out on the old Cold Spring Church Road. He said they almost run into a well-kept Nash, black and red. They couldn't see the driver, it happened so quick. They were coming toward Sulphur Springs and the Nash was going south toward Harris County," said the chief.

"We were out there and searched around the old church," Heather said. "We saw a lot of tracks, but none led to any definite interest. We saw where a heavy truck had been there, and even loaded or turned around, on the south side of the church. There were signs that a vehicle, maybe a car, had backed into the cover of a large root ball, where a red oak had fallen in a bad storm. A farmer told us about the place. There were few folks out on the roads today. Troup County has a good case," Heather advised. Jasper looked at the clock on the wall.

* * *

Jailer Curley Jones came into the Meriwether County Sheriff's office, huffing and puffing under the loaded cardboard box in his outstretched arms. "Dixie! Look here! I've rounded up some food for ole Bo Bob," he said, pushing the door fully open with his butt. He placed the box on the nearby desk. "Whew! That was heavy," Curley announced.

"Why not flowers?" she asked smiling, knowing full well the old Negro would not want flowers. He would rather have a pint of good liquor.

"My ass!" Curley said, laughing at her remark. "Canned food from the grocery and some from my wife's pantry. She'll want the jars back. I worry about him bein' all right. That was a hell of a beatin'." Dixie sat and watched Curley pull out various cans to show her. "Where's tha sheriff?" he asked.

"Him and Watkins went to lunch over at the café."

"Which one?" he asked.

"Becky's," said Dixie.

A car door closed outside. They both looked out the window. It was Sheriff Gilbert and the Solicitor General, Ambrose Watkins. Sheriff Gilbert was unwrapping a new cigar. Watkins brushed crumbs from his shirt and tie. Their conversation was a low whisper from behind the thick red brick walls of the jail building.

"Doc Hubbard's ta be here by now," Dixie said.

"Oh, is he goin' too?" Curley asked, sitting back down. He did not want to be seen looking out the window like some busybody.

"Sheriff wants Bo Bob evaluated," Dixie replied, as she started to type.

The screen door moaned loudly as it opened, then the office door joined in as Sheriff Gilbert pushed it open. "Damn Curley, can't we get some oil on these damn hinges?" he asked. Doc Hubbard's car pulled up. "Move out!" cried the sheriff, turning to go back out. "Dixie, we'll all be at old Bo Bob's place, hour or so."

"Dixie," smiled Ambrose Watkins. Doc Hubbard waited by his car.

The three men were in suits and ties, open collars, but neckties, nonetheless. Curley was the only one in uniform, white shirt and khaki pants. Curley once again grasped the heavy box and headed out the door.

"What's that?" asked the sheriff.

Curley huffed along, breathing deep. "Food box for old Bo Bob," he replied.

"Is he starvin' ta death?" the sheriff asked, looking at the full box.

"No, but I thought it would be nice to show good will, sumthin' other than flowers," said Curley, setting the box on the car's front bumper.

"Pint of liquor'd be more ta his liking," replied Watkins.

"Remember, no drinkin'!" said Doc Hubbard.

"Yeah! I guess that was part of the conditions," said the sheriff.

Sheriff Gilbert opened the boot for Curley. The box was almost too large to fit, but with some moving around and rearranging, the lid finally closed. Doc Hubbard and Curley rode in the back seat. The sheriff drove and Ambrose Watkins rode shotgun. "Bo Bob ain't moved since we arrested him last, has he?" asked the sheriff, looking in the mirror at Curley.

"Same old place," Curley replied. The loaded car backed into its own sweet-smelling exhaust. Curley coughed.

Doc Hubbard and Curley rode in silence listening to the shop talk of the two men in the front seat. Curley remembered the loyalty displayed by the old Negro and smiled. It was probably the most responsible task the old guy had ever done, bossing around prisoners and tending to daily activities in the cell block. Curley observed the blooming fruit trees in the distance. Peach orchards were abundant in the county. He remembered the wonderful taste of his mother's deep peach cobblers, teeth crackin' hot from the oven, granules of sugar glistening on the top crust among golden spots of buttery goodness. The sudden odor of a dead animal along the road shocked him back to the present.

Doc Hubbard sat resting his left arm on top of the leather satchel next to him. He prayed that Bo Bob would have on the restraints when they arrived. Doc Hubbard was thinking about Bo Bob's condition. He felt that the old Negro might lose sight in one eye. Doc Hubbard was not an ophthalmologist by any means. He only understood the basics of the eye, enough to treat sties, viral infections, and the like. All medical students understood and should be able to recognize the eye's signs of a concussion.

The rain from the night before had left standing puddles along the road and especially in the deeply worn drive to the old house. The marked car of the High Sheriff caused quite a ruckus as it turned into the yard, much as the doctor's new teal blue Chevrolet had done. Watkins and Curley had never been to the house of Bo Bob Huggins. They did not know what to expect, but being a Negro of his caliber, they did not expect much. The yard full of mixed chickens scurried about, once again taking cover under the house. Emma and the retarded son looked out from behind the dark heavily oxidized screen door. Tom stood on the edge of the porch next to his father. The retarded son hurried onto the porch and eagerly watched the arrival of the sheriff and his guests.

"There he sits!" said Sheriff Gilbert, stopping the car even with the opening in the hedge row. The three dogs went under the porch. "Them dogs bite?" he asked Doc Hubbard.

"A cold biscuit," he replied, opening the car door. "Two daughters, Tom on the porch, and Emma the wife. The eager one is slow, retarded," added the doctor, closing the door.

Doc Hubbard and Curley led the way. The doctor had his leather bag at his side and Curley struggled with the heavy cardboard box of canned foods. Sheriff Gilbert and Ambrose Watkins walked a few feet behind.

"Dismal, ain't it?" whispered Watkins to the sheriff beside him.

"Pretty bad," Gilbert replied. "But neat and clean, as clean as old can get," he whispered back. The three dogs began to venture out, greeting them with tails wagging.

Tom stepped forward, extending his hand to the doctor and then Curley. He did not know the sheriff or the other man. "Doc Hubbard, Sheriff," he said. The badge gave the sheriff away. "You must be Curley Jones?" Tom said, shaking hands.

"Ambrose Watkins, Solicitor General for the county," said Doc.

Emma and the two daughters stood to the side. "This is my mother, Emma Huggins, and my two sisters," said Tom.

"Will you have a seat?" Emma asked.

"I need to see Bo Bob," said the doctor.

Bo Bob sat on the edge of the high porch holding a fiddle, his legs dangling. He watched and smiled. One eye was glazed. Curley set the heavy box in a chair.

"Bo Bob, where's yer leg irons?" asked Sheriff Gilbert, looking down at him.

Bo Bob smiled. "On the hearth. Cain't go far, I'd run in circles. Cain't see good from one eye."

"Can you play that thing? Or do ya just hold it?" asked Ambrose Watkins. Bo Bob rolled his neck and worked his chin in and out. The ancient fiddle found its place and the dark leathery hand brought a horsehair bow to bear upon the taut strings and he began to play. The eerie melody brought a feeling of calm to the yard. The three dogs lay down and watched Bo Bob as he played. Chills and shivers ran the spine of the solicitor general and the sheriff. Doc Hubbard smiled. He could sense that there was something special about the old Negro. On the last gentle note, the dogs' tails wagged in the yard dirt.

"Well done, well done!" said the doctor.

"I'ze ain't mounts ta much, buts mize playin' hopes," replied Bo Bob.

"Come up and sit in a chair, I need to look at the stitches and check your eyes," said Doc Hubbard.

The examination was as thorough as Doc Hubbard was qualified to do. The old Negro sat still on a cane bottomed chair that had been sat upon for so long it was sagging beneath the patchwork cushion. Doc Hubbard's breathing could be heard as he stooped, looking into Bo Bob's eyes. The reflective disk strapped to the doctor's forehead cast a bright circle of light, accompanied in brilliance by the small flashlight that bathed the bad eye. After a minute or two, the doctor stood looking at both the sheriff and the solicitor. "He needs to see an ophthalmologist in Columbus or Newnan, maybe Atlanta. You need to see a specialist and soon," said Doc. "I'll see that you get to one. Let me do a few telephone calls and I'll be back."

"Bo Bob, Miss Emma," said Curley. "This food box is from us at the jail, and friends. We wanted ta show our concern. Hope you all enjoy it," Curley added. "I'd like the canning jars back," he smiled. "They belong to the wife." The couple and their children thanked Curley for the gift of food.

The return trip was mainly an argument between the doctor and the sheriff as to who was responsible for the medical bills. It went back and forth so long that Curley leaned on the window and dozed off. After Sheriff Gilbert had made his stand, it was overruled by Watkins.

"The Negro was injured on county property, by an inmate in our custody. The county will pay for all his needs and it will come from your budget," said the powerful solicitor. Sheriff Gilbert was visibly unhappy.

Doc Hubbard watched Curley sleeping, but when the solicitor overruled the sheriff, the sleeping man smiled. The doctor knew he was right in his thinking. He too was pleased. In due time a recognized ophthalmologist in Newnan would see Bo Bob Huggins and determine that he was in fact close to losing the use of the glazed eye. Bo Bob wore a patch during the daylight hours for the next several months, giving the injured eye a chance to rest and heal. Curley would miss Bo Bob while he was gone.

When the sheriff's entourage returned to the jail, young Alfred Huffman was waiting. The newspaper man sat quietly at Curley's desk, watching out the window. Dixie saw excitement come across his young face when the sheriff's car rolled onto the gravel yard. "They're here," he said, watching like an eager child. The doctor left and Ambrose Watkins walked across the street to his office in the courthouse. Sheriff Gilbert and Curley approached the office. Soon the doors opened. "Fine lady!" said the sheriff.

Dixie's look gave indication to someone waiting. Alfred Huffman had walked from the newspaper office a short distance down the street.

"Alfred!" said the sheriff, tossing his fedora on his desk.

"I wanted to see if there was any follow-up on the story of the escaped prisoner," said Alfred, standing behind Curley's desk.

"Nothing but the Hambyville burglary," replied Sheriff Gilbert.

"And what now was that?" Alfred asked, pulling out his pocket tablet.

The sheriff shook his head. "You'll need to call Sheriff Jacob Ector for that story," he replied.

"How about uh, Huggins, Bo Bob?" Alfred asked eagerly, letting Curley have his desk.

"I'd rather not add to that at this time, he'll survive," said Sheriff Gilbert, sitting down. "You know if we're doin' our job right, we won't tell you a lot," he said, fumbling with a cigar piece.

"Sheriff, please call me when something breaks," Alfred pleaded.

"I'll do that," assured the sheriff.

The young reporter smiled at Dixie and quietly left the office. Curley watched as he walked toward the newspaper office.

* * *

Heather walked from the Police Department to Mrs. Blakely's place. She looked at her small watch. The time was ten minutes into the evening meal. It was paid for, so Heather expected it to be there, even if it was on the stove. Out of old habit, she checked the doors along Main Street as she walked toward her place of rest. At one door a loud yell came from within. She cupped her hands and looked into the dark store, to be greeted by the wave of the merchant still at his desk. The detective waved back and went on her way. The same old cat that had run the dogs earlier was now lingering around the porch of Mrs. Blakely's place. It ran when she turned down the side alleyway.

The large dining table was a roar of laughter mixed with the sound of flatware clanging against plates. The aroma of turnip greens filled the back of the store. The burnt oil of side meat soon mingled with the greens. "Evening, Detective!" called the first boarder that saw her in the dimly lit hallway, coming to the table. Heather smiled and waved. The men started to stand.

"Please keep your seats," she said. "I'm honored that you made the gallant effort. I don't require that." She smiled as she took her seat. "Just a hello is fine."

"Any luck?" a man asked, off to her left.

"Quite a bit, but still far away," Heather replied, taking the first bowl that was passed.

The meal was satisfying, as simple as it was. Rendered side meat, turnip greens, stove top cornbread, wedged onion, room temperature canned whole tomatoes, and sweet tea. "My compliments, Mrs. Blakely," Heather said, being the last to finish. The other boarders had finished and excused themselves. "Did I get any calls?" Heather asked.

"Dear, if you get any calls you will be told as soon as I see you," Mrs. Blakely said. She stood at the sink washing dishes with her back to Heather.

"Can I dry?" asked Heather, still seated at the table.

"Thanks, dear, but I'll let them air dry."

Heather found herself thinking of where James Lee could be, even though she did not know the countryside. The recollection of a prior case brought her around to believing he was going into hiding with someone he knew and he had to get there. If only someone knew the Negro and his acquaintances. She slowly climbed the painted stairs. The table in the hallway just outside the bathroom door held a bright arrangement of early pink camellias. Mrs. Blakely was outdoing herself to make the upstairs hallway womanly. As Heather drew closer coming off the stairs, she noticed a lacy handkerchief folded in a triangular shape. The fancy note card that stood upon it bore her name. As to whom it was from, there was no signature. She folded the card backwards and wrote "Thanks".

The door to Heather's room had always bothered her. The slightest opening and someone could watch her in the bed. She spent an hour or so rearranging the room, being careful not to disturb anyone. Her bed was now behind the door so anyone would have to fully open the door and step in to see her. There was a slight dust pattern where the furniture had been moved. Heather mopped it carefully with a damp towel from the hamper in the bath and then sat enjoying her handiwork. The evening breeze gently moved the curtains about. The occasional sound of a passing vehicle was heard. She wondered if Edgar Peterson was taking the escaped prisoner seriously. He had struck her as being disinterested, intending to make his normal rounds. She hoped that Edgar would not be taken by surprise.

The clock moved to the ten o'clock hour. Heather had settled back in the upholstered chair and dozed. The events of the long day came upon her once more in her deep thoughts. She reflected on the root ball and the fact that Holly could have picked up on at least a sign, even from urine in the wood line or the tall briars and grasses. Heather remembered the feel of the dog's soft jowls in her hands as she would often cup the dog's head in her hands and talk to it.

* * *

Darkness had befriended James Lee and the moon was approaching its third quarter. The open fields were brightly lit with a blue hue from the large Georgia moon, making the darkness of the shadows deep. Alert and rested, James Lee cranked the Nash and gently rolled from his hiding place in the woods, high on the hillside close to the Cold Spring Chapel, where he had hidden the night before. The crafty Negro drove by moonlight past the old ruins of the church and back to the main road. Lula Road would take him east to the community of Midget. He knew that from there Seven Branches Road went directly into Warm Springs. Little piss ant towns like Warm Springs had no patrol at night, or if they did it would be only one, and he would probably be hidden in the darkness, asleep. Lee's confidence was building as he rode through the sleeping community of Midget. It was just a crossroads and the County Line Church. When he arrived by the ambient light of night, he saw two houses on opposing corners. One looked to be a store in the front and a residence in the back. There was no light anywhere. There was no sign of life other than the sleeping dog that raised its head from the porch as he passed almost silently in the Nash. The headlights almost touched the walls of the church as Lee turned right onto Seven Branches. For the first two miles, James Lee rode in the silence of the isolated countryside. Not a single house sat along the lonely road. To the south, the towering shoulders of Pine Mountain rose toward the velvety dark blue sky.

James Lee knew where he was, as he was passing directly where he had been just before the Warm Springs officer got after him and the long chase began. He was in hopes that the same alert officer was not working on this night. "Maybe dat bitch won't beez on tha road that turned on me and held me at gunpoint," he thought. He stopped the Nash at the forks of Seven Branches and Durand Road. He was half a mile out of Warm Springs. James Lee dropped his right hand to the seat and felt the revolver at his side. It gave him confidence. A little further over he felt the new box of cartridges. He was committed to not being taken alive with the charges he had already built up. His foot with the heavy brogan eased off of the clutch and the car quietly moved forward. James Lee was knowledgeable enough to keep the car in high gear as often as he could, and keeping a delicate balance with the powerful second gear, he quickly moved ahead.

The quiet car was stopped at the intersection where Greenville-Manchester Road took over. James Lee was fearful, but with determination he took a deep breath and continued into town. At the four-way intersection just prior to the railroad tracks he paused, glancing about for the law. There was none to be seen. The escaped Negro's mouth was cottony and his hands began to sweat. From the darkness of the street, James Lee saw a light come on in the small police department across from the café. The light was comforting. He knew that was the only law in the small town, and he was clear to go about his business of passing through, unless he ran into a county car. He realized the chances of that were highly unlikely. The same cat that toyed with the town's dogs was lying on the bench at the café, watching the Negro as he passed through the intersection.

* * *

Heather was restless. She slipped from her bed to stand at the window that looked down upon the main street. The street was quiet, not a light or a person to be seen. The trash fires of the brick men softly glowed in the back lot of the police department.

As James Lee drove the Nash across the last spur track, the sound of a loose crosstie popped in the night, causing him alarm should anyone be out in the night to see. The next four miles were as straight as a cheap arrow. James Lee turned on the large bullet shaped headlights and pushed the touring car hard. It rose and fell beneath him with a floating grace as he hurried ahead. His help was only four more miles away.

Sheriff Gilbert was restless. He stood naked behind the sheer curtains of his bedroom, as his wife lay sleeping in their bed. The bright moon washed the countryside in brightness, giving him a good view from the second floor of the jail building, just off of the Greenville square. In his years of experience and hunting down men, he too knew that the son of a bitch was out there moving somewhere. "But where?" he thought. He looked below at the small glow of the night jailer's cigarette that lit his face in the archway to the intake below. Sheriff Gilbert returned to bed and the company of his wife. Out of habit he moved his hand to the night stand, touching his revolver. Knowing where it was gave him great comfort.

Young Buddy Cotton tossed and turned in the warm night. His small puppy moved about upon hearing his master's restlessness. The puppy rolled from side to side on the rag rug beside the high iron framed bed. The boy read the newspaper every time he got a chance at the store and listened to the talk of the customers. He knew there was a dangerous man out there, and that it was his new friend Heather's job to try and bring him in.

* * *

Bulloch-Bonner Road eventually crossed Hurricane Creek. It was one of the last grizzly swamps in the area. James Lee hoped to find a ridge he could drive on or even a deep place to sink the car. How to get from the bridge down into banks he was not sure, he would have to wait and see. By the moon it was close to one o'clock or maybe later. As James Lee crossed the Manchester-Raleigh Road, he saw headlights on the horizon. He slowed to see if the car turned with him, but again he was a lucky man. The car continued south, toward the Miller Orchards. They too were on a branch of Hurricane Creek.

The headlights shined brightly upon the wooden bridge and its structural steel railings. A fishing float hung from a green line and swayed with the night winds. The locals had a well-worn path, wide enough to drive down to the banks. This was his only plan to rid himself of the stolen automobile. The frame dragged as it raked to the side and rolled down the steep lane toward the black waters. A musk rat dove from the bait littered and well-worn bank, taking safety in the water. It was quickly out of sight long before the headlights stopped over the waters. James Lee was not stupid. He recognized the white horizontal markings and numbers on the rock embankments as Corps of Engineer markings for high waters. At one time the water had been up to fifteen feet. It was now rushing by at ten feet. He turned the headlights out in fear of being discovered by the rare motorist in passing.

In the deep shadows of the road banks, James Lee removed his belongings from the stolen car. The dead man's car. The food box, the revolver, and ammunition were safely placed on the worn path. In the darkness he removed his clothes and shoes. The polished horsehair fabric was slick under his bare skin as he backed the Nash up the path. He pushed the car into first gear and ran it into the black waters with the headlights on. The heavy boxy car floated, drifting downstream as it began to sink. The bulbs in the headlights were the first to go, and then steam rose in clouds toward the dark sky, while bubbles churned around the engine compartment. The naked Lee sat until the water swirled around him and began to rush in the open driver's side window. That night he would safely swim to shore and leisurely dress for his continuing journey. His help was now only a mile and a half away, an easy walk just after daylight.

James Lee hurried along the railroad tracks, south to where they crossed Cove Church Road. There in the high brush he would rest until daylight and then continue on his way. The critters of the night moved through the brush, keeping the skittish Negro alert to the mysterious noises about him. He could only see a few feet in the tall grasses. A rabbit almost ran into him as he sat listening. That was the closest sound to a man he had heard in a while. His rushing heart thumped in his chest.

The beautiful 1925 black over red Nash touring car sank into ruin that dark morning. In some ways the spirit of veteran Ellis DeFoor was there on the bank as his pride slowly went under. The law could not track James Lee any better if he had just walked away from the beautiful machine. To sink it was James Lee's ultimate insult to the old man he had killed among the fragrance of the baskets of fruit as they exchanged blows, the polished cane against his fist.

At some point in the dark night James Lee fell asleep. He was awakened by the calling of the morning birds moving about in the grass. He had slept longer than he planned. A small bird sat nearby, turning its tiny button eyes as it studied the dark Negro. James Lee lashed out.

"Shoo, lil' shit! Git!" he scolded. The little bird flew away. The evilness of James Lee's way with the harmless bird brought out the more aggressive birds that would not pay his anger any mind. "Caw! Caw! Caw!" The black crows circled above the hidden man. One swooped low and took a seat on a limb nearby. "Caw! Caw! Caw!" called the crow. It too turned and looked at the Negro. The aggressive bird's eyes were as black as its feathers. James Lee sat watching the crow and then looked at the ones circling overhead. If a good tracker was in the area, the escaped prisoner would be found. Lucky for him there was not one.

"Git!" Lee said, louder than he intended, but he was irritated. The calling crow only switched limbs and talked some more. "Caw! Caw! Caw!" James Lee quickly gathered his belongings and headed up to the road. The lone crow was answered by the ones overhead, creating an awful noise.

The sound of an approaching car carried on the morning wind. James Lee pulled back into the cover of the brush. The car sped by, so close he was pushed by the gust of wind. He made it across the Woodbury Road and down into the deep cover of the thick new growth pines. He was crafty, entering where the grass on the shoulder had already been disturbed. By the sky ahead, Lee could tell the cover of the woods would soon run out. The dew on the grasses and leaves dampened his clothing and even the items that hung from the wooden box. He had worked from time to time on the Miller orchard that was behind him. His help lay ahead on Pigeon Creek.

* * *

The morning sunlight cast its bright rays down upon the vast thicket of native holly trees. They were covered in bright red berries and feeding birds. Under the cover of the beautiful evergreens a horde of hogs lay, some grunting, some rooting, socializing and talking with the occasional argument or disagreement that led to a fit of loud squealing which could be heard for a great distance. Anyone that knew hogs, even domestic ones as these were, stayed clear, especially on foot. The boars were fierce and territorial. Even a sow with nursing piglets was often aggressive. It was an hour after daylight and they were restless, anticipating their slop. The hogs got up and moved about, working closer to the feeding troughs. A few had already checked, moving their large pink snouts over the empty vessels and expressing a desire to be fed with loud squeals. The sharp bite of ammonia nipped at the clean morning air, as the hogs moved through the ankle high mud, manure, and urine puddles.

The barn door opened and a Negro man of medium build stepped out. He had a heavy galvanized bucket in each gloved hand. His strong dark brown arms were taut with the heavy load. The hog farmer was Theo Jackson, the hog man of Chalybeate. As far as local Negroes go, Theo Jackson was rather unusual. He was a heavy one hundred and ninety pounds. He had curly black hair, bright clear white eyes, Anglo facial features, and wore a coarse stubble beard. Few Negroes in the area wore beards. Jackson was an unmarried loner. He was known to keep a woman for a short while, but they would soon leave. Theo Jackson favored bibbed overalls and wore them until they were almost threadbare. The overalls piled up on the tops of his Wellington boots. His long-sleeved Union suit top was stained with sweat and unwashed. A clean railroad bandanna filled his hip pocket every morning..

Theo Jackson slopped the hogs. Their squeals of joy and aggression blocked out almost every other sound until they each had a full belly of slop. The crows flew high overhead this morning and seemed to be taunting something far away in the back hog lot. Jackson paid it no mind. "Anything that could get through the hogs deserved to be whatever it was, wherever it was heading," he thought, dumping another bucketful over the sturdy fence. Jackson glanced at his new 1929 Fargo flatbed. It was made by Chrysler, a fine vehicle for a Negro hog farmer. He was proud of it. The green hog manure he hauled off was already cutting through the paint on the bed.

"Caw! Caw! Caw!" the crows called in the distance.

Jackson stopped to look at the distant woods line. Maybe it was a fox or something, maybe a bobcat. One had gotten to a small piglet a while back. "I'll get my shotgun, keep it in the truck," he said aloud to himself. A large sow looked up, as though he was addressing her. "Wipe yer mouth, ya pig!" he said loudly. The sow grunted and went back to eating. There was silence except for the wet smacking sounds.

James Lee saw signs of the large number of hogs and decided to walk around the outer edge of the fence line. The crows still found him interesting. He hurried along holding the box with both hands. At one point the mud and manure were so deep he chose to cut across the much drier field and work around the mess. The crows still circled. "Son of a bitch!" Lee said out loud, hurrying before an alerted boar chose to see who was in the lot. He could see two huge boars at the crest of the hill. They were rooting about in the soft field, tossing goodly amounts of dirt about. At that point James Lee remembered the escaped prisoner from a road detail that was brought back half dead after he had gone face to face with a wild hog. The man eventually died. James Lee ran for the fence. The two boars began to trot. They appeared to be a team and he did not want anything to do with them. The small caliber .32 revolver would be child's play to these two bruisers.

James Lee made the wire fence just in time. The two charged right up to the wire, even pressed their spotted pink snouts against it, sniffing him. Lee sat on the dry leaves. "Beat ya fat boys!" he bragged. The flapping of wings startled him. He was being watched by two crows with blue eyes sitting in the slash bark hickory overhead. "Blue eyes!" he thought. He looked again. "God damn!" He shivered. "Blue eyes!" he mumbled. "May be demons or haints," he thought, gathering up his wooden crate. He hurried ahead toward the farm that surely lay ahead in the distance. The two crows stayed with him for a long time. They flew gracefully from one limb to the next to sit and wait for his arrival. He was beginning to sweat.

He was actually scared. Old man DeFoor had blue eyes. "Nah! It can't be his spirit," he said to himself.

Theo Jackson loaded his truck with empty tubs and buckets for his morning harvest from all the obliging restaurants and groceries. The banging and scrubbing sound of the empty vessels was loud, but his hogs had learned to love it. They knew it was a meal in the future. With the side bodies secure, Jackson scrubbed the mud from his boot soles and climbed into the truck. The light blue Fargo truck rocked from side to side as he traveled the winding narrow road. It eventually joined a county-maintained road, opening up to a much wider and smoother road. So good that Theo Jackson was able to shift the Fargo into high gear. The stocky Negro occupied a good portion of the small boxy cab as he sat under the large black steering wheel. The large wheel made the truck easy to control.

The hog farm was supported by a group of merchants that welcomed the pick-up of waste by the dependable and jovial Negro. Jackson always enjoyed the quiet lonely drive from his place north on Cove Church Road. There was always a strong breeze at the gap between the foothills to Pine Mountain. On some occasions several faster cars would overtake his vessel loaded truck and the strong wind pushed the foul odor of the trace remains of slop upon them. He watched in his mirror and laughed as they quickly fell back. There had always been laughter about following a chicken truck, but he held fast to the belief that he had all the chicken trucks beat. The first morning stop was Mac's Grocery in Woodbury, then over to The Home Place Café. There he would take his breakfast of coffee and a beef steak biscuit. Theo Jackson sounded the horn as he backed into the loading dock in the back alley. That was the signal for Chloe, the Negro cook, to hurry up. She was a heavy woman about the same age as Theo. Chloe would meet him with a wrapped biscuit and a large mug of coffee. Jackson would busy himself with the exchange of the tubs and buckets of table scraps.

The screen door opened and Chloe stepped out. Jackson moved the vessels about hurriedly. He knew the sound of her walk, more of a shuffle. From the corner of his eye he saw her blue shoes that were side split at the little toes. "Mornin', pretty lady!" he said, as he bent over moving the heavily loaded tubs. "Good day yesterday, I see." He stood up slowly.

"Sho' nuff! Busy day, good money. Had a busload to stop. Dey on de' way to a big meetin' in Manchester," she said, holding his food out to him.

"Thanks!" said Theo, giving her a wink. "Pack yer bags and leave that old man, come ta see me," he said, making kissing sounds as he climbed down from the truck bed.

"Wash yo' mouff!" Chloe said, laughing.

The next stop in his large circle was Greenville. He had tried to get the small amount of waste from the jail kitchen, but Miss Jewel saved it for the county farm. They took it to the farm for their own hogs once the bucket was full or started to stink. Becky's on the square gave him a one bucket stop. Her place was small and not a lot of customers, just mainly courthouse employees and business men around the square. Odessadale was the same as Becky's, but Willard Boykin usually offered him a drink of good whiskey. He never refused. The small store at Tigner's Crossroads gave him a chance to call on Chester Grubbs at the feed store in Hambyville. Sometimes a bag of feed would get wet, too damp to sell. That was a good stop. The hogs always enjoyed grains. Durand had several places. One was the store owned by Herman Pickens, and then three places that sold to the lumber men and passing salesmen. By this time of day his truck was usually almost loaded. Theo would take the top road coming out above Meriwether Inn and get their waste, and finally the two small café's in Warm Springs, and a little at Blakely's boarding house. This was a six day a week route. Theo Jackson would find himself driving ever so carefully, trying not to spill his load as he eased back to his farm in the late afternoon.

James Lee had wandered onto the farm yard shortly after his friend Theo had left. Theo had probably not even reached the gap when Lee stood in his side yard. Lee was greeted by a timid specimen of a dog. The dog approached the stranger with its tail tucked deep between its legs and its head down.

"Come boy, come!" Lee said softly to the dog.

It eventually came close to the stranger. "Good dog, good dog," Lee said, gently petting the dog's head. The tucked tail soon came out and wagged. James Lee looked around. There was not a sign of anyone else on the property. The house was locked and the chimney had no signs of a fire in the early morning dampness. Lee slipped around looking in the windows. The dark house was lifeless. The sudden sound of what he believed to be a broom handle falling on the floor caused suspicion. He stood still and listened. Lee was afraid. The single door on the barn was ajar. He grabbed his box from the yard and hurried for the barn.

The dog followed and beat him inside. The barn was cluttered with feed bags, some full and many empty. A layer of hay covered the floor. Several pigeons fed on dropped grain. They flew up to the loft when he came inside. James Lee hurriedly climbed the steep ladder to the loft where he found two escape routes, a front and back loft door. He brought his box up and settled in for the duration, waiting on his friend's return.

James Lee found himself wondering again if the two blue-eyed crows were really the spirit of the old man. He wondered if the car sank completely, and if the gasoline film drifted downstream, making the sinking spot harder to find.

Theo Jackson had completed his trip without spilling too much along the way. His hog farm touched the city limits of Chalybeate Springs. There had been a squabble for years about putting a road through his property and a bridge over Pigeon Creek. The local whites slaughtered the city's name down to "Chip-lee", in spite of the fact he had always considered it as French in origin, "Chal-i-beat-e". He thought of the bewildering pronunciation and shook his head from time to time.

The hogs recognized the sound of the Fargo as it approached the entrance to the small complex. They hurried to the trough area, knowing there would be nothing until the next morning, but they came out of interest and sociability. The conversational noise of various squeals and grunts aroused James Lee from his slumber. He opened the back loft door ever so slightly to look down on the muddy, smelly hogs below. He too heard an approaching vehicle. Lee hurried to the front. This time the door swung wrong for an easy look. He had to find a wide crack in the vertically planked barn. It was Theo. James Lee could tell that by the little free space in the small cab. They had not seen one another since a card game that went bad, several years back. James Lee and Theo ran when the shooting started. He smiled at the thought of that night, back in Booger Bottoms, in Coweta County. James Lee was in the eighth grade and Theo was in the tenth. They both dropped out, not returning the next year.

The load on the small truck caused the mechanical brakes to squeal and scrub as the pads managed to hold the truck back. The land sloped toward the west, keeping drainage and animal liquids slowly wicking away from the main house and small barn. The timid dog sat at the bottom of the ladder, looking up once in a while. James Lee would look down and the dog would turn its head to the side and whine. The loaded truck stopped close in front of the barn. Theo Jackson, believing he was alone, went about his routine. He opened the double doors. The left door sagged and had cut a trench in the sandy soil. Theo Jackson gave no thought to repairing it, since the earth below was forgiving. James Lee heard the cab door close and the groan of reverse gear commenced to sing out. Once in place, the truck began to move toward the barn. Jackson was ingenious in some ways. He had constructed a sturdy overhead hoist from scrap ropes and pulleys. This saved his back, at the truck anyway.

Theo Jackson pulled slop seasoned leather gloves onto his hands and began to hoist one vessel at a time from the loaded truck. James Lee watched from above, as he lay flat down on the floor, looking through a substantial crack. The timid dog still sat at the base of the ladder.

"How did you get in here?" asked Theo, still moving the heavy loaded vessels. The dog sat quietly and looked at him. Theo saw that the side door was open, but that was normal. It too was warped and would not latch. The strong odors were rising, all the way to the loft and out the center cupola. At first it was strong, but eventually James Lee began to get used to it.   Theo Jackson had just finished removing the last number two tub when the small straw pieces fell from the loft. He paid it no mind until he heard a board pop. Theo lowered the tub with care to its place of rest and stepped to the cab of the truck. He now brandished a sawed-off single barrel shotgun. He stepped back toward the open doors pointing the twenty-inch barrel toward the falling hay.

"Who's there?" he barked. The dog stood up.

James Lee did not respond at first, until the crisp sound of the flat mainspring engaged the hammer spur on the old gun. It was loud in the quiet barn. "Wait, wait!" he called out.

"Wait! My ass! Who's up there?" Theo barked. Whoever it was, he was coming toward the ladder, by the trail of falling hay and small trash.

"It's me! James!" a voice responded.

"James Lee?" asked Theo, still holding the shotgun at the ready.

"Yes!" James Lee replied, as he started to climb down the ladder. The dog stood and wagged its tail.

"You're wanted!" replied Theo, lowering the gun a bit.

"You goin' ta hold it on me?" James Lee asked, at the bottom of the ladder. The revolver was stuck in the front of his pants. James Lee saw the hesitation in his friend's eyes, as Theo carefully lowered the hammer.

"I can't risk my place. What do you want from me?" Theo Jackson asked right off.

"Put me up a few days and then help me get a way out of here," James Lee replied, walking close and hugging the aromatic man. "The Millers, are they still in money?" Lee asked.

"I still haul manure to the orchards," Theo replied. "Church folks say John's in poor health. I deal with Gertrude for my money. I don't see him anymore," said Theo, returning the shotgun to the cab. "Look, I can't put you up in tha house. If the law does come here and find you in my house, they'd burn it ta get to you. I just can't go that far. But the loft is a good place. I can get food out to you and water."

"I understand," nodded Lee.

James Lee and Theo Jackson visited in the safety of the barn until the wee hours of the night. They laughed and played cards, just like old times.

CHAPTER TWELVE

The morning was hurried with the preparation of pallbearers for veteran Ellis DeFoor. All who were asked to serve were too old to carry, so younger and stronger alternates were sought. The preacher at the Gold Mine Baptist Church of Luthersville paced from one end of the office to the other in deep thought. "Who can we get at the last minute?" he mumbled. He looked at his watch. The funeral was set for eleven and it was half past nine. DeFoor had been a loner, keeping to his own generation, which had aged and gradually died out. There were no young folks stepping forward to serve. Nigger Jenny came into the office.

"Oh, my lawd! Yous heres," the Negro woman exclaimed, setting down her mop, bucket, and broom. Her head was tied up like the pirates of old in a starched white cloth. Delicate gold wire frame glasses clung to her keen nose bridge by a twist of "hcezy tape". The preacher heard what she said and rushed to her with his arms open.

"Bless you, dear woman! Bless you!" he said, hugging the thin woman. He almost lifted her from the wide plank floor. "You have solved my problem. Why I didn't think of it myself, I'll never know," he added, reaching for the telephone. His first call was to the Sheriff in Meriwether County. Sheriff Gilbert promised two men, himself, and jailer Curley Jones.

"Dixie! I'm callin' a car to the square. If these prisoners make a sound other than piss in a bucket or the dealin' of cards, you call the deputy on the square. He'll be instructed to watch this office door for you and come a runnin'! Me and Curley are goin' to a funeral," said Sheriff Gilbert. The slobber from a stubby cigar hung heavy on the corner of his mouth.

The next call was to Chief Howard Hawthorn in Warm Springs. It was the only town other than Manchester with a department. The Warm Springs Chief promised three, if he could get Sheriff Gilbert to get a car down on the south end. Though they were stretched thin, the other county car was moved down to their verbal command center at Claude Allen's filling station downtown. Everyone looked there during the day for a patrol car before they came to the police department.

"Two from Sheriff Gilbert, three from Chief Hawthorn, that makes five," said the preacher, rubbing his face. "That makes five, who else?" he asked out loud. Jenny heard him.

"Big Sam was always friends wid' Master Ellis," she said, dusting the window sills. "Dey beez talkin' mos' days," Jenny added.

"Fifty cents ta go see if he can do it today," said the preacher. "Starts at eleven!" he shouted, as the woman hurried out of the church.

Exactly at eleven o'clock the organist pushed hard on the pedals causing the upright pump organ to give a deep groan and wheeze as it gradually came up to tone. Rock of Ages soon rang from the rooftop and the pigeons left the rafters in the attic for the yellow maples that lined the yard. The small, elderly congregation was made up of a landlord, two widow women, and a few Confederate veterans wearing suits. The old men sat rigid with hats in hand. They reeked of White Lily hair tonic and witch hazel. The faint drift of bourbon blended in somewhere.

The young preacher stood beside the closed casket. "Amen!" he said loudly, as the last chord was pushed through the Montgomery Ward organ. The law enforcement pallbearers were quietly standing outside the small chapel in the crowded foyer. Sheriff Gilbert smelled like a cold cigar. Curley Jones was wearing soiled pants from a jail detail that went wrong. Chief Hawthorn was in a pressed suit coat and wrinkled pants. Detective Duncan stood in her brown suit with a pale blue blouse. Officer Jasper Brown was his usual sharp self, laundered uniform and polished black Sam Browne belt. Chief Hawthorn was proud of his department.

"There's only five of us. Who's missing?" Sheriff Gilbert asked, leaning and looking around the cramped room. In the quiet, someone heard the grind of a shoe on the top concrete step. Curley Jones gently pushed the door open.

"Yes, sir!" he said to the huge Negro man who stood with his hat in his hand.

"I'ze heres fer de funeral. I'ze asked ta be a pallbearer."

Curley, being a smart ass, asked "You sure it wasn't a wheel bearer?"

The polished black man smiled, his bright teeth gleaming. "Naw, suh! I'm heres fer Master DeFoor."

Curley Jones pushed the door fully open. "Well, sir! Please come in."

"Thank yous, sir," said the giant of a man.

Sheriff Gilbert peeked into the chapel. "Come All Ye' Saints is when we go down," he whispered, with his face against the door crack.

The sermon was short, no soul saving, just a simple eulogy of the old man's life. That day the law and Big Sam ushered Ellis DeFoor to his grave, where they laid him next to his wife and infant twins. The old veteran's casket went down lightly, with Big Sam on the box. All the old soldiers walked behind, as one tried to call cadence. On that bright clear morning, the wind began to blow and a rainbow without rain arched in the east.

Sheriff Louis Gilbert wiped his hands with his tobacco flecked handkerchief. "If I find that god damned nigger he won't come in alive, like a god damned deer over the hood. I will by God, I will," he said, as he walked along folding his handkerchief and gently put it in his hip pocket. Detective Duncan cleared her throat. Sheriff Gilbert looked around. "Sorry, Big Sam. No offense," he said, looking ahead.

"Nun took, Shuriff," the big man said in a deep voice. "Kin I duz tha same?" he asked.

Heather motioned for Sam to come up beside her. He hurried alongside.

"Sam, best kill him by hand and toss him on the road somewhere," Chief Hawthorn answered.

"I sho' kin," whispered the Negro.

"Big Sam, if you get him be careful and don't even call us. Someone will find him on the road, eventually," said Sheriff Gilbert, licking the stub of a cigar.

* * *

While Ellis DeFoor was being laid to rest on the north end of the county, John Miller on the south, feeling somewhat better, chose to walk out among his two-year-old pecan trees. They were his pride and joy. They had been brought back all the way from east Texas, handpicked by him. The young seedlings had taken a place of prominence on the back seat of his shiny black Maxwell. John Miller insisted that he needed no assistance in his leisurely walk. The short new grass in its fragrant youth was an Easter grass green. "And it was a wonderful Easter this year." He smiled as he recalled the church service and the bountiful dinner on the grounds.

Gertrude Miller softly kissed her husband on the cheek and gave him a gentle hug as he pulled away to his new orchard. John's long black tonic coated hair was combed ever so neatly to the back. His sparkling gold tooth caught the faintest ray of sun when he smiled. This morning he had dressed in his new dark blue bibbed overalls, and even slipped his feet into his Sunday brown oxfords. His everyday sage green Fedora sat cocked to one side. "Like a young sportin' man," Gertrude thought, as he walked off the front porch. She watched him go out of sight through the oxidizing screen door. She saw him stop to cut a tiny red rosebud with his treasured Case brand pen knife and wedge it between the brass gallus catch and the yellow pencil loaded bib. Gertrude noticed the dog ran ahead to catch up to him and they walked along together.

"What a blessing and peace," she thought, turning to go about her housework, and pay a few bills for the company. "And to think my daddy just couldn't see what I saw in him."

John Miller walked among his young saplings, touching each one and rubbing the healthy ribbed leaves between his finger and thumb. He could tell when a tree was healthy, and these were. He smiled and shook his head. "Hog shit, just plain old hog shit, done just right," he bragged aloud, moving among the trees. The sunlight caught the young tender leaves giving them a glowing, almost translucent look. He soon stood in the middle of the new orchard, where he had placed a cast iron sundial. The business man turned and looked all around, pleased with what he had done. This was his daddy's land, and his granddaddy's place before that. Hurricane Creek formed on it and had three strong, clean flowing streams. The gentle wind blew in his face and he raised his chin a little higher, almost believing that he could hear the voices of those beloved men. The young saplings swayed gently and the sun's rays came down from the bright blue sky filled with cottony clouds. The dog sat beside the man and they both looked toward the beautiful sky. John Miller softly and silently met God's calling.

The loyal dog laid his head on his master's chest and remained at his side. Gertrude, who was busy drying a large white earthenware bowl in the kitchen, experienced a jolt to her soul like she had never felt before and never would again. Her arms suddenly opened and the heavy bowl shattered on the wood floor. Every broken piece, every tiny shard of the broken bowl slid in the direction of the new orchard. "John!" she screamed, as she ran to the front of the dark house toward the bright opening of the front door where her love had departed.

* * *

Before the sheriff and Doc Hubbard could arrive, the deacons and preacher of the church gathered around. John Miller's body lay covered with a royal purple choir robe. It looked so peaceful against the green grass. Gertrude sat nearby sobbing. The deacons softly hummed a tune from time to time. The sheriff's car hurried down the long drive covered over by the strong limbs of pecan trees that John Miller had planted as a young man. Flickering shadows passed over the men as they approached the side orchard.

"This ain't good," said Doc Hubbard, as he left the car. He closed the door gently and approached with hat in hand. His bright striped tie flagged in the gentle wind. There were blood spots on the cuffs of the long sleeve white shirt. Out of courtesy he hurriedly folded them back a turn, hiding the spots.

"Mrs. Miller," he said gently. "May I ask that you leave us to do our job, just for a few minutes?" he asked, taking her hand.

A couple of deacons walked with the wife to the house. Doc Hubbard and the sheriff began to examine Mr. Miller's body. "He'd been under the weather for several weeks," advised the preacher.

"I'll take this as a natural death," said Doc Hubbard, moving the stethoscope over several places on the deceased man's chest and neck. "I'm pleased with that, Sheriff," he said, looking up. The doctor covered the man with the purple robe.

"I'll sign off on it," said Sheriff Gilbert, standing over the doctor.

"Preacher Simpson, you may remove him," said Doc Hubbard, placing his stethoscope into his leather satchel.

John Miller was a deacon of the small Pilgrim's Rest U.N.M.C, on Pilgrim Church Road southeast of Raleigh. Miller had been a member all of his life, you might say he was born into the church. The wood from the trimmed pecan trees went to heat the church. It was never cold for the lack of wood. John Miller and Gertrude were married in the church. Their infant daughter, Polly Sue, had been baptized there. The Millers always gave to charitable causes and the needy. Miller's orchards employed several dozen local Negroes. John's death would have an impact upon them.

* * *

Theo Jackson soon learned of John Miller's passing. Miller was so well known that if telephones could not get it told, they drove in cars or in some cases walked to tell other Negroes. Theo Jackson was momentarily taken back wondering what impact this would have on his livelihood. Theo hurried to the barn. "Lee!" he called in a loud whisper. Theo saw tiny hay pieces falling from the loft as James Lee came to the ladder opening and looked down.

"Yep!" James Lee answered.

"John Miller's dead," Theo said, looking up.

"For real?" James Lee replied.

"This morning," Theo replied. "I'm due money for my last load of manure," he said, looking around the barn with his hands in his pockets.

"Go first chance and see if his old lady'll give it to you," James Lee said. "I'm hungry," he added.

"We'll eat early tonight. I'll go tomorrow on the way to the church and try ta get my money," Theo said.

John Miller's funeral was set for three o'clock the next afternoon, followed by a covered dish social in his memory and afterwards a sing. James Lee played mumblety-peg with his knife, whittled, and slept to pass the long hours. He had watched the hogs from the back loft door so much until he had begun to sort them out in a social order. Although it was one large herd, there were actually five different social groups, each with a matriarch sow and a king bore.

* * *

James Lee had seemingly vanished. Heather fully expected him to be hiding somewhere locally. Why she did not really know, just a gut guess. The funeral for Ellis DeFoor left the better half of the day to try and locate the wanted Negro. Jasper Brown drove his patrol car. Chief Hawthorn drove on his own as he needed to get back to the city.

Officer Jasper Brown and Detective Duncan found themselves sitting at the stop sign in downtown Luthersville. They sat blocking traffic a fraction of a second too long and a horn sounded behind them. Jasper looked in the mirror. He motioned, "come around, come around", waving his arm out the open window.

"There's the post office! Take me over there," Heather said, pointing to the sign on the brick front of the General Store and Hardware. "I'm curious."

When he got a chance, Jasper hurried the car across the intersection and coasted to a stop in front of the sleepy store. "I'll be right back," Heather said, looking at her partner, "Unless you want to come in," she added.

"I can wait," Jasper replied. "I'll look for women," he said, smiling.

"And at my butt as I get out," Heather said. She struck the bonnet with her fist and pointed at him. They had parked close to a fire hydrant.

The coiled bell sounded on the old store's front door. Sunlight had never made it to the back of the retail room. "Hello!" Heather called out, waiting for a reply.

"Over here, in the post office," a woman's voice responded.

Heather walked to the ornate steel barred teller window. "I'm Detective Duncan, from Warm Springs Police Department. We're Special Deputies for Meriwether County." She was interrupted.

"So, yer the woman hired to find the nigger, James Lee. Didn't you catch him once already?" the woman asked. She sat behind the wall of tiny wooden mail boxes, sorting.

"I did," replied Heather. "But he escaped. I was wondering if you might have some addressed mail that would interest us."

"Oh, and what would that be?" asked the woman, still in the shadows.

"Any mail addressed to Lees, in general?" Heather asked.

The envelopes bumped against the finely cast bronze doors as they were thrust into the tiny boxes. There was a long silence as the woman continued sorting mail. Heather stood patiently, looking at the display of dishes in the front window.

"And why do you need to know?" asked the woman.

Heather pulled the badge from her belt and pushed it as far into the customer window as she could, and then pulled it back. "I'm doing my very best to be a good representative for your sheriff and my chief. Please answer my question or I'll have reasonable basis to take other actions, which I'd rather not have to do," she said, trying to keep other customers that had slowly gathered from hearing.

The woman finally revealed herself. "I don't know you," she said.

"I told you who I was and my badge should be enough," Heather replied.

"We don't get many women through here in law enforcement," said the woman, in a sulking tone.

"I'm sure that in the years to come there will be more," replied Heather. "Please answer my question. I've already checked tax records and the telephone directory for Lees, but I can't tell from a name if they are Negroes or not."

"We have a few Lees, they are all kin to my knowledge and they are white folks," the woman replied.

"Thank you. That wasn't so hard now, was it?" Heather asked, working her badge back onto her belt.

Jasper was beginning to wonder what the holdup was. As he looked toward the store impatiently, Heather came out. It was mid-afternoon. Luthersville folks noticed the Warm Springs Patrol car on their Main Street. Jasper acknowledged with a casual assuring wave.

"Rocky Mount or Primrose," Heather said, looking at Jasper.

"Both. Rocky Mount first, then Primrose," he said, pulling the car away from the high sidewalk. "If a drunk told me he'd fell off tha sidewalk here, I'd have him checked out for hurts. The highest damn things I've ever seen. Where we were was over a foot tall," he said, looking back in the mirror. Heather smiled at his amazement.

"How far's Rocky Mount?" Heather asked.

"About five miles," Jasper replied.

"If the chief said you could get out of that uniform while we work this case, what would ya think?" Heather asked.

Jasper smiled and shook his head. "I'm use ta it. I'll wear it," he said, brushing it off. The pride in his face was obvious. Heather thought it came from his stint in the military. A uniformed presence on the scene really did not hurt anything.

They rode a few minutes in silence. "Miss home yet?" Jasper asked, turning toward his pretty partner.

"Sometimes, but not enough to pine over it," Heather said. "I miss the family and old Holly," she added. "My room, the comfortable chair and the ice box," she said, smiling. She looked far ahead, out the windshield. "Say, that gatherin' at the funeral. That was the last of a generation."

"Those old men will fade away and take a world of experiences with them," Jasper said. "Look!" He applied the brakes. They both leaned forward with the sudden force.

"Damn, what a snake!" Heather exclaimed.

"I'll get it!" Jasper announced, speeding up, turning the tires to cut the

192

snake in half.

"No!" Heather said, striking Jasper hard on the chest. She pulled the steering wheel back. "It's a king snake!" she exclaimed. "A good snake!"

"Only good snake is a dead snake!" Jasper said, missing the large slow-moving reptile.

"I'll beat yer ass if you kill a good snake," Heather said, giving Jasper a look that he did not want to challenge. "I'll tell you the bad snakes," she said.

Jasper gave a loud sigh. "I think the post office is in the small store," he said. "Not a lot to the place. I guess a hundred people live out here. They had a school at one time, one of the teachers was a McLendon guy. One of them Sacred Harp singers," Jasper said, slowing to find the store among the few buildings.

"There it is!" Heather pointed. The old building was red brick with painted bars covering the windows. A single gas pump sat on a raised island, next to a kerosene barrel and pump. The front door was guarded by three healthy cats, a solid orange Tom, a Calico female and a Tabby. They never moved to get out of the way, just made acknowledgement by raising their heads from their sleeping posture. The front wall was covered with enameled signs, Coca-Cola, Pepsi Cola, Nehi, Merita Bread, Nabisco, Butter Cup Snuff, and Tops Sweet Snuff. "I've never seen so many signs! There's not a place for another one!" Heather exclaimed. "Do you listen to the *Lone Ranger?*" she asked.

Jasper blushed. "I wouldn't miss it," he said, stopping the car under the shade of the awning. A heavyset man wearing an apron stepped into the doorway.

"Hi y'all?" he said loudly. He held a fly swatter in one hand.

"This should go easier than Luthersville," Heather said, as she opened her door. Jasper followed her up the steps.

"Oh, my! You're that gun totin' woman I've heard about. Honey, ya can arrest me anytime," laughed the man. His short clipper cut white hair stood on his round head like frost on a melon. The telephone rang. "Just a minute!" he said, as he hurried to answer it. The two officers walked in.

"Yeah! They're already here," said the store clerk.

Jasper and Heather listened as they looked about in a curious, polite manner.

"I'm trying ta get arrested by her now," he said to the caller. He hung up the telephone. "Postmaster from Luthersville," he said. "She's -- uh! I think she fell in tha yard and -- well, she got a stick hung," he said, laughing.

There were no customers in the store. The man leaned on the counter. "Piece of cheese?" he asked, as he opened the cover that protected the large quarter hoop of red rind. He indexed the slicing gage ever so slightly and pushed the sharp carbon steel blade through the bright orange goodness.

The slice gently rolled onto the waxed paper he had placed to catch it.

"I'll take a piece," Heather said.

"Me too," replied Jasper.

The cheese was free, but it led to a drink and several soda crackers, every little purchase helps. "I do the mail. There's my boxes, and the carrier runs a short route, couple hundred boxes." The clerk talked between bites of cheese. He pointed to several rows of tiny mail boxes just to the right of the front door. "We were talking yesterday as we read the Vindicator. Old granny Negro, Thelma Lee, she passed last year. Her place is down in the Andrew's Mill area. She lived in a small house up a narrow lane, back behind the old mill site. Her mail was put in an open lard bucket strapped to a red cedar post, not even a lid, just open to the world," said the clerk. Heather took a seat on a stool at the counter. She was interested. "After she passed, the mail was kept out of the so-called box, never saw anybody get it, but it was always gone. I'm Henry Markham!" said the man, extending his hand, first to Heather and then to Jasper.

"I'm Detective Heather Duncan, glad ta meet you," she replied.

"Jasper Brown, Warm Springs Police Department! We're Special Deputies for Sheriff Gilbert, Meriwether County." Jasper shook Markham's hand.

"The mail carrier's Melvin Haralson. He should be in soon," said Henry.

"We'll wait, if we're not in the way," Heather replied.

"Oh, not in the way, be my guest. It's slow out here," Henry said, suddenly taking a swat at a fly that lit close by. The wire mesh swatter had seen its better days. The binding was coming off of the edges. A loud muffler was heard in the distance. "That's Melvin now!" Henry said. Bap! Henry struck another fly. "You know we ain't had a post office since November of '09," he said.

"What?" Jasper asked.

"November 30, 1909, shut us down. They said we were dying," Henry said, looking about at his store. "This was my dad's place back then. He left us about ten years ago. Melvin comes out of Primrose, and then old Joe gets some of us out of Alvaton."

Melvin, the rural carrier, was able to tell the officers that the mail would build up, but not more than a week. She did not get a lot, but it disappeared. He had taken a package once to the small house and handed it to the old woman at her front door.

"What did the house look like, one big room, that sort of thing?" Heather asked Melvin.

"Keepin' room and bedroom all in one, then the kitchen was across the back. Toilet outside behind the large clumps of pampas grass. A chinaberry or two in the yard, most everybody's got those." Melvin smiled. He was a small wiry man, late in years, and wore thick glasses. He was missing a tooth or two in the front and smoked a curved briar pipe.

Heather was busy making a sketch of the house as Melvin described it. "Is this what you think the floor plan would be like?" she asked, showing him the sketch. Melvin nodded his head.

Henry had been watching. "That's it! I've been inside," said Henry. "Took groceries a number of times."

"Jesus! We should have been talkin' to you all the time," Heather said, laughing. Henry shrugged his shoulders.

"Never been through this sorta thing before," he said. The three cats sauntered in and walked between any sets of legs that would stand still for it.

"How can we find Granny Thelma's place?" Heather asked.

"Right there at the corner go south, and in about three miles there'll be two dirt roads that intersect the highway. Be the bottom fork, cross the bridge, and the old mill was on the right. Her mail bucket is there, ya can't miss it," Melvin said, before Henry could.

Jasper spoke up. "How far off the road is it?"

"Oh, hundred yards," Henry said. "The grass was always high on the steep banks, if that's any help," he added.

Melvin watched the female detective. He had never seen one before.

"You haven't seen us. Do you understand?" Heather asked, with a stern expression. "And we two don't know you," she added. Out of gratitude Heather bought another slice of cheese and a couple of orange Nehis.

"Please come and arrest me if ya get bored," Henry said with a wink and a smile, as they started to leave.

"I'll chain yer ass to a ball," Heather replied, as she headed toward the door.

"Oh, my! I'm in love," Henry said, laughing loudly.

Jasper kicked the tires waiting for Heather to finish talking. She finally settled in the car. "You certainly know how to get 'em on yer side," he said. "They'll be so excited they'll stay up late," he added, checking for oncoming traffic in the crossroads of Rocky Mount.

Heather was gleaming, she was all smiles. "You know what we just got, don't you?" she asked, looking at Jasper.

"A place to work just after daylight tomorrow," he replied.

"That's right! This will give us James Lee or possibly let us know who he is," she said.

* * *

"Dixie!" Get me young Huffman!" barked Sheriff Gilbert. He lowered his desk chair to the floor and placed both elbows on his desk top.

"We're goin' ta toy with this sum bitch," said the sheriff. "I'll keep him wonderin' at least," he said.

Alfred Huffman came to the jail from his office a short distance away almost at a run, with his leather satchel in hand. The front door opened without the slightest knock.

"Yes, sir!" said the young reporter.

"Pull up a chair! I've got a request," said Sheriff Gilbert.

The chair scrubbed the floor.

"Take it down, craft it as you like ta get in proper terms, but don't add to or take away," said the sheriff. "Do ya understand?" he asked.

Alfred shook his head vigorously. "I understand," he replied enthusiastically.

Curley Jones was having a row with a prisoner. All kinds of profanity spilled into the booking office. Sheriff Gilbert removed the cigar from his cheek and looked out the window. Alfred sat ready to write.

"The Meriwether County Sheriff's Department has received an overwhelming number of sightings and leads on the escaped Negro, James Lee. All available law enforcement is following up on a round the clock basis," said the sheriff. "Not much of a story, but it is that, just a story. We ain't heard jack shit!" snarled the sheriff. "Not a god damn thing!" He sat with his arms folded and looked at the puzzled reporter. "It's a ploy, son," the sheriff said. This nigger'll do one of two things; move about or go under harder. Let's hope he moves about."

It was time for Dixie to leave. She quietly eased up from her desk and waved goodbye to the two men. Curley still cursed in the cell block. The reporter looked perplexed. "You hurry over to your old boss, you know who I mean, tha old fart over in the back corner. Ya show it to him, tell him the sheriff called him 'ole souse meat' and I'll bet we get it printed," said the sheriff, with an evil vindictive look in his eyes.

* * *

"What did you two discover this afternoon?" asked Chief Hawthorn, sitting at his desk.

"Check the halls and lock the doors," Heather said to Jasper. He hurried to do as she had asked. After a minute or two of doors closing and knobs rattling, he came into the staff office and took a seat. Heather was already seated and waiting. "We came up with a lead on where this Lee might have been staying. You know they don't live anywhere, they stays here and they stays there," Heather said. The chief stopped what he was doing and gave her his full attention.

"What is it?" asked the chief.

"He may have been living at a Thelma Lee's house at the old Andrew's Mill, between Greenville and Rocky Mount. We've got information of the layout of the small house and the driveway goin' in," Heather said.

"I've heard of it, hadn't been there but know of it," replied the chief. He listened intently.

"I'd like ta hit it about daybreak," Heather said.

"We need a warrant," replied the chief.

"The old woman has been dead for over a year according to our sources. But the mail has been removed from the box; however, it has stopped coming. Up home we always say the door was open." She smiled.

The chief shook his head and sucked through his teeth. "I see, a wise expression. We've used it down here too." He smiled. "Can you two handle it? I'll need to be in town for a council meeting."

Heather looked at Jasper. He nodded.

"We can," answered Heather.

"I'd like for you to come too," she said to the chief.

"I can't miss the meeting," he replied. "It's important."

"Oh, what is it about, if I may be so bold?" Heather asked.

"Hiring a female officer," he said, looking down. He said it very low.

"The mayor approved it," she replied, in a defensive tone. Her anger was visible.

"He's answering to the council too," he said, picking at his fingers.

"God damn!" Jasper said loudly, as he jumped up from his seat. "She proved herself at the capture of the son of a bitch and they let him get away," he yelled.

The chief motioned for him to settle down. "I've got it under control. They're as narrow minded as I was," he said. "And after you put that big wife beatin' monster down, that's somethin' else." He smiled.

"You tell them that if they've changed their minds, I can pack my things and go home. I've other things I can do," Heather said, shaking her finger at the chief. "Four thirty sharp! Right here!" Heather said to Jasper, as she stormed out, slamming the door. Heather walked to the boarding house, where she did push-ups and a few sit-ups before going down to dinner.

* * *

"Sum bitches!" Heather mumbled to herself, tossing a magazine to the side. The council meeting in the morning was really gnawing at her. She paced back and forth in front of the windows, occasionally looking down onto the street. Heather had dressed for bed earlier, in hopes that sleep would rid her mind of the anger she felt. The cotton gauzelike fabric clung to her feminine features, resting on her bosom and buttocks. The gown moved gently with the slightest breeze.

Her impatience got the best of her. She hurriedly put on her suit pants and hurried downstairs to the telephone. The stairs creaked as she bounded along. The small downstairs hall foyer was dimly lit by a small lamp on the telephone table. Click! Click! The receiver sounded. "This is Detective Duncan with the police department. Get me Alfred Huffman in Greenville," she whispered.

"With the Vindicator?" asked the operator.

"Yes," replied Heather, in a whisper.

The switching made several mechanical sounding clicks and then the telephone rang. "Hang up, operator," Heather said. The circuit was closed, bringing the snooping three-way to a secure line.

Burr-ing, burr-ing, burr-ing! Heather looked about the foyer and through the French doors leading into the store. She could see the headlights of passing cars through the front door of the store. Her gown was tucked part way into her slacks. The sleeveless openings provided little coverage for her.

"Hello!" said a man's sleepy voice.

"Alfred Huffman?" Heather asked.

"That's right. Who is this?" he asked, sitting up on the edge of the bed.

"Detective Duncan, Warm Springs PD," she replied.

"Oh!" Huffman said, sitting fully upright.

"Be at the Flat Rock Church in the morning before daylight, two Warm Springs units will head north. Follow, but stay on the road, don't follow them in. You'll get a story," she whispered. "Bring no one, no one. Do you understand?" she said softly.

"I --- I understand," he stuttered. "Just before daylight at Flat Rock Church on the road ta Rocky Mount," he said.

"And yer camera," she said, just before hanging up. Heather was not well pleased with her deed. She ventured into the kitchen where she got a small glass of cold buttermilk and took it back to her room. Heather rested well.

* * *

The large faced Big Ben suddenly hammered its hellacious noise that would arouse the dead. The small brass hammer flailed in a blur against the two brass domes, as Heather's sleepy hand explored in the early morning darkness to turn it off. "Three o'clock, crap!" she mumbled, sitting up and yawning. She lay claim to the bathroom, where she hurriedly applied her light make-up. The clothes from the day before were good enough as she expected them to be soiled in just a few hours. This morning was different, it was of her planning and not of her father's or a county call for help. Most entries she had been involved with had always been messy. Most fugitives do not stay in the best environments. Her slacks were loose fitting so she had plenty of room to move. Kicking in a door was not her strong point, and certainly not laying a shoulder into one either, there were tools for that. "Save the body," Sonny always said, as he came forward with a chop axe or a sledge hammer.

This morning would call for her 1911 and the shoulder rig. The .38 was a good cartridge, but the heavy, slow moving .45 was a man stopper. Heather placed the canvas satchel on the unmade bed and pulled the 1911 semi-automatic pistol out in the dim light. The magazine was full, but the chamber was empty. She racked the heavy slide to the rear. As it pulled from her hand it made a distinctive clacking sound as it cycled a round into the empty chamber. Her thumb pressed the magazine catch and the heavy loaded magazine fell to the covers. It was topped off with another round, six in the magazine and one in the chamber, making a total of seven rounds, one more than the revolver. Heather dropped two additional loaded magazines into her hip pocket. The aroma of coffee was wafting into the upstairs rooms from somewhere. It could have been from the café nearby or even Mrs. Blakely's kitchen. The young woman slid the leather holster rig onto her torso and locked the door of her room behind her. Heather passed Mrs. Blakely in the downstairs hallway.

"Good morning!" said Mrs. Blakely, as Heather hurried by.

"Good morning! Tell Buddy Cotton to keep his mind sharp, if I don't get back," Heather said, pushing the door open with her butt. Her hands were full with two flashlights and the belt rig with her revolver.

"What? Why?" asked Mrs. Blakely, looking surprised. She stood watching Heather leave, with a pound of unsliced bacon in her hand, taken from the refrigerated case in the store.

Heather cranked the city car and hurried down the street to the front of the police department where she had arrived before Jasper Brown. He was pulling up before she could get out.

"Beat ya!" she said, smiling in the pre-dawn hour. Jasper had stopped close enough for them to touch, had they reached out the open windows.

"Not by much," he said, yawning.

"Bring yer shotgun?" she asked.

Jasper raised the barrel just high enough for her to see it. "And some of my own shells," he added.

"The reporter from the Vindicator will get behind us at Flat Rock Church. He's goin' ta do a story after we make sure the house is clear, or capture James Lee," Heather informed him. "When we get there, we'll go in without our headlights on, and walk up the path to the house. You hurry to the back and I'll go in the front," she said. "If anyone comes yer way, make sure it's James Lee before you shoot," she added, holding the top of the steering wheel. Heather leaned about looking at the morning sky. "I see a smidgen of sun, we'd best be going," she said. "But you lead," she added.

Jasper Brown went down the street and swung wide, making a U-turn in the middle of Main Street. He quietly passed Heather and she pulled out behind him.

Alfred Huffman had not been up before daylight since he started at the Meriwether paper. He moved slowly, and really did not know what he was wearing, it just felt right to his early morning touch. The eager reporter hurried northeast to his destination with a breaking story, in his own car.

He was as excited as he was sleepy, but his adrenalin kept him going. The headlights of his car shone brightly against the sides of the old church. It was just like so many in the south, painted white with green trim. The back side of the church yard had a spring box, large and moss lined. It was a starting tributary for the large Red Oak Creek that wandered aimlessly for miles all the way to the Flint River. He had been there before, for a story on the homecoming and baptism service all in the same day. Huffman was eager. The morning sun was just about to make itself known, declaring the new day. Huffman watched and waited, looking to the south.

The two Warm Springs patrol cars popped the loose crossties on the train tracks in downtown and were in high gear as they passed the turnoff to the Meriwether Inn. Jasper was driving like a policeman. Heather believed that when you are on a mission, then act like you own the road and drive with authority. When they were just south of Harris City, Heather flicked her lights then turned on the police lights. Jasper did the same as they went through small crossroads in a roar leaving a cloud of dust for the early folks to see and wonder until they read the Vindicator. She killed her lights and Jasper followed suit until they got to Greenville and he took the initiative to run through town with them on. Jasper was beginning to believe he was a police officer. He had never been on a hunt like this before. His excitement was growing.

Alfred Huffman was getting blurry eyed, keeping himself awake was hard, but he was willing to wait. Jasper led Heather to the turn onto Rocky Mount Road, less than five miles and they would be close to James Lee. In a few minutes, between his fuzzily focused eyelids, Huffman saw two cars coming from the south at a high rate of speed. His heart began to race as he cranked his car, and rolled slowly toward the road. The two speeding cars roared by, tossing loose sand and gravel toward him. "This is it, shit!" he said out loud, as he tried to pull out and catch up with the patrol cars. He was so excited he could hardly work the clutch for his shaking leg. He even missed second gear. Huffman was so sleepy he could only count intersections, four until Andrew's Mill. He was at least a quarter of a mile behind the speeding cars. They suddenly killed their headlights and he saw them turn in the dim morning light. Huffman followed, turning out his headlights.

Jasper stopped short of the mail box and Heather stopped a couple of car lengths behind him. Jasper was out quickly and on the narrow grass covered lane. Heather joined him at a jog. "Back door," she whispered.

"Yep!" Jasper moved ahead and carried the pump shotgun at port arms. The sudden burst of a rabbit startled him.

Heather moved just behind him with her pistol controlled by both hands. The two officers swarmed upon the silhouette of a house in the dawn light.

Alfred Huffman quietly stood by the back of the first patrol car with his camera in his hand. There was not a sound to be heard. The small rural house sat on raised pillars of mixed stone and bricks. Jasper hurried to the back and watched the only door. He was hidden behind the tall scraggly privet hedges. Heather saw him get into place as she squatted down in the cover of a large clump of pampas grass. She was in fact correct, there was a small opening. The front door was ajar. Taking a deep breath, she charged up the steps and opened the door with a swift kick. It slammed against the wall.

"Sheriff's Department! Sheriff's Department!" She yelled in the darkness of the small house. Her flashlight cut through the dusty darkness and hanging spider webs. Heather took the first door opening and quickly fired a round into the person standing before her with a gun pointed at her. Bam! Bam! The big bore pistol reported. Jasper jumped and looked about. He racked the shotgun and held it on the back door, expecting someone to rush out. His heart raced.

Alfred Huffman's ears perked up at the sound of the two gunshots. The person in front of Heather suddenly disappeared. It was a full-length hall tree mirror. Embarrassed, Heather continued to move on through the house with her flashlight slicing the stale air. She checked the rooms for people, and even the large chifforobe. The house was clear of anyone inside. "Come ahead!" she yelled loudly, to Jasper.

Jasper rushed the back door to find it hard fastened, so he went around to the front. "You all right?" he barked.

Yes." She pointed to the hall tree with the two thumb sized bullet holes in the backer board of the mirror.

Jasper grinned. "I'd done it too and messed up my pants," he laughed.

Heather stood before him with spiderwebs hanging from her blouse. "May I?" Jasper asked, pointing to them. "Ugh!" she shivered. "Get 'em off!" Jasper eased closer to her bosom with finger and thumb and quickly plucked the smoky spider webs that hung on her. The two officers took the two rooms one at a time and searched for anything that would help tell them who James Lee was and where he might be. There was very little left that would give the faintest idea that Thelma Lee had lived there. The place was full of papers and trash, food wrappers, empty cans, and beer bottles. The morning sun was not fully up when the patience of Alfred Huffman got the best of him. He eased up the same path the officers traveled. He could see their footprints where the tall grass was matted down. Their flashlights moved about in the dark house.

Alfred stopped outside. There were no officers to be seen, but he had heard two gunshots. "Hello! The house!" he yelled.

"Shit!" Heather said suddenly, standing up from the interesting papers that she had found on the dusty sofa. "It's Alfred Huffman!"

Jasper stood in the kitchen doorway hoping for better light soon. "So that's who was tailing us this morning," he said.

"Yep!" she said, hurrying to the door. Young Huffman stood in the tall grass watching for his cue.

The detective stood on the small front porch in all her feminine splendor. Huffman looked at the attractive woman. She knew he was there, she could see him, crouching in the grass with his camera poised. Heather pulled her pistol from her shoulder holster and did a quick magazine exchange, one that was two down for one that was full. It was the fastest thing Huffman had ever witnessed, in regards to the pistol crafts. He was smitten with her beauty, spiderwebs and all.

"Come ahead!" Heather motioned with the big pistol.

Huffman stood and stepped lively to the steps. "In the house too?" he asked

"Certainly, let us do the plundering," she said, as he came up the steps.

"What was the shootin'? Did ya get Lee? Anybody hurt?" he asked, one question right behind the other.

"Slow down, nobody's hurt and Lee ain't here, but this is a good find," she said, holstering her pistol. Heather saw the reporter watching the big pistol.

"Here's a light cord!" Jasper called out. He pulled the cord and it snapped, falling down on his uniform hat. For once he actually laughed, standing with the pull cord hanging on him. There was no electricity.

Alfred Huffman would make more pictures than his boss, Buford Stokes, would be pleased with. No matter how hard the young man worked, it seemed to always either be wrong or too much to suit the old timer who controlled the paper. The eager reporter stood in the nasty house and wrote his article by the sunlight that bathed him at the open front door. Jasper and Heather carefully explored the drawers in the remaining furniture and every piece of paper was carefully moved to reveal names and addresses, after the morning sun had risen to the point of being bright. Into the second hour, Heather discovered a bank draft made out to James Lee, on the Bank of Moreland. While the officers searched, Huffman stood and read his article aloud for them to hear and approve.

"I'd like for you to only use a picture of us on the front porch and get close so no one can readily tell where it is," said Heather.

Alfred Huffman posed the two officers and took the picture. He smiled. "First one on the second roll. I'll buy another roll to replace the first one and Buford will never know."

"I'm ready for a cup of coffee," said Heather.

"Me too!" Jasper said eagerly.

"Will you join us?" she asked Huffman. Heather looked at the young man, socks not matching and blue pants with a black suit coat, his straw

Fedora on backwards, and his necktie tied wrong side up. She was too polite to make fun of the young man.

"Greenville? Becky's!" she barked.

The city hall and the café both roared with conversation. The Vindicator sold out and was being shared from one person to the next. The sheriff's article was incorporated with Huffman's own, and the photograph of Detective Duncan and Officer Brown was larger than a post card. The resolution was outstanding. Mayor Cunningham and Chief Hawthorn swelled with pride as they shook the hands of citizens congratulating them on the work of the two officers.

Buddy Cotton met Heather at the breakfast table at Mrs. Blakely's and asked her to autograph her picture. The lad acted as if he had met Greta Garbo for a kiss. He lingered at the door watching Heather until Mrs. Blakely called him down and sent him about his paid tasks. Heather winked at him and he stumbled over the three-legged hat rack near the telephone table.

* * *

The deacons of Pilgrim's Rest U.N.M.C. were dressed in their finest. They directed cars and a few small trucks into the church yard and then up and down the road. Brother Hammett was counting cars. "Ninety-eight!" he called out to the other six deacons. Gertrude Miller and her daughter had not yet arrived. The preacher and his wife were to pick them up in a borrowed Cadillac. A parking spot was held in the order of events, placing Mrs. Miller's ride at the front door, right behind the hearse.

The deacons checked their watches in anticipation of the bereaved widow's arrival. It was ten minutes until the service was to start. "Thar they beez!" yelled Brother Jones, pointing to the main road. The Cadillac was approaching with its headlights shining and the sunlight reflecting from the polished chrome trim. Gertrude Miller and her daughter Polly Sue sat in the back seat. It was a solemn moment when they arrived. The deacons stood reverently in two rows on the steps leading into the church.

John Miller's casket lay at the altar, closed as he had wished. The congregation stood as the preacher led the widow and daughter in. Polly Sue was a year old, her father taken in the needy years of her life. The service was long, and in the tradition of the Negro customs, it went on into the night, even after John was laid to rest in the family cemetery on Hurricane Creek. The plot contained ancestors from over two hundred years.

Preacher Ulysses Simpson prayed. "Brothers and Sisters, it is late in the hour and we have seen Deacon John Miller to the other side. Let us pray. We thank thee oh Lord fer the blessed brother thad has gone on. Takes him into yo' care as he stands by yo' side. Bless his dee-voted wife and liddle Polly Sue, in dis hour. Amen!"

The congregation gave a rousing round of "amens".   Gertrude and Polly Sue returned home to a warm but empty house where the Millers' Orchard business would continue to provide for the many Negro employees.

* * *

"I was given the authority to run the police department as I saw fit!" barked Chief Hawthorn, as he stood looking each one of the councilmen in the eyes.

Mayor Cunningham stood leaning on the edge of the large rectangular conference table, "This is my third term as mayor of this town and I damn sure didn't just step into this position. I had to be elected each time. Yes, I know I'm a talker and a womanizer, but I only like 'em and enjoy the art of conversation," he said, holding up his hands defensively.   Several men laughed. "I encouraged the hiring of this young woman. She's qualified or she wouldn't have been sent down. Even Sheriff Louis Gilbert thought it was a good fit," said the mayor.

"It just ain't traditional! And we're a small traditional town," one man said.

"No! You're a clannish little back stabbing town that can't stand outsiders," said the chief. Several looked around. They didn't like that remark. "Hell, if I wasn't from here, I wouldn't be where I am," he added.

"A speeding car comes at you, you get a bullet bustin' through yer windshield damn near striking yer head. Would you turn around and run the son of a bitch down and take him to tha ground after firing a shot in a defensive manner? Tell me now! Would ya?" the mayor asked, looking at the council. "Hell no, you wouldn't! You'd suck it up and get the hell out of there. The store, wife and kids would race through yer hard head, you damn right it would," he added, taking his seat.

"Did you know the county hasn't got enough deputies to cover the county and investigate this additional tragedy? This female detective and Officer Jasper Brown, an old man, are out this mornin' kickin' down doors and hopefully arresting this wanted man James Lee. Did you know that?" asked the chief, pounding the table with his fist and yelling. A little spittle sprayed from his angry mouth. He pulled his revolver and tossed it on the table, sliding it toward one councilman. "There's my gun, are you goin' out to hunt for this killer?"

The man gently pushed it away. Chief Hawthorn pushed it to another. "Are you goin' out?" It was pushed away again. "That's what I figured! Let us run policing and you run the city business," he said, holstering it again. The men looked down, expressionless.

"There's been -- no, let me tell you this first. We didn't know this was a woman coming to us until she got here. The library lady, and according to the chief's sources, there's been women in law enforcement since the

1850's. Big towns had them to deal with whores and the like who were arrested and put in jail. Thank God we're not planning to keep women in our small jail," said Mayor Cunningham. "Gentlemen, will you smile at this police woman when you see her?" he asked, taking his seat.

"I think we've got our answer," said one councilman, softly.

"When this case is over, she will be gone. She's from Campbellton," said the chief.

* * *

The allure of James Lee there in the hog farm overpowered Theo Jackson. He fed the hogs and made his morning run for scraps, and then pulled up a chair and socialized with Lee. They played cards and talked of old times, as old as younger men can have, laughing and joking as they passed a bottle around. They even had a meal among the full buckets of stored slop. The evening hours arrived and then darkness fell upon the fragrant bottomland and the sleepy, comfortable hogs. The two men were starting to get loose under the influence of the spirits.

James Lee had just tossed down the third winning hand. "Ha, ha! Got ya again, nigger!" he said, laughing heartily. Theo Jackson frowned, he had only won one game. The loser leaned back on the sturdy wall. "Oh, what a day, dem cards marked," he said, feeling his head throb.

"No, nigger, yer just a bad player," James Lee said, stomping his feet as though he were doing a jig in his chair.

Theo Jackson leaned forward over the small makeshift table. "How long you beez here?" he asked Lee.

"As long as I needs ta be," replied Lee, pulling up his shirt to reveal the revolver. "I'll shoot yo' black ass," he laughed.

Theo reached behind him in the deep shadows and pulled out another sawed-off shotgun. "And I'll kill yo' black ass too!" he said, laughing.

James Lee began to shuffle the cards again. "Old John Miller, now he was a rich nigger, or I sees it that ways," he said, tossing a card to Theo.

"He was a workin' man," said Theo.

"A rich nigger!" James Lee said, smiling.

"Watch who ya calls a nigger, nigger!" Theo laughed uncontrollably. He laughed so hard under the influence of the spirits that he fell to the floor and rolled around.

"Fool! Get up here and plays yer hand," James Lee said. He was going to let Theo win this hand. "The ways I see it, if I can gits some mo' money from Miller's pile, I could git to Alabama, to my folks. Get a car from the Miller place and haul my black ass to Choctawhatchee River, over on the swamp near Elamville," he said, tossing down a card.

Theo Jackson tossed down the winning card, and grinned. "How ya 'spect ta get to tha Miller place?" he asked.

"It's five miles by road like it use ta be and mile through the woods?"

James Lee asked, getting up and stretching.

"Still is by road, and harder cause I've got mo' hogs. Dey's jus' gots ta knows ya," Theo said, smiling over his win. "Lots uh' sloppin' ta raise all 'em hogs, pay good this fall." He realized he might have said too much, giving Lee the impression that he had money there on the property.

"I dos best at night," Lee said, looking out the front door of the barn. There was not a light to be seen for miles other than the bright twinkling stars above.

"So, I could get you over there, day or so, and you'd be good ta go?" Theo asked, trying to grasp the understanding of his dilemma. James Lee being an old friend, he did not want to alert the law while he was in town, though he had plenty of opportunity to do so in his thirty-five-mile route over the last couple of days. He had even wondered if there was a reward, but he would not turn in a needing friend. He would be gone soon. Theo sat and thought a minute while he rubbed his throbbing head. "I can run another load of dry manure over tomorrow afternoon, 'bout dinner time. You can slip out of the cab, down into the plums along the creek. I've got to unload there for the hoppers ta fertilize the peach trees."

James Lee stood tall, moving his head forward and back, thinking to a rhythm. "Thad be fine, thad be just fine," he said, smiling.

CHAPTER THIRTEEN

G ertrude Miller held her young daughter in her arms early on the morning after the funeral. The widow stood on the back porch of the home and looked down into the hollow eyes of men who had carved out a living with her dear John. Many of these men were second generation workers. They too had based their existence on the success of the orchards. The warm morning sunlight pierced the openings in the green leaf canopy with golden rays, raising a soft gentle mist from the dew-covered land. The foremen stood with hats in their hands expressing a feeling of loneliness and loss without a single spoken word. Some were wiping away tears.

Gertrude asked that they keep the place running until she could have a grieving period, maybe a week or so. She trusted they had done their jobs so long that all would go flawlessly. The grieving widow spent her time alone in the house, holding the lovely Polly Sue and reflecting over her beloved John. Gertrude asked for her privacy, requesting that no one come to the house unannounced. There was a line of neighbors paying their respects to John Miller by parking along the roadway and quietly walking in to the Miller Cemetery to place flowers. The women of the church offered to help in any way they could, but Gertrude thanked them kindly and advised that she would call on them soon, which she never did.

The orchard office, located in the oldest section, was over half a mile away from the residence. The telephone in the small weathered building seemed to ring constantly with concerns and well wishes, and most importantly inquiries of the incoming harvest and orders for the retailers who had purchased from them for decades. "A good fruit sold at a reasonable price," John Miller's father used to say, when he was alive. He too had passed away on the property, right there in the orchard's office.

Gertrude realized that pay day was coming in a few days. "There will be no checks missed. I will gather myself to the task. Oscar, you may come and pick them up for everyone. This time there will be a list, have everyone to sign or make their mark. Make a mark and have a witness to sign too. I may underpay or I may overpay, so make it clear if that is the case there will be adjustments made. Don't come to me with a row," said Gertrude. Polly Sue looked around and watched with her big brown eyes sparkling in the morning sunlight. She sucked on her thumb for added contentment.

"Yessum," said Oscar, the senior employee of the orchard.

* * *

James Lee grew restless as he walked the loft like a caged animal, from one end to the other. When Theo Jackson spoke to Lee that morning, he saw in his eyes a lingering beast. Lee had become so impatient that he was aiming his revolver at the hogs below the back loft door and making like he was shooting at them, ker-pow, ker-pow. He even blew the imaginary smoke away from the end of the muzzle. The food box was still heavy since Theo had been feeding him. There was not a lot for him to gather before he could slip into the cab.

Theo Jackson had left on schedule to pick up the waste on his route. He felt uneasy, but it would be over this evening, with the haul of dry manure. The truckload would be light, since the moisture had dried away. He planned to hide James Lee in the cab, down in the floorboard covered with an old black coat. It should be fine for the short distance.

In the warmth of late afternoon, Theo Jackson shoveled the dry hog manure onto the sturdy flatbed. The Fargo was a strong truck, taking the load until the springs slowly began to straighten. It was almost five o'clock and the evening sun was setting in the west. Theo pulled the loaded truck to the front of the barn doors and gently blew the horn. James Lee hurried outside, carrying his box of food and the extra pants and ammunition. The stolen revolver was secured in the front of his pants. Lee sat in the floorboard and was covered by the old black coat as Theo Jackson had planned. The items Lee had carried were placed on the truck seat. James Lee had left nothing behind to his knowledge, but a single dollar bill had fallen from his pants pocket. It lay hidden among the hay bales where he had slept.

The loaded Fargo moved slowly ahead, leaving the hog farm. Theo Jackson was eager to make the manure run, for additional money and to assist James Lee in moving on. The small truck gently rolled from side to side as it climbed in and out of the rolling dips in the rural Meriwether county road. James Lee rode with his hand close to the revolver.

"Expectin' trouble?" Theo Jackson asked, holding the truck in his lane as a car approached and then passed.

"If I get any, you'll be the first to know," James Lee sneered.

"I'ze ain't told a soul," Theo replied. He was beginning to feel uneasy.

"Bet yer black ass I could have," he added, glancing down at James Lee in the floorboard.

"Where's we at?" asked Lee.

"Turnin' onto Cove Church Road," said Theo, working the gear shift. Lee moved his foot to accommodate the shifting.

"I'm crampin'," said Lee, as he moved about.

"I can let you out!" snapped Theo.

"Hurry when ya kin!" snarled Lee, moving about and moaning. "If I'ze a lard ass like you, I couldn't git down here," he added.

"If you had brains like I got, you wouldn't be in the fix yer in," Theo Jackson thought to himself, waving to a farmer in the edge of a field.

"Who's that?" snapped Lee.

"I don't know, just an old white man and a mule. We always wave in passing," replied Theo Jackson. "I'm leavin' tha road here. It'll get rough." Theo downshifted and brought the truck to a crawl as it gently left the road and rocked over the narrow pathway in the peach orchard.

The sun was behind the trees in the west casting a haunting yellow hue over the orchard. The bobwhite quail called out from the briars along the edge of the orchard. "I'll unload and you can just disappear. There's a thick clump of wild plum trees to your back," Theo Jackson advised James Lee, as he sat looking ahead. "Good luck!" he added, turning off the engine. The peach orchard was quiet, only the evening birds calling for their nesting partners, as the light quickly grew dim. "I've got to hurry or I'll be in the dark. I don't like the dark," said Theo, as he opened his door. He looked back at James Lee one more time.

"Thanks!" said Lee, covered with the old coat. Theo Jackson remembered his evil looking eyes. He shivered as he hurried to unload the manure and get away.

The flat shovel scraped the bed of the truck, and then the manure thumped as it landed on the ground. One hurried shovelful after another, scrape-thump, scrape-thump, scrape-thump. Theo Jackson was working up a sweat between his nerves and fear. He pushed himself to finish. At some unknown time between the scrape-thumps, James Lee slipped into the shadows of the wild plum. Theo Jackson saw a red fox run across between the rows of peach trees in the fading light. He wiped the dripping sweat from his forehead with his shirt sleeve and hurried along.

It was dark enough for headlights as he made the drive around loop in the lonely orchard. An occasional rabbit ran as the headlights cast a bright wedge upon it. There was nothing left of James Lee but the old coat in the floorboard. Theo Jackson's conscience began to work on him. What little beliefs between right and wrong he had were gnawing at his core. "Do right, son, always be honest, tell the truth," he could hear his dead grandparents say. His grandparents had always been poor folks, but good churchgoing people. The light was still on at the Tumble Weed Grocery. An old man from Texas had opened it a year or so ago. It was a nice place, with damn near everything. Theo Jackson pulled on to the edge of the lot. He sat quietly for a moment, thinking of what he had done by helping James Lee.

The old man appeared in the doorway. "Makin' a buy?" he called out. "Dinner time's close!" he yelled at Theo.

Theo Jackson hurried right in. "Late," he said, looking about.

"You that hog farmer, ain't ya?" asked the old man.

"Thad be me! Do I stink? I just delivered a load of manure," Theo said, holding a grape Nehi in his hand. The cold water droplets dripped from his fingers.

"Nah! Ya don't stink," the man replied.

Theo Jackson set the bottle down on the counter. He looked glazed as he ran his hand into his pocket for change.

"Ya all right?" asked the old man.

"Tired," replied Jackson, but his conscience was really working on him. "Tired," he repeated.

"A nickel, two cents for the bottle deposit," said the old man. His three-day whiskers looked like young cactus thorns. Theo Jackson placed exact change on the counter. "Thanks! Have a good evening," said the old man.

The empty Fargo truck retraced its route back to the hog farm where it was parked at the dark house. Theo Jackson set the empty Nehi bottle beside the front door steps and retired for the night. He continued to think about his deeds in the darkness of the night.

* * *

At a few minutes past eight o'clock, James Lee watched the lights in the house across the orchard. Gertrude Miller and her daughter, Polly Sue, were enjoying the evening together as well as they could with the absence of a loved one. Gertrude hummed and occasionally broke into song as she washed dishes. Polly Sue held onto kitchen chairs and periodically grasped the hem of her mother's dress for balance. The cooing of the child was occasionally overpowered by the mantel clock that chimed on the hour and half hour.

James Lee waited in the darkness like a stalking tiger, creeping closer and gaining on its prey. The lights were out except for the kitchen and the back sitting room. He was convinced that she was alone and moved closer to the house. The only dog was nowhere to be seen. Apparently, it was in the house. From time to time the old dog raised its head and looked around, feeling that someone or something was lurking about. The stalking Negro moved closer to the residence. He had now located the barn where the vehicles were kept. James Lee's eyes had adjusted to the night and he could see well enough to move around without stumbling as long as he was not in the deep shadows. His hand carefully turned the wooden keeper on the barn door and gently opened the single door. The gable windows, one on the east and one on the west, allowed the moonlight to rush in, flooding the barn with light. The nesting pigeons flew about, darting from one rafter to the other, as their peaceful domain was invaded. "Wapple, wapple, coo, coo!" called the pigeons, flapping their wings and walking the rafters above.

The almost new yellow Ford Model A truck sat with a key in the ignition. The painted art advertising the orchards on the doors caused James Lee to lose interest in the truck immediately. "Shit!" he said to himself. He saw the black car in the next stall over. "My, my! Looks here," he said out loud, touching the square bodied Maxwell that sat partially covered with a tarpaulin. James Lee pulled the tarpaulin from the car. The key was in the ignition and there was a full tank of gasoline. Wilted and drying gardenias drooped over the tops of the hanging vases mounted inside on the door post. "Only a rich nigger," he thought. He put the key in his pocket. "I'll gar-un-tee this 'un," he said. The heavy food box was soon loaded in the front floorboard.

The barn was a gold mine. There were kerosene cans, some full and others almost. He eventually discovered the gasoline cans and moved several around until he found one that was full. "Five gallons! Ole' Ironsides! A good can," he mumbled, loading the can into the back floorboard of the Maxwell. The car was not the fastest thing on the road, but it was in good shape and would fit in without drawing too much attention.

James Lee stood in the open doorway of the barn and watched the silhouette of Gertrude Miller at the kitchen sink. He started his move. The dog raised its head again and looked around, giving a soft whine.

"Old Dog, what's up?" Gertrude asked, as she turned from her sink of dirty dishes to look. "Settle down," she said softly. Polly Sue lay on the floor on her back looking up. She chewed on a rubber toy.

James Lee quickened his step, repositioning his revolver to the back of his waistband. He bounded up the back steps. The wooden steps popped and moaned. Gertrude stood still, somewhat startled at the sound. Knock, knock! The fastened screen door reported loudly. The solid inside door was also locked. Gertrude dried her hands and started quietly toward the door. Knock, knock, knock, knock, knock, knock! James Lee pounded on the screen door.

Gertrude turned on the porch light. The yellow bulb's brightness hurt James Lee's eyes. "Hey! Open up!" he cried out.

"Who's there?" the frightened woman asked through the door. Polly Sue was still lying on the floor, playing.

James Lee's eyes moved about as he tried to think of a name to use. She might recognize his real name. "Jim Lee!" he said.

"We don't have a Jim Lee working here. What do ya want?" Gertrude asked through the closed door. Old Dog had come to the door too.

James Lee thought quickly, he had expected this. "I started work today. They said I could get my first day's pay," he said, leaning close to the dark screen door.

Gertrude's made her last mistake. She opened the door. "Will he bite?" James Lee asked, looking down at the dog.

"No, he's goin' out," she said. She unhooked the screen door and pushed it open, letting the dog leave.

"Can I come in?" Lee asked. His tone was now polite and courteous.

Gertrude was never able to tell anyone her feelings at that moment, or why she had let him in, but she did. "Sit at the table," she said.

James Lee sat down at the table, his back to the wall, his face toward the sink. "Let me finish a few dishes. I'll get you some money. I'd like to write a check," she said, with her back turned.

He sat watching. She was not a bad looking woman. Sex crossed his mind, but hurried, he would not enjoy it. She looked to be the type to like it long and slow. He could work up a sweat with those hips, he thought, as a mild erection came upon him.

"I'd like to make it a check," she repeated.

"I'd like cash, if ya can. I need ta get some food and pay on my room," he said, still watching her back.

"Did you work here in the past?" she asked, washing the last plate.

"Years ago," he said.

"I thought I recognized you," Gertrude said, as she placed the plate in the wire dish drainer. Gertrude heard a clicking sound. She turned to see James Lee standing at the table with a revolver pointed at her. Fear caused her heart to race and her eyes grew large. "What is this?" she stuttered, picking up Polly Sue.

"You scream and I'll shoot you!" James Lee said, gritting his teeth.

"I won't, I won't!" she said.

"I need money, all you got here!" he barked. His eyes were wild and animal like.

"We got very little here! We don't keep it here anymore, w-w-we keep it in the Moreland Bank." She stuttered from fear.

James Lee rushed her. She closed her eyes and held the child close, with her hand over the child's face. "Lie ta me bitch! I'll blow yer brains out! Get me tha god damn money!" he yelled.

"We don't have any money, maybe twenty dollars. It's in the bank," she said again, her voice cracking from fear as she trembled and shook. "Please, please, don't hurt us, please." Gertrude wept.

James Lee waved the revolver about. "Get me what ya got!"

The frightened woman hurried toward the small home office, which had been used for the business for years. James Lee was right behind her. "How much?" he asked, poking her with the muzzle of the gun. She screamed. "Stop it bitch! I'll shoot you!" he yelled, poking her again, only harder. She began to cry. Polly Sue followed.

Gertrude opened a Hav-a-Tampa box that was on the desk. "Here!" she said, handing it to the intruder.

"Shit!" he yelled, as he grabbed the small clump of bills, not amounting to thirty dollars. "Where's the rest?" he yelled. The baby began to cry louder. "Stand in tha corner and don't move!" James Lee screamed, as he waved the revolver about.

The terrified woman and child did as they were told. Gertrude's face was wet with tears. James Lee angrily pulled one desk drawer out at a time, rifling through each one and smashing it on the wall. "God damn it!" he yelled. "Got any liquor?" he barked, almost sounding breathless.

"Y-y-yes," she stuttered.

"Where's it at? Get it!" he yelled, poking her in the ribs. The frantic woman, still holding her child, hurried to the kitchen with the intruder right behind. She bent down at the sink cabinet and brought up a bottle of Four Roses.

"Here," she said, holding it out. It was ripped from her hand.

"Get me a glass, bitch!" Lee yelled.

Gertrude Miller turned to get a glass from the dish drainer, still holding her infant daughter. Gertrude would never get a glass again. James Lee, with cold, calculated thought, aimed his stolen revolver and fired a slug into her shoulder blade. Just like being struck by lightning, her world suddenly turned black as she was thrust against the sink cabinet. She lost her sight and fell to the floor, still holding the screaming child. The strength in her arms was gone and she lay paralyzed as her daughter rolled from her arms. Gertrude's world was now viewed from the floor. She saw James Lee's brown brogans rushing up to the screaming child. Her daughter suddenly disappeared from her field of vision, only to reappear as the face of the child struck the floor beside her. The mother wept harder as she lay lifeless, helpless. James Lee continued to hold the child by the ankles and swing the tiny girl hard against the floor, like swinging a baseball bat. Gertrude could hear the child's bones breaking. After the first strike, the child did not make a sound. Gertrude passed out, lying in a pool of her own blood.

James Lee's anger over the lack of money kept him swinging the child until he was exhausted and sweat ran down his face. He then dropped the child like a rag doll on the floor beside Gertrude, her mother. Lee took a long, slow swig of liquor and then corked the bottle. With a heavy fire poker from the kitchen hearth, he then continued to beat and curse the woman and child, striking them over and over. He tossed the poker down on the kitchen floor, took another swig from the bottle, and carried it with him into the darkness.

The kitchen light burned over the two dead bodies, mother and child. The yellow bulb on the back porch continued to burn through the night. James Lee opened the barn door, cranked the pristine Maxwell, and drove into the night. Lee had now added two more counts of murder to his head, and robbery. The law would find him.

*   *   *

Old Dog had gotten his feet muddy, but went back into the house anyway, where he expected to find a warm welcome, since he did not have to be let in. The screen opened easily and the back door was open. Things were not right. The faint odor of spent gunpowder still hung in the house. Then he discovered Gertrude and Polly Sue on the kitchen floor. The dog sniffed about, as the hair stood up on the back of its neck. The dog was so moved by the bloody sight that he ran to neighbor Moses Finley's and lay on the doorstep until daylight when the old man came out. "Hey, Old Dog," the old Negro neighbor said to the shaking dog. He gave the dog a brisk rub, but the shaking did not stop. "Yo' sick?" he asked the dog. Moses fed the dog and let it stay on his back porch out of the dampness.

Moses kept thinking of what he had heard during the night when he went out to the toilet. His toilet was his pride and joy, a new one-holer, beaver board walls inside and painted a warm pink with turquoise trim. The outside was covered in new tar paper, to match his rental house. He rented from the Millers. "Good folks! Fine peoples!" Moses would always say about the Millers. He had worked on the orchard until he was taken with arthritis so badly, he could hardly get about.

Before midnight, Moses had taken his flashlight and headed for the toilet with a magazine article in mind. The kerosene lamp gave gentle warmth to the small room and a bright light to read by. He heard what he thought was a gunshot, but he was not sure. "I'll see about it in the morning," he thought to himself, as he shuffled along with his cane in hand.

After breakfast Moses Finley encouraged Old Dog to accompany him on the walk through the orchard to the Miller house. The walk would take a non-afflicted person fifteen minutes, but it would take Moses a little over thirty minutes, a walk he probably should not have taken due to his health, but he headed out anyway due to neighborly concern. The dog easily kept up with the old man. Moses was up in years, and in dog years they were probably close to the same age. The bluebirds darted about catching bugs in mid-air and on the leaves of the orchard's trees.

"Dat beez bluebuds!" Moses said to the dog, pointing with his cane. "Puddy 'lil buds," he said, as they moved along slowly.

Old Dog stopped at the edge of the yard and refused to go any farther. That alone gave Moses pause, but he continued onto the back porch. At that point he noticed the barn door was standing open.

"Miss Gertrude!" he called out, leaning on his cane. There was no reply. He went closer to the steps. "Miss Gertrude!" he called again, pumping on the bottom step with the base of his cane. It made a loud knocking sound. Moses stood still and listened. Still there was no reply. Moses held to the side of the house for balance and took one step at a time, his cane bumping once on every step. He continued to call out. "Miss Gertrude!"

The back door was open. "Miss Gertrude!" he called again. Moses was beginning to feel that something was not right. "Miss Gertrude," he said again, only softer this time. The old Negro's hair stood up on his neck. He realized something was not right. The screen door squeaked as he pulled it open. "Miss Gertrude, old Moses here, are you home?" he called out. The back door was ajar. He pushed it wide open with his cane and stepped into the short hallway. "Miss Gertrude! Liddle Polly Sue!" he called. The house was silent, not a sound was heard. The light in the small office was burning, as was the yellow bulb over the back porch door. That was a waste of current and the Millers were thrifty people, so that was not right. The old man's shoes shuffled a few steps into the hallway approaching the kitchen door. "Miss Gertrude," he whispered. He was growing more scared by the minute.

Moses Finley shuffled to the open kitchen door. "Miss Gertrude," he whispered again, hoping for a reply, but there was none. The next step took him to a horrid sight that he would never forget. Gertrude Miller and the baby lay in a pool of old blood in front of the kitchen sink. Moses stood horrified. He gasped for breath! The air was not there for his lungs! Moses grabbed his chest as he tried to turn around and get out of the house. His arthritic feet and legs could not move him fast enough. Moses began to yell and cry out as he got to the back porch. The old man screamed from the top of the steps. "Oh, God! Oh, God! Hope me Jesus! Lard God! Oh! Jesus! Help!" he cried in his weak and breaking voice. Oscar, some distance away, heard the old man's cries and knew something was wrong. The senior foreman grabbed a cane knife and started running for the house. Oscar was not a young man either, but he hurried along as Moses cried out, getting weaker and weaker.

Oscar finally made it into the yard and ran up on the old man down on his knees crying and screaming loudly. "What is it, Moses?" he asked, shaking the wailing man.

"Ins de house, oh, lawd, ins de house," he sobbed. Other orchard hands were arriving on the scene.

Oscar entered the house as Moses had done to find the horrid, terrible, bloody bodies of the beloved woman and the little Polly Sue. He ran back out and joined Moses in the yard.

"What is it?" called Billy Bishop, as he ran up.

"Call the law, call the law!" Oscar cried out. "Don't go in!"

Billy Bishop was a thin, strong, and younger man. He ran swiftly to the office, almost to the road. He was winded by the time he burst in on Mrs. Loretta. "Call tha law, sumthin' turrible at tha house," he said, bent down holding his hands on his knees. He was panting hard.

Mrs. Loretta looked at him trying to catch his breath, while she dialed for the operator.

"Operator!"

"Send tha law! Sumthin's happened at the Miller house at Miller's Orchards," she said excitedly.

"What's the trouble?" asked the operator.

"Sumthin's happened at the Miller house, it's terrible!" she repeated.

Ring, ring! Sounded the telephone. "Warm Springs Police Department. Secretary speaking."

"This is Paulette. A call came in about something terrible at the Miller house. That's the John Miller residence at Miller's Orchards on Cove Church Road."

"Any details?" the secretary asked.

"None! Just a horrified Negro woman," said Paulette.

"That's county, you know," the secretary said.

"I'm calling them next," said the operator.

"We'll start our unit in that direction!" assured the secretary.

It was a lucky day. The secretary looked outside and hoped to see a patrol officer or even a car. There was none to be seen. Then she ran to the back door and the detective was sitting under the shade of the old chinaberry tree working on her report from the entry that morning. Jasper Brown was rinsing his patrol car, where he had just washed it amid the brick making and laying on the new jail expansion.

"Got a call!" the secretary yelled loudly.

Heather began to fold her notes and tablet. Jasper looked pissed off and gut shot, over the hard work he had just put into cleaning his car. "Where's it at?" Heather yelled back.

"Cove Church Road! The John Miller place!" the woman yelled.

"Let's go!" Heather said, as she got in on the passenger side. Jasper jumped under the steering wheel.

"Best run with siren and lights 'till we get through town," Heather suggested. Jasper turned on the headlights. Heather turned on the police lights and the motor driven siren. It began to wind slowly, moaning its low mournful sound. It was at a full wail as the police car headed east. People on the sidewalks and in the streets stopped to watch as they passed. The chief was out of the city on a business meeting.

CHAPTER FOURTEEN

Officer Jasper Brown took every known shortcut to trim time off the trip to the John Miller house. The two had no idea as to what they were getting into. "Always expect the worst," someone had said, and they did. The shiny clean Model A Ford was gathering dust; it was sticking to every damp spot. The car gradually changed from green to a dusty reddish tan.

"What do ya think we're in for?" asked Jasper, working the gears to his advantage, taking second in tight curves and then going back into third.

Heather held on tightly as she was bounced about. "I have no idea, but if it's in progress we're too late!" she replied loudly. The sound of sand and small pebbles roared and knocked as they hit the underside of the body and running boards. Heather was doing her best to work the siren in the tight blind curves and at the intersections. As always, folks stopped to watch the patrol car go by, especially the children. There's something about the allure of a siren and a badge that makes young boys stop and wish. They could see the distant pecan trees across the vast flat land, and then smell the faint fragrance of peach blossoms. "How much farther?" Heather asked.

"We're there by land, but another mile by road," Jasper replied. "Bump it! Let 'em know we're close! Yer beginnin' ta grow on me. I'll be a spoiled boy before you leave." He smiled, cupping his right hand to his ear, gathering in the mournful tone. "Chief has urged in the past that we don't use the lights and siren. It seems to tell folks that the community ain't safe." He made the last turn before the short drive into the orchard up ahead.

"My sheriff said if you get over the speed limit goin' ta a call, you'd best have everything available on and running in case you hit a child or another car gets in yer way," Heather said, pulling her pistol and checking the chamber for a round. She felt sure there was a round in the chamber, but for a good feeling she checked again. Jasper saw once more that she was an outstanding female and had the true mindset of a survivor.

Jasper remembered a female in Muscogee County Sheriff's department, a matron, who had been retained for some unknown reason. Maybe she gave a good lay or oral sex. She could not handle her revolver well enough to qualify on a consistent basis. True, there were no State of Georgia standards, just those set by the sheriff himself. Jasper had attended their qualifying sessions, just for his own satisfaction. He too was a little slow, but damn sure better than the female.

Mrs. Loretta and Billy Bishop heard the distant siren and it brought relief to them, just in knowing the authorities were almost there. They felt that nothing else could happen with them on the scene. They ran from the office and stood in the sandy yard, ready to wave them down once the patrol car got in sight.

"Nice sign!" Heather said, looking at the advertising board for the orchards.

"Hold on!" Jasper barked, downshifting to second and taking the turn quickly. The light Ford slid in the deep sand. Billy Bishop's eyes grew large at seeing the car slide into the yard. Mrs. Loretta stood with her hands folded, changing her grip frequently, all from fear and nerves. Neither she nor Billy Bishop had been told what had happened.

Billy hurried to the car as it drew closer to where he stood in the yard. "Where's the house?" asked Jasper. Heather was already checking out the surroundings.

"Down a ways! Can we get a ride?" Billy Bishop asked. Upon hearing that, Mrs. Loretta pulled the door to and closed the old iron-bodied padlock.

"Meez toos!" she said.

"Stand on the running board!" Jasper replied, working back through the gears down to first. Mrs. Loretta and Billy Bishop clung to the door posts by way of the open windows. Bishop was sweaty and Mrs. Loretta smelled like snuff and honeysuckle perfume. Heather shut down all the emergency equipment and they rolled quietly into the yard.

All of the Millers' employees had gathered in the yard around Moses Finley, who was now sitting in a rickety wagon chair. Someone had given him a small glass of whiskey. Oscar stood next to Moses, the cane knife stuck in the soft ground at his feet.

"Watch the knife," Heather alerted.

"I see it," Jasper said calmly.

"Can we have only one person to tell us why we're here?" Jasper asked, as the two officers approached the large gathering of Negroes.

"Oscar, my name's Oscar. I'm senior employee here. I speak for us folks," he said, moving toward the officers.

"Detective Duncan! Officer Brown!" Heather said. She looked at all the Negroes for signs of weapons in their hands or on their persons.

"Is he all right?" Jasper asked.

"He be bothered about what we found," Oscar said.

Heather whispered, "Oh, shit! What is it?" she asked, looking down toward the open barn doors.

"It beez bad. I'll show you, but I ain't goin' in again," said Oscar, starting toward the house. Old Dog lay in the yard where he had abandoned Moses that morning.

"In the house?" Jasper asked.

"Yessa!" Oscar replied, walking ahead.

"You stop here and we'll go in," Heather said. Oscar gladly stopped.

"In de kitchen," he said, in a trembling voice.

The two officers went ahead. "We need to search the house first," Heather said, pulling her pistol at the bottom of the steps.

Just as Moses and Oscar had found it, the back door and screen door were open. The two officers saw the bloody scene in the kitchen, but pressed on to the remaining rooms in the house. They saw the shambled office room. The other rooms in the modest house were seemingly untouched.

"They've been there a while," Jasper said. "By the color of the blood," he added.

"Early last night, maybe," Heather added, as they went back to the kitchen. "Dog tracks," she pointed out. "Probably came in and found it."

The distant sound of a siren was heard. It was coming closer quickly. The Negroes in the yard moved about at the excitement of two police cars. Oscar also met the sheriff's car.

"Dey in de house," Oscar said to Sheriff Gilbert. He had driven hard all the way from Greenville.

"What they got?" asked the sheriff.

"Dead folks," said Oscar.

Sheriff Gilbert tossed his stubby wet cigar from his mouth and hurried inside. Heather and Jasper stood waiting for the officer. They were in hopes that it was a county unit. Sheriff Gilbert hurried into the kitchen. He abruptly stopped between the two Warm Springs officers and looked at the bodies.

"God damn o' mighty!" he said, with his hands on his hips. "Son of a bitch!" he added, moving about at a distance to get a better look.

"Talked ta anybody?" the sheriff asked.

Heather shook her head and replied, "No!" There was a second or two of silence. "I think the old man in the chair might have found them," she added.

"Let me use the telephone." He started toward the home office telephone. "Not this one. I guess there's another one in the office," said

Sheriff Gilbert as he stood in the hallway. "I'll call Troup County, he's got more equipment for this than I do," he said, walking off the porch.

"Where's tha telephone, boy?" the sheriff asked Oscar.

"My name's Oscar," he replied.

"My name's Louis," the sheriff replied. "Where's tha god damn telephone?"

"At the orchard office, you passed it comin' in," Oscar said.

"Sheriff, can I ride back?" Mrs. Loretta asked.

"Get in," Sheriff Gilbert said. "In tha back."

Mrs. Loretta moved her hand to the rear door handle and got in quickly. "Thank you," she said.

"Mrs. Miller and Polly Sue wuz found dead this mornin' by Mr. Moses," Oscar said. "We mus' do our jobs, things will work out," he added. "Go back to your jobs, see me at the office quarter before quittin' time. Remember! I sez when id's quittin' time."

There was the loud sound of shock at hearing the bad news. Questions were asked. "They wuz found dead in the kitchen, looks like dey wuz beats ta deaf," Oscar said. Moses Finley began to cry out loud. Several of the women employees sobbed. "Dat's all we knows. Git on backs ta work, git on now!" Oscar said, waving his hands about.

Heather and Jasper had gone back out into the yard. "I'll talk to the old man," Heather said, pulling out her tablet. "I'm glad you sent them away," she said to Oscar.

The two officers began to interview the witnesses. Heather talked to the old man and Jasper spoke to Oscar.

"Sir! I'm Detective Duncan, specially assigned to assist the Meriwether County Sheriff's Department. How are you?" Heather asked, standing a few feet in front of the man.

"Not so goods," he replied, looking down.

"Do you need a doctor?" she asked.

"I beez fine adder while," he mumbled.

"I need to know what you heard and what you saw," she said, holding her small tablet and pencil, ready to write. "Why did you come down here?" she asked.

"I wuz checkin' on Miss Gertrude," replied Moses. He wiped a tear away with his sleeve.

"Do you normally check on the Millers?" she asked.

"I had gone out to the toilet 'foe midnights and I thawd I hud a gunshot," Moses said.

"Just once?" Heather asked.

"Just once," Moses replied. "I sez ta myselves, I sees 'bout dat in da' mawnin'. Nest mawnin' de old dawg is at my house. He's actin' skittish. Weez walks down together. I'ze calls out fer Miss Gertrude over and over, bud she don'ts answer," he said, looking at the back porch.

"Then what?" Heather asked.

"Olds Dawg, he stops right yonder," Moses said, pointing to the dog lying in the edge of the yard. "Dat old dawg knows who dun' it," he said mournfully, followed by a deep sigh. "I'ze seen de house barn do' open, bud I'ze goes in de house," Moses said, moving his fingers about, his hands beginning to tremble.

"Did you go anywhere other than the kitchen and the hallway?" Heather asked, writing quickly.

"Alls I coulds do ta get up de steps, my old body done gives out, bud I gits on de poach. De screens do' is unlocked and de backs do' is open. I'ze calls out agin and no answa', so I'ze goes in steel callins' outs. No answas. I seez dem in de flo'. I wuz skeered and I hurried outs hollering fer hope," said Moses. He was growing more visibly upset. Heather stopped questioning and gently touched his shoulder.

Jasper Brown questioned Oscar. "What did you see?"

"I was in the orchard when I heard Moses yellin' for help. I grabbed my cane knife and come a runnin'," Oscar said. "Moses was about there in the yard, on the ground cryin' out. He told me ta go in the house. I found Miss Gertrude and the little baby on the floor in the pool of blood," said Oscar.

"Anyone else go in?" Jasper asked.

"No, but Billy Bishop ran up to me and I told him to go call for y'all," said Oscar.

Sheriff Louis Gilbert returned from using the telephone. His car slid to a stop. The angry sheriff slammed the car door. "They can't help us!" he barked loudly. "Can we do it?" he asked Heather.

"You don't have anyone on the force that can do it?" she asked.

The sheriff stood with his hands tucked in his hip pockets, another cigar in his mouth. "No!" he replied, kicking the dirt.

"Thank you," Jasper said to Oscar. "I'm cuttin' him loose," he said, looking at Heather, and then the sheriff. They both agreed to release him.

"Sir, Mr. Finley, would you recognize that gunshot if you heard it again?" Heather asked.

"I sho' would," he replied.

"Thank you," said Heather.

"I've got a crime kit, what little it is, some distilled water, cotton swabs, tweezers, and such," said the sheriff. "I think there's even some small sealed sterile collection bottles, and some envelopes. There's a print kit too! Y'all got a camera?"

Jasper answered before Heather got the chance. "I've got a box Kodak in my car, only the film that's in it."

"I have a print kit too," Heather added.

No one had checked out the house barn. "Sheriff? Will you check out the barn?" Heather asked. She wanted to get him out of the way for a moment or two.

"I'll be glad to, Detective!" He pointed his wet cigar at her. Sheriff Gilbert headed toward the open door with his revolver in his hand. "I hope there's some son of a bitch in there! I'm goin' ta shoot hell out of 'em!" he said loudly, as he walked away. Moses sat looking at the sheriff and wondered if he really meant what he said.

"Mr. Finley, I'll ask that you go with the sheriff back to Greenville and be seen by their doctor. I want his opinion of you. Then the sheriff will have you to give a written statement," Heather said.

"Yessum."

Sheriff Gilbert entered the barn and was unable to find anyone hiding. He noticed the kerosene and gasoline cans that had been moved around. There was a circle left behind where the five gallon can had been removed. The stall where the Maxwell had been stored was empty except for the tarpaulin that had covered it. At the time they did not know what type of vehicle was stolen.

Heather pulled Jasper aside, out of the hearing range of Moses. "We can do this scene. Will you help me, by just doing what I ask?"

Jasper looked surprised. "Certainly. Can we?"

"We'll be slow, but as good as anyone close that would show up," she replied.

Jasper smiled. "All right."

"Not a damn thing, Detective! A vehicle of some kind is gone, and a five gallon can of gasoline, or at least one was moved and I didn't see it anywhere," reported the sheriff, wallowing his cigar around in the corner of his mouth.

Heather stepped closer to the sheriff. "Sheriff, you asked me to work this case," she said, looking him in the eye.

"I did!" he replied, somewhat shocked by her approach.

"I need someone to take Mr. Finley to a qualified doctor for their opinion on his mental health, and then I need a written statement. I think it would be best if someone wrote it as he tells it," Heather said. "He'll need to be brought back home and I don't think he's had any food today," she added.

"I can handle that," the sheriff replied.

"Thank you."

"Mr. Finley, come with me. Let's me and you go eat, and then see Doc Hubbard. We need a statement from you," the sheriff said loudly.

"My ears ain't deaf," said Moses, as he struggled to his feet.

Sheriff Gilbert left the equipment that he had and the two men drove out of sight. The sheriff was behind the steering wheel and the small Negro man was barely visible above the seat on the passenger side.

"Put these on when you touch anything," Heather said, handing Jasper a pair of cotton gloves. "Give me yer camera and then go see if you can feed Old Dog." Detective Duncan gathered the kits they had assembled between the two agencies and placed them on the chair where Moses had sat. Jasper soon returned from feeding Old Dog. The officer had found a stash of canned dog food on the back porch. Heather watched the lonely dog whine and wag its tail as Jasper dumped the food on the green grass.

"First I want to photograph it," Heather said. She held out the camera to him. "Get a picture so we will know in later years this was the John Miller house." Jasper moved about composing his photograph.

"Make one of the back steps and the porch, then if light allows, we'll make the next one of the open doors into the hallway. I'll hold the screen open with something; we want to see inside. Shit!" Heather said loudly.

Jasper jumped. "What's wrong?"

"These bodies need to be removed, and given the time it'll take to get anyone out here, we need to call now. Can I have the car? I'll go to the telephone at the orchard office and call the Sheriff's Department, maybe the secretary can get someone started," Heather said, holding her hand out for the keys.

"And leave me here?" Jasper asked, looking surprised.

"Stand at the porch steps. I won't be long."

Heather left for the orchard office while Jasper stood guard over the bodies. He sat on the top step and eventually Old Dog came over and joined him. The dog placed his head on the officer's thigh and sighed.

"I didn't know dogs sighed," said Jasper, petting the dog's head.

Mrs. Loretta heard the patrol car coming and went to the door to see who it was. Heather stopped the car and hurried toward the door. "I need a telephone!" she called out.

"Right here!" Mrs. Loretta said, holding the screen door open. Billy Bishop was sitting inside, sharpening pruning tools with a smooth cut file. Mrs. Loretta pointed to the telephone.

"Thanks!" said Heather, snatching the handset from the brass yoke. Click! Click!

"Operator!" a voice said.

"Get me Sheriff Gilbert's office," Heather said. "And clear the line!"

There were a considerable number of switching sounds before the phone rang on the other end. It was most likely being routed through the Warm Springs station.

"Sheriff's Office! Dixie speaking!"

"Ma'am, this is Detective Duncan with Warm Springs. The sheriff's been gone a few minutes and we forgot to request that he get someone started to get these bodies," she said.

"Bodies!" snapped Dixie.

"Yes, ma'am, two of them. One adult female and one infant female," Heather said.

Mrs. Loretta wailed, broke into tears, and ran out of the office into the yard.

"Myself and Officer Brown are working the scene and will be finished in an hour or so, but someone needs to come on, they are getting worse by the minute," she whispered.

"I'll call Michael Cargile's Mortuary at No. 4 Terrell Street. We've used them in the past," Dixie replied.

"No, I mean to get an autopsy done, before they are released to the funeral home," Heather clarified.

"That will be Dr. Hubbard in conjunction with Michael Cargile's funeral home. Dr. Hubbard does them for us at the funeral home, as they have cold storage. Dr. Hubbard is the coroner.

"The sheriff is on the way with an old man who needs to be evaluated, and then have his statement taken. I kinda suggested a person of your ability," Heather said.

Dixie sighed. "All right."

"We've got a lot to do, please get them started," Heather urged.

Jasper was glad to see Heather when she arrived, this time parking closer to the back door. "I see you found a friend." She smiled as the old dog raised its head and looked at her. "Let's get started. The kitchen first," she said, donning her cotton gloves. Jasper hurried behind her, picking up his Kodak from the porch.

There was a bloody presence in the stuffy air, a smell one does not forget. "Make one from the door, right there." Heather pointed. "Then one from as high up lookin' down as you can." That one was a little tricky. Jasper ended up on a chair next to the Monitor refrigerator, leaning over the warm coils.

"What's it look like?" Heather asked, standing out of camera range.

"Like two dead people on the floor," Jasper answered, as he balanced precariously to compose the photograph.

"Now we need to do it from the other side, showing their faces," Heather instructed.

Jasper moved the kitchen chair to the other side. "Here, you do it. I can't, it's bad," he said, holding the camera out to Heather.

"Oh!" said Heather, taking the camera from him. "You just can't stop because you don't like to look at the dead," she said, stepping onto the chair. She composed the photograph. "If James Lee jumps out and says boo what are ya goin' to do?"

"I plan ta say bang!" Jasper replied, looking into the hallway. "I would like ta shoot tha sum bitch." He was standing with his back turned to her.

"Get the cotton swabs and a small bottle, make it two." Heather motioned with her hand for him to hurry. She had already noticed a fly. She carefully took samples from each of the bodies, using the swab to gather the coagulated blood. "There," she said, tightening the lids. There was one bottle for each victim. "Put them in the refrigerator." She handed the bottles to Jasper.

"Here, take this fire poker. It's bloody and was most likely used to beat them with," said Heather. "It certainly needs to dry before it's stored in evidence. Give me another bottle and a swab, I'll get blood samples from it too." Heather placed it on the table and gently took samples where the blood appeared to be the thickest. "Refrigerator!" she said, handing the bottle to Jasper. "Take a tag from the kit, fill it out and tie it to the end." Heather pointed to the poker. "Blood, poker, photographs," she said aloud, then stood thinking. "Fingerprints! Hand me the soft feather brush and the black powder." Heather began to dust for prints. "Oh! Film left?" she asked.

Jasper looked at the count through the small enlarging lens on the back of the camera. "Four!" he said.

"Make some of the office, from the room going in, and then the rest inside, desk, drawers, you know, but don't touch," she said, continuing to dust. The light black haze of the carbon-based dust clouded around the objects she explored. The use of the flashlight was futile, as it was not bright enough to make a difference. Heather stood at the kitchen door that led to the hallway. Her eager eyes explored the possibilities of anything whoever did this might have touched. She saw dirt under the chair that was pushed back from the far end of the table. "Why would it be where it is?" she asked herself. "The shot! The bastard shot from there!" she said to herself.

"Ya say something?" Jasper asked from the office.

"Thinking out loud," she replied. She dusted the table top in the area where the chair would have been if someone was sitting at the table. The brush gently moved about in a swirling motion, clockwise and then counterclockwise. A left hand print appeared. Heather was excited. "I've got a set of four prints!" she yelled out. Jasper hurried from the office to look. He had used all of the film anyway.

"If Moses heard a shot, then there must be a bullet in Mrs. Miller. I missed it," she said, looking over at the stiffening woman. "You don't make a lot of sense, she's face down," Heather said to Jasper.

"I heard a car!" Jasper said, standing tall and listening.

"You lucky bastard! It must be the doctor," said Heather, listening. They heard a car door close and footsteps on the back steps, then on the porch.

"Hello!" A man's voice called out. Heather motioned for Jasper to see who it was.

"Yes, sir!" Jasper said, looking at the man.

"Dr. Augustus Hubbard, the Sheriff's Department sent me."

"In here!" Heather called out.

The doctor followed Jasper into the kitchen. "My!" said Dr. Hubbard, looking down at the two bodies. "Several hours ago, I'd say."

"We have a time frame. I'd like to see what you come up with on the autopsy," Heather said. "I was just in need of turning her over," she added.

Dr. Hubbard took rubber gloves from his bag and worked his hands down into them. "Now!" he said. "Let's turn her over. Who is she?" he asked, as they rolled the woman over.

"Gertrude Miller. The child is Polly Sue, about a year old, maybe a few months past, but not much," Heather said. The woman was rigid. Her eyes were open, looking into nowhere.

Dr. Hubbard took over with his examination there in the kitchen. He ran his gloved hands over the woman's torso. "They say the eyes are the path to a person's soul. I've always wondered if the brain records the last thing they saw." The doctor rolled Gertrude back over. His hands stopped on the bloody spot and he tore the cotton dress away at the small hole in the fabric. Jasper jumped at the sudden ripping of the fabric. Dr. Hubbard's finger quickly found the bullet hole. "Looks ta be a thirty-eight, too small for a forty-five and too large for the tinky shit; twenty-fives, twenty-twos, or even a thirty-two," he said, exploring the area with his finger. "It damn sure didn't come out," he added. "You're not squeamish, are you?" he asked Heather.

"No, I'm all right. It has to be done," she said, not having dealt with death before, not in this forte', anyway.

"Officer Brown! Would you care to wait outside and bring in the ambulance crew when they get here?" asked the doctor.

"I'm sure he'd like that," replied Heather, before Jasper could answer.

"That's what I need to do," Jasper said. He hurried out of the kitchen.

"Her husband passed several days ago," Heather said, helping the doctor roll Gertrude over again.

"This is the hard part," Doc Hubbard said. A tear rolled down his cheek and dropped into the drying pool of blood that covered the kitchen floor in front of the sink cabinet. "God damn! I'd kill tha bastard that did this," he said, wiping the tears on the shoulder of his white shirt. "God damn!" he said again, shaking his head in disbelief.

"I think it's the escapee, James Lee," Heather said. "He's got ta be caught! Damn, this is a killing spree!" she said, standing over the doctor as he examined the child. Her small body was rigid. "If I could, I need to be trying to get some prints," she said softly.

"I've got this," he said. "Any sexual assault on either will be looked at in the lab," he said.

"I would expect that," Heather said. She had removed her bloody gloves and taken on another pair.

Heather did not dust the refrigerator because there had to be many prints, and overlapping ones at that. The small office was in shambles. Several of the drawers had been thrown against the wall so hard they had come apart on impact and lay in pieces. The contents were strewn from one wall to the next. Heather dusted the edge of the varnished wood desk in hopes of finding more prints, but there were none. One by one she picked up the drawers and dusted them, but they too revealed nothing. The eager woman stood and looked down at the mess, thinking of what she had to that point: An old man and an old dog that were alerted between maybe nine o'clock and midnight by a single gunshot. Four good prints from the edge of the kitchen table. Blood samples for typing to the victims. The bullet in the body, most likely a thirty-eight, and a bloody fire poker.

Dr. Hubbard had walked up behind her. "Are you all right?" he asked. Heather jumped as his voice brought from her trancelike spell.

"Oh!" she said. "I was just thinking of what we have to work with." She put the lid back on the wide-mouthed jar of powder.

"I believe the bullet tumbled, turned, and passed through her lung, then struck her heart, maybe the edge. Not sudden death, but a slow bleed out. She most likely saw the child die," he said. He looked down for a moment and wiped a tear with his sleeve.

"Damn!" Heather said, stepping toward him, needing to pass into the hallway. Suddenly the screen door loomed in her sight as an additional place to dust. There the detective was able to find a partial palm print.

Jasper saw the ambulance coming and hurried up the back steps. "They're here!" he called out, not entering the house.

"Bring 'em in!" shouted Dr. Hubbard. He walked down the hallway to the kitchen door. Looking in, again, he shook his head in disgust.

The heavy-built hearse came quietly into the yard. Jasper motioned for them to back up to the steps. Two well-suited men emerged and opened the rear door, sliding out a rolling gurney.

"Best get two rubber blankets, one woman and a little girl," Jasper said, as he stood on the edge of the bottom step.

Dr. Hubbard looked at Heather. "Give me until this time tomorrow. I'll do my best," he said, moving aside for the transporting crew.

"I want everything you can do. Can you do blood type?" Heather asked. He nodded his head, "Yes."

"I have three blood samples in the refrigerator. You want them now or later?"

"Now is fine, with a chain of custody sheet," said the doctor.

Heather went to the back door. "I need a chain of custody sheet," she said to Jasper.

Jasper turned and looked puzzled. "Uh, what?"

"I need a chain of custody sheet," she repeated.

"I've never seen one," he replied, still looking puzzled, as if he should have known something and missed it somewhere along the way. He shrugged his shoulders.

"Shit!" Heather said, turning back into the house. "We ain't got a form like that. Can we do some kind of letter of receipt?" she asked the doctor.

"This is a little deep for me too. I'll take it and these gentlemen can sign as witnesses," he suggested. The problem was solved with a sheet of tablet paper and a carbon.

Later that afternoon as the two Warm Springs officers rode back to the police department, Jasper was silent, visibly affected by the bloody scene. Heather shook her head at herself now, looking back on all the print powder and time she had wasted, not having a way to photograph the latent prints found on the table or the door. She shook her head in disbelief.

* * *

"Frances, have you heard or seen the officers today?" asked Chief Hawthorn, as he hung his hat before taking a seat at his desk.

"They are at the Miller house," she said, looking up from her alphabetizing of papers to be filed.

"Where?" he asked, arching his eyebrows with a puzzled look.

"Operator called several hours ago and I sent them down, since they were closer than the county. It's the John Miller place, the house in the orchards down toward Manchester and Chalybeate Springs," Frances replied.

"Do you know anything about it?" asked the chief.

"Some Negro woman was screaming to get the law, something terrible had happened," she said. "That's all I know. I hope I did right."

Chief Hawthorn stood up. "Maybe I should go down," he said, looking at the clock. He jingled his keys. "How long, do ya think?" he asked.

"I'd think the county took it over. They should be back, I would think," replied Frances, her fingers hesitating between sheets.

"I'll call Miss Dixie," said the chief, going to the telephone.

Sheriff Gilbert answered the telephone. "Sheriff's Office!"

"Sheriff! Where's my officers?" asked the chief.

"On a call at the Miller place, south end of the county. Good thing they went. Just right for the detective," said the sheriff.

"What was it?" asked the chief.

"Double murder!" snapped Sheriff Gilbert. "Bloody too!"

"Damn!" replied Chief Hawthorn.

"Gertrude Miller and the little girl, Polly Sue," the sheriff said, taking the wet cigar from his cheek. Curley and Dixie were listening. "I called the newspaper, they should be at your place 'fore long," he added.

"Thanks!" said the chief. "What's yer thoughts?" he asked.

"Maybe the work of the sum bitch we're all lookin' for," replied Sheriff Gilbert. "Just can't tell. But I'm confident yer two can handle it," he barked.

"I'll stay here and wait on the newspaper," the chief said.

"The young guy, Alfred Huffman," said the sheriff. "I've got Negro Moses Finley, a neighbor that said he heard a single gunshot when he was walkin' to tha toilet. I'm gettin' him evaluated and then Miss Dixie's takin' a statement. It's goin' ta be a long day. That was at the suggestion of your detective, and that was a good one. Me and Moses, we're goin' ta eat somethin' before Miss Jewel gets gone. I asked him if there's anything he couldn't eat. He said anythin' thad don't eats him fuss." The sheriff chuckled.

* * *

The loud closing of the lobby door startled Frances and Chief Hawthorn as they were working silently in the staff office. It was Alfred Huffman. The young man smiled and waved as he continued toward the locked staff room door. Chief Hawthorn watched. "See how hard he pushes on the door," he said, looking down at his desk. The eager reporter did as the chief expected and almost ran his nose into the glass from stopping so quickly. The chief smiled and let the man in. "Well, yer back!" he said, turning his back and returning to his desk.

"I'm here for the story on the Miller murders," he said. "Sheriff Gilbert sent me down, said it was your officers that worked it under the mutual agreement. What happened?" he asked, pulling up a chair.

The chief continued his work, never looking up. "My detective and Officer Brown will be here soon," he said.

Jasper turned the Ford north toward the main street. "Shit! There's the newspaper guy!" he said. Heather looked at the department, and sure enough there was Huffman's car, a newspaper car. He had suddenly been allowed to drive a company car by "old souse meat".

Heather gave a loud sigh as Jasper stopped the car. "I'll tell the chief what the newspaper should know, and the case details later, after he's gone," she said, as she got out. Buddy Cotton saw Heather down the street and stood watching to give her a wave. She responded, making him smile. "Do you know Buddy Cotton?" Heather asked Jasper, as they were gathering what little evidence they had from the scene.

"I know they are a poor hard-hit family, just like a lot of folks, but not as bad as some others," he said, following her to the door. "I heard that Giles & Eiseman Grocery are holding a food shoot," Jasper said, trying to hold the door for Heather.

"A food shoot?" she asked.

The two managed to get inside before Mayor Cunningham saw them.

"Like a turkey shoot, they have it every year this time. Old Giles puts a new No. 2 pencil eraser on an ink pad and touches it to an index card, near dead center, hangs it at a distance Eiseman paces off, about seven yards. The person who shoots it out, with one shot for a dollar, wins," Jasper said. "That's a rifle round, whatever caliber ya bring." They were now at the staff room door.

Alfred Huffman stood and greeted the detective. He was all smiles after his success from the combined articles. "My boss was pleased with my coverage!" he said to the detective.

"I'm glad," she replied. "Leave for a few minutes, we'll come out for you. I promise," Heather said. The chief had stopped his work once he saw them coming in. He seemed to be pleased at her telling the reporter to leave.

Jasper put his Kodak on the chief's desk, along with the bloody fire poker. Heather spoke up. "You already know there was a double homicide at the John Miller place, the huge pecan and peach orchards close to Manchester. Gertrude Miller and the infant girl, Polly Sue. Moses Finley found them dead in the kitchen this morning. A car is gone, and we think a five gallon can of gasoline. We can't account for anything else." Heather grinned. "Like a fool, I dusted for prints. I did give blood samples to Dr. Hubbard. I hope he can at least type the blood. There's a poker used to beat them with, and the woman was shot once, most likely a .38, so believes me and Doc Hubbard."

"Yes, we can't photograph them with our budget, no one else except maybe Atlanta or one of those larger cities, well, maybe Columbus," said the chief. "It made the scene look worked anyway," he said, taking his seat.

"Jasper! Frances! Get together and check the tag office in Greenville for whatever vehicles John Miller owned. Hurry before they close. When you do get them, keep them there until they give us what we need. Pull Sheriff Gilbert's name if ya have to," said the chief. Jasper joined Frances.

"I plan to tell Huffman as little as possible, for right now," Heather said. "Please listen," she added.

In a few minutes Huffman stood making notes for another article. He listened to the detective, in a deep stare. "On today's date, during the mid-morning hours, the bodies of two people were discovered at the John Miller residence," she said. "You can find out the correct address." Huffman shook his head. "They were bludgeoned to death. The deceased adult was Gertrude Miller, mid to late thirty years of age. The infant Polly Sue, less than 16 months," Heather said. "You can go down and make a photograph of the outside, if you like." Heather looked at Chief Hawthorn. "Anything to add?"

"No, I believe you've covered it well," he said. "Sheriff Gilbert knows yer here, he sent you, so don't play us against one another," he warned

Huffman.

"Oh, no sir!" Huffman said. "Thank you! Detective, Chief. Thank you. Got a deadline!" He hurried to the door, waving and leaving the lobby.

"Now, tell me the rest," said Chief Hawthorn.

"We think that maybe between 9:30 and 11:00 p.m. Moses Finley, a neighbor, was on the way to the toilet outside when he heard one gunshot. He thought it came from the Miller place. He rents from them. Being in the shape he's in, he said to himself that he'd see about Mrs. Miller in the morning. He found the screen door unlocked and the back door ajar. He found them in the kitchen floor dead. The woman was shot once in the shoulder blade with a .38, and the child was beaten to death. Both were beaten with this fire poker," she said, pointing to the tagged object on the desk. "There's a vehicle gone, maybe five gallons of gasoline. Maybe money, we don't know, but the small office was destroyed, trashed," Heather said. The chief motioned for her to take a seat beside his desk.

"Do you ever see the chief in Greenville, or a police car?" he asked.

Heather replied promptly. "No! Not on the street anyway, parked in front of their office," she said, occupying her hand with the twirling of a pencil. "I've wondered why."

Chief Hawthorn walked about the office looking into the dark lobby. "It's all political. All political," he sighed. "What's next?" he asked, turning to her.

"Before this night is over, I'd like to see if Moses Finley can tell the difference in gunshots. Maybe if he can hear several of different calibers, he could narrow it down for us. Maybe we can tie it to James Lee on suspicion anyway," said Heather.

The chief took his seat. "What do you need?" he asked. Jasper and Frances had the tag office on the telephone line.

Frances covered the mouthpiece. "They ain't happy," she said to Chief Hawthorn.

"I don't give a damn about their happiness! We need answers!" he said. "Y'all are doing a good job, don't let them hang up before you get what we've asked for," he said, pointing his finger at both of them.

"I need a .32 revolver and -- well, that's it, other than two bags of sand," Heather said to the chief.

"Two bags of sand?" he asked, arching his brow.

"I'll put them in the hearth, in the kitchen, and shoot into them with a .32, my .38, and then the .45," she said. "I need to borrow a .32," she said.

Jasper was listening. "I've got a .32," he said to Heather.

"You need to keep it on yourself," she replied. "I'll try to borrow one."

"We've got an extra one here somewhere," replied Chief Hawthorn, as he began pulling open his desk drawers. After opening a couple of drawers and rifling through them, he found the extra revolver. "Here it is!" he said, laying it on the desk. He continued to rifle through the same drawer. "Here's a box of ammunition." He brought it to the desk top.

Heather took the revolver and swung the cylinder out. It was empty. "Now for the two sandbags."

"I think we can get some of the bricklayers to accommodate us on that," said the chief. "Jasper, go out back and see if the bricklayers can put two bags of sand in yer car," he said. Jasper welcomed the chance to leave, as about all he was doing was sitting next to Frances and listening to her conversation.

"Let me call the sheriff," said Chief Hawthorn, walking to the occupied telephone. "Shit!" he mumbled. "I'll go down to the mayor's office." The chief stopped short of the staff room door. "Y'all come in late tomorrow, maybe ten o'clock, since you'll be working overtime," he said, smiling at Heather. He left the room and disappeared down the sidewalk.

"Hold on!" Frances said, getting her pencil. "Go ahead." She started writing. "3, 2, 1, dash, 6, 8, 9. 321-689! And that's on a black 1925 Maxwell owned by John Miller?" Frances asked.

"That's correct. Do you want the other vehicles?" asked the woman at the tag office.

"No, this is all that's missing. Thanks!" said Frances, hanging up the telephone. "5:26, I'll bet they're happy," she said sarcastically. "Here!" Frances held out the piece of tablet paper to Heather.

"Thanks!" Heather replied, folding the paper and placing it in her pocket.

Chief Hawthorn had managed to contact Sheriff Gilbert as they were finishing the statement by Moses Finley. Miss Dixie had done a remarkable job on her shorthand and translation of his words. She read the statement back to the old man. He agreed with what he heard and made his mark, witnessed by Miss Dixie, Sheriff Gilbert, and jailer Curley Jones. Sheriff Gilbert sent Curley to the café on the square and brought back a plate of food for the old man. Moses ate his meal in the kitchen in the company of Miss Jewel, who was busy with the prisoner meals. She always enjoyed someone to talk to. It was almost dark when the sheriff brought Moses into Warm Springs. Chief Hawthorn and his two officers, Jasper and Heather, caravanned to the Miller place, where they set up the test.

The two commanding officers, Sheriff Gilbert and Chief Hawthorn, took Moses home and stood in the side yard awaiting the signal from Jasper. They could just barely see the light from the Miller house. The brown crickets serenaded and the small shrubbery loving frogs joined in the evening sing. The two heavy sand bags were wrestled into place in the cold fireplace of the bloody kitchen. The night was dark, very dark. Clouds had filled the night skies. Old Dog was on the steps of old Moses' place. Jasper and Heather carefully moved the kitchen table from its usual place in order for Heather to have a clear shot at the stacked sand bags.

"I'm ready," Heather said to Jasper.

"I'll sound my whistle long and loud, then I'll call out to you and you can start," he said, as he stood at the back door.

"The first will be the .32, then I'll go up," Heather said, holding the revolver furnished by the chief. Jasper hurried down the back steps and stood at the bottom. In the pitch blackness he touched the whistle to his lips, took a deep breath and blew. The shrill of the pea whistle could be heard by all three men at the Finley place.

"Listen to all of them, then tell us which one it was," said the sheriff.

"There'll be three," added Chief Hawthorn. Old Dog had wandered over and sat among the men.

Detective Duncan plugged her ears with cotton from her satchel. The cotton had been brought all the way from home. It was from an aspirin bottle. The single lightbulb swung ever so slightly in the center of the kitchen. "Here goes!" she cried out to Jasper.

"Let 'er rip!" he called back.

Heather raised the small framed revolver and aimed it at the sand bags. She squeezed the trigger and boom! A single round was dispensed into the sandbags. The revolver was placed on the table and she pulled her .38 Special and did the same. Boom! Sand flashed from the hole made in the cotton bag and dusted the nearby area. The single hanging lightbulb swayed. Jasper noticed that it changed the shadows on the window shade and there was silence as the crickets and frogs stopped their socializing. Moses stood listening. The last round was the big .45. When it was fired, the sand blew back on Heather, stinging her face even at a distance of eight or so feet.

Jasper hurried back into the kitchen. "They sounded pretty loud," he exclaimed, smiling. "But that forty-five was awesome!" He looked at the bullet holes in the bag, all close together. "Do I clean up?" he asked.

Heather shook her head, "Nah! Someone will have a hell of a job ridding this place of the blood. A little sand won't matter."

"Did you recognize any of those?" asked Chief Hawthorn.

"Beez de second one," said Moses, nodding his head. "Beez de second one," he repeated. "Sho' nuff!"

"Can we help you into the house?" asked the sheriff.

"Woods ya see if deys ain'ts nobodies in there?" asked the old Negro.

"We sure can!" said Chief Hawthorn. "Where's the first light?" he asked.

"Insides de' do' on de' right, a string to de' hangin' bulb," said Moses.

Chief Hawthorn pulled his revolver, went up the back steps, and pulled the light on. He quickly searched the small house. There was no one inside.

After seeing Moses safely into his place, the sheriff and the chief drove down to the Miller house where the two officers were waiting. "So, what's this tell us?" asked the sheriff.

"Which one did he identify?" Heather asked, standing out in the yard.

Chief Hawthorn went inside and looked at the scene. He had not seen it before. He was visibly shaken by the bloody kitchen.

"He said it was the second one," answered Sheriff Gilbert.

"Did the sheriff in Troup say a thirty-eight was stolen from the store in Hambyville?" she asked, knowing the answer.

"Yes, he did!" said Sheriff Gilbert. "I believe a .38 blue steel, break top."

"In my mind, that gives me belief that the person who stole the revolver in Hambyville ties to this. And we know that person was James Lee," she said, as the chief walked up.

"I'm tired. That's good logic," said the sheriff. "God damn! Two more killed by the sum bitch!" he said, kicking the tire on his car.

"We found out that the person who killed these two also took a black 1925 Maxwell. The tag number is," she pulled the note from her pocket. "321-689!"

The law men and Heather stood around the cars talking quietly as the night grew even darker. They discussed ways of trying to catch the killer.

"I'd like for someone to get in the office and try to find out if James Lee was ever hired here, even for a day," Heather said.

"Can Frances do that?" Chief Hawthorn asked.

"Hell! Miss Dixie can take some books too!" barked Sheriff Gilbert.

"All they're doing is looking for a name," Heather replied. "On the ledgers and in the pay book."

"There were only two filing cabinets. Let's manhandle the son of a bitches out and each agency take one," suggested the sheriff.

That night the sheriff's back seat carried a filing cabinet, as did Chief Hawthorn's. The two women in their respective offices would busy themselves searching the records first thing the next morning.

Moses Finley had been a deacon of the Pilgrim's Rest U.N.M.C. until his age and declining health took away his ability to attend regularly and be active in the Negro community with visitations and such. The church had all but forgotten about him except for the usual Christmas basket of canned foods and commercial candies the week before Christmas. The old associates at the orchard did check on him daily, if nothing but a shout from their work nearby and a friendly wave. After the discovery of Gertrude and Polly Sue Miller, his aging hastened. He never recovered from the traumatic experience. He frequently sobbed over their loss.

CHAPTER FIFTEEN

James Lee had left the Miller residence in the stolen Maxwell that belonged to John Miller. He was bold and drove with the headlights on. He was a Negro and so was John Miller. If he was seen in the car, he had only to be courteous and reply with a hand wave in passing. Lee's face and body were covered with the spattered blood of the victims. The blood on his hands was drying and becoming sticky. It had transferred to the car handle and the steering wheel.

Lee had left the large orchard and taken the Cove Church Road northeast toward Woodbury. This took him to downtown Woodbury, where it intersected with Warm Springs-Woodbury Road. The wanted mad man now traveled in the safety of darkness to the small community of Cedar Rock. The hours were dwindling and daylight was coming soon. The dried blood on his face now felt like dried egg, making his skin feel tight. James Lee could not see the amount of blood on him, but no matter how little or how much, he wanted to get it off. At this point in time he was unsure of his location, but could see that he was heading in the right direction, west toward Alabama.

The bright headlights soon shone upon the black and white hand-lettered sign of the Cane Creek Baptist Church, isolated and surrounded by thick woods. Lee slowed down to investigate. The Maxwell was running warmer than it should, but he had pushed the car for all it was worth. Whenever possible, the speedometer was pegged. The manufacturer boasted a speed of fifty-eight miles per hour.

James Lee was pleased with his findings and the ability of the dense brush to hide the stolen car. He backed the boxy black Maxwell into the thick brush. Lee forced the door open in order to get out of the car. By the light of the moon and stars, he saw what appeared to be a springhouse or a baptismal pool. The skittish man investigated in the darkness. Every snap of a twig in the woods caused him alarm, even the ones broken under his own foot. "Damn, nigger! Whad yous so jumpy 'bout?" he said aloud, approaching the water. It was a baptizing pool after all, concrete block steps leading up on the outside and then down into the clear running water. Lee timidly touched the mirror surface of the water. It was warm from the bright sunlight, and tempting. "Lawd! Whad a blessin'."

In the darkness James Lee stripped naked, walked boldly up the steps, and then down into the sacred waters, where many had professed their life to Christ. As he descended the water covered steps, the dried blood was lifted and laced from his dark skin in crimson swirls. The felon, now cleansed of blood, slept peacefully in the back seat of the Maxwell hidden at the rear of the Cane Creek Baptist Church. He was relatively clean and comfortable, well-fed with the box of groceries from the Hambyville store. He had money in his pocket and an extra five gallons of gasoline. The tank was almost full and with the reserve he could make it to Alabama. The morning sun rose with its golden rays touching the bountiful earth. A curious gray squirrel explored for an early meal, digging about in the edge of the church yard, while the yellow finch and Carolina wrens serenaded.

* * *

The Miller Orchard was closed due to lack of management and for the mourning of the tragic deaths of the entire Miller family, first John Miller, and then his wife Gertrude and infant Polly Sue. Oscar and Miss Loretta would take over the business until further notification, by order of the courts, in months to come. Many continued to work out of loyalty and habit. The orchard business had gone into "cash only" terms for worker survival. The Negro community was deeply depressed, some talking about vigilante actions against the wanted Negro after the burial. There were no family members that could be located for funeral arrangements or notification, other than a long-term death notice in the Vindicator, and the Columbus and Atlanta newspapers, in hopes of locating a relative.

The two filing cabinets taken by the sheriff were searched by the secretarial staff for the name of James Lee. Oscar was picked up and brought in for questioning by the sheriff, after discussing the tactical move with Chief Hawthorn and Detective Duncan. The Greenville Police Chief, John Nolly, and his small department remained uninvolved.

Sheriff Gilbert stopped his car at the orchard office. The heavy car door closed with a thud. Oscar walked to the dark screened door where he was met by the sheriff.

"Mornin'!" Oscar called out from behind the screen door.

"Mornin'!" replied Sheriff Gilbert. "We need to talk," he said, pulling the door open. The older Negro looked shocked. "You're not in trouble, just puttin' heads together," said Sheriff Gilbert standing in the shack of an office. "Let's go!" he said, with hat in hand.

Miss Loretta looked surprised. "I'ze be all right. You close up when you want to," Oscar said, getting his hat and lunch pail.

"I hope you'll be back before lunch," said the sheriff.

Oscar set the pail back down. "I'ze be all right," he said again to Miss Loretta. There were a few cars pulling onto the orchard lot.

The sheriff cranked his county car and Oscar closed the passenger side door. "Am I supposed to be up front?" he asked.

The sheriff did not say anything for a few seconds, then he looked at the Negro man. "You help us catch this son of a bitch and I'll let you sit in my rockin' chair at my house." He smiled. Oscar felt more at ease. "Ain't there a Negro café in Raleigh somewhere?" the sheriff asked, as he drove up the Manchester-Raleigh Highway.

"There's a small place, the only place, down among the houses up around the church," Oscar said, not looking at the man.

"The Pilgrim's Rest, nigger church?" asked Sheriff Gilbert.

"Yes, sir!" said Oscar.

The sheriff's car twisted and turned down among the Negro houses and narrow dirt lanes, dogs and chickens running about, as well as children that should be in school. Some of the locals saw Oscar, and thinking he was arrested, walked behind the car. Sheriff Gilbert watched in the mirror. "Trouble?" asked the sheriff.

"Naw, sir! Dey be nosy," Oscar said. "Dere it be," he said, pointing to a weathered, unpainted store, bearing a hand painted sign, "Marigold".

"Marigold. A woman or a flower?" asked the sheriff, pulling the car to the side of the dirt yard.

"A granny woman," Oscar answered.

The sheriff got out, as did Oscar, much to the surprise of those who had walked down the street. "Go on, nows! Nuttin' ta see, just talkin'!" he said, motioning for them to go about their business. The street soon cleared.

The double screen doors could not contain the aroma of deep lard fried fruit pies and the strong coffee that boiled in the large enameled pot. An occasional spit from the curved spout sizzled on the hot stove top.

The dark café and store combination was a good place for the High Sheriff to talk to a Negro on his own turf. The old granny raised the prices when she saw the sheriff. Coffee was a nickel, it went to a dime. The fruit pies doubled too. The sheriff sat so he could watch his car. Oscar knew what he was doing.

"To your memory, did John Miller ever hire a Negro by the name of James Lee?" asked the sheriff, followed by a sip of hot coffee. The granny woman set a pie in front of each man. "Thanks!" said the sheriff.

"What kind, today?" asked Oscar.

"Dried abble," she said, walking away.

Oscar sipped his coffee and looked out the window. His expression was one of deep thought, trying to remember. "Not to my memory," he answered.

Oscar turned to Marigold. "You knows of a James Lee?" he yelled out.

Her back was turned to them. She was turning more pies in a deep cast iron skillet. "Thelma Lee's kin," she said, just barely loud enough to be heard. Sheriff Gilbert leaned forward to better hear the old woman. Her shuffling slippers were louder than her voice.

"Where's he from?" asked the sheriff.

She did not answer. "Where's he from?" asked Oscar.

"Chicago, or there 'bouts," she said, still with her back turned.

"And Miss Thelma?" asked the sheriff.

A yellow cat walked from the back toward the screen doors. It sat down in a spot of bright sunlight. The sunlight gave reflection to the dust that was disturbed on the unpainted wood floor.

"And Miss Thelma?" asked Oscar.

"Right here, deez parts," she said.

"Fine coffee and pie!" said Sheriff Gilbert.

The old Negro woman did not reply. She kept tending to the pies. A crowd was gathering. "Yous takin' money frum me," she said softly.

"I'll fix that," said the sheriff. He hurried to the screen doors and held one open. "Come right in! Come on in!" he said loudly, waving the people inside. They acted uncertain for a moment. Oscar stood behind the sheriff and waved them in. "I'll bet they don't pay double," laughed the sheriff.

"I bets dey ain't white neither," Marigold replied, just barely loud enough to hear.

The Negro customers lined up, still looking uneasy at the white sheriff in their small private place. "You all knows that Gertrude and Polly Sue Miller, dey wuz kilt last night," Oscar said loudly, as he stood looking at his own standing there in line. Some were shocked, as they had not heard. "Shuriff got questions. He thinks its tha Nigger James Lee, on tha run escaped days back. Beats Bo Bob Huggins, up Greenville way."

"Anyone know this James Lee? Anyone know of who might?" the sheriff asked, holding his coffee cup and half a pie. No one had an answer, but an old Negro man did leave for a moment. The sheriff thought he was going to take a piss, for the short time he was gone.

The sheriff did not get any information from the Negroes. He drove Oscar back to the orchard office and headed north to his office in Greenville. The open windows moved the fresh air through the cab. A small piece of paper drifted up from the front floorboard. It was almost taken out the driver's window, but fell to the seat beside the sheriff. He captured it with a slap. He had not had anything in the way of paper in the car in a long while. He tried to keep it cleaned out. He picked it up out of curiosity. The torn piece of paper had a name scribbled in soft lead pencil.

Hog Man. "Hog Man?" he mumbled. "Hog Man? Who tha hell is Hog Man?" he asked aloud, pushing the paper into his shirt pocket. "Hog Man." He kept running it through his mind. He was north of Harris City, heading to the office.

The office door was open as the sheriff walked toward the screen door. He could hear Curley talking to Dixie. The door moaned as he pulled it open.

"Sheriff!" greeted Curley.

"Curley! Dixie!" he replied, tossing his hat on the desk. "Who's Hog Man?" he asked.

"Stinkin' ass Theo Jackson!" Curley quickly replied. "Huge stinkin' place close to the Miller Orchard and Chalybeate Springs," he added. "Why? Did ya get hog shit on yer car?" Curley laughed.

"Dixie! Get me the detective in Warm Springs! That Duncan woman!" the sheriff snapped.

"And tell her what?" Dixie asked, as she was already busy raising the operator.

"Just get her, please!" smiled the sheriff.

"You know anything about this guy?" asked the sheriff. "Oh! He's the one that hauls slop from Becky's," he smiled, leaning back in his chair.

"It's Frances, Chief Hawthorn's secretary," said Dixie.

The sheriff took the telephone from Dixie. "Sheriff Gilbert, here! I need the detective," he barked.

"They are on the road," Frances replied.

"When you find her, tell her to call me at once, even after hours, got a lead," he said. "Operator can raise me," he added.

"I certainly will, Sheriff," Frances Goulding assured.

* * *

It was the morning of the Food Shoot held by Giles & Eiseman Grocery. The small vacant space to the side of the store was set up with hay bales and a plank target frame. There were ten shooters to the chance, and in the event of a tie the food would be split equally. The sidewalk was boiling over with men of all ages. It was the biggest thing every year except for the Masonic Turkey Shoot. It was early and there was a line of almost forty entrants. Young Buddy Cotton found Heather still in the boarding house.

His knuckles rapped on her door. "Hello!" Heather called out. She was taking the final steps in getting dressed for the long day ahead.

"Buddy, ma'am!" he called out.

"Yes!" Heather replied, from behind the closed door.

"I need yer help, just a split second and I'll pay for it," he said. The boarder across the foyer was listening to Buddy from an open door.

Heather was dressed and opened her door. "And what would that be?"

she asked.

She was wearing a sky-blue suit. The woman was strikingly handsome. Her shoulder rig was worn over a white pleated front blouse. A deep red handkerchief accented the suit coat lapel pocket. The young boy stood stunned for a second. "Yes?" Heather inquired again.

"It's Food Shoot Day. I've put up flyers all over town and as far out as I could get rides or cared ta walk, got fifty cents for it, and now Mrs. Blakely has let me work with the grocery today. She said I was caught up." Buddy smiled. He was neat and clean, in his ironed blue bibbed overalls and a starched white shirt. Heather stood listening with her hands folded in front of her belt buckle. "There's a family bad off, worse than any down the road from me. If I pay the dollar, will you shoot for the prize?" he asked. His eyes were sad and beckoning for her skill. "I took up money from the school kids, some gave a nickel and most come up with a dime," he said.

"I've got to go to an autopsy," Heather answered.

"Uh, what?" Buddy replied.

"An autopsy, where the doctor explores a dead person to see what killed them," she explained.

"Oh!" he said. "Just a minute," he begged.

"I don't have a rifle," she said.

"It's seven yards, at a pencil eraser dot," said Buddy. "Please? The rules don't say nothing about pistols," he added.

"Only if I can get in and out. I can't be late," Heather said.

"Do you know where it is?" he asked.

"Between here and old Bullochville," she replied.

"Where the crowed of men is," he said excitedly, going down the stairs.

Jasper Brown had decided to wear his Sunday suit for the meeting with Doc Hubbard, who served as Coroner. He had walked from the police department to the front porch of Mrs. Blakely's. Mrs. Blakely had discovered him and gave him a cup of coffee and the last buttered biscuit. She had whispered to him how pleased she was to have the detective staying at her establishment, and especially long term, where salesmen come and go. Jasper sat on the front porch and waited.

Heather had a walk that was virtually silent. She almost glided along, light on her feet, the sand under her shoes refused to grind. The young woman had the walk of a sleek cat. Heather cleared the door and stepped into the shade of the porch.

"Mornin'!" Jasper said, sitting to her left.

She looked twice. "A suit!" she exclaimed.

He smiled, his head turning pink. "My only one, Sunday suit. Wore it for the meeting," Jasper said, with a look of confidence.

Heather looked at her watch. "I'm in a fix," she said. "Buddy Cotton and his school mates have taken up money for a ticket at this food shoot.

They want me to shoot," she said, looking past Jasper toward the large gathering of men and boys. There were rifles cradled at a field carry and some resting on shoulders. "We don't want to be late for the autopsy."

"He can't start without us," Jasper reassured her. "Whose gun ya usin'?" he asked.

"My .45," she replied. He blinked several times in disbelief.

"Yer pistol!" he said out loud. People on the sidewalk heard him.

"I'd like to help these kids, they are trying to get food for a family," Heather said.

"Well, let's go do it. I'm glad I'm not shootin'," Jasper said, as they walked down the steps and started toward the alley. The loud shots filled the town, with several echoes from each round feeding off of the brick buildings.

"Who's on duty?" she asked.

"Edgar and the Chief and Frances; remember, nobody's off until this sum bitch is caught," Jasper said, walking beside her. They made an impressive pair for the small town, two officers in suits, badges and pistols. Heather naturally drew a crowd of lookers as they walked along, especially the young school boys and the young men.

Buddy Cotton saw Heather approaching, making her way through the crowded sidewalk of men waiting to pay for a chance. Buddy hurried toward his idol with a smile he could not contain. This time he was wearing a paper hat sporting the name of the grocery.

"Hi!" he said, grinning. Heather looked about, sizing up the shoot. The target distance was as he had said, seven yards thereabouts, no more than twenty-five feet. The targets had a place for the shooter's name, and they were held securely in place on the target boards with thumb tacks. Several boys his age were with him and three strapping girls, ones that could hold their own.

Heather made a point to speak to the girls. They returned with a polite reply. "I'll need to shoot ahead of this crowd, remember I've got the autopsy to attend," Heather reminded.

"I can handle that, wait right here," Buddy said. He hurried over to the grocery man wearing a white and red striped promotional vest. Heather and Jasper watched as Buddy talked with his hands. There was a lot of head shaking and raised brows. Heather felt there was a problem developing, but there was not.

The grocery man waved his arms before the next round of shooters and yelled so everyone could hear. "We've got a shooter, Detective Duncan from our police department, and she's to shoot for the school kids. They're trying to get food for a very needy family here in our community. I'm sure you gentlemen won't mind if she gets up here and shoots so she can keep an appointment with the Coroner."

241

Many voices from the group were in agreement, based on the purpose. The grocery man motioned for Heather to step up, as the next line had taken their places. She and Jasper heard whispers about where her rifle was, but they soon got their answer. "Where's yer rifle, missy?" asked the man.

Heather opened her coat and revealed her pistol. "I'm using my pistol."

The grocery man rolled his eyes and stepped back. She was shooting against some of the best shots in the county. "Everyone gets one round, and has to cut out the dot. All of the dot, before there's a win. If there's two that shoot out the dot, then the prize food is split," he said. "Load yer rifles and commence ta fire. Step back one step when you've shot," he said. The shots soon rang out, everything from .22 Shorts to Lee Enfield's. Then there was the last shot. Heather's sturdy two-handed hold and her squared stance toward the target gave the last round to be fired. The loud thunderous report of the forty-five rumbled down the alley. Jasper had not been watching, he felt that she was going to embarrass herself and he did not want to see it.

"Son of a bitch!" someone called out. The crowd moved closer to look at the target. Jasper took an elbow. "Ya lookin'?" a man barked. Jasper looked up and moved about to see the target. There was no sign of a dot, just a clean hole, damn near a half-inch in diameter, so clean the printer could not have punched one so neat. Jasper's eyes grew wide and his jaw dropped. A large smile spread across his face. "Son of a bitch!" someone else called out, shaking his shoulder.

The grocery man and Buddy walked down the line and looked at the targets. "We have a winner!" the man yelled. "Detective Duncan!" The school girls clapped and bounced around with joy. The smoke from the spent round gently drifted from the barrel of Heather's pistol as she held it down. The others who had fired on the line shook her hand and congratulated her. Buddy Cotton gleamed with joy.

Heather saw Buddy digging in his pocket. He had been paid for the flyers and for working the entire day, seven o'clock until six o'clock, closing. He lacked a dime having a dollar in change. The boy had the nerve to ask Jasper if he had a dime and told him what for, just like the policeman did not have an idea. Jasper was reluctant in giving the dime, because the shoot was luck, but he contributed anyway. Buddy handed the grocery man another dollar. Heather was ready to go, until Buddy rushed her again.

"Do it again!" he said. "I've already paid my money, except for a dime from Officer Brown. We'll give the winning food to the family," he said, almost bouncing where he stood.

"I don't know if I can do it again," she whispered. She felt relatively sure she could, as she and Sonny shot groups and acorns from the fence for practice and they shot a little further out, but not by much.

"Please," he said. This time he was joined by the school girls.

"For the school girls," Heather said.

"Nine more!" yelled the grocery man.

"Nine?" a man barked.

"The detective's shootin' again, then she's got to go," replied the grocery man. The line was now double down the sidewalk, even blocking the front doors to the grocery. "Everyone gets one round, and has to cut out the dot. All of the dot, before there's a win. If there's two that shoot out the dot, then the prize food is split," he said. "Load yer rifles and commence ta fire, step back one step when you've shot," he said. The shots soon rang out.

The smoke cleared and Buddy and the grocery man checked the targets. "We have a winner!" the man yelled. "Detective Duncan!" The school girls clapped and bounced about with joy as they ran up to Heather. She holstered her pistol after exchanging the magazine that was two rounds shy for a full one. The others who had fired on the line shook her hand and congratulated her again. Buddy Cotton gleamed with joy.

"It ain't luck! She can do it again!" Buddy bragged, as he stood close to her. Alfred Huffman appeared from the crowd and made a photograph of the detective and the school kids that were gathered around. Jasper was in there somewhere. The story and the photograph would be on the front page the next morning. Heather got a hug from all the school kids that supported the project, even the bystanders that dipped snuff and chewed tobacco. Heather waved and made her way to the sidewalk, with Jasper right behind.

Several old men made comments about Jasper's shooting and how he could not have performed the feat they had just witnessed. The hungry family would be well-fed for a while. Ten dollars of food went a long way. Rice was three cents a pound, yams one cent a pound, side meat five cents a pound, and Eight O'clock coffee was twenty-one cents a pound. Buddy was so proud of knowing Heather that he stood on top of the hay bales to watch her walk away.

* * *

The booking photograph had come back from the drugstore and Sheriff Gilbert held the black and white photograph of James Lee in his hands. "God damn bastard!" he mumbled at his desk window as he looked at the criminal.

'How'd I do?" asked Curley. He was sitting at his desk playing solitaire.

"Ya did good. Take the negatives and go now and get a dozen more made," said the sheriff, handing the envelope to Curley.

Dixie dug for a nickel in her purse. "Bring me back a limeade," she said, holding out the nickel. Curley hurried on foot toward the drug store, just beyond the courthouse on the square. He often ran errands on foot since the business district was around the courthouse square.

The sheriff pulled his pistol and checked it, something he was seldom seen doing. "I'm goin' down toward Chalybeate Springs on Pigeon Creek to a nigger's place. A hog farm, Theo Jackson's," he said. "If ya can locate a deputy, send them toward me, drive 'till they get there. If I'm already gone, then they can patrol on back," said Sheriff Gilbert. Dixie heard his revolver yoke close and the cylinder roll into place. "He may know about this nigger," he added, as he stood at the front door. "Don't go far tonight, I may need you to take a statement," he said to Dixie.

"I'm a homebody, we seldom leave town," she replied, looking up from her stack of paperwork. The sheriff tossed the short, wet cigar out the screened door and stepped back to his desk where he took another one from the center drawer. "May be tha last one," he said, pointing it at the longtime employee.

* * *

Jasper and Heather hurriedly left Warm Springs and headed north to Greenville where the meeting was to take place. Dr. Hubbard was the one who seemed to never be on time, but they were attempting to be professional and keep the appointment. Jasper drove and Heather sat quietly, basking in her recent accomplishment, two in a row.

Jasper remained quiet until they were north of Harris City. He could hold it no longer. "Damn!" he said loudly, looking at Heather. "Some shootin'!" Heather did not say anything. She just sat quietly, like it was an everyday occurrence.

"I'm glad I could help the kids out. They are to be admired for wanting to help out an unfortunate family," she said, looking ahead.

"We never drive yer city car," Jasper commented. "Maybe tomorrow," he said.

"You do know where we're going?" Heather asked.

"Been there many a time, except not for this," Jasper said, slowing the car down to drive around the square. The Greenville police officer sat outside the front door, enjoying the shade and the company of the old men and the unemployed. The officer waved as he watched the Warm Springs car passing around the corner.

"I'm glad I'm workin'," Heather said. "I'd lose my mind, wasting my life just watching the world go by," she said, shaking her head in disbelief.

"Some can do that," Jasper said. "I was a mix of too much ta do and nothing until you exploded my life," he said, smiling at the pretty woman. "I'm glad ya did," he added.

"You know yer tie is dark blue?" Heather asked.

Jasper looked down. "Damn it!" he said, bending his neck down to look at his mistake. "Shit! Maybe in the dim light they won't notice." He shook his head in disbelief.

"My handkerchief is red," said Heather, trying to help him out.

"They ain't looking at yer handkerchief," said Jasper. The funeral home came into view. "Michael Cargile, Mortuary, No. 4 Terrell Street. Lots of loved ones and friends went through here," Jasper commented, pulling the car alongside the curb.

A suited man met them at the front door. "Yes, may I help you?" the man asked, holding the door open.

"Officers for the autopsy with Dr. Augustus Hubbard," Heather answered.

"This way," said the man. He led them through several doors and hallways, and then down into the basement. Dr. Hubbard stood in his white lab coat, drinking a cup of coffee. Heather and Jasper detected the odor of whiskey on his breath.

"You are on time," greeted the doctor. "I'm having a little nip, settles my stomach for this kind of work. Have ya been to one before?" he asked both officers.

Heather knew what to expect. She replied, "No". Jasper shook his head, also indicating "no".

"The sight doesn't bother me as much as the smell, that works on me. Animal slaughter bothers me too!" said Doc Hubbard, as he took the last long sip of his spiked coffee. "I'd suggest you suit up. There's a couple of lab coats on the rack." He pointed to the wall. "The last officer puked during the examination of the skull," he added. Jasper was already feeling queasy. "It's the heat and the fluids that generate the odor, somewhat like a primeval fear. Then I knew an old doctor who would eat a pimento cheese sandwich and a glass of milk, should lunch fall during the process," said Doc Hubbard. Heather was keeping herself under control, but it was not pleasant. Jasper was already a ghostly white. "Jar of carbolated salve on the counter. Some folks put a dab of that in their nose to help with the odor. She'll be a bad one, as long as she's been dead. We won't do the child, will we?" he asked, looking at Heather.

"No, just the adult," she replied, putting on a smock.

The cool, tile finished room was well-lit. A roll-around lamp stood close to the examination table. The table was an old one, enameled with deep formed troughs around the edges and a drip corner to a five-gallon bucket below. The doctor moved the catch bucket with the toe of his shoe. It chattered across the floor, getting Jasper's attention. "Anybody has ta puke, there's the sink," said Doc Hubbard, pointing to the large sink on the wall. "The water's left at a trickle to help keep the odor from coming back on us." Jasper's gut tightened. Heather found a stool, pulled it close, and sat down. The small mortuary had only four cold storage vaults. The name of the occupant was hand printed on a piece of paper and slid into the metal bracket to identify the body within. G. Miller was in the top right vault. The mortuary personnel helped Doc Hubbard remove the woman and place her on the gurney which would transport her to the examination table. She had been removed from the bloody rubber tarpaulin that had wrapped her for transport. It was a brutal sight. Gaping wounds from the fire poker covered her face and head. The blood had dried around each wound where it had come to rest on her. Her hair was matted. The green day dress was soaked.

It took all three to attach the scales and weigh Gertrude Miller. "One hundred and thirty pounds," said Doc Hubbard. "Hold this at her feet!" he said, extending a measuring tape to Jasper. "Sixty-seven inches! I'll change that to the metric equivalent on the report," he said, making a note on a tablet which lay a safe spatter distance away. The doctor looked at her scalp, her teeth, in her mouth, and before it was over, he looked into every body cavity except her rectum. This was all before he picked up a scalpel. He closed Gertrude's legs and looked at Jasper, who was growing increasingly pale. The doctor knew Jasper would be the most apt to puke, based on his appearance. "Well, I rectum that does it!" he said, slapping the corpse on the upper thigh. Heather caught the pun, Jasper just looked down.

"Help turn her over. You want to know what killed her. We know it was the bullet," said Doc Hubbard, as the three of them rolled the rigid body. Very little blood or other fluids were present on the table when they turned her. The doctor made a line down the center of the corpse's spine and then took a yard stick and began to make notations of distances which would locate the entrance wound. The findings were noted. The cold room and the lack of fresh air were beginning to work on both officers.

The lengthy process of exploring for exploration's sake seemed to be the only reason for an autopsy after the determination of the cause of death, which was the bullet. For a moment the doctor left the room. His messy rubber gloves were left lying on the end of the table. The slow seepage of cavity fluids dripped from the end of the table and into the five-gallon bucket below. "Think of something pleasant," Heather whispered to Jasper. He looked violently ill. She expected him to puke at any minute. "Worse than the battlefield?" she asked.

"Hell, yes," Jasper replied. "Men were shot and we moved on, nothing like this, exploring for entertainment." They heard a toilet seat clang in another room nearby. "Maybe he's pukin' too."

"I doubt it," Heather said.

A renewed scent of whiskey pervaded the room when Doc Hubbard returned. "Help me turn her again, to her back this time."

Jasper stepped forward to save his masculinity. "Now for the 'Y'," said Doc, smiling at Jasper. "And I ain't talkin about them places," he said, looking at the pale officer. "This one is armpit on each side ta the center of the chest, at the sternum and down the gut, all the way to the bladder," he said, holding a larger glistening scalpel. "I'll miss her navel." Jasper hurried to the sink, his hand over his mouth while en route. Vomit was beginning to escape from the cracks of his fingers when he gave it up at the sink. The poor man hurled then stood on his tiptoes and hurled some more. He sounded as though his navel would pass through his mouth before it was over. The doctor kept on with his work.

Heather looked down at the floor during the cutting and the folding away from the rib cage. There was a different odor with every procedure. They could hear the metal tools making their distinctive sounds as they came to rest on the enameled table in some instances, and on the standing tool tray at other times.

"Someday we'll be able to record this and then get it transcribed," said the doctor, stopping to make notes. He studied the body and organs for several minutes. "Gunshot wound to the shoulder blade, back to front, upward and rightward through the soft tissues of the left posterior back, entering the body through the 10th intercostals space posteriorly with laceration to the left kidney upper pole, left adrenal, spleen, liver and through the right 6th rib into the soft tissue of the anterior right chest," said Doc Hubbard. "Here is the deformed lead bullet," he said, holding it up secured in long forceps. Heather came closer, looking at the bloody bullet. "Thirty-eight?" she asked.

"I'd say so. I'll measure it," said Doc, putting a Vernier caliper on it. The doctor looked over his glasses. "Tissue on it and it's measurin' three, no four hundred thousandths. Let me clean it off." He dropped it into a tiny pan of alcohol. Blood laced away as the tissue separated from the lead and the grease grooves. "Now let's see," he said, holding it in his hand. "Three hundred and fifty-six thousandths. Yep! Three hundred and fifty-six thousandths. It's a .38!" confirmed the doctor.

Heather slowly gleamed. "That's the same caliber as the one taken from the Hambyville store," she said out loud. Jasper, still pale, wiped his bitter mouth. "I really believe we're after James Lee," said Heather. "Can we go?" she asked.

"I'm finished except for placing the organs back into the cavity and stitching her up," answered the doctor. Jasper ran to the sink again. This time he was louder than the first.

"Get him out," said Doc Hubbard, motioning with his head toward the door.

Heather took Jasper by the arm and tugged him toward the doors leading upstairs, where the mood was lighter and the air fresher. They hurried to remove the lab coats. "Drop 'em on the floor, I'll take care of 'em," said Doc, still standing by the examination table.

"When can I get the official report?" Heather asked, holding the door for Jasper.

"Couple of days," Doc replied. Jasper was in the doorway. "Hey! Maybe next time we can have that pimento cheese sandwich I talked about!" said Doc, laughing. Jasper held the railing as he climbed the stairs with wobbly legs.

* * *

Sheriff Gilbert stopped by the telephone company where he spoke to the supervisor and operator on duty. There was no listed telephone number for Theo Jackson, a/k/a in the Negro community as "Hog Man". The sheriff headed south in hopes of catching the Negro at the hog farm. He had no way to tell what slop hauling schedule the Negro was on, but he knew he was going to be interviewed before night fell. The morning sun pressed through the windshield as the lawman hurried southeast. Somewhere between Woodbury and Buck Creek he passed a light blue Chrysler flatbed loaded with tubs and buckets, giving off an odor that would twitch the nostrils of a turkey buzzard. The truck was driven by a heavy Negro. It lumbered along northward on the Cove Church Road. The marked sedan driven by Sheriff Gilbert slowed quickly, took to the sandy shoulder, and soon gave chase to the blue truck. The driver gave no resistance and stopped at the very next suitable shoulder.

Theo Jackson pondered as to why he was being stopped. He did recognize the man as Sheriff Louis Gilbert. Theo Jackson got out of the truck and began to walk toward the sheriff's car that had just barely stopped. The sheriff did not like that. He called for Jackson to stop. The Negro stood at the back of his truck, his hands tucked behind the overall's galluses. Sheriff Gilbert got out of his car and walked forward to talk to the Negro. "You tha hog man?" he barked as he approached.

"I'm a hog farmer," replied Theo Jackson.

"Where's yer place?" asked the sheriff.

"Down on Pigeon Creek," replied Theo Jackson.

"Yer the one I'm lookin' for."

"What'd I do?" asked Theo.

"I'll ask the questions!" said Sheriff Gilbert. He pulled the photograph of James Lee from his coat. "Ya know this nigger?" he asked.

Theo Jackson looked at the photograph for several seconds. The sheriff saw in his eyes that he knew the man. "Do ya?" he asked again.

"I've seen him before," replied Theo Jackson, glancing away.

"I'd say ya know more of him than you'll admit," Sheriff Gilbert said, pulling the photograph back. "Where'd ya see him last?"

"Uh, several days ago at a card game," replied Theo Jackson.

"Oh! Where was that, and you and all them card players knew he was wanted, didn't y'all?" Sheriff Gilbert barked.

"Really?"

The sheriff stepped closer. "Get on my bad side boy, I'll take ya down!"

The sheriff put his back to the sun. "Look at me when you talk!" he barked.

Theo Jackson was looking into the sun. The law was a huge black shadow.

"I'll give ya the benefit of the doubt. You be in my office in the morning or walk in to the Warm Springs Police Department and talk to the detective, you've got a choice," said Sheriff Gilbert. "You think about it. Sleep on it," he said, as he walked to his car.

Theo Jackson said, "I'll be there, early."

The sheriff opened the car door and looked back at Jackson. "Tomorrow!" he said, pointing his finger, then he drove off. Sheriff Gilbert watched Jackson in the mirror. He had planted the seed of fear in this Negro. Theo Jackson would lose a night's sleep and be ready to talk in the morning. Sheriff Gilbert opened all the windows that he could reach, including the vents, and sped up to push the sting of tainted air out of the cab.

* * *

Detective Duncan worked on her case file that afternoon and Jasper sipped Milk of Magnesia to ease his stomach, in spite of the fact that Heather told him it was mental. Jasper would not eat lunch with her. He just sat in the patrol car around town, but stayed close and chased the shade. Most of the foot traffic thought he was off duty, dressed in his Sunday suit.

Before shift change the sheriff called and advised that he had made contact with a Negro named Theo Jackson, a hog farmer who possibly had information on James Lee. The news was exciting to the detective. Her case file was growing larger.

The next day came and went. Theo Jackson did not report to either of the two law enforcement agencies. A sheriff's deputy saw Theo Jackson in Durand and asked if he had talked to the law. Jackson assured the deputy that he had not but intended to come in the next day. The dutiful deputy called his findings in to the sheriff by telephone and did the same to the Warm Springs Police Department, leaving a message with Frances Goulding. The third day passed and still Theo Jackson had not come in.

On the fourth morning, the Meriwether County Sheriff and the Warm Springs Detective were waiting, hidden around the Greenville square. The morning was warm and patience was thin. The gentle breeze that passed through the open windows of the parked cars was pleasant, but the reflective heat from the car body quickly offset any comfort from the breeze. Theo Jackson's second stop on his slop haul was Becky's Café. The law officers watched as the light blue Fargo truck backed into the alleyway at the tiny café. Sheriff Gilbert pulled a patrol car across the alley. Detective Duncan and Officer Brown showed their badges and hurried through the restaurant, coming out on the rear dock. Theo Jackson was taken in for questioning. His partially loaded slop truck was pulled clear of the alley and parked on the street. Jackson was hurried into the sheriff's car and carried to the jail for the interview.

The screen door of the booking room popped behind Sheriff Gilbert as he literally shoved Theo Jackson into the office. The Negro was not under arrest, but being held for questioning. "Sit down!" barked Curley Jones, pointing to a chair along the red brick wall, the one that separated the booking room from the cell block. Jackson sat down. The rickety wooden chair moved under the man's heavy weight. He sat tense, wondering if the chair would give under his weight. "Back in my youth, a man was as good as his word!" the sheriff yelled out. "Ever heard that?" he asked loudly.

"Yes, sir!" replied Theo Jackson. "And why am I here?" he asked.

Sheriff Gilbert scratched his head vigorously. "I'll be god damned!" he said, looking around the room as though he had lost something. "Did ya forget that you were told three times to come in and let's talk?" he asked. The sheriff took a deep breath and sighed as he released it, then he pulled at his right earlobe. Jackson sat silently. Sheriff Gilbert looked at Detective Duncan and nodded.

Detective Duncan stepped forward. "I'm Special Deputy, Detective Duncan," she said, walking back and forth in front of Theo Jackson. He looked up at her as she moved around. "Now, you are Theo Jackson," she said, stopping and looking at her fingernails. "You're a business man."

"Yes," replied Theo Jackson.

"How long?" she asked, standing with her arms folded, looking down at him.

"Since high school, fifteen years, more or less," he replied.

"Good business?" she asked.

"I do all right, better in the fall and winter than in the warm months," said Jackson, smiling.

Detective Duncan held her hand out to the sheriff for the photograph of James Lee. He turned it face down and placed it in her hand. "Do you know this man?" she asked. She leaned down, still out of striking range, and held the photograph in front of the detained Negro. "Be sure now, I don't want you to say later that you made a mistake," Heather said. "And this lady," she pointed to Dixie, "And this man," she pointed to jailer, Curley Jones. "She's taking down what you say and he's a witness. Do you understand?" Heather asked.

"I understand," Theo Jackson replied. He looked around the room like he was looking to run.

"You're not under arrest," said the detective. "Do you know this man?" she barked loudly. The sheriff did not know she had that much of a bark in her.

Theo Jackson jumped. He shook his head.

"Records can't hear head shakes!" Heather said loudly, moving the photograph about. "Do you know this man?" she barked again.

"I know who that is," Jackson answered.

"So, who is this?" the detective asked.

"James Lee!" Theo Jackson said, dropping his head down.

"Can you read?" Heather barked.

"I can," mumbled Theo Jackson, looking everywhere but at her.

"Do you listen to the radio?" she asked, as she began to move about, handing the photograph back to the sheriff.

"Yes!" replied Theo Jackson.

"What stations? Be general!" she barked.

"The local ones," he answered.

"Read the newspaper?" she asked loudly, pacing back and forth.

"Yes!" replied Jackson. He was beginning to sweat.

"Wipe yer face, we ain't hardly started," Heather said. She took a sip of water. "Would you say you were raised right, Mr. Jackson?" she asked. This time she was looking out the window, her hands resting on her waist. "I'm sorry, what?" Jackson had not answered the question.

"I believe I was," he replied, putting his plaid handkerchief in his back pocket.

"Tell me in your words, loudly, I don't want to misunderstand. Did you know James Lee was wanted?" the detective asked loudly.

"I knew he was wanted!" said Theo Jackson.

Detective Duncan pulled up a straight chair and set it in front of the detained Negro. She sat in it, backwards like a man. "You knew he was wanted?" she asked, looking him in the eyes. "How long did he stay at yer place?" she asked, in a slow, deliberate sounding tone. Sheriff Gilbert was impressed so far. He shook his head with pleasure at how this detective woman was getting in Theo Jackson's ass. Large beads of sweat rolled from his face. Jackson looked shocked at the question about how long Lee stayed. His eyes began to move from one side to the other. He would not look at the woman in front of him.

"How long, Mr. Jackson? How long?" the detective asked coldly.

Theo Jackson was not responding. "Lost yer hearing Mr. Jackson? How long, Mr. Jackson? How long?" she asked louder.

"Two, three days," Theo Jackson stuttered.

"My hearing's goin'! You knew James Lee was a wanted man, and you put him up for two, three days. Is that what I heard?" Detective Duncan barked.

Theo Jackson nodded his head, "Yes."

"I can't hear a head shake!" Detective Duncan barked loudly.

"Yes! I put him up for two or three days!" he said, gritting his teeth.

"Did he show you his revolver?" she asked.

There was a long silence. "Yes!"

"You got a gun in your truck too, don't you?" She went out on a limb in asking.

The Negro looked shocked. "A shotgun," he said.

Detective Duncan walked to the sheriff and whispered in his ear. The Negro thought it was about the questioning, but it was not. She asked if Miss Jewel had left any tea cakes, and did he have any questions. Sheriff Gilbert smiled, nodded, and whispered that she was doing a great job.

"Can I go?" asked Theo Jackson, "Since I'm not under arrest?"

"Just a minute! Let me cover again, quickly, what you told us," Heather said. She began to pace back and forth. "You knew James Lee was wanted; you gave him shelter for two or three days; you saw a revolver. Do you know what caliber it was?"

"Thirty-eight," Theo Jackson said.

The detective showed no emotions at hearing the caliber. "You knew he was wanted; you gave him shelter for two or three days; saw a revolver." She stopped, placing her hand over her mouth, and stood in deep thought. "And you took him to the Miller house. Didn't you!" she barked, leaning down close to him, looking him in the eyes. "Didn't you?" she asked louder. Theo Jackson looked away.

"What would you say if I produced two workers that saw you there?" she asked loudly. "You took Lee to the Miller house, didn't you?" she asked again. "Didn't you?" she yelled.

There was a long silence. "I took him to the Miller property," Jackson said, looking down. "Can I go?" he asked.

"Stay close. We'll need you again," Detective Duncan said calmly.

The sweaty Negro stood up. "Don't let the door hit ya in the ass when ya leave!" said Sheriff Gilbert. "Yer truck is on the street at Becky's. Here's yer key!" The sheriff held out the small ignition key.

The frightened Negro closed the screen door gently and was last seen walking toward the square.

"Dixie, call Ambrose Watkins, see if he'll see me and this wonderful detective," said Sheriff Gilbert.

Dixie made the telephone call and advised the sheriff that the solicitor general would see them now.

Sheriff Gilbert and Detective Duncan walked to the office of Ambrose Watkins, where they covered what Theo Jackson had admitted to.

"So, this hog farmer knew James Lee was wanted by the law, and he put him up for two or three days, and saw a revolver. Then took him to what he said is Miller property," said the solicitor, as he stood with his back to them, looking out the tall window in his second story office. His nicotine stained fingers held a cigarette. He mumbled again, "Knew he was wanted, put him up for two or three days, saw a revolver and took him to Miller property." He was still standing with his back turned.

"That's right!" said Sheriff Gilbert.

"I feel sure he's under the definition of aiding an escaped felon and would be under definition of an accomplice to the killin' of the woman and the child, since this Negro drove the escapee to the property," said Watkins.

"We saw it that away," said Detective Duncan, sitting in a high-backed upholstered chair.

"Man drives for a hold-up, is the same as if he went in and held up the place, ain't he?" asked the sheriff.

"In Meriwether County," said the solicitor general. He sat down at his desk and started typing the arrest warrants. Sunlight flooded into the smoky room. A pigeon cooed as it sat in the open window looking in at the figures moving about, the window screen keeping it safe.

"I need ta fill out an application, don't I?" asked Heather.

"Yes, here's the forms," replied Ambrose Watkins. He stopped typing long enough to pull the blank forms from the top left desk drawer and pushed them toward her.

"Dixie got all this on shorthand. She'll type it up tomorrow," bragged the sheriff.

The detective used her notes, kept safely in a pocket tablet, to fill out the warrant applications. The solicitor walked in the company of the detective and Sheriff Gilbert, taking the arrest warrants to Judge Erastus Cobb. They were signed by the Superior Court Judge of Meriwether County. The stick pen scrubbed over the bond paper forms in the silence of the chambers. Judge Cobb signed the first one and pushed it to the female detective. "That's for aiding an escaped felon," he said. The pen was then guided across the next form. "That's for accomplice in the two murders," said the Judge. "And this one is for the burglary in the Miller house," said Judge Cobb. He counted on his fingers as he spoke. "Aiding an escaped felon, two for accomplice in the murders, one for the burglary of the residence and the theft of the automobile. That's four felony counts," he said, resting his pen on the decorative rack with his name engraved on it. "He should be easy, bring him in tomorrow," said the Judge, pulling a small mint from a crystal jar on his desk.

* * *

The afternoon sun was setting in the western sky where James Lee yearned to be, in Alabama. The work traffic had come and gone. He did not notice the small leak in the brass radiator of the stolen Maxwell. Lee was refreshed and chanced moving westward. If he could get to the old Parks Plantation there would be plenty of field roads to hide on. It was a distance of only seven miles, but he had to pass through Harris City, a busy settlement in the afternoons. Lee took a piss near the hidden car and cranked the once pristine vehicle. The brush that he had forced the car deep into made loud squeals as the limbs bit and gouged into the paint when the vehicle pulled away.

"Character," he mumbled, as the car pulled itself free of the dense brush. The revolver was lying on the seat next to him, reminding him that he was one round down from a full cylinder. Lee took the time to remove the spent round and replace it with another cartridge. The spent hull of the round that had killed Gertrude Miller was tossed out the window.

James Lee was very confident that he could get to his next hiding place before dark. He planned to eat food from the box on the seat and gather his thoughts for the Alabama run.

"Money in my pocket, gasoline in the tank, and a can full in the floorboard, a pistol and food." He smiled as he hurried toward the woods of the Parks Plantation.

* * *

Theo Jackson finished his slop pickup for the hogs. It was late, some stores and cafés had closed. He left them wondering. He seemed to always be counted on rain or shine, but today he was late.

CHAPTER SIXTEEN

James Lee drove toward the bright orange setting sun as he approached the Harris City intersection. He was only a mile from where he had been captured the first time. A rabbit scurried across the road in front of the car. The temperature gauge on the Maxwell was rising as the straight block engine began to labor from the excessive heat. Escaping water found its way to the engine block and the intake manifold, turning it into white steam.

The late gathering sawmillers at the Harris City store stood around the heavy trucks and socialized, bringing the day to a close. Westbound cars were seldom seen that time of day, most were headed north or south. The approaching car driven by Lee drew attention as a cloud of white smoke boiled from the underside. The needle of the temperature gauge was lying against the high side's stop, as far as it could possibly go.

"Damn it!" Lee exclaimed, as he glanced down and discovered white smoke in the mirror. "Damn it!" he said again, pounding the steering wheel with his hand. "Damn it!" The gathering of men watched as the skipping car came and barely passed.

Tom Baker, a Negro saw filer, looked at Henry Jones who stood nearby. "That looks like the Millers' car," he said, lowering his Nu-Grape drink. The two men watched as the overheated Maxwell passed with white smoke rolling.

"That is John's car!" Tom Baker said, leaning around Henry Jones, who was also looking as the car passed by.

Henry Jones began to recite, "321689, 321-689." Tom Baker quickly wrote the number down in his pocket tablet. He kept money amounts, saw set angles, and the like in it.

The two men quickly agreed to call the law. Neither had a dime between them, just pennies and quarters. The two strapping men took the steps to the rock store like eager school boys. Their heavy brogans made a thunderous rumble as they hurried across the plank porch. Bill Sullivan stood behind the counter in the dimly lit store. It was not quite dark enough to turn on the electric lights, but barely light enough to see small print on labels and advertisements. Several men were sitting around, exchanging lies and laughing. They looked up when the two Negroes rushed in.

"We saw John Miller's black Maxwell go by!" said Henry Jones.

"We passed up the pay phone outside 'cause we ain't got a dime, just pennies and quarters," explained Tom Baker.

The two excited Negroes stood in front of Bill Sullivan. "You sure?" Sullivan asked, looking toward the road.

"As my palms are pink!" Henry Jones snapped back.

The liars and storytellers hurried to the porch and looked both ways. "321689!" recited Tom Baker.

"I'll call the sheriff!" said Bill Sullivan, moving the telephone from the back shelves to the front counter. He finally got the operator out of the Warm Springs exchange. "Get me the sheriff!" he said quickly. "Ya damn right! The Meriwether County Sheriff, you know where I'm callin' from!" he said, rolling his eyes at the two Negroes.

One man opened the door and called back. "There's a reward on that nigger! We're goin' ta try and catch him!" Several cars were heard leaving the sandy graveled lot.

"Sheriff! Bill Sullivan, here! It's not? Well, see that he gets this!" Bill said, looking toward the road. "Two Negro gents that saw a black Maxwell pass said it belonged to John Miller. Said the tag was 321689," Bill Sullivan said excitedly. "Headin' west, just a minute or two ago!"

The person on the other end of the line was Curley Jones. "I'll see that he gets it, and I'll start tryin' to get a deputy headed that way." There was a patrol car on the square. Curley went outside and stood on top of the granite capper that boxed in the front steps. He yelled and waved, trying to get the deputy's attention. Curley soon gave up and started walking toward the square, waving his hat now and then. The deputy eventually rolled the patrol car toward him. "That Miller car, the black stolen Maxwell, 321689, was seen heading west as it went through Harris City," Curley said, as he held the window opening and leaned into the car.

"I'll start that away!" said the deputy. "Start another car! We may have that nigger this time," the deputy said, as he pulled away. Curley called the local operator and asked that she call about, trying to locate the sheriff or another car. The car in Greenville was four miles north of Harris City. It rounded the square with the cotton cord tires growling as it leaned on the thin sidewalls. Curley stood in the middle of Greenville-Luthersville Road with his hands in his hip pockets. "I bet I'd catch that sum bitch," he said to himself, with a gleam of excitement in his eye. He seated his hat and slowly walked back to the jail.

Detective Duncan worked on her case file in the staff room. It was getting late in the day. Jasper Brown and Chief Hawthorn were in the office when Frances got the call. Everyone sat quietly, listening as Frances took the call. "Thanks! We'll get a car started!" she said. "That was the operator. Two Negroes saw the Miller car passing through Harris City a short time ago, headin' west. They want us to start a car. She said it was an official BOLO, put out by jailer Curley Jones, he took the call. They've got a car started from Greenville," Frances added.

Heather began to assemble her case file, as she was already standing while she heard the words from Frances. "Jasper and I'll get it! Finish yer report," said Chief Hawthorn. He grabbed his shotgun from the nearby corner. "Jasper? Got yours?" he barked.

"I do!" Jasper replied, standing with his ignition key in his hand.

"Head to Durand and then go north on the Durand Road. I'll take Greenville-Manchester to the old Pea Field Road. I think I can make it through there," said the chief. "Then I'll head north! Meet me at Bill Sullivan's," he added.

Heather's mind was not on her report. She might as well have gone too! The two patrol units left town with the sirens bumping to clear the evening traffic. It was just dark enough for the police lights to look bright and exciting.

Pong! Pong! Pong! Pong! Pong! The slow striking clock in the lobby sounded off. "Five o'clock!" Frances Goulding announced, as she stopped where she was in her typing. "Not a word more!" she said, gathering up her purse.

"Me too!" Heather announced. She stacked the case file and placed it into the wooden filing cabinet that she had been afforded for the time she would be there. "If I was at home now, I'd be soaking in the tub, with my old hound dog Holly layin' outside the door," Heather said, as the two women walked to the door together. Edgar Peterson met them on the sidewalk.

"Anything happening?" he asked, his flashlight and lunch pail in hand.

"Some Negroes saw the Miller car westbound at Harris City. The sheriff's got a car comin' down and Jasper and the chief left to try and find it too," Frances said.

"Hubert Jennings found me last night. He said it looked to be a car or something reflecting light from the woods behind the Cane Creek Baptist Church. It was so far out of the city 'till I just let it go," Edgar said to Heather.

"I'd have backed you and we'd have seen about it," she said, thinking of how dumb his actions might have been.

"We ain't got jurisdiction up there," Edgar said.

"No, but I do. Jasper does," Heather replied. "Roust me up if you get something like that again," she said, as he headed for the office. "Good night, Frances." Heather smiled at the older woman.

Frances had mellowed out and found that Heather was not there to take anyone's job or show anybody up. She saw that Heather was an officer of the law and would not hesitate to act, where others would, based on who the offenders were. Heather had typed a letter once as Frances read it aloud. It was astonishing to the woman for someone to be that good.

* * *

Henry Jones and Tom Baker lingered into the early darkness in hopes of seeing the sheriff's car as it passed. "Maybe he took the other road from the square," Henry said to Tom.

"He sure has had time to have passed here," Tom replied, as they sat on the running board of a truck. Bill Sullivan was closing the store across the way. The men waved at him for his kindness and help in raising the law. Bill Sullivan pulled his car over to where they were sitting.

"Hope they catch the sum bitch!" he said, rolling down his window. The distant whip-poor-will called from the marshy woodlands, down in the bottomland. "See you guys tomorrow," Bill said, as he slowly headed west. He lived on a small parcel cut from the old Parks Plantation.

The two Negroes were right. The deputy had taken another road from the Greenville square. The eager deputy had intersected the Ogletree Road in the middle and turned west, hoping to overtake the troubled vehicle. He had a bullet with that killin' nigger's name on it. The thought of a throw down had entered his mind in the past, but not on this one. Everyone had a license to kill. Jasper and Chief Hawthorn had about the same distance to travel. The chief's might be a little slower, if the old Pea Field Road was washed out. Chief Hawthorn was counting on the two tenant farmers that lived on the narrow road having kept it passable. He did know there was one place that could be muddy, as cattails had always grown there.

Jasper bumped his siren as he went into the sleepy town of Durand. There were a few motorists on the streets, but for the most part everything was boarded up and the sidewalks rolled and tucked away. He chuckled and smiled at that expression, but the little town emulated the saying. The experienced officer thought of his detective partner as he rolled through the intersections with his police lights on, using due caution. A young boy stood on the porch of the closed store at Herman Pickens place. The boy reached for the sky and pulled down hard several times making a whistle blowing motion with his arm, wanting the officer to hit the siren. Jasper leaned down and switched it on. The large bullet-shaped, chrome-plated device slowly moaned and built up to a full wail. The excited boy waved as Jasper drove out of sight.

"Every boy's dream," Jasper said to himself softly. "Every boy's dream" he whispered again. For the time being Jasper had forgotten about the possible danger. "Hell! I've been through a war and now an autopsy, all I can do is ta get killed," he thought, shutting down the siren and the police lights. "Maybe on the next car we'll get a foot operated siren switch," Jasper thought, as he steered in the growing darkness.

Chief Hawthorn had been lucky so far. The first half of Pea Field Road was well-kept with deep established ruts in the sand. He could almost let go of the steering wheel and let the car guide itself. The deer alerted and raised their heads from their stolen meals in the early fields. They stood chewing and flipping their tails as he passed along the sandy road. He was right, the cattail portion was muddy, but only enough to get his car dirtier than it already was. As he turned onto Durand Road heading north, his headlights washed over the patrol car driven by Jasper Brown. Jasper was now in the lead. Neither man saw a car on the road, nor had they seen any sign of a car off the road. It seemed to prove out that they were the only two cars on the road at that time of night. Out of the three lawmen, all converging to one place, James Lee had not been seen.

* * *

Aunt Thelma, as she was called, had worked on the Parks land at one time. Like most Negro women, she had a good hand at the stove, making wonderful simple meals from almost nothing. She had fed the sawmillers when the south half of the land was being timbered. The old plantation was ten miles square, many acres and plenty of rattlesnakes that had not been introduced to a human, much less bitten one yet.

James Lee cursed angrily. He had never had a damn thing that worked out or did not go bad. "God damn it!" He pounded the open window ledge as he looked for a place to ditch the spent car. The overheated engine had gone from the smell of super-heated steam to the odor of burning oil. He recognized the area where the old Clemens Cemetery was located. He had played there as a small boy waiting on Aunt Thelma to leave. The small pond should still be there. Back then it was a beautiful place with the alders, lilies on the deep green water, and lush green grass before the pine thicket. The Maxwell, like all the Millers, was gone. It was on its last leg. There was a loud knock coming from under the bonnet. The cemetery was an easy transition from Ogletree Road.

"Damn bastard! I'll push the piss out of ya!" James Lee said, gritting his teeth in anger. His heavy foot slammed the clutch for the last time and his strong arm forced the transmission into second gear as the dying car left the road and headed toward the woods past the cemetery. The engine locked up and dropped the drive shaft. The strong shaft hung in the hard ground and sent the boxy car airborne. It landed sideways against several small pines. The gasoline can in the back seat turned over in the process of

259

putting the car into the woods. Lee still held the large steering wheel with both hands as he saw flames coming through the ventilation louvers that covered the sides of the engine. The headlights went out upon impact as the side thrust broke the filaments in the reflector mounted bulbs. The darkness amplified the orange flames that licked skyward. The gasoline revealed itself with its powerful warning odor as it ran forward along the rubber floor mat, pooling against the firewall.

Lee scrambled out of the passenger side door just before the engine compartment burst into flames, followed by the ignition of the pooled gasoline in the floorboard. The night sky provided a backdrop for the leaping orange and yellow flames as the stolen car burned. James Lee had lost his food box and his ammo, except for what was in the revolver and his front pocket, maybe a couple dozen rounds. He was feeling sore from bouncing around as the car came to rest. The ball of fire would surely attract attention, as it could be seen for miles around. The family cemetery was on a knoll, like so many in the Deep South. Lee scurried north, toward the Parks property. Like a nasty, evil rat he ran into the deep shadows of the woods. He stood on the opposite road bank and laughed to himself at how much better the car burned with almost a full tank of gasoline and the five gallons spilled from the back seat.

The clouds passed and the moon gave him good light for walking on the narrow, abandoned logging road. It was the same road he had taken up to the camp's kitchen where Aunt Thelma worked. Since the days when it had fallen out of use, several large pines had died and fallen across the road, making it difficult for anyone to drive up looking for him. He was pleased. The old road followed a high ridge. Below was a finger of Flat Shoals Creek. From the ridge James Lee noticed the lights of a house about a half mile west, out on the main road. That would be his goal for tomorrow. Maybe they would have a car or something he could steal to get to Alabama, he thought to himself.

* * *

The sheriff's deputy was never seen by the two Warm Springs units. They drove to the store at Harris City, where they sat for a few minutes and talked from car to car. The half barrel on the porch of the store had contained drinks during the business day. Bill Sullivan kept them iced down for the thirsty laborers that came by. Every brand of drink was in the barrel, any one for a nickel. The melted ice found its way to the volunteer zinnias and giant marigolds that come up each year along the underpinning of the porch. Jasper Brown sat facing the store. Chief Hawthorn sat looking south, away from the store, but he glanced at it now and then in his mirror.

"I see Sullivan's store cat is drinking from the cold water left in the drink barrel," Jasper said. He watched the crafty cat balance on a wide rocker arm with its hind feet and touch the rim of the half barrel with its front paws. The chief bent down to find the cat in his mirror and smiled at the creature's ingenuity. The wind blew from the southwest. Jasper took his hat off and let the cool breeze rush through his white hair. He looked at his watch. "Past quittin' time," he said.

"And I'm here too!" said Chief Hawthorn. "What's the Bible say about the wicked?" he asked, looking around and sniffing hard enough to be heard.

"They'ens shall be with us forever and take over the place," Jasper quickly replied.

Chief Hawthorn smiled. "That's the meek shall inherit the earth," he said, correcting his officer.

"Oh!" Jasper grunted low. "Smell tires?" he asked the chief, as he raised up higher in his seat, looking around.

"I thought I did," said the chief. "Jesus!" he said, pointing to the southwest sky.

Jasper finally moved about to look through the chief's car, parked next to him. "Hell of a fire!" he exclaimed.

"Heck, we're here! Let's go see, you do have a flashlight?" asked the chief.

"Two!" Jasper proudly replied. "That new woman detective, one of her things," he said, grinning.

They cranked their engines. "Hey!" the chief said, before pulling away. "I'm glad yer here. You've certainly changed since she came."

"Thanks!" replied Jasper, eager to go to the fire. The two curious officers sped away, south on Durand Road and then due west on Ogletree Road. The chief led the way. The burning smell grew stronger and the glow in the distance brighter.

James Lee was so far into the Parks property that the car fire was a small glow behind him. He looked about in the overgrown timber country for the main road, where he knew the old cook house was. Lee expected it to be in bad shape, maybe even fallen over, but it was a place he knew well. The operation was so large they had hand dug and curbed a well. There should be the remains of a boiler, unless the surplus steel mongers had stolen it away.

The last of the burning Maxwell bent and buckled under the extreme heat of the gasoline fueled fire. The roof was gone, melted. The metal frames in the seats still held the coiled springs and the hand wired connectors. The burning upholstery flamed in small clumps, occasionally falling to the earth below. The wooden boards making up the floorboard were long since gone. Chief Howard Hawthorn pulled his car head-on toward the burning automobile. Jasper, thinking of what he should do for safety, swung wide and put his headlights on the burning car from almost ninety degrees to the chief's. The chief stood watching. Jasper burst out of his patrol car with a flashlight in hand, but not on, and went even deeper into the cover of the brush. The veteran officer quickly looked for others in the woods around the car. Maybe the nigger had set up an ambush. After riding with the Campbell County officer, his partner Heather, he did not want to take the chance by just sitting in the car with such a bright light source.

The two pines the Maxwell sat against were burning all the way to the very tops. Jasper looked quickly in the front seat and then the back. The flames were still hot. "Nobody in it!" he yelled to the chief, who had just gotten out of his car.

Jasper walked toward the chief. "Ya scared?" the chief asked.

Jasper holstered his revolver. "No! Just givin' that nigger a sportin' chance," he said, watching the fire.

"You've gone local on me," said Chief Hawthorn.

Jasper looked at the chief. 'What do ya mean?" he asked.

"A man who's been to a World War and come back, politically correct, you've been using nigger a lot. It was Negro," smiled the chief. The flames, reflecting from their uniform buttons and badges, felt warm on their faces.

Jasper spit a wad of mucus, trying to rid his throat of the nasty odor of the burning materials. "This sum bitch ain't no Negro, he's a god damn nigger. Not that I'm an educated man, but I looked it up in the dictionary. Mine said anyone low down, slovenly, lazy, applying to any race," Jasper said, watching the car burn. The sound of glass breaking from the tremendous heat broke the silence of the dying flames.

"That's the Maxwell car," said the chief. "See the tag? 321-689. The sum bitch is around here somewhere," he added, looking around in the darkness.

"We know he's on foot," added Jasper. "Tomorrow?" he asked.

"I think so, get a posse out here and see what we can find. Maybe some dogs, too," said Chief Hawthorn.

The two officers drove back to their jurisdiction, one behind the other. Chief Hawthorn called Sheriff Gilbert with their findings and the location of the burned car.

*   *   *

Heather's evening at Mrs. Blakely's was unusually quiet, with the feeling there was something lurking about. She tried to read, but it could not hold her interest. Heather was restless. Jasper had stopped by, unbeknown to the chief, and told her of their findings up at the Clemens Cemetery, and that the chief thought the sheriff would get up a posse to search the woods in the morning. She was excited. Back home her father, Sonny, and the dog, Holly, would be tracking even in the darkness. In some ways she wished it was home, but it was not, and things happened a little slower down here. Heather burned off energy with her sit-ups and some push-ups. The telephone rang downstairs. The harsh bell resonated up the stairwell. She laid back from her sit-ups and listened.

"Hello!" said Mrs. Blakely. "I'll get her."

Heather brought herself to a full sit-up, rose to her feet, and hurried into the foyer, where Mrs. Blakely yelled for her to come to the telephone. Heather took the steps, skipping every other one, in her bare feet.

"Thanks!" she said, taking the telephone. Mrs. Blakely returned to her room. "Detective Duncan," Heather said.

"Detective my ass!" a gruff voice said on the other end.

"Dad!" Heather's face gleamed with happiness.

"You all right?" Sonny asked.

"Sure! Why not?" Heather asked.

"Grandmother Margaret elected me to call," he said.

"Tell her I love her!" Heather said.

"We've heard radio coverage on this case and read about it in the newspaper. That sum bitch is dangerous," Sonny said.

"Is that Holly I hear close to the telephone?" Heather asked.

"Right here under my arm. She can hear you," he said, rubbing the loyal dog's head. "Should me and her come get the bastard?" Sonny asked.

"If it were up to me, yes, but the sheriff is calling the shots, unless we run across him," Heather answered.

"Well, you know me and her can pull him out," Sonny said. Holly barked!

"I can't say much, the line could be open," Heather said.

"I know that," Sonny said. "You be damn careful. If ya have to shoot someone, shoot ta kill," Sonny said in a stern tone.

"I will. I will," Heather said.

"Don't even blink once you start, shoot 'till they drop," he said. "Yer Grandmother's saving the articles," he added.

"I don't doubt it," she replied.

"This is expensive," Sonny said, letting out a loud sigh.

"I love y'all," Heather said.

"We love you too!" replied Sonny. "Good night," he said softly.

"Sleep tight!" Heather whispered.

* * *

The lawn of the jail house was noisy with the yelping of dogs and the moving of cars and flatbed trucks for the purpose of hauling the specialized dogs about the countryside. Miss Dixie was irritated over the fact that someone was in her parking space and she had to park on the far side of the court square. She carried her lunch sack high to keep the sniffing dogs from exploring it as she wormed her way through the maze of animals, both men and dogs. In some cases, she was hard pressed to tell the difference. Miss Dixie had been told for years that trackers were a breed of their own. This morning was like walking through the midway at the fair with these men as the main viewing attraction. Some were polite and tipped their hats as she passed by. Others, like their dogs, looked at her with a hungry, meat stalking look about them. The youngest appeared to be in his late teens, probably would not know what to do with a criminal if he caught one. Some looked like criminals themselves, unshaven, ill-kept, dirty clothes, and every one of them either wore a pistol or had a rifle of some sort.

Miss Dixie finally made it to the front door of the sheriff's office. "Damn it!" she mumbled as she entered, the screen door slamming behind her. She gave the lunch sack an angry toss and it slid across her desk.

"Forget something?" asked Sheriff Gilbert, looking up from his desk when she came in.

"No!" she replied sharply, dropping into her desk chair. The telephone rang. "Hello!" she said, grabbing the telephone. "Sheriff's office! Dixie speaking!" she corrected herself, noticing that her boss, the sheriff, was watching. "Telephone!" Dixie said, holding it out for Sheriff Gilbert.

"Who is it?" he asked, rising from his desk chair.

"Chief Hawthorn," she replied.

The sheriff hurried to the telephone. "Sheriff Gilbert," he said, sitting on the edge of Miss Dixie's desk.

"We're at Bill Sullivan's store now and should be at the burned-out car in fifteen minutes," said the chief. The Warm Springs officers had begun to gather a crowd of onlookers, especially since Heather was there. "We plan to keep a distance until you can get down here and see it for yerself," said the chief.

"I've got a yard full of trackin' dogs and men! We'll see if we can get a sign, maybe we can find this sum bitch," said Sheriff Gilbert. "We'll come in there on the road in front of the cemetery," he added, looking at his watch. "Should be there on the hour."

The kitchen cat that Miss Jewel fed had wandered around to the front steps, where it sat in the morning sun, eyes squinted, watching the dogs. They began to bark and tug at their leashes. The thirty or so dogs that barked and yelped were bothering Miss Dixie. She got up and closed the office door, muffling the noise a little.

"Curley! Dixie!" yelled the sheriff. Curley came from the cell block, the heavy steel door moaning. Dixie stopped what she was doing. "All the deputies are on patrol. These dozen or so trackers will be sworn in just a minute, they are armed and can back me if we find this nigger. I use that loosely, I think he's lower than dog shit," snarled the sheriff, as he unwrapped a fresh cigar.

"Long day?" asked Curley.

"One day, one cigar!" the sheriff replied. He checked his revolver for a full cylinder of shells, just as if he had fired it recently. It was a mental thing, a comfort. He turned toward the door. "Oh! Miss Dixie, would you be so kind as to contact Doc Hubbard and see if the autopsy report is ready? If it is, please tell him we'll pay him to take it down to Warm Springs, to the woman detective. A copy for the county will be fine," he said, with a slight smile at his secretary. The door closed behind him.

"Peace!" Dixie said out loud. "I can get something finished."

The waiting trackers stood by, smoking and spitting. The eager dogs, mostly hounds, were sitting or lying about on the grass and under the shade of open tailgates. Everything began to stir when the High Sheriff came out. "Use yer truck Jed?" the sheriff asked an old man who was parked close to the jail steps. The old man nodded. The sheriff stepped onto the running board and then into the back of the Model T Ford truck. The men knew that a short speech was next.

The sheriff removed the cigar from his cheek and held it in his hand. "Gentlemen! Dogs! Thank you fer comin'!" he said loudly. A few people had stopped on the square to watch what was happening at the jail. "Warm Springs Special Deputies found a burned-out Maxwell last night, just good dark, at the old Clemens Cemetery on Ogletree Road. Road other side of the square drops right down to it, should ya get separated from the group." He looked about at the faces, some young and some terribly old, and the same for the dogs that were gathered. "The pay, well, it's slim," he said. That got a chuckle from the crowd. "There is a reward. Whoever lays hands on the sum bitch, I'd say he should get at least a third, then everyone else can split it, the other two-thirds, evenly. We've always done it that way," said Sheriff Gilbert. "I'll swear you in and I'll swear at ya too, 'fore the day's done!" he said.

"I think I got shot at last time," a man called out.

"I'm sorry I missed," smiled the sheriff. The old ones laughed and the new faces did not know what to do. "Raise yer right hands!" said the sheriff, doing the same. "I, state yer full name, accept the duties assigned and appointed to me as a Special Deputy for Meriwether County. I will perform this to the best of my ability, so help me God," said the sheriff. The sea of voices repeated the oath. "Look around ya fellers. Them with badges have captured more than five men in their volunteerin'," he said, pointing to a very few men wearing them. "Load 'em up!" he yelled, waving his fedora and giving a rebel yell. The dogs went wild, barking and baying with excitement.

Sheriff Louis Gilbert cranked his car and slowly lugged toward the stop sign on the courthouse square. The trackers' vehicles fell in behind and they all headed out, like a parade of excited boys. The sheriff bumped his siren, the vehicles behind him sounded their horns, and the caged dogs barked and yelped as they went around two sides of the square and out of sight. Old veterans and old men stood and waved with their hats as the parade passed.

"If I'ze that sum bitch, I'd put it in high gear and get gone," said one old man, braced on a cane, to his checker playing friend standing next to him in front of the hardware.

Chief Hawthorn, Detective Duncan, Officer Jasper Brown, and Officer Edgar Peterson were waiting in three cars, as the chief had said they would, on the edge of the road at the cemetery. Everyone was in uniform except for Heather. She was in her suit with her heavy .45 pistol tucked under her coat, nesting in the shoulder holster. Jasper sat patiently, cleaning his fingernails with a small penknife, one arm resting in the open window. Edgar Peterson sat with his car door open, feet squarely on the running board, carefully peeling a Red Delicious apple. He tried to keep the peeling from breaking as it spiraled from his knife blade. He was really not interested, he would rather be at home, or sitting in town, maybe watching the bricklayers in the back finishing the addition.

A single car pulled behind the three Warm Springs marked police cars. It was the newspaper reporter, Alfred Huffman. He sat waiting on the sheriff and the trackers. The deputy who went out to search for James Lee had tipped him off about the sighting. Frances Goulding was a big help too; she had told Huffman over the telephone that there was a search taking place in the area of the Clemens Cemetery. When the reporter saw the first tracker and his dogs arrive at the jail's yard, he drove ahead. He had lots of film, his film. If there was not a story with photographs, then he would have them for his collection.

*   *   *

James Lee had found his cook house, what there was left of it after all these years. He slept out in the open, on pine tops that he had pulled off in the light of the moon. The old house, even though it was only one large room, looked too spooky for him to enter in the darkness. He was damp, but the morning sun felt good as it began to slowly dry him out. A fire would have been grand, but the smoke would drift too far, arousing those who might live around the property. He was beginning to feel hungry. The marble sized green plums that he managed to find along the overgrown road were bitter, but better than nothing. Lee gradually ate them from his hand and the shirt pocket that he had filled. This Negro was smart. He knew the trackers were next, but when?

Lee quietly backtracked almost to the road. He was so close to the cemetery that he saw the four cars parked along the shoulder. He took a small pine bough and began to dust out his tracks in the sandy dirt. Before the sheriff arrived, he was already sitting high on a hill top watching the activity below. He laughed at every mistake the trackers made. "Dum' ass white folks," he giggled to himself, hidden in the warm sun.

* * *

The sheriff arrived along with all the trackers and dogs. They were loud enough to wake the dead and alarm the deaf. The sheriff stood in the middle of the road and the Warm Springs officers gathered around. "I want an old tracker and a young tracker to work together," the sheriff yelled. "Pair off then get yer dogs!" he said, chewing his cigar. He counted teams. "Four teams and an odd lot," he said, so everyone could hear. "The four teams, see if you can get a sign around the car and work it. The odd team work the road, quarter mile back and a quarter mile ahead, talk to folks, maybe someone saw the sum bitch," said Sheriff Gilbert, spitting on the dusty road. "Warm Springs will put a sworn man with every team," he added, looking at Chief Hawthorn.

Hawthorn pointed out a team to Jasper and Edgar. "I'll take one," he said.

Heather spoke up. "I'll take the road," she said, walking away to catch up with the young man and his dogs.

James Lee stood up. He thought he recognized the suited one on the road. "It's that bitch!" he said aloud.

The trackers circled the burned-out car and got a sign. Little did they know it was three school age boys that had come down after seeing the bright fire in the evening sky. They wanted to see what was burning, then they headed off to the deep holes along the creek to fish, giving no thought that they would be caught.

Heather caught up with the tracker on the road. "Hey! Wait up!" she called out, jogging along. The young man, just barely past eighteen, pulled up his dogs. There were three. "I'm to work with you," she said, walking up.

"I'm Toby Sims," said the young man. "That's Sam, Judy, and Sheba," he said, pointing to the three dogs. The male was in the lead.

"Detective Duncan," Heather said, extending her hand.

"Glad ta meet ya!" he said.

Heather touched each of the dogs. "You like dogs?" Toby asked.

"I'm a tracker, with my Dad, from Campbell County," she answered.

"Campbell County!" he said excitedly. "Sonny Duncan?" he asked.

"That's right, and our dog, Holly," Heather replied.

"Y'all are legends!" Toby said eagerly. "They don't know that. They been talkin' 'bout you and how a woman's taking a man's job," he said low, like they would hear.

"Let 'em talk. We'll see," she said. She had settled on Sheba. "This is yer best dog," Heather announced.

"Oh, why?" Toby asked. Heather rubbed the dog's head and larger

267

boxy nose. "Larger nose cavity than the other two, processes the scent better," she said. "We've only had one dog at a time," she added. "They are like family 'round our house. I think we're just walking for the hell of it," Heather said, giving her opinion. "This Negro's heading west, for some reason. Seen any signs?" she asked, walking along.

"No," Toby said.

"You from here?" she asked.

"Odessadale," he replied, pulling the dogs to a stop.

"Think of where there's a place to hold up, or a small dry place to hide," Heather said. "He may be hurt. Did he wreck the car, or did he do it deliberately?" she asked, as they turned to walk back in the other direction. "Any Negroes live around close?" Heather asked. Sheba was tracking next to Heather.

"Your Holly, what kind?" Toby asked.

"Big feet, wrinkles, a registered bloodhound, red in color," Heather said proudly.

"These, well, you know, blueticks," he said.

"Any dog beats a human's nose," Heather said, not wanting him to feel bad. She dropped her hand down, touching Sheba. "Here's yer best dog," she said again. "The other two trot and pull along. Sheba, watch her. She thinks and smells, with her head up, reads tha wind. Best dog. Our Holly can sign from the car," she bragged.

They walked silently, looking at the ground. Eventually they passed the cemetery where the Maxwell had left tracks when it left the road. "Do we go down to the car?" Toby asked.

"No need, the smells will cloud the dogs' noses. Best walk in a circle out around it," Heather suggested.

The four tracking teams had rushed up around the burned car and then hit on the school boys that came through. The teams were now working both sides of the small pond and one even a ways down the creek bank. The boys could hear the dogs, but had no idea as to what they were in for. Sheriff Gilbert was with the team down on the creek bank.

"You never answered my question," Heather said, unbuttoning her top blouse button and taking off her coat. The bright sun was warm.

"No Negroes," Toby said. They walked a little further looking closely for sign. "I've heard there was a sawmill on the old Parks Plantation, maybe thirty years ago. There was a wood fired boiler and some outbuildings, so I've heard," Toby said.

Toby had a lever gun slung across his shoulder. The strap was a homemade leather and canvas contraption.

"What caliber?" Heather asked.

"44-40," he replied. "It's my first gun," he added.

"Model 92's are good guns, strong, smooth actions," Heather

commented. She could tell he was taken back that she would know what he was carrying.

James Lee had grown tired, bored, and hungry. He had watched the trackers take to the other side of the road, out of hearing range. The curiosity of the house he had seen last night gnawed on his mind. "There could be another car or something to steal, get tha hell out of here. Maybe something to eat or even water," he thought, as he stood up to wander in that direction. The woods floor was covered with damp leaves and it was almost silent walking. When he would squat down, he could just barely make out the small unpainted house in the distance. He could take a chance and dart across the road a ways down and then silently come up on it.

"Let's give this road trackin' to that house in the distance, maybe sumthin'll turn up," Heather suggested. "Look!" She pointed down at a heel print. Toby looked and then got on his knees examining the heel print.

"Looks ta be goin' to the road," he said.

"That's what I thought." Heather nodded in agreement. They got on the dusty roadway, but the tracks seemed to vanish. "Lots of cars been by. I'll look on the other side ta see if they crossed," Heather said, walking alone on the opposite shoulder.

* * *

The four teams began to bay and the trackers were becoming excited. They felt they might have the wanted Negro on the run. Sheriff Gilbert hurried along with the trailing pack. His cigar was growing wetter, slobber dripping from the corner of his mouth. Jasper Brown was doing good to keep his team in sight. Edgar was not much better; he too was older and slower. The chief was wiping sweat with his handkerchief as he quickstepped behind the tracker and his team.

The schoolboys sat quietly on the creek bank and watched the deep green waters of Flat Shoals Creek pass by. An occasional lingering fall colored leaf fell from the sycamore and drifted to the mirror surface of the waters below to be swept away. The voices of men and the barking of dogs grew louder.

"Is that the truant officers?" one freckle-faced boy asked his friends.

"There's someone!" yelled the first tracker.

"Turn 'em loose!" a man yelled. The men's voices and the barking dogs were enough to strike fear in anyone's heart. The schoolboys, who had done nothing more than skip school just to fish, instantly related the sound to the chain gangs seen on the cinema screen.

"R-u-u-n-n-n!" one boy screamed, as a huge dog broke the brush line, yelping and baying as it loped forward. The three young boys dropped their cane poles and took to the woods. One went downstream. He kept ahead of the five dogs and the sheriff almost to the road bridge a mile north of

Durand. The other two boys went up the steep banks and took to the first trees they could find, climbing to the very top. They watched the men with the packs of barking dogs below. The terrified boys clung to the tree limbs as the wind blew the limber treetops about. They rode the treetops and looked down like treed raccoons.

"Quiet tha dogs!" yelled Chief Hawthorn, trying to catch his breath between deep pants. The handlers soon calmed the dogs.

"They're worse in groups like this," called out one tracker.

"Hey! Boys! You white?" the chief yelled out, looking up in the tall tree, where one boy swayed.

"Y-y-yes, s-s-sir!" the scared boy yelled back.

"Ain't seen a nigger here 'bouts?" called the chief.

"No, sir!" the other boy called down from another tree.

"Damn! There's another one, up there!" a tracker yelled, pointing to the top of another tall tree.

"You boys go around that burned car at the cemetery?" asked the chief, yelling up into the tree.

"Yes, sir!" the boy called down.

"Are we in trouble?" the other one yelled down.

"I'm the Chief of Po-lice! You be in school tomorrow!" yelled Chief Hawthorn, with his hands cupped beside his mouth.

"Tomorrow's Saturday!" yelled down the other boy.

"Don't piss me off, boy! I'll shoot you out of there like a God damn 'coon! Be in school, next school day!" Chief Hawthorn yelled back. The tracking men chuckled and took the chance to catch their breath too.

Sheriff Gilbert and his trackers had grown tired. "It's him, boys!" yelled the sheriff. "Fast as he's runnin' it can't be a white boy!" he called out, still running along as fast as a man in his late fifties could. The sheriff's voice broke and quivered with each rough spot and hole that jarred him. All the dogs were on a pleasurable summer run, pink tongues showing. They seemed to laugh and giggle at the men who tried to run with them.

The young schoolboy could see the road rise and fall alongside him as he ran. "It's time for a diversion," he said to himself. "Damn! Truant Officers from hell! Where did they come from?" he thought, as he suddenly took to the top of a weathered poplar log that ran to the creek bottoms, then up to the road. It was steep, but his re-soled shoes bit into the weathered trunk with the surefootedness of a raccoon. At that moment, the lad thought of his trip to Peter Street in Atlanta, a long ways for a haircut from the Shaw Brothers, but it was close, all the way to the white and lasted for months. The trip was really to get Grover Shaw to put one more set of soles on the brogans that the local man said were too far gone. The miracles of Mr. Shaw had just proven themselves. The nails and maple pegs might look funny when he showed his shoe soles, but they bit into the slick barkless tree trunk in his time of dire need. Traction was certainly better than the "cat paw" rubber ones.

The dogs would have to be disciplined to take the log one at a time, and that would create a problem for a few minutes. His legs were beginning to burn. He needed a place to rest, or better yet, to hide and lose them. The young boy was now on the Davenport property, cotton one year and corn the next. He was tired and his lungs were starting to burn. "Oh, God! What a blessing!" he said out loud, when he saw a water filled ditch and a culvert pipe. The splashing water spotted him with mud to his elbows and then the wet culvert pipe finished him off. The young boy was dirty from head to toe as he took to the pipe on his hands and knees. There was a treetop that had hung about six feet in. He tore the gnarly limbs loose and managed to force himself past it. If he had a hard time, then he knew the dogs would too. The lad forced the treetop into place and pulled several limbs from nearby to shore up the entangled mess. The tired and winded boy was still and quiet. He could hear his heart beating and his own breathing there in the darkness of the long concrete pipe.

The dogs and men were eventually heard splashing about. "Sum bitch's here somewhere!" a man's voice said. The dogs sniffed, even up inside the pipe. The sounds echoed. The better dogs kept hitting on the culvert.

"Boy! We know yer in there!" yelled the sheriff, his damp cigar held in his hand as he looked up into the dark pipe. The scared boy lay quietly. "Give up!" the sheriff yelled out. "Don't make us fire up in there!" he yelled. "Make it easy on yerself! James Lee, come out!" yelled the sheriff.

The young boy was lying on his side. "James Lee? Who's James Lee?" he asked himself.

"I ain't James Lee!" the boy yelled back.

Sheriff Gilbert stood looking bewildered with his hands on his hips. "Don't try that shit on me, boy!" he yelled back into the pipe.

"But, I ain't James Lee!" the boy yelled back.

"We been in the business too long for that trick," the sheriff replied. "If you ain't James Lee, count to five for me," he commanded.

"One, two, three," counted the tired and muddy boy.

"Here it comes," whispered the sheriff.

"Four, five," continued the lad.

The sheriff was shocked. "One more time!" he yelled back.

"One, two, three, four, five," the boy counted loudly.

"He didn't say fo'," said the sheriff. "Who are ya?" he yelled.

"Jimmy Benson, fifth grader!" the boy called back.

"Jimmy Benson!" the sheriff barked. "You ain't no Negro?"

"No, sir! Not the last I looked!" the boy called out from the echoing pipe. The trackers laughed.

"Did you go around the car in the cemetery?" asked Sheriff Gilbert.

"Me and two more," answered the boy.

"God damn it!" said the sheriff, spitting a piece of wet cigar from his mouth. "Shit!"

"Come on out here," the sheriff said, looking up into the pipe with a little less caution. He could see the small boy lying on his side in the shallow water.

The young schoolboy eventually crawled out. He was wet and muddy. "Why did ya run?" asked Sheriff Gilbert.

"We thought ya was Truant Officers," Jimmy replied.

* * *

Della Cummings was doing laundry. The wringer washer churned the soapy water about as the open electric motor hummed, drawing its power from the overhead receptacle. It was connected by a screw-in adapter right into the light socket. The midday sun warmed her nicely behind the dark oxidized screens that covered the upper half of the back porch. The wash water that splashed from the enameled tub ran down the outside and dripped onto the worn board floor, finding its way to the small crack under the wall, dripping to the ground below. The yard chickens were bewildered by the sparkling domed bubbles of all sizes that floated on the surface of the water. They pecked at the bubbles just to see them suddenly disappear.

Della Cummings had a cat and a tiny dog that could not get along, so the cat took the front porch and the tiny dog got the back porch. The cat napped in peace, while the tiny dog sat on the porch ledge and looked toward the Flat Shoals Creek bottoms. The baying and barking of the tracking dogs called him to wander.

"Pud' yer suitcase down, ya ain't goin' nowheres." Della laughed at the tiny dog as it shook with excitement.

The Elberta peach crop had come in a little early. Della had always canned, but this year she was trying her hand at drying some. The rehydrated fruit pie was something to behold in the hands of a good cook and clean new lard. Cobblers did all right with the canned ones. Between washer loads she was busy working down a bushel to place on the window screens she had traded for at the church flea market. They were the very dinkum for supporting cheese cloth and the uniform sliced peaches in the bright sun that she had committed to chasing around the porches. It took about three hot days of full sun to dry a screen load. She was finishing off the first two screens out of six.

James Lee had worked his way zigging and zagging through the new growth woods, mostly sweetgums, hickory, and dogwoods. The old lumber site was littered with rotting pine tops, making it hard to make time without raising a noise. At first, he thought the house was across the roadway, but it was not. It was across a small cow branch and green open field, then past the outbuildings. It was perfect for a rat like James Lee to scurry from one to the next. Lee came out of the woods by sliding down a steep red clay bank, right into the small branch. The two milk cows kept the rich manure laden mud churned up.

The blue jays called out when they discovered him. Even over the sounds of the washer, Della heard them fussing over something. "Must be a snake in the pasture," she said to the tiny dog. Its keen tail wagged as it looked from behind the screens. The dog saw the Negro dart between the leaning barn and the old blacksmith shop. He gave a short ruff!

"Another cat, huh?" Della said, pulling the hose from the side of the washer and placing it on the crude floor drain. The soapy water rushed out. The poor woman drew her wash water from the well, located on the back porch. She had an electric pump, but that was more money spent, to run it. The galvanized bucket rode the cotton rope into the darkness, from the well curb to the water below. Then she would crank the windlass and bring the full bucket to the top, dumping it into the washer's tub, one bucket at a time. The dog continued to show interest in something. Della joined in and looked too, but she could not see anything unusual.

James Lee was able to open the back door to the blacksmith shop with the blade of his pocket knife. The whittled down peg was no match for the skills of the Negro that handled the knife. He lifted it from the rusty hasp. The old building was well ventilated by the vertical cracks on the rough planks that covered the sides. Sunlight beamed in through the tiny nail holes in the tin roofing, casting bright circles of light on the old equipment and the coal dust covered floor. James Lee could check on the house by looking through the many cracks. He had all the time he needed to explore.

The old shop was now used for storage. Dusty tarpaulins covered stacks of wooden crates and trunks. In the space in front of the double door sat a vehicle of some kind. The Negro could only see four inflated wheels. His leathery hand pulled back the tarpaulin and a 1922 Willis glistened, stored with spit and polished pride. James Lee smiled. Even in the darkness, inside the cab he could see that the ignition key was there. The Negro checked the house once more, as he heard the tiny dog bark.

Della had eventually filled the washing machine and began the rinse cycle. The loud machine sloshed the soapy clothes back and forth in the deep tub. Della went to the front porch to check on her peaches. One screen full was ready to be stored. "After the wash," she thought, and then returned to the washer. She stood watching. The next dreaded step was the rollers, mashing the water from the wet clothes. It made her fingers sore to just look at the damn things. She had run her fingers in there on more than one occasion. During the waiting time, Della drew a bucket of water for the chickens. A cast iron spider was sitting outside, next to the steps. They drank from it during the day. She set the bucket just outside the porch door, on the top step.

James Lee crawled inside the cab. He tapped on the fuel gauge. It was showing empty. The ignition switch in the operating position did not make any difference either.

"Damn it!" he said, hurrying out of the dark shadowy cab. He totally removed the dusty tarpaulin and found the fuel cap. It was chrome plated and unscrewed easily. He took a slender piece of river cane and explored the tank. It came up with the slightest trace of gasoline on the tip end. "Damn it! Sum bitch!" he said, striking the car body with his fist. "Damn it!"

The sun had changed and he could see the silhouette of the woman on the porch. She would go and come. Whenever she left, the tiny dog followed. The old buildings were shaded by chinaberry trees, and many of those were ill-kept with young sprouts growing up from the surface roots. The sprawling magnolia close to the back porch touched the ground. James Lee continued to watch the woman as she went about her work. The water bucket was most tempting. When Della left the back porch, Lee made his move. He hurried to the chinaberry closest to the magnolia, before the yard chickens clucked and moved about. Della and the dog stopped to listen.

"Chickens!" she said to the dog. Its tail wagged as it looked up, hearing her words. "They'll cluck at an acorn," she remarked, setting the ready screen of dried peaches close to the steps. "I'll do the clothes and then we'll put these away." The woman and her dog went back to the washing.

* * *

Detective Duncan and tracker Toby Sims were slowly working the shoulders of the road, but still far from the home of Della Cummings. Toby's dogs raised a cotton tail. It scurried away in leaps and bounds, finding cover in another clump of budding blackberries.

"It took the longest to get chase out of 'em," Toby said, holding the three dogs that had stopped to watch the critter run away.

"That's nature for them," Heather replied. She bent down looking at the ground for the slightest disturbance. "We need to go back a ways," she said, standing to stretch her back. Heather leaned forward and looked at a twig growing from a dewberry. "Look." She pointed to a small gathering of bugs. Toby came closer to see. "Ticks! Damn nasty blood suckers," said Heather, stepping back. "We comb yellow sulfur on our dog before we go out. Let's go back, I want to look again. I've missed his tracks somewhere."

Toby pulled Judy and Sam around. Sheba seemed to be favoring the company of Heather. "How far?" he asked.

"I'll know, just a little ways," Heather said. She walked stooped over, dropping to a knee now and then, but not leaving the road.

"I hear the others," Toby said. "They're comin' back."

"They struck out," Heather said, still looking for sign.

"Let's call it!" yelled the sheriff. He was covered, as was everyone else, in beggar-lice. The dogs had a good run and the men were looking tired, lacking enthusiasm. The schoolboys had given them a good chase.

The three schoolboys walked with the group of lawmen and trackers back to the road. The dogs were eager for another run but the men were finished for the day. "Come see me, boys! I'll see ya get a store-bought cane pole, a new green line, and a float," said Sheriff Gilbert, shaking hands with the sweaty boys.

The sheriff and the other lawmen saw Heather and the young man on the road. "Heck, they ain't found anything either. I didn't expect 'em to," he said. The older trackers did not comment. "Call it a day!" yelled the sheriff, waving to Toby Sims and Detective Duncan.

"When they leave, we'll stay behind," Heather whispered. "I've got sign, too many will spoil the hunt," she whispered, as they pulled off and walked toward the cars.

"Bill Sullivan's?" someone yelled.

"Bill Sullivan's!" was the reply.

Heather went to Chief Hawthorn. "I've got reason ta stay. I want to talk to the folks in the house up the road a ways," she said. "Tracker's staying too," she added.

"Not past five, hours are too many now," he replied, wiping sweat with his handkerchief.

Jasper walked up after hearing the comment. "I'd like ta stay, Chief. Not on the clock," he added.

"Why?" the chief asked.

"She's my partner," Jasper replied. "It can't be that long. I'll come out of this coat though," he said, unbuttoning it.

"I haven't heard that before she came," he said.

"That's right, I didn't know what it meant," Jasper replied.

"Be back before five," replied the chief.

"Yes, sir!" they both replied. Edgar Peterson had already left. Heather and her back-up watched as the others left for Bill Sullivan's store in Harris City.

"What's up?" Jasper asked, tossing his uniform coat on the front seat of his patrol car.

"I've found sign over here. I believe whoever wrecked the car went into the woods here," Heather said. Toby looked surprised, as he had missed it.

* * *

Della Cummings busied herself putting the wet clothes through the rubber coated steel rollers of the washer. The release and the clutch were all in the same lever. Minus the water splashing and sloshing, it was the loudest part of the laundry day. Her tiny dog took its seat back on the ledge against the screen. The dog suddenly barked and jumped up. "Sit down!" Della said, holding a dress as it fed through the rollers.

"Damn it!" James Lee said to himself, as he looked from the darkness under the heavy shading of magnolia limbs. The dry fallen leaves were like small fragile plates rustling at every step with loud crunching sounds.

Della stopped and listened. The dog looked out into the yard. "Let me finish here, put up my peaches, and I'll get my shotgun and we'll see what's out there," Della announced, as she pushed the lever forward, engaging the rollers once more. The tiny dog stood and growled.

James Lee could see the water bucket. It was an easy snatch for an experienced thief such as himself. His thirst was awesome, his mouth almost sticking together, his saliva thick and tacky. A nesting hen was company under the magnolia that he had not noticed. She suddenly gave up her nest and hurried into the dirt swept yard. The Rhode Island Red cackled and clucked loudly as she left her nest. Several of the others in the yard joined in. The large rooster strutted about, raising one foot very slowly and putting it down, one after the other, as if in slow motion. He turned his head with its yellow eyes and studied the dark glossy leaves of the huge tree. Just like the tiny dog high above the yard, the rooster was not too sure either.

"If nothing else, I'll get some water," James Lee thought. He joined the strutting rooster and took long exaggerated steps, moving quickly to the steps, where he snatched the full bucket. When the Negro's hand hit the handle, he kept on moving toward the front of the house. The chickens clucked and ran about.

"I'll bet it's a snake," said Della, to the dog.

James Lee hurried behind the gardenia bushes and nandinas, sloshing water as he ran. The defensive rooster was behind him. Not knowing the dried peaches were available on the front porch, Lee planned to cross in front of the small house and make his way back to the old cook house. He was hungry, having gone hours without a meal. His stomach growled and he chuckled at the funny joke he had heard about the stomach snappin' at the liver. The fragrance of the dried peaches suddenly filled his nose, getting his attention. His mouth watered. The napping cat was startled. It jumped down and took cover under the complex structure of the many rockers on the porch.

James Lee's eyes sparkled at the newly discovered treasure. He quickly put a peach in his mouth and proceeded to make a bundle with the very cloth the fruit had dried on. The guardians of Della Cummings' property were on a return trip from the daily pilgrimage to the dusty road ditch, where they took sun naps and bathed. The Negro ran his fingers into the bundle and got another peach, even took one that was not ready yet from another frame nearby. Della was still running the clothes through the wringers. Her screen door was unlocked. The Vindicator lay on the sofa with the wanted Negro's booking photograph on the front page. The front page moved in the gentle breeze.

James Lee was grasping the water bucket handle when the guards arrived. They were pissed! Their hair-raising, scalp tingling cries caused Lee to jump. Della stopped. "Bunky! Get tha shotgun! Sumthin's in the yard!" she shouted, striking the roller lever.

The startled Negro stepped out at a full run, as fast as he could go without spilling most of the water. The water bucket was in one hand, the bundle of dried peaches in the other, and the stolen murder weapon in his pants, weighing them down as he ran. The gray barred guineas were fast, trailing the frightened Negro less than a leap away. The African birds sounded their cry, pot-rack, pot-rack, pot-rack, pot-rack! Geeeheee! Pot-rack, pot-rack, pot-rack, pot-rack! Geeeheee! Geeeheee! If Della and the dog had gone out the front door, she would have seen the fleeing Negro, but she went out the back door.

Even though Della was up in years, she knew when someone or something was about her tiny farm. She noticed the water bucket was gone, saw the spots of spilled water on the steps, and the rooster was strutting around in the side yard like he had just run at something. "Get in tha house!" she said to her tiny friend. The dog was in the porch door first! Della locked the screen and made her way to the front porch, where she immediately saw the screen hook swinging in the gentle breeze. "Oh, God!" she whispered, taking time to look in the other two rooms before going onto the front porch. Della let her long shotgun barrel touch the black screen door, pushing it open in an aggressive manner.

The water bucket sloshed as James Lee hurried along with it. The spilled water had made wet spots in the dirt. Della could see where the bucket had been carried around the side of the house. There was even a wet ring on the bottom step, where someone had set the wet bucket down. She noticed the sulking cat under the group of rockers. Della's eyes grew large and filled with anger when she saw that the screen of dried peaches was gone, cloth and all. The woman stood on the edge of the porch and trailed the water spots as far as she could see, her shotgun held with both hands, ready to fire upon something.

"Sorry sum bitch!" Della yelled as loud as she could. "Steal from an old woman will ya! You God damn sorry trash! Trash, just sorry trash!" she yelled, her wrinkled face flushed with anger. Della shouldered the long-barreled shotgun and fired in the direction of the water spots and tracks in the dirt yard. Boom! Every animal on the small farm suddenly got quiet. The chickens and the rooster ran under the house. It was not Sunday, but they must have thought one of them was bound to die. Della opened the breach and the spent 12-gauge shell ejected into the air. Smoke rose from the barrel until she dropped another cartridge in the chamber. "Peter's Sure-shot! You sum bitch!" she yelled, her shoulder feeling numb. It would be yellow in the morning from the hard recoil. "Come git sum buckshot!" she yelled angrily. The cat had somehow taken sanctuary in the front room of the small rural house. Della was furious. "Steal my damn peaches! I'll call the law! Damn bastard!" she mumbled, hurrying into the house. This time she hooked the screen door. Della heard the guineas returning, clicking and conversing amongst themselves as they walked up from the direction of the road. "Had gasoline in my Willis, I'd run yer ass down," she mumbled, hurrying to the kitchen.

While Della was in bad financial shape, like many folks she did have a telephone. It was seldom used and seldom did she ever get a call. The last time it rang, she had jumped so hard she spilled a covered dish that she was putting into the ice box. She was saving up for a GE Monitor someday. The shotgun made a thud when Della laid it on the kitchen table. The cat and the dog gave a sigh of relief, knowing the shooting was over. "Steal my damn peaches! I'll call the law! Damn bastard!" she mumbled. She hurried over to uncover the wall mounted telephone. It was covered with several aprons and a slicker. The perfect place to hang her accessory garments for the kitchen and the barn.

* * *

Heather walked ahead hurriedly. She waved the others over to join her. "See this, right there?" She pointed to a flat rock on the road bank.

"See what?" Toby asked. Jasper bent down to look.

"The small break, where this tiny piece of rock is broken from the outcropping on the big one," Heather pointed, touching it with her pencil.

"Yes," answered the men.

"Something's been across this rock, as skilled as they were, they disturbed it," Heather said, standing and looking ahead. "Where's the old lumber camp?" she asked Toby.

They both looked around. "This is the old road here," she said, pointing to a small rise on both sides. "From the plums to those trumpet vines. That's the old camp road, I'll bet. I'll go first. Can I work Sheba?" she asked Toby, holding her hand out.

"Sure!" said the young tracker. He cut the dog from the leash and handed her to the detective. Toby felt reluctant giving his dog to someone else, but heck, she was part of Sonny Duncan's bunch.

"Walk behind us, on each side of the road, as best you can determine where it is. Watch for anything bent, crushed or broken, even slightly disturbed sand," Heather said, stepping out with the dog. "Will she bark on command?" she asked, with her back to the two men and dogs.

"When you yell b-a-y," Toby spelled out, not wanting to get the dogs stirred up.

They walked up the remains of the old road for about a hundred or so yards, watching ahead and looking down. The dogs sniffed along. "I believe they are onto the scent, but don't know to follow it, since we've nothing to address them with," said Heather, almost in a whisper. She suddenly stopped and pointed to a dead pine treetop lying across the road, blocking their path. "See that?" She pointed to a single piece of fallen pine bark, paper thin as it was. Jasper and Toby hurried ahead to see. "That's disturbed," she whispered. "And look at the ground, the tracks have been wiped out pretty good, but not good enough," Heather said. "I've seen that since almost the road," she added.

The large, boxy nosed Sheba stood with raised head looking toward the southwest. The dog narrowed her brown eyes and moved her nostrils wider. Heather pulled her pistol. Jasper did not know why, but he pulled his too. "Go see," Heather whispered to Sheba. "Go see!" The dog moved out with raised head. It could be heard sniffing as the group moved through the high grass and woods as silently as possible. Heather had seen what Sheba had found many times. The tall grass was matted down and the leaves disturbed. "Someone's been beddin' down here," she whispered. "Good dog! Good dog!" Heather said, rubbing the dog on the ears. "Sit!" Heather whispered. Sheba sat down.

"What's that?" Jasper asked. Far in the distance to the southwest they could hear the calls. Pot-rack, pot-rack, pot-rack, pot-rack! Geeeheee! Pot-rack, pot-rack, pot-rack, pot-rack! Geeeheee! Geeeheee! Toby and Jasper turned their heads to listen.

Heather knew the sound and hated it. "God damn guineas," she said softly. "Something's about that's unwanted."

The wind seemed to carry the sound of yelling, but they were not sure. "Steal from an old woman will ya! You God damn sorry trash! Trash, just sorry trash!" Boom! They certainly heard the report of the gun.

"Shotgun!" Toby exclaimed.

"Backtrack to the road and let's get to the house we never got to," Heather said, hurrying ahead with Sheba by her side.

Della was so upset she let the telephone ear set dangle against the wall. "Damn bastard!" she said, grabbing the shotgun once more. "I'll shoot at you again just for the hell of it!" The angry woman hurried to the front porch again, stood in the same spot, and fired another load of shot head high toward the road. Boom, the gun reported. "Sum bitchin' bastard!" she yelled at the top of her lungs. "Trash!" The cat and the dog were under the red velour ottoman. They had dropped all their animosity toward one another and were huddled together.

"Come on!" Heather said, as she started to jog along. Jasper, still worn out from the running of the schoolboys, lagged behind.

Boom! The second shot sounded.

The law officers and the tracker had come out so close to the cars that Jasper suggested they drive to the house, about a half mile away, a tiny speck in the distance. Heather took Sheba to the floorboard. Toby eased along with the other two tied in the bed of his truck, and Jasper brought up the rear. He was exhausted and breathing was hard.

Once again, the shotgun was tossed on the kitchen table as Della mumbled to anything that could hear. Ring! Ring! Ring! The bells on the telephone sounded as she cranked on the generating coil to raise the operator.

"Operator!" a woman's voice announced.

"Get me the law!" Della said loudly.

Heather and Sheba were first to pull into the yard. She sounded her siren just a second or two, to announce who was there.

"Hell! Forget it! They're already here!" Della said, hanging up the telephone.

Heather and Sheba got out of the car quickly. The dog ran loose, sniffing about. She worked the side of the house where James Lee had walked with the water bucket and around the front porch and steps where he had been. Heather took cover at a large pine tree until Della opened the screen door. The other two lawmen stopped their vehicles at a distance behind Heather's. Jasper got out quickly and stood at the far back corner of his patrol car, listening and watching. Toby got out on the passenger side and did the same. Judy and Sam stood sniffing and wanting to join Sheba. The guineas began to sound off. Pot-rack, pot-rack, pot-rack, pot-rack! Geeeheee! Pot-rack, pot-rack, pot-rack, pot-rack! Geeeheee! Geeeheee!

"That was fast! I just called for the sheriff and y'all drove up," said Della loudly, standing on the front porch.

"What was the shootin' about?" Heather shouted, still at the edge of the tree.

"Some son of a bitch stole my water bucket and a screen full of dried peaches," Della said. "That was me shootin' out of anger."

Heather stepped from the large tree and walked toward Della.

"Yer' a woman!" Della said.

"All the time, every month!" Heather said loudly, as she walked ahead, putting her pistol in the shoulder holster.

"You the one I read about in the paper!" Della exclaimed, with her hands resting on her hips.

"We're looking for an escaped Negro, James Lee," Heather said. She was joined by Jasper and Toby. "Officer Jasper Brown, my partner, and Toby Sims. This is Judy, Sam and Sheba." Heather made the introductions, pointing as she named people and dogs.

Judy and Sam sniffed around the house, finding interest in the guineas. Sheba was on the scent of James Lee. She was sitting at the edge of the yard, sniffing in the air. Heather pointed to her, once she got Toby's attention. "There's yer best dog," she said.

"That dangerous nigger?" Della asked.

"Very dangerous!" Jasper answered.

"We need to go, ma'am. This is our chance ta catch him," Heather said, smiling at Della.

"I want my water bucket back, forget the peaches!" Della yelled, as they hurried off with the dogs.

"I'll work Sheba! Jasper, stay here in your car and watch the road. If anyone crosses, hurry down and blow your horn if it's him," she said, as she hurried toward the waiting Sheba.

James Lee had hurriedly worked his way back to where he slept and on to the old leaning cook house. He knew he needed to hide some place where he could make a stand. He felt it might come to that. The water bucket was a little more than two-thirds full. The bundle of dried peaches gave off a very sweet and pleasant fragrance as he hurried along. The briars tore at his clothing and his skin, even tugging at the bundle of peaches, causing one to fall out.

Jasper pulled his patrol car onto the road and looked east, toward the cemetery and Harris City. "Damn! Not the man I was," he said to himself, wiping sweat. He was sure glad to be watching, there was not a good fight left in him. Heather had seen that by his pale complexion. He was where he needed to be, watching and driving.

Heather and Toby trailed through Della's yard and came out on the road. Sheba, the lead dog, was working toward the woods to the northeast, back to the old cook house and lumber camp. Heather felt of her butt to see if her two extra magazines were there, then Toby noticed she checked her shoulder holster. There was another one there. He had never worked with a woman before, especially a tracker, and one that appeared to be able to handle a gun. Between all that and the fact that she was attractive, he was on an adrenaline high as he tagged along, often working to the side of Heather and Sheba.

The land lay at a slight grade, uphill. One could get winded quickly. From time to time Heather would drop down to one knee and look ahead, under the line of green tree leaves. She could get a better look at what the woods looked like to the tracking dog. "How close to the camp?" she whispered, bumping into Toby.

"Stop!" he said, bending to catch his breath. He looked around under the tree canopy, as she had done.

"You've never been down there before?" she asked.

He blushed. "No! But I will be from now on," he said, getting up. "About a hundred and fifty yards."

"You're self-taught," Heather said.

Toby looked down for a moment and then up. "Yes," he said.

"Keep that 92 out of the dirt, and if you survive you need to get professional training," she said. "Or quit. You can get killed doin' this." Heather pulled a piece of string from her coat pocket, dropped off her suit coat, and tied the back together in a tight gathering, then put it back on. Toby looked at her and grinned.

"Don't laugh! I'm not rich and can't leave this behind," she said. "I can get some air and get to my gun," she whispered.

The wind changed. Sheba stood and gave a soft woof!

"Hold yours," said Heather. "See 'bout it, girl! See 'bout it!" Heather whispered. She could see ahead for a long way, but apparently did not see what Sheba was alerting on. Heather slacked the long leash and Sheba moved ahead, sniffing the leaf-covered ground.

Sheba nuzzled something on the ground. Heather walked up. "It's a peach!" she whispered back to Toby, just a few yards away. "She's scenting on the peaches!" Heather smiled, almost a girlish grin. She picked up the peach, covered it with her handkerchief, and put it away.

A chipmunk gave its alarm squeal in the distance. "Shit!" Heather said.

Toby looked about in the treetops. "Damn blue jays will be next," he said softly.

"It may not be alerting on us, it could be Lee," she said in a low voice. Sure enough, a few yards more and the blue jays started their alarm.

James Lee had made it to the old lumber camp. His thoughts were that if he did not come out of the old cook house, they would surround the place and burn him out. He looked around for a sturdy outbuilding. Everything else but the boiler shed was down. His sharp eyes found a standing section of the old steam boiler. "Damn!" he exclaimed, as he headed for it. "I'll hide here," he thought to himself. The ground was so hard packed nothing wanted to grow except a few white oak acorns that had sprouted. Lee felt if he at least went through the old cook house, it would draw the trackers and the dogs to it, making them good targets.

Lee hurried ahead to the standing boiler plate, setting the bucket of water and the bundle of peaches down behind it. "An excellent place," he said to himself, kicking the dead limbs away with his foot. The alarm of the blue jays got his attention. He too knew something was in the woods with him. James Lee stood quietly and listened. "Nothing," he said, heading to make his diversion and set up whoever was out there. The knowledgeable Negro circled the leaning building and then got up enough courage to enter it. The sunlight only went so far, not enough for him. Lee began to get cotton mouthed. His scalp grew tense as he continued carefully into the dimly lit ruins. The sunlight that did enter made cone-like circles on the dusty floorboards and the air was filled with floating particles of dust. The windows of the old place had been removed, probably by someone who needed them for another building. Theft from abandoned buildings was common. The empty openings were narrow and long, almost floor to ceiling, probably for circulation in the hot summer months.

Lee moved forward slowly, watching his step. The old floor had not been walked on in years. The boards moaned and creaked with every step. His eyes grew larger as he ventured into the darkness. The serving counter that his Aunt Thelma had once loaded with bowls of beans, cornbread, biscuits, and fried side meat was still there to the left. A cone of dusty sunlight fell down upon it. A small bird flew in the deep shadows, causing him to jump and duck. The rock stove flue still stood, but the large flat top cook stove was gone. For a moment he thought he heard Aunt Thelma calling. The serving counter was covered with cob webs, heavy dust, and leaves, some moving slightly in the cross-breeze. The long dark gray hoe handle that lay on the counter suddenly moved to the edge and slithered away. James Lee's jaw dropped and his skin tingled at the sight of the large snake, which had been there long before he ventured in. Regardless of the racket, he burst into a run, going out the boiler shed side of the old building.

"That's all the diversion they're gonna get," he said to himself, as he ran out into the sunlight. James Lee shivered and jumped about at the slightest sound. Not only had the snake slid from the counter, but it had crawled through his mind. He took a piss on a sweet gum tree before settling in behind the standing piece of boiler plate. In a few minutes he was not thirsty, nor was he hungry. The stolen well water and dried peaches filled the bill. Why James Lee chose to make a stand rather than running, knowing the law was near, no one will ever know.

"I'd like to circle around and get a look at the old camp before we get close. Tha sum bitch will fire on us before he'll be taken," Heather said to Toby.

"I'm sure he will," Toby replied.

Down on the dusty road, Jasper sat in the hot car, sweating. He listened intently for sounds of the chase. The time alone in the heat gave him a chance to think about his situation. The divorce, his fault, maybe hers, he really had not understood. When this was over, he was going to clean up around the place, plant some flowers and make a new start. Find himself a loving, peaceful woman.

The sheriff and his trackers were all gathered at Bill Sullivan's store, under the turning paddle fans that hung from the high ceiling. They were telling lies and downing cold carbonated drinks before going their own ways. Chief Hawthorn was on his way back to Warm Springs where he would take a discounted late lunch in the corner of the back porch of the Meriwether Inn.

Heather and Sheba walked quietly in a wide circle, frequently going out of the way to avoid making a sound. It was quieter to walk around a downed pine top than to climb over it. Toby, with Judy and Sam leashed, followed. The sniffing of the dogs was the only sound, except for the woodland birds flitting and exploring about in the leaves.

James Lee sat leaning against the warm rusty boiler plate and chewed on a dried peach, counting the money in his pockets. He arranged the bills to his liking, face down in the small stack. The thoughts of where he had been often came to mind, and how hard he worked to get to where he was, and still falling so short of Alabama. He still had hope. "White bastards!" he mumbled. "I'll get to Alabama," he thought to himself, stuffing the folded bills and loose change back into his pocket.

The sun was now high overhead, straight down in no one's favor. The trackers could see the old ruins in the distance, just as Toby had advised, about a hundred yards ahead. The curious crows ventured closer to see what was in their woods. The first crow lit in the top of a blooming tulip poplar and rode the tender limb for a minute or two as it drifted in the breeze. The glossy black crow turned its head to the left and then to the right as it looked down at the figure leaned against the rusty boiler plate. James Lee sat in the warm sun, growing sleepy. The curious bird called to its companions sitting at a safe distance away, waiting on the signal to come. Five other crows swooped in to the surrounding treetops and studied the downed figure, then began to converse. They were clear, crisp talkers, not wanting the other to have to strain to hear a single crow word that was said. At that point James Lee realized that no matter where he hid, if they could see him, they would tell his whereabouts to the creatures of the wood.

Even Jasper could hear the crows. He too knew that someone or something had been seen. Heather and Toby Sims stood still and watched the black specks in the distance. The dogs sat and panted in the heat of the midday woods. "I can't see him, but he's hidden in there somewhere," Heather whispered. Toby took a step to the side and dropped to his knees, trying to get a better look.

"Let's move in closer," Heather whispered. She stepped out quietly.

The crows continued to squawk, and the jays joined in. James Lee wondered if the crows were squawking about him or if they had seen someone else in the woods. The section of standing boiler plate was not very wide. He could lean on his hands and knees and look from either side. Lee rolled to the right and peered around the edge of the rusty plate. His dark skin almost blended with the color of the aged piece. His eyes opened wide. "God damn!" he mumbled aloud. He had seen the tracker and his two dogs. The blue overalls and white shirt quickly gave Toby away. The Negro's heart raced. At first, he thought they might pass him by, as they were still a ways out, but then he seriously doubted that. "I'll add another to my list," he thought, pulling the revolver. The crows grew louder as he moved about. "Damn it!" he mumbled, looking up at the squawking pack of forest thugs.

"He's movin'!" Heather said. "Space out!" She pulled Sheba and headed for a thicker section of trees.

"Ya see him?" Toby asked in a whisper.

"No, but he's there somewhere. He can see us," Heather added. She had pulled her pistol. Toby dropped his rifle from his shoulder and gently levered a round into the chamber. The smooth polished action of the quality crafted Winchester was as silent as greased glass.

"See the thicket of sweet shrubs?" Heather asked Toby.

"Yes," he replied.

"Take the dogs and tie them up. We'll move ahead. We're in this deep, we've got to finish it."

Toby gave his rifle to Heather and tied the three dogs to the sturdy new growth trees. The dogs whined and moved about after being restricted. "Sit! Down! Quiet!" said Toby, making hand movements to the three dogs. Sheba sat down, then Sam and finally Judy.

"The crows are not around the old cook house," Heather said, looking at the birds floating on the treetops, flapping their wings to keep balance as they rode the limbs under their feet.

Toby took his rifle and got a good distance away. "The old boiler shed," he said, in a minute or two. "Be good cover," he whispered loudly.

Heather moved forward, working from one tree to the next. Toby did the same. Neither really knew what would happen or when, but they knew that the escaped Negro was there somewhere, and had no problem killing again.

Jasper had listened to the crows and his patience was growing short. He cranked the car and moved slowly down the road until he was even with the loud nosy birds. Jasper stopped the car, waiting for something to happen. He could look all the way back to Della Cummings' house in his rear mirror, so he was doing his job as Heather had asked.

James Lee looked from around the edge of the boiler plate again, only from the left side. He could not see the white boy. "Damn it!" he said to himself. The crows finally became silent. James Lee's hands were sweating. He felt the bullets in his pocket, about a dozen he figured, by feel. "Let 'em get close then kill 'em, one shot. "Six in the revolver, twelve, eighteen rounds. Hell of a pile of white folks!" He grinned. "They got here in something, I'll take it and get on to Alabama," he thought, bolstering his confidence.

Heather and Toby had come to within forty yards of the clearing where the old cook house and the remains of the lumber camp wasted away. The crows suddenly left. Heather covered behind a sturdy oak tree. "James Lee! James Lee! Come out into the clearing with your hands up!" she yelled, aiming her pistol, expecting movement at any second. Lee moved about behind the steel plate, trying to get a look at where the voice was coming from. "I took ya once! I'll take ya again!" Heather yelled. Toby's thumb rested on the hammer spur of the rifle, which was shouldered. He was ready for a quick shot at anything that popped up, or worse, fired on them.

"Move up," Heather said softly, as she darted to another tree, getting closer to the clearing. Her experienced eyes searched for the slightest clue as to where the Negro was hiding. "If I were out there, where would I be?" she asked herself. Heather soon realized that the standing, rusty tombstone looking shape was a section of old plate, maybe some rusty equipment or something. "Can you put a round on that thing that looks like a rusty tombstone, or maybe a section of old plate?" she asked Toby. "Before you do, how many rounds you got?" she asked.

The young man ran his support hand into his bibbed overalls and proudly displayed to her a white drawstring bag, which had been a Prince Albert tobacco bag. "That many!" he said, smiling.

"Thirty rounds or so," Heather replied.

"At least!" he said, putting the bag away.

"Take aim and just ring it. Shake him out if he's behind there. It'll let him know we mean business," Heather said.

Toby Sims moved ahead to the next tree. He did not stand, but waddled like a duck, in a hurry. He used the side of the tree to rest his hand while he took careful aim at the standing plate. James Lee sat behind it waiting for whoever it was out there to walk a few feet away. He planned to make an ambush. The Negro sat holding his revolver in both hands, resting it between his knees. He had done it before, he planned to do it again. Boom! The rifle's blast echoed across the rolling hills. Tha-wong! The lead bullet slapped against the rusty plate. James Lee felt the bullet's energy and the gritty dusting of years of rust that exploded from the side where he sat. "Shit!" he said aloud.

James Lee hurried to look around the left side of the plate. He looked across the woods, but he saw nothing. "Give it up!" Heather yelled.

The excited Negro dropped to his left elbow and fired toward the sound of the voice. Boom! His revolver sounded, leaving a cloud of smoke. Heather quickly saw the white of his shirt and fired a round. The report of her .45 sounded deep, like an angry storm coming.

The lead ball hit the side of the plate and rode the gentle curve, striking James Lee in the right ear. It punched a hole the size of an index finger. It bled, free flowing and bright, through his dark fingers. "God damn it!" he exclaimed, pressing his hand hard against his ear.

"Give it up, James Lee!" Heather yelled out once more.

Lee was hurting and pissed off from being shot. He hurried to the other side, just as Heather figured he would, so she was waiting, and aiming her weapon. The bleeding Negro rolled out and took aim. "Take him!" Heather said loudly, as she dropped another heavy pistol round toward him. The target was truly out of range for the pistol. Toby began to shower the steel plate and the ground around it with rounds from his rifle. He got off at least four rounds before the Negro was able to pull back to cover. The rounds that struck the rusty plate caused a cloud of rust to hover in the sunlight.

"Some shootin'!" Toby said, looking over at Heather. The dogs were lying in the leaves, not making a sound.

"This wasn't designed for much more than forty yards, Philippine conflict," she said, exchanging the magazine for a full one. "If I get in the old house, I could get a bead on him," Heather said. Toby was busy pushing cartridges into the loading gate. He could hear the spring in the magazine tube compressing with each added round. "If he shows fire, take him," Heather said. "I'm goin' into the old house," she said, as she moved toward the ghostly leaning building.

Heather did not have time to be cautious about snakes, bugs, and crawly things. In a few seconds she was leaning against the side of the old house. A quick look-see into the room, and then she made a hooking movement into the open door, taking cover in the darkness. The nesting sparrows darted about, startled by her intrusion. The sudden flicker of movement by the tiny creatures was to be expected. Heather did not react. The bright windowless openings across the way were sharp to her eyes. From the left window she could see the rusty boiler plate. Stepping to the right, just a step or two, she could see James Lee. She could see that he was hit. The blood had run down onto his dirty white shirt. The detective shifted her grip on the heavy pistol. Her heart beat faster. The walls of the house were only structural framing and the outside planks. She knew that the stolen .38, if that was still what he had, would come through the outside plank. Heather had no cover.

Toby rained bullets down on the Negro whenever he made himself visible. Heather watched the wanted man as he moved from side to side trying to get a shot off at Toby, who was knowledgeable enough to move after each round. When the Negro was not trying to fire on them, he sat holding his bleeding ear. Heather calmed herself and gathered her wits. She watched as James Lee took another shot at where he thought Toby was. Heather took the opportunity to cross the open window. James Lee kneeled and fired. The smoke from the black powder round drifted away on the gentle wind. Toby saw it rising from behind the rusty plate and held his fire. It would have been a wasted shot.

"Drop yer gun!" Heather yelled out, holding a bead on the wanted man.

James Lee kneeled, motionless.

"Drop it! I'll kill you where you kneel!" Heather barked loudly. Her voice reflected her desire to kill, him then and there. "Drop it!" she yelled. Toby rose and hurried closer. The killer's finger was still on the trigger. "I took yer ear off! I'll take yer head off! Drop it!" Heather yelled once more. Her eyes grew more focused on the sights and her finger began to take up the slack. Lee's eyes moved about quickly. Heather knew he was thinking about what he could do next. James Lee touched the revolver's muzzle to the ground and then tossed the gun away. "Hands on yer head!" Heather yelled, as she hurried toward him, still holding a bead.

Toby saw her come out of the deep shadows of the old house and ran to assist her. The three dogs barked. Jasper left the car on the road and hurried into the woods, running up what he believed to be an old roadbed. Heather stood behind the Negro. "Don't move!" she said.

Toby arrived quickly, pointing his rifle at the captured Negro. "I've got him covered," he said, panting.

"Move his revolver, first," Heather said, changing her location slightly. She knew that by her voice James Lee could tell where she was, if he decided to lunge at her and make another attempt to escape.

Toby moved the revolver, placing it in his deep front pocket. "I've got him covered," he said again.

Heather holstered her pistol and pulled out her handcuffs, quickly forcing the ratcheting half over James Lee's right wrist and then the left. "Get up!" she said, pulling on him. The Negro gradually stood. He was testing the strength of this woman. "That big ball did a job on yer ear," she said. "Little higher and ya might not hear too good," she added, pushing him toward the overgrown road.

"What's that?" Toby asked, standing straight and listening.

Heather and Toby stood listening for a moment. "It's Jasper!" Heather said. "Come ahead!" she yelled, knowing that Jasper was wanting to know if she was all right. The dogs barked and yelped. The loud rustling and breaking of dead dried tree limbs soon revealed Jasper. He was covered in seeds and pestilence of all types, not taking time to pick and choose as he hurried ahead toward the gunshots.

James Lee shook his head. "My ear hurts," he said, as Heather pushed him along.

"Do you think Gertrude Miller and little Polly Sue hurt, when you beat them with the poker?" She replied. "Toby, get yer dogs."

Jasper was close enough now that he could hear them talking. He was in the clearing, but still on the other side of the old cook house. "Over here!" Heather called out. Jasper ran through the shadowy house to get to her, his revolver drawn.

"Ya got him!" he said, holstering the gun. Heather motioned for Jasper to get behind the prisoner. "I see he got shot in the ear, somebody missed," Jasper said, tugging at his gun belt.

"That was me," Heather said.

"How far out?" Jasper asked.

"At least fifty yards," she said.

Jasper shook his head and smiled at her feat. "Toby do all right?" he asked, looking into the woods at the tracker and his three dogs coming toward them.

"Just fine!" she answered, pushing James Lee along. Heather jerked the handcuffs violently. "God damn it! You son of a bitch, I'll not push your black ass all the way to the god damn road!" she said loudly. Heather jerked again, so hard that the prisoner fell backwards on the ground. The keen toes of her shoes quickly found favor in his ribs as she kicked him hard over and over again. Jasper and Toby stood wide-eyed, watching Heather in her fit of rage. "You get up and walk! You piece of shit! Get up!" She yelled, kicking him again and again.

James Lee was lying on his back looking up at her. "Yessum," he mumbled, in a slow beaten down tone.

Lee blinked and found a pistol in his face. The muzzle pushed hard into the thin skin above his nose. "You get up and stop this beat down shit. You bastard, I'll kill you where you lay. I put the cuffs on you, I can damn sure take 'em off. Shit like you is why God gave up dry wells," she said. He rolled over and eventually got to his feet. "Walk ahead, you got in here, you know the way out," Heather barked.

The walk was hot, almost fifteen minutes. The path that Jasper had made running in was easy to follow. "Toby, can you get to the Cummings place and get a clean rag for his head, and tell her we got the escaped prisoner?" Heather asked. "Call the chief in Warm Springs and tell him to come to the Greenville jail, lights and sirens," she added.

"Yes, ma'am, I can do that," Toby said, following the three eager dogs.

The open roadway was a welcome sight, moving air and almost journey's end. "Sit down!" Heather said, pushing James Lee toward the ground in front of Jasper's patrol car. Toby quickly loaded the dogs and left for Della Cummings' house. Jasper stood off to the side and rear of James Lee and guarded him. Heather walked a short way to her car and moved it up, placing the prisoner between the grills of the two patrol cars.

The guineas alarmed on the strange truck coming into the yard. Della met Toby at the door with her shotgun and tiny dog. "Didjya git 'im?" she asked loudly, through the screen door.

"Sure did!" he answered. "The detective asked if she could have a clean rag to bandage up the nigger's head. She shot his right ear damn near off from 'bout fifty yards," he added, swaying on his heels, his thumbs resting behind the bib of his overalls.

"Sure can!" Della replied, disappearing from the door. In a few minutes she returned with a white strip, apparently ripped from an old bed sheet.

"Best I got," she said, handing it out to the young man.

"Thanks!" Toby said, bowing slightly. "Can I use yer telephone?"

"Can I do the call fer ya?" Della asked.

Toby thought for a moment. "That'll be just fine," he said, smiling. "Call the chief in Warm Springs and tell him to come to the Greenville jail, lights and sirens. Tell him we got James Lee."

"And my bucket?" Della asked.

"Well, I don't know anything about yer bucket, but I'll pass it on to the detective," Toby said. His dogs sniffed and whined from the cage in the truck.

"You do that. It cost me a case dime," Della said.

"Yes, ma'am! Thanks!" Toby said, backing away.

Toby was only gone about twenty minutes, but it seemed to be longer. The clean cloth was placed around the bloody ear. It was already clotted and had stopped bleeding, but for issues of care for a prisoner, Heather and Jasper made an attempt to wrap his wound. The snug bandage made the ear start to bleed again. It soon soaked the bandage, making a bright red spot. Heather appeared from her patrol car with a set of Tower's leg-irons. James Lee sat on the ground and began to resist. He moved his feet about. Jasper tried to catch an ankle to get a cuff on. The loud click of Heather's pistol broke the spell of resistance.

"Keep yer feet still!" she ordered. James Lee dropped his legs to the ground and Jasper was able to shackle the man. Jasper stood up, breathing hard from having his breath cut off.

"Now here's the plan. Jasper, put him in your car. My second set of leg-irons, we'll attach to the handcuffs, and the other end to the seat frame somewhere. Mr. Lee! You will ride in silence. We're not paid to listen to your mind games and psychology shit. You are here because ya chose to be," Heather said, pushing the prisoner toward the passenger side of the car. Jasper and Toby secured the prisoner under the detective's supervision. Heather told Jasper to put his revolver in the left side of his gun belt, just to reduce chance and temptation.

Della Cummings made the telephone call, and Chief Hawthorn and Mayor Cornelius Cunningham were on the way. Frances Goulding called Alfred Huffman at the Vindicator and tipped him off to be at the jail standing by with his camera. The chief left town in such a hurry that the mayor's straw hat almost blew out the open window.

Chief Hawthorn had not told the mayor of the importance to get to the jail. "What's the hurry?" asked the mayor, holding his hat with the arm that rested in the open window. The wind pushed the thin brim up in front.

"The detective that we were not to hire and Jasper got the escaped prisoner," Chief Hawthorn said, grinning as he passed a slower car, the siren wailing.

"James Lee?" asked the mayor.

"That's right!" said the chief.

"Oh, boy! This ought to be something!" said the mayor, with a huge smile.

The time had slipped away. It was later than they thought. Jasper drove ahead and Heather followed. Toby Sims and his dogs were behind. Jasper was given instructions to drive with all his lights on, and Heather would add the siren when needed. "Stop for no one, and nothing," Heather said, before they left the roadside. She gave Jasper a pat on the forearm, assuring him they were doing a good job. "Hold on," Heather said, walking around to James Lee. "If there's any trouble, I'll be the last thing you see. I'll blow your brains out." She whispered, but Jasper heard her. He believed she would do just that. James Lee did not blink, he just looked straight ahead.

Jasper made sure he had on his uniform cap and waved as he passed motorists and walkers along the way. In short flashes, he remembered the parade when he came back from war with the boys. Jasper smiled. James Lee sat in misery, handcuffed in the rear. He was ankle cuffed and rear cuffed to the seat frame. In a few minutes the three cars passed through Harris City, Heather's loud siren echoing off the hills and buildings. Toby Sims's dogs were barking like they had had a taste of the Negro. People inside the stores hurried out to look, and those in the parking lots stopped to watch. There were cars coming from the north and the south, but with caution and trust, Jasper pushed into the intersection and turned north to Greenville.

Bill Sullivan stood speechless in the window. "Sum bitch! They got the nigger!" he said. "I'll call Louis!" He turned to the telephone. "If he don't know it, he'll be damn shocked." Sullivan giggled to himself as he raised the operator.

In a minute or less, the sheriff answered, his wet cigar riding in the corner of his mouth. "Shurriff! Greenville!"

"Hey! Louis! Bill Sullivan, here. They're comin' in with that nigger y'all were lookin' for," he said proudly.

The sheriff snatched the short, wet cigar from his mouth. "Who?" he snapped.

"Y'all!" Bill Sullivan exclaimed.

"We got run ta ground and called it," replied the sheriff.

"Two Warm Springs cars come by here lights and sirens and Toby Sims's dogs, barkin' and yelpin'," Bill Sullivan said, glancing over at customers in the store, who were listening to his conversation.

"I don't believe it 'till I see it," replied the sheriff, "but I 'pre-shate ya callin'". He hung up the telephone.

Bill Sullivan looked at the customers. "He don't believe it!" he exclaimed.

Mayor Cunningham leaned over and looked at the speedometer on the chief's car. "Damn! How fast we goin'?" he asked, sitting up and looking at the chief.

"Sixty-two!" the chief replied. "I want the next car to do eighty," he added.

Mayor Cunningham shook his head in disagreement. "Oh, no! Too much liability," said the mayor, still holding his hat.

The three capture vehicles were overtaken by the chief and mayor just south of Walnut Creek. They were almost in the city limits of Greenville. Toby Sims saw the marked unit coming up behind him. He sounded his horn and blinked his headlights. Heather acknowledged with a wave. Alfred Huffman stood on the street, hidden in the shade of tall camellias, stalking to get a photograph.

The late afternoon traffic around the square was heavy. Heather could see that Jasper was slowing as if he was going to stop. She sounded her horn and waved him to go ahead. The loud mechanical siren on her car wailed as they came up on the square from the south. For once Jasper pushed his way through the traffic, forcing motorists to yield and move to the side. Chief Hawthorn and Mayor Cunningham gleamed with pride. The mayor was wiping tears he was so damn pleased with the two Day Watch officers.

"Son of a bitch! What a proud day!" he said loudly to the chief. The siren on his car was running too.

Miss Jewel was walking home in the excitement. She saw the police car approaching with the captured Negro. Miss Jewel took it upon herself to shake her fist at James Lee as they slowly passed. "You see me! You yeller-eyed fool!" she yelled. "Satan awaits!" she yelled at the top of her lungs. "Satan awaits!"

Alfred Huffman was taking photographs as fast as he could. He was able to run ahead and get a photograph of the cars pulling into the jail. Sheriff Gilbert and Curley Jones burst from the office doors.

"I'll be God damned!" the sheriff said slowly, in disbelief.

"Got company tonight!" Curley said. "Welcome home!" he yelled, as he ran up alongside the open window where James Lee sat.

"They're glad ta see ya!" Jasper said, setting the brake on the car.

"Keep him there! I've got a big ball for him," Curley said, running back inside for a forty-pound ball. The jailer hurried back with the heavy iron ball and chain balanced on a set of freight trucks.

The newspaper reporter swarmed over the group making photographs. He soon started asking questions. Chief Hawthorn, Mayor Cunningham, and the sheriff shook hands, slapped one another on the back, and talked to the crowd that was gathering.

"Sheriff! Keep 'em back so we can work," Heather said, opening the car door for Curley. She handed Curley the key to her restraints. Jasper and Curley took the prisoner out of the car.

"You'll never get me to trial!" yelled James Lee. "Dumb ass white boys, you'll never get me to trial!" he yelled.

CHAPTER SEVENTEEN

The angry crowd jeered and yelled racial slurs at James Lee as Jasper Brown and Curley Jones walked him to the booking room. "Nigger bastard! Hang him! Piece of shit!" Even motorists stopped to see the excitement created by the mob. Detective Duncan walked behind the prisoner with the stolen revolver in her hand. Mayor Cunningham, Chief Hawthorn, and Sheriff Gilbert stood by, gloating over the capture.

The Solicitor General, Ambrose Watkins, pushed his way through the crowd and stood with the politicians. "I see tha woman who took tha job of a man brought him in," he said, loud enough for the sheriff to hear over the mob.

"She got it done," Chief Hawthorn replied, defending his detective.

"It ain't right, folks expect a man," added Watkins. He took a drag on his Lucky Strike. The package printed under his white shirt.

Heather heard the remarks and felt gut punched after the job she had done. As she took the first step onto the shallow porch, she heard Mayor Cornelius Cunningham's defense. The short, robust man stepped closer to the solicitor. The mayor's pastel yellow shirt pulled on his belly and made his bright blue bowtie pop. "I hear the deputy that went down on the lookout didn't even get a glimpse," he said, with a flushed face. The mayor leaned closer. "And it's out that the trackers, except this one, ran three schoolboys to ground and up two trees, then called it a day. The newspaper's been down asking around about them facts," he said, with a tight lip. The mayor nodded his head. "Been asking around about them facts," he repeated.

Several men in the crowd heard the conversation. "So that's the woman y'all hired, rather than a man," said one burly, ill-kept man.

"I guess ya did it ta save money, pay 'em less than a man," another man said, leaning through the crowd.

The mayor stormed toward the chief. "Let's go inside! I'll regret my tongue 'fore this is over with." He turned to walk to the office. Chief Hawthorn followed. "Get after me for my chicken grease spots on my shirt, at least it ain't yellow fingers from nicotine," the mayor said sullenly, as he led the way.

* * *

"What's tha noise?" Oliver Queen, a Negro prisoner, asked a newcomer in the black cell.

"Dey beez comin' in wid sumbody."

Oliver strained to look over the top of the two cell blocks across the way. He could only see the evening sun as it crested over the steel cells. The setting sun was so bright it was impossible to make anything out, even if he could see what was out there. "Lawd has mussy! I wonder whad it is?"

"Shut up, damn it!" snapped Lewis Dumphey. "Ssshhh! God damn it! Listen!" he barked. The prisoners got deathly silent. Dumphey could barely make out a few words by leaning against the back air grate in the very top corner of his cell.

The crowd jeered and shouted racial slurs. "Bringing in some nigger!" he said, with his ear still against the steel grate. "Say he's been shot!" he informed the others. Lewis Dumphey had come in after James Lee's escape.

"Thad be James Lee!" Oliver said. "Sho' hopes dey don't puts him in heah," he said, leaning his face against the cell bars and grasping one in each hand. "Bad man!" he mumbled. "Bad man!" There was silence for a few minutes as everyone strained to hear. "Satan don't take dat nigger," said Oliver. "He best hungs hisself and goes on toos de unknowns." Oliver sat down on the steel bunk that hung from the wall.

It was a chore for James Lee to carry the forty-pound ball that Curley had placed on his ankle. There was just enough chain to cause a prisoner burdened with the restrictive device to stoop when walking. Lee breathed deeply as he set the ball down on the linoleum covered floor. The heavy ball made a thud. The bandaged ear was starting to bleed again, the blood trickling down his neck

Curley Jones kicked James Lee in the leg. "Get that damn ball up! Who said ya could put it on my floor?" Curley barked. He was almost up against the face of the restrained prisoner. James Lee picked the ball up and held it, slightly stooped. "Officer Brown, there's a telephone call, and get Doc Hubbard ta see about this ear," Curley said.

Heather came in and busied herself with tagging the recovered weapon. "He's got a knife in his front pocket," she said. "I can see if from here. We didn't take everything when we cuffed him in the rear. There was three that wanted ta just kill him where he stood." She filled out the rectangular card that sported two cotton strings.   The detective tied the form card to the trigger ring of the revolver and placed the spent shells along with the unfired ones beside the revolver on the sheriff's desk.

Jasper raised the operator. "Officer Brown, here at the county jail. Can I get Dr. Hubbard, please?" He looked out the window at the crowd.

"Dr. Hubbard's office," a man's voice answered.

"We've got a shot prisoner over here at the jail and Curley wants him to be seen after," said Jasper.

"Where's he shot?" asked Doc Hubbard.

"Most of his ear's gone. Well, a good part anyway," he replied.

"I'll be there, hold him out of the cells," said Doc Hubbard.

"Said he'd be here and hold him out of the cells," Jasper relayed to Curley.

James Lee was growing tired, his upper body beginning to tremble from the static load. "Put it on yer feet, but not on my floor," Curley said to Lee. The Negro cautiously lowered the ball to his feet. The rattle of link chain was heard from a small closet nearby. Curley appeared with a three-foot piece of chain and two all steel padlocks.   The jailer dropped links around the handcuffs and snapped the heavy lock in place. "Put yer gun on him," Curley said to Jasper. "If he moves, kill 'im." Curley kneeled down to secure the other end of the chain to the ball.

Heather shoved a chair to the prisoner. "Sit him down for the doctor." She picked up the stolen pocketknife and the money from James Lee's pockets. "Do y'all have property receipts?" Heather asked Curley.

"We do, but he won't need it. He's not comin' out," Curley said, isolating the two different keys to the chain he had just applied.

"You'll never get me to trial," snarled James Lee. "Dumb ass white boys!"

Curley pushed Jasper aside, grabbed the Negro by the throat with one hand and held his leather club in the other. "You piece of shit, you may not live ta get in a cell," Curley said, showing his teeth and gently rubbing the club around the side of the Negro's face. "Keep it up!" he said, pushing Lee away.

The crowd had died down and the sheriff walked Dr. Hubbard in. The chief and Mayor Cunningham had entered and were sitting in the nook that Miss Dixie called her office. They were watching the activity of booking in the prisoner. "Should have killed him in the woods," whispered Mayor Cunningham to the chief, sitting next to him.

The heavy leather medical bag, tossed by the doctor's hand, slid to a stop on Miss Dixie's desk. Doc Hubbard stood and looked down at the prisoner. "I was sure I'd do an autopsy on yer evil ass. Planned on usin' a machete or maybe a chop axe," he said, with a most sincere expression. "Throw a piece of ya about, here, there. Spread the evil poison in yer soul.

Kill some kudzu along the roads." Doc Hubbard pulled a leather-bound surgical knife set from his bag. The snap of the cover filled the silent room as he opened the case. The largest of the silver mirror polished scalpels was lifted by his steady, skilled hand. Doc Hubbard placed the knife against the bandage that covered the wounded ear. He held it there for a while. "Maybe cut it off," he said, quickly pulling the silver knife back. James Lee flinched. The doctor knew that the detective had shot the Negro, the sheriff had told him. "Whoever shot at ya missed," he said, putting the scalpel away. He winked at Heather.

The bloody bandage was removed and dropped into the trash can by the desk. The earlobe was missing from the antitragus down. "You'll still hear, but nothing to tug on when yer an old man, but that won't happen anyway." James Lee gave the doctor an evil look. "This will help," said Doc Hubbard, raising a bottle of witch hazel and pouring it on the ear. The dried and clotted blood turned loose and washed down the prisoner's neck. James Lee flinched, almost crying out from the burning sensation. "Damn near bad as bein' beat with a fire poker, ain't it?" asked the doctor, putting the lid back on the bottle. "There now, not enough to make a mess, not even on the floor." He stepped back to look. "Don't sleep on it, keep it clean and dry. Let it air," he added.

All the while, Sheriff Louis Gilbert stood with his back to the outside door and watched. The day's cigar was growing shorter. "Send a bill!" said the sheriff, opening the door for the departing doctor.

"Is the autopsy ready?" Heather asked.

"Yes!" said Dr. Hubbard pointing to her. "Here it is." he pulled the Warm Springs copy from his coat pocket, along with the copy for the sheriff and the solicitor general. "Sign fer these," he said, holding out a written receipt to Heather. She signed and then passed it over to the sheriff.

"Anything we don't know?" asked Sheriff Gilbert, cutting his eyes toward the Negro.

"Not a thing," replied Dr. Hubbard, folding the signed receipt and putting it in his pocket. "Tell Miss Jewel I love her," he added, with a grin.

"Not unless there's tea cakes involved," replied the sheriff.

"Jailer Jones! Can we go?" Heather asked.

"I think me and the sheriff's got it from here, and night shift's comin' any minute," he said.

The evening sun was setting as the Warm Springs bunch walked to the cars. "I'd like ta ride back with Detective Duncan," said Jasper.

"I'll drive yer car back," volunteered the mayor. Jasper handed the key to him.

"Thanks!" Jasper said.

"Chief! We're off the clock," said Heather.

"After drivin' time. I'll note it," he said. "Oh! Keep up the good work," he added.

Chief Howard Hawthorn, the mayor, Heather, and Jasper drove into the dusk of the new evening.

* * *

The official autopsy report was held by the detective until the next morning. Chief Hawthorn, Mayor Cunningham, Jasper, and Heather took the liberty to eat breakfast at the café. The autopsy report was carefully passed around in pecking order, with Jasper last. "Nothing surprising," said Heather, spooning strawberry jam onto her sausage biscuit.

"The whole thing is bad," said Jasper, looking away by means of the front window.

"They certainly get into a body, don't they?" commented the mayor, just loud enough for those at their table to hear. "I don't care to read another one." He pushed his runny egg back from the grits on the plate. The waitress poured another cup of coffee for everyone. "Can I get this egg cooked hard?" he asked with a smile.

"I saw ya readin' that autopsy, make you sick don't it?" the waitress said, removing his plate.

Heather read over the report, her eyes moving swiftly over the lines. The men's talking soon became a soft noise in the background of her absorbed mind.

MERIWETHER COUNTY
CORONER'S OFFICE
Postmortem Examination of the Body of: Gertrude Miller
Case No. MWC-003-1931

A postmortem examination of the body of a 32-year-old Negro female identified as Gertrude Miller, performed at the Meriwether County Coroner's Office, joint facility with Michael Cargile, Mortuary, No. 4 Terrell Street. Examination conducted by Dr. Augustus Hubbard, M.D.

IN ATTENDANCE: In the performance of their customary duties, Detective H. Duncan and Officer Jasper Brown were present during the autopsy. They are acting as Special Deputies for the Meriwether County Sheriff.

CLOTHING: The body is received clad in a green cotton dress, white brassiere, white underwear, white socks, and black shoes.

PROPERTY: A yellow metal wedding band is on the left ring finger.

IDENTIFICATION TAG: There is a Meriwether County Coroner's tag, affixed by myself, Dr. Augustus Hubbard, at the scene.

EXTERNAL EXAMINATION: The body is that of a well-developed, well-nourished adult Negro female, 130 pounds in weight

298

and 67 inches in height, whose appearance is appropriate for the stated age of 32 years. The body is cold. Rigor mortis is present. Livor mortis is purple, posterior, and blanches with pressure. This in the slightest form is hard to see due to contrast with the dark pigmented skin. The head hair is black, 8 inches in maximum length. The irises are brown. The sclera and conjunctivae are bloody. The nose and ears are not unusual. The teeth are natural and well-kept. The tongue appears normal, with surface blood present. The neck is unremarkable. The supraclavicular, cervical, axillary and inguinal lymph node regions are free of palpable adenopathy. The thorax has a normal anterior-posterior diameter. The abdomen is flat. The upper and lower extremities are well-developed and symmetrical, with evidence of severe clubbing and edema. The head and facial areas are heavily marked with evidence of blunt force trauma. All the markings, based on my professional experience, were left by a round, cylindrical rod. Of the numerous markings, the smallest is estimated to be 1.5 cm and the largest 3.7cm.

IDENTIFYING MARKS: Identifying marks and scars include a small scar on the right knee, 2.5cm in length. The scar is raised, comparable to a childhood accident.

EVIDENCE OF INJURY: Gunshot wound to the shoulder blade, back to front, upward and rightward through the soft tissues of the left posterior back, entering the body through the 10th intercostal space posteriorly with laceration to the left kidney upper pole, left adrenal, liver and through the right 6th rib into the soft tissue of the anterior right chest where a deformed lead bullet is recovered and retained.

The back of the green dress has a 1.27cm diameter defect with torn edges. Upon inspection with the naked eye, this is not a contact wound, no powder burns or circling of muzzle contact are present. The weapon used is believed to be a .38 Smith & Wesson Long. I bring to the attention of the judicial system that the round is of the black powder type.

INTERNAL EXAMINATION: The body is opened with a "Y"-shaped incision, revealing the described gunshot injuries.

CARDIOVASCULAR SYSTEM: The heart is 241 grams and has a described evidence of injury. Coronary arteries arise normally, following a right dominant pattern with no significant atherosclerotic stenoses. The pericardial surfaces are smooth, glistening, and unremarkable. The chambers and valves have the usual size position relationship. The cut surface of the myocardium is uniform dark, red-brown. The atrial and ventricular septa are intact. The aorta and its major branches arise normally and follow the usual course with no significant atherosclerosis. The aorta is perforated, a hole size comparable to a .38 caliber projectile is present. The vena cava and its major tributaries are thin-walled and patent in the usual distribution.

RESPIRATORY SYSTEM: The left lung is 232 grams; the right lung is 263 grams. The tracheobronchial tree is patent and the mucosal surfaces are intact. Pleural surfaces are translucent, smooth, and glistening. The pulmonary parenchyma is pink-tan to dark red-purple and exudes slight amounts of blood. Pulmonary arteries and veins are normally developed and patent.

DIGESTIVE SYSTEM: Not tested

ENDOCRINE SYSTEM: Not tested

GENITOURINARY SYSTEM: Not tested

HEMATOPOIETIC SYSTEM: Not tested

MUSCULOSKELETAL SYSTEM: Other than the described and/or noted injuries, the bony framework and supporting musculature and soft tissues are not unusual.

NECK: Examination of the soft tissues of the neck and connecting muscles and large vessels reveals nothing abnormal. The larynx and hyoid bone are intact.

NERVOUS SYSTEM: Not tested

OPINION: The 32-year-old woman, Gertrude Miller, died of a gunshot wound to the back. The circumstances are not clear, with investigation pending by joint efforts of this office and law enforcement. It appears that the wound was sustained while holding her infant daughter with the right arm in front of the kitchen sink. The autopsy examination revealed a penetrating gunshot wound to the chest, by entry through the shoulder blade, changing direction, which damaged the left kidney, left adrenal, liver. At this point the range of fire can't be determined with a definitive accurate distance. However, with past experience in such wounds, it would lead one to make an educated approximation of less than ten feet, (3.04 meters).

Remembering that with the naked eye there appears to be no soot on the skin around the wound, no spent powder (soot) on the clothing, in regards to the entrance hole, other than a few points of adhered spent powder granules. There is no tattooing nor red abrasions on the skin. The spent powder granulations led the examiner to believe at this time (without laboratory testing) that the gunpowder was of the "black powder" type.

The table guests soon came back into Heather's world. She leaned forward to the chief. "They don't do as thorough on Negroes, do they? A lot was not done," she commented, folding the report and carefully placing it in her clean suit coat.

"Do you need it for the case?" replied Chief Hawthorn.

"Not really," Heather replied.

The waitress brought the mayor a fresh plate of food. This time his eggs were well scrambled. "There ya are," she said.

"The report caused a queasy stomach," he said, smiling.

"I hope there's not another for me," said Jasper, eating his breakfast.

Heather leaned toward him and said softly. "If ya do, you'll take a pimento cheese sandwich," she said, teasing.

"Jesus shit!" said Jasper, dropping his fork. "I'll be like the mayor now."

* * *

Jimmy Benson rode to town with his grandfather, who had to pick up a few items at the hardware and then the grocery on the square in Greenville. Jimmy advised the old man of where he was going and ran toward the Sheriff's Department. After the run yesterday, the three city blocks were not worthy of bragging. Jimmy was spotlessly clean, bibbed overalls and a cotton T-shirt. His only shoes were cleaned and polished. The screen door to the sheriff's office reported with a loud pop each time the boy's knuckles knocked. Seldom if ever did anyone knock. Miss Dixie went to the door.

"Yes, sir," she said, holding the door open.

"I'm here ta collect!" said Jimmy, big as day.

"Collect?" Miss Dixie asked.

"From the sheriff," Jimmy Benson said, his hands in his front pockets.

Miss Dixie sniffed the morning air. "Is that whiskey on you?" she asked.

"No, ma'am! Tonic water!" he replied. His hair was greased and combed close to his head.

"I'd have sworn whiskey," Miss Dixie replied, just to get a rise from the young boy.

"All in due time!" he snapped back.

Miss Dixie thought that reply was just grand. "Well, come in!" she said, extending her hand.

Jimmy Benson stepped boldly into the cool office. "Sheriff Louis Gilbert, I believe," he said, looking around.

"I'll get him for you. Would you have a seat?" Dixie asked, standing at the narrow door that opened into the hallway of the sheriff's residence. "Sheriff! Sheriff Louis Gilbert!" she called out.

"God damn! It must be trouble!" he yelled back. His footsteps could be heard upstairs. Sheriff Gilbert hurried down the long staircase.

Miss Dixie stood in the doorway. She made eye motion that the person was close, and a hand gesture to say that the person was short. The sheriff acknowledged with a grin.

"Hello, young man!" he said loudly, extending his hand to Jimmy Benson.

"Hello, sir!" Jimmy replied, shaking the official's hand. "I'm here to get all our new poles. They elected to send me, since I'm the oldest."

"And just how old are the other two?" the sheriff asked, taking a seat on

301

the front edge of his desk.

"I'm three months older than one and five months older than the other boy," Jimmy replied. "Can I get the new poles? My grandpa's waiting."

"I'll call the hardware and tell Frank what to get for you, he can put it on my bill," said the sheriff, heading for the telephone. Dixie pushed the telephone to the front of her desk, so the sheriff would not get into her space.

"Mornin'!" said Sheriff Gilbert, when the operator answered. "Connect me with the hardware."

"Hardware!" answered Frank.

"This is Louis! How are ya?"

"Could always be better, short on seed 'taters and seeds," Frank replied. "And yerself?"

"Tired and sore from yesterday. I've got an associate that was involved with us on the hunt. I need ta get him fixed up with three new varnished cane poles, green lines, and floats. Yes, and hooks too!" he said, looking at the young boy.

"I can do that," replied Frank. "This the ones that run y'all?" Frank asked.

The sheriff sighed. "Yes! Yes, keep it low if ya can. Let him pick out the poles, and whatever floats, make the hooks the small packs, whatever size he needs," said the sheriff. "Thanks!"

The sheriff hung up the telephone. "Well, sir! You should be fixed up, go right over and see Mr. Frank at the hardware." Sheriff Gilbert walked to the screen door.

"Pleasure doin' business," the young boy said, as he pushed by and went on his way.

Sheriff Gilbert smiled and shook his head. "That's a future politician if ever I saw one," he said, tugging at his pants.

"Five more years, he may take your job," Dixie said, looking over the mail.

* * *

Della Cummings worried over her stolen well bucket, from the time it was taken all through the night. "It ain't the bucket or the dime, but the principle of it," she thought to herself, lying in bed.

Neighboring farmer Homer Hopkins had lost his pick-up truck to the bank, but was able to keep his tractor since it was paid for. He had gasoline, but no way to town. In his loyalty to Della for helping him with his transportation needs, he paid her with gasoline and vegetables. Della had walked over the evening the Negro was caught and visited with Homer and Paulette, telling of her adventures and how she had fired on the escaped prisoner twice before calling the law. Being that she was out of gasoline, and the carburetor bowl full would only get her a mile out, Homer was obliged to siphon from the tractor tank and carry a gallon over to get her into town. The two neighbors opened the blacksmith shop doors to discover that the Negro had been in there, pilfering in her storage boxes and looking at the Willis. Della was enraged.

"That nigger!" she said, dusting the door handle with her apron. "Of all things!" she said, gently folding the dusty tarpaulin that had once covered the car.

Homer saw the back door ajar. "There's how he came and went." He pointed. The whittled peg, held by a red string from the head of a worn-out store-bought broom, swung gently in the cross-wind against the door casing.

The light dust around the fill cap was printed by James Lee's hands. "Looka here! He's been up on the car messing with the fuel cap," Della said, wiping what might have been left of the Negro's handprints away. "Ya can't have nothin'!" she said.

"Let me get it, Della," said Homer, nudging her aside as he opened the fuel cap. The one-gallon Old Ironsides can formed a finger-sized stream of red gasoline as he poured without spilling a drop. "I'll fire it with the hand crank. The battery can charge up 'tween here and town," he said. Della was a short woman. Homer was well over six feet and it took a red brick in each hip pocket to keep him on the ground on a windy day.

Homer opened the double doors wide and propped them with stones that had been there since the first day of the shop's completion some fifty or more years ago, back when her husband was alive. Della sat patiently waiting for Homer to give the signal. The house was locked up, the cat on the front porch, and the tiny dog watching from the ledge on the screened back porch.

"Get her set!" Homer yelled from the front of the car.

Della set the spark advance and the choke, as Homer pushed the hand crank into the seat. "Give it hell!" Della yelled. Homer's strong bony arm jerked the crank skyward, the sitting engine sparked, and the sweet smell of burned gasoline was pushed from the exhaust pipe. The crank jumped from the seat and Homer secured it in its bracket. Homer walked out into the dirt yard and began to flag the Willis forward, like an airplane hand he had seen on the Merlin Theater screen in Manchester. Della looked the part of an aviator. Her hat was pinned in place and then bound by a yellow silk head scarf. She grinned as Homer stood there with her driving toward him, then stepped aside as she passed. The Willis circled the yard and came back to rest close by the shop.

"I'll take ya home!" Della said.

Homer waved her on as he closed the double doors. "I'll check my fences," he said.

"Get in!" she yelled. "I'll take the pasture," she said, knowing where the opening was. Della drove the Willis through the bright green chickweed with its tiny yellow flowers in bloom, onward through the manure and gentle grass covered ruts.

Homer held to the open window as he looked at his barbed wire fence. "Makes me think of Texas!" he said.

"They ain't got nothin' on Georgia!" Della called back, as they rolled and bounced along toward the Hopkins house just over the rise.

Della Cummings and the Willis were always a conversation at Allen's Garage. Della was a creature of habit, always coming and going the same way, never taking a different road. Today, as always when the corner gasoline station was in sight, she sounded her horn.

"Della's coming!" a bench warming local called out.

Claude Allen waved from under a hood in the yard. "I'll flush the lines for her!" he yelled back. That always brought a laugh from the men who were sitting around. Claude did as much in peanuts, tobacco, and soft drinks as he did gasoline. Somehow Della was told that Claude flushed the hose before she got there so the gasoline would always be good and fresh. The bright yellow Willis with black running boards gleamed in the bright sunlight. Della had ordered wooden wheels, stained a dark oak, with a red steel rim. She was proud of her baby.

Della slowed the Willis to a crawl before leaving the pavement and coming onto the oil-soaked lot. "Three gallons!" she said, stopping the car in front of the faded globe style pump.

"Splurge today!" Claude said, pumping her three gallons into the glass reservoir. "It's normally two."

Della tapped on the windshield. "Fresh?" she asked.

Claude smiled as he leaned over the side of the car, careful not to scratch the paint. "Always, Miss Della!"

"Where's the police department?" Della asked Claude.

"Where it's always been, Miss Della," Claude answered, pointing to the building several doors away.

Della Cummings soon stormed the lobby of the police department. The Day Watch was on the street, the chief was gone to Manchester, and Frances was alone when the angry little woman came in. "I want my bucket replaced!" Della yelled, closing the door rather hard. It startled Frances, who was finishing the investigation into the ledgers from the Millers' office. Della looked through the glass at Frances, sitting in the staff room. "I want my bucket replaced!" she repeated.

Frances got up and went to the small framed opening. "What bucket?" she asked.

"Tha one that escaped nigger stole yesterday," Della replied, still very loud. It must have been the illusion of the glass.

"I don't know anything about it," replied Frances.

"Well, ya better! That detective said she'd either get my bucket or y'all would get me another one!" Della yelled out. Her knuckles were turning white from clutching her purse so tightly.

"I can't replace yer bucket without an authorization letter," Frances said politely.

Della shook her finger at Frances. "I want my bucket!"

"Ma'am, I can't replace it without a letter of authorization," Frances said again.

"Well! I ain't leavin' here without it!" Della said, looking around. "I'll just sit right here!" She stomped over to the short sofa. "What's all the banging?" she asked, sitting on the sofa.

"A jail expansion," Frances replied.

"That's just some more government money wasted," Della said, followed by a loud, "Huh!" She sat bolt upright, feet and knees together, clutching her purse on her lap with both hands.

"Ma'am, you could be here a long time. They don't come in here on a regular schedule, except beginning and end of shift," Frances said, leaning down to the opening.

"I'm in no hurry. I'll be right here," said Della, followed by another, "Huh!"

Frances went about her work, but slipped in a telephone call trying to find the chief or the detective. After an hour or so, Heather and Jasper walked in. Neither noticed Della sitting in the darkness.

"I want my bucket!" Della said loudly.

Heather and Jasper turned to see who was yelling. "Oh! Mrs. Cummings," Heather said.

"I want my bucket!" Della repeated loudly.

Heather knew better, but she said, "I think I shot a hole in it."

"Well, ya can just buy me another one!" Della barked.

Jasper leaned close to Heather, his nose touching the fuzz on her ear. "Bossy little woman, ain't she?"

Della sprang from the sofa. "I'll boss yer ass, old man!" Della said, ready to square off with the officer. Jasper hurried inside the cover of the windows, leaving Heather to handle the old woman.

"Do you still want it with a hole in it?" Heather asked, needling.

"No!" Della stood looking about, her chin raised.

"You said it cost a dime," Heather said, pulling her suit coat closed.

Della looked at Heather's bosom. "I thought you was terribly lopsided," she said, "Until I saw that, that," she waved her hand about. "Pistol holder."

"If I get you a bucket, will you go to Mrs. Blakely's and pick it up?" Heather asked.

"I certainly will!" Della said, looking about the room, as if she had just smelled something.

"I'll be right back," Heather said, as she went into the staff room. The telephone was almost hidden by the Miller books and papers. "Operator, connect me to Blakely's Store," she said, keeping her back to the angry little woman.

"Blakely's!" a voice answered. It was Buddy Cotton.

"Are you not in school?" Heather asked.

"This the movie star?" he asked.

"No, Buddy, it's Detective Duncan," Heather replied.

"Oh!" he said, disappointed.

"I'm sending down a Della Cummings, see that she gets a water bucket, and it can't cost more than a dime. Put it on my tab, and make a detailed note as to what she got. I'll have to fight to get my dime back."

"I'll do that," Buddy said. "Hey! That bad off family, they were overjoyed at the food, all two rounds of it," he said. "I told 'em who shot and how it went down with the menfolk." Buddy leaned close to the mouthpiece and whispered. "They said you couldn't shoot with yer pistol next year."

"Buddy, I won't be here next year," said Heather.

"Don't talk like that. Send her down and I'll get the bucket."

"Thanks!" Heather went to the window opening. "Mrs. Cummings, see the young lad, Buddy Cotton, at Blakely's. He's waiting for you. You're good for a dime bucket."

Della knocked on the glass with her gloved hand. Frances looked up. "I told ya I'd get my bucket!" Della said loudly, shaking her finger.

"Detective," Frances said, closing the last ledger a few minutes later. Heather looked up from the autopsy report. "I haven't found any names that would possibly tie the Lee subject to the Millers and the orchard business."

"I thank you for looking. I know it was a long and tedious job," Heather said. "Let me help put them back into the filing cabinet."

"Lot of fuss for a dime bucket," Jasper mumbled, sitting at his desk.

"Strange little woman. Totally different from yesterday," said Heather, stacking ledgers and loose papers from the desk and the nearby counter. "Now there's a woman for ya!" she said to Jasper.

"No thanks!" he said. "I'm goin' ta whisk out our cars. After that I need some fresh air."

"I'll call Dixie Van Wormer and see if she's found anything," said Frances, clicking the telephone.

The telephone call was very brief, as there was an office argument in the background, leaving Frances and Dixie struggling to hear one another. "I'll call you back!" yelled Dixie.

It was close enough for Dixie to leave work. Grabbing her purse and lunch sack, she emerged into the busy city streets. Even with the clatter of heavy trucks passing, the cry of produce vendors selling from the back of small trucks, the barking of dogs, and the play of children, it was quieter than the jail.

"Good day, Miss Whitehead," Dixie greeted another woman on the sidewalk. The courthouse was still open, but only for fifteen more minutes, as Dixie looked at the clock tower.

The marble steps were dished, having been trod upon for almost a hundred years. About the only thing that had changed was the replacement of the original door hinges, now cast bronze. The originals had been ornate cast iron. The dimness of the dark foyer was a shock to her unadjusted eyes, only to be offset by the brightly painted plaster walls in a stark white. The Clerk of the Inferior Court was still in. Dixie tapped gently on the glass of the gold and black lettered door. Sarah Oglesby motioned for Dixie to come on in.

"Hello!" Sarah said, smiling.

"Can I use your telephone? We've got a ruckus in the jail and I couldn't hear it thunder," Dixie said, with her hand already on the telephone that sat on the counter.

"You go right ahead," Sarah said, smacking on her chewing gum.

"Get me Warm Springs PD, please," Dixie said to the operator.

"You're not at your office," the operator said, while the telephone was ringing.

"I couldn't hear, so I came over here to Sarah's," Dixie said.

"Warm Springs Police," Frances answered. A click was heard by both women as the operator hung up.

"This is Dixie. I walked over to Sarah Oglesby's office. As I was trying to say, I found only one mention of a small pay to a 'J. Lee' almost five years ago. I did find a Thelma Lee too, just ahead of, well, the very name above the J. Lee," Dixie said.

"It goes without saying, please hold the books out, and I assume we can return the rest," Frances said. "Again, I didn't find anything."

Heather had almost finished placing all the ledgers and loose papers into the filing cabinet. "Can I talk to her?" she asked, waving her hand at Frances.

"Detective Duncan wants to talk to you," Frances said, handing the telephone to Heather.

"Hello!" Heather said. "Have you heard when the sheriff plans to serve the warrants on the hog man, Theo Jackson?"

"I'm not sure, but I would think soon. I'm sure he's planning on you to assist. He talks about the interrogation you did," said Dixie.

"I hope it is positive," Heather said, standing tall.

"It was," Dixie replied.

"Have a good evening," Heather said.

Jasper returned from whisking the cars out. His jacket was covered with shiny little specks from the sandy dirt on the rubber mats. "It's almost a day. My ass is finishin' right here!" he said, sitting down.

Clang! Bang! Clang! Something was striking the lobby window. "Sum bitch!" Heather said, hurrying to see what it was. She left the staff room door open as she hurried and pulled up the venetian blind. It sounded off with a metallic fluttering as it rushed to the top under her strong hand. "I see ya got it, Mrs. Cummings!" Heather said loudly. Jasper hurried to close the staff room door. "Yer welcome! Have a good trip home!" Heather said, smiling as she lowered the blind. "Don't let the bed bugs bite, nor tha well go dry, nor the cow. Don't let the cow get in tha bitterweed," she said, getting lower and lower. That was a side of her that neither Frances nor Jasper had ever seen. They laughed at her handling of the proud old woman and the bucket.

The evening was pleasant at Mrs. Blakely's table. Many of the old faces had moved on, except for the man across the hall from Heather's room. "I was goin' ta move him, but I thought how y'all had gotten accustomed to each other's schedule and I let him stay. It is a higher priced room he's in, but he's lookin' like he'll be here a while longer. It's the coming and going that hurts me," Mrs. Blakely said, passing a large dish of green beans around.

"An attractive bowl," Heather said. "The look of corn ears is different. Will it hold up after washings?" she asked, taking the bowl.

"It should, it's fired in," Mrs. Blakely replied. "I'm selling them now. They'll be in the display window tomorrow."

All the men had to hold up the bowl and look at the detailed ears of yellow corn with shucks that adorned it. The final dish was an egg custard with a layer of dried apples. "This is why I always stay here," said a guest Heather had not met before, holding up his last bite of the dessert.

"There's a surprise in your room," Mrs. Blakely said to Heather, as the table was being cleared. "I think you'll enjoy it," she added. "I needed a place to put it, since I got me a new one."

Heather wondered what it might be, but whatever it was it was fine, there was plenty of room for her and whatever. "Buddy Cotton should have put a dime bucket on my tab," Heather said to Mrs. Blakely.

The hot soapy dish water sloshed about as Mrs. Blakely washed the last of the dishes. "He did, I saw it. He's a good worker," she said, placing a wet plate on the drainer.

"Is it a radio?" asked Heather.

"Yes," said Mrs. Blakely. "It's ready to use. The antenna is connected to the screen of the window. It even picked up White Columns today. It must be because it's up so high."

Heather took an early bath and sat in the plush upholstered chair. The wool blend fabric was hot against her skin. An extra single bed sheet did the trick of soothing the heat transfer. She trimmed and painted her toenails, thinking of Holly, who would sniff the drying polish and sneeze. Those were pleasant thoughts. Maybe being on your own was not so great after all. It was lonely once the work day was over. The alarm clock on the bed table was climbing on to the hour and the last news cast for the evening. The bullet topped radio was more speaker and tubes than anything else. The tiny dial was hard to read. It made the listener go by association with the broadcaster rather than the numbers, since they were so tiny.

There was a Glenn Miller song and then the news. She sat listening with her toes separated by twisted tissue as they dried. The small lamp's eight-watt bulb, along with the radio tubes, gave gracious plenty of sitting light. Gentle wind from the open windows floated the light curtains. There was a bouquet of Japanese snowballs on the table by the front window. Heather leaned forward as the broadcaster covered the local news and then statewide.

"Just in! The escaped Negro, James Lee, was captured late yesterday in west Meriwether County by Special Deputies of Sheriff Louis Gilbert. Detective Heather Duncan and Officer Jasper Brown, with the help of tracker Toby Sims, cornered the murder suspect in the woods, once part of the Parks Plantation. There was gunplay and the wanted Negro was shot in the ear, bringing his run to an abrupt end. He was transported to the Greenville jail where he is presently housed. This detective is a woman, in case you didn't catch that. A woman! What's the world comin' to?" asked the broadcaster. "Hold on! This was pushed to me at this very minute. It is the front page of the Vindicator, the Meriwether County newspaper. The Negro was shot in the exchange of gunfire. Detective Duncan shot the Negro's ear from a distance of fifty yards, with a handgun! Now that's some shootin'! James Lee is being charged with numerous felony counts. There are three murder charges and a battery charge on an inmate, along with burglary and auto theft. A detailed list is posted at the Meriwether Courthouse, says the article. The low in the morning is expected to be in the low sixties with an expected high in the seventies." Heather leaned forward and turned the radio off.

CHAPTER EIGHTEEN

The morning was damp. The summer rains had already started their pattern of showers followed by extreme heat, making the skin sticky and breathing difficult. The atmosphere after a sudden shower was like standing in a gigantic humidifier. Heather decided to walk to the office, leaving her city car between Blakely's Boarding House and the police station. She had found that the children liked to slip up and look inside, never touching anything, just looking out of fascination. As she passed the front windows, she could already hear the hard striking of the typewriter keys under the pressure of the secretary's fingers.

"It's louder when she's angry, she must be angry today," Heather thought. Frances was not a typist, but an angry woman when asked to apply her slight skills to the composition of a formal letter. Heather shook her head at the sound. The young detective's hand, adorned with polished fingernails, gently turned the tarnished brass doorknob. She leaned inside. "Knock! Knock!" Heather called out, peeking from behind the edge of the open door. She was hoping to lighten the mood. The typing stopped.

Frances sat waiting for Heather to enter. "I'm glad you're here!" Frances said loudly. "What'll it take to get a letter typed in a hurry?" she asked Heather. Jasper sat in the back of the Staff Room talking to the sleepy Edgar Peterson.

"A cup of coffee," Heather replied, as she entered the room.

"Please! Here is the handwritten one, just make it work. I'll get your coffee," Frances said, pointing to the typing chair.

Heather sat down and read the letter. It was less than a hundred words, addresses included. She began to type. The carriage roller clicked and sounded the tiny bell as her skilled fingers stroked the black round buttons, laying down the lines. Jasper stood at the coffeepot as Frances stepped up. "I'm so damn glad she's here. Typing makes me nervous," Frances said, pouring a cup of coffee. Since the Day Watch had been such high achievers on the Lee case, Chief Hawthorn had brought in a percolator.

"Plays that thing like a machine gun," Jasper whispered, leaning against Frances. Her spoon was striking the side of the cup as it made its rounds, dissolving the sugar.

Before Frances could return with the cup of coffee, the paper was pulled from the carriage, making a pleasant zip sound with the geared ratchet attached to the black rubber roller. It was the sound Frances always liked, a finished letter, one less to fool with.

"Here ya are!" Frances said, setting the hot cup on the desk.

"And there's your letter and an envelope," Heather said. "All thanks to Margaret Selman Duncan," she said, taking the coffee. "My Grandmother!" she added.

Frances held the finished letter. "Oh, my! Not a spot of eraser and no errors," she said, smiling.

"Where's the chief?" Heather asked.

"He's at the county. They're goin' ta pick up Theo Jackson," Jasper said, wiping down his shotgun. "We need ta go. The chief wants us there whether we touch the fat bastard or not," he said, followed by a loud sigh. "I've grown to want to fight someone, since you've been here," he said, looking over his coffee cup.

* * *

Theo Jackson's mother, a large ebony woman, lived in Atlanta along with Theo's only sibling, a sister. The mother's name was Gladys Hightower. Those that knew her would surmise her as a boisterous woman, loud and obnoxious. In her mind she was three societal notches higher than she really was, a better person than those around her. Gladys had not always been a Hightower. There were three more before the last one walked out. In her younger thinner days before Theo, the oldest, she was a paid performer, a whore. Gladys and Theo's sister, Rhonda Jackson, were employed at the Black Derby Club in the Auburn Avenue district. Gladys was the hostess, in charge of the bouncers and waitresses. Rhonda worked at the bar, not a bartender, just a younger, large woman to take orders and help push the drinks when they were busy.

Auburn Avenue had once been Wheat Street, some older signs still bore the old name. They would eventually be corrected as they were damaged, rusted, or fell from the street post. The issue here is white and black. In the old order of the night life, whites had the Kimball House, close to the Union Station. The Black Derby Club was the equivalent for the blacks, only the music was livelier and the night life wilder. Above the street level businesses, there were apartments and single rooms to rent. Gladys and Rhonda lived above the rear of the Derby. Between the two of them they could afford an apartment, two bedrooms, bath, kitchen, and living area.

The street noise died down before daylight, but the noise and thunderous rumbling of the trains was heard all the time, seemingly louder at night. Gladys had long ago lost her girlish looks, but apparently not her tricks. She would turn one or two for an old-time associate now and then. The extra money kept her in furs, feathered hats, and costume jewelry.

Theo Jackson had felt his problems coming on ever since he drove James Lee to the Miller place. He had sent a telegraph to his mother, delivered to the Black Derby. Theo asked that she make arrangements to come and keep the farm while he might be away. He would explain it to her later. The telegraph was closed with the word "urgent". Neither of the two women had a vehicle. The doorman was Glenn Gunby, not a more timid, meek Negro would one ever meet. He had a piece of a car. It was made from several, but it did run and seemed to be dependable. During the panic of the call for a mother to come to her son, Gladys planned to pay Glenn to drive her and Rhonda to the hog farm. Glenn, having more sense than one would give him by his appearance, explained that a train ticket was the best way to go. Gladys finally gathered her large self into the cab, next to Glenn. Rhonda sat comfortably on a cushion in the back seat, a homemade wooden bench with no back. It opened to the trunk space. Two train tickets, a wave and a smile, and Glenn Gunby was soon back sitting atop his stool by the black lacquered door with the oval glass and gold trim. His black silk derby had a thumb hole where it had worn through long ago from his lifting it on and off, greeting the paying guests.

The southbound train rolled effortlessly through the switchyard of Union Station, rocking from side to side as it made the gaps in the switches from one track to the other. The two large women, built with ample posteriors, continually pushed themselves back into the oil cloth upholstered seat. They were facing north, seeing where they had been and not where they were going. After a few short stops along the way, the steam locomotive soon began to limber its legs and run at a considerable speed from Greenville non-stop to Warm Springs. Two Negro men sat across from the two well-dressed Atlanta women. Mostly they napped or looked out the window at the few remaining cotton fields.

"There it goes!" the man closest to the window would point. The women noticed it was only inside a town that he would say it.

"There goes what?" asked Rhonda, looking out the window. "There goes tha mail! Slinging tha mail! They drop a bag or more off and snatch tha hangin' one on tha pole as tha train passes," the old man said. The other one sat silently and looked down.

The train slowed to a crawl and the screech of the brakes brought it to a stop on the south side of the Warm Springs Depot. There were no white passengers getting on or off, or it would have stopped on the north side. The railings of the coach's rear stairs were well wiped by Gladys as she took one step at a time getting off, followed by Rhonda. Gladys was somebody on Auburn Avenue and at the Black Derby Club, but she soon realized that she was just an unknown flashy dressed Negro woman accompanied by her daughter in a rural Georgia town. The luggage car's sliding doors slowly opened and a man's voice called out loudly.

"Gladys Hightower! Rhonda Jackson!" cried out the voice from inside the car. The leather and veneered cardboard suitcases were tossed onto the boardwalk.

Gladys waddled over to the tossed luggage as the train puffed and chugged, pulling away from the tiny depot. "Welcome ta cotton town," she mumbled, grasping her bag. Rhonda was right behind her, picking up her luggage. A horn sounded down the street.

"It's Theo!" Rhonda said, as the bucket loaded, light blue flatbed truck pulled up.

"Lawd bless! You'ze got here quick," Theo said, getting out and putting their luggage on the back of the truck. Somewhere in the stress of the impending situation, he had forgotten how large his women were, and that there were two of them. Gladys managed to get inside the cab. Theo had to ride with his door tied with a piece of rope. Rhonda sat flat down on the bed, after Theo wiped it down with a tow sack. Her ride was windy, there among the buckets.

Theo told Gladys about helping his friend James Lee, and how the law was trying to put the charges on him, based on guilt by association. Gladys felt that her son had done no wrong and she could talk them out of it. Theo Jackson's mood was a little lighter upon hearing his mother's boastful display of knowledge and her interpretation of Georgia law.

* * *

Sheriff Gilbert had two deputies, Curley Jones, and Miss Dixie in the office when Chief Howard Hawthorn arrived. Miss Jewel had just left to return to the kitchen. The small booking room and office were crowded, and the shower did not make the odor of tobacco smoke any more pleasurable. Chief Hawthorn pulled as close to the door as he could. The rain spotted his fedora and he detested that, but a good brushing would blend it out. Alfred Huffman hurried toward the Sheriff's Department on foot. He managed to miss most of the rain puddles, but his step would get off and he would sometimes step dead center into one as he hurried.

"I see the chief is here," said Sheriff Gilbert, looking out the window. "Shit! There comes Huffman too! Damn it!" he mumbled, biting his lip.

The spring on the screen door sounded loudly as the chief pulled the door open. "Hi, y'all," he greeted, stepping in from the shower. He bumped his hat, knocking off the raindrops.

"Hold tha damn door, there's Huffman," said the sheriff.

"Come in tha house!" yelled Chief Hawthorn, holding the screen door for the running newspaper man.

"I've got a warrant here for Theo Jackson. The solicitor said one was enough right now. We'll get him in the system and add the others quickly, before a bond hearing. He'll have damn near the same as James Lee, the nigger in the back," said Sheriff Gilbert, with the tri-folded warrant in his moving hand. "If we're lucky we'll find him on the road, but we're heading for the hog farm first," he said, tossing the warrant on the desk. "I'll want a deputy to block his truck and another to block the main road in. We've looked and there seems to be no other farm roads off property. The chief and I will make the pull. He'll cover from the side of the front and look under the house in case he goes to the back. I don't expect any trouble, but that's when the shit hits the fan," said the sheriff. The telephone rang.

'Sheriff's Office!' said Dixie. "Hold on," she said, holding the telephone out to the chief. "Your detective," she said.

"Let me get this," said Chief Hawthorn.

"They can meet us on the road," said the sheriff.

"Chief Hawthorn," he answered.

"Where do you want us?" Heather asked.

"Meet us on the Cove Church Road, follow us in. When ya get there stand by, do whatever needs ta be done, if it breaks bad," said the chief. "Sorry for the interruption," he said, hanging up the telephone.

"Sheriff! Can I go along? Stay out of the way, not ask questions? Just make a story out of what I can see and hear?" asked Alfred Huffman. He had forgotten to take the paper press badge from his hat, which had allowed him access to the Municipal Auditorium in Columbus the night before.

Sheriff Gilbert stood silently looking out the window. The young reporter thought the lawman was thinking of a reply. The sheriff was watching an attractive Betty Jean Thompson walking to town, pulling a wire wheeled shopping cart behind her. He stood watching for the longest.

"Sheriff?" said Huffman.

"Oh, yes! You be the last car in, don't set foot past my car. I'll shoot you myself," replied the sheriff. Curley, you watch that sum bitch eat his meals, no fork, only a spoon. What goes in the cell comes back," he said, tugging at his pants and arranging his hip holster.

"I've got that covered," replied Curley, leaning his ear to the cold steel door, checking on the housed prisoners.

"All we need is a God damn female prisoner and we'd have a hell of a mess," said the sheriff. "Do I need ta go over this pull again?" he asked, looking about the room.

"No, we've got it down," replied a deputy.

"Here's yer irons," said Curley, holding out a flour sack that was weighted down with extra restraints.

"Dixie, we'll be back before lunch. I'd like to take you to the café," said the sheriff, as he turned from the door.

"Can't today! Miss Jewel's pintos, hocks, and onions are today. Did you forget?" Dixie asked, wanting the men to leave so she could get into her work.

"Then I'll make it another day," he said, smiling.

There was a marked unit for every man in the group. There were four law enforcement cars and the reporter's city car, then the doubled-up officers from Warm Springs. There would be six cars storming down on the Jackson hog farm. Sheriff Louis Gilbert led the way with a new cigar, followed by his two deputies, the Chief of Warm Springs, and then the reporter. The sheriff ran with his lights on as he led the small parade around the courthouse square. The bench warming locals and checker players at the barber shop gawked and commented as they took three sides of the square before dropping south out of Greenville.

"Hey! Butthead! Nigger James Lee!" Curley yelled out, looking through a small opening he had made with the heavy steel door and the red brick wall of the booking room.

"Dey beez callin' yous," said Oliver Queen, from his game of morning cards with the other Negro cellmates. "I'ze bets deys goin' ta tell yous dey goin' ta grease de rope," he said, with the other Negroes laughing.

"What?" snarled James Lee, from the darkness in the back of his cell.

"You have company 'foe dark. They gone ta get yo' hog friend," Curley said, laughing loudly as he closed the door.

"You love to torment," said Dixie.

"It's my job," Curley replied.

Back in the dimly lit cell blocks, Oliver Queen, wanting to needle James Lee, took the opportunity to do so. "Ya might add another killin' ta yer list of charges. Old Bo Bob ain't pulled out yet," he said, winking at the other Negroes as they tried not to laugh.

* * *

This morning Detective Duncan drove Jasper Brown's city car. They made it to an isolated pull-off on Cove Church Road about five minutes before the parade came by from Greenville. "Damn!" Jasper said, looking behind them. "They brought enough!" he added, turning around. Heather cranked the car and fell in behind the newspaper reporter. Alfred Huffman saw who it was in his mirror and motioned for the Warm Springs unit to come around.

"I'll bet the sheriff told him to stay in the rear," Jasper said.

"I would think so," Heather replied, as she quickly dropped the car into second gear and sped around. Alfred Huffman waved as they passed.

The standing puddles in the sandy road splashed as the fast-moving law enforcement cars turned off of the main road. The element of surprise was valuable. Huffman lagged behind, taking the puddles somewhat slower. Sheriff Gilbert's car came to a stop in front of the house, then the chief's car. The first deputy took to the rear of the house, blocking the Fargo flatbed. Detective Duncan and Officer Jasper Brown stopped midway of the long drive. Huffman pulled to the side and hurried on foot toward the sheriff's car, where he stood with pencil and tablet in hand. Before the sheriff could approach the small house, a huge Negro woman burst onto the front porch.

"What ya want wid my baby?" Gladys asked, in her normal loud volume and defensive tone. Her hands rested on her wide hips. Rhonda stood just inside the dark screen door.

"Sheriff Gilbert, Meriwether County! I have an arrest warrant for Theo Jackson," he yelled back. His seasoned hands were not far from his revolver. They rested at his waistline near his belt buckle.

"What ya want wid my sawn?" Gladys asked loudly.

"I have a warrant! For his arrest!" the sheriff yelled back. Chief Hawthorn was feeling uneasy. He stooped down to look under the house, which rested on high pillars. He could see to the back steps.

"He ain't here!" yelled Gladys. "He's gone! Yes, sir! He's gone! Come up in here arrestin' my boy," she mumbled. "I'm from the BDC!" Gladys exclaimed, her hands resting on her wide hips.

"Look, lady! If I didn't already know you were from Atlanta, I'd tell you to go do somethin' sexual ta yerself! Little goes on in this county and these small towns the law don't know about," barked Sheriff Gilbert, pointing his finger at the large well-dressed woman. "BDC ain't no Russian equivalent to the OGPU. It's the Black Derby Club!" he added, his face turning red from anger.

"It's a fine establishment," Gladys replied, in a defensive tone.

"We're not here to discuss Negro nightclubs. We're here to arrest Theo Jackson!" barked the angry sheriff. "His truck's here, send him out!" yelled the sheriff, stepping closer to the porch.

The deputy at the Fargo truck touched the bonnet with his flat hand. "It's cold!" he yelled to the two superior officers.

"I can take him," said Sheriff Gilbert coming closer. "If you don't send him out."

"You deaf or sumthin'? He ain't here!" Gladys said loudly.

"It's a felony warrant," said Chief Hawthorn. "Let's take him," he said, loud enough for only the sheriff to hear a few feet away.

"Let's go!" replied Sheriff Gilbert, taking off on a run toward the huge Negro woman standing in his way. Chief Hawthorn was right behind.

"I got her!" the chief said, as he grabbed Gladys's dress yoke and pushed her backwards, on a run. The rotund woman tried to stay on her feet, but running backwards is harder than it looks. Her feet soon became slower than her weight and she fell back on the porch. The house shook and dust fell from the tongue and groove planks that covered it.

Sheriff Gilbert pointed to Rhonda and yelled, "Get outside!" Rhonda was not stupid. She hurried out of the front door with her hands over her head. Heather and Jasper pulled up to where the sheriff had been standing, in front of the porch. The small house was dimly lit. The three-cell nickel-plated Ray-o-vac flashlight swung by the sheriff lit the dark corners of the room and under the high beds.

Gladys was lying on her back like a flipped box turtle. Her ham-like arms wiped the sandy floor as she waved and struggled to try and get to her feet. Her short thick legs seemed to find little traction on the floor. Rhonda stood in the yard with her arms still over her head. She had moved away from the porch, well clear of her cursing and screaming mother.

Chief Hawthorn stood inside and to the left of the bright opening of the front door. Both searching officers had their revolvers drawn and held at the ready, for any threat that Theo Jackson might put up.

"He's not in here!" said the sheriff.

"Didjya look for a scuttle hole?" asked the chief. He had now moved to the center of the small house. "Bad idea, without a ladder. He's too large to pull up," he said.

"Outbuildings and the barn," said Sheriff Gilbert, as he hurried out the front door, passing the chief. "Perimeter search!" He yelled to the officers in the yard.

"We'll take the barn!" replied Heather.

Jasper hurried ahead of Heather with his pump shotgun, trotting at port arms. "Inside you cover me. I'll climb up," Heather said, trotting next to her partner. "Don't get winded. He's not going anywhere," she added, as they approached the front doors. The hogs were all around the back side of the lot that surrounded the back of the barn.

"If he jumps among 'em they'll make a noise," Jasper said softly, as they went in.

The two officers searched the ground floor. The single door on the side was pegged from the inside. They looked behind the stacked empty slop buckets, even in the baled hay and inside the large wooden grain bins. Heather pointed to the loft. The two stood silently for a moment watching for any trash that might fall. Heather made a silent gesture for Jasper to go outside and look up at the hayloft door, as Theo might jump and run if he was cornered. Jasper found a sawed-off single barrel shotgun leaning against a wall stud. When he broke the action open, it was loaded. He put the shell in his pocket and moved the gun elsewhere, before going back out to watch the loft door.

Heather dropped off her suit coat and began to ease up the steep ladder. She climbed one rung at a time, trying to hold her head up, looking at the opening above and keeping her pistol ready to fire if need be. After ten tension filled rungs, she was looking into the hayloft. There were food wrappers among the hay bales. Someone had been there in the recent past. Jasper watched the loft door, like a house cat mesmerized by a cuckoo clock. The crates and hay bales were against the walls, making it difficult for a person to hide. Once the loft was cleared, Heather took a rake that stood nearby and gently pushed the loft door open. Jasper saw the movement of the small door and quickly brought his shotgun to bear. It was only Heather.

"It's clear," she said, looking down. "Come in, let's look around for any evidence of James Lee." Jasper lowered the weapon and hurried to join her.

Jasper found several empty liquor bottles in the ground level, a homemade tabletop, and a stack of cards on a lower plank shelf. He patiently waited for Heather to search the loft.

Heather moved about carefully and quickly, looking at the hay that was wallowed out, giving rise to the fact that someone had been sleeping there. A faint green corner of a dollar bill broke through the hay. She pulled it out. "A dollar bill up here!" she said loudly.

"So?" Jasper replied from the bottom of the ladder.

"It may have been one that James Lee dropped," Heather replied, looking at the bill.

Jasper scratched his head through his thin hair. "How tha Sam Hill will you tie that to Lee?" he asked, looking up through the loft port.

Heather looked a moment longer. "I don't know right now. You need to come see where it was found so I can have you as a witness. I'll want a supplemental report on it from you as well."

Jasper gave a deep sigh and started up the ladder with his shotgun held in one hand. It was a hard climb. Heather could hear him breathing. "Where was it found?" he asked, puffing loudly.

"Right there." She pointed to the edge of the wallowed-out place in the hay bales.

"Somebody slept here," Jasper commented.

"And that too goes in your report," said Heather, heading for the ladder.

Sheriff Gilbert and Chief Hawthorn stepped over the huge woman who was still lying on the porch. Her costume necklace was hung on the bridge of her nose. Her hair piece had been knocked loose from the hard fall. Alfred Huffman ventured closer to the action, but still kept his distance. Pissing off the sheriff was not on his list of intentions. One deputy pulled the toilet door open to find it empty. He even tried to raise the lid of the seat box and check inside. Desperate men do desperate things.

"Let's get the pump house," Sheriff Gilbert said to Chief Hawthorn, as they paired off across the dirt yard. The pump house was small, but large enough to hide a man. They could see where an attempt had been made to wipe out footprints around the building.

"He ain't in there! He's gone!" yelled Rhonda, still standing with her hands in the air.

Sheriff Gilbert waved her off. "My ass!" he said to the chief. "Swing wide, see if there's another way out," he said to Chief Hawthorn. The two men never slowed their stride toward the pump house. The chief quickly walked around the building and then stood by the side of the sheriff.

"Ready?" asked Sheriff Gilbert.

Chief Hawthorn nodded his head, "Yes."

The door was hinged on the outside, a little harder to enter quickly. Both seasoned men pulled their revolvers. Chief Hawthorn took the door handle and nodded to the sheriff. Sheriff Gilbert, with gun in hand, acknowledged. Hawthorn pulled the slab constructed door open quickly. Sheriff Gilbert entered the darkness with his flashlight in hand. The only noise was a gentle seeping down of the water in the reservoir. Chief Hawthorn stepped in on the other side of the door opening.

"Jackson, we know yer in here. Ya can come out with no trouble or I can send in a dog. Got one up on the road. What'll it be?" growled Sheriff Gilbert, his wet cigar held in the corner of his mouth.

The deputy held up a sawed-off shotgun from the truck. "I'd say we shoot the shit out of the place, him included, and toss the sawed off in here. He did attempt to fire on us," added Chief Hawthorn. There was a slight movement in the far back corner, behind the electric pump. Both men raised their revolvers. Sheriff Gilbert flooded the dark corner with his flashlight. They could just barely make out a Negro male dressed in a dark plaid shirt and bibbed overalls. The Negro blocked the bright light with his open hand. Heather and Jasper had walked up cautiously and were standing outside.

"I'm comin' out," said Theo Jackson. He managed to get to his feet. His legs were asleep, as he had been there quite a while.

"Hands over yer head!" barked Sheriff Gilbert. "Keep comin'!" he added, as he backed out the open door into the light of the morning.

"They got him," Rhonda said to her mother. Gladys had just been able to sit up on the porch.

Theo Jackson was searched for weapons and a small pocketknife was found, nothing more. "Theo Jackson, you're under arrest for helpin' an escaped prisoner," said the sheriff, holstering his weapon. Chief Hawthorn stood covering the Negro until he could be handcuffed.

"Can I make bond?" Theo Jackson asked, as they slowly walked toward the waiting cars.

"Up to the Judge," Sheriff Gilbert replied.

Gladys Hightower and Rhonda Jackson stood on the porch and wept.

"We tried, baby! Weez tried!" yelled Gladys.

"We should take them, or at least the mother, in for obstruction," said Chief Hawthorn to his two officers.

"It could be in the cards," Heather replied.

"Feed my hogs, Momma!" Theo called out, as the door closed on the transport car.

"Take his stinkin' ass to Curley. Here's the warrant," said Sheriff Gilbert, leaning on the car as he signed the execution portion of the arrest warrant.

"Sheriff Gilbert! Sheriff! Can I get a photo before he leaves?" asked Huffman, excitedly.

"Through the open window," growled the sheriff.

"Thank you, sir!" said the excited reporter.

"Tell old souse meat I caught him," said Sheriff Gilbert, standing in the open door of his car.

"I'll do that, sir!" stuttered the reporter, licking a flash bulb. "Mr. Jackson, look this way. This is goin' to Associated Press, be all over the East Coast papers by tomorrow," he bragged.

"Y'all be all right goin' back?" asked Chief Hawthorn, standing in the open window of the sheriff's car.

"Oh, yeah! Three guns and three cars! We'll get him to Curley," replied the sheriff. "And I thank you for y'all's help. And for bringin' that fine lookin' female detective," he said, looking at Heather walking across the yard with Jasper.

Gladys stood watching as her son was taken from the property and out of sight. The telephone for the business was the first thing she went for. "Honey chile, what's Glenn's number to de do'?" she asked Rhonda.

"Sycamore fo'-nine-three-fo'," replied Rhonda.

At first Gladys tried to dial, but that did not work, then she just tried to say "operator", but that did not work either. Finally, she dialed "0".

"Operator! Looka heah, I needs Sycamore fo'-nine-three-fo'," advised Gladys.

"What city?" the operator asked.

"Atlanter!" Gladys snapped back impatiently.

"One moment please," said the operator. The telephone began to ring. On the fourth ring it was picked up.

"Black Derby Club," Glenn Gumby answered.

"This is Mrs. Hightower. Glenn?" Gladys said loudly.

"Yessum," he said slowly.

"I need a lawyer!" she snapped. "Don't you always brag about knowin' a lawyer?"

"Yessum," Glenn drawled. "Dat beez Isaac Pittman, add-tunny ad laws."

"Got his number?" Gladys asked.

"But I'ze gots a car to tend to. Deys blowin' de hawn," Glenn replied impatiently.

"I'll find it!" Gladys yelled, and hung up the telephone.

Paulette at the Warm Springs Southern Bell office obtained the telephone number for Isaac Pittman, Attorney at Law. Pittman should have known he would have his hands full at the first conversation with Gladys Hightower.

"Isaac Pittman's office," a rough voiced man announced on the telephone. "Attorney at Law," he added. Isaac Pittman rubbed his fingers across his gray hair, patting the bald spot on top. He was a loud, heavy breather. The traffic two stories below seemed to be in the room with him, for all the noise that traveled upward and into the open windows along Mitchell Street. He had tried to get in the Kimball House, but there was a waiting list. "How may I help you?" he asked.

"Looka heres now! My son, Theo Jackson, is in de Greensville, Jawga jail and needs hopin'!" Gladys blurted out loudly, since there was a considerable distance between her telephone and the attorney in Atlanta. "Id's good money, but not a lot!" she barked. "Is yous interested?"

"Ma'am, who are you?" the attorney asked, reaching for a peppermint.

"I am Mis-riss Gladys Hightower of the Black Derby Club," she announced. Rhonda listened from the other room. She rolled her eyes at her mother's haughtiness.

"I'm a criminal lawyer," Pittman said, rolling the hard candy around in his mouth, striking his bad teeth. "What are the charges against your son?"

"Sum kind a felony warrant," Gladys replied. "They didn't say."

"Well, what was he supposed to have done?" Pittman asked, looking down at a pretty woman in a form fitting black skirt walking along the sidewalk.

"Dey say he hid a friend of his, James Lee, and helped him escape," Gladys answered.

Isaac Pittman sat straight in his chair. "James Lee, the Negro that's killed and robbed?" he asked.

"Dat beez him," she replied, sounding proud of her son's actions.

The attorney squirmed around in his seat, then leaned his elbow on the desk as he held the telephone. "You want me to defend your son, Theo Jackson, in a trial associated with James Lee?" he asked, wanting to make sure he had heard right.

"He's in de jail too!" Gladys said.

Isaac Pittman swallowed the mint. "How much money you got?"

"I got 'nuff for you to start, dey beez mo'," she said, in a boastful tone. Where the other money was to come from, she did not know.

The attorney leaned into the telephone. "It'll take two hundred up front and five hundred a week, until the case is over, win or lose," he said. "I drive a twenty-six Cadillac and I'll be put up in a decent room, not in the same town as the jail. There will be mileage of six cents a mile and gasoline, food, two meals a day. You will pay me the last draft before the final outcome of the trial," he said. "My mileage and other expenses will be paid weekly."

Gladys was silent. She swallowed hard and took a deep breath. "Did you comprehend that?" Pittman asked.

"Y-y-yes," she stuttered.

"Send me two hundred by wire and I'll be on the way," he said. Pittman actually thought she would back down, but she did not.

"If I arrange for you to get it from the Black Derby Club, can you pick it up?" Gladys asked, in the most proper use of the English language she could muster.

"Money first, then I'll pack," Pittman replied.

"Start walkin'!" Gladys barked. "It'll be there in cash when you go in, see the owner, Big Sam," she added.

An evil grin slowly grew on the aging face of the attorney, like that of a weasel with a hen house in sight.

Gladys Hightower called Big Sam next and arranged for the money to be there. They argued back and forth about the amount. A truce was called between the two with one hundred dollars in cash and a specific number of designated tricks.

* * *

The sheriff and the two deputies quietly returned to Greenville, where Solicitor General Ambrose Watkins sat patiently waiting in the sheriff's chair. Sheriff Gilbert was the first to enter the jail. "Took y'all long enough," said Watkins, still leaned back in the desk chair. He had dozed off in his silent wait. Dixie was busy with paperwork and Curley was in the cell blocks working with the prisoners, except James Lee.

"Wanted it done any faster, ya should've done it yerself!" barked the sheriff. "I see that Miss Jewel made you at home," he added, noting the coffee cup and the tiny crust of a custard pie on a saucer.

"And it was damn nice of her," replied Watkins.

"She's butterin' ya up, so if she gets in trouble, you'll bail her out," laughed Sheriff Gilbert. "She does sorta sway her hips when she walks away," he said, smiling. Sheriff Gilbert hung up his hat. "That's just big ass," he said, laughing.

Ambrose Watkins stood and looked out the window at the cuffed Negro being led up the walkway. "So that's the accomplice?" he asked.

"All two hundred hog lovin' pounds of him," answered Sheriff Gilbert, pushing his way past Watkins and taking his seat. "What brings you here?" he asked.

The solicitor general opened his leather briefcase. "All these!" he said, pointing to two stacks of warrants. "I need to see James Lee, read him his charges."

"CURLEY!" yelled Sheriff Gilbert, from his desk.

In a few minutes the jailer opened the heavy steel door. "Yes, sir!"

"Let the solicitor have at James Lee, and they're comin' in with the other one, Theo Jackson," said the sheriff.

The solicitor took one stack of papers and followed Curley deep into the dank cell block system. "There he is," pointed Curley. "Step up, boy!"

James Lee came to the front of the cell, shackled with the heavy ball. "I'm here ta advise you of your formal charges," said Watkins. "I'll be fine, Curley," he said. Curley went back to the front. "I have a stack of official charges, in the form of Arrest Warrants all made against you legally," said Watkins, fanning the thick stack of tri-folded papers with his hand. James Lee stood silently. "This ain't to the word, but me to you so you can relate to the charge as I call it out. Robbery of Herman Pickens, Durand Store, Murder of Herman Pickens, Escape from Meriwether County Jail, Murder of Ellis DeFoor, Theft of Motor Vehicle owned by Ellis DeFoor. Troup County brought this one over, Burglary of Benjamin Hill's Store, when we're finished, you'll go over there. Burglary of John Miller's barn; Burglary of John Miller's office in residence, Theft of Motor Vehicle, owned by John Miller; Murder of Gertrude Miller; Murder of Polly Sue Miller; Burglary of Della Cummings' barn, Theft of bucket and food."

"What food?" snapped James Lee.

"Peaches! And a god damned dime water bucket," Watkins snapped back. "Your partner Theo Jackson is comin' in the door now. He'll be charged accordingly," said Watkins. "These will be executed in just a minute at the front desk. You need a lawyer, think about who you will be making the one call to," he said, just before turning and walking away.

The steel door closed with a sturdy thud. "My, oh, my! Little nigger's got sum charges on his ass!" yelled Oliver Queen, several cells away.

"And tha horse ya rode in on!" yelled James Lee.

Solicitor General Ambrose Watkins took a seat at Curley's desk and began to execute the warrants against James Lee. There was very little talking done by Jackson, just "yes, sir and no, sir!" as he was booked in. Watkins noticed that the new prisoner kept watching the stack of warrants as they were signed. "These aren't yours," Watkins said. He reached into the briefcase and brought out the stack belonging to Jackson. "These are yours, not as many, but God damn sure enough. You a prayin' man?" Watkins asked, looking down at the warrants he was signing.

"Yes, sir!" Theo Jackson replied.

"Ya best get at it, some stupid shit you did, maybe yer last. Folks of all colors don't get into violence around here, especially murderin' folks of any color," Watkins snarled. "A hundred years ago, neither of you pieces of shit would have made it this far!" he said, his jaw tight. "I'll advise you of your charges now, save me a trip in tha stinking place," Watkins said, pushing James Lee's warrants aside. "Theo Jackson! Burglary of John Miller's barn, Burglary of John Millers' office, in residence, Theft of Motor Vehicle owned by John Miller, Murder of Gertrude Miller, Murder of Polly Sue Miller, Burglary of Della Cummings' barn, Theft by Taking, bucket and food. This is where ya really screwed up! It's where the whole thing started, Aiding an Escaped Felon, just dumber than shit," he said coldly, looking at the Negro. "That's where ya went wrong, that's where ya went wrong," Watkins said getting softer as he spoke.

Theo Jackson suddenly grabbed his stomach, took a deep breath, and puked all over the floor of the booking area, which was technically the same space as the office area, where everyone had a desk.

"Jesus Christ!" yelled the solicitor, stacking the warrants. "I'm goin' to tha kitchen!" Watkins said, storming out of the room.

* * *

Isaac Pittman slipped into the Black Derby Club while Glenn Gunby was at the curb, leaning into a car window, telling whoppers and laughing loudly. The closed club was dark, not a light on except for the ones over the long black lacquered bar adorned by a brass foot rail. Isaac stood for a minute as his eyes grew accustomed to the darkness.

"You need sumthin'?" a big Negro asked from the far end of the long bar.

"Big Sam!" Isaac Pittman replied.

"Who's callin'?" the big Negro asked.

"Attorney Isaac Pittman, Gladys Hightower sent me," he replied, standing at the opposite end, closest to the doors.

"I'm Big Sam," the Negro replied. He reached into his suit coat pocket and pulled out a stack of bills. "Two hundred?"

"Two hundred," replied the attorney, walking down the bar. Pittman stood with his mouth open, breathing hard and loud. His brown oxfords needed to be polished. He wore bright green suspenders and no belt. His laundered white shirt still had creases from being folded around the laundry cardboard. The Negro noticed the man's black pants against his brown suit coat. There was some evidence of re-woven spots here and there. The garish candy cane tie with gold threads brought the white male character to life. The tie bar and square cuff links were once gold finished, but that was wearing off. The smile that he displayed was spotted with bad teeth, covered by the fragrance of peppermint candy.

"Do a good job," Big Sam added, handing the bills to the white man. Big Sam had a heavy odor of cigars about him.

"I always do my best," Pittman replied, feeling two hundred-dollar bills.

"Thanks!" he said, turning to leave. He had almost reached the doors when Big Sam called out.

"You a Jew?" Big Sam yelled out.

Isaac Pittman stood with his hand on the polished brass door handle. "You a nigger?" he asked in a surly tone.

The huge muscular Negro slowly smiled. His white teeth contrasted against his dark skin.

"Me neither!" replied the attorney. Before nightfall, the Mitchell Street attorney was on the road in his used Cadillac.

CHAPTER NINETEEN

The night air was pleasant, cool and refreshing after the hot muggy days. It raced through the thin hair of Isaac Pittman as he drove into the sleeping town of Warm Springs. The Atlanta lawyer took two passes around the small town before pulling into a vacant space in front of J.C. Blakely Dry Goods & Rooms. The stiff legged man slowly climbed out of the Cadillac. The cat hissed at him as he started up the steps.

"Democrat!" said Pittman. The tired, wrinkled man tapped on the glass of the front door, having no idea there was a side entrance. There was no reply. He tapped harder. The first tapping had aroused Heather, whose room was right above the front doors. The second, louder tapping brought her to the window.

"Hey!" she called out. "You down there!"

Pittman stepped back into the street and looked for the voice.

"She's closed!" Heather said, from her window. The street lights, as few as there were, illuminated the man well enough for her to see that he was a white male, in an attempted suit.

"I need a room," Pittman called out.

"Not here! She's full," Heather said. "Go north to the Meriwether Inn, a sign on the road to the east, or the Warm Springs Hotel, down the street, or even the old Huff House, they've got rooms by the night or longer."

"Hey! Thanks! I'll try the Warm Springs Hotel," Pittman said, getting back into his car.

Pittman got a room at the Warm Springs Hotel, probably not as nice as the ones at Mrs. Blakely's, but adequate and not buggy. The next morning the attorney for Theo Jackson walked into the office of the sheriff bright and early, even before Dixie had arrived. The aroma of coffee brewing filled the cold red brick building, as it mixed with the smell of side meat soaked in water and then fried. His mouth watered as he sat quietly in a straight chair that was not assigned to anyone's desk. Pittman was wise enough to realize he was not in Atlanta, and folks out in the small towns could be touchy about their territory and simple property.

Curley was in the kitchen with Miss Jewel, but soon discovered the surprise guest. He came through the narrow hall door with his morning coffee and the latest Vindicator under his arm. "Mornin', sir! What can we do fer ya?" he asked.

The stranger stood. "I'm Isaac Pittman, Attorney for Theo Jackson," he said, extending his hand to the jailer.

"Jailer, Curley Jones," Curley replied.

"I'd like to see my client," said Pittman.

"I'd like for the sheriff to be here, that should only be a few minutes," replied Curley. "Like a coffee?" he asked.

"That's a fine idea," Pittman answered.

"I'll bring it out to you," said Curley, as he went back through the narrow door. Curley hurried up the steps and called to Sheriff Gilbert, who was shaving in the bathroom. Curley stooped down and saw the sheriff's bare feet. "Sheriff!" he whispered loudly. He tossed a penny at the crack under the bottom of the bathroom door. The coin slid under. Curley waited in the darkness of the residential hallway, still on the second step from the top of the stairs.

The door opened, revealing the half-shaven sheriff in his underwear. "What?" he whispered back.

"Theo Jackson's lawyer's downstairs. He wants to see the nigger," Curley said, trying not to wake the sheriff's family.

"Encourage him to go to Becky's Café and eat breakfast. Tell him we're close to feedin' and it's not safe for him in the cell blocks at this time. You know, bull shit us some time. I'd like to call Ambrose Watkins before he gets to Jackson," the sheriff added. A ball of shaving lather dropped from his safety razor onto the hardwood floor.

Curley saluted and hurried down the stairs but doubled back to fetch a cup of coffee for the lawyer as he had suggested. "Here we are!" Curley said, carrying a steaming hot cup of black coffee into the office on a tin tray, accompanied by a small pitcher of cream and a container of sugar. "Sheriff asked that you consider taking breakfast at Becky's Café across the square. I'm just a few minutes from doin' mornin' feed and it's not safe in the cell blocks during them times," Curley said, setting the tray down.

Pittman looked toward the courthouse. "Just over there?" he asked.

"Yes, and you can fix this cup and take it on the pleasant walk," Curley encouraged, gently pushing the tray toward the guest. "She's got the best greasy fried eggs! They slide down like fresh oysters, if ya was a mind to swallow 'em whole." Curley laughed.

"I believe I will. I'll tell her you sent me," said Pittman, as he sipped the now blonde coffee. "Boy! That's good!" he said, as he shuffled toward the door.

Sheriff Gilbert soon came down to the office, where he called the solicitor general and advised him of the Atlanta attorney's presence. Curley and the sheriff led Theo Jackson to a small secure room, one frequently used as an infirmary for the jail. Theo Jackson was shackled with leg irons as he waited for Isaac Pittman. When the attorney returned from breakfast, Dixie led him to the secure room, and the sheriff and Curley stood by outside while the two met.

Theo Jackson was not even dressed out. He was still in the clothes he had been arrested in. The sulking Negro sat on a heavy wooden bench that was bolted to the floor.

"Mr. Pittman!" said Sheriff Gilbert loudly, extending his hand.

"We've met," Curley said, extending his hand to the open door where the client waited.

"Due ta security, we'll be standing by out here, not too far away," said Sheriff Gilbert, closing the door behind Pittman.

"I need a list of the charges," Pittman said, from the doorway.

"Sure thing," replied the sheriff. "Give us just a minute." Pittman closed the door and Curley hurried back to the office to retrieve a list of the charges.

"Need a box?" asked Dixie, pulling the case folder.

"Damn near!" Curley replied.

The jailer's heavy hard heeled brogans made a loud report as he hurried across the hard wood floor toward the small makeshift conference room. Curley handed the list to the sheriff, who in turn knocked on the door. The attorney opened the door.

"Here's the charges," said the sheriff.

"Thanks!" replied Pittman, taking the list and pulling the door closed.

Isaac Pittman stood. A bacon grease spot had been added to his shirt from the meal at Becky's Cafe. "Son, I'm attorney Isaac Pittman, your dear mother hired me yesterday. I'm to represent you in this case," he said, extending his hand.

"Theo Jackson, hog farmer," the Negro replied.

"I'll need a minute to look at the list of charges," Pittman said, as he took a seat in a nearby straight chair. Theo watched as the white man's eyes moved swiftly through the information. Sheriff Gilbert leaned toward the door, listening. "I'll just read them. Theo Jackson! Burglary of John Miller's barn. Burglary of John Miller's office, in residence. Theft of Motor Vehicle owned by John Miller. Murder of Gertrude Miller. Murder of Polly Sue Miller. Burglary of Della Cummings' barn. Theft by Taking, bucket and food. God damn, how much education you got?" Pittman asked.

"Tenth grade, St. Marks Colored School," Theo replied, extending his restrained legs forward. The bench was unusually low.

"And somewhere along the way you didn't think that you should have turned in this James Lee? Passing all those chances to telephone the police or even flag one down," Pittman said. He sucked through his bad teeth and rolled his right earlobe between his finger and thumb. He sat silently for a moment or two. "That's goin' ta be hard to overcome," he added, shaking his head.

"Yes, sir," Theo mumbled, looking down at the floor.

"All these are felony charges, Superior Court," Pittman informed him. "What's your bond?" he asked.

"I ain't been told yet," Theo replied.

Sheriff Gilbert quickly moved from the door, where he had been listening. The door slowly opened under the attorney's hand. "What's his bond?" he asked.

"Curley, has there been a bond amount brought over?" the sheriff asked. "It may be on the back of the warrants, since the solicitor advised Jackson of the charges in person."

Once again Curley headed toward the office, where Dixie would have the bond amounts written down, taken from the backs of the arrest warrants. "Sheriff wants -- " he almost got it out, before the secretary handed him a single sheet of paper. "Thanks!" Curley replied, hurrying away.

"Here ya are, sir!" Curley said, holding out the list.

Pittman took the paper and closed the door. "Burglary of John Miller's barn, $1,500. Burglary of John Miller's office, in residence, $1,500. Theft of Motor Vehicle owned by John Miller, $1,000; Murder of Gertrude Miller, $3,000. Murder of Polly Sue Miller, $3,000. Burglary of Della Cummings' barn, $1,500. Theft by Taking, bucket and food, $100. Here's where ya really screwed up! It's where the whole thing started, Aiding an Escaped Felon, just dumber than shit," he said coldly, looking at his client. "That's where ya went wrong," Pittman said.

"I've been told that before," Theo replied.

"$11,600!" the attorney said, glancing up at the Negro. "Can ya make it?" Pittman asked, with his fist resting on his hip.

Theo Jackson looked down. "No, sir! The lot full of hogs won't start ta bein' that much. It's the wrong time of year ta get top price too."

Pittman reached over and slapped Theo on the thigh. "They feed ya good?" he asked.

"Grits and side meat this mornin'," Theo answered.

"It sure smells good," said Pittman, as he stood up. "Do I tell yer mother about the bond?" he asked.

"Please," replied the Negro.

Sheriff Gilbert and Curley were standing by when the door opened. Theo Jackson stepped out of the room at the direction of the jailer. Curley and the sheriff escorted the prisoner back to his cell. The attorney walked behind.

"Jackson! I'm sure that James Lee is on no bond. You're already a lucky son of a bitch," Pittman said, as the group of four walked down the narrow hallway.

It would take almost one hundred days for Gladys Hightower to raise the bail money, even with the assistance of the local churches and the organization known as the NAACP, National Association for the Advancement of Colored People. In their charter they made it plain that they were for the equal treatment of all races, just like the KKK was for seeing that all folks were treated fairly. The Atlanta churches that knew the Black Derby Club staff held dances and raffles. The Negro churches in the county and as far away as Muscogee held fish fries and other money raising events. All these efforts were based on the information that Gladys Hightower and Rhonda Jackson had told them about her son's innocence. Gladys Hightower stood in the pulpits of the rural African American churches and pounded the podium, wiped sweat, and raised her loud, obnoxious voice to the rafters swearing that that her "dear, kind, hard workin' son had been framed, doin' nothin' wrong, 'cept in the eyes of de white folks".

It was near the end of August when Gladys was invited to speak at the Greater Muscogee Temple of the Brotherhood, an African American church turned labor hall located on the corner of Earline Avenue and 36th. The sweltering Georgia heat sapped the strength from every living thing. The scents of witch hazel, anti-perspirant creams, and tonics blended as one in the huge hall as it filled late in the afternoon with those who wanted to hear what the woman from Warm Springs had to say. The stained-glass windows of the hall were open on top, as well as the bottom half, leaving the Holy Scripture scenes intact. The funeral home fans and the more expensive palm leaf fans generated a flutter like that of bird wings as they moved about. The horrid conditions brought on by the summer heat stifled those housed and working in the prison system everywhere. The brethren of the brotherhood lined the streets on both sides for several blocks. Many rode the city buses and others walked. They all came to hear the troubles of Theo Jackson, the innocent son, as told by his loving mother.

"Let us pray!" shouted a heavy Negro pastor, dressed in black from head to toe. Sweat beaded on his face and balding head.

"Amen!" the congregation responded.

"Oh, Lawd! We're so blessed to have this fine specimen of Motherhood here with us this afternoon. Lawd! We pray that yous will bless us wid some rain."

"Amen!" from the congregation.

"Help us ta beez better 'samples and stewers fo' you!"

"Amen!" from the congregation.

"Guide us to hope this po' mother, in Jesus name we prays! Amen!" The pastor closed the prayer.

"Amen!" from the congregation.

"I gives y'all Mrs. Gladys Hightower. She is accompanied by her loving daughter, Rhonda Jackson." Rhonda sat on the first row wiping sweat. The congregation thought she was sobbing as she blotted the rolling sweat from her face and eyes.

Gladys wore a white dress with tiny, pencil eraser sized navy blue dots. They moved about on her behind in a hypnotizing manner as she walked. If you followed her long enough, dizziness was likely to occur. Gladys waddled to the steps and took them one at a time, eventually making it up to the podium.

"Praise de Lawd! I'm so blessed ta beez here!" she said in a loud outburst, with her hands held high.

"Amen!" from the congregation.

"My sawn, my lovin' and only sawn, he's in de Greensville, Jawga jails," she said, looking at the faces in the crowd.

"How many jails dey got?" asked one older man of his neighbor.

"Jes' one ta my knowins," the neighbor replied.

"Almost a hundred days ago my lovin' sawn, a devoted hog farmer in de beautiful community of Chalybeate Sprungs, wuz took into arrest by the Shuriff and some five gun totin' deputies," Gladys said, with a long pause.

One man leaned to another. "I've drove out of the Miller's Orchard with a truckload once or twice. Dey ain't nothin' down there but Pigeon Creek, hog shit, ticks, chiggers, and us niggers," he whispered to his companion.

"My sawn, my lovin' and only sawn, he called me at my job in Atlanter and I axed him what was wrong. He commenced ta tells me of how he hoped a longtime friend, who was needin' a place to stay until he's could get ta family folks in Alabama."

One man leaned to another. "He sho' is a lovin' son. He beez wore out 'foe long," he whispered. The men snickered.

"Every person deserves ta beez wid dey loved wons!"

"Amen!" from the congregation.

"He's a hard workin' sawn! Got a hog farm and drives a route six days a weeks ta take scraps frum ress-a-runts and de grossery stos ta hope feeds 'em. His po' friend comes ta him askin' fo' food ands a place ta sleep. What wuz he ta do? Weez cain't tuhns one anotha' out," Gladys said, patting sweat from her face.

"Amen!" from the congregation.

"The po' boy was just needin' some hope, food, shelter. My sawn, my lovin' sawn and only sawn, hoped him outs! And dey comes and knocked me down, run through my sawn's little house and then dey drug him from out of de pump house, where my sawn, my lovin' and only sawn, was fixin' tha pumps!" Gladys said, growing louder and louder.

"Amen!" from the congregation.

"My sawn, my lovin' sawn, made this farm from his own sweat. Stopped school in de tenth grade and went ta work wid his own hands. He ain't neva' been in troubles, neva' harmed nobodies," she said, staging a sob.

"Amen!" from the congregation.

"Dem judges set him a bond of elem' thousand, six hundred dollars, like a black man's made of money!" she yelled, striking the podium with her fist. That brought many "Amens!" from the congregation and a few, "Praise God's!"

"My sawn, my lovin' and only sawn, he needs ta be keepin' up his place and caring for his hogs."

"Amen!" from the congregation.

Gladys Hightower attacked the white race with the hatred of the best clenched racists of either ethnic group during the lengthy sermon. She attacked the white culture and its people with the equivalent of Thomas Watson in his published newspaper, "The Jeffersonian", attacking the political scene of America, or Henry Ford's opinion of the Jews.

"We be askin' fo' yo' hep," Gladys sobbed. "We needs only fifty mo' dollars and he'll be out on bond," she said, wiping sweat with her handkerchief. "Been in there almost a hundred days. My po' sweet sawn, my lovin' and only sawn," Gladys repeated, looking pitifully at as many of the men's faces as she could. Rhonda sat thinking of how good a cool triple dipped ice cream cone would be. On a secret cue, Rhonda wailed out in a loud sob, adding to the pity of the two women's situation. "Thank yous so much fo' givin' me this opportunity to speaks wid jew," Gladys said, as Rhonda sobbed loudly. Gladys took her seat next to her wailing daughter.

"Praise de Lawd!" said the pastor, as he took the podium. There was discussion among the men and some women in the audience. A soft rain began to fall. "Praise de Lawd! Look a here, de Lawd has blessed us with a soft rain. How wonderful!" the pastor said, jumping about and moving his hands in the air. "Weez asks that you hope this dear, wonderful, kind woman with her sawn's troubles wid de law. We know how they can be toward our kind. We hope this situation will not be another case like de famous Moore vs Dempsey case, back in twenty-three," said the pastor, interrupted by the loud sobbing of Gladys, now reinforcing her daughter's tears.

"Praise de Lawd!" from the congregation, followed by, "Amen!"

"I axe dat yous considers them when we pass de plate," the pastor said, motioning for the ushers to come forward.

The men rocked from one side to the next to get their wallets out, shoulders and elbows inflicting strikes on one another.

"Let us sing!" shouted the pastor. "Give us one, Brother Turner!" He shouted and pointed to the man sitting at the piano.

"The Sun Will Shine! Everybody knows that!" Brother Turner yelled, as he struck the piano keys into the melody.

The first-row plate was full and there were twenty-six more rows to go. Gladys cut her eyes and looked at the offering plates rounding over. She knew Theo would soon be free. The song went all three verses, dragging more and more slowly because not everyone knew all the verses.

"Praise de Lawd! Praise de Lawd!" the pastor said, walking back and forth on the platform. "God bless ya! God bless ya! Give 'till it hurts, it's for a good cause!"

The brotherhood had filled the needs of Gladys and the pastor. The two well-dressed women stood at the pastor's side and shook hands as the men and few women left, thanking them for their contributions. Early evening, still in a blessed soft shower, Rhonda got her triple scoop at a drug store counter in the black neighborhood. The pastor got his in the back of his bright blue Studebaker with the side curtains dropped, parked in the shade of a large maple tree on Carlisle Street. He was blessed by Gladys, and she by his congregation.

CHAPTER TWENTY

Time passed, and the rigors of county business slowly ground to a conclusion in regards to the reward money offered for the apprehension of James Lee. It was argued that Detective Duncan and Officer Jasper Brown of the Warm Springs Police Department had captured the escaped Negro. Hearings were held with many hours spent debating the subject of the reward. The hurdle to be overcome in legal terms was the fact that a law enforcement officer had laid hands on the escaped prisoner first, disregarding the joint effort concept. The two officers argued that without the help of the tracker Toby Sims and his three dogs, they would not have been able to locate and capture Lee. Some county commissioners actually argued over the fact that if the Negro was shot so precisely as to be missing an earlobe, why didn't Detective Duncan just kill him, saving time and expense for the county and all concerned.

At no time was there any discussion of the misleading of the tracking posse, and how the three schoolboys had taken the professionals on a wild goose chase. At no time was the fact that three new rigged cane fishing poles were charged to the county by the sheriff on the hardware tab for the month questioned. It was as though it had never happened.

Detective Duncan was called to the stand in the courtroom once more.

"Detective, will you again recap for us what happened that mid-morning when the escapee James Lee was located?" asked the coordinating commissioner.

Heather cleared her throat. "We were at the old lumber camp on the Parks Plantation. The escaped Negro, James Lee, was captured. Officer Jasper Brown and myself, with the help of tracker Toby Sims, cornered the murder suspect in the woods. There was gunplay, and Lee was shot in the ear, bringing his run to an abrupt end. I understand it's not very pleasant," she said loudly, so the men present could hear, along with the secretary taking minutes. There was laughter. "He was transported to the Greenville jail where he is housed presently, or so we believe," she said, leaning forward.

"I believe we can do without those comments," smiled Chief Hawthorn. He had been asked to attend, for his opinion. Sheriff Gilbert looked down at the floor, holding the daily cigar in his cheek.

"This detective is a woman, in case you didn't catch that," said a commissioner.

"And what difference does that make? I believe you are a man and not a mule, but I do wonder," Heather said, with a serious cold look on her face. There was more laughter.

"A woman! A woman is an opinioned creature," the man replied, turning away from her cold look toward him.

"I'll not argue that point, and most men are driven by their penis," Heather snapped back. There was a dead silence. The secretary smiled at the comment.

"Here, here! Now, that will be enough, Miss," the coordinating commissioner said, stepping into the line of sight between the two.

"Did you lay aside your business to help locate the escaped man?" Heather asked the offending man.

Chief Hawthorn made motions for her to stop her aggression. "I think this needs an apology. No place here for personal opinions," he said, looking at the man.

"Why was the Negro shot in the ear?" asked the commissioner.

"Because I was aiming at his head with a pistol made for an effective range of twenty-five yards," Heather replied, sitting back in the chair. "Isn't the subject of this discussion who found the escaped prisoner?" she asked.

"That's twenty-five yards, three times twenty-five is seventy-five feet," advised the commissioner, pacing back and forth as though he were a lawyer.

"Had I been furnished with a rifle, things might have been different. The city doesn't budget them," Heather said. "There'll be a day coming that we'll wish we'd had them," she added. Chief Hawthorn sat quietly listening to her. "According to the newspapers, there is increased crime in the central states of small stores and gas stations."

Another commissioner got a chance to speak up. "And tell us why you were hired?"

"That's my chief's job to know why I was hired. I've done my job as well as, or better than a man. Why do you ask? Do you want my job?" Heather snapped back.

Jasper sat looking down in embarrassment at what was going on. Heather saw the top of his balding head turn pink, as it did when he was angry.

"Let's keep this discussion to related matters, so we can conclude the meeting," said the coordinating commissioner. "You are dismissed. Thanks for your part," he added. Heather stepped down. "Chief Hawthorn, Officer Brown, you may go."

The final conclusion reached by the reluctant commissioners under strong encouragement from the county attorneys was to pay the two-hundred-and-fifty-dollar reward to Toby Sims.

* * *

The month of August was one of the hottest many of the citizens could remember. The katydids were very plentiful that year. The night woods were filled with the spooky, haunting sound of their mating cry. The jail was completed. The brick men's shanty village was torn down. Buntings were draped across City Hall and the Police Department doors and windows for the grand reception on the third Friday of the month. The mayor and chief frequently stood admiring the new addition. All that was missing was prisoners. In a short time, the patrol cars would bring the arrestees to the new jail, rather than making the tension filled drive to the county jail in Greenville, where a fair fee was charged for their housing. The café was hired to furnish a light punch for the occasion, and Mrs. Blakely was to furnish tea cakes, nicely uniform in size with a golden-brown edge. The ribbon cutting was expected to be a grand affair. Even Buddy Cotton found a way to make a quarter from the event. He was paid to set up four refreshment tables, borrowed from the Christian Church, along with the use of fifty folding chairs.

Officer Edgar Peterson roped off the parking spaces in front of the police department early in the morning. Just after daylight, two city workers swept the street and the sidewalk, and even brushed the cobwebs from the corners of the windows. Buddy Cotton had the tables and chairs set up long beforehand. It was a slow patrol day, not a call one. Heather and Jasper stayed close in, only making a drive through the residential area twice, before the evening's festivities. The downtown businesses stayed open right up to the time the mayor and council assembled in the street. The local brass band played a rendition of an old favorite composed by John Philip Sousa. The walking public was already seated. There were a few wagons, loaded with old and young sitting in short-legged chairs, dogs trailing along. There were trucks of all sizes and makes carrying the same. It was shaping up to be a wonderful event for the people of Warm Springs.

Mayor Cornelius Cunningham and his wife Agnes were shaking hands and greeting the citizens. The town council was slowly gathering and doing likewise. Officer Jasper Brown and Detective Duncan mingled in the perimeter of the crowd. Frances Goulding was Sunday dressed, complete with a fruit arrangement on her dark straw hat. The brightly painted pasty fruit had an impact on the young children, who wondered if it was real.

Frances stood by in the lobby to greet as the citizens walked through to the new jail addition. The band played softly, knowing that the mayor was about to speak at any moment.

The crowd settled down as the mayor waved his straw hat over his head, and Chief Howard Hawthorn stood beside him. "People of this fair city, we, your servants, are very pleased to be here on this pleasant evening," the mayor said.

"Cornelius, ya wouldn't know a pleasant if it flew up and hit ya in the face!" a man yelled from somewhere in the standing crowd.

The mayor smiled and looked up for a moment. "Well, I could have said it's too darn hot, and my BVD's are sticking to me, but I didn't," he replied. The crowd roared.

Jasper saw a horse and wagon stop at the crest of the street, not under a street lamp. He thought it was odd. "See that wagon yonder?" he whispered to Heather. She moved to look.

"Is that the man I arrested early on, back some time ago?" she whispered back.

"It is, I think," Jasper replied. They both moved to watch the wagon. The speech and laughter were now background noise. Clapping broke the murmur of conversation. A man climbed down from the wagon and approached a store clerk who was closing. The two officers walked closer in the shadows.

"I need a pint!" the man said.

"Sir, I'm closed, done balanced my ledger," said the clerk, with his back turned to the man.

"No, God damn it! I want a pint!" said the man, getting louder.

Heather and Jasper stepped out of the dark shadows and saw the woman in the wagon was Mrs. Harper.

"Mrs. Harper," Heather whispered, surprising the woman.

"Yes," Mrs. Harper replied.

"Is he drunk? Better still is he -- " Heather started to ask, then she saw the bruise on the woman's face. " -- beating you again? Where are the two kids?"

"My sister took them for a while," Mrs. Harper whispered, with her head down.

"Hey! Ya talkin' ta my wife?" Harper bellowed from the sidewalk. He was yelling at Jasper.

"I'll handle this. He's mine," Jasper said, stepping toward Harper.

"That's my God damn woman!" he yelled. The gathering was distracted by the disturbance.

"Mr. Harper, are ya drinkin'?" Jasper asked, keeping just out of reach of the huge man.

"Maybe!" Harper replied, looking away.

"I think ya have been. Drunk, for a matter of fact," Jasper said, easing his hand back to his hard club.

"Can I go?" asked the store clerk.

"Not till I get my pint!" Harper slurred loudly.

"Ma'am, can you get back home?" Heather whispered.

"I can," Mrs. Harper said softly.

"He's goin' ta be with us for a while," Heather advised. "You may go," she added.

This woman who had attempted to dress for the occasion was still showing a hard life, like many in the area. Her clean day dress was showing its years in wear. Her clean hair did not have any barrettes that matched. Heather realized just how well off she was, and that things could certainly be worse.

"Someone will drive out to be sure you got home. We'll check along the road," Heather said, as the woman took the worn reins and nudged the mule ahead.

"Hey! God damn it, woman! Where ya goin'?" Harper yelled. By now the festivities had stopped and the citizens were watching the police in action.

"Jesus, it's Harper, again. I think he's drunk," said the mayor to Chief Hawthorn.   "Let's see how this works out, folks. I'm sure you are all curious," he said, loud enough for most everyone to hear.

"I'll bet he's the first guest," someone said.

"Probably so," whispered the chief. "Probably so."

The well-worn, field abused wagon rolled past Heather, exposing her to the drunk man.

"Hey! Bitch! Where ya been?" Harper slurred loudly.

"Givin' yer name to the Klan," Heather said, standing square to him, but several steps away.

"I saw you at T.C. Handley's store once," he barked.   Their faces were bathed by the street light.   Jasper's brass buttons shined. "So, yer still tha new lady po-lice," Harper said, swaying.

"I am that!" Heather replied.   "I think we need to hurry," she said to Jasper. "We're holding up things."

"Harper, yer under arrest for drunk and disorderly," Jasper said, stepping toward the drunk man. Jasper stayed behind the man's shoulder, in order grab a wrist and cuff it.

Heather saw the lantern light swinging from the tailgate of the wagon as it rocked along and then turned the corner.

"Step up, this'll take both of us," Jasper said, looking at Heather. Jasper touched the man, and as he expected, Harper jerked away. The older officer followed, trying to grasp the strong man's wrist. Jasper managed to thump the drunk on the side of the head, a sharp but controlled tap to get

338

his attention. Harper went wild, rushing toward Jasper and getting a headlock on him. Jasper's uniform hat fell to the ground.

Heather rushed to help. She quickly ended the fracas by pushing the muzzle of her revolver against Harper's temple. "Hurts, don't it?" she asked loudly, stepping forward to keep the painful pressure on. "Let him go! Get on yer knees!" she ordered loudly. The crowd watched.

Harper released Jasper and got down on his knees, then he sat down.

"On yer knees! You can't get up from yer butt!" said Heather.

"You ain't shit without that pistol," Harper said.

Heather holstered her revolver and promptly kicked the drunk in the face. He went down hard. "Now, he's ready to cuff," she said. Jasper hurriedly cuffed the downed drunk. "In the back, in the back," she whispered, as Jasper changed from his years of habit.

"Damn! A scene from the Old West," a school teacher said, fanning her face with a bleached woven fan. There was applause from the crowd. The drunk came to rather quickly, to find that he was under arrest.

"Excuse me," said Chief Hawthorn. He hurried to assist in getting the large man to the jail.

The three officers had to pass through the crowd with the drunk.

"Oh, Chief! When they are finished, the city has to see those two officers," said the mayor, with a big grin.

Harper hissed like a cat as he passed several women. They jumped and gave him plenty of room to pass.

The chief saw the man was cuffed in the back. "In the back?" he whispered, as they went down the side alley to the jail doors.

"Always!" smiled Jasper. "Always," he said.

They were out of sight and hearing of the public. "Mr. Harper, I told you about beating yer wife," Heather said, as the three officers dragged Harper into a new cell.

"She's my property," Harper slurred, trying to stand. Jasper pushed him back down.

"I'll get you, you old fart. I'll get ya," Harper said, looking at Jasper. The drunk man was an evil son of a bitch. "She's my PROPERTY!" he yelled, as he tried to struggle free.

Heather wrapped her strong hand around her pocketknife and pulled it from her pocket. Chief Hawthorn stood by listening to Harper's threats. "She's my PROPERTY!" he yelled, as he struggled to get free. "Mine! God damn y'all!" Harper yelled.

Heather hated the son of a bitch and felt sorry for his wife. She suddenly struck Harper at the moment he mouthed an obscenity directly at her. Then she struck him with her weak hand. The angry woman suddenly lost her senses and struck a rhythm of hard punches on his face like her punching bag that hung in the barn back home. She was drawing blood after the third set of punches. Heather spouted obscenities that one would not have expected to have crossed her mind. Chief Hawthorn and Jasper stood speechless for a moment before pulling her off.

"Do you remember the last time? What did I say? When I'm in this town, you touch the woman who bore you two children, I'd beat you senseless. You didn't believe me!" Heather said loudly. Harper remained silent and looked at her, bleeding. Heather kicked him in the chest. Harper's big chest sounded like a ripe melon as her foot found its place.

"Ugh!" he grunted.

"Answer me, you dumb son of a bitch!" Heather yelled.

Once again Heather pulled her revolver and held it to Harper's face. "This is a threat! I'll kill you before I leave this town if you don't change!" she yelled. The band had begun to play, as the jail activity was loud enough to be heard on the street.

"The mayor wants ta see you both out front," said the chief.

Heather and Jasper straightened their clothing and washed their hands from handling the drunken man. The chief stood by and all three walked out together. The mayor and the gathering of citizens applauded.

"We'd like to recognize these two officers for their hard work and for the apprehension of the wanted fugitive, James Lee. These two took him over on the old Parks Plantation. Give 'em a big hand!" the mayor said, smiling. Heather and Jasper waved at the citizens and nodded in acknowledgement of the recognition.

"We will tell you now that there's a drunk in the first cell to the left when you enter. I'd say that if a woman wants to go through, she needs to do it with an escort," said the mayor.

The citizens rushed in to see the new jail addition. Frances was greeted by women she knew. It made her feel important. The tea cakes and punch were consumed, and visiting on the street went on for several hours. It appeared that the taxpayers were pleased.

CHAPTER TWENTY-ONE

Time passed slowly for Theo Jackson. He wondered if his hogs were being cared for, and would he lose his supply of slop customers. Life was bleak in the days spent alone in the cell. The other Negroes took every opportunity to make hog sounds, rootin' and squealin' as they passed by coming from community chain gang work. Oliver Queen called him the sheriff's little piggy. Jackson had made so many small marks on the steel wall that he had lost count of the exact number. He thought it was close to a hundred.

During the lonely silent hours of the night, Theo recalled James Lee bragging about the revolver he had tucked inside his waistband. He remembered Lee's comments about, "Nobody can stop me from gettin' ta Alabama. These Georgia Crackers can't touch me there." Lee's voice echoed in Theo Jackson's head. The memory was like a bad thunderstorm. A pained look crossed his face and he sometimes flinched. "Nobody can stop me from gettin' ta Alabama." The recollection of James Lee's voice would whisper again. "Nobody can stop me, nobody." The voice grew stronger and louder in his head until he sat up in the cold steel bunk. The voice momentarily stopped when Theo struck his head on the steel bunk above him with a loud thunk. The other prisoners knew what he was going through and would laugh in the darkness. At first, they all laughed at once, but then they became sadistic and laughed one at a time, changing their voices to make haunting sounds.

Theo Jackson was glad he was in the cell alone. He was embarrassed by his sobbing in the night, as he sat on the side of the bunk. He hoped the others did not hear. Even the gray mouse that searched for morsels of food nightly avoided his cell. Jackson laid still and watched it scurry through without stopping, going to another cell. He even left food to attract it, but it never stopped, running within inches of the bait. On the morning of the one hundred and first day, at exactly ten o'clock, he heard his loudmouthed mother.

"I'm Gladys Hightower, employed by the Black Derby Club on Auburn Avenue, in Atlanter," she barked to Sheriff Louis Gilbert. Gladys stood in front of the sheriff's desk with her purse in one hand and a roll of money in the other.

The sheriff could tell the woman was impatient. He leaned back in the desk chair, removed his daily cigar, and spoke. "I don't give a God damn where ya work. State yer business," he growled.

Dixie looked calm, cold, and steely. She knew the sheriff well, and a Negro bursting in and making demands was getting off to a bad start. Curley Jones was busy with his supply order for Miss Jewel's kitchen and the jail supplies. He watched with limited vision, but open ears.

"Yous knows who I'ze is, fo' I'ze finished!" Gladys Hightower snapped back, putting her fist on her hip.

The office smelled of old tobacco ashes that remained in the ashtrays. Sheriff Gilbert carefully moved his cold cigar closer to the center of his desk. His employees knew it was not going to be pleasant as he slowly stood. "I'm sheriff of this county! I'll not be spoken to in that tone! You will get yo' black nigger ass out of my office, off my jail yard!" he yelled, and pointed to the door. He started around his desk to get to the rotund woman. The sheriff took hold of her flabby arm and muscled her toward the door. "I'll lock yo' ass up too!" he said, pushing her out the door. Gladys Hightower looked at the sheriff from midway of the walk.

"You come back with yer lawyer!" yelled the sheriff, as he slammed the door. The papers flew about on Dixie's desk. "Sorry," he said, as he picked up the ones that floated to the floor.

"No, problem," Dixie replied softly.

Curley took the opportunity to laugh. Theo Jackson moved away from the cell bars and sat down on the bunk. He wondered how long it would be before she came back.

It was 11:05 a.m. when the screen door spring gently sounded and Jackson's attorney stuck his head inside. "Knock, knock!" he said loudly, seeing the three county employees at their desks.

"Come in!" said Sheriff Gilbert, motioning with his free hand. His cold cigar was back in his mouth.

"How you good folks this morning?" asked Isaac Pittman. He looked exactly like the first time they had seen him, except the wrinkles in his laundered shirt were slightly different. "I told Becky that you sent me," he said to Curley. "They went heavy on the grits!"

"Good people," Curley replied, as he stopped running a column of figures.

"Have a seat," said the sheriff.

"Thank you, sir!" Pittman replied, as he sat down.

"By Missuss Glad-ass Hightower, employee of de Black Derby Club, way up in Atlanta, I'd say you are here to bond the hog farmer out," said the sheriff, laying down his fountain pen.

"Derby don't get ya too far down here!" replied Isaac, laughing and playing along with the game.

"Miss Dixie? Do we have the papers drawn up?" asked Sheriff Gilbert.

The wooden filing cabinet drawer opened under the weight of a fully loaded drawer. "Right here," Dixie replied, as she brought the file over.

"Thank you, ma'am!" said the sheriff. He placed the papers on the desk. "Everything is detailed on here. It will total out to a cash bond of $11,600.00," he said, pushing the paperwork toward the attorney.

"I'd like to read 'em again," the attorney said, raising the pages into his view. "Burglary of John Miller's barn, $1,500. Burglary of John Miller's office in residence, $1,500. Theft of Motor Vehicle owned by John Miller, $1,000. Murder of Gertrude Miller, $3,000. Murder of Polly Sue Miller, $3,000. Burglary of Della Cummings' barn, $1,500. Theft by Taking, bucket and food, $100. Aiding an Escaped Felon. Seems to be fine. Who do I pay?" Pittman asked, looking around.

"Miss Dixie, she will count it twice and give you a receipt," said Sheriff Gilbert, moving his cigar in his cheek.

"$11,600!" said the attorney, glancing up at the sheriff. Isaac Pittman held up a stack of bills.

"Curley, bring him out," said the sheriff.

Gladys Hightower and Rhonda sat in the Cadillac parked on the edge of the street. "I'ze ain't habby won bit!" Gladys snarled, looking toward the sheriff's office window.

"But Mama, this ain't Atlanter," Rhonda said, from the back seat.

Isaac Pittman took the receipt from Miss Dixie and stood by quietly. The cold steel doors opened and closed, starting out loud and growing faint as Curley worked his way into the bowels of the fortress-like complex, eventually bringing Theo Jackson forward. Jackson stepped through the jail door into the dim light of the shaded office. He covered his eyes, even in the dim light.

"Bright, ain't it?" laughed Pittman. "They say the snap of death is a lot brighter," he added, as he took his client by the arm and led him into the morning sunlight. The attorney waved at staff in the office, then pulled the door closed.

* * *

The afternoon was quiet, lunch had made everyone sleepy. Curley walked the fence line for holes, just to stay awake. Dixie stood on the kitchen porch and sipped a cup of hot tea. Miss Jewel had gone away for a while. The wrens hopped around on the bottom steps looking for food.

Sheriff Gilbert was cleaning out his center desk drawer.

Dr. Augustus Hubbard opened the door. "Get busy, asshole!" he said loudly.

Sheriff Gilbert looked up. "I see yer wide open."

"Just came from the Judge's chambers," said Dr. Hubbard. He had papers in his hand.

"Chamber? Pot or office?" asked the sheriff, as he continued to explore his desk drawer.

"Office," replied the doctor. "I've got papers ta be served on old Bo Bob Huggins. My medical report and his age convinced the judicial system to put the old nigger on non-reporting parole, whatever that is," he said, tossing the court orders on the sheriff's desk.

Sheriff Gilbert moved his cigar to the other cheek, rolling it across his mouth. He carefully read the order. "Lucky nigger," he mumbled, as he tossed the paper down.

"Who's goin' ta serve it?" asked Doc Hubbard.

"It'll be a deputy, Curley's not recognized by the court. This evening or tonight," he said, closing the drawer. "He'll be glad of that," he added.

The Sheriff gave the papers to the deputy that lived in the direction of Bo Bob Huggins' place. It was a little after dusk when the marked car pulled into the yard. Bo Bob was startled, as he was pouring up whiskey into smaller bottles on the kitchen table. The Negro made a dash to the front porch, where he met the deputy.

"Evenin's, deputy," Huggins said, walking through the screen door with a limp.

"Pourin' again?" the deputy asked, jokingly.

Bo Bob looked caught and replied with a stutter. "Naw, suh! Ain't beez po-in' no whuskey."

"Bo Bob! You've been placed on non-reporting parole by the judge," said the deputy. He held out the offender's copy of the papers.

"Oh, mize!" the Negro said, as he carefully took the papers. "Tank yous, suh," he said, holding them carefully. He could not read.

"Put 'em away so ya can get to 'em," the deputy said, as he turned to walk away.

The Negro was so taken over the fact that he was, in his eyes, a free man, that he sat down on the porch.

* * *

The train sounded its whistle at the north yard limit as it slowed for a stop in the small town of Warm Springs. The steam billowed cloudlike from the whistle of the locomotive as the engineer pulled on the cord. Dogs ran to chase the huge rumbling beast and children stopped to watch as it passed.

"Them new diesels will take its place someday," said one old man, as he got up from the community bench at Allen's Gas Station and Garage. The old man stood with his hand held in still reverence for the engine that passed.

"I hope that damn windshield for the woman police is on that thing," Claude Allen said, looking up from an engine he was working on.

Heather and Jasper passed the depot on a slow patrol around town. It had been a slow day. A dog call was the only thing they had responded to. The dog was off its chain and had dug up a flower bed several doors down from its rightful place. The citation Jasper wrote to the dog's owner was not well received, and a call was made to the mayor at city hall. However, Mayor Cunningham backed his officers and advised that there was nothing he could do. The offender was required to appear in court.

In the small town, everyone except the deaf heard the train. It brought freight and passengers. Most passengers went to the Meriwether Inn and enjoyed the warm mineral springs. Jasper and Heather were passing city hall by way of the back alley.

"I wonder if my windshield has come in?" Heather asked, as she leaned and looked toward the depot.

"We'll see if it did," Jasper replied. He steered the Ford across the railroad tracks and soon pulled into the freight depot yard. Among the many boxes, wooden crates, and paper wrapped packages, the windshield was certain to stand out. "There it is!" said Jasper, pointing.

"I believe you're right!" replied Heather, opening the car door.

The freight depot was busy with railroad agents logging and checking in received goods.

"Yes, ma'am! How can I help ya?" asked Titus Johns. He was counting boxes.

"Is this addressed to Claude Allen?" Heather asked, standing by a large crate.

Johns lowered his clipboard. "Yer close enough ta look," he said, laughing.

Heather bent down and read the label. "Yep! It is!" she said. "That's my windshield," she added. "I'll even go tell 'em it's here."

"Is that it?" Jasper asked.

"Yep! Take me to Allen's garage. I'm glad it finally came."

Claude Allen saw the patrol car coming. "I told ya it was probably here," Claude Allen said to the old man on the bench. "I'll be damn glad ta get her off my butt," he said, wiping his hands and stepping out to meet Heather.

"Did it come in?" Claude Allen asked.

"It did!" Heather replied, grinning.

"I'll have it replaced by noon tomorrow," said Claude.

"That's fine, just before I have to leave," Heather replied.

"Leave? Where to?" Claude asked.

"This is not for me; everyone expects to have a man when they call the law. Seems that everyone but the women and kids resent me being here," Heather said, looking toward the skyline.

"I wouldn't say that. Lots of folks think ya do a damn good job. Better than some men po-lice," said Claude.

"Nah! I finish this and I'm goin' back home," Heather said, with a sigh.

The old man on the bench was listening. "Little sister! You've cut a notch in yer pistol with lots of folks. I wouldn't be discouraged just yet," he said, pointing his aged, boney finger at her.

"We'll see, we'll see," Heather said.

* * *

Before Sheriff Gilbert could get out of the office for the night, the solicitor came in. "Busy?" asked Ambrose Watkins. He looked tired, his shirt was out on one side and his tie was loose.

"Not too busy for you," the sheriff replied with a sigh. He took his seat.

Ambrose Watkins produced a list of three attorneys to be presented to James Lee. He was to choose one. "Ya tell this sum bitch that this one is on the taxpayers and he needs to be happy with the one he picks. Damn nigger!" said Watkins. "The one he picks is the one he keeps. He can find a disliking later, but the county damn sure won't finance another one. He can do without, damn bastard," he said, kicking the desk with the toe of his oxford.

"Just come back and we can let him pick," said the sheriff, as he opened the wall mounted strong box containing the jail block keys. The heavy steel lid on the box made a horrific squeak as it opened and closed. The heavy bronze keys were very complex in design.

The sheriff turned on all the electric lights, and only six for the cell blocks. The inmates moaned as their eyes were shocked. "Shade 'em, boys!" the sheriff called out, as he and the solicitor walked into the depths and soon stood face to face with James Lee.

"The county is required to furnish you with legal representation, better known as a God damn free lawyer," barked Sheriff Gilbert. "That shit was started back in, I believe 1914 or so," he said. The sheriff tossed his cigar on the floor and pressed it flat with his shoe. The inmates moaned. "Here's a list of three attorneys. Pick one out," he said, holding up the sheet of paper.

"Read their names out loud," said Watkins.

"Albert Odom, Roger Sloss, Robert Gaskill," said James Lee.

"Which one?" asked the sheriff.

James Lee was silent for a moment. "Robert Gaskill, I guess," he said.

"Don't guess! Once you tell us who, he'll be standing here in less than twenty-four hours, like a damn bad cold, hard to get rid of," said Ambrose

Watkins. "I'll call him tonight. He's a Columbus man," he added.

The two county men walked out of the cell block. The sand under their shoe soles made a gritty grinding sound as they progressed to the door. The heavy door closed behind them.

"I'll use your telephone," Watkins said, as he picked it up. "Paulette!" he said loudly.

"No, Sue. Who do you wish to call?" she asked.

"Get me Robert Gaskill, Columbus, Georgia. The number may be Forest 4831," Watkins said.

The telephone rang. "Gaskill and Associates! Robert Gaskill speaking."

"This is Ambrose Watkins, Solicitor General in Meriwether County. Can you take a murder case, and a whole bunch of other sundry lesser charges?" he asked.

"Who's been charged?" Gaskill asked.

"Negro, James Lee. Probably read about the manhunt in the newspaper, and heard about it on the radio," replied Watkins.

"What's the charges?" Gaskill asked.

"I'll recite 'em. Burglary of John Miller's barn, burglary of John Miller's office in residence, theft of motor vehicle owned by John Miller, murder of Gertrude Miller, murder of Polly Sue Miller, burglary of Della Cummings' barn, theft by taking bucket and food, escape, aggravated battery," Watkins said. "Pay is scale," he added.

"I can take it. I'll be there in less than forty-eight hours," replied Robert Gaskill.

"See Sheriff Louis Gilbert, at the jail. Red brick building off the square in Greenville, can't miss it," said Watkins.

"I've been in Greenville before, several small cases before you took office," said Robert Gaskill. "I believe y'all claim ta have the best trackin' dogs in the Southeast," he added. "Well, let me take that back, second best. I hear there's a damn near saint of a dog in Campbell County, a Duncan man out of Campbellton owns her. They cost me a case once," he said.

Solicitor Ambrose Watkins did not associate Detective Duncan of Warm Springs with the Campbell County tracking dog.

* * *

On the second morning, a new deep black Chevrolet, glistening in the sunlight, pulled into the jail yard. The sound of the gravel under the tires was heard inside. Dixie looked out the window. Most people did not come to the jail for pleasure and she wondered who it was. The dusty lace curtains rode the warm breeze. In a few minutes a short skinny man stood by the car coughing into a folded handkerchief. "Jesus! A Jew!" Dixie thought to herself. She had nothing personally against the race or religion, she just acted off of the opinion of others. In some parts of the great land, Jews were considered to be a race. Most locals were a mix of everything

European, showing no particular identifiable traits. Both men and women were a mixed breed, like running dogs, no one of certifiable origin. They were either Baptist or Methodist, foot washers and snake handlers, and very few Catholics in the mix.

If the man stepped into a puddle, he would cry out that he was in deep water because he was so frail. His black hair was long, greased down with tonic and combed from front to back. It cut a sharp, very neat line about his ears and neck. His cheek bones were sharp and his nose was crooked. The crooked nose supported tortoise shell glasses. She chuckled, as they were the round, thick drinking glass variety. He stopped and coughed once again before arriving at the steps. Dixie saw his shoes, black wing-tips they were, new or well taken care of, as they had a brilliant reflective shine that contrasted fiercely with his white socks when he took a step. Unlike Theo Jackson's attorney, this man's white shirt had no laundry fold wrinkles. His bright blue bowtie was almost electrifying against the dark blue suit with a faint thin gray stripe. Dixie quickly took her seat.

The door opened. "Hello!" the man's voice called out.

"Come in!" answered Dixie, from behind her typewriter.

"I'm Robert Gaskill, the appointed attorney for James Lee. I'd like to meet with my client," said Gaskill. He stood in front of Dixie's desk, holding his black leather satchel.

"That has to be scheduled," Dixie replied. "But that can be arranged, the jailer's here somewhere," she added, rising from her desk.

"Thank you. I'd like to wait." Gaskill took a seat near the outer door.

"Where ya from?" Dixie asked.

"Columbus, 9th and Broad Street, close to the courthouse. I can see the river from my office window," Gaskill answered. He clutched the black satchel in his lap. "Fourth floor, it's quite a climb," he added.

Dixie knew not to keep an attorney waiting. She excused herself and headed into the private residence portion looking for Curley. He was where she expected him to be, in the kitchen flirting with Miss Jewel. Everyone liked to kill time with Miss Jewel. She was easily amused by whites and laughed often. The Negro cook was busy with the preparation of the evening meal.

"Curley! We need to get James Lee and his attorney together. He's up front," Dixie said, standing in the doorway.

"I'ze glads he's gettin' his time killin' ass frum heres," the Negro woman said, as she peeled potatoes. She laughed loud but meant it. Curley kept her mind from her church and Bible study.

Curley carried the jail keys. He chose to take another route through the jail complex and bring James Lee forward to an empty cell, closer to the front. Dixie returned to her desk.

"Lee's being brought up," she said, taking her seat. The attorney smiled.

The jailer's ring of keys tapped and swung against the heavy steel door that divided the free world from the confined hell of ill-kept conditions and shadowy darkness. He soon emerged. "He's in the first cell on the right," Curley said, seeing the attorney for the first time.

Robert Gaskill set his leather satchel on the floor, pulled all the papers from it and fanned them for the jailer to see, then let him look inside. "How's that?" he asked. The thin man raised his coat and turned about. "Nothing on me but a business card, wallet, keys, and penknife's in the car."

"Just fine, sir! Just fine!" Curley said, as he held the door. "I see you've been working in the system," he said, holding the heavy door.

"A time or two," replied the attorney. The darkness and stench overtook him as he headed inside.

"I'll have to leave the door open. I'll be sitting just outside, house rules. Prisoners have been known to attack their lawyers," Curley said, pulling the nearest straight chair to the edge of the open door.

Robert Gaskill walked inside. His eyes were struggling to adapt to the darkness and deep shadows. In some of the cells beyond he was able to make out the figures of prisoners. The odor of urine filled the morning air. "James Lee?" he asked, looking into the cell he thought his client was in.

"Yes!" A voice responded, from the back of the cell.

Gaskill stepped closer, but never came within reach. He peered inside and eventually made out a Negro, sitting on the back edge of a bottom bunk frame. There was no mattress, as the cell was unoccupied. It was only being used for this meeting.

"I'm your attorney, Robert Gaskill."

James Lee did not say a word.

"I see you've got a long list of charges. Are they all correctly made?" he asked right off.

James Lee still did not speak.

Robert Gaskill chose to stand. The wooden bench looked as though it were soiled and nasty. "My concern is the murder charges, or the homicide charges, to be technically correct in the wording of the court. Do you have anything to tell me about these?" he asked.

The Negro sat silently, sulking.

The attorney removed his glasses. James Lee saw the large dark eyes change to tiny glassy spots on the field of the white face. Gaskill rubbed the glasses on the shirt fabric between two buttons on his white shirt. He put the glasses back on and his eyes were large again. The thin attorney leaned forward. "Mr. Lee, will you not speak to me? I need to hear from you," he said.

The other prisoners lay quietly. Some had been pulled to take duty on the chain gang detail. The others were not so lucky, they had been left behind.

"I see your ear has stopped bleeding, it looks to be healing," the attorney said, as he leaned forward, peering into the dark shadows. He could see the whites of the Negro's eyes as they blinked and followed him about. Gaskill looked at his watch. "If you're not going to help me to help you, then I shall go," Gaskill said. He started toward the outer door that was ajar. It cast a bright wedge of light into the darkness. Gaskill felt it to be a holy light, one sacred in nature. Before he was out of sight, he turned. "I'll make your case from the case reports and whatever I can come up with." There was nothing but silence from Lee. "Good day, sir!" Gaskill said softly, as he continued toward the light.

James Lee rushed to the front of the cell and looked out with his face touching the bars. The heavy steel door made a loud harsh clang as it seated in its steel casing. The cell block was darker once again. The street traffic soon became the saving grace for those left behind. It gave them something to imagine as they heard the vehicles pass and occasionally the laughter of passing children.

"Don't piss away yo' chance," a Negro voice said, just above a whisper.

James Lee sat back down, waiting to be returned to his own assigned cell. The leg restraints and heavy ball tired him greatly.

"Thank you, sir!" Robert Gaskill said, looking at Curley. "Ma'am," he added, looking at Dixie.

"Anytime, 'tween daylight and dark," Curley said, turning the heavy bolt on the huge box lock mounted on the steel door.

"I'd like to see a complete case file," the attorney said, looking at Dixie.

"The most complete file is at the solicitor general's office, over in the courthouse," she replied, pointing to the square.

Robert Gaskill nodded his head, acknowledging what she had said. "And where's a good place to stay?" he asked.

Dixie thought a moment. "I think you'd do well for yourself and your client to go to the newspaper," she said, pointing to the red brick building across the way. "See Alfred Huffman, he's better able to recommend than I am. He has guests from out of town often, other reporters and the like."

"Thanks!" Gaskill replied, as he gently opened the door and left. The Columbus attorney took his car and circled the square, parking along the curb in front of the Vindicator office.

Alfred Huffman had just made his first pot of coffee and old Souse Meat was running late. Robert Gaskill took the time to gather all the past issues of the paper that covered the events of his client. The young reporter suggested that he take a room at Ransford's Boarding House in Moreland. It would be away from the noise of the city and the curiosity seekers who were following the trial's development. Huffman felt sure that Ransford's could accommodate him with a room located in the rear where it was quiet. He could take his meals there in the dining room, where there was no one but boarding guests. Huffman watched as the shiny Chevrolet drove out of sight.

Old Souse Meat was coming up the sidewalk as the attorney left the newspaper office. Alfred returned to his desk, where he took the quiet time to gather his writing tasks for the day. His boss was heard entering the business. "Alfred! Who was that? Did ya charge him for those back copies?" he barked, as he turned out the light and opened the blinds as full as they would go.

"He's Robert Gaskill, the court appointed attorney for James Lee, and he paid for the copies," Alfred answered, pushing the money toward the corner of his desk.

The old man picked up the coins and placed them in a metal coin box. Alfred heard each coin as it dropped.

"Get a story out on that!" said Souse Meat, slamming the drawer and hiding the money box.

The stage was set, all the needed actors were now accounted for, both offenders had attorneys, and evidence was assembled by the prosecutor, Ambrose Watkins. The announcement of the court date would soon be published in the Vindicator.

CHAPTER TWENTY-TWO

Claude Allen finally replaced the bullet punctured windshield for the woman detective. He was relieved to get her off his back, as she had been checking on it every third day. The few stolen items that he occasionally bought were apt to be discovered if she continued to come around. The sellers were taken at face value and a paperwork trail was often non-existent.

The city council and businessmen had passed notice by word of mouth of a secret meeting in the old Sunday school building at the First Baptist Church at seven o'clock in the evening. The city council was one hundred percent, and the most powerful and influential businessmen were there. Three businesses in town were owned by women. They were not informed of the gathering. Police Chief Howard Hawthorn was not made privy to the gathering either.

The warm breeze of the summer night felt dry, not a drop of rain had fallen in several weeks. The dust was easily carried by the slightest wind. Heather was ready for bed, attempting to keep reasonably comfortable. Nothing would ever offset the pleasure of winter in her opinion. Edgar Peterson was seen making his rounds on foot in the downtown district. The night was so still Heather could hear him rattling doors several stores away.

The churchyard was circled with automobiles, not a buggy on property. The attendees were established enough to afford motorized vehicles. The windows and the yellowed shades were raised in an attempt to capture the slightest breeze. The secrecy of the meeting demanded the use of a kerosene lamp. It gave a soft glow to the men's faces as they sat around the rectangular table. Red wasps darted about the yellow flame, to be joined by a candle fly. The hand fans were quickly deployed by each man. The heat was nothing to be macho about. Perspiration rolled down their temples, as much from their temperament on the subject of a woman officer as the heat.

"Call to order," one councilman said, as he stood at the rickety podium, tapping hard on it with the end of his closed pocketknife.

Mayor Cunningham sat quietly to the speaker's right. He was unsure of this assembly. He looked slowly around the table at the powerful men's faces, bathed in the flickering lamplight. They sparkled with beads of sweat, occasionally wiped with a handkerchief. Every councilman was there, Bob Johnson, Albert Swanson, Herbert Akins, James Howard, William James, and Buford Sims. There were certainly more businessmen, but apparently those who chose not to attend had made a statement as to their beliefs. There was Claude Allen, of the gas station; Emmet Sikes, from the café; Frank Block, one of three hardware owners; Charles Fairbanks, a grocery man, along with Addison Mitchell. Tom Haygood from the pharmacy looked glassy-eyed, and then there was Daniel Flynn, in building materials. Mayor Cunningham could not remember who in this gathering was in the Klan, but he knew their presence was here. He actually wished he had stuck to his first reaction and not attended.

The mayor was brought back to the moment at the speaker's comment, "And that's why this outsider woman should not be allowed to occupy the job of a deserving man!" The mayor actually jumped. He hurriedly scratched his ear with the end of his little finger and then pulled out a soft peppermint candy and placed it in his mouth.

"What do you say, Mayor?" asked Herbert Akins, from the podium.

"I'm sorry, what was the question?" the mayor responded.

"This woman y'all hired should not be here in her capacity. It needs ta be a man in that job," repeated Herbert Akins.

The mayor sat silently, almost giving the impression he was sleeping with his eyes open.

"Mayor?" Herbert Akins inquired.

"Anyone in here ever been shot at?" the mayor asked. "Not in the service at some great distance," he added. "But up close, see the other person's eyes. See the determination, the evil within," he asked, looking around the room. The men's ghostly lit faces, in the continually changing shadows of the lamp's flame, looked ahead.

"What's that ta do with the situation?" asked Emmet Sikes.

"We advertised, and not a man applied," replied the mayor.

"Maybe not long enough," someone said.

"Damn near a month. Crime and killin's was takin' place, y'all was singin' a different tune back then," said the mayor.

"It still isn't right!" barked Charles Fairbanks, seconded by Bob Johnson.

"Any of ya sons ah' bitches want my job can have it, too old for this

353

shit!" said the mayor, as he looked at the faces of each man again. "My wife's got family elsewhere and she's wantin' ta move. God damned pissy ass politics! This town'll never amount to a God damned thing, you mark my words. There's always going ta be men like y'all ta keep it down, good old boy politics," he said in a steely tone.

"Well, now! Mayor, we don't want ya to feel that away. We just want ta do what's right for the community. Don't y'all pay her what a man would make?" asked Claude Allen.

"We did! Charles, Addison," he looked at the two men. "Tell everyone how she shoots," said Mayor Cunningham. "Cleaned y'all's profit plow, didn't she? And that was with a pistol!"

The two grocery men looked down, knowing Heather had done just that at the food shoot.

"So, what are you going to do about it?" asked Councilman Bob Johnson.

"We actually let the ad run for more than a good week in the Vindicator, you couldn't wrap a field hand's sandwich in the applications we got, there was only two after she was hired. One admitted ta havin' a criminal record," said Mayor Cunningham. "The other bastard couldn't read or write!" The mayor was silent for a while. He was somewhere between deep thought and just damned angry. "This will work itself out in due time. After the trial, I'm sure she'll move on. A single woman in a town she's not from. I suspect she's growing homesick. And other than that, the gist of this meeting will be written down and placed with my important papers, sealed in an envelope. So, if any of you brilliant sum bitches do harm to me, there'll be a base to work from. You need to kill me between here and tomorrow at ten when the bank opens," he said, standing and blotting sweat with his wadded handkerchief. He walked to the darkness of the screen door. "Oh, by the way! I'm not running for another term, you assholes!"

The mayor stepped out into the night. He came back to the screen door. "The detective will teach me how to shoot. I'll be armed pretty damn quick!" he said, looking in through the screen door. The mayor's face floated about like a ghostly spirit as he yelled out his message. The room was silent as the men listened to the mayor's car crank and leave the gravel lot. The mayor did his best to sling loose gravel on the other cars as he left.

"I thought he was one of us," said Emmet Sikes.

"I guess you don't really know a man until he's faced with choices," said Claude Allen.

The secret meeting soon disbanded and the old building was once more silent. Bob Johnson yelled to Herbert Akins, "Maybe we need a bought editorial in the Vindicator."

"Maybe so, maybe so," Akins replied, as he sat down in his car and closed the door. "We may have just made matters worse," he replied to Johnson, who stood smoking by the rear of his sedan. The quarter moon hung just above the treetops. The night birds called to the crickets below as midnight approached.

The mayor drove in a hurry, just to put space between himself and the assholes he had just discovered. "God damn bastards! Hire a person to do a God damned dangerous job and this is what I get. Ungrateful sons of bitches!" He steered with his hands at the ten and one o'clock positions. The brim of his soft straw fedora rose in the front as the wind rushed in through the open window. He glanced in his rearview mirror frequently to see if he was followed. All he could see was the cloud of sandy dust reflecting in his red taillight. "I bet I get me a damn pistol," he thought to himself. "Chicken shits!" he mumbled aloud.

CHAPTER TWENTY-THREE

Georgia was hot and dry that summer, and some crops failed. Crime was down, except for the bootleggers and the still operators with their car chases from the law, if the law cared. Local jurisdictions tended to close a blind eye to the speakeasy clubs, what few there were. Most folks continued to pour in the comfort of their own homes. It was known that locals had made corn liquor since the land was settled. A way of life since the early 1700s would be hard to change. The law was not up to the challenge of putting a stop to it, based on manpower and the political upheavals that would certainly follow. When the government agents came around, local law showed great interest and passed on information as to where the clubs and stills were said to be located.

Officer Jasper Brown and Detective Duncan had no intentions of interfering with the local still operators. They had taken it upon themselves to break the mundane heat of the long summer days by sitting in the shade of the huge oaks on the north side of town and stopping delivery trucks, or trucks in general, to examine their cargo, as they headed into Warm Springs without thought of speed. Trucks with loads of sugar and yeast among the cargo were noted as they created a pattern. The two officers marked the load with a small "x" on the front of the sugar bags and yeast cartons. The marked bags and cartons were seen in loads leaving the rear of the grocery stores. The officers established the fact that there were several councilmen who were either running a still or participating in the covert steps to supply one. Sometimes there were several layers of involvement before the actual kingpin could be identified.

The mid-afternoon sun had finally given way to a heavy cloud cover. It was a welcomed affair. The temperature under the shade of the thick canopy of oak leaves had dropped by ten or fifteen degrees.

"I think a cloud's comin' up," said Jasper, as he leaned out of the open window and looked at the darkening sky.

"Let it rain!" Heather replied, as she puffed her white blouse in and out. "Shew!" She blew from the heat.

A large raindrop struck the windshield. "Here it comes!" said Jasper, as he started to roll up his window. "It's apt ta be a gully washer."

Lightning struck nearby. They jumped in reaction to the bright flash. "Best move from these trees," Heather urged. "Let's go to the gazebo at the Inn. We can sit there." The rain was washing the road dust from the windshield.

Jasper cranked the car and carefully climbed back onto the roadway. The dusty road was already shedding water as the rain fell. "You've said, but I'm old and forget. When's tha court for the two niggers?" he asked, turning into the long roadway to the Meriwether Inn.

"You forget quickly. It starts next week, the second Monday in September, in case you've forgotten the month," Heather replied.

"Don't be a smart ass," Jasper said. He circled the large gazebo and parked looking toward the roadway. The rain was falling harder. The windows were beginning to fog.

"It's a good one," Heather commented, as she wiped her windows with her handkerchief.

"I saw Theo Jackson getting scraps and garbage at Becky's last evening after work," Jasper said, trying to keep his windows clear. The outside mirrors were useless. They were small, round, and covered with thousands of raindrops.

"That son of a bitch is lucky," Heather said, gritting her teeth. "Tha bastard been elsewhere he'd still be in jail." Jasper could tell she was angry over his release. "Back home we call what he did aiding and abetting. My father'd say contributing to the completion of a crime."

"So, at what point do ya think I'll be called to testify?" Jasper asked.

"I have no idea," Heather said. "Maybe not at all," she added.

The conversation was broken by a car coming out of the property. Jasper flashed his headlights. The passing car sounded its horn. "Who was that?" Heather asked.

"I don't know," Jasper replied, "but they know we saw them," he added. "Look! A God damned leak!" Jasper pointed to a pin drop coming from the outside vent between the engine and the windshield. The raindrops dripped slowly and began to puddle on the rubber floor mat. "There's another car," he said, flashing his lights again.

"Listen!" Heather said, as she lowered her window and leaned into the opening. The occasional rain wet her face and hair as the wind shifted. "Hear it?"

Jasper lowered his window, only to take on more of the forced rain water and high wind. Heather watched his expressions. He turned his head several times. "Yeah, I do! It's a siren. A fire siren!" Jasper said, cranking the car. The hot engine's exhaust rushed into the cab, by way of the open windows. The sweet smell of raw leaded gasoline and a trace of engine oil made for a recognizable smell. Two vehicles passed down on the highway, one was a sedan and the other a pick-up truck. They were sounding their horns. The cars already on the road were yielding to the horns. "It's a damn fire somewhere!" Jasper pulled the patrol car into gear and carefully rolled toward the private roadway.

"I guess lightnin' struck a house or something," Heather said, as she held on to the car. "Should I drive, old man?" she joked.

"I could make a ham sandwich and go on this call," Jasper responded. "Nothing to it," he added, but Heather turned on all of the available police lights and began to bump the siren, for what it was worth. When they turned toward town, they could hear the fire siren and caught a glimpse of the volunteer truck turning the corner in old Bullochville. Several more volunteers joined the small parade. "It's the old Powell house!" Jasper said excitedly. He pulled the car to a stop.

"I'm not a fireman," Heather replied. "I'll stay right here and keep the traffic moving," she said, from the dry inside of the car. She watched the mirrors for oncoming vehicles, but there were none other than volunteers.

The old house had been vacant for several years. High weeds and kudzu had grown over it. It was much like the one the officers had gone into hunting for James Lee. The falling rain caused steam to rise from the hot, intense orange and yellow flames. The fire captain had already made the determination that the house was a loss and would be allowed to burn out. The 1917 Oldsmobile fire truck was the first one the city had. It had an open cab, allowing all the weather conditions to rush down upon the driver. The business owners had pooled resources to purchase it. The four extension ladders could easily work a one-story fire in the trained hands of the volunteers. The used truck had been equipped with a 150-gallon chemical tank. It was expensive compared to water. There were four hundred feet of two-and-a-half-inch cotton hose on board, in hopes of a local water source, and a sturdy pump to pull it to pressure.

The first six volunteers were suited in the only fire clothing the city had, fire retarded slickers that were well below the knees of most of the men, and heavy leather molded helmets with long protective bills that protruded down the backs. A number of onlookers appeared and drove slowly past. The heavy rain put out the hot fire once the walls met the floor system. The stone chimney toppled at the midway point and fell into the house. The only thing left on the inside was metal framed items, bed frames, sinks, tubs, and mattress springs.

Jasper sat in the car with the rain still falling, although it was lighter now. "This is one time I'm proud ta be right where I am," he said, pointing to the firemen slopping around in the rain and the smoky mess. "Done any fire work?" he asked Heather.

"Held a bake sale with my grandmother to raise money to help get our equipment, back home," she replied.

"What'd y'all get?" Jasper asked.

"We helped get a converted White truck for Fairburn. It's got a chemical tank and a large pump too. Most of our city has hydrants. Our truck is closed in, unlike this one. We have extinguishers mounted everywhere one can be placed," Heather said, as she watched the sooty men.

* * *

The trial date came quickly. Jasper Brown was in his best uniform, not a thing was out of place. He was a fine example of the Warm Springs Police Department. Detective Duncan wore her cleaned and brushed brown suit. She dropped her heavy gun belt in favor of the shoulder holster and the 1911, under her coat. Her darker fedora made a pleasing combination for the observers. She held it in her hand as she walked with her partner into the crowed courthouse. The Greenville square was crowded with spectators.

"It's a setup for a killing," Heather thought to herself. She quickly dismissed it from her concern since she was not involved with the transport safety of the one Negro. Theo Jackson knew he was to be there. He and his mother and sister calmly walked in through the colored entrance to the building along with Isaac Pittman, his attorney. Sheriff Gilbert had a full staff of deputies. He intended to get James Lee there and back in spite of the verbal shouts and cat calls of threats made by various white men known to be associated with racial organizations.

The Vindicator was first to be noticed. The reporter Alfred Huffman was at the very top step, making photographs of the crowd and officials as they came up the steps.

"Huffman!" a deputy shouted.

Alfred looked around as his name was called out. He finally spotted the deputy serving as courthouse security. "Yes!" he replied.

"The solicitor general, judge, and the sheriff said for me ta tell you ta keep these god damn reporters under control. There will be no photographs in the courtroom, at all! Every one of 'em needs to display an I.D. Badge or we'll put 'em out," the deputy barked from a distance. "You clear?" he yelled, pointing to the young reporter.

"I'll pass it on," Alfred yelled back. There was the Newnan paper, the Manchester, Columbus, and even as far away as Atlanta. Alfred finally got the attention of the reporters. Some had even brought a photographer along. "No photos in the courtroom! I.D.'s must be visible!" he shouted. "Be extra cautious about rushin' up for questions," he added. There were disgruntled moans from several.

The foyer doors were propped open due to the massive crowd. Most of the people in attendance were in dress clothes. A few presumed locals wore clean bibbed overalls and white shirts. The balcony where the Negroes sat was full, with some even standing along the walls and sitting on the steps. They were there to see justice served for the victims Gertrude and Polly Sue Miller. The deputies made a profound presence at the white entrances and none at the colored.

"Hug the wall," Heather said to Jasper, who was in front of her. He took her advice and moved quickly.

"Law enforcement! Move, please! Move!" Heather said loudly. They were able to move along ahead of the curiosity seekers.

Every odor from alcohol to perspiration was to be found in the massive crowd. The courtroom was full and the line for seating was down the steps and onto the grassy yard. Jasper was able to worm his way into the courtroom and get a reserved seat for those that were issued subpoenas. Jasper's was tucked into his uniform shirt, while Heather had hers in her suit coat pocket. It was required to get a seat, or to be known by the deputy serving as bailiff.

"Jesus! It's nice ta have a ticket," Jasper said to Heather, leaning close to her as they sat down.

He looked along the wall, where the judge's bench sat high above the crowd. A single door was slightly ajar. "There's the judge," Jasper pointed. "That's the face of Erastus Cobb. His wife's name is Emma. She's a looker for an old gal," Jasper said. "Ain't no judge could handle this without an appeal but him. It don't look good for the accused," he whispered.

A bailiff took the judge's bench. "Hey! Hello!" he shouted, just before blowing his traffic whistle. The loud murmur instantly stopped. "The rule of the court is that if you can't find a seat, then you must not stay standing. No one sits in the aisles, by order of the fire chief. Work it out and be quick about it. The court will start in less than five minutes, at the stroke of nine."

* * *

Curley Jones and the night jailer, along with a deputy, stood by while James Lee bathed, unrestrained, in the close confines of the cell block. The two jailers had secured their hard leather clubs to their wrists so that it would be impossible to take one from either of them. The deputy stood in another cell block where he could get a shot at James Lee should he overpower the jailers. "Wash yo' stinkin' ass! We've got twenty minutes to be in the courthouse. Nine o'clock ain't far off," barked Curley Jones.

James Lee bathed with the tepid water that came from the brass-finished shower head hung above the steel cage. The water ran over the cell block floor until it reached the central drain. The journey to the volunteer zinnias was a long one, all the way to the rear of the jail.

"Hey, boy! Could yous scrubs a little mo' on de nuts fo' me? I'ze imaginin' I'ze takin' a baf too," laughed Oliver Queen. Several other Negroes joined in. Every prisoner was on lockdown during the trial.

"Ya could always roll over and admit," said a white prisoner. "Then we could all get back on the road." The other prisoners joined in. Curley raked the cell bars with his club. They knew to knock the chatter off and they did. It was dead silent.

"What clothes, boss?" asked James Lee, as he stood naked.

"The taxpayers of this county sprung for a new suit. They don't want you to look like a prisoner," snarled Curley, as he revealed the suit. "They forgot the dress shoes. Yer brogans will do fine. Looks like the pants are too long, anyway," he said, holding up the black suit.

"If it'd been brown, you'd looked like the shit ya are!" said Oliver Queen.

"Knock it off!" yelled the night jailer, as he slapped at Queen's knuckles that were grasped around the cell bars.

"We'll go out the back and get into a marked car," the armed deputy said, as he watched Curley put the cuffs on James Lee. "That plated chain is twisted. It's smaller and lighter, but stronger than it seems," he said, for the benefit of the prisoner, who might have thoughts of escaping. "The car's down there. Miss Dixie's watching it from the kitchen window, so nobody's ta mess with it. We'd hate ta have a bomb."

"Me too," mumbled James Lee. "I'm ready."

As planned, Lee's attorney, Robert Gaskill, was standing at the bottom of the kitchen steps waiting to ride with his client. The two jailers walked Lee out of the cell block, stepping into the long maze of passages to the back door.

"Don't forget ya can pleas guilty right off!" one prisoner yelled.

"Knock it off!" yelled Curley Jones. His voice echoed off the hard steel plate and thick interior walls.

The armed deputy took a quicker route than the way the prisoner was taken. He cranked the car and waved Dixie and Miss Jewell off. They stepped inside the kitchen and looked out the pantry window.

"Morning!" Robert Gaskill greeted the deputy.

"Morning!" the deputy replied, now standing in the driver's door of the running car.

Sheriff Gilbert had coordinated a tracker to be on the side of the jail building with a pack of dogs should anything go awry. The tracker's lever gun was at the ready as he stood by the caged dogs. The dogs began barking at the sight of the Negro. The deputy gave a wave to the tracker, who exchanged a dead serious look at the task at hand.

Gaskill sat next to James Lee in the back, along with Curley Jones, who was armed with a revolver this morning. "He'd kill my client if he tried to run, wouldn't he?" asked Gaskill, as he leaned down looking at the older, weathered white male. The years of roughness and the stain of tobacco on his chin cast a solemn shadow.

"He'd flip the cage latch and kill yer nigger before the dogs could jump to the ground. He's killed several," the deputy driver said, as he looked in the mirror at the passengers in the back seat.

"I believe he would," the attorney said faintly. "I believe he would," he repeated, even lower.

The marked car pulled the grassy hill in low gear and never got out of second as it rounded the courthouse square. The jeering white males yelled and struck the side of the car with their open hands. The prisoner's window was covered with tobacco and spit as it came to a stop in front of the main entrance. Sheriff Louis Gilbert stood at the top of the steps with a Winchester '97 pump and a holstered revolver. His first load was hand packed. It was full of rock salt and dried black-eyed peas. The car was swarmed by the unruly white men. A gathering of black men stood at a distance and read scripture aloud from the book of Revelations, some praying aloud for justice. The canopy of oak trees was suddenly shattered by an enormous blast from the twelve-gauge shotgun. Pellets cut through the tree limbs and showered green leaves and trash down upon the stopped car and the angry mob.

"Not another sum bitch touches my car! Back off! The next round goes into the crowd," yelled Sheriff Gilbert.

Everyone inside the courthouse flinched and became silent after the shot rang out. "Keep yer seats!" yelled the bailiff.

One white male started to step forward to the car, but several arms went up and stopped him, as others grabbed him by his clothing. Sheriff Gilbert racked the forearm to the rear, expending the spent red paper shell, and they knew another one went into the chamber. "He's bluffin'," said a man in the crowd.

"He's killed three in his first term. He ain't bluffin'," another man said.

Sheriff Gilbert motioned with the barrel of the shotgun for the men to step back, and they did, allowing the deputy and the jailer to get the prisoner and the attorney out of the car. The reporters outside were certainly surprised at the display of authority by the rural sheriff.

"There's always tomorrow," someone yelled.

A stray leaf occasionally floated to the ground as the attorney hurried along beside his client. The deputy moved from the patrol car as Curley Jones escorted the two men to the steps where the sheriff stood.

"Nigger lover!" a man's voice yelled out.

The gathering of blacks continued to read the scripture and pray aloud.

Shackled James Lee walked at the side of his attorney, taking one step at a time into the crowded courthouse. The people still packed into the foyer and halls were silent as the three men passed, followed by the sheriff. The double doors swung open and the four men made their way to the respective seats of the defense. James Lee made eye contact with Theo Jackson, who sat close by.

"All rise!" the bailiff cried out. The sheer numbers of people created noise, just by the act of standing. Jasper and Heather looked around. There were very few women in the white seating area. Their eyes ventured to the balcony where there were a goodly number of colored women.

"This is the Superior Court of Meriwether County, Special Session. It is under the control of Honorable Erastus Cobb," said the bailiff. "Be seated! When your name is called, it is because you were ordered to be here. It may have been by involvement or by a subpoena, nevertheless please answer the cry with 'here' and be recognized before being seated. There will be no talking, no tobacco use, no presence of alcoholic beverage on your person. That is on your breath and in your clothing. You will be charged with contempt!" said the bailiff.

"This is a high-profile case and there will be no exceptions for sheathed knives or pistols," said the bailiff, as he looked around at various men. "Don't piss me off or try us by being technical in definition. Any handheld device that discharges a cartridge is considered a pistol!" he yelled. "The sheriff has instructed me to advise you that if you are determined to possess a gun, you will be arrested immediately and serve a sentence of seventy-two hours in the county jail. The gun will be the property of the county and sold at auction."

Several men slowly stood and wove their way to the nearest aisle and headed for the door.

"The names of the ordered will be called first, and then the special calendar will be discussed between the parties involved," said the bailiff. Two more bailiffs appeared from the door behind the bench.

"All rise!" yelled the bailiff, as the Judge entered the stuffy courtroom.

"Be seated!" said Judge Cobb. He struck the gavel. "Call the names," he ordered, leaning back in the upholstered chair. He listened and read the case file once more.

The calling of names proceeded, with those who had been summonsed standing for recognition for the next forty-five minutes. Jasper and Heather were lucky, as they had an aisle seat with room to move about. Judge Cobb lowered his chair and looked across the desk at the attorneys for the accused, and then the solicitor general. "I will address each of you. I want to hear your voice, as we will be here working together for a considerable time. I will introduce our County Coroner, Dr. Augustus Hubbard," said the Judge. The doctor stood for a moment and then sat back down.

"Robert Gaskill," the Judge called.

The attorney sitting next to James Lee stood. "Your Honor," he said, with a smile.

"Be seated," said the Judge.

"Isaac Pittman, representing Theo Jackson," called the Judge, looking around.

The tall attorney stood in his mismatched suit. "Your Honor," he greeted, with one hand resting on the lapel of his suit coat.

"Be seated," said the Judge. "Ambrose Watkins, Solicitor General for Meriwether County."

Ambrose Watkins stood, at the table next to Robert Gaskill.

"Be seated," said the Judge. "These are the men who will try this case," said Judge Cobb. "We will be as courteous as we can be and follow correct protocol," smiled the old judge. Erastus Cobb was a large man, six feet tall. Some would guess him to be in his late sixties, some in his middle seventies. All of his trials were by the book and he was noted to be a hard man when it came to sentencing. Sweat beaded on his forehead. His white handkerchief moved over his sharp facial features, almost disappearing against his snow-white hair. His tiny blue eyes sparkled. Some said it was from the evil within, others said it was from the vigor of the challenge for justice. Erastus had excellent hearing; the slightest sounds were gathered in by his large ears. The suit of the day was a steel gray highlighted by a faint vertical black stripe.

"You surely notice that I do not wear a robe, but ya can bet yer ass I'm in charge," said Judge Cobb, looking at various faces in the room. There were several chuckles.

"I want to hear and see the accused. Stand when your name is called," said the Judge. "James Lee!"

Gaskill elbowed his client. Lee slowly stood. "Here!"

"You look nice in the county furnished suit," commented Judge Cobb. "Be seated. Theo Jackson!"

Theo Jackson and Isaac Pittman both stood. "Here!" said Theo Jackson.

The Judge looked puzzled. "Who is the accused?"

"Me, sir!" said Jackson.

"My apology, your Honor" said the attorney, taking his seat.

"Be seated, Mr. Jackson," said the Judge.

The Judge picked up the thick stack of papers pertaining to the trial. "I see that there are charges pending in another county, Troup County. Sheriff Ector, I see that you are here, representing your interest. These charges will certainly not be tried in the court of this county, as I have no jurisdiction. Go on record please, that I acknowledge the request for transfer to Troup County when we have finished here, all pending the outcome," said Judge Cobb. "Sheriff Ector, you may go, if you like."

"Thank you, sir!" said Sheriff Ector. He placed his hat on his head and walked out the doors.

"Please come forward, Attorney Pittman, Gaskill, and Solicitor Watkins," said the Judge. The three men stepped before the Judge's bench. "I present to you a list of names, read them carefully and agree if these are the witnesses you intend to call, as I would like to thin the courtroom of those who are not necessarily needed. We can bring these subpoenaed people back with notice," said the Judge. He handed the sheet to Watkins, who read the list then passed it on to Pittman, and Pittman to Gaskill.

"These are correct, your Honor," advised Gaskill, as he looked at the other two attorneys.

"Very well, then," said Judge Cobb, holding out his hand for the list. "The following persons will need to remain as part of the trial, others may leave, but be sure to give a contact means to the bailiff as you leave," he added. "We need Moses Finley, Billy Bishop, Curley Jones. Jones, you can be at the jail. Bo Bob Huggins." The Judge looked around and found the Negro high in the balcony. "Come down here, sir. There will be a place made for you and one family member," said Judge Cobb. Those seated in the reserved rows moved about, trying to make room. "Doc Hubbard, Alfred Huffman, Officer Jasper Brown, Detective Heather Duncan," the Judge continued.

"That's her. I don't think the arrest is legal," someone whispered.

"Silence!" shouted the Judge, as he held the gavel at the ready. Heather heard the remark.

"Sheriff Louis Gilbert, Audrey Pickens and young Albert Martin. I'd like a parent to be with the young man," said the Judge. "Normally I ask a bailiff to read charges, but I will do that in this case. James Lee, I will read yours first. If I have failed to list any, then it is to your benefit, as there are certainly many. Stand up, as I read," he directed.

James Lee and Robert Gaskill stood.

"James Lee comes before this Court with the following charges," said the Judge. He fanned the thick stack of tri-folded papers with his hand. James Lee stood silently.

"Murder of Herman Pickens, escape from Meriwether County Jail, murder of Ellis DeFoor, Theft of Motor Vehicle, owned by Ellis DeFoor. Burglary of John Miller's barn, burglary of John Miller's office in residence, Theft of Motor Vehicle, owned by John Miller. Murder of Gertrude Miller. Murder of Polly Sue Miller, an infant. Burglary of Della Cummings' barn, and last, Theft of Property of Della Cummings, and First-Degree Battery on inmate Bo Bob Huggins." Judge Cobb sat silently and looked at James

Lee for a moment. "These are serious charges," he said, tossing the stack aside. "Be seated. Think of these charges and how you wish to enter your plea."

"Theo Jackson, stand up, as I read," directed the Judge. He wiped his face with his handkerchief. "Theo Jackson comes before this Court with the following charges," said the Judge. He fanned the thick stack of tri-folded papers with his hand. Theo Jackson stood silently.

"Murder of Herman Pickens. I hesitate, as I wonder if you know why you are here. You are charged based on the fact that you assisted the accused James Lee to accomplish his crimes." The Judge gave a deep sigh. "Aiding an Escaped Felon. Burglary of John Miller's barn, burglary of John Miller's office in residence. Theft of Motor Vehicle owned by John Miller. Murder of Gertrude Miller. Murder of Polly Sue Miller, an infant. Burglary of Della Cummings' barn, and last, Theft of Property of Della Cummings." Judge Cobb sat silently and looked at Theo Jackson. The Judge shook his head in disbelief at the Negro's stupidity. "These are serious charges," he said, tossing the stack aside. "Be seated. Think of these charges and how you wish to enter your plea."

Gladys Hightower, sitting next to her son and his lawyer, mumbled. "I knows how's my sawn's gwine ta pleas. He ain'ts guilty."

Bang, bang! The oak gavel sounded. "One more outburst from you and I'll have you charged in contempt of this Court, twenty-five dollars and three days in jail!" barked Judge Cobb.

"My baby's -- " Gladys started.

Bang, bang! The oak gavel sounded again. "Bailiff, place her in custody and charge her accordingly!" shouted the Judge.

"Dis coteroom ain's hurd tha las' of dis!" Gladys Hightower yelled, as the strong men hurried her out.

Theo Jackson looked shocked, as did his attorney, Isaac Pittman. Two bailiffs had swooped down upon Gladys and escorted her out.

"Let this be an example as to the severity of my control in these proceedings. We must have order," said Judge Cobb. He held the gavel in one hand and caressed it with the other. The Judge appeared to be enjoying the smooth finish as he sat in deep thought. "Lord, at the cases I've sat on. This is the most complex of the hundreds. It's not about stealin' hogs or cattle, runnin' liquor, but about multiple deaths, heinous murders," said Judge Cobb. He sat and looked far off into the distance, beyond the circular spun glass window panes. "We're all in financially troubled times, salaries are hard to get and prices are up. A pint of honey is a dime, sliced bread is a nickel. Heck, a steak is eighteen cents a pound, and new shoes ten dollars!" He looked at the faces in the crowded courtroom. "I believe that we should hear the case of store owner Herman Pickens first, and if the jury delivers a guilty verdict, that could overrule the need to hear all the others, with the exception of Theo Jackson. Are we in agreement on this?" the Judge asked, looking at the solicitor general.

"Yes, your Honor," replied Ambrose Watkins.

"We have our plan of action. Let us recess in preparation for this until tomorrow at nine o'clock," said Judge Cobb. "Court is adjourned!" he said, striking the gavel.

The bailiffs and transport deputies surrounded James Lee and walked him to the side of the courtroom, where they stood until the majority of the citizens had left.

"Keep yer ass clean," Curley Jones said, standing close to Lee. "Same suit, dress out by eight. I'll let you know."

As the white mob stood waiting for the Negro to be transported by the car that had brought him, he was taken on foot out of the north side door and hurried down the sidewalk and into the front door of the jail. It was done so covertly that the angry mob never saw it happen. Sheriff Gilbert stood on the top step and saw the escort group make it to the jail without incident. "Okay, gentlemen! I need my car," he said, as he walked down the steps.

The angry men were disappointed by the sudden disappearance of the chained Negro.

CHAPTER TWENTY-FOUR

Sheriff Gilbert shook his head in disgust upon realizing the loud Atlanta bitch was in his custody. After a few devious payback thoughts, he called Sheriff Banks of Coweta County. He had a larger jail staff and housed women frequently. Before nightfall, Gladys Hightower was suited out and incarcerated in the neighboring county. Sheriff Gilbert was sure she would have plenty of company willing to listen to her bitching.

Into the late evening hours, Robert Gaskill sat outside of James Lee's cell and discussed the facts of the case. The other prisoners listened out of interest, as they played cards and other made up games until it was too dark to see.

"Tell me about this robbery in Durand. How far is that from here?" asked Gaskill.

"About twelve miles, almost into Troup County," said James Lee.

"Did you shoot the man?" asked the attorney.

"I did," James Lee said, just above a whisper.

"Why?" asked Gaskill, taking notes.

"After I had the money, he ran out after me in the street. He had a gun, him or me," James Lee replied. "Nobody saw me do it."

"Oh, but you're wrong. There was a witness who will testify that he saw the whole thing," said Gaskill. The attorney sat still for a moment in deep thought. "I'll see you in the morning," he said, as he stood holding his leather satchel. The darkness was so solid he had to touch the cell bars to feel his way to the exit door, where a jailer sat in a straight chair.

"Ready to go?" the jailer asked, lowering the chair to all four legs.

"As ready as I can be," Gaskill replied.

Sheriff Gilbert, upstairs in his living quarters, heard the screen door open on the office door below his open window. He pushed the lace curtain aside and watched the well-dressed attorney leave. Sheriff Gilbert wondered if the attorney had a chance at a defense case for the Negro housed below. Robert Gaskill sensed that he was being watched. He looked around and then up. Gaskill saw the ghostly image of the sheriff behind the heavily oxidized window screen. The skinny, well-dressed attorney raised his hand in friendship and held it for a moment, until the sheriff returned the same.

"Like a snowball in hell," the sheriff thought to himself. He watched as the young man left the property and headed north toward Moreland. Radford's Boarding House was the right place for the funny little man. There were few if any troublemakers known to stay there. It was a very quiet place.

* * *

Curley came in just after daylight. There was a yellow, stormy hue to the morning sunlight as it washed over the countryside. Sheriff Gilbert was up and dressed. He was waiting for the jailer. The first cup of coffee was still warm when the sheriff spotted Curley on the walk below.

"Curley!" Louis Gilbert cried out from his second story bedroom window.

"Yes!" Curley replied, looking up.

"Roust the nigger out. Get him over there thirty minutes early, go ahead and set him in the courtroom," said the sheriff, as he looked around for any possible scouts sent by the racist groups. "Don't let yer guard down. You know what we've talked about," he added, looking down on the man. "I'll be close with the shotgun." He moved away from the open window.

* * *

Heather and Jasper were so deep into the Lee case, they might as well make the best of it. Cases were often long, drawn out and complex, making for hours of discomfort during the time spent waiting to be called to the stand. They ate a good breakfast and then moved on out to court, allowing themselves plenty of time. Mrs. Blakely had suggested they dine at her place more often. Jasper had become quite a hand at setting the table. Mrs. Blakely was getting used to his morning company. She put down a good meal for only a nickel. The same meal at the café was about eight cents by the time coffee was added.

Jasper had taken it upon himself to creek rinse the patrol car every evening. He wanted it to look neat and clean when they pulled into Greenville. His pride in himself and the department was quite evident. Jasper changed into his cut-off bibbed overalls and drove back to the creek within sight of his house. He took a small pail and dashed creek water on the dusty car until it was clean. Jasper placed his wet feet on dry tow sacks and drove slowly back to his residence. The Greenville Police Department was not fazed by the intruding agency as it occupied their town. The chief and his few officers were quite content to watch accidents almost happen due to everyone struggling with parking, and the merging into traffic that was always there due to normal commerce.

Buddy Cotton discovered Heather and Jasper that morning as he was heading off to school with several friends. The young boy was excited as always to see the pretty police woman. He was almost breathless when he was around her.

"Who's winning?" Buddy asked eagerly.

"There's no winning Buddy, the jury decides," Heather said. "The trial hasn't even started yet. The jury has to be picked." The two officers stood in the store room.

"Y'all will do fine!" Buddy said, smiling. The other three boys were checking out the candy and making selections.

"Can you polish all my shoes this afternoon?" Heather asked Buddy.

"Leave 'em with Mrs. Blakely and I'll get 'em 'fore I go home," he replied. The other boys were waiting at the front door.

"Dreamer! We'll be late! Let's go!" a boy called out.

"How much?" Heather asked.

"I never washed the car. They'll be free," Buddy replied, hurrying to catch up with his friends.

* * *

By 8:30 a.m. the prisoner James Lee was in the courtroom. His attorney was there shortly thereafter. The escort guards backed away and gave the two space to converse before court started. Sheriff Gilbert walked the halls quietly with his shotgun. A crowd had already gathered outside. Those who had not been able to get a seat inside yesterday were at the front of the line for a chance today.

"Let's park in the back of the Vindicator," Heather suggested.

"After I washed the car?" Jasper asked.

"Get in and out quicker," Heather said.

"All right," Jasper said, as he turned up the grade to the back lot of the newspaper office. They walked under the shade of the large oaks and hurried across the busy street. The Warm Springs officers took to the colored entrance where there were fewer people to displace in their efforts to get inside.

At exactly nine o'clock the chime in the clock tower struck.

"All rise!" yelled the bailiff, as the Judge entered the already stuffy courtroom.

"Be seated!" said Judge Cobb. He struck the gavel. "I hope we are blessed today with less excitement than yesterday. I'll put up with no outbursts. This list is the jury pool," said the Judge, handing the papers to the bailiff. "Call the names," he said, leaning back in his upholstered chair. He listened as he read the case file once more. The list for the jury pool had been drawn up by the random selection of names of property owners,

370

taxpayers and voters.

"Each jury name called shall count off, and remember your number," said the bailiff.

"State your name and your occupation," said Judge Cobb. "This will be a lengthy process, so many of you may choose to leave," he added. There were a few who took this opportunity to exit. "Go ahead," the Judge said to the bailiff. "Oh, one more thing. As your number is chosen at the end of the process, gather together here in the jury seats. Race has no place in this Court," said the Judge, as he turned a yellow pencil about between his hands. He gave a nod to the bailiff.

"Oscar Carroll," called the bailiff.

"Here, number one. Tailor."

"George Adair," called the bailiff.

"Here, number two. Railroad worker."

"John Badger," called the bailiff.

"Here, number three. Painter."

"Jack Brown," called the bailiff.

"Here, number four. Barber."

"Lee Brown," called the bailiff.

"Yes, sir! Number five. Machinist," replied Lee Brown.

"John Cosby!" called the bailiff.

"Here, number six," Mr. Cosby replied.

This went on for the longest time. Heather was about to drift into a nap when Jasper nudged her and whispered a suggestion that they go to Becky's Café, for coffee and a more comfortable seat. The two officers quietly left the courtroom for the fresh air of the beautiful morning.

* * *

The angry white mob was dwindling a little more each day as the trial continued. The gathering of blacks stood fast in their numbers, even though the victim was a white man at this stage of the trial. In spite of the large mob gathered under the trees that grew around the courthouse square, the birds still gathered and went about their lives as though there was no distraction. Their calls and songs filled the air. The outdoor air felt refreshing as the two officers descended the marble steps.

"How long?" asked Jasper.

"At the current rate of progress, maybe two hours and then a recess," Heather replied, as they pushed their way through the gathering. Heather could feel the angry stares as she stepped among the men.

The morning crowd at the café was gone, mostly empty tables, except for a single elderly couple occupying a corner booth. The coiled bell rang as the framed glass door opened under Jasper's control.

"Hello, stranger!" a woman's voice called out.

"Hi!" replied Jasper, as they stood looking for the best place to sit.

"Here for the trial?" the woman asked.

Jasper took a deep breath and gave a loud sigh. "Yes," he replied, as he placed his uniform cap on the table.

"And you're the woman detective everyone talks about," she said.

Heather set her fedora on the table, brim up. "That's me," she replied, as she slid into the booth.

The woman laid down a spoon and paper napkin for each of them. "The women are glad you're down here," she said, smiling. "We feel like the menfolk have an obligation to react rather than ignore our crimes," she said, holding the order tablet.

"Thanks!" Heather replied. "An iced tea, please."

"Coffee," said Jasper.

"It'll be right out," said the woman.

The café soon began to fill with the tired mob that stood in protest of a Negro being tried like a white. At first Jasper and Heather had felt as though they were not a hindrance to Becky's business. It was close to noon. The highbacked booth hid them from the white males who had come in. The room was filled with loud crosstalk. The conversation in the booth behind Jasper was soon loud enough that they could both hear the subject was the woman detective from Warm Springs.

"I think the case won't hold water when the Judge realizes that a woman made the arrest. Only menfolk are made to be police. That stupid mayor pays her the same as a man," said a man's voice. This led to more negative crosstalk and opinions about the legality of the case, once that part came up. It seemed that no one cared if Heather heard their negative opinions or not. The more they talked, the more they revealed their level of hatred for a woman doing a man's job for a man's pay.

Jasper saw the disappointment in Heather's eyes. He had grown to like her. She had brought him around to thinking that he was a police officer, rather than a referee. The comments that were affecting her now affected him. He stood abruptly.

"No! Let it go," Heather said, loud enough for him to hear. She saw the tension leave his body. He shook his head in disbelief at the room full of biased and racist men. Heather stood close beside him. "Let's go down to the pharmacy, a hot dog or an egg salad at the counter. They've got overhead fans, come on." Heather picked up her fedora and placed it on her head. She gently tossed her shoulder holster and settled it again.

Jasper motioned to the waitress for the check. She smiled and waved him on. He blew her a kiss and blushed. The woman was half his age. Together they walked out of the crowded café and turned toward the pharmacy on the opposite end of the block.

"Still got it, huh?" Heather said, smiling.

Jasper grasped his rig and settled it on his hips. "Still got it," he replied, blushing again.

In the short walk to the pharmacy counter, several women spoke to Heather and acknowledged Jasper as well. "That in itself makes me come to work," Heather said. "I'm known up home. It's not like this, to my face anyway," she said, as they walked along. "I guess I ride on Dad's reputation up there."

The pharmacy doors opened easily and the cooling air greeted them. There were customers at the pharmacy counter in the rear, and very few at the refreshment counter up front.

"Hello!" said a cheerful woman.

"Hello!" replied Heather.

"Here for the trial?" the woman asked.

"Here for the trial," Heather replied, as she took a seat. Jasper sat down next to her.

A beaded glass of cold water and a paper napkin were quickly placed in front of them.

"Menu?" asked the woman. "Or can you order from the board?"

"Board's fine," Heather replied.

The other customers were reporters from out of town. They busied themselves eating and writing, before time ran out.

"Any specials?" Jasper asked.

"Chicken salad on white bread and a serving of chips," the waitress replied. "Or pimento cheese."

"One of each, we'll trade off," Heather answered quickly.

Jasper looked surprised. "That's a good idea."

The food was good, and the sweet iced tea was even better. There was no upsetting conversation, mostly silence from the reporters. Refreshed and reinvigorated, they returned to the courthouse and resumed their reserved seats.

* * *

The solicitor and the attorney for James Lee, Robert Gaskill, had agreed on a list of jurors. There were equal numbers of whites and Negroes. The chosen Negroes had joined the whites in the jury pool. The selected Negro jurors were George Adair, railroad worker; John Cosby, miller; Isaac Gibson, gardener; Robert Hardee, track hand; Frank Mattox, musician; Hiram Leathers, carpenter; and William Young, a laborer. The whites were Jack Brown, barber; James Latham, pulpwooder; James Osborn, school teacher; Robert Shields, printer; Robert Young, stump and rock remover; William Yancey, laborer; and John Zent, cement laborer. Alfred Huffman and other reporters stood by noting the jury that was selected. Two of the men would serve as alternate jurors in case one of the main twelve became ill.

"The Court finds that Theo Jackson is not needed for this case as he has no involvement. It is so taken that he is dismissed until further notification. Mr. Jackson, do not leave the county, and be close to the telephone," said Judge Cobb. "Recess until 1:30!" he said, sounding the gavel. "Hold the jury over!" yelled Judge Cobb, as he stood behind the bench. "Jurors, assemble in front of me."

The jurymen were standoffish but gathered loosely as the Judge had directed. "Everyone here seen his own blood?" he asked, looking at each man. "Answer me!" he snapped. There was a "yes" from everyone. "You will become men on speaking terms, not one is less important than the other. You need to find a common ground with those around you. This county and the victims cannot suffer a mistrial on any problems that you may have. When we're done here, you can revert back to being yourselves. I hope you will remember this event and hold your efforts and decision in an honorable way. Have a good lunch, do not discuss the case. Becky's Café has a cold sack lunch for each of you, at my expense. There will be an urn of cold sweet tea at the rear of her business, under the maple tree. The city moved in a sturdy table and benches. I'll eat with you shortly," he said.

A few of the men, white and black, who were neighbors, began to speak to each other. Those who were unknown to each other were leaving the courthouse talking about the warm dry weather and hopefully better days to come. The afternoon heat was beginning to drive the crowd of angry whites away. The black protesters were prepared with chairs, hand fans, and food. They sat around their vehicles and on the sidewalk.

* * *

Over in Coweta County, Gladys Hightower was verbally delivering a double helping of hell to any women in the cell block who would listen. Her cotton suit was too long, the sleeves were rolled up about nine inches, and the pants legs were turned up a good foot. The sobering experience was not calming her verbal assaults on the people of the county, black or white.

"Dem sum bitches ain't hurd de las' of my baby," Gladys said to anyone who would listen, as she sat in the small common area of the cell block. There were five other Negro women incarcerated, and three white women in an adjoining cell block, all within hearing distance of the loud, bragging woman. Gladys was even talking to the jailer when she made her rounds. Everyone counted the days until she could be released.

* * *

"All rise!" called the bailiff, as Judge Erastus Cobb entered and took the bench.

"Be seated!" said the Judge. "Solicitor, are you pleased with the jury selection?"

"I am, your Honor," said Ambrose Watkins, as he stood.

"And Mr. Gaskill?" asked the Judge.

"I am, your Honor" Robert Gaskill replied.

"Reporter, note that the jury is official and meets the satisfaction of the attorneys," said Judge Cobb. "Solicitor, present the case."

The solicitor general stood and began to give his account of the incident. "The accused James Lee, to my right, is said to have entered the store of Herman Pickens. This store being located in the town of Durand, and in this county, Meriwether. The accused is said to have fired the shots that struck and killed Herman Pickens. It is the intent of this Court to prove this fact, asking for the harshest of penalties," said Solicitor Watkins. "That's all, your Honor."

"Solicitor, call your first witness," said the Judge.

Ambrose Watkins stood at the front of the bench and looked out into the courtroom. "The State calls Audrey Pickens!"

Audrey Pickens was the wife of the deceased, Herman Pickens. "Place your hand on the Bible," said the bailiff. "Repeat after me, stating your name. I, Audrey Pickens, swear to tell the truth, the whole truth, and nothing but the truth, so help me God," said the bailiff. The widow recited the oath.

"You may be seated," said Judge Cobb.

"I'd like to ask the Court's permission for this widow to give her account of the day of her husband's murder," asked Watkins.

"That is fine," replied Judge Cobb. He turned his chair to look at the woman as she testified. The courtroom was silent.

"I was down the street on an errand. I had gone to the bank to conduct business. Herman always took the money. He didn't want anything to happen to me," she said, with a sniffle. "The day was slow, there was hardly any traffic out after nine o'clock. I was at the bank counter." She was interrupted by the solicitor.

"What bank?" asked Watkins.

"The Durand Bank," she replied. "The town was quiet. I could hear the ink pen rubbing against the surface of the paper as I filled it out. We all reacted to hearing a gunshot. The first teller looked out and yelled it was a shooting. When I got into the doorway, I saw him," she said, pointing to the Negro James Lee, sitting at the defense table. "He was putting our money bag into the front seat of a car. I couldn't see the tag number, as it was parked with the tag toward the hardware store. Herman was lying on the boardwalk. The Canada Dry sign above the door was swinging. I can still hear the squeaking sound in the darkness of night as I am lying there alone. We were together forty-two years. I screamed and started toward my husband. He was already dead when I got to him. He was shot twice in the chest. I know the shotgun was empty, it was a single shot and Herman had dropped two shells from his hand when he fell dead. The nigger pulled away before I could shoot at him myself. I never fired the gun. He killed my husband, Herman Pickens!" said the distraught wife.

"Did you see the Negro well enough to identify him again?" asked Watkins.

"I did. He was driving a black sedan. I'm not that much of a fanatic about cars, but I thought it was a late model Star. We don't see many of them about," answered Mrs. Pickens.

"Did you see the murder weapon?" Watkins asked.

"The Negro had a dark finished revolver in his hand. That's all I can tell you. I heard the pistol go off twice," she said, clutching her purse in her lap.

"That's all," said Watkins. He took his seat.

Robert Gaskill stood and approached the woman on the stand. "Where was the shotgun kept in the store?" he asked.

"Under the counter, close to the cash register," she answered.

Gaskill walked back and forth for a moment in deep thought. "Hidden from the customers?" he asked.

"Yes," she answered, looking puzzled.

"One might say y'all were planning to kill someone," he stated.

"Certainly not," she said, looking offended at the thought of lying in wait for someone.

"But nevertheless, you did have a gun hidden for such events? Yes or no?" Gaskill said.

"Yes!" she replied.

"And to your belief, in your late husband's intention, he would kill anyone who appeared to be robbing him, the store?" Gaskill asked.

Audrey Pickens looked confused and turned to Judge Cobb. "Answer the question," he said softly.

"Yes!" she said, looking down.

"That's all, your Honor," Gaskill said, as he took his seat.

"State wishes to call Officer Jasper Brown," Watkins said.

"Officer Jasper Brown," called the bailiff.

Jasper stood and gave a deep sigh. "You'll do well," Heather whispered, as he wormed between her knees and the bench in front of them. His white hair and blue eyes were captivating against the darkness of the raised wood that made up the bench. Jasper carried his uniform cap under his arm in a very formal military manner.

"Place your hand on the Bible," said the bailiff. "Repeat after me, stating your name. I, Jasper Brown, swear to tell the truth, the whole truth, and nothing but the truth, so help me God." Jasper repeated the oath after the bailiff. "Take your seat!"

"I may ask for information slightly out of the order of events, but please bear with me," said Watkins.

"All right," replied Jasper.

"Where were you when you first saw the car driven by the defendant?" asked Watkins.

"On the eastbound road, Bethsaida Church Road out of downtown Warm Springs. I was sitting in my patrol car at the Sulphur Creek Primitive Baptist Church," Jasper replied.

"Are you the oldest officer in your department?" asked Watkins

"I am. I'm the oldest of the few officers that our small town has. Only one officer on duty at any time," Jasper said.

"And just how old are you?" asked Watkins.

Jasper's ruddy round face, covered by a head of thinning white hair, made him look older than his actual age. "Sixty-seven," he replied.

"Good vision?" asked Watkins.

"These two sharp ice blue eyes ain't failed me yet," Jasper remarked. There were a few laughs in the courtroom. Judge Cobb cleared his throat loudly.

"I'm establishing here that you as an officer of the law have no physical impairments that would keep you from doing your job. Give me your opinion of how you see yourself in the profession," said Watkins. He stepped to the center of the bench and rested his arm on it.

"For a man of my age, I still think I can hold my own. I'm still looking at womenfolk and flirting, nothing wrong with my manhood, everything still works. My legs are a little bowed from years of hard work, and this left arm, I carry it out to the side since it was shattered during the World War," he said proudly. "I'm a better officer now than back then, because of Detective Duncan," he added.

"Oh, how is that?" asked Watkins.

"More safety alert, use my head more," he said.

"What type of car were you on the lookout for?" asked Watkins, as he moved from the bench.

"A black 1925 Star two door sedan driven by James Lee, a black male," Jasper answered. "I was looking for any black car of the general size driven by a Negro male," he added.

"Go on," said Watkins.

"Over the crest of the slight hill came a black Star sedan, driven by a Negro. I was not too sure if it was James Lee or not. The black sedan passed without incident and appeared to be a citizen of non-interest. The slim Negro and the vehicle fit the bulletin's description of Lee. I pulled the patrol car onto the dusty dirt road and sped increasingly closer to the suspicious vehicle. My actions soon turned into a high-speed chase," Jasper said.

"That's all," said Watkins.

"Attorney Gaskill, do you wish to cross?" asked the Judge.

"Yes, your Honor," replied Gaskill. He stepped up to the bench.

"In my field investigation, I spoke with a witness of the car chase. Did you in fact kick my client in the ribs while he was on the ground?" asked Gaskill.

Jasper felt the fear of being caught rush over him. He sat quiet for a moment. "Answer the question!" barked Gaskill.

"Yes! I kicked the nigger! Good and damn hard too! Tha sum bitch!" Jasper yelled back.

Judge Cobb sounded the gavel several times. "Here now, here now!" he said loudly.

The Negroes in the jury looked shocked.

"And why was that?" asked Judge Cobb.

"Careless -- uh, person, was shootin' out the car window. Houses along the road, folks out workin'. Could have hit someone. He'd run me off the road and shot the windshield of an oncoming car," he said, looking at the Negroes in the jury box. "I kicked him. If it hadn't been for my good mind, I'd probably tried ta stomp him ta death," Jasper said, looking at the jury and then at James Lee.

"Nothing further," Gaskill said, as he took his seat.

"You may step down," said the Judge.

"The State calls Doctor Augustus Hubbard," Watkins said.

The doctor, who was not expecting to be called, had dozed off in his seat. He stood and swayed a bit, but quickly took the stand, where he stood to be sworn.

"Place your hand on the Bible," said the bailiff. "Repeat after me, stating your name. I, Augustus Hubbard, swear to tell the truth, the whole truth, and nothing but the truth, so help me God," he said. Doc Hubbard repeated the oath. "The doctor is in the capacity of County Coroner. Take your seat!"

"Doctor, did you examine the body of Herman Pickens?" asked Watkins.

"Yes," replied the doctor.

"In summation, what did you find?" asked Watkins, standing at his table.

"Herman Pickens was a physically fit man for his age, white, average build. From his center chest I removed two .32 caliber lead bullets. Under microscope examination they matched to the best of my ability one that was fired from the revolver taken from the accused," said Dr. Hubbard.

"Tell the Court how you retrieved this comparison bullet," said Watkins.

"I've got a rain barrel out back with a circular mesh screen in the bottom. I fired the projectile into it and then pulled it up. Being over about three feet deep, pistol rounds are slowed a lot, they've never hit bottom yet. I looked at the sample and the retrieved bullet under a microscope."

"Was the pistol you tested -- where did you get the pistol you tested?" asked Watkins.

"It was brought over by Sheriff Louis Gilbert. He stood while I fired it into the rain barrel, then he took it back," replied Dr. Hubbard.

"That is all," Watkins said.

"Defense?" asked the Judge.

The defense took the floor. "Why did you compare the bullets?" asked Gaskill.

"May I ask who else would do it? It is a matter of visual comparison," replied the doctor. "They are available if you'd like to review for yourself. The evidence room has them," he added.

"That's not necessary," said Gaskill. "How many have you compared to this point?"

"I've been coroner for three terms. Oh, six to eight," advised the doctor.

"No additional," said Gaskill.

"You may step down," said the Judge.

"State calls back Jasper Brown," Watkins announced.

Jasper hurried to the stand. "You are still sworn," said the bailiff.

"I show you this revolver. Will you give a detailed description to the jury?" Watkins asked, handing it to Jasper.

"This is a blue steel, 32 Smith and Wesson revolver. It is a break top action. It was taken from the defendant at the time of arrest, just south of Oakland Plantation. It was turned over to the Sheriff's Department for evidence," Jasper said. "This is the same one that was taken in the home burglary, along with money and the Star automobile."

"That is all," Watkins said.

"Defense?" asked the Judge.

"No, your Honor," Gaskill replied.

"State calls Albert Martin," Watkins announced.

The young boy and his father, Horace Martin, stood and slowly walked to the bench.

"Son, this is no more than addressing the class in school. Tell the truth and it will be over in no time. I've spoken to the attorneys and they have been instructed to treat you according to your age," said Judge Erastus Cobb.

"Thank you," said Horace Martin.

"Place your hand on the Bible," said the bailiff. "Repeat after me, stating your name. I, Albert Martin, swear to tell the truth, the whole truth, and nothing but the truth, so help me God," said the bailiff. The young boy recited the oath. "Take your seat!"

"Albert, what school do you attend?" asked Watkins.

"Durand, sir," replied the young boy.

"What's your favorite class?" asked Watkins.

"Reading."

"What was your last book?" Watkins asked.

"*Tom Swift and His Wireless Message*, and *Tom Swift and His Air Glider*," young Albert replied eagerly.

Heather was familiar with the two books, as they had crossed Margaret's desk.

"Who wrote those?" asked Watkins.

"Victor Appleton," said Albert.

"Were you in school on the day of the shooting?" asked Watkins.

The boy looked caught. He glanced at his father standing a few feet away. "No, sir."

"Why not?" asked Watkins.

"I was bored," replied the boy.

"Where were you?" asked Watkins.

Albert Martin began to squirm about in the large chair. "I was in the storage cellar of the Durand Hardware store," he said, looking down.

"How did you get in?" asked Watkins.

"I go in and look over the candy display. I buy a penny's worth and mingle with the early morning crowd. When they're not looking, I slip down the stairs," said the boy.

"What was the weather like that morning?" asked the solicitor.

"It was cloudy, like it was apt to rain. The colors were deep. I thought they looked like the ones on the theater screen, rich and pretty," replied Albert.

"You're very astute," replied Watkins.

"Thank you, sir," the young boy replied.

"What did you do down there?" asked Watkins, as he sat down on the edge of the table.

"Finished the last book," he replied.

"That was *Tom Swift and His Air Glider*," said Watkins.

"Yes, sir," answered Albert.

"Do you have a favorite hiding place down there?" asked Watkins.

"Yes, sir," answered Albert.

"Where's that?" Watkins asked.

"High on the cotton seed bags, on the front side of the store," the boy answered.

"Go on," said Watkins.

"I can see the main street from the window beside me. It's dirty, but a theater seat for things outside. The depth of the boardwalk above it hides me. Maybe I shouldn't have been there," he said.

"Let's not deal with that right now," said the solicitor, with a smile. "What did you hear that day, what did you see?"

The jury leaned forward and looked at the young white boy. "I saw that nigger y'all call James Lee. He came out of the store owned by Mr. Pickens into the street. He had a bag of money in one hand and a revolver in the other," Albert said.

"Do you know the difference between a revolver and a pistol?" asked the solicitor.

"One turns like a wheel and the other one has the bullets up in the handle," Albert replied.

"I'll buy that!" smiled Watkins. "Go on."

"Herman Pickens ran out with a shotgun. Mr. Pickens got to the steps and started to draw down on the nigger when he was shot twice in the chest. The shotgun went off and filled the hanging Canada Dry sign full of holes. I saw the porcelain pieces fly everywhere. I could hear the men upstairs in the hardware store running after the shots rang out. They ran out to see! When they got to Herman, Mr. Pickens, he was already dead. I think Mrs. Audrey was there too. I didn't come out until the deputies got there. That was Sheriff Gilbert, and I'm not clear on which deputy," said Albert, all excited.

"Anything else?" asked Watkins.

"The car driven by him," he pointed to James Lee, "was parked with the tag toward the hardware store. I can't remember what the tag number was, but it was Georgia plates."

"Once again, are you sure that is the man you saw shoot Herman Pickens?" Watkins asked, as he pointed to James Lee.

Albert Martin made eye contact with the Negro and stuttered out his final reply. "Y-y-yes, sir! He shot Mr. Herman!"

The jury whispered among themselves.

"That's all, your Honor, the State rests," announced Ambrose Watkins.

"Defense?" asked Judge Cobb.

"Yes, your Honor," Robert Gaskill said, as he stood and walked toward the young boy.

"How many colored people do you know?" Gaskill yelled.

The boy jumped. "Lower your tone, counsel," said Judge Cobb.

"How many colored people you know?" Gaskill asked, walking back and forth.

"School or big folks?" Albert asked.

"Let's be grown up for a moment. Big folks," Gaskill said.

"'Bout ten," Albert said.

"And what's your reason for knowing them?" Gaskill asked, standing and looking out the tall window behind the jurors.

"Family," the boy replied.

Robert Gaskill jumped. "Family?" he asked.

"Yes, sir," Albert replied.

"How do white people have coloreds in the family?" Gaskill asked.

"Daddy works them in his business. He says they're family. We do sings and dessert socials down at the mill, spring and fall. Big Fanny and Uncle Henry, they split hog profits at killin' time," young Albert said proudly.

"So, you don't put much store in the white folks' comment that all them coloreds look like a sack of 'taters. Meaning it's hard ta tell one from the other," Gaskill said, as he started walking back and forth.

Albert sat still and thought about the question. "No, sir. I can tell the difference," he said.

"If I put my client in a group of coloreds, you could pick him out?" Gaskill asked, leaning in close to the young boy.

"Yes, sir," Albert said.

Robert Gaskill struck the bench with his hand. "No further!" He stomped back to his seat.

"I feel that due to the hour we should be considering a recess," said Judge Cobb, as he leaned back in his chair. He tapped a yellow pencil against the desk pad in front of him. "Are there anymore witnesses or call backs either side wishes to do?" he asked.

The Solicitor General Ambrose Watkins stood. "The State rests, your Honor."

The Judge looked at Robert Gaskill. "None at this time," he said. "But tomorrow may bring another witness."

"The Court will allow that. However, I suggest that each side have their final argument ready for tomorrow at nine o'clock. Court is adjourned!" said Judge Cobb, striking the gavel.

CHAPTER TWENTY-FIVE

The morning started with a horrific clap of thunder about daybreak. The roosters returned to roost and gave up on the morning's greeting. A bolt of lightning struck somewhere between Greenville and Primrose, shaking the earth for several miles around. Sheriff Gilbert and his deputies brought out their long slickers and rubber hat covers. The day looked like it would be a wet one. The racist spectators waiting for James Lee to be transported got to the square early. A few stood on the courthouse steps, others sat in their vehicles. Sheriff Gilbert did not give a second thought to knowing that they had a stout rope and guns among them. This was not the sheriff's first time dealing with these types of men. Some men are driven by hatred, it can far outwit their brains.

Louis Gilbert had been a very young Cobb County Deputy when he saw firsthand the strength of a mob during the 1915 Leo Frank execution. That day still lived with him, in the darkness of night and in the largest of unruly crowds. Only eighteen years of age, he had been pushed against a building front and held there by the passing horde of angry men, on that hot humid day of August 17, 1915. Gilbert often heard the angry voices shouting as the ghostlike faces argued about where they should hang the Jew. From a distance he saw the slender man swing from a rope hung over a strong limb in the community of Frey's Grove. Louis was marked for life. Emotional scars often run deeper than those of the flesh. The trial of James Lee would not imitate the one of Leo Frank. This time there would be bloodshed. His hand would not be called and go unanswered.

The patrol cars were parked on the kitchen side of the jail as they had been on the first morning. This was the fifth and final day of the trial. Judge Erastus Cobb expected to hear from the jury before noon. If James Lee was found guilty of the murder of Herman Pickens, a white business man, there would be no need to hear the other cases. The maximum penalty for murder was death, the sentence that Judge Cobb expected to deliver. A jury finding of not guilty would trigger all the other cases into motion.

It was about 8:15 a.m. Dixie stood at the pay phone on the south corner of the new motor court, just out of Moreland. She looked at her watch. "Five minutes," she said to herself, then four minutes. "Operator! There's a bad wreck between Luthersville and Rocky Mount," she whispered to herself, as she threw her voice. The early morning breeze blew in her face coming from the southeast.

Sheriff Gilbert had gathered the deputies in the booking room, with the exception of one. The single deputy stood guard from the kitchen porch, watching the cars. The sheriff looked at his watch. "It's 8:20! Remember our plans. Curley! You lay on the nigger on the back seat and stay down until the siren's turned off. That'll be yer signal to come up. Cut across the old Granny Turner Road and then turn back toward town. Slip in through the basement door, on the west side. I'll be there to open it. I'll have ya covered," said the sheriff, as he held up his shotgun. The Model 97 was a force to be reckoned with, in the hands of a man who could use it and ride its recoil out under fire. Sheriff Gilbert was considered an expert at close range among his associates, as he had mastered the skill of slam-firing. Five rounds in just under two and one-half seconds!

"If anything starts, you get to the basement door, no matter what. GET TO THE DOOR!" said the sheriff, pointing to Curley. "You join me from cover of the car, remember the motor block's where ya want to be. Have ya got yer carbine?" he asked the deputy.

"In the car, against the seat split," the deputy replied. "Shoot and feed. I'll remember, shoot and feed," he said to the sheriff.

"It's 8:25! Load him out," said the sheriff. "I'll leave after you head out." He held the heavy door for Curley and the others to enter and take James Lee out. The sound of the heavy door was loud, no matter how easily one tried to close it.

* * *

The sound made by the case dime jingled and signaled the operator.

"Operator!" The voice was broken, muffled, like someone talking over a comb with a wax paper sheath over it. Dixie set her mind to the task and threw her voice. "There's a bad wreck between Luthersville and Rocky Mount!" she said quickly.

"What kind of vehicles?" asked the operator.

"I couldn't tell! They're off in the woods! Hurry!" said Dixie. She hung up. "Jesus, I hope that worked," she said to herself.

Dixie headed her car back toward the office. Her heart raced at the excitement of her small part, but that little bit should trigger a cover to get the Negro into the courthouse.

* * *

Ring, ring, ring! The telephone rang in the sheriff's office.

"Sheriff's Office!" answered Louis Gilbert.

"Sheriff! This is Paulette at the telephone company, I've got the Coweta operator on line."

"Go ahead," the sheriff said loudly, in case there was a bad connection.

"We received a report of a bad wreck between Luthersville and Rocky Mount," the woman said.

"Anyone hurt?" he asked. "What types of vehicles?"

"Sir, that's all we have, just a bad wreck between Luthersville and Rocky Mount," replied the operator.

"We'll be en route," said Sheriff Gilbert. "Thanks, Paulette!" he added, just before hanging up the telephone. He hurried to the back porch of the jail kitchen with shotgun in hand and flagged for the men to head out.

The watching deputy guarded from above, while Curley Jones and the driving deputy hurried the suited James Lee across the small, sparsely covered grass yard and into the waiting marked car. Sheriff Gilbert gave a wave to the driver. Suddenly the official lighting came on and the mechanical siren was heard winding up to its maximum operating speed. The low groan gradually achieved a high pitch that caused every dog in town to howl and moan. Sheriff Gilbert waved as the car pulled the short grade and emerged onto the city street. The deputy took the corner in second gear and hit third within a few more yards. The powerful straight block engine growled with excessive power as it transferred thrust to the cotton cord tires that gripped the paved road. They were headed north.

"Step one." Sheriff Gilbert smiled at the deputy next to him. "Remember, nobody in the office today, unless you know they are with our court system or one of our own," he said, as he hurried with the deputy to the front door. The trip through his residence was obstructed by children's toys in the hallway. The sheriff had sent his wife and children out of town under cover of night.

"Yes, sir!" the deputy replied. "No one! Remember to lock Miss Jewel in the building," he added.

"Yer a good man," Sheriff Gilbert said. He touched the deputy's shoulder, and then took to the front porch of the office. The vest pockets of his suit were full of shotgun shells and several more were dropped into his suit coat.

The lone deputy watched as the sheriff walked toward the courthouse. His shotgun was at a low ready. In the momentary silence, chills ran down the deputy's spine as he realized the seriousness of the job.

The early comers watched as the patrol car moved through the small town and headed north at a high rate of speed. A gathering of schoolboys stood waving and tugging in the air with their closed fists, acknowledging that they liked the siren and lights. Little did they realize the significance of the day to come. The car was a distraction for the sheriff as he hurried toward the square. He noticed the white mob had split into two groups, one on the south side of the square and one on the north. The sheriff quickly realized that the men were well organized. They wore khaki wash pants and white shirts. The ones that wore suit coats were probably armed. The occasional back pocket revealed a slapjack profile under the fabric. Sheriff Gilbert walked ahead, remembering his experience years ago. It would not happen in his town as long as he was alive. He was confident of that, right or wrong, he would draw blood.

The few women on the sidewalk spoke as he approached. Sheriff Gilbert tipped his hat and smiled. "Morning, ladies!" He took the first step leading to the foyer of the large building. Out of habit, the shotgun was quickly swung to his shoulder as he hurried ahead. His strong hand was still on the grip, his trigger finger just a short distance away. He read the faces of the men. They were watching for James Lee.

* * *

Curley Jones, who should have been a road deputy but chose not to, was lying over the Negro as the car left town in a hurry. "We're out of town," commented the driver. The siren still wailed.

"You remember, if we're jumped, I'll kill yer ass before I go down," Curley said to the prisoner. "I've got less regard for you than a green dog turd," he sneered. Curley held the revolver close. The Negro could see the weapon from the corner of his eye. James Lee's eyes grew large as he looked around at the quickly changing shadows and the back of the front seat. They were meeting other cars on the road.

"Folks are pullin' off," said the driver.

Eventually there were no more cars and Granny Turner Road was up ahead. The Ford's suspension worked hard as the vehicle left the pavement and pulled onto the dirt road. The brush had grown to the point that the old road was hard to find. The old county road sign had fallen over and was now resting against a post oak, held there by a late blooming yellow jasmine vine. The prison camp had driven the old road the afternoon before, at the request of the sheriff. He said there had been complaints of a downed tree about midway. That was a fabrication on the sheriff's part. He wanted to make sure the less traveled road was passable. The old road was a mile and a half long, thereabouts. There was good green grazing land with several small streams. Alders and sycamores lined the banks, providing shade for the cattle owned by the county farm.

The winding, narrow road was lined with cedar and locust posts that were weathered to a soft silver. The rusty barbed wire between the posts provided a place for the ruddy breasted bluebirds to gather as they called the quiet countryside home. The siren went silent. Curley and James Lee sat up in the seat.

"Such a short distance ta seem so long," Curley grumbled. He looked out the small back window. There was little dust raised, due to the light rain the night before. "Anyone see us when ya turned off?" Curley asked.

"No!" the driver replied. "When I get close, I'll knock it out of gear, coast the last bit."

James Lee sat quietly. His eyes explored the car door. Curley saw him. "Watch them thoughts, boy!" Curley said, with the revolver in his right hand. "Not on our watch!" Suddenly Curley pivoted slightly and slammed his left foot against Lee's face. He pressed hard. "Ya sum bitch!" The driver looked at the two in the small rearview mirror. Curley pushed hard, pressing the Negro's face into the raised window. "Get them thoughts out of yer head!" Curley said, pressing harder. He slowly released the pressure from James Lee's face. "Not on our watch! Ya bastard!"

James Lee looked straight ahead, his eyes watering from the force that had been exerted on his neck. His mind raced, knowing his chances of escaping were better since his legs were free. "It'd be a bitch to run with my hands bound to my waist by this twisted link chain," he thought to himself.

The patrol car slid to a stop at the end of the road, where it met North Depot Street. A small cloud of dust drifted over the stopped car. The fast-tuned car loped from side to side as the engine began to smooth out. The county would not spend the money to trick out the cars with aftermarket parts, so the local garage did all it could in timing and idling tricks. The straight exhaust pipes had a sound of their own, very similar to those of the liquor runners. The driver raced the engine and pulled the transmission into first gear. It made a slight groan as it seated in.

"I can tell you ain't a whisky runner," said Curley, from the back seat. "What are we waitin' on?" he asked.

"Gettin' my mind right. There's liable ta be trouble," said the driver. He reached for the lever gun that was propped against the seat.

"What did ya get? The 94 or the 92?" Curley asked, watching James Lee.

"The 92, always!" the deputy replied. "It's smoother, quicker," he added, as he released the clutch. The Ford jumped up onto the road. "You ready ta die, boy?" he asked James Lee, by way of the mirror. "Them crazy bastards'll do anything ta get ta you," he said, smiling.

"I'm real worried, white boy," the Negro replied. "Real worried," he repeated.

"Any of us goes down, you'll go down too," said Curley. "My loyalty goes only so far, when old death comes a knockin'," he said, still looking at the restrained Negro. Luck was with them, there was not another car in sight.

* * *

Sheriff Gilbert hurried down the dark hallway. Every step could be heard, no matter how easy he walked. The morning light that entered around the pulled down window shades gave a faint ghostly shadow to the doorways and ornately framed portraits in the tomblike hall. The heavy wooden door that opened to the basement was found locked. The sheriff's hand shook the knob fiercely. "God damn it!" he mumbled. "Damn!" he said, gritting his teeth. "Shit!" He stood motionless facing the door, in a state of great frustration. "What next?" he asked himself.

The sound of a falling metal pail handle broke the silence. His eyes moved about quickly, then he heard a faint humming coming from an office down the way. "Sum bitch, old Clarence," he said to himself. The sheriff's footsteps quickened as he moved toward the soft melody. Tap, tap. His knuckles gently broke the silence in the dim hallway. "Clarence?" said the sheriff. His face was close to the door, so close the brim of his fedora was bent.

The old man's eyes grew large. "Dat' yous Gawd?" the old Negro asked, as he stood still and listened.

"No, Clarence! Sheriff Gilbert!" replied the angry sheriff. His shotgun muzzle bumped the bottom of the door.

Clarence hurried to open the locked door. He did not like to be in the huge building alone. The large brass box lock echoed in the hallway as the strong steel mechanics functioned, retracting the bolt. The heavy wooden door slowly opened. The dark Negro's face appeared in the narrow opening.

"I need to get in the basement. In a hurry!" said Sheriff Gilbert.

"Oh, yes, sirs! Yes, sirs!" Clarence said. The ring of keys jingled as his fingers moved about trying to find the key to the basement door, as they hurried down the hall. "Here it beez!" he said, as he shuffled ahead of the sheriff. "Mighty big gun," he mumbled.

"Winchester pump, made famous durin' the World War," replied the sheriff. "Outside door open?" he asked.

"Id opens from de inside," replied Clarence, as he opened the basement door.

"Trip the light and let me pass," said the sheriff.

Clarence pushed the top protruding button on the wall switch. It gave a sturdy click and a dim circle appeared at the bottom of the steep steps. The crippled old man shuffled aside, allowing the law man to pass. The sheriff's oxfords made a thunderous rumbling sound as he hurried down into the stale air.

"No business of mine," Clarence mumbled, as he gently closed the door. He went back to his cleaning task.

* * *

388

"Comin' up!' yelled the deputy. The Ford was almost silent except for the dusty brakes. They squealed terribly every time they were applied. "Damn it!" the driver exclaimed as he downshifted, trying to hold the heavy car back as they came up on the square.

"We're close! Get ready!" Curley said. He holstered his revolver. The belt holster fit loosely on his pants belt. It was designed for a wider Sam Browne garrison style belt. No matter how tight he had the pants belt pulled, the revolver holster sagged.

"I see the door!" said the driver.

"Can ya jump the curb without ruining the rim and cuttin' the grass too bad?" asked Curley, as he sat up and looked over the seat.

"I'll drive right to the damn door," the deputy replied. He skillfully eased the soft-tired car at a graceful angle and it rose onto the grass, then onto the cement walkway.

The sheriff stood with the door ajar. "This is good!" yelled Curley, as he opened his door and got out while the car was still rolling. Sheriff Gilbert had hurried up the steps and was opening the prisoner's door. The sheriff's large hand grabbed the Negro and pulled him out.

"Hurry! To the basement door," he said, pushing the suited Negro along.

"They're comin'!" yelled the deputy.

"We're good!" replied Sheriff Gilbert, as he pushed the prisoner into the dimly lit basement. Curley Jones was right behind, the last one through the door. The deputy pulled away, laughing and pounding the steering wheel. He circled the square before returning to a reserved parking spot.

Sheriff Gilbert pushed the basement door closed as the angry white, testosterone driven mob rounded the Stone Mountain granite foundation wall of the building. Curley held James Lee at a safe distance from the frosted window glass while the sheriff shook the door, making sure it was securely closed and locked. There was a metal side chair nearby that Clarence had not thrown away. "Bless old Clarence!" Sheriff Gilbert said loudly, as he pulled the strong chair close and wedged it under the door handle.

James Lee stood quietly in the dim light. The only bulb was a clear twenty-five watter that hung at the bottom of the steps. The only other light that could get in was by way of the heavily grated air vents around the basement. The men could see the mob's feet and legs as they moved about on the courthouse yard at street level. "James Lee," the sheriff said calmly. "Our job is to get you to court alive," he said, looking at the Negro with a stern face. "Them men would like to pull ya high up in a tree, let ya swing and watch the crows and the buzzards peck out yer eyes, yer ears, then yer lips and yer tongue. They don't like folks killin' in their county, 'specially niggers. Mr. Lee, you are a nigger. Yer about three notches shy of making it to the definition of a Negro," said the sheriff, as he stood in front of the prisoner, his shotgun cradled in his arms. "We'll do another trick, once I come up with it this afternoon. Take him up, Curley. Let me go first," he added, motioning with the shotgun in his hand.

Sheriff Gilbert took the steps more slowly this time. He carefully checked the hallway. The county employees had arrived, and the curiosity seekers were beginning to fill the hallways, lining up for a seat. Today was the day the jury would deliberate and announce their findings. The Greenville Police Chief realized that his fellow associates had more to do than they could handle. He had gotten off his ass and had his small force escorting the jury as they made their way from the street to the courthouse. "Curley," said the sheriff, standing at the top of the steps. "Come ahead." James Lee started up the steep steps, taking one at a time.

Attorney Robert Gaskill saw the sheriff and hurried down the hall. "I went to the jail. They wouldn't let me in!" he said excitedly.

"That's today's orders," said the sheriff, as he gave a hand to the prisoner one step below. "Here's yer client," he said. "I hope you realize the danger in today's events," he said to the attorney.

The Columbus attorney gradually turned a waxy pale color. "That bad?" he asked.

"That damn bad," replied the sheriff.

"Thank you for taking care of my client," said Gaskill, as he took James Lee by the arm. "What's this dirt on his face and neck?" he asked.

"A discussion," replied James Lee, before Curley could answer. "Just a discussion."

The mob of white males was determined to take the first opportunity should justice not be served their way. They stood strong on the front lawn. The gathering of blacks conducted their own show of support for the victims of the crimes, and faith in the judicial system.

* * *

The courtroom was full, just as crowded as the previous days. The jury filed in led by a bailiff, with two Greenville officers in the rear. The low murmur of the people seated in the courtroom was hushed as the mixed jury entered single file and took their seats in the jury box. Jasper and Heather were in their reserved seats. The clock in the tower indexed from 8:59 to 9:00 a.m. and the mechanics within the clock triggered the loud bronze bell signaling the hour.

"All rise!" the bailiff called out. The Judge's door behind the bench opened and Judge Erastus Cobb entered the courtroom. His suit was black, as plain as one would ever see. His shirt was bright white and the bowtie was yellow ocher.

"Be seated!" the Judge called, as he took his seat. "I remind you that all who have been sworn are still sworn," he said, moving the thick case file on the bench top before him. "I am in hopes that today will bring this case to a close, with the exception of sentencing. However, I will not rush a decision. We will take as much time as necessary to do the job right." He took a small piece of orange peanut candy from his pocket and tucked it in his cheek.

Jasper leaned toward Heather. "Ya think today will wind it up?" he asked.

"It probably will," she whispered back.

"The closing arguments will be next," said the Judge. He pointed to the solicitor.

Ambrose Watkins stood. The chair legs chattered against the hard floor. His posture as he walked toward the jury was one of deep thought. One arm was resting across his chest and the other held his chin. He cleared his throat. "Gentlemen of the jury, the State thanks you for being here and serving your civic duty. Without men like yourselves, our great nation wouldn't be what it is today. The state has shown you that the accused -- " he pointed to the Negro at the defense table, " -- was at the scene of the crime, Herman Pickens' store in Durand. We have shown that he was armed and driving a stolen automobile. He was seen with the money bag that belonged to the deceased. The revolver rounds, two," he held up two fingers, "were proven to have come from the stolen revolver. It was a .32 Smith and Wesson. Those two rounds were found in the chest of Herman Pickens."

Audrey Pickens began to weep.

"The State has presented an eyewitness telling you what he saw. There is no reason to place any doubt on the young boy. He will remember the shooting for the rest of his life. He, in fact, should be a victim in the case as well," said Watkins, as he moved about in front of the jury. "We need not place a shadow of doubt regarding the race of this man nor the victim. A human being is dead, one at the hands of the other. You have heard the testimony of the widow. In your assembly, the State trusts that you will consider all that was presented and make your decision based on the definition of the charges," said Ambrose Watkins. The solicitor took his seat. "I give the floor to the defense," he said, sitting with his legs crossed.

"Thank you, sir!" replied Attorney Robert Gaskill, as he stood and walked toward the jury. "My predecessor has taken the wind from my formal greeting, so I will forgo that."

Sheriff Gilbert moved about the courtroom, never staying in one place for very long. He watched the audience and the doors.

"The defense has shown that the store owner, Herman Pickens, had hidden a shotgun under his counter, WAITING to use it on a person, ANYONE who happened to appear that they were robbing him. HE was waiting, BROODING over the opportunity to kill someone, should this opportunity arise," Gaskill said. He slowly moved about in deep thought. "The fact that the State had believed to establish is irrelevant to the fact that Herman Pickens was about to kill my client, James Lee. It WAS a situation of kill or be killed. The young boy, HIDING in the cellar of the hardware store, only establishes that HE is an uncontrolled juvenile, a seed to become a VAGABOND! If he cannot be trusted to attend school, HOW can he be trusted to tell the truth?"

Young Albert Martin's father, Horace, began to stand. "Counsel, I address you to calm your attacks on the young witness!" said Judge Cobb, pointing his finger at the attorney. Horace Martin slowly sat down.

"Sum bitch," Heather whispered to Jasper, referring to the attorney.

"What we have here is NOT a murder trial involving my client, BUT a trial that should be trying the late Herman Pickens for attempted murder! Gentlemen, consider that when you weigh the facts," said Robert Gaskill. He took his seat. "Nothing further, your Honor," he added.

Judge Cobb was seen shaking his head at the defense's closing argument. Some who were standing nearby thought they heard the Judge mumble, "I hope not."

Judge Cobb proceeded to read the charges to the jury and give instructions for their deliberations based on state law.

"The Court will be cleared for the length of time necessary for the jurors to deliberate. Jury, please walk with the bailiffs to the jury room. The bailiff in the hallway will have whatever you need brought to the door," said Judge Cobb. He stood behind the bench as the jury was escorted out. The courtroom broke into loud conversation as the curious filed out the nearest door.

* * *

The jail was quiet. The prisoners napped, played cards, and talked. Dixie and the only deputy were in the office, while the night jailer slept inside the cell block in a straight chair. Dixie's typewriter tapped and clacked away at the letters and other assorted correspondence required by Sheriff Gilbert. The deputy sat reading the newspaper and watching the yard and the street beyond for anyone passing or approaching. Miss Jewel was finished with the meal for the day. It was held safely in a warming state on the stove. She had cleaned the kitchen well beyond her normal attempts and found solace in sitting in the office with the others. The fifty-pound bag of dried beans soon appeared between her feet. Her nimble fingers carefully picked through the beans for trash and small stones. When she would find either, the sound of the hard object striking the white enameled wash pan interrupted the concentration of Dixie and the deputy.

"Bear wid me's now! It could beez worse," Miss Jewel said, followed by a chuckle.

* * *

Judge Cobb emerged from his chambers and walked down the hall toward the guarding bailiff.

"How's it look?" asked Judge Cobb.

"It's been awful quiet. They've asked for nothing, but it's only been a little over an hour," the bailiff replied.

Sheriff Gilbert sat on the bench. His shotgun was lying in front of him. The stillness had made him sleepy, along with the implied stress of the mob outside. The second bailiff and deputy stood just inside the doors that led to the front steps. Now and then they peeked out the door to see the white mob growing stronger in number. At first the racist group had stood filling the sidewalk. Now they were spilling over to the lawn. The black supporters had ceased their soft songs and Bible scriptures and had either gone back to their homes or took refuge in the balcony, waiting for the outcome of the jury's decision.

Sheriff Gilbert appeared at the door. "How many?" he asked.

The deputy, looking through a small opening, was surprised. "'Bout triple," he replied.

"Any visible guns?" asked Sheriff Gilbert.

"I haven't seen any, but they've got ta be there," said the deputy. He gently closed the door. "We're damn sure outnumbered," he added.

Sheriff Gilbert stood holding his shotgun at his side. "What we need is a downpour, some good lightnin' strikes," he said. He wiped his face with his handkerchief. "Never seen too many angry men who could last through hard rain and lightnin'," he added, putting away his handkerchief.

Heather and Jasper sat in the pharmacy, slowly spending on drinks to keep their seats. The reporters had been occupying space since day one, but their money and tips were good. There seemed to be no locals waiting for a seat. The floor trade, along with the brief meetings with the pharmacists, went smoothly. The overhead paddle fans turned slowly. One could follow the blades with one's eyes, counting the revolutions. A mechanical swish made a relaxing sound as they ran from a single power shaft connecting them all. One large open framed motor sat on an ornately cast metal bracket and suspended a leather drive belt to the first fan. The skylights above cast a flashing shadow as the five paddles turned.

A young reporter watched Heather. Their eyes locked on more than one occasion. The seat next to her came open. The young man moved to it before the next customer could get it. Before moving, he had noticed how nice her butt looked on the round top, backless chrome plated stool. "You from here?" he asked.

"No," Heather replied, looking at him in the wall mirror, mounted over the prep counter.

"Me either," the young man said, smiling. He could detect a very faint fragrance of perfume about her. "We wanted to see if this case was close to the Moore versus Dempsey case, back in twenty-three. That's back a few years, I guess you've heard of it, bein' in the law profession," he said.

Heather surprised him. "That was about a Negro in Phillips County, Ark-can-saw. A shooting and a riot broke out," she said.

The reporter leaned and looked out the store front. "Looks just like the same day in Helena-West Helena," he said. He sat up straight and looked at Heather in the mirror. He smiled. "And I didn't stutter," he said.

"That's quite a name," she said.

The young man agreed, nodding his head.

Jasper watched the waitress as she cleared the counter of dirty dishes and raked tips into the uniform dress that fit snuggly around her hips. He leaned out and looked at the courthouse. "Big crowd gatherin'," he said. "I hope they're here for the results and nothing else," he whispered.

Heather leaned out and looked too. "It looks bad. More than the sheriff can handle safely," she said, watching the men. There appeared to be several in the group that were talking, working the group up.

"I've seen that kind before. They're not here for something ta do. I did apprentice in Philadelphia and finished in Chicago. I know the signs," said the young reporter.

* * *

The secluded room that held the jurors and the extras opened. "Bailiff! A juror called out.

The bailiff sitting in the dim hallway stood and moved toward the jurors. "Yes, sir!"

'We're ready," the juror replied. "Do we hand you the results?"

"Oh, no! Hold it for the Court, you'll be asked for it," the bailiff replied. "Sit quietly. I'll tell the Judge y'all are ready."

The foreman of the mixed jury looked at the other members. "I feel good about our decision, we've worked well together," he said.

Robert Hardee, a Negro, spoke up. "Yes, we've done well. I feel as though I've made new acquaintances. I hope you will speak to me in public, as I will speak to you."

The bailiff opened the door. "The Judge is ready for you," he said. The jury stood, chairs chattering on the hard floor. The men lined up in the order of their seats in the jury box. Judge Erastus Cobb was already on the bench and the sheriff had his bailiffs at the ready for disorder. The hall door opened under the hand of the sheriff.

"All rise!" cried out the bailiff. The people in the courtroom stood in deathly silence.

The jurors filed into the jury box. "Be seated!" called the Judge.

This time there were two suited men from the white mob standing at the front entrance to the courtroom. The jury had passed the defense table and the State table on the way to their respective places. The mixed-race group was somber in appearance. Heather and Jasper were in their seats. "This doesn't look good, and it damn sure don't feel right," Heather whispered to Jasper. "Come on, the sheriff needs us now, not when it happens," she said, getting up. The sheriff saw her rise. Jasper followed right behind. His revolver struck the back of the courtroom bench. The loud thud got the attention of those waiting on the verdict. The two Warm Springs officers hurried toward the sheriff. He was pleased to see them coming.

"Where do you need us?" Heather asked. She put her hand on her waist, pushing her coat back and revealing her 1911. Jasper stood close with his hand on his revolver. Chief Howard Hawthorn slipped in the side door, where the blacks were expected to come and go. Heather saw him. "Our chief's here too," she added, indicating with a head movement.

"See them sum bitches at the door? One's Jake Satterfield. He's the big fat one. Mostly mouth, but he'll use a gun. The other one is Sam Butterfield, what Jake does, he'll follow. They are armed. I'd bet my life on it," said Sheriff Gilbert.

"Want us to shadow 'em?" Heather asked. "We can work tha bastards!" she said, looking at the two men. She felt sure the sheriff was right, by the way a suit coat was printing. Belt holsters seldom fit properly, being mass produced, unlike shoulder rigs. They always profiled the pistol under a coat, especially one that was too small. Judge Cobb sat quietly as he realized there was a security issue brewing. He too had his own .38 caliber revolver pulled from his pants waist and placed on the bench. No one but the balcony could see the top of the bench. The balcony was packed with blacks, many different faces this time, from what had been observed in the days before. Judge Cobb knew they had seen his pistol, by the way they looked and whispered to one another. There was a small black girl dressed in a bright yellow sun dress. Her hair was braided with small ribbons. She gave a timid wave to the Judge. He smiled and waved back. The pretty young girl jumped into her father's lap and hid her smiling face.

"Please stay on those two," said Sheriff Gilbert. He held his shotgun down by his side. The public was moving about, wondering what the delay was.

Jasper and Heather hurried up the aisle and stood just behind the two questionable men. The detective could tell that she was making Jake Satterfield nervous by her presence behind him. Jasper was on Sam Butterfield. The sheriff heard the front outside door slam and hurried footsteps coming down the hall. The north courtroom door opened. It was the deputy assigned to the courthouse.

"They are assembled in the front yard," he said, breathing deeply from excitement. "Must be God damn near a hundred of 'em," he said, as low as possible to Sheriff Gilbert.

"Go back and watch 'em. Keep me posted on what they do," replied the sheriff. "They don't get inside!" he whispered to the departing deputy.

Jake Satterfield stood waiting for the jury to deliver a verdict that he and his group would not agree with. He looked at the detective who stood behind him on more than one occasion. "Sumthin' botherin' you?" he asked Heather.

"You," she whispered.

"I know you. Yer that bitch Warm Springs hired ta do a man's job. You'd be like shit under a shoe if I wanted ta take ya down. Don't mess with me. I'll hurt ya," he said, looking rather evil.

"I'm sorry, what did ya say?" Heather asked.

"I'll hurt ya," he said, still looking evil.

The fat man blinked, slowly. Too slowly! Heather grabbed his collar and ran him backwards down the aisle. His feet worked hard to keep up, but he finally fell over backwards. The windows shook from his weight hitting the wood floor. The courtroom was a roar of excitement. Jasper pushed Sam Butterfield against the floor and handcuffed him. All the while, the small woman detective stood with a foot on Satterfield's nuts and barked out orders.

"Hands behind your back!" she snapped.

Sheriff Gilbert was pleased. He stood his post and watched for others in the mob to come in.

"Way back!" Heather yelled, grabbing one arm and applying a cuff. "Hold the other one up!" She grabbed the other arm and secured it.

"You bitch!" Jake Satterfield yelled, as he lay face down on the floor. His revolver had slid down the aisle a few feet.

"Disorderly conduct!" the detective barked. "Roll over and sit up!" She stepped off his manhood.

The heavy man grunted and groaned as he rolled over on his back and then eventually, after several attempts, sat up. "Shit!" he said.

Judge Erastus Cobb was standing at the bench. "Here, here! That's enough of the language!" he yelled to the cuffed man.

"You and yer God damned pussy court!" Satterfield yelled at the Judge.

"Contempt of Court!" Judge Cobb yelled, pointing at the handcuffed man. "You with him?" he asked, pointing to Sam Butterfield, who was not as vocal. He was under control of Officer Jasper Brown.

"This bitch officer ain't got jurisdiction in this court!" snarled Satterfield.

Heather kicked him in the butt, almost causing him to tumble forward. "Special Deputy!" She replied loudly. An old man handed Heather her fedora that had rolled toward the bench during the altercation. "Thank you," she said, smiling.

"You can come arrest me anytime," the old man said, winking.

"I may have ta do that," Heather replied with a slight smile. He took his seat, but never took his eyes off her.

"That's two counts of contempt! Both of ya!" yelled the Judge.

"This was the woman who arrested James Lee after he almost ran head on into her personal car and shot a hole in her windshield," said Sheriff Gilbert, from where he stood against the wall. "She and Officer Brown there have been Special Deputies all along, so they could arrest outside of their city."

Judge Cobb once more took the stand, but he remained standing. "Put them two over there so we can keep an eye on 'em."

Jake Satterfield and Sam Butterfield were seated along the inside wall of the courtroom. "Any of your bunch comes in here shootin', I'll kill you before their bullet stops," Heather whispered.

"Bitch!" Jake said, spitting at Heather.

Heather reacted inappropriately and quickly from her stance with her back turned, bringing her left foot around and kicking Jake Satterfield in the face, knocking him out. The courtroom roared from the sudden dealing with the simple assault on the woman officer.

"No, no!" muttered Sam Butterfield. "It wasn't me," he said, looking surprised at the woman's lightning actions.

"Doc Hubbard, will ya look at him?" asked Judge Cobb.

Doc Hubbard was sitting a few chairs away. He leaned forward and looked. "I've seen him. Tha big bastard's all right, time will bring him about," he said, laughing. The courtroom roared again.

Bang, bang sounded the gavel. "Let us begin!" the Judge said, taking his seat.

Heather and Jasper went to the doors where the two mob members had been standing. The sheriff whispered to several in the nearby crowd who were still discussing what they had just witnessed. Chief Howard Hawthorn smiled at Heather and made indications that he was very pleased with their actions.

"Gentlemen of the jury, have you made a decision?" asked Judge Cobb. He turned in his large chair and looked at the group of racially mixed men.

The foreman of the jury stood. "We have, your Honor."

"Would you like to announce to me your decision, or prefer for me to read it to the Court?" asked the Judge.

"We'd like to ask that you read it, your Honor," the foreman said.

"Bailiff, hand me the sealed envelope," said the Judge.

Curley Jones sat close behind the accused. He was ready for any sudden outburst or attempted escape.

The foreman handed the envelope to the bailiff, who in turn gave it to the Judge. The courtroom was deathly silent. Satterfield was just coming to.

"The jury of this case finds the accused, James Lee, guilty of murder in the first degree," read Judge Cobb. There was still silence in the court.

Some faces grew smiles, while others were stone faced at the serious decision, regardless of race. "Take this and read it, Mr. Gaskill," said Judge Cobb, holding out the jury decision.

Attorney Gaskill quickly stood and stepped up to the bench, where he took the written notice and read it. "I'm satisfied, your Honor," he said softly.

"Well, I ain't!" yelled James Lee. "They'll never get me sentenced!"

The nearby bailiffs hurried to subdue the raging Negro, who was standing and yelling his discontent. Curley had already laid hands on him.

"You Uncle Toms ain't no better than them home boys, just white niggers, butt lickers!" James Lee yelled, as he fought the bailiffs. He kicked one bailiff in the groin, rendering him useless for a time. Curley was at a disadvantage, as he was at the Negro's back. Jasper rushed to help, kicking the Negro's leg from under him. James Lee hit the floor and continued kicking. Heather also rushed to help. The rows of citizens around the brawl stood and moved back in fear and disbelief. The old man who had handed Heather her hat sat still and watched the pretty woman.

James Lee's legs kicked about fiercely. Curley was trying to get on the Negro's knees but was still in reach of his powerful kicks. His head was the only thing that seemed to remain in the same place. Heather shucked her large pistol from her holster and pulled the safety off. The click was heard, like magic. She placed the muzzle against the thrashing Negro's temple. "Remember me?" she said loudly, pressing the muzzle hard so he could feel it. The muzzle against the thin skin of the temple quickly got his attention as she continued to push. The fighting Negro stopped.

"Shoot me, bitch!" he said loudly.

James Lee could see her from his side vision. Her trigger finger slowly moved from the side of the slide to the trigger ring. Gasps were heard from the citizens. Judge Erastus Cobb watched in wonder. The still Negro was sweating now. His heart raced and his breathing quickened again.

Click! The hammer fell against an empty chamber. James Lee jumped at the sound. His legs dropped flat against the floor. "Maybe later," Heather said softly. "Get in your seat!" she said in a low growl. Curley had managed to sit on his knees.

Judge Cobb wiped his forehead with his handkerchief. "Order! Order!" he said loudly. "James Lee, do you understand the jury's decision?" he asked.

Attorney Robert Gaskill jumped to his feet. "Yes! My client understands."

"Place this prisoner back in the county jail. I will announce a meeting with the State and the Defense within the next week. I must review the transcripts," said Judge Cobb. "I ask that the courtroom be cleared except for those assisting with security and the transport of the arrested, Satterfield and Butterfield."

The courtroom quickly emptied, leaving law enforcement and the three prisoners behind. The watching deputy hurried back to report to the sheriff that the gathered mob had gotten word of the decision and had slowly dispersed, leaving only a few to wonder where Jake Satterfield and Sam Butterfield had disappeared to. Judge Cobb motioned for Heather to come closer. He still sat on the bench, eating candy from a brown bag.

"Was that a misfire?" he asked Heather, as she looked up at him.

"No, deliberate. Empty chamber in case someone gets it in a struggle, here in these close quarters," she replied with great confidence.

"You do know I jumped when the hammer fell?" he asked.

"I'm sorry, sir. I didn't know that," Heather said, holding back a smile.

Alfred Huffman and the group of reporters had quietly entered the courtroom, from the foyer. "And the rest is history!" yelled Alfred, from the Vindicator. "Pictures?" he asked loudly.

"Yes, you may!" replied the Judge. "I'd like one with this fine woman officer," he said, smiling. "It's for myself," he added. The flashbulbs lit the room, one burst after another. "Sheriff!" called the Judge. "Come here!"

Sheriff Gilbert hurried over to the bench. "It was a fine ending. I just knew it was goin' ta be a terrible one," he said, cutting his eyes to the two cuffed whites awaiting transport.

"It was a good day. Once we get these three in lockdown, it will be better," said the sheriff.

"Bitch!" yelled Jake Satterfield. Sam Butterfield flinched and rolled his eyes at hearing the remark.

"Three counts contempt!" yelled Judge Cobb, pointing to the two.

"God damn! Shut up!" said Sam, as he turned away from Satterfield.

* * *

Dixie was finishing up. She had planned to leave early in case there was trouble. The armed deputy sat watching the courthouse from the office window. Miss Jewel had fallen asleep. "Hey! It's over! They're all leaving," he said.

Dixie stood and looked out the window next to her desk. "Finally."

This time all the lawmen and women walked the three prisoners across the short distance to the jail, where they were dressed out, and those that needed booking were booked in.

"How did it go?" asked the jail deputy.

"These two, three counts of contempt, and one each disorderly conduct," said the sheriff.

James Lee stood with a deputy on each arm and his attorney close behind. The Negro looked down in silence. "How 'bout him?" asked Dixie.

"Jury found him guilty," answered one of the deputies that had served as a bailiff.

"Umm," said Dixie.

"Curley, I want Lee dressed out jaybird, nothing longer than his dick in the cell. You know the usual. We have ta see that he gets to the sentencing part," said Sheriff Gilbert.

Curley noticed the cut and the bruise on Jake Satterfield's face. "How about this?" he asked.

"Doc Hubbard's already blessed it. He's good ta book," replied the sheriff.

The newspaper reporters had followed them from the courthouse, making photographs along the way. "Can we get a few words?" asked a reporter, looking in through the oxidized door screen.

Sheriff Louis Gilbert set his shotgun in the rack and smiled. "Yes, you may," he said, very pleasantly. "Ready?" he asked, as he walked to the open door.

"Oh, yes, sir!" the reporter replied.

"Have a good evening," the sheriff said softly, as he gently closed the door.

CHAPTER TWENTY-SIX

During the coming week, Judge Cobb sat in his chambers. "I'll not sit here and listen to your outrage about the legality of your client being arrested in my court by the woman detective or any other officer. I find that highly offensive and accusatory," said Judge Erastus Cobb, his face blushing with anger as he spoke to the attorney. He pushed back from his desk. "Where did you get your degree in law, Montgomery Ward? You may be attorney Dempsey Perkerson, someone of importance in your town, BUT in my county you're just another face!"

The man sitting in front of the desk was beginning to feel as though the battle to get the charges against his clients, Jake Satterfield and Sam Butterfield, dropped before the next court was a lost cause, and at his embarrassment. "Had fat Jake touched his revolver in court, I certainly feel that he would be dead and I wouldn't have to listen to your foolishness. Do these crazy bastards actually pay you to try and sell their logic to sane people?" asked the Judge. He took a piece of orange candy from the center drawer and bit into it. "I'll tell you where I'm at with your antics. I'm just about ready to call the sheriff and have you arrested for bribery," he said, glaring at the attorney from Franklin.

"But my group tells me that the woman was not a legal officer of the county, and being a woman doing a man's job is certainly not ethical with most Christian beliefs," said Perkerson.

"And I tell you that the woman was hired because she was the best qualified candidate that applied, and she came highly recommended," Judge Cobb said, leaning across the large desk.

"Can you prove that?" asked Attorney Perkerson.

"You sum bitch! You calling me a liar?" snapped Erastus Cobb.

"Well, not in certain terms. We just want to be assured that she was legal in her actions," replied Perkerson. He tugged at his buttoned shirt collar.

Erastus Cobb stood up. "When you think I've finished, you best be heading for that door," he said, pointing to the closed office door. "If the jury had decided that the Negro, James Lee, was not guilty, just what would your clients and their followers have done? Shot him? Strung him up? Were they ready to do another Leo Frank?" he asked, turning redder and redder. The Judge had removed the telephone receiver and both men could hear the local operator speaking. "You and this mob you represent will be the downfall of this country," he added, shaking his finger at the attorney angrily.

Dempsey Perkerson stood and started progressing toward the door. "I shall consult higher authorities in Georgia, and even Federal law on this issue," he said, holding the doorknob. "There will be consequences."

"You can consult God for all I care!" Erastus Cobb shouted.

Dempsey Perkerson left and closed the door rather hard. "Sum bitch!" yelled Judge Cobb. He quickly grabbed a bound copy of Georgia laws, a hefty leather-bound book of some eleven hundred pages, and threw it, striking the closed door. "Good riddance!" he yelled. "Prejudiced, ignorant bastard!" The rest of the day was a blur for the aging Judge.

* * *

It was Saturday morning. Buddy Cotton had reported to work early. He wanted to dust and rearrange store displays. Mrs. Blakely pretty much turned him loose to do whatever he saw fit. The store was in sparkling condition, free from dust and the clutter of items that did not sell. He had suggested that every Saturday they have a sale table close to the register, displaying any items from canned goods to large garden tools that were not moving quickly. This was proving to be a great help. Buddy was on his knees dusting and washing off the bottom shelf when the rolled-up newspaper struck him in the ribs and fell to the oiled wood floor with a thud. His curiosity got the best of him. He sat against an opposing display and opened it to the front page. The lad's eyes grew large and his face turned red with anger. "Hey, hey!" he yelled, as he hurried toward the kitchen where the Saturday boarders, including Heather and her guest Jasper Brown, were eating breakfast in shifts. The grits and meats were on the stove top keeping warm, and biscuits were inside the warm oven. Mrs. Blakely cooked eggs to order. Buddy's yelling was heard over the loud cross talk that was taking place around the large table.

"Jesus Christ! Look what's in the damn paper!" Buddy exclaimed, as he stood in the hall doorway. He held up the newspaper so they could see.

Mrs. Blakely stood at the stove cooking two fried eggs. "Watch yer mouth, young man!" she barked, pointing a spatula at him.

"Yes, ma'am, but it's important," he replied.

"Go on, what is it?" she asked.

"They're questioning the legality of the detective," Buddy said, getting lower in volume as he spoke, his head seeming to drop.

"Assholes, what they need is a dose of big city," one boarder said, waving his fork in the air as he talked.

"Jesus!" Jasper said, as he leaned closer to try and read the headlines.

Heather sat quietly and continued to enjoy her warm breakfast. "It won't be the first time a Duncan's been challenged," she said, not even looking at the newspaper that Buddy was still holding up. "Buddy, do you doubt me? Do you have a different opinion of me since that was published?" Heather asked.

Buddy looked sad and replied, "No, ma'am."

"Sit down and read it to us," said Mrs. Blakely, as she plated hot eggs for a waiting boarder.

"Forget about the name of the paper and the date, we know all of that," said a nearby man.

Heather pushed a vacant chair out with her foot. "Sit here," she said.

The young boy sat down and began to read. "It has come to the attention of the press by a paid submission, that there are questionable legalities which concern many citizens of the county, in regards to the hiring of the woman by Warm Springs. As most know, she is serving in the capacity of a detective for the police department. While she has done a quite remarkable job, she is taking the job of a man. These concerned citizens feel that she is overpaid, due to the fact that she is doing the job of a man, and tradition has it that women do not deserve the same pay as their male counterparts. Clerical jobs, nursing, home-making, child rearing, teaching, waiting tables, the more traditional tasks as ordained by God's definition is where this aggressive woman should be, rather than in the capacity to answer calls for service, make arrests, and fight with the unruly. Maybe there's something to the old saying, barefoot and pregnant.

While the work place has appropriate jobs suitable to women and young children, it is best that they confine themselves to those tasks. The agricultural environment is brimming with jobs for this group, hoeing, weeding, harvesting, the jobs requiring bending and stooping. Women are proven to be more flexible. By taking such jobs, it frees up the valuable, skilled men to do other technical, mechanical tasks.

We wonder about the legalities of this woman and her arrest powers. If or when she was sworn in as a Special Deputy by the local sheriff, did he have the power to do this under Georgia law? We seem to find that Georgia law reads that law enforcement officers are intended to be men. So, were all these actions in the city of Warm Springs and out in the county legal? Were her arrests right in the eyes of the law? In the State versus James Lee case, with the victim being Herman Pickens, if it is challenged, will it stand up in the Supreme Court's eyes, especially since the arrest wasn't made by a male officer?

It is the opinion of this group that if challenged it certainly will not hold up. Therefore, all the time put into the case will be for naught, wasted. The accused will walk scot-free. We feel that this woman should be relocated to a clerical position immediately, before she does more damage to the city and county's image. This should also result in a pay adjustment. Leave law enforcement to men!" Buddy sat reading the paper, holding it up with both hands.

Suddenly a biscuit struck the newspaper. "Shit head!" yelled Jasper, as he threw the whole biscuit, striking the center of the newspaper. Buddy jumped, thinking he had done something wrong. Jasper sprang to his feet and stood mumbling, turning in a small circle. He was visibly more upset than Heather. She sipped her coffee, holding the thin cup with both graceful hands. "Ya finished?" Jasper snapped.

"Well, no," replied the young boy.

"Finish the shit up!" growled Jasper. The top of his head was red.

"Sit down," said Heather.

Jasper took his seat. "Excuse me," he said. "It's hard to listen to a bunch of opinionated crap."

Buddy laid the newspaper across the dirty plates before him. "Let me see," he said, finding his place. "First Timothy 2:8 through 11, I will therefore that men pray everywhere, lifting up holy hands, without wrath and doubting. In like manner also, that women adorn themselves in modest apparel, with shamefacedness and sobriety; not with broided hair or gold, or pearls, or costly array; but with good works. Let the woman learn in silence with all subjection," he read.

"I guess they're saying don't kick the shit out of helpless big sum bitches in front of their wife and neglected children," said a male boarder. He leaned and looked at the nice checkered grips on Heather's Colt pistol. "And not ta have nice pistol grips," he said, laughing.

Buddy looked at Heather and the man. "What's this mean?" he asked.

"Men are to lead, women are to be modest, learning quietly and in submission. By doin' that they, the woman, proves her way to claim godliness. I wonder if God would think that away if he were gettin' the shit beat out of him, pinned down, and the hard fists strikin' like lightnin' bolts, one after another?" Heather said. "Go on."

"First Timothy 5:9, 10 and 14, be faithful in home related activities. First Corinthians 14:34 and 35 says, women are to look upon men for leadership, and Ephesians 5:22, wives submit yourselves unto your own husbands as unto the Lord. What's that mean?" Buddy asked, looking at the faces around the table for answers.

"Keep an aspirin between yer knees and be faithful, just as yer cheatin' husband," one man said, pushing his plate away.

Jasper leaned forward. "Don't screw around."

"Much more of that?" Heather asked.

"No, ma'am," Buddy replied.

"That's good. Just stop there unless they had the balls ta sign it," Heather said, setting her cup down.

Buddy looked at the bottom of the article. "There's no name."

"All this is based around women not being equal to men," Heather said, looking at Buddy.

"It's not right," he replied, folding the newspaper and tossing it on a clean place on the table.

"Say goodbye and finish yer work. I hear people up front," Mrs. Blakely said, with a smile at the curiously upset boy.

Buddy disappeared down the hallway, toward the store. He reappeared at the kitchen door. "What's broided?" he asked, peeking around the door casing.

"Not to have fancy hairdos, wearing jewelry, fancy combs, be a plain Jane," Heather answered.

"Oh!" replied the lad.

"We don't get this up home," Heather said. "Folks generally concentrate on subjects of better pickings. Drunk men who neglect their families for the bottle, whorin' around." She slid her chair from the table. "I've got your breakfast," she said to Jasper.

"No, I've got ours."

"Shall I kick your ass in front of these men?" Heather asked, with a big grin.

"No, I'm just fine!" Jasper replied, holding up his hands in surrender.

Mrs. Blakely rattled dishes as she took them from the table. Breakfast plates stacked easily. The only obstruction was the occasional ham bone ring, or the hard rind of a slice of streak o' lean. "Heather, I'm always available for listening. I do know the difficulties I've had running this place," she said.

* * *

Mayor Cunningham and Chief Hawthorn were in the café when they discovered the front-page article. "Look at this!" pointed the mayor. His eyes hurried to read it. He laid the newspaper out so Chief Hawthorn could see it too. Neither man could believe what they were reading. The mayor tapped the newspaper with his knuckles. "How in the hell did this get printed?" he asked, leaning close to the chief.

"Freedom of speech," said Chief Hawthorn, shrugging his shoulders. "We're on the money. We've done nothing wrong."

Mayor Cunningham tossed his hat on the table. "Damn!" he said low, gritting his teeth. The two friends sat silently for the longest time. They were into their third cup of coffee, glad it was a Saturday and most folks were at home for breakfast. Things in town were slow. The mayor looked around to see who could hear them. Most of the other patrons were in booths. "That fat beer guzzling son of a bitch! He should be visited by his own kind. Loud mouthed bastard," said the mayor. "All the effort we put into filling the opening and this is all we get. Why, only the womenfolk have openly supported us, tellin' me how good she was. Damn, damn, damn!" he said, rubbing his head vigorously, leaving his hair mussed. "Who all's in that mob?" he asked.

The chief took out a small pocket tablet. "Let me think. There's Fat Jake Satterfield, and Sam Butterfield," he whispered, as he wrote. He thought a moment. "Then John Hawkins, down at the lumber yard. Henry Saxon, ain't he with the telephone company?"

"I think he is," replied the mayor. He was looking at a menu, just like he did not know what he would order.

"Bill Gibson and Albert Howard," said the chief. He took a look around. "They're running liquor down on Cane Creek, over toward Woodbury. We should turn 'em in. Tim O'Neal, maybe that's where the crosses come from. Isn't Lathem Humphrey one of 'em?"

"Yes, he runs the laundry, down in Manchester. Shit that ain't picked up, maybe that's their wrapping rags," replied the mayor.

"Brad Collins and Bud Bradley," whispered the chief. "I don't know what they do," he said, putting the tablet away.

The waitress walked up. "The usual?" she asked. "Or something different? I see ya got the menu,"

"The usual," replied the mayor. He blushed like he had been caught.

"Me too!" replied the chief.

"It'll be right out," she said, pouring the fourth cup of coffee.

"It'd be funny it Brad and Bud were infiltrators," laughed the mayor, elbowing the chief. The two men chuckled at the evil thought.

A car pulled up and Sheriff Gilbert got out. His heavy, sandy footsteps could be heard coming up the steps, into the café. "I see the damn telephone cord don't run over here!" he said, pulling out a chair.

"Well, sit down, take a load off your mind," said the mayor. "Oh! Yours is in your butt, I forgot!" he laughed.

"My old butt is gettin' tired," Sheriff Gilbert replied, as he took a seat. His hat joined the others on the table.

"What brings you down here?" asked the chief.

"Your detective. Seen the newspaper?" he asked.

"Ruined our day, first thing," replied the chief.

The mayor turned the newspaper over and handed it to the sheriff. "No, I've read it several times," replied Sheriff Gilbert. He made motion of a coffee cup to the waitress, who was at another table.

"What brought it on? We thought they got their way on this case," said the mayor.

"Their mob attorney, Dempsey Perkerson, tangled with Judge Cobb over the issue of legalities and the woman detective making the arrest. We heard the Judge threw him out and tried to hit him with a four-pound Georgia law book, or something to that effect," said the sheriff. "Thanks!" he said, as the waitress set down a cup and poured hot coffee.

"Be eatin'?" she asked.

"Will ya brown me a split buttered biscuit?" asked the sheriff.

"That was started by that new woman detective," said the waitress.

"I don't care who started it. I'll have one, if you please. Oh, and some sorghum!" he added, as she was walking away. "The Theo Jackson trial is Monday, 9:00 a.m.," said the sheriff. "Can ya tell the detective?" he asked.

Chief Hawthorn looked out the café window. "Here she comes now! You can tell her." The chief waved for Heather. Jasper was soon right behind her. "Damn! It's Jasper Brown. He tails her like a pup in heat. Shit!" he said.

"He can hear it too," replied the sheriff.

Heather and Jasper came into the cafe. "Morning!" she said. Jasper just nodded. "Did ya want me?" she asked.

"Sheriff wants ta speak to you. Jasper, you can stay," said the chief. "Pull up another table." Jasper helped Heather join the tables.

"Did you see the article in the newspaper?" the sheriff asked Heather.

"I did," she replied. "What of it?"

Sheriff Gilbert looked puzzled. "So that doesn't bother you?" he asked.

"No. Offended a little, but I've got folks waiting on me, apparently them folks don't. I can make a living off of what my father and grandmother haven't finished yet," she said. "I'll see these types in hell before I go down. Two teas, please!" Heather flagged the waitress. "I'm fortunate in the fact that my dear mother saw fit to get us away from my father to a better environment. I was raised hard and worked for all I've got. Being disliked is second nature to my family, second generation law enforcement. My grandfather was Marshal Mathew Duncan. It's said that those who liked him would do anything for him, even turn themselves in, those that didn't like him avoided him. The family is still that way," said Heather. "I was hired to do a job and it's almost over. Things are too slow here to keep me busy, I'll probably move on," she added.

The men sat and listened in silence. Jasper looked surprised at the possibility of losing his admired partner. "I don't think leaving's necessary as long as I'm mayor," Cunningham said.

The waitress brought out the sheriff's food. "Thanks!" he said, smiling. "Nevertheless, court for the Theo Jackson case is Monday, same time, 9:00 a.m.," he said. He poured a thin stream of amber colored sorghum over his browned biscuit. "I think the article is pretty lowdown, but those kinds are." He took a bite of the biscuit.

The mayor shook his fork at the sheriff. "We'll all be there," he said coldly. "While the Millers were not city voters, they were nice black folks. They ran a wonderful and successful business down there and nobody deserves ta be shot and beat ta death," he said. "I'd like ta kill that fat, stinkin' sum bitch myself!" he snarled. "Shoot him dead myself, yes, sir!"

* * *

The heavy barred doors screeched and moaned as the jail matron brought Gladys Hightower to the bonding area. Her own clothes waited in a large brown grocery sack. The walls were painted black along the bottom half and a light blue to the ceiling. There were printed signs and contact information for every bondsman for miles around. The jailer, a man, stood in a caged area hurrying the paperwork to relieve the jail of the loud arrogant woman. Her rolled up pants struggled to stay up around her sagged waist.

"Gladys Hightower!" the jailer called out. Before she could answer, he pushed the bag of clothes across the metal topped counter. The heavy sack fell to the painted floor. A path had been worn from the outside door to the counter opening, and then into the jail. The concrete floor was slick and polished from years of heavy wear. The heavy sack fell to the floor with a flat thud. "Dress out! In the stall, make sure ya lock the door. Nobody wants to see yer naked butt," said the jailer, as he checked blocks on the release form. "HURRY!" He shouted without looking up. The matron stood close by the small changing room.

"She's the loud bitch, first ta talk in tha mornin' and last to hush at night?" he asked, to assure himself that they were ridding themselves of the problem.

"That's her," replied the matron.

The small room was cramped, not much more than a telephone booth. Gladys's elbows and knees bumped the walls. The jailers could hear her mumblings about the small space, and how she should not be treated the way she had been in jail. Finally, the door opened and Gladys stood in the clothes she had been wearing when she was arrested. The jail clothing was dropped and wadded at her feet.

"Put the jail suit in the laundry bag," barked the matron, pointing at the dark gray canvas bag, hanging from the metal roll-a-round frame.

Gladys bent down in the open doorway to pick up the soiled prison suit. Her fingertips barely grasped the clothes between her small feet. In the struggle, she lost her balance and fell forward into the room, saved from a face first fall by her wide hips that lodged tightly in the door opening. There she hung, not down, and certainly not able to get up. Both jailers tried not to laugh at the heavy woman's predicament.

"What's tha hold up, Mrs. Hightower?" the jailer asked. He placed her release forms aside and watched the large woman. Her huge breasts hung like two Christmas mail bags. Gladys mumbled a reply, sounding breathless. The matron covered a laugh with her hands.

"Hope me ups!" Gladys struggled to get out, spittle dripping from her mouth. The matron placed her hands on Hightower's rounded shoulders and pushed hard, eventually freeing the wide hips from the door frame. The short heavy woman fell against the back wall, where she tried to catch her breath.

"Try it again," said the matron, pointing to the laundry bag.

Gladys gasped for air as she carefully stepped out of the door, sideways. The prison suit fell to the bottom of the bag, since very few inmates had been released.

"Sign here!" said the jailer.

The Negro woman shuffled to the counter. "Wheres?" she asked, looking at the form.

"Here!" he said, pointing to the signature line close to the bottom of the third and last page.

Gladys Hightower headed toward the door. "Hey!" the jailer yelled. She stopped and turned. "Don't come back!" he said, pointing in a threatening posture.

"Huh!" Gladys huffed as she stepped into the morning light. A small bird flew from the doorway as she opened it, and a stray dog trotted up the street. The morning was heavy with dew. The small patch of grass between the jail and the sidewalk was sparkling with the dew drops. A late brown cricket scurried ahead of her down the walkway.

There was no one to pick her up, not a car on the street. Somewhere a tower clock chimed for the seven o'clock hour. The sturdy bench provided by the city of Newnan was covered with the heavy dew, so she tried to resist sitting on it. Eventually the foot pain created by the poorly fitting dress shoes and the concrete changed her mind. Her heavy body could feel every dew drop as it wicked through the dress, chilling her skin.

The tower clock eventually signaled another hour passing. A knee-high fog hung over the ground. "Eight o'clock," she thought. She sat with her arms crossed at first, looking up the street and then down. There was not a sound except for the activity in the jail behind her, and only that which escaped through the open windows behind the heavy steel bars. The morning sun eventually flooded the back street, erasing many of the deep shadows. Her eyes spotted what she thought was a pay phone across the street, hiding in the shadowy inset of an old warehouse building. Gladys Hightower waddled toward the telephone as she dug for a dime in her purse. Her opinion about her son was changing with every step, thinking about how he had left her standing on the sidewalk. "Gwine ta gives him a piece of my minds," she mumbled. The six-inch high curb seemed taller today than when she had come in to the jail. "Maybe it was that thin mattress and the woven steel straps spring loaded on each end, sorry excuse for a bed," she thought, pushing herself up onto the sidewalk from the cobblestone street.

The coin dropped into the smooth slit and fell through several mechanical switches, giving a signal to the local operator.

"Operator!" a voice said.

"I'ze needs ta beez connected to Theo Jackson between Wahm Sprungs and Manschester," said Gladys.

"One moment, please," the operator said. Gladys could hear others in the background waiting on callers.

The telephone rang several times before it was answered. "Hello!" Rhonda said.

"A call to Theo Jackson," said the operator.

"I'll take it," Rhonda said.

"You're connected," replied the operator, as she hung up.

"Theo Jackson's Hog Farm," greeted Rhonda.

"Where yo' ass at?" Gladys shouted.

"Here at the house," replied the daughter.

"I'ze ups heres on de street! I'ze wuz ta beez picked up!" Gladys yelled.

Rhonda held the telephone away from her head, as her angry mother yelled.

"Theo knows you're ta be picked up. He's making rounds toward you. I'm surprised he's not there, maybe he's got a heavy load," Rhonda said.

"I beez waitin'," said Gladys, slamming the receiver to its hook. "Sorry, sawn!" she mumbled to herself, as she headed back to the damp bench. The back of her dress was wet, where it touched the wooden bench. Gladys stopped halfway of the street. She sniffed the air for a foul odor coming from somewhere. Before she reached the curb at the jail, she heard Theo's truck.

The Fargo truck pulled the slight grade in second as Theo tried not to slosh his load onto the street. The police had gotten after him once for splashing the spoiled slop on the city streets. It seemingly lay and stunk in the sun, regardless of the weather. The brakes squealed as Theo brought the loaded truck to a stop. The horrid odor drifted. "Mornin'!" Theo said, smiling.

Gladys kicked the front truck tire as best she could with her thin poorly fitting dress shoes. "Wheres yo' beens? Keeps yo' ass out of jail and yous do me dis' away!" she said, hurrying around to the passenger side. Gladys eventually worked herself into the cab. She held the door closed with her arm, since her butt pushed against it. "Sorry, sorry, just plain sorry!" she said, looking at her son in disgust.

"The trial is Monday," Theo said, trying to ignore her angry insults.

The slop loaded truck pulled into the yard about fifteen minutes before good dark. This left only Sunday for Gladys to get her clothes ready for the trial on Monday. Sunday was a bad day around the small house. Isaac Pittman's black Cadillac entered the yard about eight o'clock. The few chickens scurried about as the large car pulled up to the front porch. Pittman had not changed anything but his shirts since he had been on the case. Today he wore a pale yellow shirt, complete with laundry folds, which formed large squares. His gray hair contrasted against the pale shirt. His pants sagged around the top, being supported by the fading striped suspenders.

"Who dat?" Gladys asked Theo, who was sitting in the small front room.

"It's my attuhney," he answered.

"Lawd, haves mussy! I ain't even dressed fo' company," Gladys replied, as she began to hurry about getting herself presentable.

Isaac Pittman had not been to the farm before. He soon covered his nose with his handkerchief as though he had a cold. He closed the car door and headed up the porch steps. Theo opened the door before he could knock.

"Mornin'!" Theo greeted. "Come in," he added, holding the screen door open. Isaac Pittman hurried inside, hoping the odor did not follow him into the house.

"Thank you, we've got to discuss the case," said Isaac, shaking hands with Theo and smiling at Rhonda, who was reading a magazine in the sitting room.

"Have a seat," said Theo. "Gladys will be out eventually."

Isaac Pittman sat down in a red oil cloth upholstered chair. He set his leather briefcase at his feet. "Trial's Monday. We need to be there and in our seats by 8:30," he said, removing the handkerchief from his nose. Theo sat across from him on a dark green sofa. A framed picture of Jesus hung over the sofa. It came from a magazine, but Isaac Pittman could not make it out from where he sat, just the indications of a magazine's name in the lower corner. He chuckled. "Where was He when you did all this stuff?" he laughed. Theo was not catching the humor in the remark. He sat stone-faced and silent.

"As you've told me in the past, you did take James Lee to the Miller place and let him out. You did put him up in your barn loft and give him food and drink, and you were aware of the fact that he was wanted by the sheriff," Isaac Pittman said. "You did tell me that?"

"I did," replied Theo.

Gladys could be heard shuffling about in the other room, getting herself presentable for the attorney. "I'ze beez out in a few minutes," she called out to the attorney.

411

"You take your time," he called back politely. "God, I hope I'm gone before she comes out, unless she's got money in her hand," Isaac thought to himself.

"They have charged you with these crimes because you were a party to them. You helped James Lee achieve these horrendous deeds. If you'd called the law and got out of the way and they had captured him, everyone would be ahead of the game," Isaac Pittman said. "Uh!" he groaned, shaking his head. "They are working off of 16-2-20. Any party who did not directly commit the crime, but was involved with the achieving or completion, is as guilty as the man that did the deed, and held accountable, just like the person who directly committed the crime. If you drove the car and waited on the gunman to go inside and hold up the business, then you're as guilty as the gunman," he said.

Theo wiped his brow with his red railroad style handkerchief. He was clean and dressed in newer bibbed overalls and a white shirt. His body had the powerful fragrance of some clove and ginger based concoction. "Oh, my" he said, folding his handkerchief.

"I'll be in the kitchen," Rhonda said, as she excused herself. "I'll fix some fresh tea." She gracefully left the room.

"Do you know what duress means?" asked Isaac Pittman.

"Down and out, hard up," Theo said.

"That's close," replied the attorney. "That's the defense we're taking. I hope I can meet with the Judge and the solicitor and keep it out of court. That's not a guarantee," he said. "Do you have a Sunday suit?" asked Isaac Pittman.

"No," replied Theo. "Just good overalls and a white shirt. Do I need to wear a necktie?" he asked.

"That will be fine, if you have one," replied the attorney. "Tell your mother I'm sorry I missed her. She owes me money and it's due in the morning. She pays up or I walk," he said, standing.

"Yes, sir!" replied Theo, as he showed the attorney to the front door.

"Remember, tomorrow at 8:30. Walk in the front door, bailiff or not. I'll be there," said Isaac Pittman. He drove off thinking how lucky he was to have escaped Gladys.

* * *

Heather spent the rest of the day Sunday in her room. She spent time on the girly things, keeping herself with a neat feminine touch. She even dusted her room a little more thoroughly than Mrs. Blakely had done. She gave herself a pedicure and painted her nails a bright red. Home loomed in the background of her thoughts. She remembered the long straight section in the dirt road that passed the home house. Her grandfather's picture came to mind. She smiled with misty eyes. "He must have been quite a character," she thought to herself. The light lace curtains that covered the windows in her room floated on the gentle breeze. Every suit was brushed and lay neatly across the bed. She even polished her shoes that Buddy had missed.

The trip downstairs to the closed store yielded a pint of vanilla ice cream, some of the finest around. It was made by Moore's. The mascot was a royal looking sentry, black pants, red jacket, and a bear skin hat. There were no evening meals on Sundays at the boarding house. Most everything in town was closed, so the men boarders ate cold items, meats, crackers, beer. The pint of ice cream was hers. She thought of how much Grandmother Margaret liked good vanilla. The evening sun gradually set in and the soft darkness of night filled the room. The electric advertising signs that hung in the store fronts lit the sidewalks with their combinations of colors. From Heather's window she heard a whip-poor-will calling in the woods a short distance behind the boarding house. The dark sky was eventually filled with bright stars and Monday morning finally came.

Theo Jackson, Gladys, and Rhonda drove into Greenville in the empty Fargo truck. The slop tubs were gone and Rhonda sat in a short-legged chair held against the cab with a cotton rope. Gladys sat in the cab with the door held tightly under her arm. Theo was driving. Isaac Pittman said he would be there, and he was. He stood on the sidewalk awaiting their arrival. The attorney held a parking spot next to his Cadillac. The tall man stood grinning, baring his bad teeth.

"Good morning!" He greeted his client in the loaded truck. He offered windblown Rhonda a hand. "We're here as ordered by the court, follow me in the front door," Isaac said, as they walked down the shady sidewalk.

CHAPTER TWENTY-SEVEN

The racist mob had gone about their business elsewhere, but the Negroes still gathered in support of the Miller family. Their numbers were as strong as ever. The balcony was already full, and others were waiting for their turn to sit and listen. This black on black trial did not matter to the racist group.

Alfred Huffman of the Vindicator hurried toward the courthouse with a stack of morning newspapers. "Ink's still stinky," he said, holding them out to passersby. "STATE VS THEO JACKSON! ACCOMPLICE!" he shouted, selling the papers quickly. Detective Duncan and Officer Jasper Brown walked toward the front steps, where Alfred hustled to sell his craft. The line of citizens was solid all the way back to the sidewalk. Alfred saw the female detective ahead. Her neatness and beauty excited him, creating a bright spot in his day.

"Here," Alfred said, holding out a newspaper to Heather. She looked at it. "It's free, me ta you," he said, smiling.

Jasper grabbed it. "Thanks!" he said to the young man.

Sheriff Gilbert had swapped out deputies, giving those who had been bailiffs last time a chance to get back on the road. The new group was excited to work the trial. Sheriff Gilbert had relaxed his armament to just his sidearm. This time he had pulled a soft gray suit out of mothballs, but his fedora was the same. It was a stark contrast to his suit. He stood at the top of the front steps greeting the public. Heather and Jasper soon worked their way to him in small steps. "Can I count on you two?" he asked, extending his hand to Jasper who was first, and then Heather.

"Always!" replied Jasper, as he shook the sheriff's hand. Heather shook hands and smiled as she passed.

"Is that her?" someone was heard to say.

"That's the one," replied the sheriff.

414

The Jackson crowd had already taken their seats. Isaac Pittman asked that the row behind the defense table be reserved for Gladys and Rhonda. The presence of blacks on the main floor of the courtroom generated curious looks among the locals. Ambrose Watkins hurried in from a side door off of the hall. He placed his briefcase on the table and began to pull out heavy stacks of papers. Ambrose had little to say to Isaac Pittman. The air around the defense table carried a faint scent of peppermint and Theo's cologne. All the windows were open, and the morning was quite pleasant, a gentle breeze blowing almost continually. Gladys was already working a hand fan. She turned to look at the blacks in the balcony. Her large wandering eyes were unable to detect a single person who had supported the cause during the fundraiser to get her Theo out of jail. Nevertheless, he was bonded out. Rhonda, as well as her mother, sat on the hard, polished bench and seemed to want to slide forward. The roundness of their butts certainly did not fit the sharp corner where the seat and the back joined.

"All rise!" cried a bailiff, from the side of the judicial bench.

The standing of the full house generated noise. Judge Erastus Cobb walked into the courtroom and climbed the steps to his chair. "Please be seated!" he said.

"The Superior Court of Meriwether County, Jaw-ga is now in session, under the authority of Judge Erastus Cobb," said the other bailiff. Sheriff Gilbert sat next to Doc Hubbard, along the side wall. The two men frequently whispered.

"I'll ask you to stop the side talk the first time I'm able to hear what you say," said the Judge, looking at the two.

"Sorry, your Honor," replied the sheriff. "Talkin' about the case," he added.

"My ass!" said Judge Cobb. "Crops, watermelons, fried chicken, socials, and women," he said, smiling. The courtroom had a good laugh. "Settle down," said the Judge. He struck the gavel. "This is the State of Georgia versus Theo Jackson. He is charged with being an accomplice in the James Lee crimes. Being that he assisted, Georgia law provides that he can be charged with the same crimes as James Lee," he explained. "This trial like any other is important, and we will follow rules of order and the safety of the accused will be at all cost," he added. The Judge leaned back and began to quickly read over the case file. The defense and the solicitor sat quietly, both ready to begin.

"Mr. Theo Jackson, do you understand what you are charged with?" asked the Judge. Gladys began to move about as though she were going to speak. The gavel was quickly struck. "Mrs. Hightower! I remind you again that there will be NO outburst in this court," said the Judge, pointing his finger at the large woman. She looked down at the floor.

"Once again, Defense, how do you wish to plead?" the Judge asked.

The chair scrubbed as Theo Jackson stood, along with Isaac Pittman.

"We enter a plea of not guilty," Pittman responded.

"Yes, Judge," Theo agreed.

"Very well," said Judge Cobb. "The jury selection is next. All those called for jury duty, please stand." There were some forty mixed men that stood. "Jury selection is expected to take a few hours. If you were not called for jury duty and wish to leave the building, please do so now. If you were called for jury duty, please work your way to the front rows," the Judge said loudly. The roar of the crowd eventually subsided as citizens left the courtroom.

"I'd suggest that you enjoy the square, as it will be a long and tiring day," said Judge Cobb to Gladys and Rhonda. They spoke to Theo and Isaac Pittman, and then left to wander about in the shops.

"Law enforcement officers, please come to the bench," called out the Judge.

Jasper rolled his eyes. "This has got ta be trouble," he whispered to Heather, as they stood.

The bailiffs and the sheriff, along with the two Warm Springs officers, stood at the Judge's bench. "There's a room for you in the hallway, Room 103. There's a radio and refreshments. I'd like to be able to find you there," said Judge Cobb.

"My officers will be in the courtroom during any official business," said Sheriff Gilbert.

Jasper and Heather were excited about having a secluded place to hang out. They hurried down the dimly lit hall to find the room.

There were a varied number of professions represented in the list of jurors, along with a good spread of income levels. They ranged from suit and tie men to bibbed overalls. The interview and selection of jurors took until one o'clock, with the solicitor and defense lawyer asking questions of all forty potential jurors. The selection was reduced to twelve jurors and three alternates. The three alternates, two whites and Adam Favors, a Negro, were separated from the twelve. Judge Cobb was already seeing a lengthy trial based on the time required to select a jury. The clock in the tower rang out the hour when the bailiff was sent to get the officers from Room 103. The second bailiff went to the courthouse steps, where he blew his brass whistle and waved his hands, motioning that court was about to begin. The dull roar of the gathering citizens once more filled the hallways and courtroom.

"All rise!" cried a bailiff from the judicial bench. "Court is now in session!"

Gladys and Rhonda were the last two to come in. Judge Cobb tried not to show his impatience with the large woman and her tardiness. She eventually took her seat behind the defense table. Judge Cobb motioned for a bailiff to pull the window shades down on the west side of the room.

"Now," said the Judge, leaning back in his seat. "Are the defense and the state unanimous in the jury selection?"

"We are!" replied both men.

"Very well," said Judge Cobb. "Solicitor Watkins, the floor is yours." The Judge made eye contact with the stenographer, who indicated she was ready.

"The State calls Theo Jackson," said Watkins. "Just a moment. Bailiff, are all the subpoenaed parties here?" asked the Judge.

"They are, your Honor. They were checked off at the doors upon entry. There are several who weren't subpoenaed, as well," a bailiff answered.

"Thank you," said Judge Cobb. "Proceed with your opening statement," he added, looking at Solicitor Watkins.

"The State will place the defendant, Theo Jackson, with the accused, James Lee. We will show that he gave him shelter and assisted in the transporting of James Lee to murder the woman and her infant," said Watkins, as he stood center of the bench, looking at the jury. "We, the State, will show that the efforts of Theo Jackson," Watkins pointed to the Negro. "AFFORDED James Lee the opportunity to commit these heinous acts!" He moved about, as he spoke loudly and distinctly. "May we read from the interrogation of Theo Jackson, as done by Sheriff Gilbert's qualified officers, what was admitted by Theo Jackson?" Watkins asked the Judge.

"If it is relevant, please do so," the Judge replied.

The stenographer proceeded to read from the interrogation.

"Did you know James Lee was wanted?" asked Sheriff Gilbert.

"Yes," replied Theo Jackson.

"How did you know that?" asked the sheriff.

"I heard it on the radio, and read about the escape in the Vindicator," answered Theo Jackson.

"How did you discover James Lee in your barn?" asked the sheriff.

"I was workin' in the barn when he -- " said Jackson.

"He who?" asked the sheriff.

"James Lee. He made himself known to me. He was in my loft," answered Theo Jackson.

"So, James Lee, the wanted criminal, was in your barn," said the sheriff. "Do you own your property, the hog farm?" asked the sheriff.

"Yes," answered Jackson.

"How long did this go on?" asked the sheriff.

"About a week," replied Jackson.

"Hold up, there!" said Watkins, loudly. "The escaped prisoner was in the care of the defense for about a week, per his own admittance." Walking to the other side of the jury box, he signaled the stenographer to continue reading.

"You gave him food, drink, and shelter during this time," said the sheriff.

"Yes!" replied Jackson.

"During this time, how many times did you go and come from the hog farm, with the opportunity to contact law enforcement?" asked the sheriff.

"Out and back, every day except Sunday," replied Jackson.

"Say, 'bout six to eight times?" asked the sheriff.

"Yes," said Jackson.

"So, the defendant sitting right there," Watkins pointed to Theo Jackson. He followed his finger quickly to within inches of Theo Jackson's face, where he sat next to his attorney. "This adult Negro, right here! In his mind, qualified enough to run a successful hog farm, but NOT willing to contact the law!" he barked. "The State rests."

Judge Cobb sat silent for a moment. It was as though his mind had wandered, perhaps to a good cigar and a brandy, or a shaded fishing hole. "Mr. Pittman, the floor is yours."

Pittman rose slowly and cleared his throat loudly. "The Defense will forgo the opening argument."

"Solicitor, you may call your first witness," said Judge Cobb.

"I call Sheriff Louis Gilbert to the stand!" Solicitor Watkins said, as he got to his feet.

The sheriff hurried to the witness box, where he turned and raised his right hand.

"Do you swear to tell the truth, the whole truth, and nothing but the truth, so help you God?" asked the bailiff.

"I do," replied the sheriff. He took the stand.

"Sheriff, the stenographer just read a portion of the interrogation as transcribed, done by yourself and other officers. Is this a true account of what you heard the defendant say?" asked Watkins.

"It is," answered the sheriff.

"If your department had been contacted early, let's say at first, would it have saved the lives of two people?" asked the solicitor.

"Objection! Not relevant, opinion!" barked Isaac Pittman.

"I uphold that motion," replied the Judge.

"Nothing further," replied Watkins.

"Cross-examine?" the Judge asked Pittman.

Isaac Pittman walked up to the sheriff. "Did my client tell you that James Lee had a gun?" he asked.

"He did," replied the sheriff.

"Did my client express to you that he was afraid of James Lee?" Pittman asked, leaning on the witness stand.

"I don't recall," replied Sheriff Gilbert.

"Nothing else, your Honor." Pittman took his seat.

"State calls Detective Duncan!" said Watkins.

Heather worked her way to the witness stand, where she too was sworn in. "State your name and capacity with your agency," said Watkins.

"Detective Heather Duncan, Warm Springs Police Department, as the title says, detective, and a Special Deputy for the Meriwether County Sheriff's Department, when pertaining to the case of James Lee," she said.

"On the morning of Theo Jackson's arrest, were there any problems?" asked Watkins.

"Yes, sir!" Heather said loud and clear.

"Oh, what were they?" Watkins asked.

"When law enforcement arrived, we were met by Gladys Hightower, who identified herself as Theo Jackson's mother. She said he wasn't there. Chief Howard Hawthorn with our department had to take her down so the house could be searched. We found Theo Jackson in the well house, hiding behind the pump, in the dark."

"And the sister, Rhonda?" asked Watkins.

"Very cooperative," the detective replied.

"That's all," said Watkins.

"Cross-examine?" the Judge asked Pittman.

"Nothing of this witness," Pittman replied.

"Very well," said Watkins. "State calls Moses Finley!"

Moses Finley was way up in the balcony. He began to work his way down the row of seated blacks.

"Any other blacks to witness, please follow Mr. Finley down. This takes time from the Court." Bo Bob Higgins got up with the assistance of his eldest son and came down with Moses Finley to the main floor.

"Make room for these people!" said the Judge. The Hightowers moved over to make room on their bench for the two men.

"Mr. Finley, up there," Heather said politely to the old man. She motioned for him to come forward and sit closer. He looked surprised but changed his location as quickly as possible.

"State calls Moses Finley!" Watkins repeated. The old Negro shuffled his way to the witness stand.

"Mr. Finley, raise your right hand," said the bailiff.

Moses Finley raised his right hand, but then looked closely at the bailiff. "Yous de Wilkerson boy, ain't yous?" he asked, leaning toward the bailiff.

"Yes, sir!" whispered the bailiff.

"I'ze knowed yo' granddaddy," Moses said.

"Mr. Finley!" called the Judge. "Keep us moving along, please," he said, smiling and shaking his head at the old man.

"Do you swear to tell the truth, the whole truth, and nothing but the truth, so help you God?" asked the bailiff.

"I do!" said the old Negro, as he took his seat.

Ambrose Watkins walked to the stand. "How do you know the Millers?" he asked.

"I'ze de neighbor, wuhked fo' 'em toos!" he said. "Long times," he added.

"Tell the Court how you found Mrs. Miller and the little girl?" said Watkins.

"I hurd a shots in de night. Next mornin' I comes out of de house and de old dawg wuz on my do' steps. I walked downs ta see 'bout Miss Gertrude," said Moses.

"By Miss Gertrude, you mean Gertrude Miller?" asked Watkins.

"Yes, suhs!" Moses answered.

"What does this have to do with my client?" interrupted Isaac Pittman.

"I'm showing the brutality of the crime and hope to establish the fact that without the help of Theo Jackson it might not have happened, and if it did eventually happen, it would have possibly been a while longer," replied Ambrose Watkins, showing his impatience.

"Go ahead!" said Judge Cobb, slipping a candy from his drawer.

"What did you see?" asked Watkins.

"Miss Gertrude wuz deed next to de little gull. De blood was awful," said Moses. He began to sob.

"Thank you. That is all," said Watkins.

Defense Attorney Pittman approached Moses Finley. Finley's eyes were keen, though dimmed by age. His old eyes took in the stranger before him.

"Mr. Finley!" Pittman said sharply. Finley jumped. There were a few chuckles in the audience, but Judge Cobb's gavel quickly struck and his eyes expressed a seriousness understood by all.

"How's your eyesight?" Pittman asked. "Can you tell me with detail what colors are in the necktie of the large man there on the back row, in the brown striped suit?"

Moses Finley narrowed his eyes and squinted. "GA 348 dash 773, soft gray background and black words," he said loudly.

Pittman looked about for this GA 348-733. "What?" he asked.

"Yonder, Ford at de curb, cross de street." Moses grinned, looking up the aisle and out the open courtroom doors.

Pittman hurried up the aisle to see for himself. Judge Cobb sat quietly, with a large grin on his face. Moses sat straight and smiled serenely. "Well, I see your vision is good," Pittman said, now back at the witness stand. "My original question, please."

"Yeller background, navy stripes, and red ones too," Moses said.

Pittman's anger was obvious in his face. "No further questions!" he exclaimed, slapping the high front rail of the witness stand.

"Mr. Finley, you may step down," said Pittman.

"State calls once more Detective Duncan," said Watkins.

"Detective, tell us what you found when you, as officers say, cleared the barn?" Watkins asked. He took a stand at the jury box.

"Officer Brown and I were clearing the barn, that's making sure there's no one of a threat capacity in the building. I found a dollar bill in the loft. We searched the serial number and found that it was a recorded serial number for the Troup County burglary of a store owned by Benjamin Hill," she said.

"What relevance?" Attorney Pittman shouted.

"The state will tie James Lee to it!" Watkins said, pointing to Pittman.

"Go ahead," said judge Cobb.

"Sheriff Ector and the case deputy advised that the serial number was one of the small bills that the store owner always left in the cash drawer. That was the location where torch cut restraints were found in the weeds around the work shed at the side of the store. There were numerous other small things that tied James Lee to the burglary," said Heather.

"So, a prudent person, a reasonable man, would be led to place James Lee at the burglary of Benjamin Hill's store in Troup County, and say that that identified dollar bill placed James Lee in the barn loft of Theo Jackson," said Watkins.

"That's correct," said Heather.

Watkins stepped to his table where he picked up a brown envelope that contained the found dollar bill. "I'd like to admit this into evidence," he said, as he carefully opened the metal clasp on the sealed envelope. The bill fell toward the envelope, meeting his waiting fingers. "Is this the dollar bill?" Watkins asked Heather, as he handed it to her. She looked at it carefully.

"I'd have to refer to my filed notes for the exact serial number," she said, moving her hand toward her suit coat pocket.

"Go ahead," Watkins replied, waiting patiently.

Heather hurriedly turned through the spiral bound pocket tablet. "Yes, that is the one found in the loft," she replied.

"You may cross," said Watkins to Pittman.

Pittman stood and thought for a moment. "Nothing at this time, right to recall," he said.

"You may step down," said Judge Cobb.

"The state calls Dr. Augustus Hubbard," said Watkins, looking around for the doctor, who was also the county coroner.

Dr. Hubbard appeared from the hallway door, which stood ajar. In moments he stood at the witness box. The doctor turned and raised his right hand. "Do you swear to tell truth, the whole truth, and nothing but the truth, so help you God?" asked the bailiff.

"I do," replied the doctor. He took the stand.

"State your full name and occupation, including any positions held here in the county," said Watkins, as he leaned forward at his table, resting on his elbows.

"Augustus Samuel Hubbard, local doctor of internal medicine and elected county coroner," he replied. His face was flushed from drinking the evening before. "Coroner, I think three terms," he added.

"What caliber of bullet did you recover from the deceased, Gertrude Miller?" asked Watkins.

"A .38 caliber pistol ball," Dr. Hubbard quickly replied.

"Were there any other disturbing attributes to her death?" asked Watkins, as he sat back in his chair.

"Objection, relevance!" shouted Pittman. He was so sudden and loud, Theo Jackson jumped.

"I want to hear this," said Judge Cobb. "Go ahead," he said, looking at the coroner.

"Gertrude Miller and her infant daughter were bludgeoned with a fire poker, to the point of a closed casket," Dr. Hubbard replied, looking down and flicking his fingernails. "It was bad," he added.

"That is all, cross," Watkins said.

Isaac Pittman stood for a moment and then walked to the witness box. "Are you known to drink?" Pittman asked the coroner.

"I am," replied Dr. Hubbard.

"Does this hinder your ability to make sound decisions?" asked Pittman, as he looked at the jury.

"No!" replied Dr. Hubbard.

Pittman jumped in surprise at the answer. "And why do you feel this doesn't affect your ability?" he asked.

"It helps steady my hand," said the doctor.

"Haven't you been observed sleeping on a bench, here on the square?" Pittman asked quickly, making eye contact with the doctor.

"Everybody has ta sleep somewhere," the doctor replied. There was laughter in the courtroom.

Judge Cobb sounded his gavel, smiling at the answer himself.

The cross-examination gave Watkins a witty thought.

"That's all!" Pittman said, taking his seat.

"State calls Bo Bob Huggins!" barked Watkins.

"Here!" Bo Bob called out, as he stood.

Bo Bob was dressed in his Sunday best. He even had a red rosebud displayed in his lapel. Watkins met the old Negro and guided him to the witness stand. "Raise your right hand," Watkins whispered. It took the old man two attempts to get the correct hand up, first it was his left and then his right.

"Do you swear to tell the truth, the whole truth, and nothing but the truth, so help you God?" asked the bailiff.

"I do," replied Bo Bob.

"Be seated," said the bailiff.

"Mr. Huggins, what was your occupation up until about a month or so ago?" asked the solicitor.

"I'ze wuz de lead trustee in de county jail," said Bo Bob. "Nod that I'ze proud of it, buts everybody gots ta beezs sumwheres."

"And why did your situation change?" asked Watkins, standing close to the witness box.

"De bad Nigger James Lee escaped and beats meez bad, left meez fo' dead," replied the Negro.

"Whose skilled hand examined you and stitched ya up?" asked Watkins.

Bo Bob pointed his leathery, crooked fingers at Doc Hubbard. "He did."

"Objection!" shouted Pittman. "What has this to do with the case?" he asked.

"I want to hear this," said Judge Cobb. "Go ahead," he said, looking at the solicitor.

"Did you almost go blind?" Watkins asked.

"I'ze sho' did," Bo Bob replied.

"Tell us about it," Watkins said, leaning close to the Negro.

"Doc Hubbards saw in mize eyes de problem. He gots mize eyes checked. Drove me hisself to de special doctor. He sewed up my cuts at de kitchen table. I put down a pint and then he took a shot or twos, we finally got the fixin' done," Bo Bob said, gently rubbing his head that still had soft scars.

"That's all, your Honor," said Watkins. "Cross!" he said loudly.

Pittman stood. "Nothing at this time," he said.

Judge Cobb struck his gavel. "Recess for ten minutes!"

Loud moans came from the citizens that had been seated for a long while. Many hurried out to smoke, while others headed for the restrooms, where a line quickly formed.

* * *

"Three Minutes!" cried out the bailiffs. The courtroom began to fill.

"Court is now in session!" called a bailiff. "All rise!" Judge Cobb hurried to the bench.

"Be seated!" the Judge said. "Call the next witness."

"Officer Jasper Brown!" said the solicitor.

Jasper looked surprised, but hurried to the witness stand. He raised his right hand. "Do you swear to tell the truth, the whole truth, and nothing but the truth, so help you God?" asked the bailiff.

"I do," replied Jasper. He took the stand.

"When did you discover the tracks that matched up with the truck driven by the defendant?" asked Watkins.

"The morning after the bodies were found," Jasper answered.

"Who assisted in this?" asked Watkins.

Isaac Pittman sat quietly, knowing better by now than to object, based on all his prior attempts.

"I was asked to scout the orchard by Detective Duncan. I took three longtime employees of the Millers with me. That was one Negro man, Oscar, Billy Bishop, and Mrs. Loretta," Jasper said. "They had all worked the orchards, and even the layout of the fences and the planting of the earlier trees."

"What did you find?" asked Watkins.

"They knew it was time to manure the peach trees, so they took me to that portion of the orchard. There we found indication of a set of tire tracks in the crushed grass and the dirt trails, with the measured width, both outside to outside of the tires, but the tire width and the tread pattern matched that of the truck driven by Theo Jackson," he said.

"Are those employees in the courtroom?" Watkins asked.

"Yes. Stand up!" Jasper said, pointing to Oscar first, up in the balcony. Oscar stood. Then Jasper called Billy Bishop and Mrs. Loretta, and they stood up too. "That's them," said Jasper.

"So that, those findings would lead a reasonable man to believe that Theo Jackson was in the orchard delivering manure," asked Watkins. "Yes," replied Jasper.

"Cross-examine," said Watkins, as he returned to his seat.

Isaac Pittman stood and rubbed his chin in thought. He walked to the jury and looked about for a moment, then turned to Jasper. "Did my client ever admit to saying he didn't deliver a load of manure on the evening in question?" Pittman asked.

"I don't know, sir. That's more of a question for Sheriff Gilbert's office. They did an in-depth interview with Jackson," said Jasper. Heather was proud of Jasper not cowering down to the attorney.

"Thank you, you may step down," said Pittman. "Mr. Watkins, Judge, may I deviate from protocol and call a witness?" asked Pittman.

The solicitor flipped a number two pencil, eraser over point, several times in deep thought for consideration. Judge Cobb looked at Watkins. "State is allowing deviation, if approved by the Court," Watkins replied.

"Court gives way," Judge Cobb said, with open hand extended toward the defense attorney.

"Defense calls Sheriff Gilbert!"

Sheriff Gilbert took the stand. "Remember, you're still sworn," said Pittman. The sheriff nodded, acknowledging his swearing. "The question was, did my client ever admit to saying he didn't deliver a load of manure on the evening in question?" asked Pittman.

"No, he never denied going there to the peach orchard on that date," said the sheriff.

"That's all!" barked Pittman. He walked away.

"You may step down," said the Judge. He looked at his watch. "It is getting late. We will pick up again at nine o'clock in the morning," he said, striking the gavel.

"Tomorrow, same time, same door," said Isaac Pittman, gathering up his papers.

"It's not looking good," said Theo.

"There's always tomorrow. I've got a plan," replied Pittman.

* * *

"All rise!" cried a bailiff from the side of the judicial bench. "The Superior Court of Meriwether County is now in session." Judge Cobb took the bench once again.

"If we do not finish today, I will need a day long recess for tomorrow, as the convicted James Lee was promised his sentencing. I will not keep a guilty man waiting," said Judge Cobb. He started the morning out with a soft stick of peppermint. "State, call your first witness!" he said, leaning back in his chair.

Solicitor Ambrose Watkins stood. "Judge, the State was about to advise that we have called all our witnesses when you called for a recess last evening. I am ready to present closing to the jury," he said.

"And Mr. Pittman, are you needing to call or cross-examine any more witnesses?" asked Judge Cobb.

"I'd like to put my client on the stand," Pittman replied.

"That is unusual, do you really think it advisable?" asked Judge Cobb.

"I do," replied the defense attorney.

"Very well," replied the Judge, taking a small bite of the soft stick candy.

"The defense calls Theo Jackson," said Pittman, who was already standing at the witness box.

Theo Jackson looked surprised, but he hurried toward the stand. Theo raised his right hand.

"Do you swear to tell the truth, the whole truth, and nothing but the truth, so help you God?" asked the bailiff.

"I do," replied Theo Jackson. He took the stand. Jackson had worn the same clothes, only changing his necktie.

"Do you know James Lee?" asked Pittman.

"I do," replied Jackson.

"How long?" Pittman asked.

"Off and on 'bout seven years," Jackson replied. He wiped his face with his white handkerchief.

"What was your relationship?" asked Pittman, moving about in front of the jury.

"We had worked together time ta time. Latest was at the Miller Orchard. James worked there, I had the hog farm," stuttered Jackson.

"Were you afraid of James Lee?" asked the attorney.

"He was bullish, pushy ta get his way," Jackson said.

"When you found him in your barn, were you afraid of his actions if you didn't cooperate?" asked Pittman.

Theo Jackson thought for a minute. "Yes," he replied, looking down.

"I ask again. Did you feel that James Lee would do you serious bodily injury if you didn't help him?" asked Pittman.

Theo Jackson thought for a minute. "Yes," he replied, looking up in the balcony at all the Negroes.

"That is all, your Honor," said Pittman. "Cross!" he yelled out, as he passed Watkins sitting at the State's table. Pittman returned to the defense table, but before sitting down he looked at Gladys Hightower who was behind him. He pointed his finger and turned red in the face. "Shut up!" he said, gritting his teeth, before he sat down. Gladys gave a loud huff. Pittman turned and looked at her again, shaking his head.

Watkins stood quickly and hurried to the bench. He put both hands on the edge of the witness box and looked into the large brown eyes of the Negro. "Just how big are you?" he barked.

"Objection! Not relevant, opinion!" barked Isaac Pittman.

"I uphold that motion," replied the Judge.

"I argue that it is relevant, your Honor. May I?" asked Watkins.

"Very well," replied the Judge. "But it better show relevance!"

"'Bout five foots eight and 320 pounds," Jackson answered.

"Whoo, a big boy! I'd say if you had a mind to, ya could take most any of these deputies in here. Well, except for the Warm Springs detective. She's got a damn mean kick!" Watkins said, waving his arms about as he walked up and down in front of the bench. "Sheriff, can ya cuff this big boy?" Watkins asked.

"It'd be a chore," the sheriff replied.

The Judge picked up the gavel. "Get to the point!" he said to Watkins.

"James Lee's half your size. And you were scared of him?" asked the solicitor, looking fiercely at Jackson. "Let me do something unusual, with the Court's permission. That's ask a single question from a sworn person in the audience," asked Watkins.

"Mr. Pittman?" asked Judge Cobb, looking at the attorney.

"A single one!" Pittman replied, wiping his face fiercely.

"State calls to the floor Detective Duncan," Watkins said loudly.

Heather rose to her feet. "What did you reflect in your report that you found in the ground floor of the barn? Did you find a gun on the main floor of the barn?" Watkins asked, pointing to Heather.

"A sawed-off shotgun, but legal length," she answered.

"Thank you!" Watkins replied. Heather took her seat.

"Do you own a shot gun of that description?" asked Watkins of Jackson.

"Yes, sir!" Jackson replied.

"How many?" asked Watkins. "Where do you keep them?" he snapped.

Theo looked at Pittman. Pittman shook his head to answer. "One in tha truck and one in tha barn," Theo Jackson answered.

"James Lee's got a pistol and you had two shotguns. Seems like this could have been alleviated," Watkins barked.

"Counsel! Counsel! Pull your opinions back!" said Judge Cobb, as he struck the gavel.

"Yes, sir!" Watkins said. He walked the floor for a minute or so. "So, your defense is you were acting out of duress?"

Theo Jackson looked surprised. Pittman stood quickly. "Objection!" he shouted.

Watkins touched Jackson on the hand. "Po' thang, I wouldn't want ya to be afraid of someone half your size," he said.

"Objection!" Pittman shouted.

"Are you ready for closing?" asked the Judge, looking at each attorney.

"The State is!" snapped Watkins.

The Judge looked at Pittman. Watkins returned to his seat.

"Yes, your Honor," replied Pittman. "Defense rests."

"Return to your seat," said Judge Cobb to Jackson.

Gladys Hightower made wide-eyed, evil looks at Ambrose Watkins, as she sat with her arms crossed.

"Defense, are you ready?" asked the Judge. "Please go ahead."

Pittman wiped his face with his handkerchief before walking to the jury. "The State has placed my client, Theo Jackson, a business man in this county, at the scene of the crime. We have never said that he wasn't." Pittman put his hands in his pants pockets. "My client is a mild-mannered individual, a follower, NOT a leader. He is one of the playground's nameless rabble, NOT a bully!" Pittman began to move about slowly. The eyes of the jury followed him. "Is it NOT the duty of the State to prove that my client intended to commit these crimes that he is accused of? IS IT NOT?" Pittman said, removing his hands from his pockets and pointing at the jury. "My client was in fear of receiving bodily harm if he did not comply with the desires of the dangerous James Lee," Pittman said. He was silent for a moment. "I ask you to keep in mind the fear my client must have felt during those days when he was housing and feeding James Lee. God's blessing be upon you as you make your decision," he said softly. The attorney returned to his seat.

Ambrose Watkins stood and walked to the jury box. He suddenly spun around, pointing to the jury. "Ever been bullied? Most of ya took it so far, then probably beat the hell out of 'em, didn't you?" he said. Several chuckled. "The State has put Theo Jackson at the scene of the crime, by the fact that he had all KINDS of chances to TELL THE LAW and DIDN'T!" Watkins moved back and forth before the jury. "That man, that healthy MAN, and ARMED, delivered the killer in his work truck to the residence of the deceased, both GERTRUDE MILLER and little POLLY SUE, a mother and her child. SO, he was acting under DURESS. DURESS MY ASS! A cowardly man, a CHICKEN SHIT of a man, that couldn't help prevent the killing of these two dear souls," Watkins said loudly. The blacks in the balcony were visibly shaken; some were heard sobbing. "HE WAS ON THE CRIME SCENE and did NOTHING to help prevent the killing of those two lovely people." Watkins pointed his finger up and down with each word as though he were shooting a gun. His voice grew softer like a Baptist preacher on the last plea for building funds in a half full church. "A COWARD! And did nothing to stop it after he was free of James Lee. A COWARD! Watkins stood with both palms resting on the jury railing. He gave a loud sigh. "He was on the scene; he took the killer to the crime. He did nothing after he was free of the threat. God help you in your decision," he said. Watkins returned to his table. "State rests!" Watkins took his seat.

At this point, Judge Cobb proceeded to read the charges to the jury and give instructions for their deliberations based on state law.

"I'd ask the jury to follow the bailiff and the sheriff to the jury room. Remember, if there's anything you need, a bailiff will be right outside the door," said the Judge, as he stood and struck the gavel. "Court is in recess until the jury reaches a verdict"

* * *

"Let's get a sandwich at the pharmacy and eat it in the room the Judge set up for us," Jasper said, as he and Heather waited in line to get out of the courthouse. They ordered two specials, one chicken and one pimento cheese, and returned to the private room. Sheriff Gilbert was there, having brought something from Becky's Café. Chief Hawthorn stopped by.

The sudden influx of hungry people would create a line at Becky's Café and maybe at the pharmacy. The newspaper reporters were smart, they remained at the back of the courtroom and could tell when a recess was about to happen. They hurried ahead and took seats at the lunch counter. Business was always good when court was in session. The curious citizens often ate a sack lunch from home at their cars or on a bench in the shade around the square.

The heavy raised panel door opened slowly. It was Chief Hawthorn. "How's it goin'?" he asked, standing in front of his two officers. He waved at Sheriff Gilbert who was eating at the far end of the long conference table.

"I think he'll be found guilty," replied Jasper. "The solicitor did a good job, especially at the closing."

"Have a seat," Heather said, pointing to a chair.

"No, I've got to get back in the city. You two are up here playing," Chief Hawthorn said, winking.

"My ass!" Jasper replied. "I been up on the stand several times," he said, pointing to himself with his thumb, bragging.

"Someone let me know, even if you have to call the house," said the chief. He closed the heavy door behind him. As he left, he saw Judge Cobb in his office. The door had not closed all the way. The Judge was busy with a stack of law books, one on top of the other, along with loose papers.

Judge Cobb was quickly absorbed into the sentencing of James Lee. Lee would get everything he could legally put on him. Judge Erastus Cobb already knew the penalty was death, but as always, he read over the law several more times, and even had former cases that were similar pulled from the county files. The old Judge read hurriedly over the law books in front of him. His finger moved down the thin pages quickly. "God damn bastard worked hard ta get what he did. I won't cut him shy of his just reward," he mumbled to himself. He pulled the top left desk drawer open and retrieved a wrinkled paper bag that contained a sandwich and a slice of pound cake. The water pitcher nearby would serve him well, and the shot of bourbon from his pocket flask. Judge Cobb ate while he continued reading. From time to time he picked up a pencil and made notes on a ruled tablet.

The jury deliberated hour after hour, longer than the jury had spent on the fate of James Lee. Each hour sounded with the clock in the tower striking hard and echoing across the hillsides. It was almost three o'clock when a knock broke the Judge's concentration. "Yes!" he called out.

"The jury is ready," said the bailiff, peeking inside the Judge's chambers.

"I'll be right there. Take 'em on in," Judge Cobb said, marking his place with an index card. He stood up, loosened his pants, and tucked his shirt tail in. "Damn," he whispered out loud. He had discovered there was no more orange candy, only hard peppermint. Judge Cobb remained in his chambers until he heard the jury go by. He followed several steps behind. The public was called and began to hurry to their seats. The balcony was hot. The Negroes worked the hand fans from local churches and funeral parlors hard. Some of the handles failed, giving out a sharp crack before the paddles fell to the floor.

Erastus Cobb, as a man, was as ordinary as the next. Out of a suit and his environment, one would have a hard time determining he was a judge. As he walked behind the jury, the sky became overcast, taking the light from the hallway. In his heart, he knew it was the soul of the condemned James Lee leaving, getting a head start. The evil Negro would need it as soon as he was officially told he was to die on the gallows. Judge Cobb felt his decision in his bones. While it was a very dark decision, his heart soon became warm thinking of the two lives James Lee had taken. Judge Cobb shed a tear. It rolled from the corner of his eye to the end of his chin. He caught it with the back of his hand before he could pull his wrinkled handkerchief from his pocket.

Sheriff Gilbert stood in the dark hallway waiting for the jury to enter the courtroom. He saw the eyes of Judge Cobb. "You all right?" he asked, placing his broad hand on the older man's shoulder.

Judge Cobb stopped and looked up into the eyes of the sheriff. He nodded his head indicating that he was, and then blotted his eyes. "Little Polly Sue, little Polly Sue," he began to sob. The sheriff gently closed the door, separating them from the courtroom. Judge Cobb sniffed hard and tried to compose himself

"Give me the papers and I'll kill the sum bitch myself, white or black he's a piece of shit, breathin' too much air," said Sheriff Gilbert. "Too much air," he whispered.

"It's a hard job," said the Judge, as he straightened his tie. He wiped his eyes again. "I'm ready," he said softly.

"All rise!" cried the bailiff. Judge Cobb entered with the sheriff and took the stand.

"I wonder if you rise for me or the respect you have for this Court? I have finalized the fate of James Lee and it disturbs me, but it has to be done," said Judge Cobb. "Gentlemen of the jury, are you ready with your decision?" he asked, looking at the foreman.

"We are, your Honor," said the foreman, as he stood at the rail.

Ambrose Watkins sat with his hands in his lap. He felt he had won another case, taking down both men in the killing spree. The anticipation was tense. Isaac Pittman sat with Theo Jackson, who wiped sweat from his brow. Gladys Hightower created a breeze with her hand fan. She gave out a loud "whew" as she looked at the bench. Her heart raced. Rhonda sat twiddling her thumbs. The Warm Springs officers were backing the handiwork of Ambrose Watkins. They too felt that he had proven the case. Heather especially felt that she had done her job in bringing the killer and his accomplice to justice. Sheriff Gilbert sat next to jailer Curley Jones, who had slipped in to hear the verdict.

"Would you like to tell us, or do you have it sealed and prefer for me to read it?" asked Judge Cobb.

"Read it please, your Honor," the man said, dropping his head. The hearts of all the law enforcement officers pounded.

Judge Cobb made motion for the sealed envelope to be brought to him.

"Here, your Honor," said the bailiff, as he handed off the envelope.

The letter opener kept on the bench sailed through the sharp crease of the envelope's top. The courtroom was silent, only the growling of a nervous stomach and the movement of the hand fans. The outside traffic could be heard through the open windows. Heather watched as the Judge's eyes read the decision to himself and then aloud. "The jury finds that the State has failed to meet the burden of proof in the case of Theo Jackson. NOT guilty," said Judge Cobb. He tossed the paper on the bench and leaned back in his chair.

The sudden release of tension was overwhelming to Theo Jackson. At first, he sat with his mouth open and then held his face in his hands and sobbed. Gladys Hightower jumped to her feet and began to pray, thanking Jesus out loud. Sheriff Gilbert stood in total shock at the decision. He almost became vocal, but Curley Jones pulled the powerful man back into the chair. Ambrose Watkins was in total denial from the loss of the case. The heavy oak gavel earned its keep. Judge Cobb, shocked himself, hammered the gavel over and over, calling the Court to order.

Jasper Brown, sitting next to Heather, gave out a loud, "What?" He sat with his mouth open in disbelief. Heather was stunned. She slowly turned a pale color and began to feel sick. The young woman excused herself from her partner and hurried to the public restroom. The afternoon sunlight struggled to make it through the heavily frosted outside window. It only made a rectangular spot of light on the small white octagonal tile nestled in black grout. Heather hung onto the wall mounted sink and bathed her face in cool water. She went through the dry heaves as she flashed to the Negro woman who had been shot, and her small child lying on the kitchen floor in a blood pool, bludgeoned to death. The woman she could handle, but not the small child. Heather began to cry. The brass doorknob rattled.

"Go away!" Heather cried out. "I'll be a few!" she shouted. Heather ran the water louder.

A faint voice called out. "You all right?" It was Jasper Brown. He stood in front of the women's restroom door, feeling very out of place as people walked by.

"I'll be fine," Heather said.

Jasper stood for a moment or two. "I'll be in the car, when you're ready. They've shut it down," he added.

Judge Cobb had left the bench and was heading to his chambers. He was followed by Sheriff Gilbert. "Can I appeal this? God damn it! Tha sum bitch is guilty! GOD DAMN GUILTY!" he yelled behind the Judge.

"No, and lower your voice!" said the Judge. Ambrose Watkins was already driving off.

Theo Jackson walked beside Isaac Pittman to the shiny Cadillac parked on the curb. "Well young man, you're free," said Pittman, tossing his briefcase into the back seat. The attorney stood and pointed his finger to Theo and Gladys. "There's blacks and whites that didn't take this well. You'd best be alert," he said. He put another mint in his mouth. "My money," he said to Gladys. She started to pull bills from her large sweaty bosom and then from other wrinkles unknown. "Go to the restroom and get up my money, make sure it's dry," he said, in disapproval of her actions there on the sidewalk. "I'll fill out a receipt." Pittman pulled out a receipt book and placed it on the hood of the car. Gladys eventually came back.

"Heah yo' monies!" Gladys said, handing a stack of bills to the Atlanta attorney.

Pittman took it smartly and counted it. "It's here. Here's your receipt," he said, holding it out to the sweaty Negro woman.

"Cans weez ride ta 'Lanter?" she asked.

"OH, NO! I'm on the way to, uh, Montgomery!" he said in a stutter, hurrying to get in the car. The heavy, solidly built car door closed. "There's a bus station! See tha sign at the gas station?" he said, cranking the car and backing out. "Call me again," he said, as he drove away. "Jesus Christ, help me," he mumbled to himself.

Jasper waited patiently in the car. Heather eventually came out of the restroom. He was visibly upset. Sheriff Gilbert still stood in the doorway of the chambers talking loudly to Judge Cobb. Heather approached quietly. "A good job!" said the sheriff. "A damn good job!" he said, shaking Heather's hand. "We couldn't have gotten it this far without your good policing," he added.

"Thanks," Heather said in a whisper.

Newspaper reporters still lingered in and around the courthouse. Alfred Huffman shook hands and exchanged information on the events. Heather walked alone. Old Clarence was already cleaning up the courtroom. His wide oiled string mop pushed cedar shavings along the wood floor. Heather pushed the outside door open and walked down the steps that were showing years of wear. Jasper came from the patrol car to meet her. "Win some, lose some," he said softly, walking by her side.

"The sum bitch is guilty," she said.

"He knows he is, and God knows he is," Jasper said softly. They walked along the shady sidewalk. There were calls from passing cars as to how the case went. Everyone seemed to be disappointed. "I'll drive," Jasper said, pulling out the ignition key from his pants pocket.

Heather took her seat and slammed the door. "I don't care!" she said, still puffy eyed and flushed.

Jasper started to pull the car into traffic. "Don't we have somewhere ta go?" he asked, smiling at Heather.

"That's for damn sure!" she replied, holding her hand out for traffic to stop. "Make it legal!" she said, sitting back in the seat.

Jasper turned on the siren and all the flashing lights, made a loop around the courthouse square and headed south. Sheriff Gilbert and Curley Jones walked toward the jail. The sheriff knew what they were doing, as Jasper took the square in second gear growling. Sheriff Louis Gilbert stood with his hat held high and smiled.

CHAPTER TWENTY-EIGHT

The Warm Springs Police car headed south out of Greenville, both officers riding with the windows down. Jasper drove with his hands in the ten and two positions. Heather sat slouched on the edge of the seat and rested her arm in the window. She was laughing inside at how much Jasper looked like an old woman with his hand position. She had been taught to hold at eleven or seven with one hand and shift with the other. The wind blew her short hair where it stuck out from under her fedora. Jasper's uniform hat was folding up from the harsh wind that rushed in through his window. They rode in silence all the way through the intersection at Harris City. The marked Ford took the slight rise on the gradual hillside and seemed to go airborne for a very short distance. Heather reached over and turned off the lights. Jasper turned off the siren. The powerful electric motor's life was lost. It instantly depleted the shrill of the device down to a low growl before dying.

"GOD DAMN IT!" Heather yelled, striking the dash with her flat hand. "Damn it, damn it, DAMN IT!" she yelled, striking the dash over and over again. Jasper was silent. They were approaching the Oakland Plantation, where James Lee had been taken the first time. "Stop, right here!" Heather said, sitting up straight and pointing. Jasper applied the brakes and the car slowed to a stop.

"Right here?" he asked. He knew they were very close to where she had taken the Negro down.

"It's fine," she said, getting out and walking in front of the car.

"Why are we stopping?" Jasper asked, as he gently closed the driver's side door.

"Right here. Right here it all started," Heather said. She stood with her hands on her hips, her suit coat pushed back. The shoulder holster revealed the heavy 1911 pistol. "Damn!" she said, kicking the ground. The dry dust rose and drifted away. Jasper watched silently as Heather walked in a small circle on the road. "Son of a bitch!" She gritted her teeth and her jaw tightened. "Jasper, I come from a family of poor losers." The young woman kicked the dirt again. She struggled to muster up a smile. "My Grandfather, the marshal, he'd stop eatin' pork to keep the money from that piece of shit," she said, looking into the distance. The wind gently blew her hair. "See the sumac? Fall's comin'. Seasons change," she said, sniffing.

Jasper held his hat in his hand and just listened. He had never lost a major case. Hell, he had never worked a case this massive before. He was glad he had met her.

"Listen!" he said softly. He looked around.

"The old Negro woman's comin'," Heather said, pointing toward the plantation house. The woman waved a white handkerchief to get their attention. Heather opened her hand wide as she held it high over her head and waved.

"Jesus!" Jasper said. "It's been ages since I saw a wave like that. Why, it was old man Peter Lynch that waved that away. He was over a hundred when he passed away. He was a Confederate Veteran," he said. "A Confederate Veteran," he repeated, just above a whisper. Jasper waved at the approaching woman. "Yessum," he greeted her.

"Can yous tells me 'bouts de hog man's trial?" she asked. Her medium brown floor length dress had gathered cockleburs as she came across the field rows. The yellow calico bibbed apron had kitchen stains on it.

"We sure can," replied Heather, motioning to Jasper to oblige the woman.

"He got off, not guilty," said Jasper, looking down at the ground.

The old Negro woman was silent for a moment. "He be guilty in de eyes of de Lawd," she said. "He be guilty in de eyes of de Lawd!" She shook her head in disbelief. "Judgment Day cometh!" she shouted, looking at the setting sun.

Jasper put his cap on. "We were surprised too," he said.

The Negro woman pulled the front of her dress up slightly and turned toward the house. "I thank ya so much," she said, as she started back to the house. She mumbled as she walked. "Judgment Day cometh!" she yelled, about halfway.

"Do you know how to get to the graves from here?" Heather asked Jasper.

"I do," he replied.

"I want to be the first to tell them that one of the God damn killers walked scot-free," Heather said, arranging her hair and setting her fedora again. Her mood was beginning to lighten. Jasper was glad of it.

"It'll be almost dark 'fore we get there," he said, closing the car door.

"Hurricane Creek's a good ways off." He shifted the gears quickly and moved along. The remote cemetery was a lonely, spooky place during the day, much less at night. Jasper knew why Heather was going. Sometimes talking to the dead helps the soul to be at peace. They both had tried hard on this case with the two Negroes, especially Heather.

"There's a flashlight on the back seat," Jasper said, pulling on the headlights. It was not dark yet, but the deep shadowy curves made it difficult to see clearly. Gradually the wide yellow wedges of the headlights grew to be a bright white as the darkness of the night came upon them. He took every shortcut he could think of. The full moon was breaking over the treetops. The night bugs flew in the path of the headlights. Occasionally one would strike the windshield with a loud thump. Heather held on and sat quietly. "Here we are," said Jasper, as he turned off the roadway and drove up a narrow lane overgrown with tall grass. "Grass takes over quick," he said, pulling the car into low gear. "I'd bet Oscar or some of them would come cut it, if they realized it was this high." The headlights bathed the three freshly covered graves.

"This is fine," Heather said, holding the door handle. The flashlight was a three cell, silver-plated Ray-o-vac. It was a good one. The hot exhaust pipe sizzled against the wet grass that was crushed under the car. The two officers got out and walked in the cemetery. "Nobody's been here since the funeral," Heather said, coming back to the graves. They cast large black shadows on the distant woods as the night birds called. Jasper remained quiet, letting Heather do whatever she had come to do.

Heather held her hat in her hand. Jasper quickly removed his hat. Small dry limbs snapped in the distance, making the cemetery that much spookier. "I wanted you to know that we tried our best for you folks. We had tha sum bitch in the bag, but the jury let the driver off. It was the hog farmer, a neighbor, Theo Jackson," Heather said. She looked down for a moment. "Why they chose ta let him off we'll never know." Jasper looked around every time a twig broke. "Mr. Miller, we'd have killed both them sorry bastards if we'd had the chance. I think they'll hang James Lee," she said. Jasper looked at her. He thought Lee would probably get life. "I'm sorry about your wife and little girl," Heather said, catching a stray tear that fell. "I'm sorry," she whispered again, pulling out her handkerchief. Heather turned and started for the car. Jasper hurried behind her. He had had enough of the snapping twigs and the night sounds.

The car doors closed and Jasper found reverse with a slight groaning of the gears. Heather blew her nose and put away her lace edged handkerchief. "My Dad said his father, my grandfather, could sit and tell ya all the sounds and who or what was makin' 'em. He too was a Confederate Veteran." She rested her arm in the open window. "Can you tell the chief?" she asked. "I want to go home."

"I can do that, a little out of the way, but it can be done," Jasper replied.

Heather began to nod off, from the stress of the situation. Jasper was starting to see a softer side to his partner. She dozed off before they got close to Warm Springs. Her coat had fallen away and her pistol rode in its holster against her firm youthful breast. The white pleated front blouse made her all the more attractive as Jasper glanced over at her, asleep on the seat.

The sounds of the city woke Heather as Jasper gently crossed the railroad tracks, just a few blocks from the boarding house. She sat up on the seat. The illuminated store fronts filled the cab with a flash of light as they passed each one. The movement of cars on the streets bathed them in the glare of headlights. Some drivers sounded their horns and waved out the window. "Side door," Heather said. Jasper stopped short of the front doors.

"Breakfast?" he asked, looking at her as she sat with the door open, one leg on the street.

"I'll buy," she replied with a smile.

"I'll see you then," he said. "We've got to patrol tomorrow, same old grind." Jasper sighed.

Heather got out and closed the door. She looked back through the open window. "Tell the chief I'm whipped," she said, slapping the car.

Jasper sat watching her go down the side alley and enter the boarding house. Car horns blew as he was holding up traffic. He waved them around. "Move along!" someone yelled.

"Hey! I'm the God damned police!" Jasper yelled back. "Damn asshole," he mumbled, easing the car toward the street the chief lived on. He thought he might see Edgar Peterson, but he never did. Jasper suspected he might be in a store watching a card game or listening to a radio program before the town became a graveyard until daylight. Night watch was lonely after bedtime came and the stores all closed.

Jasper thought of how he would tell it to the chief, but when he saw the house up ahead, he forgot his rehearsed approach. Jasper saw a faint light around the parlor curtains, and another from the bathroom on the back of the modest house. He parked on the street. There were still some folks sitting in robes and pajamas on their front porches. Electric fans were expensive to operate, while the God given cool air was free. He caught the glow of a smoker's cigarette across the street. A voice called out, "Good job, good job!" Jasper waved in the direction of the compliment. The chief's small dog soon stood at Jasper's feet. "Hey, pup!" he said softly, as he started up the walkway. The small dog's tail wagged as it hurried ahead of him.

He was lucky, the chief met him at the front screen door. "How did it go?" asked the chief. He was in his underwear and undershirt, a glass of ice water in his hand. "Water?" he asked Jasper.

"No. I won't be long," Jasper replied.

"Seat?" asked the chief, as he sat down in a metal chair, comforted by a homemade cushion.

"I'll stand," Jasper replied. "It ain't good. The God damn jury let Jackson go," he said, holding his uniform cap.

"What?" the chief responded, looking up at Jasper.

"Let the sum bitch go, not guilty," replied Jasper. "Detective Duncan and the sheriff took it hard. Ambrose Watkins grabbed his papers and was seen driving off soon after the court was dismissed."

The chief almost dropped the glass of water as he stared blankly. "Let him go," he said in a low voice.

"Yep!" Jasper replied.

"Jesus," the chief whispered. "Thanks for coming out. Y'all be on the street tomorrow?" he asked.

"On the street," replied Jasper.

Jasper walked to the patrol car with a great deal of pride in the contribution he had made toward the case. The small dog sat watching Jasper from the steps of the porch. "Two shots tonight," he said to himself. He was tired. The full moon bathed the countryside of the rural Georgia town as he headed to his home.

Heather walked softly past Mrs. Blakely's door. She was light and could displace her weight like a cat. "Have ya eat?" Mrs. Blakely's voice asked from somewhere. The woman sat in the moonlight at the kitchen table. "Drink?" she asked. Heather heard the clink of glasses.

"No to food, and yes to drink," Heather replied, as she stepped into the kitchen.

"There's a plate on the stove for you," said Mrs. Blakely. "Ain't it a bitch?" she said, pouring Heather a drink.

Heather uncovered the plate of food. It was good warm fried field corn, green butterbeans, corn bread, and a piece of fried chicken. "So, you heard the sum bitch got off," she said.

"I did," said Mrs. Blakely. "I know y'all are pissed."

Heather sat down where she could see the hallway, her back to the wall. "I'm so sorry for the Millers, an entire family gone, and the little girl. That is so hard for me, a life wasted," Heather said, taking a bite.

"My late husband always said what goes around comes around. Jackson'll get his sometime," said Mrs. Blakely.

"Thanks for the plate," Heather said, getting up for a glass of water to cut the dark bourbon. "Time heals all," she said.

Mrs. Blakely was bathed and wearing her gown, covered by an open robe. She smelled of witch hazel and bath powder. Evening sponge baths were common among the rural folks, and a tub bath for everyone on

Saturday night, starting off fresh for the Lord's Day.

"I'm glad yer in. I'm headin' ta bed," said Mrs. Blakely. She placed her glass in the sink. "Bottle?" she asked, holding it out to Heather, who was still sitting at the table in the moonlight.

"No, thanks," Heather said. "A long bath will help."

Mrs. Blakely entered her room and closed the door to the world within her business. The moonlight was so bright Heather never turned on a light. Some admirer within the house had left a token at Heather's door, a chocolate bar and a yellow silk rose, bearing a small note. "Give 'em hell; a job well done."

The bathroom was heavy with the fragrance of Dixie Dew. It was mixed with the humid steam from a recent bath. She bathed by the light of a candle in the large tub and wondered if the candy and flower came from Buddy Cotton. She would eventually find out they did not. Heather soon drifted into sleep thinking of how her father would rant and rave over the jury's decision. She still hurt for the family that had been lost.

The failure upset her so much that she kept the largest suitcase open on the dresser top. Her clean folded clothes soon found themselves within. She yearned for things to reason out and the chance to return home to Campbellton.

CHAPTER TWENTY-NINE

Curley Jones and the available deputies had James Lee pulled from his secure cell. The Negro was once again suited out in the finest the county budget could buy. "Today's tha day," Curley said in a chipper tone, as he secured the handcuffs to the waistband. James Lee looked straight ahead, not saying a word. "I'd like for ya to break and run," said Curley. "I'm second to the sheriff with my pistol skills," he bragged. "They took me off the road gang, one nigger run and I forgot ta shoot ta stop. I shot him in the back of tha head. He dead." Curley laughed, setting the final lock on the belt.

The heavy door moaned as Sheriff Gilbert pulled it open. "Y'all ready?" He called out from the dim light of the cloudy morning. "The mob's back, but we'll walk right past 'em. They know he's guilty and there's lots of cameras and newspaper men already gathered."

"Move out," said Curley, nudging the prisoner and pointing to the door where the light entered. The silhouette of the waiting sheriff filled the opening. "Walk or ride?" Curley asked.

"Walk," replied the sheriff. "Them two and the chief are here from Warm Springs," he added.

The three officers stood at the open screen door watching the traffic and the gathering crowd on the courthouse lawn. Jasper pulled his revolver and carefully checked the cylinder. It was full. Heather had checked her pistol prior to leaving her room that morning. James Lee's untied brogans scuffed along on the hard floor. The slightest amount of grit or sand made the loudest racket. Lee stood with his hands cuffed in front and secured to the waistband. His dark brown eyes grew large. His ear muscles pulled his round ears back. The one that had been shot off did not pull as far as the good one. Facial muscles always gave away the intentions of a man before his actions.

"Don't you start that rabbit shit!" said Sheriff Gilbert, as he grabbed the prisoner's arm. "I see them thoughts!" he added, shaking the Negro. "Best shots in the county in this room, one took yer ear damn near off. You wouldn't get to the edge of the yard," snarled the sheriff, moving his wet cigar from one side of his mouth to the other with his tongue. James Lee's face lost the muscle tension. He looked down and gave a loud sigh.

The small posse huddled around the prisoner, walked down the cement steps of the jail, and cut across the dew-covered yard. Heather motioned for Jasper to switch sides since he was right-handed, getting his pistol away from the prisoner. Sheriff Gilbert and Curley walked in front. Jasper was on the right side, Heather on the left, and the deputy in the rear with a carbine. Miss Jewel watched from the second story porch of the sheriff's residence. Miss Dixie watched from the cover of her window curtains.

"Here they come!" yelled someone in the white mob. They stood their ground, not moving from the area where they had assembled. The newspaper reporters rushed to meet the escort posse. Cameras were flashing front page photos as they walked along. Soon the air was filled with questions, which the sheriff answered short and to the point. Once on the square, the deputy walked, guarding their backs, staying turned as much as physically possible. Sheriff Gilbert had watched the lever gun being loaded with a spent shell in the chamber. The deputy shucked the finger lever once the white mob started to follow. The spent brass-hulled cartridge stripping from the receiver made a recognizable sound of its own, especially when the live round struck the loading lever and began to enter the chamber. The empty hull struck the cement walkway with a unique sound, bouncing several times before coming to rest in the worn grass. The arms in the front row of white protesters went up, holding the members back. James Lee was successfully marched into the courtroom and placed in his seat.

Attorney Robert Gaskill stood waiting. The young man's hair was greased and combed to the back. His tortoise shell framed glasses rested on his sharp featured face. The dark blue suit with thin gray stripes contrasted against the snow-white shirt and gold bowtie.

"Thank you, Sheriff," Gaskill said, shaking the sheriff's hand.

The Warm Springs group took a seat behind the prisoner, as did the carbine armed deputy. The sheriff and Curley sat along the hall wall. Ambrose Watkins walked in. He looked a little more chipper than when they had seen him last, at the end of the Theo Jackson trial. He took his seat.

"All rise!" called the bailiff. Judge Erastus Cobb opened the door to the right of the bench and entered the full courtroom.

"Thank you, be seated," he said. "This is the sentencing portion of the State versus James Lee case. It will be very short. I see that everyone that means anything is present, those that ain't just missed it," he said, with a soft chuckle. "Does the Defense or the State have anything they wish to ask or present in my consideration of this sentence?"

Robert Gaskill stood. "No, your Honor."

Ambrose Watkins stood. "Same here."

"Very well. Do you have anything, Mr. Lee?" asked the Judge.

The Negro sat silently, looking down. He shook his head, indicating there was nothing he wished to say.

"In my years of service to the public from this bench, all these portions come hard to me. I have to give great consideration into the reading of the Georgia law and its meaning. I refer back to other similar cases before my decision is finally made," he said, rubbing his finger under his nose. "Upon my delivery, there will be NO outbursts of any kind. Contempt still rules in my Court. I ask the solicitor, the defense attorney Robert Gaskill, and the accused James Lee, to please stand," he said, loud enough to be heard, but in a soft tone. The bailiffs both motioned for them to stand. "It is the ruling of this Court, the Superior Court of Meriwether County, that the accused, James Lee, be sentenced to death, by hanging from the neck until dead," said Judge Cobb. He sounded the gavel.

James Lee was not surprised. He stood still and looked down. The sheriff and Curley Jones slowly stood in the event he might try to escape. The courtroom was silent. The announcement was soon being yelled around the courthouse square. Car horns sounded and there were shouts of glee, as though it were a celebration.

"Be seated!" said the Judge. The courtroom was still at order. "Is there anything the defense would like to say?"

"Yes, your Honor," said Gaskill. The young appointed attorney stood. "My client and I have discussed the possibility of this outcome and have drafted this letter for the Court," he said, pulling it from his suit coat pocket.

"Please read it," said the Judge.

"In its lengthy body, it essentially asks that the Court have leniency on this sentence and conduct it as quickly as possible, as it is perceived as undue cruelty to prolong it, and I do realize the heinous crimes that have been committed," Gaskill said, looking down at the table.

Judge Cobb looked at the attorney, and then leaned back in his chair. He bit on the body of a pencil, but only for a moment. The powerful man pointed the pencil at the attorney and then at James Lee. "For all the harm, heartache, and disruption you've caused, if it were within my power, I wouldn't tell you the day you'd die. But then I would be held to higher authority for cruelty," he said, looking at the accused wide-eyed.

A small but distinct voice was heard from the balcony, where the seats were full of supporters for the Miller family. Judge Cobb looked up. "Yes, who spoke?" he asked.

A well-dressed man stood. "You're Pastor Prather," said the Judge.

"Yes, yo' Honor, I am," replied the man. He was sharp, dressed in a well-cared for black suit and a starched white shirt, with a white rose in his lapel and a beautiful blue bowtie. The pastor moved to the railing.

"Pastor, what is it?" asked the Judge. The people seated below on the main floor looked up at the man.

"I speaks fo' de majority of de black community. Weez thought dey wuz to be two hung," he said, holding up his hand expressing that he understood the court system. "Mos' hangin's always been fo' de folks ta see. But nows wid one, we figure he be hung in de tower of de jail," said Pastor Prather.

The sheriff raised his hand and stood. "Not necessarily, if there's public demand and lumber at the county farm, it can be done outside," he said. "With the Judge's permission," he added.

"Lots of de timber men dun got up mo' dan enough timbers to build a double one," said the pastor. He stood still for a moment, looking down on the Court. "De' Millers wuz fine folks and lots had counted on seein' dem hang," he said. "Thank ya, yo' Honor." The pastor took his seat.

"Well, Attorney Gaskill and James Lee, it looks like you will go with the eyes of Heaven upon you. It is approved by this Court that you be executed in the yard of the Meriwether County Jail's property. I will expect that you, Mr. Gaskill, will draw a last will and testament for your client and give us notification as to who shall be contacted to claim the body," said the Judge, striking the gavel. "Execution in fourteen days, at ten o'clock in the morning, rain or shine," said Judge Cobb.

Jasper leaned toward Heather and whispered. "I hope his God damned head comes off." Heather gave him a hard elbow. "I'll kill him now with the right papers," she replied in a whisper, her lips almost touching Jasper's ear.

"Court dismissed!" called the Judge. He hurried off the bench.

James Lee sat with his head down, his chin on his chest. "I'll be over tomorrow to draw up your will and get the other information," said Robert Gaskill.

Sheriff Gilbert and the deputies surrounded the prisoner to take him back to the jail. "Move out," said the sheriff, taking James Lee by the arm and turning him toward the main doors.

Pastor Prather and two other Negroes had hurried down from the balcony and took the chance to enter the courtroom. "Sheriff!" the pastor called out.

Sheriff Gilbert looked around for the voice that had called out to him. He saw the three Negroes just a few feet away. "Yes, pastor," he said.

"Weez don't want ta rush, but de lumber's outside on de trucks," Pastor

Prather said, smiling with his bright white teeth showing.

"Well! You mean business," said the sheriff, with a smile. He still held tightly to the prisoner's arm, as they made their way toward the doors. "Curley!" called the sheriff, only to jump when Curley answered right behind him. "When we get him secured, show these good men where to unload. Let's do it between the office and the main road."

"Thank you, sir!" replied one of the men with the pastor. They followed at a distance as the accused shuffled toward the doors.

The citizens who had attended the sentencing portion of the trial gave the sheriff and his guarding deputies a wide berth. No one spoke to the accused or the sheriff and his officers. The walk back to the jail was quick and very solemn. The street traffic stopped to allow their crossing. The sheriff walked the prisoner down the center of the side street. The blacks in support of the victims gathered and sang a church song in their honor. All this took place while the accused was walked to his cell. The small mob stood silently as they passed. The clock in the tower tolled the hour.

Dixie and Miss Jewel saw the posse coming. Dixie opened the screen door and the solid door, propping them both open. Miss Jewel hurried out of the way and stood at the narrow hallway door leading to the private residence and on to the kitchen.

"Lock him up!" said Sheriff Gilbert, when they got into the booking room and office. The two women were stone-faced and very quiet. "Last lock up, son," he said, as the sturdy key was turned in the jail door.

"I'm not yer son," James Lee replied.

"Conversation, conversation. Hell, at this point if ya were, I don't know if I'd claim ya," Sheriff Gilbert replied, nudging James Lee into the dimly lit cell block. "Curley, you know to dress him out, get the suit to the cleaners and get it brushed only, unless Miss Jewel wants to make the quarter," he said.

Miss Jewel heard the sheriff. "I'ze take de quarter," she said loudly.

"Very well, give it to Miss Jewel," replied the sheriff.

"Black sorry ass. I'ze gots a black silk rose jus' right for de lapel," she mumbled.

* * *

Ambrose Watkins hurried through the crowd in the courthouse to find the Warm Springs officers. He spotted Jasper Brown in the crowd by his sharp uniform, and the detective by her fedora and haircut.

"Hey! Brown!" he called out. Jasper looked around and waved at the approaching solicitor.

"Sheriff has some papers for the both of you," Watkins said. "How did this turn out for ya?" he asked.

"It's a shame it's not two," Heather replied. Several citizens standing nearby heard the solicitor and joined in with a reply of the same.

444

"Jury works in strange ways," Watkins replied. "Strange ways."

Jasper and Heather hurried to the sheriff's office where they found Sheriff Gilbert at his desk. His cigar was in its place and a glass of iced tea beside him.

"Did you want to see us?" Heather asked.

"I did, have a seat," the sheriff replied, pointing to two nearby chairs. Heather took the one right in front of his desk and Jasper pulled up to the side. The two officers wondered what he wanted. The sheriff picked up a nearby sealed envelope and tapped it on his palm. He was hesitant. "The county commissioners, Judge Cobb, and Solicitor Watkins have agreed with these contents," he said, handing the envelope to Heather. She took it and opened it carefully. Her eyes quickly read the body and handed it to Jasper. She was pleased, for what it was worth.

Jasper read it and then smiled. "That's something!" he said, smiling.

"We'd like for you two to be able to work with the county when things arise on that end of the county," said Sheriff Gilbert, leaning back in his chair. "As full-time deputies!"

"I'm sure the mayor and the chief are aware of this," replied Heather.

"They are, and very proud of our agreement," the sheriff added. Sheriff Gilbert stood. "Thanks for your hard work," he said, shaking both their hands.

"We're happy to do it," replied Heather. Jasper smiled.

"I must see to the prisoner," said the sheriff.

Jasper and Heather left the office and soon headed for their jurisdiction.

Sheriff Gilbert walked to the back of the cell block where Curley and a deputy were watching James Lee dress out. "I'll take the suit," said the sheriff. He draped it over his arm as it was taken off. "Curley, shoelaces and only drawers. This sum bitch might try to hang hisself," he said. No one was in the cell with the prisoner but Curley. He handed out the suit and gave the jail uniform back to the deputy.

"Shoe strings, quickly!" Curley said. "So I can get to lunch."

James Lee removed the shoe strings and handed them to Curley. Curley backed out, leaving the Negro in his underwear and stringless brogans.

"Don't forget the trucks," reminded the sheriff.

"They can unload it," Curley replied, as they walked to the front.

"Yes, but show them where you want it," said the sheriff, pushing the heavy door open. "Miss Jewel, here's the suit. Hand it in to the office when you're finished. Tell Dixie and she will get your money," said the sheriff.

Pastor Prather leaned against his Studebaker, talking to the other two Negroes. Curley hurried outside to meet them. "Right here!" he pointed. "Here against the fence'll be fine," he said, pointing. The two Negro men had removed their coats and ties and were ready to unload. "My, that's mighty nice lumber," Curley said, as he looked at the new cut pieces that were being taken from the two trucks.

"Nothin' but the best for the Millers," replied one Negro. The sound of board slapping against board filled the neighborhood around the jail, rousing the nearby dogs to bark.

Curley stood by watching. Pastor Prather walked over. "If de county needs this built, we can do it, wid a simple drawing of what dey want. It is de least de community can do for de Millers," he said.

"I'll certainly pass that on to the sheriff. Do you have a telephone?" asked Curley.

"Just tell the operator Pastor Prather. She can ring me at the church or at home."

"Thank you, sir!" Curley said, extending his hand.

In a relatively short time, the two trucks were unloaded. Curley waved once again from the front steps of the jail as they pulled out.

* * *

Mrs. Loretta at the orchard office cut a check to pay Theo Jackson in full for the last load of manure. She yelled for Oscar to come in and sign it too. "Havin' two of us sign it, makes it mo' 'fissial," she said, as Oscar leaned down over the old desk and signed under her name. They had both signed small amounts for the Millers for many years.

"My, my, that looks nice," Oscar said, holding the check up. He was proud of his handwriting, especially with a fountain pen.

"I'ze thought of dis," Mrs. Loretta said, holding out a letter. Oscar read it, slowly. His eyes and mouth followed his finger.

"So, dis says he don't duz business heah and nots ta come on property no mo'," he said, looking down at the letter.

"Git it served and gits him paid," said Mrs. Loretta, pulling the letter from his hand, folding it in thirds, and putting the check inside. "Calls de Shurriff and ask hows ta git it done," she barked, tossing it on the desk in front of Oscar.

Oscar called the sheriff's office and Dixie answered the telephone. She was just about to leave. "Dis beez Oscar at de Miller Orchard. I'ze got a keep off letter and a finals check ta have given, officials like, ta dat sorry Theo Jackson. Howz I gits it dun?" Oscar asked.

"Hold on!" Dixie said, laying down the telephone. She had just seen the two Warm Springs officers at the corner talking to citizens. The screen door spring screeched when she snatched it open. It was so loud Heather heard it and looked toward the jail. "Hey, hey! I've got papers ta serve in your area!" Dixie yelled so loud that Oscar could hear the commotion. He felt important at all the sudden attention he was getting. He began to rock on his feet. Heather tugged on Jasper's sleeve.

"Excuse us. We've got a call," she said. Jasper signed off in a hurry and went with Heather to the jail.

"What is it?" he asked, hurrying along.

"Some kind of papers ta serve," Heather replied.

Dixie waited on the steps. "Oscar at the orchard wants criminal trespass papers served on Theo Jackson, and his last check given to him. Can y'all do that on the way in?" Dixie asked.

Heather smiled and pointed to Jasper. "He's got tha keys!" she said.

"Sure we can!" replied Jasper. They followed Dixie inside.

"Oscar, the new deputies can get it in just a few minutes," said Dixie. "Got it ready?"

"I sho' dos," he replied.

"Read it to me," Dixie said.

"She wants it read tos her," said Oscar to Mrs. Loretta.

"Wells, opens it and reads it," she replied.

Dixie could hear the conversation on the orchard end of the telephone. Oscar cleared his throat. "The business knowns as Miller's Orchards and all property connected tells yous ta stay off, from now to de' end of time, signed Mrs. Loretta and myself. De check is in heah," he added.

"Let the two deputies witness it and they will get it done," replied Dixie. "Now stay there, they're on the way to you," she added, before hanging up. "Miller's Orchard wants to give Theo Jackson his last check and have him served with criminal trespass warning," said Dixie, as she gathered up her purse.

"Piece of cake!" Jasper said.

"You'll think that when you deal with his mother, Gladys Hightower," Heather laughed, as they all went out the door. It was late afternoon and the Sheriff's Department was quiet for a change. Curley was finishing paperwork on the status with James Lee.

Jasper's patrol car was covered with bugs and road dust. Heather could tell that he was concerned about getting it clean again. He placed his uniform cap on the seat between them. There was not much room after he put the hat down, just an inch or two on each side. His tie was loosened and his collar unbuttoned. He had come out of the uniform coat long ago. The black Sam Browne belt had stained the shoulder of the white shirt on one side, revealing that he had worn it like that once before. "It's comin' on fall, but it's still warm," Jasper said, riding with the window down.

"Ya wouldn't know it by the bugs," Heather said, as another one popped on the windshield.

"Someone said the last thing a bug sees is its asshole," Jasper commented. "When it hits the windshield," he continued, smiling.

"I think it's the knees," Heather said, looking at Jasper. "They're probably dead by the time the asshole comes by." She tried to keep a straight face.

Jasper wished he was thirty years younger; she was quite a woman. He took every shortcut he knew to get to the hog farm. "I'll bet they're out celebrating at Miller's Orchard," he said, as he worked the gears from taking a southbound turn.

"Maybe not," Heather replied, removing her hat and running her slender fingers through her short hair. The air felt good. "My dad talked about weather like this once, when he was a boy. He said that his dad put the horse in the barn and it was a breezy wind from the northeast, then next mornin' was a heavy freeze, real sudden like." She leaned forward looking at the sky. "Maybe this could be another."

The two officers pulled into the Miller Orchard office. Oscar hurried out and Mrs. Loretta watched from the screen door. Jasper killed the motor. The warm ride had become tiresome and it felt good to get out. The air helped cool their damp clothes. "Oscar!" Jasper held out his hand in greeting. Oscar wiped his hand on his overalls before he made contact with Jasper. He shook Heather's hand too. She had a fierce grip.

"My old Pappy said a firm hands shake is a sign of good character," Oscar said. He held out the envelope that contained the check and the letter of warning. Heather took it, hurriedly read the letter, and looked at the check.

"Let me use a pen," she said to Oscar. Mrs. Loretta heard her and brought out a fountain pen and inkwell. "Thanks!" Heather said to the woman. She hurriedly signed the letter as a witness and one of the serving officials, then handed it to Jasper. It took him several attempts to get situated on the car. He was looking for just the right place to get his best signature. He was funny that way. His hand moved about in a circle several times before settling down on the paper. Oscar and Heather watched his antics and smiled. The smooth writing pen was returned.

"It'll be done in just a few minutes, if we can meet up with him," Jasper said. They signed off and got in the car. Though they were in a hurry, Jasper showed respect by not raising a dust to drift onto the Negroes. The two officers waved, as did Oscar. The hog farm was down on the opposite side of the large tract of orchard land, about a mile and a half across. Jasper looked with due caution at the stop sign, where the orchard road met the main road to Manchester. He saw no one coming or in sight as he rolled through the intersection.

"Fine example!" Heather said, riding with her hand out the window, playing with the cooling wind.

"Can't be an example if nobody's around," he said, defending his actions. "Jesus!" Jasper blurted out. "Damn, I can smell the damn place!" He tried to breathe through the fabric of his shirt covered elbow on his free arm.

"There he comes!" Heather said loudly, pointing to a small light blue spot up ahead. "He must have just pulled out. Slow down, let him pass," she said. "Get him alone on the road, it's a hell of a lot better for us than dealing with his damn mother."

Jasper slowed the patrol car and dropped a set of wheels onto the grassy shoulder. They were there long enough for the dust to settle. "I can smell the place," Heather said, wiping her nose.

"I think he's alone," said Jasper, as he watched the light blue spot gradually turn into a passing Fargo truck.

Heather held the papers that Oscar had given them. They sat still waiting for him to overtake. The light blue Fargo truck passed at a fast clip. They noticed there were no tubs, and the bed appeared to be washed out. Theo Jackson passed, looking straight ahead. They knew he saw them, he was not stupid, nor was he blind. "He knows it's us," said Jasper, as he pulled the car from neutral to first and released the clutch. The narrow road caused the Ford to require two attempts to maneuver in the direction of the truck.

"Just wait it out. There's a house or two up the road. Let's pull him over there. If there's any trouble, maybe someone can see what happened," Heather suggested.

"Do ya reckon that's him we smell?" asked Jasper.

"No!" Heather said, laughing. "He's a piece of shit, but not that big," she said. She took her coat off and laid it on the back seat. She was beginning to show sweat too. The shoulder rig had lightly stained her blouse. She pulled her pistol and checked for a shell in the chamber by moving the slide ever so slightly to the rear. The brass shell body revealed itself.

"God damn! Ya goin' ta shoot him?" Jasper asked, glancing at his partner.

"Did ya forget that he rides with a sawed-off shotgun?" she asked, returning the large pistol to the holster.

"Oh, yeah!" Jasper answered. "I forgot about that." He unsnapped his holster strap.

"Forget'll get ya killed," Heather said loudly.

A desirable location was up ahead. There were people in the fields and around the houses. "Do it!" Heather said, as she turned on all the police lights. Theo Jackson continued to drive. Jasper sounded the car horn. They saw the Negro look in the tiny rearview mirror, but he did not slow down.

"Kick tha siren!" Jasper exclaimed. Heather turned on the siren, still keeping her hand on the switch. The powerful siren slowly grew to a climactic growl.

"Grrrrrr, grrrrrrr!" the siren sounded, each time Heather bumped it.

"Get close to that sum bitch! Let him see us and we can see his eyes in

449

the mirror," Heather said.

Jasper punched the Ford and gained on the small truck. He drove straddle of the center, knowing the Negro could see them. Jasper waved for him to pull over. Heather turned on the siren and left it on. Finally, the small truck pulled to the shoulder and stopped. The folks around the houses stood and watched, just what Heather and Jasper needed them to do.

"Get him out, hands up," Heather said, jumping out when the car stopped. Her pistol was drawn. Jasper did the same, but remembered to swing wide, into the oncoming lane.

"Sir, get out of the truck! Hands where we can see them!" Jasper barked loudly. Heather had taken a spot at the rear corner of the small truck. She kept her pistol on Theo Jackson.

Theo Jackson was slow to get out. "What I dos?" he asked, still sitting in the cab.

"Get out of the truck!" yelled Jasper. This time he had the man in his pistol sights. Jackson slowly opened the truck door. Heather ran up to the passenger side and looked in. There was the shotgun leaning against the seat.

Jasper yelled for Theo to walk to the back of the truck, which he did. Heather pulled the shotgun from the truck and took the round from the chamber. "It's empty!" She called out from the passenger side of the truck. Jasper holstered his revolver. "I should take ya in!" he said loudly, pointing his finger, just out of arm's reach. "Why didn't ya pull over?" he asked.

"I'm scared," Theo mumbled.

Heather stepped up. "This is your last check, and this letter," she held it, and waved it about, "is a trespass warning. From here forward and FOREVER, stay off the Miller property." Heather handed the envelope to Theo. She snatched it back and pulled a receipt of service from the same envelope. "Sign this! It says you've been served. It will be on file at the Sheriff's Department."

"Have a good day," said Jasper. The two officers backed away and left Theo Jackson standing in the road. Jointly they turned off the police lights. Jasper looked at Heather. "Dumbass!" he said.

Heather looked at her watch. "Quittin' time! Take me home! I can't play anymore," she said, laughing.

They were tired, and Jasper took every chance to get back to Warm Springs as quickly as possible. The clouds were forming like a weather front was coming. "I thought he would come out with the shotgun. Surely one of us could have killed him. I might rest better knowing he had got what he deserved. We both know he helped kill the Millers, by taking James Lee over there and not calling the law," Heather said.

"I'm sure all this is for a reason," Jasper said, glancing at her as he drove.

"Old folks say what goes around, comes around."

* * *

Gladys Hightower was busy packing and scheming. She had already arranged for Glenn Gumby to pick them up at the Greyhound Station and bring them home. Bothering Glenn was cheaper than a cab. Gladys folded her clothes and talked to Rhonda in the next room about big plans and returning to work. Theo was on a slop run; he would be gone for a while.

"We beez leavin' soon as I gits de bond money back. Maybe tomorrow," she said. Rhonda sat listening to the radio, just outside the small makeshift bedroom. "We gits ourselves backs to de Black Derby," Gladys said, all excited.

"Shouldn't we give the money to Theo, or to a church? It was all done in good faith, charity," Rhonda questioned.

"Lawd child, yo' brother don't knows de' diffrunce. I put dat money ta use," Gladys cackled.

* * *

It was the first evening in a while that Heather and Jasper had gotten off the clock and back to their respective homes before dark. Buddy Cotton was seen at the depot with his family. The young boy yelled and waved eagerly at his favorite and only police woman. Heather sat up straight and waved back. The young growing boy stood and watched the patrol car as they drove out of sight.

"He's a fine boy," said Jasper. "He's been smitten with you from the first day." He reached over and poked Heather on the thigh with his fingers. "He'd fight me ta get ta you. He's got a crush on ya," he said, smiling.

"I know that," Heather replied, grinning. "And you do too," she said, looking at Jasper.

He blushed a deep red. "I do," he said slowly. "I've never met a woman with such an independent streak," he said, stopping in front of Mrs. Blakely's boarding house. "If only I were a younger man," he sighed, looking down.

Heather had opened the door and started to get out. "Stay for dinner," she said. "Who ya goin' home to?" she whispered, as she closed the door gently.

"I'll do that!" Jasper said.

Heather pointed to an open parking space. "There's one!" she said, walking ahead into the open space. It was right next to her Essex.

The old boarders and a few new ones were already gathering in the hallway and foyer, just outside the large kitchen. "Well, Warm Springs' finest!" one boarder said. Heather remembered the face but had let the name slip. "Got 'em all but one, I see," he said, smiling and rocking on his heels.

"I don't know about the finest part, but we got one to the gallows. The jury had a brain fart and let the hog farmer off," Jasper defended, as he stood close to the boarder. "My old grandma used ta say what goes around comes around. He'll eventually get his," he said. "Yes, sir! He'll get his!"

Heather counted heads with her finger, pointing to each man standing in line. She then counted the chairs around the table. There was one extra. She walked in and put her suit coat on the end chair, which would allow her to see the doors, and claimed the one to her left for Jasper. She pulled her handcuffs and placed them in front of the plate.

The same man spoke up again. "Well, I'm glad you didn't get my seat."

"You stay here long enough, and you'll earn the right to claim a seat," Heather said.

The salesman who was upstairs with Heather spoke up. "Your place is the middle seat, here on the front," he said, pointing to the exact chair. "The man who made that available took double helpings and was too loud. He was eventually asked to move on." None of the longer boarders made a comment to the lie they had just heard, but the man was already not fitting in, unless he quickly changed his ways. Mrs. Blakely heard the conversation as she dished and set the hot food on the table. She was glad they had called the man down. She liked to have a quiet homely table. It was good for the digestion. Mrs. Blakely wiped her hands on the thin cotton towel hanging from her apron band.

"Someone please say grace," she said, bowing her head.

The room was silent for a while. A throat was cleared and a man began to speak. "Our Heavenly Father, bless this food to the good of our bodies and the fellowship to the mind and spirit. Bless this gathering of the tired and those away from home. In thy name we pray, amen." Several soft amens followed. The hungry men rushed to the table. Jasper held the chair for Heather. One of the other boarders saw him do it for Heather, so the he held the chair for Mrs. Blakely. She always sat next to Heather. Jasper removed his gun belt and hung it on the back of the chair, keeping the revolver between him and Heather. The food was passed in a sudden sea of low conversation, from the weather to sales made on the open road.

"I'm certainly proud of these two officers. They did their best to make a strong case on the two murdering sons of bitches. They got the trigger man for damn sure, but the driver and provider of shelter, well, the jury let him go. It was a marvelous job!" said Mrs. Blakely.

"Thanks!" replied Heather. Jasper gave a smile and a nod.

The mid-week meal was good, but a thrifty one, vegetable gumbo of garden tomatoes, okra, and corn, butter peas, fried side meat and corn bread, buttermilk or iced tea, simple and good. "How much?" Jasper whispered to Mrs. Blakely, as he and Heather helped clear the table. There were still several men sitting and talking.

"Not a thing, just shop here more," she whispered in return.

"Oh, my! I'll certainly do that," Jasper said, placing dishes on the sink cabinet.

The cool breeze floated the curtains over the sink and poured in the screen door, which opened onto the small dark back porch. "I can dry," Jasper said.

"I can wash!" said Heather.

"I'd love that! I can put them away," replied Mrs. Blakely. The dishes sank and rose under Heather's hands and the hot soapy water moved about by a coarse woven dish rag made them sparkle. "Buddy Cotton was in today, after work," Mrs. Blakely said, putting a stack of plates in the cupboard. "He thought ya might be in," she added.

"I saw him in passing when we come by the depot. His whole family was there," replied Heather.

"He's got an aunt comin' in on the bus," said Mrs. Blakely.

"That's nice," replied Jasper.

"No, her husband recently passed, up in Detroit. Their small house will be even more crowded," Mrs. Blakely replied, with a deep sigh.

The three busied themselves with the dishes and the kitchen chore was quickly finished. Jasper once again thanked Mrs. Blakely for the meal and was out the side door. Heather watched as he pulled away. The lonely man took every opportunity to watch her in the rearview mirror, as it vibrated and shook from the car itself and the rough surface of the city street. She was quickly out of sight. Jasper gave a loud sigh, but no one heard but him, as he continued toward the small place he called home.

CHAPTER THIRTY

There was a nip in the morning air. The sharp odors of the hog farm had a heavy acidic bite. Rhonda struggled with a suitcase under each arm as she came down the front steps. Theo was in the toilet taking his time. Gladys eventually came from the front door for the last time. She took shallow breaths, hoping they would be the last she would ever take of the malodorous farm. She set her suitcase on the step, waiting for Rhonda to return for it.

"THEO!" Gladys yelled. Her shrill voice startled some of the hogs. They replied with loud squeals. "Git yo'sef heah! We'ze ready ta go!"

Rhonda placed the suitcases on the truck and secured them with a cotton rope. She was not too concerned about them, due to the fact that she would be sitting in the back where she could watch them. The coiled spring on the toilet door made a faint creaking sound as Theo pushed it open. The lightweight door gave a loud pop as the spring pulled it closed. He hurried toward the house, working his arms into the galluses of his bibbed overalls. The magazine he emerged with was quickly folded cover first and tucked into his hip pocket. It was not suited for a mother to see. His cuffs hung on the tops of the high boots he wore. It was the last day that his mother and sister would be with him. He would welcome the silence once more, and the ability to sit around the house in his underwear.

"Twenty minutes 'till theys opens. I wuz plannin' on fust in line," Gladys said, taking one step at a time as she hurried to the truck. She dreaded the trip. The small cab was cramped, as she had to ride with the door pulled almost closed under the force of her arm. She lost a shoe, as the heels were too small and would barely slip onto her foot. The aggravation of stepping back to get it made her all the more eager to get to Atlanta. Rhonda sat quietly on the short-legged chair in the bed of the truck.

"Yes, ma'am," said Theo, as he hurried to get in the cab.

Gladys was packed in, the gearshift rubbing her thigh and butt when Theo moved it about. He sometimes skipped a gear to keep from having to work it past her.

"Hurry when yous can!" Gladys said, looking straight ahead.

"Yes, ma'am," said Theo, cranking the truck. Some of the younger hogs squealed and ran the fence line as he circled around the yard to leave.

"Noisy thangs!" Gladys mumbled. "Yous retarded," she added, almost sneezing from the odor.

"Dem's my chillens," Theo replied.

"Wuh!" Gladys said.

Theo parked the truck as close to the clerk's office as possible. The weather change had brought about an early falling of tiny water oak leaves. Large trees grew in many places around the square. The leaves drifted and twirled as they fell to the ground. Several struck Gladys's hair before she reached the door. "Gwine gits my money," she said to herself.

Rhonda, who had been riding in the back of the truck among the empty tubs, carefully moved to the front seat. The upholstered seat felt better to her large sturdy frame. The front posts of the short-legged chair that she had been sitting on had dimpled the backs of her thighs. Brother and sister sat silently watching Gladys as she entered the clerk's office. The two were as different as daylight and dark. Neither actually knew that much about one another, since Theo had struck out to rural Georgia and Rhonda had chosen to follow their mother.

"Thanks for comin'," said Theo.

"It's been different," Rhonda replied.

They sat in silence. Theo felt there was something awry, but he could not imagine what it might be. The gas station where the Greyhound pulled in was on the corner. He could actually make out the schedule board. "Atlanta bus is 10:30," he said, looking toward the store. The truck windows were down and the cooling winds felt good.

"I'm sure we can make it," Rhonda replied.

"I wish I could pay y'all back for your troubles and for comin' down to help me. I gives Mama cash for the lawyer. Dey 'spensive folks!" Theo said, watching the courthouse.

"I didn't knows ya paid Mama anything for the lawyer," Rhonda replied.

"She told me how much she'd put out and I got it up. I keep it here 'n there around tha place," Theo said. "All cash," he added. "I'ze wouldn't be rude and axe her for a itemized bill, she's my mama."

"She my mama toos, but you duz what yo' heart says," replied Rhonda, looking out the open side window, toward the jail. "What wuz it like in there?" she asked.

Theo saw that she was looking at the jail. "Food wuz all right, twice a day. Dey beds be hard, but I had lots time ta think and sleeps. Most left durin' tha day fo' de' road gang," he said.

The clerk's office door was half-glassed with a heavy frosted effect. Gladys could make out shadows inside as people moved about. She opened the door and looked inside. A woman's voice greeted her. "Come in!" Gladys stepped in and stood at the heavy raised panel counter. The twisted steel grill work kept anyone from entering the restricted area. The setup looked much like a bank, with only four desks and a chest high rolling safe located in the corner with the door slightly ajar.

"May I help you?" a woman asked, walking to the open section of the grill work. The other two openings were closed by inset grills. The woman was old. Her almost white hair was pulled into a tight bun on the back of her head. The dark green dress she wore looked to be from the twenties. "I'm Roberta Houston, the county clerk," she said, smiling slightly.

"I'ze Gladys Hightower. I pud up de munnies fo' my dear sawn, Theo Jackson, fo' his bond," Gladys said, resting her heavy arms on the counter. The polished Stone Mountain granite felt cold to the touch. "He's cleared, whiles back, maybe even yesterdays," she said. She batted her eyes several times. "Times gits aways," she added. "Here's my receipt," Gladys said, pushing it across the counter.

Roberta Houston took the receipt and read it carefully. "I have the carbons of it in my books. I'll have to look them up," she said, walking away from the counter. Roberta pulled out her desk chair, which had a homemade patchwork cushion. She sat down gracefully. The large book that Gladys vaguely remembered from the sheriff's office was the one Roberta was working from. Gladys looked about the office. None of the faces were young. Her eyes gradually settled on the safe door. She noticed the ornate painting around the heavy combination lock. From where she stood, it looked to be a farm scene with barns, rail fences, and cows by a small stream. Nevertheless, it intrigued her as to how the details could be done so well. Roberta flipped the pages several times and then settled on one receipt. She checked the number and the contents carefully before closing the book.

The slender woman stood, holding Gladys's ticket to lots of money. "Mrs. Hightower, this amount will be in the form of a check. The bank is across the street, and down a few doors. They will cash it if you like. I'd tuck it away until I got to my own bank and deposit it, but do as you wish," Roberta said. She walked to another desk, where she handed the receipt to a clerk. The woman opened a large ledger type check book, selected a fountain pen, and began to write a check for the full amount less thirty-five dollars court costs.

"The full amount less thirty-five dollars court costs," said the woman. She worked a tabulator quickly to calculate the exact amount.

"Thurdy-fives dollars! Whad tha cote does?" Gladys blurted out.

Roberta, who was seated at her desk, stopped her paperwork and looked at Gladys. "The amount is legal for this type of transaction. It is in our operating rules and by-laws."

"Don't seems right ta meez!" Gladys said, creating a scene over the thirty-five dollars. "Uhm, uhm, uhm!" she said, in a loud huffy tone.

"If you like, I can get Sheriff Louis Gilbert to step over and explain it again for you," said Roberta.

Gladys had already met that son of a bitch. She had no desire to see him again, nor the Chief of Warm Springs. "Ta hell wid bof dem whide sum bitches!" Gladys thought to herself. "No, thad's all right," she said. "Whatever's de rules say is fine."

The woman writing the check carefully folded it along the creases and tore it gently from the book. It closed with a loud thud. The check was handed to Roberta for her signature. Gladys's heart began to pound with the anticipation of having the money in her care.

"I'll need you to sign here that you received the check," said Roberta. She pushed a receipt book forward to Gladys. A fountain pen rested in the depths of the open pages. Gladys hurriedly made her mark and the clerk of court handed her the check.

Gladys Hightower stood and looked at the large check. She shook her head at the excitement of feeling it in her thick hands. "Uhm, uhm!" she said, folding it and finding a place for it among the depths of her large, heavy bosom. "Y'alls has a nize day!" she said, as she headed to the door behind her. Sheriff Gilbert was coming in as she was leaving. At first all she saw was the shoes of a man, then she looked up at the face and jumped.

"Miss Hightower!" he barked loudly, holding the door. "Got your check, I see."

Gladys looked down at her bosom, thinking he saw the check. "I'ze sho' do!" she said, in a huffy tone. "We be goin' ta home," she said, hurrying to the outer door.

The outside door closed and Sheriff Gilbert watched to see that she was out of hearing range. "And don't let the door hit yer big ass when ya leave my county!" he said, glancing at the women in the office. "Don't spend it all in one place!" he added, as he stepped in and closed the door. The women looked surprised. "Bitch!" he yelled, shaking his head.

"Here she comes!" said Theo. He cranked the truck.

Rhonda got out and decided to walk the short distance to the bus station, or actually the gas station, where the bus stopped. She walked past the front of the truck but turned and came back to Theo's open window. "I love ya," she said, looking at her brother.

"Me too!" he quickly replied, but then laughed. "I meant to say, I love you too," he said.

"Be careful. Come to see me sometimes," she said, touching his arm.

"I will," he said, almost breaking up.

Rhonda walked toward the gas station. Theo shook his head. "She'll be just like mother," he said to himself, as he watched her leaving.

The truck door suddenly opened. "Gits me ta hell frum dis place!" Gladys said loudly. Several passersby on the sidewalk heard her and looked. The small truck shook as the large woman wormed her way inside.

Theo carefully backed out and circled the square, coming closer to the bus stop. "10:30's when it leaves next," he said, struggling for second gear as he forced the shift stick past Gladys's leg.

"Jus' as longs as it goes nawth!" Gladys replied.

The light blue Fargo truck had a parking place at the gasoline station. Theo purchased fuel on a regular basis when he was on the north end, and at a regular place on the south end, down in Manchester. A few locals waved at Theo, but most got up and walked away when he drove up. He was slow to notice, but as time would go by, he would take note. Rhonda had beaten them there. She was already standing under the awning at the colored ticket window.

Theo began to unload the suitcases and arrange them on the sidewalk. "Leavin'?" shouted a man, wiping the grease from his hands.

"Two, one-way ta Atlanter," Theo said, setting the last bag on the sidewalk.

"That's three dollars for both," the man replied, holding out his hand for the money.

"Mama!" Rhonda called out.

Gladys seemed to overlook the three dollars. Theo eventually pulled it from his pocket. "Three dollars!" he said.

"And here's your tickets," the man replied, as he punched a hole in one corner. "Lose this, you'll pay again. It's about an hour 'fore it arrives. Sit anywhere but the white lobby."

Gladys took a deep breath. "Yes, sir!"

"Mama, I'm glad you come to help me out of this situation," Theo said softly, as he hugged the large woman. He was almost on his tiptoes to reach around her neck. "Thanks!" he said softly.

"Yous my good sawn, my luvin' sawn," she replied.

"I've got work ta do," Theo said, releasing Gladys. "Calls me when ya gets there."

"Yous my good sawn, my luvin' sawn," Gladys repeated, wiping tears.

Theo waved at Rhonda, who was standing under the shade. She waved back. The hog farmer quickly lost sight of his kin as he drove away on another slop run. Gladys pulled the check from its hiding place, deep within her brassiere. "Leb'n hunderd, no, leb'n thousand, five hunderd and sixty-five dollars," she whispered, as she quickly glanced at the bond refund once more. Rhonda believed that the money should have been divided among the various churches that helped raise it, or just give it all to a non-profit charitable group.

The tranquil setting of the slow town was broken by the shrill sounding of a horn, coming from the south. Rhonda watched with curiosity. It was the Greyhound bus. As it pulled the hill into town and circled the square, a roll of black smoke drifted across the downtown area. There were no other passengers to board, just the two Negro women.

The bus driver could see how large both women were, especially Gladys. "Could ya move to another seat so I can get these two seated right quick?" the driver said, talking to a couple behind him that were occupying one to the seat. The man directly behind the driver leaned to the woman behind him and asked if the lady cared to join him. "Big Negro woman and another one, he wants to get 'em seated up front," smiled the man, to the younger woman. The woman gave a loud sigh and moved to the seat.

"Ain't they supposed ta sit in the back?" asked another man. That question could be read on all the white faces. The bench seat in the back already had four Negroes on it.

The bus was stopping in front of the gas station. The driver motioned two cars into the street. The large bus blocked the entrance and exit to the business and obstructed the vision at the side street. "Have ya seen that one on the street? She can't get to the back without swiping everyone," said the driver, as he stood up with his hand on the door lever. Several looked up and down the aisle. That seemed to justify the placement of the new passengers within the bus's seating arrangement. The door gave a loud hiss when it opened. "All aboard!" called the driver, as he stepped to the ground. "These your bags?" he asked, pulling a key from the large bundle on his carved belt.

"Dem's ours," Gladys replied, as Rhonda walked up. Rhonda was already carrying bags to the side of the bus for the driver to secure in the cargo bay underneath.

"Thanks!" he replied, taking two bags from Rhonda. She went after two more and Gladys shuffled forward with the last one. "Climb aboard," said the driver, closing the large door. The driver stood back and watched Gladys wipe most everything with her wide hips. "Second seat on my side!" yelled the driver.

"Ain't thad fo' whide folks?" Gladys questioned, as she looked into the sea of faces.

"Not today! Sit down!" replied the driver, taking one step at a time. The door closed with a clap and a hiss, blocking most of the exhaust fumes. "I need your tickets," he said, as he stood behind Rhonda. She soon handed the tickets over her shoulder. The quick snapping sound of his ticket punch was heard cancelling the Atlanta bound tickets.

The driver took his seat and tapped the horn. A helper at the small bus stop went into the busy street and stopped traffic, waving the bus driver to pull ahead, a custom in small towns.

"Missa Glenn pick us ups and weez be home, home sweet home," Gladys said, as the bus floated from side to side. The next stop was Luthersville, unless the flag was down at the Primrose crossing.

* * *

Heather did not feel well. She was almost to the point of calling the chief and asking for a sick day. The boarders were gone. Mrs. Blakely had finished the dishes and was ready to open the store. Heather was ready for duty, but still sat at the table. She felt so bad that she actually dreaded the inevitable confrontation with Buddy. As soon as the thought had crossed her mind, she remembered her mother's saying. "Be careful what you wish, and remember that you make a difference in someone's life, whether you know it or not."

Heather was drinking hot tea this morning, something she frequently did when the cramps rolled around. She still walked in on discussions here and there about the case and Jackson being freed, and whether the woman detective was even legal. The young woman still found herself drifting into deep thought about the dead woman, and especially the infant, the blood pools, and the fire poker speckled with pieces of flesh from the savage beating. Heather was in need of support, and there was no one to turn to. She took a sip of the steaming hot tea and watched the sky to the north through the window in the side door. The last of the zinnias were arranged in a cobalt blue vase. The bright colored flowers gave a burst of excitement to the dimly lit foyer. She heard the front store bell sound. Just by its tone she knew it was Buddy. His hurried footsteps could be heard coming to the kitchen. Heather quickly gathered herself.

"Hi!" Buddy said, as he stood in the hallway. His big smile was almost contagious. Smiles were something the Duncans seemed to struggle with, even in their brightest hours.

"Hi!" she replied, nursing her tea.

"Time of the month?" he asked.

"You think that's something to ask a woman?" Heather snapped.

"My mama and all the females at my house drink hot tea when it is," he said, looking down. He was embarrassed.

"Yes, and it's not to be broadcast," she replied, with a stern look.

"My aunt's moved in, my uncle died. She didn't have any place to go, up north. Dad took it pretty hard. Mama doesn't like it," Buddy said, looking at the chair across from her.

"Sit down, but don't get into trouble with Mrs. Blakely," Heather said.

"She said I could come back, just for a few. My aunt says she's got some money and will give it for an addition on our place," he said eagerly.

460

"That's nice," Heather replied.

"Industrial arts teacher said I could use the planning and drawing of the plans as my quarterly project. Do you know anyone that can help me get started? I've read the chapter and it's got me stymied," he said, scratching his head.

"I never knew my grandfather, but he was a draftsman," she replied, sipping her tea.

"And a marshal?" Buddy asked.

"Yes. I'll bet he'd say determine what the room is to be used for, take into consideration the furniture to go in it, doors, windows, and draw it to scale. Maybe make the addition in keeping with the roof line," she said.

Buddy looked surprised. His eyes sparkled. "Hey, that's a good start. When I get it sketched out, would ya look at it?" he asked. Mrs. Blakely was calling for him. "Be right there!" he yelled. The eager boy hurried to the front where customers were gathering.

Heather managed to overcome the last cramp. As she sat watching the telephone it rang. "I'll get it!" she yelled. "Blakely's Store and Boarding."

"Collect call for Detective Duncan," said the local operator.

"That's me! I'll pay!" Heather said.

"Hey, Daddy!" she said, excitedly.

"How did ya know it was me?" Sonny asked.

"Because I wanted it to be," she said, sitting down in the chair. "I want ta come home," she said, trying not to cry.

"It's just like you left it," Sonny replied.

"I need a helper!" Grandmother Margaret yelled in the background.

"I failed. I failed the woman and the baby," Heather said, as she began to sob.

"We've kept up with it. You and Jasper did a fine job. It was the court that gave it away, but ya got the gunman," Sonny said, in a defensive tone. "Don't leave yet. See the bastard swing."

There was silence for a moment. Heather wiped her eyes. "What's Margaret got?" she asked.

"Life, some speaking engagements, and manuscripts underway," Sonny replied. "She's not gettin' any younger, ya know," he whispered.

Heather took a sip of tea and the cup rattled on the saucer. "That time?" Sonny asked, upon detecting the distinctive rattle.

"Yes," she whispered. "How's Holly?" Heather asked.

"Holly! Sing for Heather!" Sonny said. The bloodhound sat up and began to howl several different tones. The dog knew it was Heather. She finished singing and placed her large head on Sonny's thigh as he sat at the telephone table.

"Oh, my! That's music," Heather said.

"We saw the date in the newspaper," Sonny said. "Shall I come down and ride back?" he asked.

"No, I'll close it out and hurry home," Heather said. She was feeling like there was hope.

"Ya can type, file, run an office, shoot, track. There's plenty to keep you busy," he said.

"I love y'all," Heather said.

"Remember, there's always home," Sonny said. His voice almost cracked from missing her. He saw Polly in Heather, even more so after Polly's untimely passing. Sonny now knew how his father had felt about Maybell and Margaret. "We'll see you soon," he said softly, just before hanging up.

Heather wiped away tears and took her teacup to the sink. It was a new day, with a brighter outlook.

* * *

Time was passing. Robert Gaskill had met with James Lee in his cell and obtained the information required by the court. There was no property, and therefore no will. There was no designated family to claim the body. The cooler months were close at hand. Doc Hubbard met with Sheriff Gilbert and discussed plans for the sturdy gallows for the public hanging. Being the coroner, he had a few books with suggested illustrations for the structure, and those were of his own interest and curiosity. The books specifically discussed the calculations of the correct knot, and the effects of too much or too little. It seemed to be a rather scientific thing. There was even a paragraph and illustrations on where the long knot should strike when the subject fell. The two men agreed upon a detailed sketch and it was passed off to Curley Jones. He would get it done with prison labor. From daylight until almost dark for the next three days, the strong massive structure was the only project for the county. Curious motorists slowed to look, while the old men in town moved their chairs to the shady side of the street and watched the gallows slowly grow.

Sheriff Gilbert drew a purchase order from the county clerk's office and walked across the square to the hardware store. The doors, both front and rear, were open. The cooling weather was comforting. Cold weather was always welcomed in the South. For the farmers it was a reward after the long hours of intense labor. It allowed a time for renewal of equipment and rest for the harvest bearing land. There was a homemade sign already in the front window advising that the current hunting licenses were available. The State of Georgia had been taxing the citizens since the 1890's with a professional hunter's tax. It permitted and limited the number of animals and the types that could be killed. Hunters sold the dressed meat for a profit. The general public and game limits came a few years later.

"Howdy!" greeted the store clerk, as he stacked new boxes of shotgun shells into the glass fronted display case. "Shells?" he asked, looking up at the sheriff.

"No, not today. Pre-stretched rope, hemp or cotton if there's nothing else," said the sheriff. He leaned over the counter and looked at the new boxes of shells. "I see the duck's been changed a bit on the new boxes," said the sheriff. "I've always wondered why they don't ever put a rabbit on one," he added.

The hardware clerk continued to stack just a few more to finish the display. "We've got no pre-stretched rope," he said, glancing up at the sheriff.

"What do ya suggest?" asked Sheriff Gilbert.

The clerk stood up. "Wet it down and pull it till it's dry, I guess," he said, shrugging his shoulders. The glass door silently slid closed.

Sheriff Gilbert looked perplexed. "Give me fifty foot of half-inch hemp. I'll make it work!"

The clerk started toward the back of the store. "We may have only manila," he said, with his back to the sheriff.

"I don't give a damn if it's chocolate, just sell me some strong rope," said the sheriff, with a chuckle.

"I need not ask for what," replied the clerk. He handed the sheriff one end of the rope. "Walk to the wall, that's forty feet, then the marks on the floor each indicate one foot. I'd leave it coiled and soak it in a tub, then pull it between a car and a sturdy tree. Let the sun get to it. It won't stretch much anyway," he said, cutting the rope.

"Doc said stretched rope. I think he's goin' ta wax it in the knot area. He don't want any suffering," advised the sheriff. He handed the purchase order to the clerk. "I need a ticket."

"I'd raise money for a charity, sell tickets ta shoot his sorry ass," said the clerk. He priced out the rope purchase on a small tablet. Several customers came into the store. The sheriff moved his cigar in his mouth, raised his hand in a form of salute, and left.

"When do tha new huntin' licenses come in?" a customer was heard to ask, as the sheriff walked out. The sheriff drew attention walking from the hardware to the jail with the coil of rope hanging from his shoulder.

* * *

Jasper pulled up to the front door of Mrs. Blakely's store. He did not have to sound the horn. Buddy Cotton saw him and yelled out for Heather. She hurried through the busy store and down the front steps. Heather opened the car door and eagerly sat down. "Let's ride!" she said, looking at Jasper.

"My, you're chipper today," he replied, as he watched the mirror for oncoming cars.

"I got a call from home this morning," she said excitedly. "I'm convinced there's hope yet."

"I think we need to stay on the outskirts, see the countryside," Jasper said, as he pulled into traffic.

* * *

The sheriff entered the office and dropped the length of rope by the heavy steel jail door. "Is that it?" asked Dixie, working at her desk.

"That's it!" replied Sheriff Gilbert. "Where's Curley? The gallows is looking good," he said, taking his seat.

"He's in the back of the yard with the prisoners. They're getting some cold water."

Curley sat on a stick of stove wood watching the prisoners he had chosen to build the gallows. They sat around under the large chinaberry tree. "Today'll get it done, boss," said one of the prisoners.

"I hope so," said Curley.

* * *

By law, the sheriff was responsible for the ordered execution of the condemned person. This was Louis Gilbert's first. On the night before, as he tried to sleep, he had given thought on the best way to stretch the rope. It should not be that hard, soak it and put tension on it until it dried.

"Mornin'!" he said to Miss Jewel, as he came into the kitchen with the rope. "Where's the foot tub?" he asked. The Negro woman had bacon grease on her hands, as she was loading the large skillet. Coffee was making on the back burner.

"Hangin' on de wall down below," she answered.

"Oh, yeah," he replied, as he passed on through.

The kitchen door closed. "Jus' likes it's been theres all de time," she said, shaking her head. "Men folks, couldn't fine dey ass if it wasn't growed on," she said, smiling and shaking her head. Through the narrow opening in the back window, she heard him leave the wood steps and then heard the tub striking the ground, and the sound of splashing of water.

Breakfast was soon ready. The prisoners and road gang had already been fed. The Negro cook had fed them biscuits and side meat, with black coffee. They seemed to enjoy it. Miss Jewel heard their excitement as Curley Jones handed it through the bars. Maybe for anyone left on Christmas Day, she would try and get them some sorghum syrup to sop. Miss Jewel always thought it was sad for folks to be in prison during Christmas. She had heard that the big house in Atlanta served a piece of white bread, a boiled turkey neck, and an orange on Christmas Day.

"I'll let that soak till after while," the sheriff announced, as he came in for breakfast. There was enough time for everyone to sit around the kitchen table and eat together, even Miss Jewel.

"Calls 'em in," she said to the sheriff.

He hurried down the narrow hallway to the door that separated his residence from the jail office. He banged on it and called out like he was

464

calling the hogs. The lingering deputy, Dixie, and Curley hurried back to join him. The nip in the morning air told them that fall was near. It made all the food aromas that much more tempting to one's nose. Jewell made the greasiest biscuits in Greenville, but they certainly went down well, especially when they were hot.

"Shurriff, hope ya don't mind me joinin' in," the deputy said, as he passed the plate of hot biscuits on around.

"Just let some of the others get a chance," the sheriff said with a smile, as he cut the syrup off with his finger.

"Oh, I will, I will!" said the deputy.

"How far from the chinaberry tree to the toilet?" asked Sheriff Gilbert.

"Hundred feet or more," the deputy replied.

"At least seventy-five," added Curley. "Why?"

"The hangin' rope is soakin'. I need to stretch it. I'll tie it to the tree and pull it tight with a patrol car. It's downhill. I won't set the brake. The rope can hold the car back. It should dry by good dark," he said. That was a chore for the sheriff after breakfast. He could often be seen looking out the kitchen door at his handiwork. The rope turned from a medium brown to a light tan. He knew it was ready then.

Sheriff Gilbert had borrowed the book from the coroner showing the detailed tying of the hangman's knot. He and Curley Jones had spent considerable time tying and re-tying. They placed it on James Lee's neck whenever they thought it was the right number of turns. They pulled it down snug and held it straight up, as it would be when he dropped, trying to get the top of the knot to be against the desired skull spot. The sheriff stood outside the cell and admired his final handiwork. The trial and error attempts worked on the accused, but he did not show it until they left. James Lee had become unnerved from the ordeal.

The sheriff lowered the knot, slowly realizing the deadline. "I need to see Old Souse Meat and get an announcement run," he said, quickly looping the rope neatly. "Tonight's yer last meal," he said to Lee. "What would you desire?" Sheriff Gilbert. James Lee stood with his back to the lawmen. There was a long silence. "Fried chicken, pork chop, watermelon?" the sheriff asked, laughing.

James Lee turned and rushed to the front bars. He grabbed the bars and snarled his reply. "A freedom sandwich! Asshole!"

"Touchy," Curley said.

"If ya decide, call the jailer," said the sheriff. "I've got a deadline."

The sheriff tossed the rope on his desk, then hurried out the door and across the street. He was headed to the Vindicator office. He looked at his watch. He should have twenty minutes before they closed. His hand turned the door knob at ten till five. Things inside were visibly slow.

"Sheriff," greeted Alfred Huffman.

"Where's the old man?" asked Sheriff Gilbert. The young reporter motioned with his head that the old man was in the back. "Thanks!" the sheriff replied, as he walked back. The room was dark except for the dim glow of a one bulb desk lamp on the man's desk.

Sheriff Gilbert sat down. "Have a seat!" said the old newspaper man.

"Thanks! I did!" said the sheriff. "I need a legal announcement put out in the morning edition."

"What would that be?" the old man asked. "An execution notice?" he asked, before the sheriff took a deep breath to reply.

"Yes!" he said. "Y'all got his correct name, and he drops at 10:30 tomorrow," said Sheriff Gilbert, moving his wet cigar.

"We've got it set," said the old man. He pulled a proof from his desk and handed it to the sheriff. "Approve it."

"Superior Court of Meriwether County has sentenced the accused, and found guilty in a court of law, James Lee, Negro, to be executed by hanging, until dead. The location is at the grounds of the sheriff's office. Civic organizations and religious groups wishing to participate afterwards should contact the sheriff's office by eight o'clock on same morning, for consideration. This is for the murder of Gertrude and infant Polly Sue Miller."

"Sounds good to me," the sheriff replied, handing it back.

"Young Huffman can get it on the radio stations tonight, if you'd like," the newspaper man said.

"Same words?" asked the sheriff.

"That's what we'll get to them. He'll do it by telephone," said the old man.

The sheriff walked out the door at exactly five o'clock. The window shade was pulled behind him. By the time he got back to his office, the Manchester station was broadcasting. He stood still and listened. It was word for word as the old man had presented. Jasper and Heather were standing at Claude Allen's garage with a Nehi when they heard it on the table top radio.

"The time is nigh," Heather said softly.

* * *

The day before the execution was busy for the sheriff and his deputies. The telephone was in constant use, and marked cars were coming and going on related errands. The telephone rang in Doc Hubbard's office.

"Doctor's office!"

"Sheriff Gilbert. We'll need ya ta be over here at ten o'clock for the hangin'," he said, moving his wet cigar about in his mouth. He stood at the front of Dixie's desk and looked at the gallows on the front yard. The massive structure was natural and unpainted. The thin curtains hanging over the window moved about with the slight breeze.

"I'll be there earlier if Miss Jewel's feedin'," replied the doctor.

"I'm afraid it will be so hectic that she'll just put out a plate of biscuits filled with somethin' and a pot of coffee on the stove. I'm not feedin' tha world. Just those who are here to pull this thing off," said Sheriff Gilbert.

"Rope ready?" asked the doctor.

"Yes, tied and lying on my desk," answered the sheriff, looking over at it.

"Got a box?" the doctor asked.

"God damn it! I'm glad ya said something. I'll get someone over to the county barn and see if there's one in the loft," said the sheriff. "We'll be up and about by daylight," he added.

"I'll be there, early," replied Doc Hubbard. The men ended the telephone conversation.

The sheriff yelled for the deputy who was in house. He was sent to the county farm to see if there was a coffin in the storage loft. The deputy forgot the key to the chain lock and had to return to get it. This added time to the chore, making his day on the lonely road a little shorter. At one time the barn had been painted red with white trim. The cupola centered on the top ridge was still sporting an iron and copper ball and a wind arrow. It moved with the slightest wind, making a squeaking sound.

The patrol car's brakes squealed as they brought the car to a stop near the large double hung doors. There was a single door that the key fit. All the doors were secured with a rusty colored link chain and a surplus railroad lock. The keys were a little harder to come by, which kept them from being purchased off the display board in town at the hardware, or the feed store along the railroad tracks. The deputy turned off the engine. He sat for a moment and looked around at the surplus farm equipment and a few pieces of road machinery that were to be auctioned off. A lot of it was mule drawn, outdated stuff. There was seemingly a fenced off section for everything. Before a prisoner could get off county property, he would be tired from climbing hog wire fences topped with a strand of barbed wire. The vast majority of the fence posts were crossties. There was not a person in sight. The only living things were several crows watching him from a safe distance as they sat in the top limbs of a dead pine at the edge of the woods line. Spider webs were thick in the sheltered eaves and the door frames. The yellow and black garden spider clung to its web, moved about only by the slightest breeze.

The car door moaned from a lack of oil on the hinges as it swung open under the power of the deputy's hand. The dust rose when his black Wellington boot struck the ground beneath the open car door. The car's hot engine hissed as a tiny coolant leak dropped onto the exhaust. The dirt yard that surrounded the large lonely barn was without tracks. Maybe a small field mouse had left its tracks as it came and went from the opening under the single door, but it was hard for the deputy to tell, with all the pieces of straw and grass that lay about. His hand guided the key into the opening of the lock. The innards of the lock were dry from the lack of oil, but a good shake managed to break it free. The cast iron hinges cried out under a light coat of rust as the lone deputy pushed the door open. The cold air inside stood like a dark wall, bearing all sorts of mixed odors, guano, old leather collars and harness that covered one wall, the last animal waste that had dried, and a hint of coal oil, a familiar smell but a lonely one.

The only light came from the door he had just opened and from the cracks along the vertical boards that covered the back wall. The side walls had been covered earlier with surplus weather boarding, which had been painted forest green years ago. It was wind tight and almost light proof. The shadowy steps without a hand railing were before him, leading to an even darker loft. "Maybe there's a hay door. That will let light in," he thought. The deputy got up enough nerve to take the first step up into the darkness of the loft. The sudden movement of loose boards and the sound of claws on tin raised the hair on his neck. His hand went to his revolver, as he looked about in the darkness of the main floor. He never knew what had made the noise but convinced himself that it must have been a tenant animal, a stray cat, a fox, maybe a 'possum. The deputy held his baton out in front of him to break the spider webs as he went up the steps.

The loft was a large open space. Tiny holes in the sheet tin roof gave small tapered cones of bright sunlight, falling to the dusty plank floor under his feet. The circles of light were the best he would have to find the coffin. The loft door was also chained, from the inside. A bird swooped past and left through a bright hole at the top of a far wall. His heart raced as he wondered what else was up there with him. The moisture in his mouth was almost gone. His tongue was sticking to his cheeks from fear of the unknown. The deputy's eyes eventually became acclimated to the poor light that was available. He could make out various stored objects. For the longest he overlooked the coffin. He thought it was a work table with feed sacks and buckets sitting on top, but it was not. It was a coffin, resting on sawhorses. The lid served as a surface to lay things on. Inching his way from one bright circle to another, he soon came close to the coffin. Hurriedly he set the paint buckets on the floor and began to rake off the feed bags and papers that were left with his baton. The disturbed dust drifted in the still air. He coughed a couple of times and thought he heard something move when he did. He stood still and listened. There was nothing moving but the loose sheet tin, which groaned when the wind blew, and something that scraped against the back wall down below.

"Holy, Jesus! Get this damn thing down with me," he said, taking hold of one end, setting it on the floor. Once he got it off of the sawhorses, he dragged the box toward the rectangle of light afforded by the steep stairwell. The sliding of the coffin caused loose dirt to be raked over the cracks in the loft planks. It drifted into the still air below. Soon he reached the stairs.

"Front ways or behind?" he asked himself. "Behind," he reasoned. Each end had a sturdy handle to hold the coffin off of him. The deputy went down several steps and reached back, pulling the box to him. It soon dropped, taking the angle of the steep steps. Another step or two and he pulled the box toward him. In the midst of pulling the box down behind him, something fell in the loft. The deputy stopped in his tracks. His heart raced once more, pounding in his chest from the sudden sound. He stood holding the box off of him and listened. All was quiet. Eventually he reached the single door where the bright sunlight rushed in. Sweat was running from his hair, down his forehead. A small gray mouse sat in the corner of the door. It quickly scurried away when they made eye contact.

"Did the sheriff ask me to check on a coffin, or to bring one back if I found it?" the tiring deputy asked himself. He scratched his head and carefully found the car key in his pocket with his dirty hands. The large trunk lid opened with the turning of the keyed lock. There was not much in the trunk, just a scotch block for a wheel, a length of pull chain, and a bumper jack and handle. Removing the coffin's lid lightened the load a bit. The deputy managed to slide the box into the trunk all the way to the back of the rear seat. The lid had room to settle in. Now that he was in good light, the coffin had been brush painted with dark oak, probably flooring color from one of the government buildings. The inside was whitewashed. The trunk lid was fully open and nothing to tie it off with. "The damn barn's got to have something, a plow line, cotton twine or something," the deputy mumbled, as he stepped back inside. He was lucky, someone had saved twine from various objects and hung it on a nail along the stairs. The long piece of sisal twine was all he needed to pull the trunk lid down and tie it off for the trip back to town. The traffic was always light between town and the barn. The deputy was able to cruise along without incident.

He sounded the car's horn when he pulled past the gallows and close to the steps of the jail doors. Beep, beep! Sheriff Gilbert was resting his face in his hands at his desk. He had closed his weary eyes for a moment and dozed off. The car horn startled him awake. "Jesus!" he said, looking out the window. He saw the patrol car with a coffin tied into the back. "Curley!" he yelled. "Hurry!" Curley was in a storage closet, pulling inventory. He hurried to the sheriff's calling. "Sum bitch brought it down here. I thought he'd just let me know if it was there," replied the sheriff, putting the damp cigar back into his mouth.

"Hell, sweep it off and prop it on the front steps," Curley said, as he pushed the door open. Sheriff Gilbert followed.

"Here it is!" said the deputy. The sheriff put his hands on his waist and walked around the dusty box looking pleased. The deputy was sweaty and dusty from his efforts.

"Let's put it here on the stoop," said the sheriff, as he began to untie the twine.

"Little dusting and it'll look all right," replied the deputy. Curley agreed as he took the handle of the exposed end. The three men carried the coffin easily to the stoop and leaned it against the building.

"It'll get a corn broom to it, and that's all," said the sheriff. He was right, that was all the coffin got. Doc Hubbard pulled up in his car and got out.

"So that's the final box," said Doc, walking up and looking at the dusty coffin. The sheriff did not respond. The doctor looked it over carefully. "No government requirements. There's no embalming either," he said, pushing his straw fedora back on his head.

"Can the public see him be put in the box?" asked Curley.

"They can see him hang. I don't see why not, if they want to stay until that time," replied Doc Hubbard. "Where's the grave?" he asked, looking at the sheriff.

"There's no one ta claim the bastard. I guess we'll put him in pauper town cemetery," said Sheriff Gilbert. "Curley, get the road gang supervisor on the telephone and have him to get the next spot dug by eight o'clock in the morning. Tell him I know it's close, but this is a close profession," grumbled the sheriff. "A full six feet down, not four!" he reminded. Curley hurried away to get the crucial task under way. "Curley!" yelled the sheriff, motioning for him to come back. "Whoever he takes out, chain 'em without the ball, and here, give him this ta get 'em a drink at the store before they come back. The sheriff dug into his pocket and pulled out a dollar bill. "That should buy a lot of drinks," he said, smiling.

In less than an hour, a heavy Dodge truck pulled up. It was the road gang warden. He was left to pick his diggers from the men in the jail. Curley walked him inside the cell block. "I'm here to get volunteer diggers!" he called out, as he walked in through the heavy steel doorway.

"Niggers? How many, boss man?" yelled Oliver Queen, with his black face against the cell bars.

"He didn't say niggers! He said diggers!" replied a new white prisoner. "Dumb ass!"

"Don't make no difference, weez do de wuk mos' all de time," yelled back Oliver Queen. He wanted to be part of this historical moment, burying the notorious James Lee.

"Three teams of two," said the warden.

"Oliver and those other three," he called out, pointing to the blacks in the one cell. "Curley, two whites that can work with these blacks," he barked.

Curley looked into the three cells and pointed to the men he wanted. "No trouble. He'll put ya in the hole under James Lee. No trouble!" he repeated, opening the cells and allowing the two whites to step out. "Sit on the floor!" Curley ordered, as he brought leg restraints in and dropped them at their feet. "Shackle up!" He brought up Oliver Queen and the other four Negroes. "Same thing! Shackle up! No talking unless yer spoken to by a badge!" Curley reminded.

Oliver Queen sat on the floor, fastening the chains on his ankles. He looked at James Lee, who sat slumped on his metal bunk. Queen made hand gestures to Lee that implied he was seeing him buried. James Lee replied with silent explicit words, then got up and walked to the dark end of his cell.

"Load up!" Curley ordered. All the prisoners stood, with the whites first in line. The road warden wore a large double-action revolver and kept a shotgun in the cab. All the prisoners rode in the back of the large flatbed truck. The special detail gave them something different to do, even if it was hard work.

The pauper town cemetery was located close to the property where the large storage barn stood. Both were off of Granny Turner Road. The warden parked the heavy truck along the eastern side of the growing rows of graves, mostly prisoners who had died in the system or persons who had been found with no one to identify them. The truck was high, only the youngest could jump down. No one jumped in this detail. The men were well beyond their prime years. The warden knew all the Negroes by name. He did not know the two whites. There was a rusty quart oil can at the end of the rows.

"Hold yer ears, boys!" The Negroes knew the warden was about to shoot something. They held their ears and watched. "See that oil can?" asked the warden, pointing to the end of the row of stone marked graves. It was some seventy feet away. The large revolver was hefted from the hip holster and careful aim applied, along with delicate trigger control. Bam! The revolver reported. The rusty can jumped high and exploded into several rusty pieces. The Negroes bragged on the warden's shooting ability. They knew it helped to their betterment of the task at hand. The fired shell was quickly replaced from several in the warden's pocket.

The new grave's location and size were indicated by a spade point as the warden stepped it off and scribed a line in the dirt. "Dig 'er here, boys," he said.

"Yessa, boss!" said the Negroes.

Even working in teams of two, two on the shovels and four resting, it was tiring work. Sweat soon dripped from their elbows and brows. "Speaks boss?" asked Oliver Queen.

"Go ahead," replied the warden, standing at a distance as he watched the progress.

"Darks gwine cotch us," Oliver said.

"Headlights'll get us through," the warden replied. Dark did catch them. The Dodge was cranked and the two large bullet shaped headlights cast a bright light over the men and the dark hole at their feet.

The digging crew missed feeding time. The shovel dug hole was a work of art, true sides, a clean bottom, and six feet deep as the sheriff had specified. The warden declared the dig done and ordered the prisoners back on the truck. The darkness and the moving air were chilling to their wet skin as it rushed over them on the ride back. The Negroes hoped this detail would be like the other special ones. The last store to stay open late was Thames Grocery, a tiny place on the west side of the square. The heavy truck pulled in and stopped. The horn sounded loudly and the store owner knew it was a prison detail. He came to the front door and looked out. The warden stood at the back of the large truck.

"Can I feed six?" he asked loudly.

"Tha usual?" asked the store clerk.

"That's fine!" the warden said.

Oliver Queen smiled. Those who had been in the system long enough knew this meant a grape or orange Nehi drink, a small pack of soda crackers, a large can of Underwood's Deviled Ham, and a Moon Pie.

The clerk brought the food out and the warden took his and set the box on the truck. Each prisoner took his share and passed it on back. "I do believes it's wuff de wuk to git dis meals," Oliver whispered in the moonlight.

The prison truck pulled into the jail yard after lockdown. The night jailer was sitting on the stoop in a cane bottomed straight chair in the dark. He stood in the headlights of the truck as it pulled up. His boys were home.

"Dug and fed," said the warden. "Get down, boys."

"Gittin' down boss," they all replied, as they dropped from the high truck. They formed a line on the cement walkway.

The night jailer walked the line and looked at the faces. "All here!" he yelled out. "Sleep in yer drawers, baths tomorrow," he said, as he motioned for them to go inside. The prisoners who were inside were aroused by the noise of shuffling feet and clinking chains. The warden covered while the jailer locked everyone down where they belonged. The jail was quiet after the bosses left. The sparse street lamplight combined with the moonlight sieved its way inside the jail.

Oliver Queen stood at the bars in his drawers. He could make out James Lee in his bunk. "Hey, nigger! Yous wid blood on yo' hands. Tomorrow's de day," he said softly. "Sweets dreams," he whispered.

The day before the hanging had been quiet and peaceful as far as policing. There were pleasant conversations and rides on the city streets, pointing out the changing leaves. Buddy Cotton had stayed over to show Heather his sketch of the addition to his family's small house. The boy was enthusiastic about the project. Heather made a few suggestions, mostly in window placement and door swings, practical things a teenager would not normally consider. The Have-a-Hank display of fall colors had come in, along with the new heavier billed caps for the upcoming colder months. Heather, at Buddy's insistence, had to go and see the window display that he had created.

Officer Edgar Peterson was in early. He had stopped by Mrs. Blakely's store for a few personal items. Edgar took it upon himself to ask if Buddy wanted a ride home. Heather was very pleased at that gesture as it was a good ways out, and besides, the lad had many times proven his worth as a growing good citizen. Heather watched and waved at the teenager hanging out of the patrol car window in his efforts to get another look at her and wave goodbye. He was unaware that it would be Heather's last night in Warm Springs. Tomorrow, with God's Grace, she would be in her own home.

Mrs. Blakely locked the cash register and placed her sign on the counter, "In back - ring bell". Closing the store and finishing the evening meal was always difficult, as her time was split between the two tasks. Heather caught her in the hallway between the kitchen and the store room. "I'd like to pay in full through tomorrow," Heather said. She had turned and walked along with the busy woman.

"And why all of a sudden? We're fine on money," Mrs. Blakely replied, wiping her damp hands on the kitchen towel that hung from her apron. She looked at the advertisement clock for Moore's Ice Cream that hung on the front wall. It was ten minutes until closing time. The second hand moved smoothly, but the minute hand suddenly indexed with each passing minute. The afternoon sun coming through the front windows had a yellowish cast about it. There was possibly a weather change coming soon.

"No one knows, but I'm resigning tomorrow, just as soon as James Lee drops and swings with no signs of life," Heather whispered to the woman, as they stood at the store counter. Mrs. Blakely had already pulled the boarding house ledger and was beginning to calculate to the time that Heather had requested.

"I noticed you had your suitcases up and opened," said Mrs. Blakely. "A dollar and forty-five cents," she advised, closing the ledger.

"It should be more than that," Heather reminded.

"My records show that is a fine price for us to part on," smiled the woman. "I must stir the corn!" she said, hurrying to the kitchen.

Heather followed. "I'd like to keep this between us, no one knows," she said, walking right behind her.

"I can do that," Mrs. Blakely assured, pushing a spatula under the corn that bubbled in a large cast iron skillet.

Heather stood just inside of the kitchen's preparation area. "You're a wonderful cook," she said.

"I know, I'm very simple," Mrs. Blakely said, smiling. Beads of sweat were forming on her brow. "Let's call this our goodbye," she said, tapping the spatula against the edge of the skillet. "I've really enjoyed it. The women in town will miss you. Maybe you could come back and speak to our women's groups sometimes," she added.

"Between my Grandmother and me, I'm sure we could be of some entertainment," Heather said, smiling.

"So, Buddy doesn't know?" asked Mrs. Blakely.

"No one but you," Heather said.

"The boy will be crushed," Mrs. Blakely replied, looking at Heather.

"Hopefully he'll have fond memories," Heather said, looking down at the floor. "I'll load out in the darkness."

The two women walked back to the front, where Mrs. Blakely turned the sign on the front door and gently closed it for the night. The large barrel bolt slid into its keeper on the top and the bottom bolt through the metal plate in the threshold. The surface mounted Yale deadbolt gave its loud click, throwing the set of rectangular bolts into the opposing fixed door. The aging narrow window shades were pulled well past the midway point of the door glass. The two shades were curled badly on the edges from the heat of the sun over the years. "I take it that you're leaving because of the negative opinions, and the fact that in the horrible bloody murder cases, the court only found the one Negro guilty."

"Pretty much so," Heather said. She stood a few feet away in the main aisle. "The personal attacks are taking me down."

"Times are hard to change. Maybe you are a pioneer for women's rights. You damn sure are in these parts," Mrs. Blakely replied. She walked back to the kitchen with Heather still following. "I'm sure this case put changes into play in many a relationship, especially the arrest of that wife beater here in town, twice I believe. Mark my words, there's a time coming when womenfolks'll save this country." Mrs. Blakely turned and looked at the much younger Heather. "Remember me fondly," she said, smiling.

"I will. Oh, I will," Heather said softly. "It's been a pleasure to stay here."

That evening, the boarders were quiet. It appeared that everyone was tired. There was small talk about avoiding the Greenville square and the traffic until noon. Heather packed her belongings after laying out her suit for the execution. The last thing before bed, she loaded the suitcases and checked the fluids of the Essex with her flashlight. She was dressed in her nightgown and housecoat. She was unaware that Edgar Peterson was admiring her from a distance as she worked in the moonlight.

In the cool air of the night, under the dim lamplight, Heather carefully wrote a notice of resignation for Chief Hawthorn, and a letter to Jasper. She felt more obligated to Jasper than she did the chief, even though he had given her the chance. She sealed the envelope for the chief and then wrote the letter to Jasper. *"Dear Jasper; I take this moment to express how pleasurable it was to have worked with you, all these days. I wish you the best of luck with the department and your career. Sincerely, Heather Duncan."*

Heather took the time to express to the newspaper man Alfred Huffman her opinion of his negative coverage of the trial, and for the publishing of the racist group's article. She fully intended to hand it to him before she left, maybe even tacking it to his breastbone to make sure he received it.

CHAPTER THIRTY-ONE

Sheriff Gilbert was up before daylight. He appeared downstairs with a small tablet containing a list of things to be done. He would be obligated to everyone within the department. The narrow door between his residence and the jail office was open. He lay in wait, listening for Curley as he hurried about getting himself ready for the day. The screen door moaned and he knew the familiar sound of Curley Jones arriving for duty. He heard the night jailer signing off duty and the small talk about the prior shift. The sheriff overheard that James Lee had not asked for a special last meal but had picked over the cold sack meal that was delivered, along with the ambient temperature sweet tea.

"Curley!" The sheriff yelled from his toilet located upstairs. He stood at the sink in his suit pants, shaving his face. Curley hurried in to the bottom of the tall steps.

"Sir!" replied Curley, from the bottom newel post.

"Offer Lee a shower, and then get him dressed out, all by 9:30," said the sheriff, with his face stretched tight, to pull the safety razor over it. The blue razor blade would chatter and bite if the handle was not tightened. The blade had a bite that revealed itself after the deed was done.

"Reverend Prather called last night. They want to pray and sing after the drop. Said it was to memorialize the Millers and the other victims," Curley yelled up.

"I said in the paper to call me today. It's fine by me," he called down.

"I told 'em ta come ahead. I thought you'd agree," Curley said.

"Rope on the desk, coffin on the stoop, grave's dug. Doc Hubbard's to be here," said the sheriff.

"Say, who -- " Curley started to ask, only to be quickly answered.

"I'll drop the bastard," said the sheriff, buttoning his dress shirt. "I've shot 'em, I can hang 'em!" Now he looked down the stairs at his longtime

476

employee. "Get the box on something waist high, we don't want to carry him too far. Them that show get seats behind the dignitaries and law enforcement. I expect Troup County to show, all their victims, the family of Ellis DeFoor, maybe a lot of the old veterans. Them War Between the States fellers stick together. They get all our over and above consideration and hospitality. Miss Jewel will be here to cater to them, show 'em a seat and a cool drink of water. They'll like that. I need the votes next time," he said with a wink. "A bunch of blacks for the Miller family, Herman Pickens's family and friends. There'll be every mayor for cities around. I want the Warm Springs folks together up front. That female detective, my Special Deputy, was instrumental in this," said Sheriff Gilbert, puffing out his chest. "Since the wife's gone, she'd make a fine woman for some man," he said, jerking his head sideways and giving a loud click.

Curley thought for a moment. "Maybe borrow chairs from the church around the corner?" he asked.

"I'll see Oliver Queen and threaten him," said Sheriff Gilbert. "There's too much to get done for the people we've got. Go on with the tasks," he said, sliding a suspender onto his shoulder.

The aroma of coffee, biscuits, and a slight trace of smoked meats soon filled the jail complex. Miss Jewel was working magic in her kitchen. She wore a black cotton dress with petticoats and had a straw hat for the occasion outside. Doc Hubbard appeared in the kitchen door. Jewel was bent over the hot oven door. Her butt, with the dress, was as wide as the cast iron stove. "My, what a woman!" Doc Hubbard said loudly.

Miss Jewel's eyes grew large as she bent down and rubbed butter over the tops of the baking bread. She was aware of her size. "Who dat?" she asked, almost breathless.

"Yo' luvin' man," he replied.

"Luvin' my ass, Doc Hubbard!" she exclaimed, standing up.

"I'm here only because of you," he said, smiling.

"Fo' mize biskits!" she laughed. "Go on now, Misser Curley, he be needin' hope."

Doc Hubbard heard some kind of bumping on the front stoop and went to see what it was. Curley was attempting to get the coffin to the sawhorses he had brought up from the back yard. "What ya need is a strong trustee," said the doctor. Sheriff Gilbert appeared at the jail door with Oliver Queen.

"Oliver's been read the law, my law. He's ta help today without restraint. We have an agreement, let him get chairs set up from the church if they will allow, and anything else, but he'll be locked up when the crowd begins to gather," the sheriff said.

Oliver stepped outside waiting for instructions. "Ya hear me now?" asked Sheriff Gilbert.

"Yessa, boss!" Oliver replied.

Reverend Prather and his following had already gathered at the church. The people attending the event numbered to a couple of hundred, almost all dressed in black. They had a covered dish prayer breakfast at daylight, and then worshiped and sang the songs they intended to sing at the execution. They were planning to put as many in a car as possible. Some would ride in trucks to save parking problems in town. It was a wonderful pleasant morning.

The veterans who had known Ellis DeFoor were assembled at the Luthersville church, where he was buried. They too had a prayer breakfast. They numbered about forty-five to fifty. From a distance, all the old men looked alike, dark suit, white hair and a cane.

The Warm Springs government had assembled at the café in town, the usual gathering spot. Most all the councilmen, the police chief, the mayor, and any wives that wanted to attend the gruesome event, were there. The small café was crowded. Pastor Bigalow from the hard-shell Baptist church on the Southside gave the prayer. Detective Duncan and Officer Brown did not attend.

The Greenville city government assembled at Becky's Café. The police chief had chosen to attend.

"I'm sure you are prepared to handle the additional traffic today," said the Greenville mayor. The chief looked surprised. "With that look, I'd bet the woman detective could easily get your job," said the mayor. He was talking and pointing at the surprised chief with his fork. "Cut everyone slack. I wouldn't give out any parking tickets," said the mayor. That brought a loud roar of laughter from the council, since the chief and his department hardly did anything at all, other than watch. "I'd expect y'all to work an accident and cover the city's ass on that," said the mayor.

"I second that," replied one of the councilmen. The chief was visibly embarrassed.

Heather and Jasper knew they were expected to attend, but patrolled a little longer before they left. Jasper laced through the downtown district. There was not a lot of conversation, but that was normal. It picked up when there was an event or an open case. "I'd like to drive my Essex up," Heather said suddenly.

Jasper looked surprised. "My drivin'?" he asked.

"No, it needs ta be run," she replied, looking ahead. The short note she had written to hand to him just before she left was in her suit pocket.

Jasper looked at her several times. "My, what a handsome, neat woman," he thought to himself. He truly regretted that he was so much older.

* * *

Oliver Queen had carried about a hundred chairs from the nearby church, under the watchful eyes of the old pastor who lived nearby. Curley had closed off the street in front of the jail and the chairs spilled over all the way to the shady sidewalk on the other side, after the benches the jail owned had run out. The neighboring business owners watched from their windows and steps, grumbling about the street closure and disruption.

The gallows were lubricated and set to drop the single trap door with the least amount of effort once the sheriff pulled the lever. Additional barrel bolts had been installed to give the trap door added support during the process of securing the hangman's knot. The bolts would be hammered away, and then only the true trigger would remain.

Oliver Queen, with the sheriff watching now and then, saw that the grounds were ready, except for the tying of the rope. The coffin was close by, resting on sawhorses. There were enough seats gathered for about two hundred people. Oliver sat quietly on the front steps for a few minutes until Sheriff Gilbert put him back in his cell. Curley stood by while James Lee took his final bath and then dressed out of the cotton prison suit. He exchanged black and white horizontal stripes for a county furnished suit. Appointed attorney Robert Gaskill and Reverend Prather appeared in the office.

"We're here to see the accused," Gaskill said to the sheriff.

"Certainly," he replied, as he stood up. "Curley is in with him. He may not be dressed," the sheriff said, as he turned the key on the jail door. Out of humanity, the sheriff had turned on all the lights, all six. The prisoners sat silently. There was not a sound other than the one-sided conversation of Curley Jones and a deputy coming from the cell where James Lee was dressing. Curley took the damp prison clothes from Lee and tossed them behind him, not noticing that the attorney and the preacher were there.

"My apologies!" Curley said. "Who let you in?"

"The sheriff," replied Gaskill.

"He'll be able to meet in just a minute," Curley replied. He made sure the cell door was locked, as he stepped back allowing the two men to come closer.

"James," said the attorney. James Lee sat in his final clothes and looked down at his feet. He never made eye contact.

"I've passed on the information to the court and the sheriff. They know what to do," the young attorney said, as he too looked down. The prisoner never said a word. "Reverend Prather's here. Do you want him to say a few words with you?"

The Negro finally sniffed and wiped his eyes with the sleeve of the cheap suit. "No!" he said, not looking at the preacher.

"Gawd loves ya son," said Reverend Prather, softly. He stood behind the attorney and looked over the young man's shoulder.

"Go away!" James Lee said loudly.

The older Negro jumped at the sudden response. He tugged on the attorney's sleeve. "Let's go," he whispered. The two men stood for a moment, hoping the accused would change his mind, but he did not. They turned and slowly walked away. The old reverend began to recite. "De Lawd is my shep-hurd, I'ze shall nots wants. He makest meez ta lays downs in green pastures. Lo, he be with us'ins always, eben ta de ends of de earth."

Curley and the deputy opened the door, allowing the two men to return into daylight and fresh air. The prisoners sat quietly in their cells. Oliver Queen stood against the bars, listening and watching. "Yous ta be gittin' on ta wheres you'ze goin'. If you'ze between Heben and Hell and I'ze pass throughs, I'll finish yous myself. Dat lovely woman and dat little baby. I'ze hopes de wurms crawls ends and outs yo' head, shit in yo' eyeballs, and dance in yo' skull. You evil bassard!" He whispered just loud enough for James Lee and the nearby prisoners to hear. They were on lockdown and there was to be no talking. Queen watched the smaller man become short of breath as he sat on the metal bunk.

* * *

"We need to switch out cars and head on. We don't want ta be late," Heather said, looking over at Jasper as he drove.

He headed to the Blakely Boarding House where the Essex was parked. Jasper stopped the patrol car quietly at the back of Heather's car. She looked back at him as she got out. "You're leaving, aren't you?" Jasper asked, looking her in the eyes.

Heather stood silently and looked down for a moment. "Yes, after the hanging," she replied.

"I won't ask why," he said. He was getting teary eyed. His round face was flushing.

"I was goin' to leave you a note," Heather said. She pulled it from her coat and placed it on the seat. "I couldn't bring myself to say goodbye," she whispered.

"I understand," he said, as a lone tear rolled from his eye. "I'll miss you," he whispered. "I wouldn't let ya go if I was a younger man."

"If you were a younger man, I'd be ten," she said, with a broad smile.

"Yeah, I guess so," he said, looking ahead. "Anyone else know?"

"Only Mrs. Blakely. She's been paid up. We've got to go," Heather said, closing the door.

"I'll always remember you," Jasper said, as he tried to pull the car in gear. He was visibly upset and missed the gear. He tossed his uniform cap on the seat and wiped his tears. "I'll follow you," he sniffled.

Heather closed the door on the Ford for the last time. It felt as though she had closed the door on a part of her life. She was sad, but she missed home. Jasper would hold the sealed note for several weeks before he was able to open it. It remained on his mantel for a long time.

The Essex was slow to start. It had not been run in several weeks.

Once it cranked it gave a soft, vapor like cloud of gasoline from the exhaust, indicating a rich mixture. The warming of the engine and a choke adjustment would take care of that. Heather backed the bright burgundy car into the street and headed carefully out of Warm Springs. Due to the ill feelings that remained in her heart, she would never return. She waved at the old men on the bench at Claude Allen's Service Station and Garage. Claude slowly stood from working under a hood and watched as she drove north past his place. Jasper followed at a distance and watched the car leaving with the woman who had probably saved his life on the road the day James Lee was chased. He remembered the skill with which the woman, unknown to him at that time, had spun the big Essex around and given chase, eventually holding the Negro at bay. He shook his head and smiled. That was some day. "There weren't really any days policing with her that weren't pleasurable," he thought, wiping his eyes with his handkerchief. She was worth knowing, a highlight in his life that he would never forget.

About half a mile south of Greenville, the Warm Springs officers encountered parked cars and folks of both colors walking toward the square. The parking on the square had been saved for law enforcement and political officials. Heather pulled the Essex into the first available space and Jasper parked beside her. Greenville Police officers were walking the town at the request of the sheriff. Heather placed a business card inside her driver's side window in hopes of avoiding a citation, since she had no official tag or markings displayed, and worst of all, a soon to expire Campbell County tag.

Jasper stood in front of her car on the busy sidewalk. He looked like a disappointed schoolboy. His pain was visible. "Lots of folks," he said, with a faint crack in his voice.

"A lot of folks," Heather replied. "I told the chief in his letter that I'll send money back for the badge. I'd like ta keep it," she said softly, as they walked along. Jasper was a proud man. He had polished his uniform buttons, buckles, and even the brass pea whistle that hung from a pocket flap. Heather wore her brown suit and her shoulder rig. She had placed a tiny white rosebud in her lapel out of respect for the Millers. They could see the top of the gallows above the gathered crowd. The sidewalk was crowded with silent people dressed in everything from dress suits to plow clothes.

Miss Jewel was out and about watching for the old men who looked like Civil War veterans. She had already seated about ten of them. She talked to the old men and laughed at their funny comments. She appeared to be enjoying herself. Doc Hubbard and Sheriff Gilbert walked to the gallows at 9:45 and began to mount the official rope. Sheriff Gilbert measured from the trap door to the open knot, making it swing very close to the height of James Lee's chin, and then added a calculated amount for the drop. All whispers stopped while the two men secured the prepared rope. A deputy stood by and watched. The task was soon done. "No one comes up here but the party," said the sheriff, as he and the doctor descended the steps.

"Yes, sir!" the deputy replied, as he moved to the bottom of the steps.

Reverend Prather arrived so early that he had established the seating area for the Negroes. In many places there were whites and blacks seated side by side. The sturdy built choir leader for the black church handed out small song books to his singers, gathered on the end closest to the jail.

Jasper and Heather found the saved seats and joined other law enforcement officers who were already seated. Small notes lay secured in the seat of the chairs by the weight of small stones, holding places for Judge Erastus Cobb and Ambrose Watkins.

The public was barred from the sheriff's office at this point. Sheriff Gilbert, accompanied by Doc Hubbard, entered the cell block by way of the heavily guarded intake door. The jail complex was deathly silent, only the sandy footsteps of the walking men could be heard. James Lee heard them coming. His heart must have raced, knowing the moments were fleeting. Curley Jones and a deputy stood by, just outside of Lee's cell. They were there to insure he did not harm himself. Sheriff Gilbert tossed his wet cigar into a trash can in the center of the cell block. All prisoners were against the bars, wanting to see the evil son of a bitch pass on the way to his death. Sheriff Gilbert worked a small piece of tobacco from his mouth and spit on the floor. "Let him out," he said to Curley and the deputy. The words seemed to echo from the steel cages and cold red brick walls. Reverend Prather and Attorney Robert Gaskill stood at the door looking into the dimly lit dungeon-like room.

Curley turned the heavy bolt on the cell door with the complex key, specific to that cell alone. The mechanical click was loud. Curley's hand pulled the barred door slowly open. James Lee looked down at his feet as he continued to sit on the metal bunk. "Lee, stand up!" ordered the sheriff. Doc Hubbard wiped sweat with his handkerchief. His pocket flask was certainly handy, as he quickly took a long drink. "Cuffed in front, and the waist chain, take a set of leg irons for the act," the sheriff said. The guarding deputy looked pale. He had seen hangings after the fact, on calls and such, but never one like this. He had heard stories of all sorts of mishaps; strangling, heads coming off, gurgling sounds. He shivered.

James Lee stood and placed his hands together in front. Curley applied the handcuffs. The mating of the hardened gear shaped teeth was loud. The prisoners looked on. The twist chain waistband was applied. Curley pulled a small lock from his pocket and secured the handcuffs to the ring on the twist chain. "He's ready," Curley said softly. "I won't wish ya luck, it's too far gone for that," he said to Lee, as he pointed to the open cell door.

Doc Hubbard noticed James Lee's brogans were untied. "Tie his shoes," he said, pointing to the prisoner's feet. "A little dignity can't hurt," he added, wiping his brow. The guard deputy pointed for the prisoner to place his foot on the edge of the lower bunk, where he tied the man's shoes, first one and then the other. The sheriff looked at his watch, "10:24," he said aloud. "Let's go." He pointed to the open door across the cell block.

The jail yard and the street were full of people. Deputies armed with side-arms and shotguns were standing along the cement walkway from the sheriff's office to the gallows. There were four armed guards, two of them Greenville Police officers. They were without shotguns. The cool winds of fall blew strong. The city street sounds seemed to fade away. Dogs no longer barked and the birds did not sing. The world awaited the departure of the evil bastard.

James Lee took one short step after another behind Curley Jones and the jail appointed deputy. Sheriff Louis Gilbert and the coroner, Doctor Augustus Hubbard, followed. When the small group cleared the intake door, it closed hard behind them with a loud clang. The waiting public hushed upon hearing the signal given by the heavy door. The guard deputy turned the key in the heavy box lock, giving the prisoners the chance to talk. By court order there was no returning by the accused, his welcome had run out. He surely must be destined for the arms of Satan. The sky grew dark and overcast with heavy clouds. An unseen owl gave a single hoot. Those who believed in omens shivered. There was a pause at the office door.

The sheriff looked at his watch again. "Hold up about a minute," he said. He saw Miss Jewel outside, standing close to the old veterans. He was very pleased. "All right," he whispered. Curley moved ahead, first through the door. Doc Hubbard was last. The armed guards received them on the walkway. "Form up, keep it neat," whispered the sheriff, as the men hurried to organize their escort. James Lee still looked down, not making eye contact with anyone. His hands formed tight fists. Robert Gaskill and Reverend Prather had hurried ahead and stood at the bottom of the gallows steps.

"Woulds yous like for me to say a word?" asked Reverend Prather, as the condemned man came close.

"Damn you, old man!" said James Lee, as he took the first step. The reverend looked shocked at the reaction to his final attempt.

"Four minutes," Sheriff Gilbert whispered, as he climbed the steps. Curley Jones and the deputy stood off to the side. "Step up!" said the sheriff, pointing to the spot where James Lee was to stand. The Negro took two steps and stopped dead center on the trap door. Sheriff Gilbert held his hand out for the leg irons. The rattle of the irons was the loudest sound in the yard as everyone looked on. Sheriff Gilbert kneeled down and secured the irons on Lee's ankles. James Lee looked into the distance without the slightest expression on his face. Sheriff Gilbert motioned for Miss Jewel. She hurried forward, pulling a small washed flour sack from her apron pocket. The sheriff was too high and the heavy Negro woman was too short. A deputy on the ground took the sack and hurried it up to the sheriff. The courthouse clock was moving to 10:28. Miss Jewel hurried back to her place near the old veterans. She mumbled something about sending his soul to hell, holding her dress up as she moved along. "Takes him, Satan!"

Sheriff Gilbert raised his hand. "James Lee, do you have any last words?" he asked. The Negro stood silently, giving no reply. The sheriff popped the thin cotton sack open. The waiting crowd jumped. His large hands held the sack open and draped it down over the Negro's head. Doc Hubbard swung the knot to the sheriff. It was quickly secured around Lee's neck. All was going well. The knot was snug, exactly where it should be for a quick kill. Many in the crowd looked away.

Heather watched every movement of the sheriff. She had never seen a hanging, but had heard tales of the only one that had taken place in Campbellton, a prisoner of her grandfather. Newspaper men made photographs all during the different stages of the event, hurrying for better vantage points.

"Kick the bolts!" said Sheriff Gilbert. He stepped off of the trap door. A deputy on the steps hurried under the gallows and hammered the three steel slide bolts away from the trap door. All the weight of the Negro sat squarely on the trigger. The deputy hurried back to his post and tossed the claw hammer on the steps.

Oliver Queen stood against his cell bars. His dark face was pressed firmly against the cold steel. The prisoners across the way could see his large white eyes as they moved about quickly in the sockets. "Listens nows!" he said, whenever someone moved creating the slightest sound.

The clock in the tower of the courthouse began to grind as the mechanics within cocked the bell hammer to strike the half hour. "Pong, pong!" the bell sounded. Sheriff Gilbert's hand was white knuckled around the drop lever. At exactly 10:30 a.m. he pulled the gallows lever hard and the accused James Lee dropped suddenly. His neck was heard snapping. There was a slight twitch of his legs. His clenched fists opened. The executed man swung about a foot off the ground. Just as Heather had always heard, piss formed a wet spot on his pants and soon dripped from the toe of his brogans. The trap door bounced off of the gallows bracing and settled into a gentle swing, until it too stopped. A slight dusting of the dry Georgia clay drifted on the morning breeze. Doc Hubbard stood by with his stethoscope. It would be at least fifteen minutes before he would check for a heartbeat.

The loud slap of the trap door striking the gallows was heard inside the jail by the other prisoners. "He's gone, boys! Dat evil sum bitch is gone!" Oliver Queen suddenly sang out. "De devil is holdin' his soul," he said, dancing about among his Negro cellmates in the tiny cell.

"God rest Ellis DeFoor!" shouted one old veteran. "Here, here!" cheered several of the old men, tapping their canes on the ground.

The lawmen left the gallows and stood by to remove the body. Reverend Prather's choir leader hummed to get the choir into key. The blacks began humming Blessed Assurance. Many people were already leaving. The deed ordered by the Court was done. Judge Cobb and Ambrose Watkins stood and walked amiably about the gallows, watching the hanging body sway slightly, turning from the twist and tension on the rope.

Judge Cobb was heard sighing loudly as he placed his fingers in his hip pockets. "Another one done," he was heard to say. Several people walked up to commend him and shake his hand.

"This is for the John Miller family," said Reverend Prather. "God wuks in mysterious ways. He gives and takes away. Lo, I am with you always, evens ta de ends uf de earths," he said, holding his tattered leather-bound bible. The choir began to sing a song. Miss Jewel clapped in rhythm and danced about. Several veterans joined her on the hard surface of the street close to the choir. They were having a grand old time.

Doc Hubbard looked at his watch. "It's time!" he called to the sheriff. Both men walked under the gallows. The doctor placed his stethoscope in his ears and placed the hard disk on Lee's shirt. Sheriff Gilbert waved for the people close by to be quiet. Doc Hubbard's eyes moved about while he concentrated on the sounds.

"He's dead," the doctor declared, removing his instrument.

The majority of the public had gone. Only the old veterans remained, and the choir, which continued to sing. Curley Jones hurried up the gallows steps and released the rope while the sheriff and a deputy held the body, keeping the tension off the gallows knot. The dead man suddenly toppled to the ground and the connected rope fell over him like a strangling vine. As small as James Lee was, he was heavy as a corpse. The fact that he was still limp did not help, as four strong men placed him in the prison made coffin.

"We need witness signatures on this," said Watkins, as he appeared with a formal form of the court.

"Well, call for 'em," replied the sheriff, as he released the dead man from his arms.

"We need witnesses for the court!" Ambrose Watkins called out. "Tell history this man's dead!" he yelled. He only needed six but ended up with eighteen. Many of Reverend Prather's church hurried to sign. "Put your race after your name," said Watkins. The signing was done on the lid of the casket, the most flat and convenient surface. All the officials from Warm Springs were in line.

Heather took the opportunity to drive a nail in the evil bastard's coffin. "There now!" she was heard to say. Jasper did not want anything to do with the coffin, but he did witness. Alfred Huffman made a photograph of the woman detective driving the coffin nail home. There was nothing special about it, just a number twelve box nail. Her skilled hand never missed as she swung the aged hammer.

Jasper's heart beat hard. He knew the time was near. "Now, that's the closing to that case," said Chief Hawthorn. Mayor Cunningham stood by his side.

"I have something for you," Heather said, putting her hand into the lapel of her coat. The chief looked eagerly at what she might be pulling out. "Here's my papers. I'm done, no more. I'm going home," Heather said, handing the sealed envelope to him. He looked surprised, as did the mayor.

"What brought this on?" the chief asked.

"It's all there, you can read it. I'll send money for the badge. I want to keep it," she said, starting to back away. She was eager to get underway. Alfred Huffman saw what was happening and came close. "Hey!" She pointed to the newspaper man. "I have a letter for you and your paper," she said, holding out an envelope. The young man slowly reached out and took it. There was surprise in his eyes. Heather timidly waved once more to Jasper. He could only nod and smile. He would miss her.

Alfred opened the envelope and quickly read over the contents. He followed after the young woman. "Hey! Hey!" he called out. Heather was already well ahead, sitting in the Essex. The big engine turned over and the exhaust made a familiar chirping sound as the engine idled. The windows were lowered on this warm day. "Hey! Hey!" Alfred Huffman called out again, as he stooped in his approach to the open passenger side window. "Hey! Are you leaving?" he asked, finally getting to the car before she drove away.

"It was a pleasure to work with you, and I am leaving. There's no place for me here," Heather said, looking at the young man as she held the gear shift lever.

"I wish you'd reconsider, folks here 'bouts were taken by your boldness -- and good looks," Alfred said, still leaning in the window. For a moment he seemed to want to express some feelings for the woman, older than him, and so attractive in her looks and bold actions. His shyness kept him from doing so.

"Print the letter if you will, maybe it'll make a difference in some woman's life," Heather said, dropping the shifter into gear.

"Heather!" Alfred had never called her that before. "I'll miss you around here, got the brass of three men, and the looks of a cameo goddess," he said, as he hurried alongside the moving car.

"The court took the teeth out of the tiger," she said, looking down. "I'd better be going, home's possible before dark." Heather looked at the young reporter. "Come to see us sometime," she said, handing him one of Margaret's business cards. "Margaret Selman Duncan, best woman writer and publisher in the state," she bragged, as he read the card.

Alfred smiled. "Ya mean it?" he asked, wiping his eyes with the sleeve of his shirt.

"Have you ever known me not to mean what I say?" she asked, looking him in the eyes, melting his emotions for her. She began to pull away slowly as the chief started toward her car.

Alfred Huffman stood straight and waved. "I'll be there! I'll be there!" he yelled, repeating his words over and over, getting lower and lower, to be repeated only in his mind as he watched her drive out of sight.

The same heavy truck that had transported the diggers to the pauper cemetery pulled into the side street in front of the jail at eleven o'clock. "I'll get the diggers," announced Curley.

"No special meal today, get back by noon for the usual, if anything," yelled the sheriff, as Curley hurried into the jail. Dixie had already opened for business. She was at her desk when Curley hurried by. The heavy steel door leading to the cell blocks was heard outside, moaning under its heavy weight on the hinges. A deputy followed Curley into the cell block. He carried the leg irons removed from the dead, along with the handcuffs and the waist chain.

"Cans I'ze tetch 'em?" Oliver Queen asked loudly, reaching out for the restraints that had been on James Lee. Curley motioned that it was all right. The road deputy held them close to the bars for the Negro. Oliver ran his large hand over them. "He's gone ta hell all right! Deys hot!" he said, letting go.

In a few minutes the diggers appeared on the stoop of the jail. Sheriff Gilbert motioned for them to come ahead. "Hurry 'em up," he said to the prison warden. "A toss and pitch," he said, smiling. "Toss tha sum bitch in the hole and pitch dirt on him. There'll be no time killed over this nigger. Same ones, Queen?" he asked, looking into the back of the truck.

"Yessa, boss, same ones," Oliver replied, sitting against the cab. Five men helped the sheriff load the coffin. The bottom of the thin box made a grinding sound as it slid over the sand and road dust on the truck bed.

James Lee was buried in an unmarked grave.

* * *

Heather Duncan had walked a line, one that would someday be referred to as the thin blue line. When it appeared to be straight it was not. When it appeared to be simple, it was hard. She was a woman in what was perceived as a man's world. While she was not the first, she was a pioneer. Her summer in the rural middle Georgia town was only a taste of what could have been a lengthy career, which she did not choose to follow. The people she met were unique characters among many, some jovial and sincere, others not worthy of breathing air.

The drive from the hanging on the square was not quick enough. The face of her partner Jasper Brown flashed through her mind, along with many others. Chief Hawthorn, Frances Goulding and her typing, Buddy Cotton and his classmates' scheme to feed a hungry family. Buddy, thinking she was like a movie star because of her suits. She smiled. She thought of Mrs. Blakely and Mayor Cunningham, Toby Sims and his dogs. Most of all, the faces of the court system that let Theo Jackson off on all the charges, even though he harbored an escaped felon and drove James Lee to the Miller residence, knowing he had a gun and was going to rob Gertrude for money and a car to get to Alabama. That was the part of the experience that made her sick to her stomach. All the chances he had to contact the law and tell them where James Lee was and he did not. The stiff bloody body of tiny Polly Sue, lying next to her mother on the kitchen floor, both in a pool of blood, her life that was taken too soon.

A loose sheet of newspaper tumbled across the road in the wind. Heather remembered the young eager reporter, Alfred Huffman. There was Doctor Augustus Hubbard and the autopsy, whiskey on his person like cologne. The last remembrance of the hanging with the Negroes gathered in their Sunday best, standing segregated from the whites. The whites, some in business attire, but most in their work clothes, were gathered to see the nigger swing. Seated down front were the families and friends of all the lives James Lee had touched and destroyed. Heather remembered the silence of the square with all the stores closed for the event. One could almost believe you could hear the ticking of the clock in the four-story tower. The clock hands indexed to ten thirty, and during the first strike of the chime, the rope around the condemned man's neck suddenly grew tight as the trap door fell away and the rope snapped taut. Theo Jackson was nowhere to be seen, or to wish his friend goodbye.

The young female detective remembered overhearing the negative conversations in the café and in the small stores about a woman taking a man's job. She smiled thinking of how Sheriff Giles had gotten one over on Sheriff Louis Gilbert and the Town of Warm Springs by sending a deputy down to help them with their plight.

The plush 1929 Essex floated along, smoothly and almost silently compared to the city furnished 1928 Ford Model A's. The colored leaves of fall twirled and drifted about on the cool air as the car passed. The dark flickering shadows quickly changing from bright to dark upon Heather and the car as she pressed northward were almost mesmerizing. The new windshield was in place and sparkling clean. Heather reached out with her lace handkerchief and wiped a faint spot of dust away from the dashboard. Her images of Sonny, Grandmother Margaret, and yes, Holly, brought tears of joy to her beautiful eyes. Home could not come soon enough.

EPILOGUE

The spring of 1938 was unusually beautiful. The weather was ideal for the fruit trees to blossom to their fullest extent. The snow white of the apple trees mixing with the pastel pink of the peach trees stood majestically over the brilliant tulips in the well-kept yards along the bus route into Atlanta. Heather rode along thinking of years past, as people often do. She thought of the missed time while she was at Warm Springs, but she was consoled by the fact that she had done the job to the very best of her abilities. In his own way, Sonny had expressed that he was proud of her. Heather clutched her purse and moved over on the seat for an older woman to sit down. The deep shadows of the city flickered across her face as she watched for indications of her upcoming point of departure.

"Going far?" asked the woman sitting next to her.

"No, just to the Rhodes-Haverty building," Heather replied. "And yourself?"

"Downtown, Rich's and Woolworth's," replied the woman. "Maybe Davison's" she added.

The bus rocked as it crossed the switch yard tracks in the West End Whitehall District. Trucks were coming and going in the busy warehouse complex. A small boy sat across the way and chattered to his mother about The Lone Ranger radio program. His gun belt carried double pistols. When the wind was right, the faint smell of burnt roll caps lingered in the bus. Heather smiled, as she too had been caught up in the adventurous episodes of the masked man and his Indian companion.

At the Lee Street underpass, traffic stopped for a red light. The busy presses of a printing company filled the air with a faint but familiar sound. Heather thought of Margaret and how they had made note of the Simon and Schuster publishing company announcing their opening back in January. Heather recalled the event of bookkeeping around the kitchen table, and how proud they both were of reading that a woman was elected to be a U.S. National Bank president. On a darker side, Heather recalled the morning paper's announcement of Hitler seizing control of the German armies and placing his key Nazis in command positions, and soon after that the invasion of Austria.

The bus pulled away, not missing a single pot hole in the worn street. The bus paralleled the railroad as it continued toward downtown Atlanta. Heather was well-versed in local history. She knew that the rambling concrete road was a Federal highway, from Baltimore, Maryland to

Pensacola, Florida. As far as the designation of Roosevelt Highway, that was recent. The president had traveled the road by car from Washington, D.C to Warm Springs many times. Few other than family knew it, but she had seen him many times during her employment at the police department. Heather realized early that he was a man who loved his women. She saw it right off.

The old red brick warehouses bore ghostly signs of weathered, almost washed away signage of what had once been. The once thriving shopping district of Peters Street and Whitehall was coming up. Heather rubbed her slightly sore hand. She had been on the punching bag yesterday. It was her first time in several weeks. "It was nothing compared to the hands of boxer Joe Louis," she thought to herself. The Fox Theater was ahead. She wanted to take Margaret to see the animated cartoon, *Bugs Bunny and Porky Pig*. "Maybe soon." She smiled as she thought of the illustrations she had seen in the newspaper of the naked chubby pig and his shotgun. Heather covered her mouth as she chuckled. The woman sitting next to her looked in wonder.

"I thought of something funny," Heather said, subduing her smile.

"I've enjoyed the company," the woman said. "Especially the part about you not smoking," she added, as she stood.

"It was a privilege," replied Heather, who still had a little ways to go.

The large Rich's building was ahead, a short distance away. It was the highlight of downtown shopping for many. The sprawling store sat at 45 Broad Street, between Alabama and Hunter. There was Davison's on Peachtree, another lovely place to shop. The gentle pull of the bell cord sounded a simple, pleasant tone recognized by the driver. He announced the stop and brought the bus to a gentle stop.

"Broad Street and Rich's!" he said loudly. The woman hurried toward the front door. Several Negroes got off by way of the back door. Everyone got on at the front and dropped change into a glass sided metering system for toll. The tall buildings cast shadows that shaded the pedestrians below. Heather saw disabled men selling trinkets to pedestrians on the sidewalks. One in particular got her attention. He was legless, from high thigh down. He was gloved and used his arms to swing himself along. A cotton cord pulled a small wheeled display cart of penny candies and assorted colored pencils behind him as he changed street corners. She realized just how lucky she was.

"Rhodes-Haverty building!" Heather cried out.

"Two stops!" replied the driver.

She moved to the front and stood, holding to a hand polished pole. "Same stop to go south?" Heather asked.

"Same stop," answered the driver, activating the lever for the bi-folding door to open.

Heather stepped onto the busy sidewalk, made up of men and women in business suits going and coming. She looked at the business card she held in her hand. *"Horace Weisberg Supply, Police Equipment, Suite 14, 18th floor, Rhodes-Haverty Building, 134 Peachtree Street."* She tucked the card into her suit pocket. The sun was beginning to feel uncomfortable as it warmed her dark suit. Her purse was heavy with the weight of her revolver. It was the antique that Margaret had carried, old but in excellent condition. Heather planned to purchase a later model given the first opportunity. The rural woman stepped quickly to the shade of the cloth awnings along the sidewalk. A small coffee shop and grill seemed to be attracting most of the foot traffic. At first chance Heather held to a street lamp pole and tried to see the top of the tall building. She had read that it was the tallest one in Atlanta, twenty-one floors. She thought about how high she was when she climbed to the third floor of the Greenville courthouse. This was seven times higher.

"Tall, ain't it?" a man called out. He had seen what she was doing. He laughed. "I did the same thing," he said with a smile, before walking on.

Heather entered through the Peachtree Street side. The soft gray stone was bright as it reflected the sunlight and its heat. The building was relatively new compared to others in the city, but none were as tall. The dim lighting gave an air of uppity about the place. The polished marble walls glistened from the light of the wall-mounted sconces beside the elevators and the hallway entrances. The ceiling of the ground floor was equal in complexity to the work in a European chapel. Heather stood against the wall, out of the way, and looked at the foyer ceiling high overhead. Her eyes explored the raised carvings of shapes surely influenced by Greek designs. There was gold paint or gilding on the majority of the carvings that encircled the crest-like motifs. She smiled. "Motifs, that was a good word for her and Jasper to play with. Just what was his motifs?" she smiled, thinking of the now old man. "He might even be gone, by now," she thought sadly.

There were two elevators running. Heather took the first one to open. "Goin' up?" asked the attendant.

"Yes, 18th floor," Heather answered. She stood to the back as others came aboard.

The elevator was fancy too. The polished expanding guard that slid across the doorway gleamed in the accent lighting within the small elevator car. The Oriental rug that was tacked to the floor with dome headed brass tacks showed a lot of wear.

The travelers began to call out numbers, "Three, eleven, six, fifteen, twenty-one, two," the different voices called out. The attendant quickly noted the numbers on a small chalkboard hung in the corner with the controls. The elevator man was dressed in a fancy suit, gold cords and embroidery down the sleeves, pants legs, and even around the cuffs of the coat and pants. The jacket looked like a Union shell jacket with three rows of tiny brass buttons and a stand-up black collar. The brimless, flat top hat was held in place by a worn black leather strap. The lever at his side was held to the rear of the semi-circular slot and the vessel quickly rose skyward. The trip to the third floor seemed to be quick, and very deliberate. It came to an abrupt stop.

"Third floor! Lawyers, Fancy Dans, all them folks," he said, as a passenger hurried off. The brass door guard closed once more, and the trip was even faster to the sixth floor, where the operator made a different announcement after the designation of the floor.

Heather finally stepped off onto the eighteenth floor. She thought she could feel the building sway, but maybe it was her imagination. "How convenient," she said to herself, seeing a directory for the floor. "Horace Weisberg Supply, Police Equipment, Suite 14," she read, was to her right. All the dark mahogany doors were closed. The faint sound of typewriters could be heard from behind many of them. For the most part the floor was very quiet. The walls here were also polished marble and the floors some sort of composite stone type material. A wool runner broke the noise of foot traffic in the hallway.

"This is it," she thought, as she turned the polished doorknob to enter the suite. The room was lined with wooden casement covered by sliding glass, protecting the merchandise from dust. She saw nothing that she did not recognize. A service bell sat on the counter. "Ting, ting!" It sounded as her palm pressed it into action.

"Yes, ma'am! May I help you?" a middle-aged man asked, as he stepped from an open office door.

"I'm Heather Duncan, here to talk about the sales job," she said, standing proud and tall.

"Know anything about our business?" he asked. "By the way, I'm Horace Weisberg," the man said, extending his hand.

Heather gave it a masculine grip.

"My, that's a grip," he replied.

"Shows a person's sincerity," said Heather. "I've policed before," she added.

"Oh, really! Where?" asked Weisberg. "Come in and have a seat," he said, opening the swinging half door. Heather took a seat.

"Campbell County Deputy, under Sheriff Benjamin Giles, then at Warm Springs as a detective. Mostly the James Lee case," she said proudly.

The interview went well. Weisberg asked that she name the pieces of equipment in the display cases and tell him about each one. That was quick and easy. "Any gun sales?" Heather asked.

"Guns too?" Weisberg replied.

"Shoot a revolver and a 1911," she said.

"My!" Weisberg replied.

As well as things were going, Heather gradually began to read into the interview that someone had already been chosen, that her day was wasted and she was there for the amusement of Weisberg. The distance was much farther than she had anticipated. She too was beginning to convince herself that it was not practical, even if she could do the job. The interview was over in about an hour.

"An hour I could have been at Rich's," she thought to herself.

Horace Weisberg advised her that he would consider her qualifications and get in touch with her in the very near future. "Thanks for coming," he said. "Say, there's an old codger on Elevator One you should meet, he was a police officer somewhere. You'd make his day. He's a talker now!" Weisberg said, as he saw her to the door.

"Wasted damn time," Heather mumbled, as she stood alone in the hallway watching the indicator lights responding over the bronze tone doors. "Ting!" the bell sounded and the doors opened. She stepped inside. "First floor, whatever opens to the street," she said, looking down.

The operator sat with one butt cheek on a wooden bar stool. "Yes, ma'am," he said, closing the doors as the car slowly started to the ground floor.

Heather felt the old man watching. She never looked him in the eyes. He too was dressed like the operator she had seen before, on the way up to the eighteenth floor. This operator seemed to be more spit and polished than the last.

"You policed before?" he asked. His voice cracked as he spoke.

"Several years ago," Heather answered, looking up at the indicator lights.

"Huntin' niggers, I guess," he replied.

Heather looked at him more closely. "Jasper?"

"Ever' damn inch of me," he replied, with a huge smile. His hair was thinner and snow white. His eyes were as blue as ever, but the sparkle was gone. He stopped the elevator mid-floor. "Give me a hug, gal!" he said, holding out his arms.

They embraced. "What brought you up here?" Heather asked.

"You!" he replied.

"Me?" she asked.

"You left, things went to hell. I told the mayor and the council what I thought of 'em. They didn't fire me, but made it so hard I left, especially after I cracked my ankle," he said. He slapped his right leg. "They put me on nights, moved Edgar to days. Told 'em ta kiss my ass, got rid of my little place and moved up here. I live in a two-room over a grocery on Whitehall, noisy during the day, but quiet at night," he said. "My, my!" he said softly.

"And I'm sure ya sleep good at night," Heather said. She was glad to see him once again.

Jasper wiped his eyes. "I do, I certainly do," he said, as he moved the lever forward. The vessel slowly dropped. "So, why are ya up here?" he asked Heather.

"Dreams, I thought I'd like to sell police equipment, but it's too damn far up here. They don't furnish a sales car either. I'd have ta use mine," she said.

"The Essex?" he asked.

"Yes," she replied, with a smile.

The elevator stopped on the ground floor. There were lots of people waiting as the doors opened. "Goodbye, old friend," Heather said, trying not to tear up. "Come to Campbellton sometime," she said, as she gave him a hug and shook his aging hand. She kept the feel for the longest time, but it slipped away somewhere between the front doors and the bus steps. Heather and Jasper Brown would never cross paths again, except in the tall tales told by one another, and those grew larger and more daring with each telling.

Heather boarded the southbound bus. As she dropped her fare in coins, she bent to look back at the Rhodes-Haverty building. It was her last look for many years. Everything she needed could come from the Southside. Even the trip to Newnan was pleasurable compared to the long trip to Atlanta. Heather almost got the same seat, just two away, closer to the front of the bus. It was loaded with housewives, their small children, and Negro maids who sat in the rear. This time the train tracks were to her left, across the bus aisle. She looked mostly at the sights along her side of the bus, out the righthand window. The bus shifted from side to side as it crossed switch tracks along the way. The shadows were not as deep, as it was well past mid-morning. The sight of a brilliantly shining red ladder truck caught her eye as they passed the red brick, multi-story fire station in the Lee and Whitehall District. Heather saw the young boys looking with a gleam of excitement in their eyes, faces reflected in the bus windows. All this bus riding was not in her childhood, being from East Texas. She still did not feel at ease with the fact that she was not in control, and the tightness of the crowd bothered her as well.

As she thought of meeting Jasper once again, she recalled the difficulties of the case, especially Theo Jackson who had gotten off scot-free. "Oh, that son of a bitch!" she growled in her mind, adding another angered moment to her mind. She managed to smile at the thought of Jasper Brown and his prideful appearance in his operator's suit. Heather shook her head in fond remembrances of her old friend. She consoled herself in the fact that Sonny, Margaret, and herself often sat and talked about religion, heaven, and hell. Heather remembered the deep conversations of afterlife and was there actually reincarnation, was it the body or just the soul? Holly would yawn during those long, late night conversations and fall over, finding a restful repose. They all thought there was something to this karma thing, which started in the Far East, India, or one of those Hindu or Buddhist countries.

"Maybe Theo Jackson will eventually get his just rewards. He was responsible for James Lee being taken to the house of Gertrude and Polly Sue Miller, where he robbed and brutally killed them both," she repeated in her innermost desires. "Maybe that supported the old saying of what goes around comes around and the belief that life revolves in a circle," she said to herself. She looked down the busy streets as the moving bus passed through the intersections. A small girl stood on the seat in front of her. The pretty girl turned around and looked at Heather. The shy girl waved, only moving her fingers. Heather smiled and did the same.

Heather saw tufts of cotton caught and hanging in the thorny bushes along the railroad, as the bus rocked from side to side on the southbound journey. It brought back memories of her childhood, her mother, and the day they had run for their lives. Memories of the strong man who saved them and the hard old woman who soon saw good in them, just a young woman and a child running along an East Texas road. Heather began to sob. The manuscript of the adventures of that Texas summer came to her mind. Heather was sure it was in a prominent place on Grandmother Margaret's desk. The old woman had dreamed of living long enough to get around to publishing it. Tears filled Heather's eyes. "Maybe that's what I'll do," she whispered out loud. The small girl in the seat ahead turned and looked at her. Heather looked far into the distant sky and remembered where she had been, and most of all where she could go under her own desires and dreams. Her thoughts soon came back to Jasper and how delighted he seemed to be at seeing her again. Heather smiled. It was a wonderful day.

ABOUT THE AUTHOR

SIDNEY A. BROWN is a native of East Point, Georgia, but spent many hours of his childhood in the Stonewall community where his grandparents and great-grandparents lived. Stonewall was originally in Campbell County until 1932 when it merged into Fulton County. His devotion to the historical town of Campbellton, the original county seat of Campbell County, leads him on wondrous journeys through times gone by. Brown was elected President of the Old Campbell County Historical Society in 2015. The Society was founded in 1971. It occupies the last courthouse of Campbell County, located in Fairburn, Georgia. The county seat was moved from Campbellton to Fairburn in 1870. This genealogical and historical research center speaks softly to the author as weekly duties are performed in the old courthouse building, along with other volunteers.

BROWN was fortunate to witness the last years of the steam locomotives that operated on the historic Atlanta & West Pont Railroad. The last few years of the Campbellton Ferry also spurred his imagination as he crossed the Chattahoochee River with his grandfather. The marvel and wonder of the Model A, Model T, and open top roadsters that his grandfather worked on as a local mechanic drew Brown further into the allure of yesteryear. He fired his first rifle at the age of six. Black powder smoke billowed from the .32-20 Winchester 1873 as his grandfather held the barrel of the long heavy rifle. Now the TV western heroes came to life! Yesteryear was in his soul.

The author's professional career included thirty-five years as a mechanical designer before becoming a law enforcement officer for fifteen years. Somewhere along the way, the calling of Southern based historical writing developed, along with his personal collection of factual information. Sidney A. Brown was recognized with Honorable Mention by the Georgia Writer's Museum for his entry in the creative writing contest of October 2015.

Made in the USA
Columbia, SC
10 September 2019